FORGED IN ASHES

The Golden One Trilogy: Book Two

NOELLE EDWARDS

For all of the women who'd go to war—and win it—to create a better future for the kids we love.

Forged

in

Ashes

Forged

in

Ashes

Prologue

890 Post Creation

To survive a massacre was to endure mankind's cruelest form of punishment.

Across the realm, many claimed that surviving a tragic event, regardless of the circumstances, was a blessing from the gods. Others argued in favor of what Iago Zanaki knew to be true: surviving while those you loved were slaughtered was, without a doubt, the most merciless curse the gods could inflict upon humanity. One didn't know true loneliness until everyone they cared for was taken from them.

That, Iago thought, was a fate worse than death.

Based on the tally marks carved into the wood beside his head, Iago had been alone for nearly fifty days. Two sunrises before his eternal punishment began, he'd been removed from his cell in the Bozari dungeons, hands and wrists shackled with iron chains, and forced to walk from one end of the kingdom to the other while being pulled by an impatient stallion. His route across Bozar was accompanied not only by furious commoners tossing rotted fruit and chunks of waste in his direction, but by the remains of his loved ones strung up on either side of the road.

The first person he saw was his mother, the six-and-seventy-year-old Dowager Queen, nailed to a stake to his left. Her severed head, eyes open and wide with terror, sat atop a stake directly across from her body. Her gray curls, the primary source of her vanity, had once been long enough to dust the floor when she walked. Now, all that remained of her infamous locks were uneven tufts scattered over her bald head. The man who'd killed her, one of Bozar's newest leaders, had the Dowager Queen's three-foot-long braided hair draped over his shoulders like a scarf.

Sasoma, Iago's beloved bride of over three decades, was next. She'd been flayed alive and dismembered at every joint, her body parts scattered on either side of the road yards apart from one another. For six miles as Iago was tugged towards his destination, his eyes found nothing but bloodied, unrecognizable pieces of the woman he loved.

Then came the children. His five offspring, their spouses, and their children lined the streets throughout the center of Bozar. The women and girls, like the Dowager Queen, had been beheaded. The men and boys met the same fate as Sasoma. The eldest of them, Iago's son and heir, was only thirty years of age. The youngest, Iago's only granddaughter, hadn't yet reached her first name day.

By the time Iago and his captors reached their destination—the province of Khaba located east of Bozar—he'd seen the corpses of every member of the Zanaki family. His siblings and their families, his cousins, his aunts and uncles, and even his wife's family, had been murdered and left for the vultures because of Iago's failure.

Upon arriving in Khaba, a shackled Iago was hefted by the underarms and tossed into a wooden crate meant to transport chickens. Other than the disgraced king himself, there was nothing in the crate besides stray chicken feathers and lingering traces of excrement embedded in the wooden boards. The only light source was a circular hole at the top of the crate, just large enough for two of Iago's fingers to slither through, that cast a singular beam of sunlight onto the opposite wall.

The lid was sealed, locked, and transported from the Khabish streets to a nearby dingy floating off the coast. The soldiers tasked with Iago's transportation taunted him by sticking miscellaneous objects into the crate's hole. At first, it was nothing more than pesky insects like a cockroach or spider, but soon enough, the torment became personal. A piece of bloody cloth was identified by a soldier as a scrap taken from Iago's daughter's underthings. A slim, polished female finger belonged to none other than Iago's wife, as it still wore the sapphire ring he'd given her on their twentieth anniversary.

When the dingy reached a ship in the distance, the crate was lifted onto the deck, where it would remain for the next fifty days. The lid was opened only once to provide Iago with a canteen of drinking water. Scraps of food were delivered to him through the small hole, only once a day, while sailors and soldiers alike continued to torment him by trading stories about how they'd tortured, raped, and murdered the former king's family and friends.

Now, on their fiftieth day at sea, the ship finally anchored. A soldier—previously one of Iago's most trusted war generals—opened the lid of the crate just enough to slip three books inside. At the very least, Iago's captors had the decency to respect Bozar's funerary customs. Prior to removing him from the dungeons, he was asked to choose three texts from his personal collection—not because they wished to express kindness towards him, but because they feared inspiring ill-will with the Almighty Dhylo. It was the Almighty's decree that the dead be buried with knowledge; failing to do so would've put those responsible for Iago's burial in an unfavorable position with their patron deity.

Iago couldn't help but wonder if his usurpers would show the same grace to his family, too, when the bodies were finally collected from the streets. Even if his loved ones were tossed into an unmarked, mass grave on the outskirts of Bozar, he hoped they'd be buried with the wisdom they deserved. They may not have been allowed to choose their burial texts, but anything was better than nothing—especially for those who'd done nothing to justify their deaths. The only thing they were guilty of was sharing Iago's blood and surname.

The general and four of his soldiers loaded the crate onto a dingy and rowed towards their final destination. Iago squinted through the hole and caught a brief glimpse of where they were headed. He couldn't be certain, but judging by the landmass's marsh-like shore and jungle trees, it was Tullweine, an uninhabited island off the coast of Quapebet.

Upon reaching shore, the crate was carried inland towards the heart of the jungle. Iago heard the unmistakable sound of shovels against sand while the general's deep, gravelly voice pierced his eardrums:

"Iago Jalhor Zanaki, Third of His Name, former King of Bozar: you are hereby sentenced to death by the will of the Four Lords. You will succumb to a slow and painful death as punishment for your crimes against the kingdom. Your remains will forever lie buried here on the island of Tullweine, where another living creature may never find you. Despite your unforgivable actions, the Almighty demands that we wish for mercy on your soul. On this day, the Zanaki name dies with you."

Iago's heart leapt to his throat as his chest throbbed, but he refused to express fear. His pleadings for mercy would be ignored, and his last thread of pride would be snapped by insatiable shame. He wouldn't give them the satisfaction of hearing him, a king, begging for his life.

Iago stared through the hole in the crate at the setting sun in the distance, knowing it was the last time he'd ever see one of the greatest wonders of the realm. As his throat thickened with emotion, something caught his eye: a twinkle of golden light that clung to the trunk of a nearby palm tree. Before he could blame dehydration or exhaustion for making him see something that wasn't there, the light faded enough for him to identify a tiny figure with stick-like limbs and a humanoid head no larger than a scallop.

Even from a distance, Iago spotted a teardrop rolling down the creature's cheek. The creature, a sprite, couldn't read the king's mind, but Iago pushed a thought toward it anyhow: *Goodbye, old friend.* As if it *could* read Iago's mind, the creature lifted one of its arms—a final farewell—before disappearing in a flash of golden light.

Not a moment later, he felt himself being lifted once again. As the crate was lowered into a freshly dug hole, he peered through the circular opening once more and saw nothing but sand. He quickly tore off a piece of his tattered tunic, bunched it up, and stuffed it into the hole. He'd suffocate anyhow, but it would've been a much less excruciating death if he managed to avoid inhaling sand granules.

As he listened to heaps of sand being poured atop the crate, Iago salvaged his last moments by feeling around in the darkness for one particular text: a blue leatherbound book of ancient Bozari scripture. He opened all three books until he found the right one—the only one whose pages had been almost entirely hollowed out.

A sigh of relief escaped him when he felt a familiar object nestled into the hollowed pages. He was grateful his captors hadn't been intelligent enough to open it. If they had, the reason for Iago's death sentence—and the fall of the entire Zanaki family—would've fallen into another's hands.

Iago curled up in the fetal position with the object clutched in his fingers. He saw nothing in the darkness, but he imagined he could see it with perfect clarity: the diamond-shaped slab of iron, thick around the edges like some sort of tray, with a small fragment of moonrock fused to the center.

He'd found it accidentally not five years earlier, and when he discovered what power the magical object held, he'd unknowingly sealed his own fate. He could've used it in this moment to free himself, but he didn't. He'd done more than enough to earn his sentence—that, and his survival was meaningless so long as everyone and everything he'd ever loved was gone.

It was only right, he thought, that the object died with him. The last remaining piece of the Lunar Staff—a scepter once wielded by the moon goddess, Edea—could turn even the greatest among humankind into monsters, hungry for power and authority. Such a divine thing was never meant to end up in a mere mortal's clutches. Maybe no living soul would ever find Iago buried several feet within the sandy hills of Tullweine, but they'd never find the reason for his downfall, either. That assurance made him certain that his death, however warranted, wouldn't be in vain.

As his lungs strained for one last breath of air, Iago's hollow blue eyes filled with tears. He instinctively brought a hand to his face to wipe them away, and when he did, he saw a shimmering golden glow emitting from his fingers.

With his last breath, Iago began to laugh. He hadn't wept golden tears since before he found the last piece of the Lunar Staff. As he lost consciousness, Iago accepted his demise and prepared for his first meeting with the gods in the heavens. The last fifty days left him wondering if the gods would welcome him home with open arms, and now he knew for certain that they would.

BOOK ONE: ALLIES

1989 Post Creation

Arian Cristos, Lord Hand of Taundosa, didn't care for the north.

Of course, one's definition of *the north* depended greatly on one's place of birth. The Isalders of Glacier Bay, for example—the northernmost continent—referenced the barren, jagged Ealair Mountains inhabited by ruthless clansmen and ravenous beasts. The people of Quapebet might've referenced either the empire's agricultural districts or its many swampy wetlands. In Carthe, Arian's native continent, *the north* referred to everything above the Ngora Valley desert.

Of the four northern territories, Arian had his reasons for frowning upon each of them. Caedia, a port province and the northernmost Carthinian territory, was a place of pure chaos. Travelers from across the realm fought tooth-and-nail to barter whatever they could with whomever they could, and when that didn't work, they did what was necessary to return home with coin jingling in their pockets. Courtesans flanked the streets at all times of the day, hoping to catch the eye of a handsome sailor or traveling merchant before they returned home. Thieves and rapists lurked in the shadows, concealed by alleyways and darkened street corners, awaiting unsuspecting victims.

The Violet Forest spanned across the majority of northern Carthe, and while its unique beauties were abundant, it wasn't like the realm's other woodlands. Native tribes prowled the land in search of travelers to steal from, rape, and sometimes eat, depending on their customs. Woodland creatures, far too familiar with being hunted, seldom left the safety of their tree or cave dwellings, forcing humans to survive on little other than berries and nuts. Criminals and predators of all kinds used the forest as their hunting ground: after all, nothing was illegal in the Violet Forest, and nobody—not even royalty or nobility—could escape those who'd become one with the land.

The kingdom of Kanibar was perhaps the nicest and most similar to the southern territories. Arian had only visited thrice in his lifetime, and with each trip, he came to the same conclusion: Kanibar resembled the eastern country of Akkinor more than it did Carthe. Its ancient history and cultural identity had been lost to time, now existing only in texts and art, just to be replaced over several decades by what the Kanish believed a stable society to be. Arian often wondered if the Kanish were aware of how closely their homelands reflected the kingdoms of Akkinor—a place most Carthinians chose to despise, even if they were unaware of the reason for their animosity.

The last of the four northern territories was the worst of them. Dofell had been the center of the world during the old days: it was the first established Carthinian civilization, the original division between the north and the south, and the magical capital of the continent. It was said that, long ago, a portal between the mortal world and the heavens existed in Dofell—a portal capable of bringing magic and divinity to the realm on the gods' behalf.

The Great City (a nickname for Dofell, as the words 'city' and 'kingdom' were used interchangeably during the old days) had fallen almost two hundred years before Arian's birth. The reasons for its downfall were as numerous as they were unmendable. Whatever magic still lingered in Carthe certainly hadn't stayed in a place marked by such dreariness. Enormous, ghastly stone walls encased the entire kingdom, breaking all ties to its neighbors and isolating it from the world.

The Lord Hand of Taundosa didn't normally travel beyond the south, but when his queen gave a command, Arian obeyed. She'd sent him to collect a package from one of her contacts in Caedia—him, not a troop of soldiers or a handful of trusted knights. Queen Reyna Caltheos hadn't told him what it was or why she needed it so desperately, but she trusted no other like she trusted her Lord Hand, so only he could make the exchange.

Traveling across the barren Ngora Valley was an arduous task for the average person, but it hadn't been too difficult for Arian. He was a mage, for one: seldom was there a problem magic couldn't solve, especially for a practitioner of his skill. For another, he'd spent most of his life familiarizing himself with his homeland and its many dangers. The continent didn't favor natives over foreigners, but one's odds of surviving were much greater when one was raised within the chaos.

Now, after a surprisingly quick and easy trip across the desert, Arian had finally arrived at the gates of Dofell. Other than a camel, he was alone, with nothing but a satchel slung over his shoulder and a gold-plated dagger strapped to his waist. About a dozen groups of people, all accompanied by Dofelli traveling guides wearing blue-and-yellow face coverings, loitered by the gates as they awaited their cue to cross the threshold into the desert.

Perhaps half of them would make it to the gates of Taundosa. The other half would die on the journey. Some would succumb to dehydration and starvation. Others would be too weakened by the boiling sun and torrid desert heat to muster the strength to press forward. The especially unlucky travelers would find themselves slaughtered by desert tribes and left for the vultures.

After trading his camel for a horse, Arian took the steed's reins and guided him towards the opposite side of the kingdom, where an identical set of gates led directly into the Violet Forest. He thought he knew exactly what to expect while passing through the kingdom: shoeless children dressed in rags, begging on the streetcorners for food; gaunt-faced adults, practically skeletons, trying to make a living while desperately fighting the urge to fall asleep—or die—where they stood; and feral hounds, limping and balding from malnutrition, digging through piles of waste in search of scraps.

Other than the hounds, Arian didn't spot anything else that normally welcomed him when he visited the kingdom. In fact, what he found was unlike anything he'd thought to expect in Dofell.

Upon passing the heart of the kingdom—the tiny, half-dead villages surrounding the Phyre family's extravagant palace—he saw hundreds, if not thousands, of people flooding the streets. Most were Dofelli, of course, but he recognized people from other Carthinian cultures, too. The steely, azurite-blue gazes of Bozari natives were impossible to misidentify, as were the broad noses and feline eyes of Kanish natives.

The Phyre family soldiers (normally stationed *within* the palace walls, not beyond them) stood in a perimeter around the palace, their shields connected like a wall of iron and their spears pointed at the crowd to keep the shouting civilians at bay. A dark cloud rolled away, allowing the sun's rays to highlight the sweat on the soldiers' brows. The civilians were armed only with stones, and so long as they neglected to use the rocks as weapons, the soldiers would leave them be.

Knowing he had a job to complete for his queen, Arian didn't linger. He pushed through the crowd, careful not to draw attention to himself by upsetting the commoners, and tried to make sense of what the people were hollering. Their garbled voices blended together, their demands fading into oblivion, as the shouts intermingled with sobs from those who recognized that their cause was a lost one.

The angry crowd hadn't been enough to stop him, but one sight *did* bring him to a halt: an adolescent girl, caked in grime from head to toe, peering into a hole in the trunk of a dead tree. Her hair was matted to her neck and back with filth, masking its true color, and when Arian turned to catch a glimpse of her face, he saw that her onyx eyes were jaundiced, her teeth were rotted, and she hadn't any fingernails.

"Pardon me." Arian approached her, keeping his steed close to his side, and cleared his throat when she didn't seem to hear him over the roaring crowd. "Pardon me, miss. Whatever are you doing?"

The girl, like so many others in Dofell, had clearly been affected by starvation-induced madness. She was muttering to herself, eyes darting in every direction, and twitching uncontrollably—either because of the bugs crawling along her scalp or the hungry voices echoing in her head. Arian couldn't be sure.

"*Alb narez lave fazeeb.*" Her hushed tone grew louder and shriller when she repeated herself. "*Alb narez lave fazeeb! Alb narez lave fazeeb!*"

Arian translated the Dofelli tongue with ease: *He has come back.*

"Who's come back, dear one?" He extended a hand, intending to set it comfortingly on her shoulder, but retracted it when he saw the louse crawling in her hair.

She grinned and pointed to the hole. "*Xib lizqe!*"

"The sprite." A frown formed on his lips. He wasn't sure he'd understood her correctly. "What sprite?"

The girl laughed so hard that her chest caved inwards, and her lungs strained against her ribs, with so much childlike wonder that it breathed life back into Dofell's sordid ambience.

When her laughter didn't fade, Arian took a few steps backwards and clicked his tongue for the steed to follow. A strange feeling had washed over him, like he'd stumbled upon something he wasn't meant to see. The poor girl was ill—mentally as well as physically—and it didn't feel right to wait around for a moment of lucidity that probably wouldn't come.

As he walked off, Arian tossed one final glance over his shoulder. The girl appeared to be playing: she crouched down below the hole in the tree, and after a few seconds, she popped up as if to scare a rodent hiding in the trunk. Had Arian blinked, he would've missed the rodent in question: a tiny figure bathed in shades of leafy greens and browns, with two arms and two legs in human form, giggling as loudly as the girl herself. When the girl looked back, sensing Arian's eyes on her, the figure disappeared into the darkness of the tree, and the girl pleaded for the creature to play with her again.

A shiver traced Arian's spine from the nape of his neck to his tailbone. He mounted his horse and galloped to the other side of the kingdom, where a handful of guards were stationed at the gates. After dismounting, he approached one of the soldiers and removed a small golden token from his pocket: a token stamped with the sigil of the Cristos family on one side, and Taundosa's emblem on the other.

The guard stared at him impatiently. "May I help you?"

"I am Lord Arian Cristos of Taundosa, Hand of the Queen to Reyna Caltheos." Arian tossed the token at the soldier, who caught it swiftly and examined both sides before returning it. "I have business in Caedia, but I must ask you to send word to Queen Reyna on my behalf as quickly as possible. You'd do well to deliver my message to your king, too."

The soldier raised a bushy black eyebrow. "I'd be most obliged, my lord. What's the message?"

Arian's dark eyes flickered over to the wrought-iron gates. The Violet Forest was visible on the other side—as were the tattered remains of Kanish flags and the still-burning remnants of campfires, just barely concealed by thick foliage. A hot, uneasy lump settled in his gut. These weren't signs of a struggle or an attack, but of scouts. Spies.

"You have a sprite infestation," Arian told the soldier. "Magical creatures are all but extinct here in Dofell, as you know, but sprites are rather common in Kanibar. They're tricky little things—some say they're the only spies in the realm who can never be captured. There's a bit of uproar happening in the heart of the kingdom, too, as I'm sure you're aware. I noticed a somewhat equal number of Dofelli and Kanish commoners making demands of your fellow soldiers. Both of these things, paired with the presence of scouts just up ahead, suggest Kanibar has set its sights on Dofell." He paused and chewed on his lower lip. "Might as well ask Queen Reyna to relay the message to Aurelia of Akkinor, too. I have a feeling we shall need her."

The soldier's tanned, golden skin turned gray. "My-My lord?"

"The people seem to know something you don't, sir. I suspect your king remains unaware of it, too. The trees in Dofell have begun to speak again—that can mean nothing if not invasion. Proceed with caution, good man, and send word as soon as you can."

The soldier barely let Arian finish before he turned on his heel and darted for the heart of the kingdom. When the other soldiers at the gates turned to Arian with panic glistening in their eyes, he forced the most reassuring smile he could muster and politely requested that they open the gates for him.

Still feeling their eyes on the back of his head, Arian mounted the steed once more and set out to complete his quest. As he stared ahead at the grassy hills and blooming wildflowers, he sensed something watching him and jerked his head to the left. There, a palm-sized figure with human limbs hissed at him while perched on a wire-thin tree branch.

He sighed and turned his gaze to the forest again. "Go home, sprite. Tell your master that I know, and soon enough, the others will, too."

Arian didn't know if the creature obeyed him or not, but that didn't matter. There were undoubtedly dozens of its kind lurking throughout Dofell, gathering intel and collecting the kingdom's secrets, at their master's behest: Willem Trevas, King of Kanibar.

I

Aurelia Brentwood had always been fond of viewing the world from above. One didn't experience nearly as much from the ground as they did from the branches of a tree or the watchtowers atop stone walls—or, for the Queen of Akkinor, from the back of a dragon.

It was as if she were gazing down at a map of the realm, able to pluck ships from the sea like they were figurines placed on a sheet of parchment. Viewing the ocean from such a vast distance made it appear as though the seas were still, like a magnificent painting rather than one of the gods' greatest creations. Islands were nothing more than squiggly drawings in shades of brown and green. Even the rolling hills, deserts, and forests seemed like nothing more than illustrations. Perhaps they *were* illustrations—not drawn by the realm's greatest mapmakers, but by the gods themselves.

If there were anything Aurelia loved more than observing the world from above, it was flying. She was one of a handful of living souls who knew what it was to cut through the air so quickly that even the wind was rendered silent, to feel her belly crawl up to her throat while diving downwards at an incredible speed, and to feel the clouds parting over her skin while she climbed towards the sun, inching so close to the miraculous ball of light that she could feel its heat on her face.

What she loved most about flying, though, was her companion. Halvor, the only full-sized dragon known to the modern world, was more than just the queen's preferred method of transportation—he was her most loyal ally. He'd be devoted to her until the day she died, and when she was gone, he'd maintain that loyalty by servicing her eldest daughter until she, too, was gone.

After leaving the Folly, her native kingdom, at dawn that morning, they flew north to Sadia and followed the coastline along the entire country. They admired Sadia's snowcapped mountains, the Laynoan bronze mines, the cliffs of Holos, and the infamous Myran vineyards. They'd even taken a brief detour inland to see the colorful wildflower fields of Omara, then south of Akkinor to admire the marshes of northern Quapebet. Now that their excursion had come to an end, they were destined, once again, for the Folly.

As always, Halvor landed carefully at the rear of the palace gardens. When she first introduced him to the world five-and-a-half years prior, she'd ordered her men to extend the gardens and the palace grounds for her most valiant protector. The newest portion of the gardens contained everything a dragon might need: an enormous grassy field for lounging and sleeping, a pond for fresh drinking water, and plenty of space for stretching his wings and running in preparation for takeoff. Halvor's sanctuary was, of course, surrounded by flame-retardant materials to protect both the palace and the entire Folly from any potential mishaps.

Despite having the freedom to leave whenever he pleased, Halvor seemed to prefer the calmness and the serenity of his sanctuary. Aurelia often wondered if he chose to remain there because he was accustomed to confinement, but her uncle liked to remind her that Halvor's loyalty demanded that he be wherever she was.

When Halvor settled on the ground, he lowered a shoulder blade and imbedded his talon-tipped wing into the dirt. Aurelia climbed over his shoulder, carefully slid down his wing, and rubbed his side in gratitude when her feet were firmly planted on the ground. He curled his long neck to the side to gaze at her and blinked his golden, reptilian eyes. Smiling, she set her hands on either side of his snout and pressed her forehead to his scales. A hot gust of breath escaped his mouth when he chuffed at her—not a sign of aggression, but of the utmost affection.

"It was another lovely afternoon," she murmured. "Rest now, sweetling. I shall see you tomorrow."

The moment she released him, Halvor yawned and stretched out on the grass. She chuckled to herself as he rested his head on his arms, closed his eyes, and flicked his tail in contentment. As she walked away, she chuckled again, wondering if her ferocious companion was actually a cat in dragon's clothing.

At the far end of the gardens, Aurelia spotted four familiar faces waiting for her by the rear doors of the palace. Ansyl Bolas, Hand of the Queen, looked stoic and serious with his hands clasped behind his back and his lips pressed in a thin line. Two members of the queen's Assembly of advisors, Henry Rudal and Megara Witton, were trying—and failing—

to mask their disapproval with forced smiles, but it was impossible to miss the way their objections simmered in their eyes.

The final face awaiting her return was (not at all to her surprise) the only one of the foursome grinning from ear to ear. Jack Ashford, King Consort of Akkinor, leaned against a sturdy marble statue with his arms folded over his chest and one leg casually crossed over the other. His teeth sparkled against the sunlight when he smiled at his wife, and as she approached the group, he maintained his stance while the others immediately bowed or curtsied.

"Your Grace." Ansyl tipped his head in greeting. "I do hope it was a pleasant trip. Now that you've returned—"

"What a landing!" Jack captured her attention by wrapping her in an enormous bear hug, spinning her as he lifted her from the ground, and smothering her cheeks with kisses. While she laughed at his silliness, the others averted their eyes. "I thought we'd need to extend the gardens a bit more after Halvor leveled that fountain, but I daresay he's gotten the hang of it!"

"His spatial awareness was nearly destroyed after so many years apart from the realm, but it's slowly returning to him." Aurelia chuckled as Jack knelt before her, set his hands on either side of her swollen belly, and pressed a kiss to her navel. "How fares our little prince?"

"*Princess*. I'm certain of it." He pressed his ear to her belly just in time for a massive kick, making him grin again. "The sound of my voice continues to rile her, so I'd say she's perfectly well."

As Aurelia laughed, Lord Rudal cleared his throat. "Forgive my directness, Your Grace, but I believe I speak for the entire Assembly when I say you shouldn't be flying in such a condition. The medics have strongly advised against it. When we heard you'd left for a flight today—"

"Our medics weren't trained to work in a world with dragons," Aurelia interrupted. Lord Rudal clenched his jaw and bowed his head. "In the old days, dragonriders took to the sky in every condition. Ancient scholars— many of whom were medics, too—believed that flying encouraged healing and increased one's stamina. A bit of fresh air and adrenaline can have wonderful effects on the human body. Dragons aren't so wild as to be indifferent to their riders' needs, either. If it were unwise for me to fly in such a condition, Halvor wouldn't have allowed it. He refused to take me out for three seasons when I was carrying the young prince, if you recall."

"We understand, Your Grace, but—" Lady Witton started.

"I won't hear another word of it." Aurelia raised an eyebrow at her three advisors. "I take it you haven't come here simply to scold me for flying, either. What do you need?"

Jack offered her his arm as the group strolled into the palace. "We have a few unexpected visitors today, my love. With the Changling coming up so quickly, it seems those in need of an audience with you have all decided to come at once. They'd like their matters resolved before the chaos begins."

"Who's here?"

"Your uncle, for one, and Duke Rilian Crew, for another. There are others, but I can't remember their names."

Aurelia cracked a smile. "Gods forbid it."

As the couple laughed, Ansyl cleared his throat. "Might I suggest a quick change of clothing before the audience, Your Grace?"

Aurelia froze for a moment—not because she took offense to his words (he was, after all, entirely in the right), but because he reminded her fiercely of the last man to stand in the Lord Hand's shoes: Linden Elliot, her dearest friend for the first five-and-twenty years of her life until her brother cut his throat. Linden had never found her stinking of smoke or covered in ash after a flight, but rather with mud staining her gown and twigs caught in her hair after reading from the comfort of a tree.

Ansyl was no replacement for Linden, but they shared many of the same responsibilities. Apparently, reminding the queen of the power of appearances was one of them.

While her four companions left to meet their guests in the throne room, Aurelia made her way upstairs to her bedchamber, where she put herself in the trusted hands of her lady's maids. Despite her wind-tousled hair and the smell of smoke sticking to her skin, she chose to save a bath for later in the day for time's sake. She swapped her filthy, ash-covered gown for a clean one, let her maids try their utmost to make something presentable out of her wild locks, and dabbed rose-scented oil onto her wrists to mask the acridity. The only jewelry she wore was her wedding ring and the golden, cylindric locket hanging from her neck—the same locket that, once upon a time, was enchanted to house Halvor in a space between the earthly realm and the heavens.

Aurelia winced when the babe kicked her bladder. Jana, the lady's maid in charge of the others, chuckled and said, "It won't be long now, Your Grace."

"Let us pray they're kinder to my body than their brother was."

The quartet of maids laughed before sending Aurelia on her way. A soldier waiting in the hall offered her his arm as he escorted her through the corridor and down the grand staircase, as he had nearly every day since her belly grew so large that she could no longer see her feet. Her last pregnancy had given everyone in the palace a fright, so now, they went out of their way to cater to her—despite her insistence that she was perfectly fine on her own.

She didn't blame them for being worried, though. The beginning of her pregnancy with her only son, Henry, left her feeling so ill that she'd lost almost twenty pounds after eating nothing but cashews and green apples for five months. Her body was so severely weakened that she'd collapsed while descending a staircase. After ensuring that both mother and babe were all right, the medics confined her to bedrest for the remainder of her pregnancy. Henry hadn't made the delivery easy, either: she'd labored for almost two full days.

It was worth it in the end when she held her son in her arms for the first time, and it still wasn't enough for her to decide against expanding her family further. Four seemed like a good number—after all, both her father and her husband were one of four children. Nobody could ever say she'd failed in her duty by not producing enough heirs, either.

Upon reaching the throne room, surprise brought Aurelia to a brief halt when she spotted about a dozen guests conversing with Jack and her advisors. She'd expected a handful of visitors that day—maybe four or five—but certainly not *thirteen*.

"Your Grace." Her paternal uncle, Lord Andren Normindi of Sadia, was the first to speak as every individual in the room bowed or curtsied in greeting. "I hope I'm not disturbing you. I assumed we'd have a private audience today, but as you can see..."

She smiled as she took her place on her throne. "I might've reserved private audiences for each of you, had you sent written requests, but this kind of thing is bound to happen when urgency is prioritized over communication." Her guests bowed their heads, wincing, as she raised an eyebrow. "Who arrived first?"

"Lord Normindi, Your Grace." Ansyl took his place on his throne to the right of hers while Jack did the same to her left. Lord Rudal and Lady Witton flanked either side of the thrones while the visitors lined up before the queen.

"It's the assassins," Andren said, cutting right to the chase.

She resisted the urge to groan. "Again?"

Her mother's eldest brother grimaced. "For whatever reason, Your Grace, the Sadians haven't taken well to your abolishment of assassins' work. My soldiers recently apprehended approximately fifty individuals who were caught training for it. They've been careful about keeping their movements quiet, but my men have heard whispers from across the kingdom about assassins looking for work. Whatever you'd have me do with the fifty prisoners is crucial for discouraging such illegal activities."

"How many worked as assassins prior to the war with my brother?"

"Uncertain, Your Grace. They're rather tight-lipped about it, despite our best efforts to acquire intel, and we don't wish to torture them into compliance. There doesn't seem to be any preference for age, sex, or status. We've apprehended Sadians from all walks of life: those just starting out in the art of death, and those who have been familiar with it since your beloved mother lived and breathed."

Aurelia set a hand on her belly for comfort. "Is there a reason they've decided to break the law?"

Andren flinched. "It would appear that most of them wish to train for defense."

"Defense against whom?"

"Mages, Your Grace."

"I beg your—"

"On that note, Your Grace, mages have stirred up trouble in Whitshear. *Again.*" Rilian Crew, the Duke of Whitshear, Holos, stepped out of line to stand beside Andren. "The six earldoms within my duchy have been battling one another since the war with your brother. The earldom of Alderwood in particular has the largest population of known mages in all of northern Holos. Its five neighbors live in fear that the Earl of Alderwood will use his newfound magical advantage to assert dominance over them. I, too, fear he may seek to conquer his neighbors— and, subsequently, the entire duchy of Whitshear. I don't wish to be usurped by my twenty-year-old subordinate."

"The earldoms in your charge have never seen eye-to-eye," Aurelia reminded him. "In the old days, their clan families spent centuries fighting over territory and power. They'll take any opportunity to pick fights with one another—magic is nothing more than the most recent instigator for their conflicts. But if you fear Alderwood so greatly, I shall write to the earl about the matter, so he remembers his place."

The red-faced duke nodded, bowed, and left as she turned her attention back to Andren. "I suspect there are hundreds of mages across the country who, even now, refuse to identify themselves for fear of being persecuted as their ancestors were. I abolished the practice of training and deploying assassins because my brother proved that even I, as queen, am not untouchable when assassins are involved. They pose too much of a threat to the peace of our nation. If assassins prevail not because they seek coin in exchange for murder, but because they wish to use the skills required of the practice as preparation for conflict with mages...They're only hindering the progress our country desperately needs to make. Breaking

26

the law in the name of defense against a nonexistent threat is worse than breaking the law for coin or survival."

"The punishment for this crime is a seasons' imprisonment." Andren raised a bushy, graying eyebrow. "Do you wish for me to enact a stricter punishment?"

She nodded. "First-time offenders will be subjected to the punishment as it currently stands, and repeat offenders will face one of two stricter punishments. Those who train and deploy assassins will face three seasons' imprisonment and a fine of twenty silver. Those caught actively working as assassins after two or more warnings will be exiled either to Quapebet or Marooner's Chain, depending on their status. We'll test this method of deterrence in Sadia first, and if the civilians in question respond well, I'll urge the rest of the country to follow suit. If they respond poorly....We'll consider that when the time comes."

Andren bowed. "As you wish, my queen."

As he left the throne room, three nobles passed him on their way inside. Suddenly feeling exhausted, Aurelia suppressed a groan as the newest guests took their places at the end of the line. She had a sinking feeling that with every matter she resolved, an additional five would take their place.

"Madam Knott." Aurelia smiled tiredly at the next person in line. "What can I do for you?"

II

"Lord Baneford was the last of them," Ansyl said. "I've asked the soldiers to close the gates—we're no longer accepting visitors today." His dark eyes flickered over to the advisors as Aurelia nodded. "Lord Rudal, inform the rest of the Assembly of the matters we dealt with today. Everything must be promptly added to our records. Lady Witton, follow Madame Knott to Elderhost to take account of the repairs she requested. We shall need an accurate report so we can request coin from the bank."

As the advisors scurried away, Jack took Aurelia's hands to help her rise from her throne. "I'll have dinner brought to our bedchamber tonight," he declared. A worried crease formed between his eyes. "You've had enough for one day."

Aurelia waved her hand dismissively. "I'm fine. There's only another hour until dinner, anyway. I can manage."

He frowned but didn't press her further. "Where would you like me to take you? Your study?"

"I don't need a chaperone," she retorted, only half-kidding. He offered her a sheepish, lopsided smile in response. "I'd like to see the children for a bit. They'll feign attention depravity when the babe arrives, so we might as well start combatting that now."

He snorted. "Clever thinking."

As the two left the throne room for the nursery, Ansyl hurried to catch up with them. "There are still quite a few matters that require your attention, my queen. You must send word to Alderwood before the duke takes matters into his own hands. The Earl of Mirador, too, was assured you'd write to Lord Tarre tonight about reinforcing its borders. Not to mention the matter in Licaid—"

"There are nine members of the Assembly, Ansyl, including yourself. Surely, one of you can craft three letters on the queen's behalf." Jack set one hand on the small of Aurelia's back as she climbed the steps leading to the second floor, while Ansyl frowned from his stance at the bottom of the staircase. "None of the concerns we heard today are urgent or life-threatening. If you must insist that Aurelia write the letters herself, there's time enough for that in the morning."

Ansyl clenched his jaw, nodded, and walked off. Aurelia flashed Jack a tired, grateful smile as the pair reached the second floor. Now that there were no more meetings to attend or highborn to converse with, Aurelia stepped out of her heeled shoes and sighed in relief when her bare feet touched the cool marble floors. She didn't see a servant rush over to collect her shoes, but when she looked over her shoulder a few seconds later, they were gone.

When they reached the nursery, they lingered in the doorway and watched the three royal children playing on the floor with their governesses, Celesse and Irina. A smile graced Aurelia's lips as she recalled memories from her own childhood when she and Linden sat on that very floor, playing with wooden knights alongside their governess, Estylle. Now, the two were both gone—Linden to the heavens, and Estylle home to Taundosa—and a new generation had taken their places.

It didn't take long for the children to notice their parents. Aurelia dismissed the governesses so she and Jack could take over, and struggled to lower herself onto the floor when her children demanded she play with them. Jack helped her to the ground, worry shimmering in his eyes, and placed a pillow between her back and the side of the wardrobe she was leaning against.

"That was *mine*, Henry!" Halle wailed.

Henry sniffed and held something out of her reach. "I saw it first!"

"You're lying!"

"I'm not!"

"That's quite enough," Jack snapped, seizing the toy in question. "I think I'll play with this today. If you start bickering over a different toy, I shall play with that one, too. Am I understood?"

Halle—who was particularly unfond of being scolded—hung her head in shame. "Yes, Papa."

She elbowed her brother in the side, urging him to respond to their father, but Henry was already distracted by another toy—the same toy Aurelia was turning between her hands, entirely unaware of what she was doing. He crawled to her like a prowling cat, set his small hands on her thigh, and blinked his pleading blue eyes up at hers.

"I play with this one, Mama?" he asked.

She smiled and pressed a kiss to his tiny nose. "Here you are, my love."

"Thank you!" He accepted the toy, then rushed over to show Halle. "Look what Mama found, Hal!"

Halle nodded. "That's nice, Henry. Sit when you play so you don't break it."

Aurelia smiled as her eldest showed her youngest the proper way to use the toy. Halle, Crown Princess of Akkinor, was rather unique: at only five years old, she was perhaps more dutiful, responsible, and well-mannered than most adult highborn in the realm. She had an ancient soul for one so new to the world, and while her worries were numerous, she was wonderfully adept at drawing a smile out of anyone—a trait she'd adopted from her biological grandmother, Katryna Cristos.

Strangely enough, she resembled her grandmother physically, too. She looked exactly like Aurelia had at that age—and Katryna, based on portraits Aurelia saw of her late mother as a child—but unlike Aurelia, she'd inherited Katryna's straight, brunette curls. She was freckled, too, like Katryna was. The only things she'd inherited from Jack's side were her long legs and her eyes: a swirling blend of blue, green, and gray, like the raging tides of the Alkamura Ocean.

Three-year-old Henry, on the other hand, favored Aurelia's biological father when it came to his appearance. Aurelia had never met or even seen Eric Haze in the flesh, but her uncle described him enough for her to know what he looked like. His eyes, like Eric's, were a clear and pale blue, like the cloudless sky. His dark auburn hair was apparently the same color as Eric's, too. He had Jack's face—down to the shape of his eyebrows and the dimple on his chin—but everyone who knew Katryna insisted that Henry had inherited her infectious smile.

For one so young, Henry was as clever as he was dramatic—a trait he'd made known from the start at birth—but very naughty, too. He was extremely intelligent, having begun speaking in full sentences just after his second birthday, but preferred using his brains to stir up trouble. He enjoyed riling and teasing his sisters, but he was stuck to them like glue, too. He liked to be silly like his father, and he was stubborn as a mule like his mother. Consequences didn't mean much to him, but he was surprisingly obedient for a child so meddlesome.

Aurelia turned to the last little face in the nursery, who sat apart from her family while trying to solve a wooden puzzle box. Hyacinth, also five years old, hadn't so much as stood to greet her parents when they arrived: she was too deeply concentrated on the task at hand, and if she knew her parents were there, she didn't show it.

The second of the three (soon to be four) Brentwood children didn't look much like the others. Her pale blonde hair hung in loose banana curls, and rarely did it obey a comb or pins. Her eyes, perfectly round and wide, were dark blue like the midnight sky and always appeared to be twinkling, as if reflecting the stars. She was the smallest of the siblings in both height and weight, and she had a small, circular brown mole below her left eye. She had rather long and slender fingers, too—*perfect for picking pockets,* as the late King Edmund used to say.

She didn't relate to her siblings in personality, either. She was far quieter than her brother and sister, and while she shared Halle's ancient soul, there was something even older about hers, as if she'd lived a thousand lifetimes before this one and remembered each of them. She was unfathomably wise, clever, and intelligent for such a young girl, and it wasn't uncommon for her to leave her tutors speechless—both because of her skill and because they were unable to answer her questions. She couldn't be bothered with most children's toys, either, but rather with hobbies and games typically made for adults.

Aurelia fell pregnant with Halle accidentally while in Carthe—likely during her stay in Taundosa, though she couldn't be sure—and gave birth several weeks early, just under six months after the war with her brother. Two months later, a heavily pregnant lowborn woman arrived at the palace from Northacre, Sadia. The woman, who introduced herself only as Sereia, claimed she'd been one of Archie's unwilling mistresses during his brief reign. After impregnating her, he'd exiled her to Northacre—the most barren and desolate territory on mainland Akkinor—with nothing but a handmaiden for company, and a bag of silver to support them.

After learning of Archie's defeat, Sereia and her handmaiden made the difficult journey back to the Folly, forced to travel in a wagon filled with animal carcasses after a kind hunter offered them transportation. Her labors began almost as soon as they crossed the border from Sadia into the Folly, so within an hour of her arrival at the palace, she'd given birth to a baby girl. She refused to hold or even look at her daughter after delivery, and begged the midwives to take the child away and leave her be. While medics were giving the babe an examination, they noticed telltale signs of an infection—typhus—and immediately opted to examine Sereia, too.

The medics found Sereia dead in her birthing bed, but proceeded with the examination anyhow. After undressing her, they found angry rashes, oozing blisters, and splotchy red spots marring nearly every inch of her porcelain skin. They found something else, too: the letter A tattooed on her shoulder blade, painstakingly etched onto her skin in a hand Aurelia immediately recognized as her brother's.

The unnamed infant faced the god of death himself in the days and weeks that followed. Everyone who tended to her was convinced she'd die, as it was practically unheard of for an infant to survive a case of typhus. Her condition bettered and worsened on a loop until finally, by some divine miracle, she made a full recovery at twelve weeks old. Priests who'd prayed for her believed her survival was a sign from the gods, and claimed she was destined for a greater purpose in the realm.

Unfortunately, the priests were the only ones enamored with the babe. While Aurelia struggled to decide what to do with her brother's bastard, everyone with access to the queen's ear told her that it was best to send the child away to be raised as far from the capital as possible. They believed it was a bad omen to have the child of a traitor anywhere near the throne—that, and they despised Archie so greatly that they wished to destroy any and all reminders of him.

Other than the fact that she herself was adopted, Aurelia remembered something her father once said to Queen Reyna of Taundosa while struggling with her decision: *It's more honorable to love another man's child than to subject the child to a lifetime without love.* Daughter of a traitor or not, the baby was a Brentwood, and Aurelia didn't wish to pretend like the child didn't exist. Instead, after a surprisingly brief conversation with Jack, they decided to raise the babe as their own. The chaos of war reparations prevented an official, public announcement when Halle was born, so the masses believed Aurelia's lie that she'd given birth to fraternal twin girls. Only those who frequented the palace were aware of the truth, and she'd sworn them all to secrecy.

She'd worried for how well she could contain the secret, but as Jack often reminded her, the urge to gossip was no match for the fear of death by dragon.

She named the baby *Hyacinth* after her favorite flower (and the grandmother of her ancestor, Oleander the Great), and after that, her second child never felt like anything but her own. Aurelia didn't know Sereia enough to see her in Hyacinth, but she didn't see much of Archie in the child, either—other than her long fingers and blonde hair, of course.

"Would you like some help, Sisi?" Aurelia leaned forward to tuck a lock of hair behind Hyacinth's ear, but thought better of it when her back strained in protest. "I think your father would be most delighted to assist you."

Jack grunted, as both knew he'd failed every one of his many attempts to solve it. She laughed, and as she opened her mouth to tease him further, the object trapped within the puzzle box—a chocolate truffle—fell onto the ground.

Jack's eyes bugged. "How did she—?"

Halle sighed as she pretended to sail her toy ship over the carpet. "She did it earlier, too. That was inside."

Aurelia and Jack followed Halle's finger when she pointed toward something on the nightstand: a small, hand-carved wooden elephant. The puzzle box had been a gift from Aurelia's uncle in Taundosa, where elephants were abundant, and after she herself failed to solve it, she'd tossed it into a chest of toys in the nursery. She hadn't expected any of her children to show an interest in it, and she certainly hadn't expected any of them to *solve* it.

"Irina gave her the truffle." Halle's cheeks turned pink almost immediately, and her voice lowered to a whisper when she added, "I promised not to tell."

"It's all right." Aurelia turned to Hyacinth, took the discarded puzzle box, and raised an eyebrow. "How did you solve this?"

The princess shrugged. "It was easy."

"That's not an answer," Jack replied.

Exhaling like he'd asked her to recite the entire Creation Story from start to finish, Hyacinth reset the puzzle box and tried solving it once again. By that point, her siblings had lost interest in their toys and were watching her alongside their parents. It took her a few moments, but sure enough, the wooden mechanisms clicked and groaned to allow the trap door to spring open. After handing the solved puzzle to her mother, Hyacinth claimed the chocolate truffle and took a bite, then turned her attention to a different toy.

Aurelia stared at the puzzle box for a moment, still amazed, before handing it to Jack. He studied every inch of it as if looking for some sort of cheat he'd missed before, then looked up at Aurelia with bewilderment illuminating his eyes. She only shrugged as if to ask, *can we really be surprised?*

"I have a bite, Sisi?" Henry asked.

Hyacinth nodded and handed him the rest of her truffle. "You may, but share with Halle."

He nodded, but the bite he took was too big, leaving nothing but a sliver of the hard outer shell for his eldest sister. Halle assured him it was all right, thanked Hyacinth for thinking of her, and politely asked their father to fetch a handkerchief so she could clean the melted chocolate from Henry's fingers.

Hyacinth, disinterested in the toy ships, instead fetched a storybook from her bedside table and began practicing her reading. Both Jack and

Aurelia stifled laughter, knowing she was too much like her mother for her own good.

Aurelia snapped her gaze from her children when a breathless messenger boy appeared in the doorway of the nursery. Jack told Aurelia to stay seated when she attempted to stand, then accepted a small scroll from the boy and brought it to his wife. She ran the pad of her thumb over the wax seal—orange and stamped with the sigil of Horscola, a small farming district in the northern Folly—and frowned.

"Horscola?" She furrowed her eyebrows at Jack. "I haven't received word from Horscola in...well...*ever*."

He shrugged as all three children, curious, gathered on either side of their mother to watch her read the message. She broke the seal and unraveled the scroll, revealing only three sentences written by the magistrate of Horscola.

"What is it?" Jack pressed.

She sighed and rubbed her belly again for comfort. "The magistrate writes on behalf of a shepherd by the name of Torbrook. He reported that several flocks of sheep were slaugh—" She stopped when she saw the three pairs of innocent eyes staring at her. "Several flocks were, uh, *seized* by Halvor this afternoon after our trip. It was a tremendous loss for Torbrook, and he wishes to be compensated for it."

Jack winced. "This isn't the first time Halvor has helped himself to farm animals, either. I assume the magistrate mentioned this, too?"

"Indeed. He urges me to find alternative means of feeding Halvor." Setting the scroll aside, she kneaded her knuckles into her temples to combat a sudden migraine. "I think I shall take my dinner in our room tonight, after all."

***

Well into the night, Aurelia stared at the ceiling with her hands splayed on her belly as Jack snored beside her. She hadn't slept a wink, despite her exhaustion, both because of the stresses of the prior day and the babe ceaselessly kicking her insides.

Too distracted and uncomfortable to lay there a moment longer, she decided a cup of warm milk and honey would soothe her. She climbed out of bed—slowly and painstakingly, and on her own for the first time in three months—and took the candle from her nightstand to light her path as she tiptoed into the hallway. A soldier standing guard nearby offered to acquire whatever she needed or to escort her to her destination, but she refused him and made her way downstairs by herself.

Though any servant would gladly fetch the milk for her, she didn't wish to wake them at such a late hour, and she was familiar enough with the kitchens to find her way around. She didn't open the door when she arrived, though. Soft, murmuring voices conversed in the kitchens, and she knew she'd have to abandon her plan; after all, the servants wouldn't let her sit with them and enjoy a cup of warm milk without feeling like they were expected to dote on her. She wasn't in the mood to be treated like a coddled child.

She lingered for a moment, wondering why they were still awake, and started to turn away before she heard something that caught her attention:

"...whispers of displeasure," a male voice said. "I've a sister in Littlegrove. She says some Omarans have been made uneasy lately: more and more mages are traveling through the kingdom to receive proper training at the monastery, and they've no problem flaunting their power to mortals."

"The queen wonders why so many people continue to train as assassins. It's because of this," a female voice replied. "We mortals can be squashed like ants under boots by mages. These people who've been caught...They know their best chance at facing mages is to train as assassins. Mages have abilities, yes, but assassins are experts in every other area."

"Not to mention the mages who have or wish to have assassins' training." This voice—a young male—Aurelia recognized as belonging to Jack's valet. "They'd be close to unstoppable."

A second female sighed. "Her Grace's heart is true. She only wishes to inspire unity and peace across the country—it isn't her fault that things haven't taken yet."

"Maybe," the first male replied, "but if we're talking about peace, there was more of that when the Scorpion sat the throne."

Aurelia sucked in a breath as the second female gasped. "Are you *mad?*"

"I should hope not."

"The country was in shambles!"

"The *economy* was in shambles. He was foolish, of course, and severe when it came to punishment, but there was none of *this*. Mages sheltered themselves as they always have, and mortals had no reason to fear being destroyed by magic. Fewer people sought to be trained in the art of death. Feuding families and territories put their differences aside to avoid conflict with the new king. The only war we saw was the battle for the throne."

"Give it time," Jack's valet said. "With every new decree comes a period of adjustment. The country will come around—especially with the dragon as encouragement."

Aurelia didn't stick around to hear the rest of the conversation. She rushed back to her bedchamber as quickly as her body would allow, head spinning and stomach churning, as she wondered how on earth her plans to better her country had led to her people comparing her reign to Archie's—with her brother as the more favorable option, nonetheless.

She skidded to a stop just a few paces from her bedroom when she saw two figures standing outside of her door: a wide-eyed and alert Ansyl, and a groggy, half-asleep Jack. Ansyl was dressed in his day clothes with his hair combed and his face already shaved, whereas Jack had his black locks sticking out in every direction, and wore nothing but his underthings.

Jack raised a tired eyebrow. "Where were you?"

"I couldn't sleep. I went for a walk." She turned her eyes to Ansyl. "What are you doing here at this hour?"

He grimaced. "There's urgent news from Clyren, Your Grace."

When she realized he was holding his cloak, she sighed. "When do we leave?"

"As soon as you're dressed."

III

A two-year-old girl squealed in delight, thrashing in her governess's arms, as she clung to the bronze fence separating them from a handful of zebras sunbathing on the grass. Her excited shrieks echoed throughout the property when two devious marmosets escaped their enclosure to pester the zebras. She clapped her little hands in delight when the monkeys darted across the zebra enclosure, only to slither through the bars separating the zebras from the tigers.

Aurelia hoped the monkeys were as fast as they looked. It'd be a shame if the child's playful visit to the menagerie was tarnished by the animal food chain.

She'd wanted to do away with the menagerie after reclaiming her throne, as it'd been just another way for her brother to flaunt his wealth and power during his time as king. He'd destroyed Sherwood Vineyards (once the largest in Myra) to construct the menagerie, which he'd then filled with various exotic animals from Quapebet. Aurelia planned to send the animals back and to reconstruct the vineyard, but the country couldn't afford it. Instead, she decided to utilize the menagerie as a financial opportunity: now, it'd become Clyren's main source of income, as Akkinorians came from near and far to catch a glimpse of Quapebet's native creatures.

Now, four years after the war, Aurelia stood in the symposium of Sherwood Manor for an entirely different reason—one far more gruesome than the destruction of a vineyard.

Voices mumbled behind her, but Aurelia paid them no heed as she watched little Daisy Sherwood marvel at the zebras from a window in the manor's meeting room. There wasn't much to be discussed amongst the nobles in the room until Daisy's father joined them, but as time passed, it became clear to all that Glenn Sherwood, Duke of Clyren, wouldn't be making the audience that day.

Sighing, she turned from the window and the menagerie to face the twelve people gathered in the symposium. Other than Ansyl, the only person she was glad to see was Silas Crowland, Lord of Myra. The others—Duke Sherwood's highborn subordinates—weren't exactly the people she'd hoped to converse with when she arrived in Clyren that morning.

"I suppose we should start without the duke, then." Nobody replied as Aurelia sunk into the seat at the head of the ovular table, struggling to lower herself while her belly corrupted her balance. "As you know by now, the duchess was attacked while traveling home to Clyren from Sadia. The handmaiden who'd accompanied her was spared, but the soldiers tasked with their protection were killed during the attack. The handmaiden managed to pay a driver to take her and Delphine to the palace—the closest safe haven to the location of the attack—but the duchess had passed on before they arrived."

Lord Crowland closed his eyes and shook his head. "She wasn't deserving of such a morbid end. Nobody is."

"The way she looked..." The Earl of Southport, a small territory within Clyren, stared off into nothingness with unblinking eyes. "I've been to battle three times in my life, and I've never seen something so grotesque."

Aurelia winced at the reminder. Before anyone could reply, a shriek echoed throughout the castle, so shrill and riddled with pain that Aurelia, too, felt as though she were suffering the same heartache as poor Glenn Sherwood.

When the duke greeted Aurelia and Ansyl over an hour earlier, unaware of the reason for their visit, he'd been full of smiles, jokes, and laughter. But when Aurelia told him what'd happened and stepped aside to show him, he'd taken one look at his wife's body and collapsed to his knees, wailing in a way Aurelia had never heard from a grown man before. He'd thrown himself over Delphine's body, and when anyone tried to pull him away from her, he responded by asking them to kill him instead. It was one of the most heartbreaking things Aurelia had ever seen—both because of the duke's reaction, and because of the horrors inflicted upon the duchess.

It'd taken everything Aurelia had not to vomit onto her shoes when she first saw Delphine's body. The driver who'd brought her to the palace had set her atop wooden crates of goods on the back of a wagon, as it was the only place for her to lay. Her hands were placed over her stomach, and her long, silky auburn hair cascaded over her shoulders—the handmaiden's doing, to draw attention away from Delphine's injuries.

Her face was ashen, and her lips were still curled in a painful grimace. If that weren't enough, her beautiful face—along with her arms—were covered in enormous welts, bruises, and splotchy red spots. One of her fingers was visibly broken, and four of her fingernails had been completely ripped off.

"The Lord Hand has already sent word to Sadia about the attackers." Aurelia kept her voice steady, hoping her composure would distract the nobles from the duke's sobs. "The handmaiden who accompanied the duchess was able to give descriptions of each of them—there's a good chance they'll be apprehended rather quickly. Lord Normindi will extradite them to Clyren to stand trial."

The duke's second-in-command nodded. "Excellent. Did the handmaiden offer any insight into what prompted the attack? Was it an attempted theft, perhaps?"

When Aurelia met Ansyl's gaze, he cleared his throat and answered on her behalf: "Delphine and the others were caught in a snowstorm while leaving Sadia. Their torches and lanterns were extinguished, so the duchess used her abilities as a fire mage to light their path. Her magic drew the attention of the attackers. According to the handmaiden, these men weren't particularly pleased to find a mage traveling upon their roads."

"Gods be good." A baron (whose name Aurelia couldn't recall) pushed his spectacles farther up the bridge of his nose when sweat caused them to slide. "Did they know she was the archmage of Myra?"

"The handmaiden didn't report any mention of it," Ansyl replied. "I assume they were unaware of it—nearly everyone knows that all reigning nobles are mortals. Delphine was the one exception. A handful of Sadian peasants wouldn't have known that a Myran duke married a lowborn mage. It isn't exactly a common occurrence."

"That's partly why I've come today," Aurelia added. "It was surprising when the duke requested permission to marry a lowborn, but even more so when he revealed that Delphine was a mage. As soon as she gave birth to Daisy, she assured the existence of magic within a reigning bloodline. That made her the perfect candidate for Myra's archmage. Unfortunately, now that the gods have called her home, Myra's coven is without a leader."

The Earl of Southport snorted. "We have more important things to address than the coven—like, say, what to do with Daisy now that her mother is gone. She needs to be trained properly, and the only other mages in Myra are lowborn. We can't hire a simpleton from the villages to train the future Duchess of Clyren in magic."

"Just because they're lowborn doesn't mean they're simpletons," Aurelia snapped at him. He flushed and mumbled an apology that she didn't bother addressing. "None of us have any control over the class we're born into, and it would do you well to remember that knowledge can be found anywhere."

"Maybe, but that doesn't change anything. Our best option is to send her to the monastery." Another baron—a dwarf, who fought alongside Aurelia during the battle with Archie—sipped from a chalice and shrugged. "She needs to be trained properly by her own kind. There are plenty of decent and honorable priests at the monastery to oversee her education. Most priests aren't mages, but they've all worked closely and privately with lowborn mages for years now. They'll have access to trustworthy mages who can assist them in educating Miss Daisy."

Aurelia pressed her lips together. "Is that the wisest idea?"

"It's our best and only option, Your Grace."

"She's just lost her mother. The duke has just lost his wife." She rubbed the side of her belly with the heel of her palm when she felt a tight cramping sensation. "It isn't right for her to be taken away from her only parent, nor is it right for the duke to be separated from his daughter after burying his wife."

Lord Crowland exhaled. "This decision is the duke's to make. He may not wish to see a living reminder of his wife each and every day. But he may not wish to see a living piece of his wife removed from his home, either."

An idea struck the queen. "If he wishes to keep his daughter in Clyren with him, then perhaps we can task a priest at the monastery—and a trustworthy mage of their choosing—with training Daisy here at the manor. The only other option I can see is leaving Daisy to be trained by Myra's coven."

"That's quite impossible, Your Grace," the first baron told her. His spectacles fogged up with hot breath as soon as he opened his mouth. "The late duchess became highborn when she married, yes, but the mages in her coven—the mages in *every* coven—are lowborn. We can't allow Daisy to be trained solely by lowborn mages. It'd be a disgrace."

Aurelia narrowed her eyes at him. "Mind your tone, my lord. I won't tell you again: being lowborn has no impact on the quality of their characters, and that's what matters most. The only reason we need a highborn archmage is because highborn have crucial experiences that lowborn, unfortunately, do not—like leadership and managing funds for a large organization. Even some highborn, as seen with my brother, lack that kind of knowledge. We're respecting tradition for now by searching for a highborn, but if we fail, we must turn to our commonfolk to save us." She cleared her throat. "Regardless of their status, mages are crucial for our prosperity in the years to come. Carthe has already surpassed us in every way when it comes to magic, and it won't be long before other civilizations adopt the western perspective, too. Akkinor would become the only place in the realm where magic continues to be scorned and ignored, and we'd lag behind while the rest of the world prospers."

"Her Grace is quite right," Ansyl muttered, shooting a look of warning at the now-cowering baron. "In places like Taundosa and Kanibar, magic has thrived for centuries because of one thing: community. Creating covens forced them to grow together, giving their homelands a nearly unbreakable military unit. Her Grace was wise to establish covens in each Akkinorian kingdom, but as we all know, every military organization needs a leader. Without an archmage, Myra will fall behind while your neighbors thrive, and soon enough, your kingdom will be the weak link that prevents Akkinor from reaching its fullest potential."

Aurelia offered him a tired smile, grateful for his support. "Precisely. In the other kingdoms, I managed to appoint highborn archmages: not individuals belonging to reigning noble families, but distant relatives of those who serve our country. They may not rule, but they're still highborn. It was a stroke of luck when Duke Sherwood married Delphine, thus offering the perfect candidate for Myra's archmage, but there are no other mages in this kingdom with highborn ties—none that I know of, anyway. When we find someone with the necessary qualifications, they can mind the coven *and* assist in Daisy's training."

When nobody replied, she raised an eyebrow and studied every hesitant, uneasy face at the table. "Well?" she demanded. "You shouldn't have needed an explanation from me to understand the importance of this. You shouldn't have needed the duchess to die for you to continue searching for other highborn mages in Myra, either. That's been an ongoing task for years now—so don't tell me you haven't found a single person who may qualify for this position."

"We've been searching, Your Grace," Lord Crowland said quickly. The bear of a man—much kinder and gentler than his appearance suggested— scratched at his neck when a nerve-induced rash formed on his skin. "Our search hasn't proved fruitful yet, but...may I be frank?"

"Of course."

"The duchess's murder, among other things, has proven that our country hasn't yet come to terms with the reemergence of magic. Some of our people may be accepting of mages and their power, but others have expressed their disapproval. They worry that Akkinor is adopting too much from Carthe. Others worry for the very thing that happened to poor Delphine."

Aurelia felt her cheeks warm. "The Assembly is currently approving an addition to the Accords that I developed last season. The new law will prohibit the discrimination of mages: any verbal or physical abuse against them, depending on the severity of the crime, will result in either a significant fine or a years' imprisonment. The punishments are subject to change if they're unable to deter crimes against mages."

That seemed to please them, though she could tell by the looks on their faces that they wished she'd addressed the other matter, too: the peoples' fears that Akkinor was becoming too much like Carthe. Aurelia hadn't the energy to discuss that, though. It was a concern that extended to all Akkinorians, not just the Myrans, and it wasn't one Aurelia was eager to discuss.

She knew Akkinor was resembling Carthe more and more with each season that passed, but she was one of few who understood the benefits of such a profound change. The others were still too blinded by Akkinor's past intolerance of Carthinian culture. Of all things, magic was the most crucial factor differentiating Akkinor from Carthe. Now that the former had chosen to welcome magic back to its shores, its people believed the country was only steps away from becoming the mirror image of Carthe—an image tainted by tales of immorality, savagery, and indecency.

"We've discussed all we can without the duke's input." Aurelia stood from her chair, using the table for support, as the nobles mimicked her. "I shall send word to Clyren after the Changling regarding the matter of Daisy's training. In the meantime, I'll offer fifteen gold to any highborn Myran mage who reveals themselves. If we're lucky, Myra will have a new archmage by the end of next season. If not, we shall have to consider an alternate path. Now, I imagine Clyren will be absent from the upcoming Changling, in which case..."

Aurelia trailed off and set a hand on her stomach when a sharp, aggressive pain struck her in the abdomen and spread to her pelvis and lower back. Ansyl was at her side in an instant, but she waved him off when he asked if she was all right. She clenched the edge of the table in her free hand, squeezed her eyes shut, and tried her best to breathe through the pain as a soft whimper escaped her lips.

As the pain subsided, she exhaled and opened her eyes. Her face burned when she saw half of the nobles averting their gazes by staring down at the table, and the other half staring at her like she was carrying a contagious disease instead of a child.

Until that moment, she hadn't realized there wasn't a single woman in the room with her.

"Your Grace?" Lord Crowland, the only man among the nobles who looked even the least bit empathetic, watched her worriedly. "Shall I summon the medic?"

"No, no..."

Ansyl frowned. "My queen—"

"Ready the carriage," she instructed. "The journey back to the palace isn't a long one, but I'd rather not deliver a babe in the back of a moving carriage. Let's not risk it by delaying our departure." As he rushed out of the symposium to obey her command, she looked around at the nobles and forced a smile. "Look after the duke, and send word to the palace immediately with any news."

The Earl of Southport coughed awkwardly. "Shall we...Shall we send a midwife to accompany you in case—"

"Good day, gentlemen."

She turned on her heel and left, and as soon as the door closed behind her, she hunched over with her hands on her knees to combat another contraction, a silent scream threatening to tear through her teeth. At the exact same time, Glenn Sherwood—wherever he was—released a howl so filled with agony that Aurelia's discomfort felt inconsequential in comparison.

As she took a few torturous steps forward, still hunched over, her eyes began to burn with tears. The droplets made a ticking sound as they fell to the floor with each step she took, leaving a trail of glittering golden tears behind on the tiles.

***

"And she has all of her fingers?" Bryan asked.

Jack grinned. "All twelve of them."

"He's only jesting." Jack's younger brother directed the words toward his eldest daughter, who'd gasped in alarm at her uncle's joke. "Would you like to hold your cousin, darling?"

Aurelia watched from her bed, smiling, as thirteen-year-old Briar sat in a nearby rocking chair while Jack placed a tiny bundle of blankets in her arms. When the babe stretched, breaking free of her swaddle, Briar took the opportunity to count the princess's fingers herself. The adults in the room laughed, and the other children—Briar's older brother, Arthur, and two younger siblings, Callum and Daphne—immediately gathered around the rocking chair to admire the newborn.

Bryan's wife, Marianna, chuckled at her children as she lay in bed beside Aurelia. "I think they should like another sibling after today. I'm afraid I can't oblige, though. My body has had enough."

"They're welcome to dote on their cousins as much as they'd like." Aurelia leaned back against the mountain of pillows propped up behind her. She didn't realize she was sharing a pillow with her sister-in-law until she felt wisps of Marianna's brunette locks tickling her face. "Speaking of their cousins—where are the children, Jack?"

"My parents are minding them." He didn't meet her eyes as he stood behind the rocking chair to gaze at their sleeping daughter. "I think they've gone to the crypt to have lunch with your parents."

A fist clenched her heart. "Even Henry?"

"He may not be fond of the crypt, but he's even less fond of being left out."

She smiled and wondered which stories her children were telling her parents' ghosts that day. The crypt below the palace wasn't exactly a place for children, but the young royals always made the excursion when their paternal grandparents visited. Aurelia was grateful for that: she hadn't the strength to talk to her children about her parents while facing empty tombs, and the Ashfords were always diligent about it.

Not long after reclaiming the throne, she'd written to the Quenosi Emperor about locating Jack's parents in exile. It'd taken over a year for the empire to track them down to a small cottage on the coast of Akharia, an agricultural district in northern Quapebet, where they'd been living since their banishment from Akkinor. They were delivered to the Folly and granted a retrial, in which Aurelia and the Assembly collectively agreed they'd been punished enough for something they couldn't control. They may have left King Edmund and Queen Cressida during the shipwreck that led to Aurelia's crowning, but it wasn't right to scorn them for wanting to survive instead of meeting an avoidable demise.

Of course, welcoming the former Lord and Lady of Omara back to Akkinor didn't mean they'd pick up where they left off. Pardoned or not, individuals banished from Akkinor weren't allowed to hold positions of power—not to mention the dishonor associated with potentially removing Bryan from leadership to reinstate his father. It'd been centuries since the last time a nobleman stepped down so his heir could rule in his place, as the line of succession was usually dependent on death alone. Alistair and Bryan had been butting heads more often than not as of late, but for the most part, Alistair seemed to have accepted that he'd never rule Omara again.

Alistair and Isobel were banished not long after Jack was declared dead. Like most Akkinorians, they spent over six years believing their firstborn son had been killed and sacrificed by religious radicals. When they visited the Folly for the first time since their exile and saw Jack at the queen's side—with his child growing in her belly—they'd both fainted where they stood. When they came to and received a proper explanation, Alistair hugged his eldest son for the first time in his life, and the shock on Jack's face was so severe that Aurelia almost laughed.

The Ashfords had been living in their ancestral home, Witton Castle, with Bryan and his family since their return, but they normally visited the Folly once or twice per season. They never left before paying a visit to their late friends in the crypt, though. Aurelia hoped it wasn't survivor's guilt that led them to spend so much time with empty tombs—her parents wouldn't have wanted that.

"Your Grace—" Briar started. When she saw the look on Aurelia's face, she blushed and tried again: "Auntie Aurelia. Have you given her a name yet?"

Aurelia smiled tiredly as the babe cooed in Briar's arms. "Not yet. There's a tradition here in the Folly: we often name our children after relatives and ancestors. I'm afraid I haven't found another name in my family tree that calls to me—never-mind one that starts with *H*."

"All three of your children's names begin with *H*. Why is that?" Briar asked.

Jack snorted. "Your aunt likes things to be orderly."

"That's one reason," the queen said with a chuckle. "I've always liked the letter *H*. It marks the beginning of so many lovely words: hope, home, honor—and Halvor, of course."

"There are a few lovely names on the Ashford side, but only my mother's family produced at least eight children, and I don't wish to name my daughter after mean old Aunt Hattie," Jack teased.

Bryan snorted into a laugh. "Horrid woman."

"I suppose the Ashford side won't be much help, then," Aurelia said playfully.

Arthur—Jack's namesake and the sixteen-year-old heir to Omara—met Aurelia's eyes. "That's not exactly true. My great-great-great grandmother was the youngest of fourteen. She married into the Ashford family."

Aurelia raised an eyebrow. "What was her name?"

"Halyna."

"Halyna." Aurelia smiled as Jack set the fussing babe in her arms. She gazed down at her daughter—who'd been nameless for the last three weeks—and gently ran her fingers over the infant's head of deep brown hair. "I think we've found your name, little one."

Marianna leaned over to kiss the babe's head before climbing out of bed. "All right, my darlings. Let's give your aunt and uncle a bit of peace."

The Ashfords said their goodbyes and left to join their grandparents and cousins elsewhere. Jack closed the door behind him as Aurelia began feeding their daughter, and while he crossed the room to join them in bed, she saw him pull something from the back waistband of his trousers. He tried hiding it behind him as he sat beside her, but when he saw the look in her eyes, he sighed and held it out.

"I was going to wait to give this to you," he muttered. "It's a letter from Reyna."

"Have you read it?"

"No. Neither has Ansyl."

She stared at the golden wax seal—stamped with the image of a phoenix—and sighed. "I'll read it later. I'm sure she's only congratulating us on the birth."

He tossed the letter onto his nightstand, but his aim was sloppy, so the letter fell between the wall and the furniture. He waved his hand dismissively as if to tell her he'd fetch it later. Neither thought about it again as he curled up against her side and watched their tiny, blue-eyed daughter fill her belly.

"Halyna. I like it," he whispered. "How shall we spell it—with an *E* or a *Y*?"

She pondered that for a moment. "Y. That's how they do things in the City of Gold, and she has Taundosan blood, doesn't she?"

He kissed her. "Just enough of it."

Aurelia smiled and looked down at the babe. "Just enough."

IV

Balor Zhoqa, Lord of Kazamir, had a particular distaste for the Nexus.

Located in southern Orestes, the fortress was crafted in the year 891 by the first Four Lords of Bozar: the same men who overthrew the Zanaki family, destroyed the kingdom's monarchy, and split Bozar into four quadrants so they'd each hold equal power within the new feudal system. The lords declared that the Nexus would serve as the capital of Bozar, where the kingdom's leaders would meet twice a year (or more, if needed) to discuss politics and other matters. No blood could be shed within the Nexus, and everyone who entered was granted full immunity from prior crimes, misdeeds, and the like until they left the premises.

Balor was the greatest and most powerful man in Kazamir: a man raised up so high that he could practically feel his fingertips grazing his seat among the gods in the heavens. In the Nexus, however, he was merely one of four equal men, and he was constantly reminded that his seat among the gods had to be shared with three others.

He was a king in every way that mattered, but when technicalities came into play, he was just another highborn.

The Four Lords weren't supposed to meet at the Nexus for another season, but Balor and Lord Jalhor Zhaaran of Orestes summoned them for an emergency audience. The others didn't know what it was about, and frankly, Balor wasn't too concerned: nothing truly worrisome ever happened to threaten Carthe's leaders, and even if it did, both Orestes and Kazamir were rather untouchable—they were allies with a dragon, after all.

When all four of Bozar's leaders gathered around the much-too-big meeting table at the Nexus, Jalhor cleared his throat. "Thank you for coming on such short notice. I would've saved this matter for our meeting next season, but it's rather urgent. Balor and I met with Reyna of Taundosa several weeks ago after she received a worrisome message from her Hand. While traveling to Caedia, Lord Cristos was made aware of what appears to be a Kanish plot to seize Dofell. I have a nephew in Kanibar, as you know, so I wrote to him in hopes that he'd provide some insight. Instead, King Willem himself intercepted the message and responded to me. He confirmed what Lord Cristos feared."

Jalaqas Zoma, Lord of Iseppa—the youngest of the four—shook his head. "That's quite impossible. I fear the king only wishes to get inside our heads by spreading this lie. Kanibar may be able to defeat Dofell in battle, but they haven't the wealth, manpower, or resources needed to maintain it. They'd abandon Dofell and leave it ungoverned within weeks of its conquering."

"None of us at this table are exactly forthcoming about our wealth," Jalhor retorted. "I know you, Jalaqas, made double the amount of coin you reported to the rest of us at the end of last year. And you, Zevir, are facing an even greater debt than you wish to disclose." Zevir Xada, Lord of Tucana, bowed his head in shame. "It's entirely possible that Kanibar has exactly what it needs to take and rule Dofell—if the rest of us can lie about our strengths, why should we believe King Willem would be any different?"

Jalaqas crossed his arms over his chest. "All right, then. Let's say Kanibar really does want to conquer Dofell, and they have what they need to do it. What does that mean for us? I say let them take it: Dofell has been this continent's greatest weakness for centuries. If Kanibar can repair it, the rest of us will benefit from its revival."

"Use your head," Zevir snapped. "Combined, Kanibar and Dofell claim the entire midsection of the continent. Bozar makes a decent amount of our coin through trade and commerce in Caedia, the forest establishments, and the valley. If Kanibar becomes the sole divider between northern and southern Carthe, they'll control all travel and trade. I assume they'd tear down the Dofelli walls, too, which would decrease—or eliminate entirely—the number of travelers passing through the valley. Need I continue?"

Balor gritted his teeth, realizing just how terrible the situation sounded when it was splayed out all at once. He hadn't been worried before, but now...

The lone establishment in the barren Ngora Valley, an inn where travelers could rest and recover from the harshness of the desert, purchased the majority of its supplies—food, drink, linens, tools, and the like—

from Bozar. If the valley was no longer the only route from northern to southern Carthe, there'd be no need for the inn and therefore no need for Bozari goods.

"Queen Reyna doesn't yet know that King Willem has confirmed his intentions," Jalhor continued. "She'll find out soon enough, but as of now, we're the only highborn in Carthe who know. I suppose he's waiting for the opportune moment to announce it to the world—and when he does, we *must* have a strategy prepared. Whatever good he might do for Dofell means little when the rest of Carthe will suffer from it. Taundosa and Krotis will understand this, too."

"We can unite briefly to keep Kanibar from seizing Dofell," Jalaqas suggested. "The combined forces of Bozar, Taundosa, and Krotis would make it impossible for Kanibar to take Dofell. Willem wouldn't stand a chance—particularly if Dofell provides us with what few soldiers they have to aid in their defense."

"It won't matter." All eyes turned to Balor as he gulped wine from the chalice before him. "When word spreads of Kanibar's plans for Dofell, it'll excite the masses. Dofell owes thousands in gold and silver to each of us, and Kanibar will have no choice but to pay the kingdom's debts if they claim it as their own. The commoners will be pleased by that, and even more pleased to know that Dofell has a chance of redemption. If Kanibar backs down, the people will want another kingdom to take its place."

Jalhor nodded. "Precisely. Whatever happens, Dofell *will* be conquered in the near future. If we can't come to some sort of agreement or arrangement with the other Carthinian leaders, we shall find ourselves at war with them—allies or not."

Zevir scratched his balding head. "What brought this on, anyway? Kanibar has had plenty of opportunities over the last few centuries to conquer Dofell. Why now?"

Jalhor exhaled. "Five years ago, we were forced to resolve some of our wrongdoings because of a foreign visitor. Lord Cristos observed a large population of Bozari peasants gathered in Dofell to protest outside of the palace alongside the kingdom's natives. It's my understanding that the commonfolk saw what decency was brought to Bozar, and wish for the same treatment to apply to Dofell."

Nobody had to ask to know who and what he was talking about, but Jalaqas mentioned it anyhow: "What about Akkinor?"

Balor blinked at him, unimpressed. "What *about* Akkinor?"

"Queen Aurelia, however responsible she is for this mess, has a dragon." The young lord shrugged as if the statement needed no explanation. "She's allied with Orestes and Kazamir. If you ask her to

49

stand beside us while we urge Kanibar against taking Dofell, Willem will be frightened into compliance. He won't risk being incinerated. And when the time comes for someone else to take Dofell...Bozar would have the best chance with her on our side."

"Unlikely. She's allied with Taundosa and Runeia, too. She won't betray two of her allies in support of others."

"What if we proposed alliances with Akkinor?" Zevir gestured between himself and Jalaqas. "That way, she'd claim the entirety of Bozar as an ally instead of half of it. She may lose Taundosa and Runeia, but her number of Carthinian allies would remain the same. It's simple: our friendship in exchange for her support."

"It isn't a terrible idea," Jalhor admitted, purple eyes gleaming with worry, "but I can't say for certain that she'd respond well. Either way, the matter of who claims Dofell is one to be addressed at a later date. For now, we need to concern ourselves with Kanibar. The king could seize Dofell tomorrow, for all we know, and Bozar's economy would suffer the consequences almost immediately. I'm certain Taundosa and Krotis would agree. Each of us has friends and allies in both kingdoms, and we must maintain those relationships for as long as we can."

"I'll write to Mekya in Krotis," Jalaqas offered. "If they've heard anything from Kanibar, Lord Keer will tell me. If not, I'll see where they stand on the matter. Hopefully, they'll tell me what the other three Kroti nobles know and desire, too."

"Iseppa has the highest population of known spies in Bozar. I'll call them to court and send them to the northern kingdoms to gather intel," Zevir said. "It may not amount to anything, but if the gods are kind, we'll have keener insight into Kanibar's strategy and timeline."

Balor turned to Jalhor. "I think it's best if you and I pay a visit to Akkinor."

The elderly nobleman frowned. "Queen Reyna—"

"She's our ally for now, but she won't be if the time comes for Taundosa and Bozar to battle one other for Dofell," he interrupted. "If there's a chance that Queen Aurelia might accept our bargain, we need to know now—*before* Reyna gets to her first."

Jalhor, weary, pulled at his graying beard. "We'll leave at dawn, then."

***

"Your Grace, I really must—"

Aurelia smiled but didn't look up from her hands in the dirt. "You needn't hover, Anna. I'm perfectly fine."

"But the Hand—"

"The Hand instructed you to accompany me, not to pester me."

"But—"

The queen laughed. "Anna, dear, if you'd like to return to your embroidery, you may. I don't anticipate that I shall need your services for the time being."

Anna, a young woman hired by Ansyl as Cicely's replacement for Aurelia's lady-in-waiting, hesitated for another moment before scurrying across the gardens towards the palace. The poor thing wasn't fond of the outdoors, and while she was meant to serve as the queen's companion, Aurelia couldn't bear to spend her leisurely time with someone who reacted to dirt like it was phoenix blood.

She sighed when she heard footsteps approaching from behind. "Anna, I've already told you—"

"Good heavens, woman! You've dirt up to your ears!"

Aurelia grinned at the sound of Jack's voice. When she glanced over her shoulder, she saw him lurking a few feet behind her while holding a bundle of white blankets in his arms. She immediately rose from the ground, wiped her filthy hands on her skirt, and greeted both her husband and their sleeping daughter with kisses on their cheeks.

"Good morning, my darling." Her dirt-caked fingers hovered over Halyna's head as the babe cooed in her sleep. "Was that you I heard shrieking for all to hear?"

Jack snorted. "Like a banshee. I finally got her to sleep a few moments ago. What are you doing, my love?"

Aurelia gestured to the flowers—delft blue hyacinths and white gardenias—scattered by her feet. "Gardening. Isn't it obvious?"

"I can see *that,* but why?"

"For Linden and Cicely. He and I used to pluck hyacinths from Mistcairn. And Cicely...Gardenias were her favorite."

He raised an eyebrow. "Why not plant Linden's favorite flower, too?"

"I did."

Now he appeared miffed rather than curious. "The two of you had the same favorite flower? Hmm. I suppose I shouldn't be as surprised as I am."

Aurelia chuckled. "I was only five when he and I snuck into Mistcairn for the first time. He insisted we stop to pluck a few pink hyacinths for Cicely—he was enamored with her, even then. He told me hyacinths were his favorite. I decided then that they'd be my favorite, too. I admired him so deeply that I wished to be exactly like him. Now...Now they've become my favorite because they remind me of him." She sighed as she glanced at the flowers. "These just arrived from Holos. They're the only hyacinths left in the Folly."

Jack smiled, but his eyes were riddled with sadness. Before their return to Akkinor, she'd often spoken to him about how eager she was to scour the Folly's villages for her favorite flower. After defeating her brother, she'd learned that Archie ordered every pot of hyacinths in the Folly to be destroyed. Now, the only hyacinths in the Folly were the very same flowers Aurelia was planting for Linden, as she'd had no choice but to request a shipment of bulbs from Holos.

Neither uttered a word as they turned their gazes to the stone grave marker placed in front of Aurelia's favorite tree—the same tree she and Linden used to climb and hide in as children. Though Linden's remains resided in the palace crypt alongside his father, and though Cicely's were lost forever to Archie's cruelty, Aurelia preferred to honor her dearest friends at their favorite place on the grounds.

She wiped her hands on her skirt again, tucked her hand into the crevice of Jack's elbow, and made a mental note to return to the flowerbed later that day. There were three weeks left until the Changling Celebration— marking the shift from spring to summertime—and her friends' little garden was among the list of things she wanted to complete before then.

"You know," Jack commented, smiling a bit, "I've yet to see *my* favorite flower adorning these gardens."

Aurelia raised an eyebrow. "Which is?"

His tiny smile morphed into a full-fledged grin—the same wicked grin she'd fallen in love with all those years ago. "Lilies."

She laughed, but warmth quickly filled the hollows of her belly and flooded her cheeks with a crimson blush. She should've known.

As they walked, the five-week-old princess awoke from her slumber and instantly reached for her mother. At the same time, Aurelia heard deafening shrieks from the other side of the gardens. It wasn't Halvor, but rather the elder Brentwood children climbing up and down the dragon's massive, scaly body like tiny, determined little acrobats.

The two governesses weren't exactly fond of Halvor, so Aurelia allowed them to take the afternoon for themselves. Now, Isobel and Alistair were monitoring the children. The sight made Aurelia long for her own parents, as she wished they could've lived to meet her children, but she was glad for the Ashfords; at the least, her children would grow up with one set of grandparents rather than none.

Aurelia and Jack stopped to rest on the lawn so the former could feed their daughter. As Halyna suckled on the queen's breast, Aurelia looked out at the horizon in the distance and imagined she could see the City of

Gold from across the sea. Her uncle had visited Akkinor once since she reclaimed her throne, but due to Aurelia's delicate (and constant) pregnant state, she hadn't managed a trip back to Carthe. Even so, she longed for the place that'd changed her life.

"Oh! I almost forgot." Jack reached into the pocket of his trousers and produced a letter stamped with the golden seal of the Caltheos family—almost as if he could sense that she'd been thinking about Carthe. "A servant found this behind my nightstand earlier today. You were meant to read it a few weeks ago."

"I completely forgot about that." The two chuckled as she traded their daughter for the letter. "I was just thinking about Taundosa, actually. I do hope we can manage a visit in the near future. I'd like the children to..."

When she trailed off as she read, Jack furrowed his eyebrows. "What is it?"

"I..."

"Aurelia? Is everything all right?"

She cleared her throat as her fingers began to tremble, causing the letter to shake violently in her grip until Reyna's loopy handwriting blurred into indecipherable black smudges. An aching pain stirred behind her eyes as Halvor, from across the gardens, lifted his head above the trees to catch a glimpse of his mistress. As always, her most valiant protector could sense her emotions as well as she could—just like Linden.

"Aurelia." Jack touched her elbow to summon her attention. "What's happened?"

She swallowed the hot, thick lump in her throat. "It would appear that my allies are preparing for war."

He raised an eyebrow. "With whom?"

She looked up from the letter to meet his eyes. As soon as she did so, he recoiled as if she'd just announced her plans to have him beheaded.

"Each other."

V

One lone candle dripped molten wax along the sides of its bronze holder as it illuminated Aurelia's study. The queen sat at her desk in her nightdress and dressing robe, knees drawn to her chest and toes curling over the edge of her chair, as she wrapped her arms around her legs and rested her chin atop her knees. Across from her, Jack was pacing from one side of the room to the other, fidgeting hands moving from his sides to his face and back again, as the furrowing of his brows caused a deep crease to form between them.

Aurelia exhaled. "Enough of that incessant pacing."

He stilled. "What's taking so long?"

"It's only been a few minutes, Jack. Give him time to—"

As if on cue, the door opened, and Ansyl slipped inside with the hood of his cloak pulled over his head of chin-length, inky black hair. Jack finally stopped moving as Aurelia planted her feet on the floor and leaned forwards.

She raised an eyebrow. "Well?"

"No ravens from Bozar or Krotis. I checked with the messengers, too, just to be sure." Ansyl removed his cloak and draped it over the back of an armchair before folding his arms over his chest. "Only Taundosa sent a plea for help thus far. The others must know you're more inclined to assist Taundosa because Reyna was your first ally—regardless of the promises you made to them, they won't wedge themselves between Akkinor and Taundosa. That's one less decision for you to make, isn't it?"

"Not exactly." She leaned her elbows on her desk and buried both hands in her hair. "We haven't received word from them yet, but that doesn't mean we won't in the near future. Until we do, there's time to spare. Unfortunately, time isn't our biggest obstacle. We shall find ourselves at odds with our allies regardless of how long it takes for them to send word."

"Our nobles will need to be informed soon, too," Ansyl reminded her. "If we'll be calling their men to arms, they'll want to know why—especially with everything else going on here in Akkinor."

She grimaced. Myra (and the other kingdoms) was still reeling over what had happened to Delphine Sherwood. As soon as the country found out about the war brewing in Carthe, they'd demand an audience with Aurelia in hopes that her attention wouldn't be split between Akkinor and Carthe. They'd throw a fit when the time came for Aurelia to favor what was happening in Carthe over what was happening on her own soil.

"This shouldn't be happening." Jack, whose nerves had only grown since having children, began to pace again. His tanned skin was flushed and clammy with worry. "They're supposed to stand *beside* one another, not against one another."

"We're all aware of what it means to be allies," Aurelia muttered. He stopped pacing long enough to glare at her, which—in spite of their current predicament—made her smile. "You saw what Reyna said. It isn't exactly their choice."

He sucked in a breath. "Read it again."

Obeying, she took the letter from her desk and unfolded it. Since reading it for the first time the day before, she'd read it again over a dozen times, and she still hadn't made sense of it.

For Aurelia Brentwood, Queen of Akkinor:

I write to you bearing grim news: King Willem of Kanibar is rumored to be planning a declaration of war on Dofell. Northern Carthinians have exceeded their patience with Dofell's negligence, and King Willem has taken it upon himself to rebuild Dofell into the Great City it once was. As you can imagine, we southern rulers aren't exactly pleased with his plans. If Kanibar succeeds in conquering Dofell, they'll become the dominant force in Carthe.

I've discussed the matter in great detail with both Lord Cristos and his fellow Taundosan rulers. Each of us agrees that we have no choice but to battle Kanibar for control of Dofell—and the Dofelli, too, if they haven't been defeated by the Kanish by the time our forces are rallied for war. As per the terms of our alliance, I humbly request Akkinor's support in the fight to come. We shall need it.

I've heard little to nothing from our allies in Bozar and Krotis since the rumors reached my ears, despite taking the liberty of informing them of our suspicions. I know the Four Lords of Bozar well, and I can say with absolute certainty that they'll do whatever's necessary to keep Kanibar from seizing Dofell. They'll seek to take Dofell for themselves, even if it means going to war with Taundosa, and they won't be swayed into sharing the spoils with us if we attempt to negotiate. I *remain unaware of how Krotis plans to respond, but they've always had a knack for waiting until the last moment to play their cards.*

I hope this letter reaches you before our allies send pleas for your assistance. I don't wish for you to lose your alliances because of our squabbling here in Carthe, and the risks will be diminished significantly if you've already promised your sword to Taundosa. Even so, I understand what I'm asking of you. This is no small feat. I hope you do what you believe is best.

Yours in friendship,

Reyna Caltheos, Queen of Taundosa.

Aurelia sighed. "Taundosa has requested Akkinor's assistance in the fight to come—the others haven't. They can't accuse me of turning my back on our alliances if I agree to help the first and only person who asked for it. They won't be pleased, but this isn't enough to warrant the dissolution of our agreements."

"One way or another, our men will find themselves fighting in Carthe." Jack gnawed on his lower lip as his eyes found hers. "Everyone knows they haven't a choice because of the alliances, but—"

"—but the entire country feels that we're becoming too Carthinian for our own good, anyway," she finished. "They can't accept Akkinorian mages simply because they associate magic with Carthe. If they won't accept and defend their own people, how can we urge them to fight for Carthinians? They may refuse to raise their swords, alliances be damned, and only the threat of punishment will be enough to sway them." She ran a hand through her hair and shook her head. "I won't threaten them into compliance. That was my brother's way, not mine."

"Regardless of how Akkinorians feel about Carthinians, they know where we'd be without those alliances," Ansyl reminded her. "It might've taken us decades to recover from your brother's reign instead of five years. Even now that we've recovered, our economy has grown to rely heavily on trade with Carthe. Nobody can deny that, and nobody can deny how awful the ramifications will be if Kanibar defeats our allies."

A shiver wracked Aurelia's body. "What would happen to them?"

Ansyl winced like she'd pierced him with a needle. "King Willem is a merciful man, but he's clever, too. He won't harm our allies, nor will he demand anything of them as punishment for fighting against him. Instead, he'll do exactly what Queen Reyna fears: control every horse, carriage, and ounce of grain that travels between northern and southern Carthe."

With her elbows digging into the desk, Aurelia rested her temples against the heels of her palms and buried her fingers in her hair. The matter in Carthe was enough to steal her attention for the next fortnight, but there'd always be plenty of domestic issues to resolve, too. It was one thing after another, and every last issue was Aurelia's to manage on her own. She could turn to her nobles and her advisors for most problems, but matters such as these were burdens for the queen to bear alone.

The anxiety bubbling up in her gut was toilsome, but with every new stressor that arose, she had to remind herself of something she tended to forget: the gods had chosen her to bring harmony back to the realm. Not her parents, not her brother, not her subordinates or her allies—*her*.

***

"Are you well, Your Grace?"

Startled, Aurelia gasped and brought a hand to her chest. In the doorway of her study, Andren Normindi chuckled and said, "Apologies. I didn't mean to frighten you."

"It's all right. Come in, please," she said. He bowed and claimed the seat on the other side of her desk. "I'm well, uncle, thank you. I was just...thinking."

He nodded in understanding. "Have I come at a bad time?"

"Not at all. What can I do for you?"

"I only wish to inform you of the progress we've made regarding the assassins in Sadia. My patrolmen have been scouring the kingdom for establishments where assassins were known to gather and train, and most have been abandoned. We've heard nothing about their activities since we altered the punishments. A total of twelve individuals were sent to Marooner's Chain, and an additional six were exiled at Vilgh-Azhor. I've brought a list of their names for your records."

He stood up from his seat enough to reach over her desk so she could accept the scroll. She scanned the names quickly, and she didn't recognize any of them.

"How many of them worked as assassins before the uprising?"

"About half, Your Grace."

"Were any hired by my brother to kill me?"

Andren winced. "Most of those who accepted the assignment from your brother were apprehended after you reclaimed the throne. Only two others—Mister Cullen and Madam Laurenia Falwell—were recently found to have been in the Folly the night of the uprising. They're among those banished to Quapebet."

"That's...That's very well, uncle, thank you."

"On another note, the men responsible for Delphine Sherwood's murder were apprehended and extradited to Clyren. They're due to stand trial by week's end."

"That's wonderful news! Thank you for telling me," she replied. He tipped his head in response, drawing her eyes to the four inches of gray hair sprouting from his scalp and corrupting his chin-length auburn locks. "Myra will certainly be glad of it, but I'm afraid that's all they have to be happy about right now."

Andren grimaced. "To be frank, I wasn't surprised to hear of it. Your decision to reintegrate magic wasn't received well by the masses. All of that aside, though, Delphine's murder has opened a door. I've heard whispers not only from across Sadia, but from across the entire continent. If I were you, I wouldn't be surprised if there's a steep increase in mages announcing their nature over the next few weeks."

"I beg your pardon?"

A ghost of a smile formed on his thin lips. "Mages are tired of hiding, Your Grace. They're tired of being targeted and butchered because of the gifts granted to them by the gods. They'll stop concealing themselves soon enough, and the rest of the country will have no choice but to accept that they've returned."

A shiver traced Aurelia's spine. "When I announced my plans for mages, I sent word across Akkinor to every highborn and lowborn household. All mages must register as such at the palace—not so we can spy on them, but so we can protect them from harm, train them properly, and assign them the positions they deserve. Just under two hundred mages have registered. That's hardly enough to populate one of Akkinor's smallest villages. Holos's coven is the largest, and there's only fifty of them."

"That number will grow in the weeks to come. One of their own managed to rise from poverty and bestow magic upon a highborn bloodline—and was killed for it. They won't forget that."

Andren tapped his fingers along his legs as if playing the pianoforte—an anxious tick that reminded Aurelia fiercely of her late mother. She wondered if he saw his younger sister in her face when he looked at her. She didn't have a drop of Cressida Normindi's blood in her veins, but she'd adopted more than enough from her mother to fool everyone—even Cressida's own brother.

"I don't know much about mages," Andren continued, "but I know Akkinorians, and there's only ever been one thing that ties us all together: honor. Our mages will honor Delphine Sherwood's memory and what her role in Myra meant for their kind. The best way to do that is to pull themselves from the shadows of fear and intolerance so magic can become what the gods intended it to be." When his green eyes sparkled, Aurelia was surprised to find a ring of bronze around his pupils. Her mother's eyes, though blue, had the same rings. "Our resemblance to Carthe won't matter much to them anymore—not when the return of magic means honoring one of our own."

Aurelia smiled. "I hope so."

She wondered if he could feel the tension escaping her body—she certainly could. Though Andren was only one of hundreds of nobles in Akkinor, his positive outlook gave her reassurance. Soon enough, she hoped, the other nobles (and the commoners) would adopt his perspective.

After seeing Andren to his carriage, Aurelia watched him disappear onto the streets of the Folly before returning to the palace in search of Ansyl. Now that she knew her method of deterrence had worked for the assassin problem in Sadia, she needed him to send word to the other kingdoms about adopting the same strategy.

She was halfway through her trek to Ansyl's study when she realized how quiet the palace was. The grounds had been bustling with noise, and while she could still hear the muffled clanging of tools and hollering of workmen from outside, the interior of the palace was silent. *Too* silent. If not the servants scurrying about in preparation for the Changling, it should've been her children running ramped throughout the corridors and hollering for all to hear.

Aurelia stopped Anna when the two crossed paths in the hallway. "Where are the children, Anna?"

"With His Royal Highness, Your Grace, and your uncle. They're taking tea in the morning room."

Aurelia frowned. Her mother's other brother, Rien, and her father's brother, Sebastian, normally arrived at the palace earlier than the other guests for each Changling (along with her many aunts, of course). They'd never arrived *this* early before, though, and neither had forewarned her about their impending arrival.

"It's no wonder they're on their best behavior, then," she muttered as she switched course toward the morning room. "They're always calmer when their aunts and uncles...Anna?"

She sighed when she realized Anna hadn't been following her. In fact, Anna had scurried away almost immediately after answering Aurelia's inquiry. The queen sighed in defeat, wondering how on earth she'd managed to find such a squirrely replacement for her beloved childhood friend.

The reason for Anna's masterful escape became clear when a soldier opened the door to the morning room. Naturally, the first people her eyes settled on were her children: Halle and Henry playing on the floor, Halyna sleeping in her bassinet, and Hyacinth perched on Jack's shoulders while pretending his dark curls were a horse's reins. Ansyl—not in his study as Aurelia had expected—was as dutiful as ever, standing behind Jack and Hyacinth in preparation to catch the young princess if she happened to topple backwards.

Sitting on the couch across from Jack, however, were two faces Aurelia hadn't expected to see: her uncle, Lord Arian Cristos, and his queen, Reyna Caltheos of Taundosa.

That foolish girl, she thought, recalling her exchange with Anna. *She didn't think to mention which uncle?*

Aurelia forced a smile as the door closed behind her. "Hello, Arian. Your Majesty. I'd say you've arrived several days early, but you haven't come for the Changling, have you?"

Reyna's azurite eyes flashed. "No, we haven't."

***

After the governesses whisked the children away, Aurelia sat beside Jack on the couch, across from Arian and Reyna. Ansyl lurked behind her, uncharacteristically silent as he waited for the conversation to begin. She wasn't surprised at his tension: he may have traded his life in Kanibar to serve Akkinor, but it wasn't an easy task to discuss his kin like they were his enemies—and what matter other than the impending Carthinian war would be important enough to warrant an unexpected visit?

"We weren't expecting you," Aurelia murmured, adjusting the way her ivory skirts fell over her legs. "I knew you, uncle, were planning to attend the Changling, but..."

"The decision to visit Akkinor was an abrupt one, I'm afraid, and I entirely forgot to forewarn you." Reyna flicked a pin-straight lock of black hair over her shoulder and forced a smile. "I hope you can forgive me."

Aurelia waved her hand dismissively. "It's all right. I assumed you'd come sooner or later after receiving your letter, anyway. I take it things have worsened since you wrote to me?"

Arian scrubbed a hand down his face, looking ten years older than he normally did, and pulled at his scraggly gray beard rather than dropping his hands to his lap. It was a nervous habit of his, as she'd noticed over the years, and it'd been her father's most obvious anxious tick, too.

"I sensed something awry in Dofell last season," her uncle began. "Magical creatures aren't extinct in Carthe like they are elsewhere in the world—endangered, yes, but not extinct. Dofell is the only exception. When the kingdom fell to ruin, its magical inhabitants fled elsewhere, and no creature of old has been spotted there since. My recent trip to Dofell revealed several oddities: the first being an angry mob gathered outside of the palace, composed of Carthinian lowborn from across the continent; the second being an abandoned Kanish campsite just outside of the Dofelli walls; and the third being a young Dofelli girl talking about a sprite—or, rather, *to* a sprite. I thought it was nonsense until I saw the creature for myself. I saw another when I crossed the gates into the Violet Forest."

"Really?" A puzzled frown formed on Jack's lips. "I saw a handful of sprites in Kanibar during my years in Carthe, but never elsewhere. They'd pull my horse's hair and jerk him around until he threw me from his back. I could always hear them giggling. Rotten little things, sprites."

"We haven't any in the south," Reyna added. "They prefer the northern climate."

Aurelia, feeling like the stupidest person in the room, flushed when she asked, "What are sprites?"

Ansyl breezed by her to sit in the armchair beside Reyna. "They're a sister-species of fairies, in a way. I don't suppose the largest of their kind is any bigger than my hand. They're known for making mischief, like a child, but they're as clever and intelligent as any educated human."

"They're perhaps the greatest messengers in the realm," Arian added. "Their speed is unparalleled—they can travel the entire length of the Ngora Valley in two or three minutes. They're nearly difficult to see, particularly when they're hiding, so we humans rarely notice them watching or listening to us. They have eidetic memories, too, but they're deceitful. Not unlike your connection with Halvor, they latch themselves onto an individual or a family line, and they're sworn to tell the truth to their masters or mistresses. They speak nothing but lies to everyone else."

"And if they only exist in Kanibar..." Jack raised a dark, arched eyebrow. "You think the Kanish are using sprites to spy on Dofell?"

"It's the only explanation. Sprites wouldn't return to a place as barren and desolate as Dofell without reason. I sent word back to Taundosa—and to the Dofelli king—when my suspicions arose, and everything I feared was confirmed by the time I returned home."

Reyna, a woman whose presence never failed to radiate confidence, flickered her gaze to Aurelia with a look on her face that made the latter's stomach churn. She looked exactly as Aurelia had felt when Aurelia learned that her brother had betrayed her.

"The mob Lord Cristos observed in Dofell wasn't the first to form, and I'm certain it wasn't the last," Reyna murmured. "Angry crowds have been gathering there for over a year now, once or twice a season, and they're composed of commonfolk from across the continent. A sizable portion of them are Bozari. According to our spies and connections, Carthe's lowborn have been rallying together to demand that action be taken in Dofell."

Aurelia frowned. "The kingdom fell hundreds of years ago. Hardly anything has changed since then. Why are the people demanding change *now*? What inspired this?"

Arian shifted in his seat. "*You*, of course."

She stifled a short, nervous laugh. "Me? What did *I* do?"

"Bozar." It was Jack who answered. As all eyes turned to him, the tips of his ears reddened, but he didn't let the attention stall him. "Don't you remember that day in Kazamir? You gave the people something to hope for by showing them selflessness and compassion. They were supposed to give you whatever they had, and instead, *you* gave them all *you* had. It was the only act of generosity they'd ever known from a highborn, never-mind a *foreign* highborn."

Aurelia, still not understanding, shook her head. "I promised them a shipment of painted glass, sacrificed one pair of earrings, and saved a handful of young girls from becoming child brides. Their reaction was unexpected, of course, but certainly it wasn't enough to inspire *this*."

"You've been away from Carthe for a long time, Your Grace," Reyna told her. "Our Bozari allies wouldn't have mentioned a word of this to you—they're a prideful people, you know—but their lowborn demanded better treatment after your time there. You showed them that it's possible for a highborn to lead with kindness, so they demanded that their rulers show them the compassion they deserve. The Four Lords made minor improvements to appease the people, and it worked. Life in Bozar is the best it's been since the old days. When word spread of such improvements in Bozar—improvements instigated by *your* actions—the rest of the continent's commonfolk turned their attention to the place most in need of salvation: Dofell."

"When one butterfly tastes nectar," Arian murmured, "the entire swarm is compelled to taste it, too."

Aurelia shivered as nausea settled in her gut. She glanced at Jack, who was carefully (and rather obviously) avoiding looking her in the eye, and then to Ansyl, who merely stared at his feet and clenched his jaw. She knew all four of them were waiting for her to say something, but she couldn't summon words. Something of a revolution had begun in Carthe, and she—however unknowingly—had been the one to start it. How could she say *anything* after receiving such news?

It felt like she'd just swallowed sawdust when she opened her mouth, but a knock vibrated the door before she could think of something to say. She nodded to the guard at the door, who opened it to allow Kaila—a handmaiden—into the room before closing it again. The shy, mousy-looking girl blushed and curtsied when five pairs of annoyed highborn eyes landed on her.

"Excuse me." Aurelia stood from the couch, adjusted her skirts, and met Kaila by the door. "What's the matter?"

"Your Grace." The maid curtsied again, eyeing Arian and Reyna as she did so, before her wide, anxious brown eyes landed on Aurelia once more. "You have visitors."

"Already?" Aurelia blinked, surprised. "Our guests weren't supposed to arrive for the Changling until early next week. We haven't—"

"Forgive me, Your Grace. It's not...They're not..."

"What is it?"

She gulped. "It's the Bozari lords, Your Grace. Zhaaran and Zhoqa."

Aurelia stilled, shocked into silence, and looked between Kaila's eyes for any sign that the maid was unsure about their guests' identities. She found nothing, but she hadn't expected to. Everyone—even a servant who'd never left Akkinor—could recognize a Carthinian leader.

Muffled voices from the outside corridor grew louder, and fortunately, Aurelia was able to move Kaila out of the way just in time for the door to swing open. Kaila gasped as Lord Zhoqa barged into the parlor with Lord Zhaaran hot on his heels. Two of Aurelia's guards were chasing after them, having apparently tried and failed to entice the lords into waiting for the queen's audience to end.

Neither noticed Aurelia loitering to the side of the door when they stopped. Lord Zhaaran only sighed and bowed his head upon spotting Arian and Reyna. Lord Zhoqa, on the other hand, snorted louder than a boar, shook his head, and released a guttural, unpleasant sound that might've been mistaken for a laugh, if one were optimistic enough.

"I knew it." Lord Zhoqa gritted his teeth. "I *knew* we should've sent word the moment—"

"Hello, Your Grace." Lord Zhaaran, having finally noticed Aurelia, offered her a tired smile. "You shall have to forgive us for barging in. We're on something of a tight schedule."

She returned his smile as best she could. "It's no bother. I take it you've come because of what's happening with Kanibar and Dofell?"

"I'd hoped to catch the first day or two of the Changling, too, but—"

"There's no time for that." Lord Zhoqa's steely azurite gaze flickered over to Aurelia. "As nice as it is to finally visit Akkinor, we haven't come to watch your jousters impale one another." He turned to the Taundosans and wrinkled his nose. "You haven't come for the Changling, either, have you?"

Reyna's lips were pressed in a thin, taut line. "No."

As if the palace were his own, Lord Zhoqa crossed the parlor to fill a chalice with wine at a nearby serving table. He chugged the burgundy liquid as soon as his cup was filled, then wiped whatever was dribbling over his chin with the sleeve of his tunic. His eyes were already bloodshot.

He raised an eyebrow at Reyna. "Would you like to start, or should I?"

VI

The group gathered in the morning room consisted of a rather interesting mix of individuals: the realm's only two female monarchs, both responsible for establishing the world's first cross-continental alliance; an elderly Bozari lord who, by all accounts, was descended from humanity's first sinners; a weathered Taundosan lord with a child's imagination and the authority of a king; and a second Bozari lord who couldn't be bothered to look into a woman's gaze in favor of ogling her chest.

The last time Aurelia was in a room with the four of them, she'd forged alliances with Lord Jalhor Zhaaran of Orestes and Lord Balor Zhoqa of Kazamir. She exchanged letters with each of them every so often, of course, but she hadn't seen any of them (save Arian) in the flesh since that day.

"You shouldn't be here." Reyna's gaze was cold and unforgiving. "You should've stayed in Bozar. The matter in the north is one that concerns the *entirety* of your country. If two of the kingdom's four leaders are gone—"

"I could say the same to you, Your Majesty," Lord Zhoqa replied. "Who's reigning over Taundosa while both its monarch and her Hand are here in Akkinor, begging at a foreign queen's feet?"

Reyna's eyes flickered with wrath. "Careful."

While the two quarreled over respect and lack thereof, Lord Zhaaran's violet eyes met Aurelia's gaze. He'd been nearing the end of his middle age when they first met five years earlier, and now he looked as weathered as a man who'd reached one-hundred years of life. She didn't remember the lines on his forehead being so deep, nor the gray of his hair and beard being so close to white. Even his warm brown skin seemed drained of life. Aurelia couldn't help but wonder if his weary appearance was because of his age or because of what was happening in Dofell, but either way, seeing him look so frail unsettled her.

"We would've sent word of our visit, but we didn't wish to risk interception," the elder lord told her. "Our enemies must assume that we'd turn to Akkinor for assistance, of course, but they'd think us rather desperate if they knew we were coming to you so soon."

Jack raised an eyebrow. "Are you? Desperate, I mean."

The corner of Lord Zhaaran's mouth twitched. "How much do you know?"

Reyna and Lord Zhoqa stopped bickering enough for Aurelia to reply. When she finished her tale, Lord Zhaaran cleared his throat. "Queen Reyna informed us of Lord Cristos's observations as a kindness. I wrote to my nephew in Kanibar after that, who didn't respond. Instead, King Willem himself wrote to me to confirm his intentions."

"The commonfolk are demanding that something be done about the state of Dofell, and King Elrin has neither the money nor the brains to fix what his ancestor destroyed," Lord Zhoqa continued. "The only way to appease the people before they engage in a full-fledged rebellion is for a capable ruler to intervene. King Willem of Kanibar has taken it upon himself. Soon enough, his men will march into Dofell, and us southern rulers will have no choice but to respond. We can't permit Kanibar to serve as the division between the north and the south."

"Why?" Aurelia felt like a fool for asking such a question, but as her father used to say, one would never learn if one was too afraid to ask. "From my perspective, Kanibar's seizure of Dofell would be beneficial for all. It will allow for safer journeys from northern to southern Carthe. Travelers won't have to risk their lives by crossing the valley. Of course, Kanibar will have the opportunity to control most trade and commerce, but that can be remedied with negotiation. It's not a terrible price to pay if it means lessening the number of bodies claimed by the desert."

Lord Zhoqa rolled his eyes. "What a remarkably Akkinorian perspective."

"I beg your—"

"Your confusion is understandable." Reyna eyed Lord Zhoqa in warning, but he ignored her. "The kingdoms of Carthe were established to wield equal power: our territories are roughly the same size, our populations close in number, and our resources of the same accessibility. If Kanibar takes Dofell, they'll become the dominant force in Carthe."

Aurelia bit the insides of her cheeks, silent. Reyna made a fair point: if the Kanish succeeded, anyone hoping to reach southern Carthe from the north would have to cross through Kanibar. While such a change seemed innocent enough, that wasn't always true. If the king so desired, he could demand compensation—in the form of coin or property—for anyone seeking to cross his territory; and, subsequently, he'd have full control over who or what went in and out. He could impose tariffs on any goods travelers hoped to trade or sell on their journeys, too. Highborn and lowborn alike would be forced to pay the Kanish monarchy simply to reach one side of the continent from the other.

Though it'd be possible for people to avoid the Ngora Valley by traveling directly from one kingdom to another, Carthe's economy would suffer. With Kanibar serving as the new barrier between north and south, there'd be no need for the southern kingdoms to supply travelers with resources meant to ensure their survival across the valley. The kingdoms would produce more goods than necessary, and if they reduced production to comply with current demands, they'd lose an incredible amount of coin.

Riches, it seemed, was the only force strong enough to incite a continental war; riches and, of course, salvation—but only if the concern for Dofell was authentic.

There was a momentary lapse in conversation when a trio of servants arrived with refreshments, forcing the allies to endure a contemplative silence. Of the two Bozari lords, only the elder sat calmly in his chair. The younger swallowed two glasses of wine in the time it took Aurelia to take a single sip, and while a serving girl fumbled to refill his chalice for the third time, he shot daggers at Reyna and Arian with his eyes. Arian, ever the peacemaker, chose not to engage. Reyna, on the other hand, returned Lord Zhoqa's expression tenfold.

It was almost summertime in the Folly, and yet, Aurelia felt trapped in the dead of winter.

When the servants left, Lord Zhoqa was the first to speak again: "One way or another, we shall find ourselves at war with Kanibar. I haven't heard a word about how Krotis feels about this, but clearly, the rest of us plan to act."

Reyna's back (already straighter than a board) stiffened. "When I sent word to Bozar before I left for Akkinor, I specifically requested that you discuss this with me before involving anyone else. I was prepared to make a deal with the Four Lords: if we stand together to defeat Kanibar and take Dofell for ourselves, we can divide the kingdom between us."

Lord Zhoqa scoffed. "You asked us not to involve anyone, but here you are, doing the same thing you requested we refrain from." The bald, prickly lord shook his head. "I won't stand for a division, and neither will the others. We may be friends, Your Majesty, but our kingdoms are quite different. Our ways of life would clash."

"No kingdom will share Dofell with another. No kingdom will allow any of its neighbors to seize Dofell, either," Jack intervened. "Whatever happens, somebody will need to rule Dofell. How do you suppose this will end if nobody can agree on what to do with the kingdom?"

"We shall cross that bridge when we come to it," Lord Zhaaran said lowly.

"Or burn it," Aurelia added.

Only her uncle smiled at that. "Or burn it."

"That brings us to the reason for our visit." Lord Zhoqa's eyes snapped over to Aurelia's. "The only deterrent we can think of is you, Your Grace. Perhaps if Kanibar is swayed to ignore their plans because of our closeness with you, then we, as leaders of Carthe, can unite to think of another solution for Dofell."

She raised an eyebrow, amused. "I've been called many things in my lifetime, but never a *deterrent*."

"This is no joking matter." The ferocity behind his piercing blue eyes prompted a deep scowl to form on her lips. If she blinked, she would've missed the way he recoiled at her expression. "That beast of yours is the only thing frightening enough to change Willem's mind."

Aurelia's temper flared, but she kept it at bay. "You won't accomplish anything by behaving like a godless *saiha*." His face turned scarlet while the others stifled laughter. *Saiha*, an Old Carthinian word, roughly translated to *jackass* in the common tongue. "You're here because you need my help—perhaps showing a bit of respect to both myself and Halvor would be in your best interest. Don't you think?"

Lord Zhoqa grumbled something under his breath about her pronunciation of *saiha*—an effort to heal his wounded pride—but nobody felt the need to address him.

Arian offered her an encouraging smile, but the worry in his eyes made it less than convincing. "For the time being, we must ensure the Kanish do not proceed. That's the only way to avoid a full-fledged war. If King Willem abandons his plans, we may invite him to assist us in finding another solution for Dofell. It'd be difficult for him to decline that offer while a dragon breathes down his neck."

Aurelia took a long, deep breath and gazed at each face awaiting her response. "King Willem knows you're allied with Akkinor, just as he knows about Halvor. He'd be a fool to think I won't stand beside my allies, and he'd be an even bigger fool to think I'd leave Halvor behind while I do so. If the idea of facing Akkinor—and a dragon—on the battlefield hasn't deterred him yet, it never will."

Lord Zhoqa narrowed his eyes at her. "He hasn't been deterred *yet* because of your reputation, Your Grace."

"I beg your pardon?"

"What he means," Arian intervened, shooting daggers at Lord Zhoqa with his eyes, "is that the realm knows you refused to unleash dragon fire during the war with your brother. They likely assume that your heart is too gentle to inflict such damage and horror—even on foreign soil. Dragon or not, King Willem doesn't currently believe you'll use your power to burn Kanibar to the ground."

"Because I won't."

Lord Zhoqa looked about ready to throttle her as he turned to his fellow lord. "What did I tell you?"

"It's difficult to recall. So rarely do I listen when you speak." Lord Zhaaran's violet eyes hadn't left Aurelia since he arrived. While his Bozari counterpart glowered at him, Lord Zhaaran continued to watch her as if she'd sprout wings and breathe fire. "I admire your compassion, Your Grace, but allow me to remind you of something: when we go to war with Kanibar, the battle will be fought on Dofelli soil. There's nothing worth salvaging there. Regardless of your involvement, men will die. We may spare our soldiers by having your dragon lay siege to Dofell and our enemies, or we can allow our men to fall until someone surrenders."

Aurelia's gaze found Arian's. She wished she could hear his voice in her head so he could provide her with the answers she needed, but telepathy wasn't necessary between niece and uncle; everything he might've said aloud or in her head was right there in his eyes.

Aurelia cleared her throat. "What concerns me is the civilian population. I doubt King Willem would provide a warning so Dofell can evacuate their commonfolk."

"Dofell will be forced to begin anew anyhow. Whatever happens, the kingdom will be torn apart from the ground up," Lord Zhoqa muttered. "It's too far gone."

Aurelia hardened her gaze. "We're speaking of the people, not of the kingdom itself."

"What difference is there?"

She bit the insides of her cheeks, silent. It ached her soul to admit it to herself, but that foul Zhoqa was right: any hope Dofell had in securing a brighter future meant ripping it apart, root and stem. Unfortunately, the Dofelli natives *were* the kingdom's roots. The modern inhabitants of Dofell were the direct descendants of those who lived in the kingdom when it was still *the Great City*. No other Carthinians, Akkinorians, or anyone else had planted seeds in Dofell in centuries. Those who remained could trace their family histories back to its founding; if the kingdom was ripped apart, its people would be, too.

Ansyl, sensing Aurelia's discomfort, cleared his throat. "Our stewardess has kindly prepared bedchambers for each of you. I imagine you must be exhausted after such a long voyage—if you'd like, I can escort you to your chambers for a bit of rest before dinner."

Reyna's smile mirrored the fatigue in her eyes. "That would be lovely."

"I shall find my way myself." Arian's eyes sparkled as he turned to Aurelia. "First, I'd like a private word with Her Grace."

As Ansyl and Jack escorted Reyna and the lords out of the morning room, Arian rose from his seat to claim the one directly beside Aurelia. A long, tired exhale escaped her as she threw her arms around his neck and buried her face in his shoulder. He chuckled as he returned her embrace, and for just a moment, her eyes welled with tears when she caught a whiff of his familiar scent—sage and peppermint, the same aromas she often associated with her late father.

"I've missed you terribly, uncle."

"I've missed you, too." He released her and squeezed her shoulder for comfort, but his smile quickly faded. "Now that it's just the two of us...I know you're displeased with what we asked of you today. Please forgive me for placing you in this position."

She waved a hand to dismiss his worries. "I knew what I agreed to when I secured my alliances. What concerns me most is what will happen to Dofell if Kanibar surrenders. Who will claim control of it? The Phyre monarchy can't remain in power. Will Taundosa and Bozar actually battle one another for it?"

"We suggested splitting Dofell in half, as Reyna mentioned, but the Bozari are unimpressed by that. Krotis, too, would attempt battling us to seize a portion of Dofell for themselves—simply to remain relevant, I'd wager. Dofell can't be split between one monarchy and two feudal systems. The government would find itself at odds over methods of leadership."

"So either way, I shall find myself trapped between allies. Is that right?"

He grimaced. "It would appear so. We've neglected to discuss the matter in detail for the sake of peacekeeping, but as soon as Kanibar is no longer a threat to us, we can't remain friendly—not unless there's a favorable solution for all. It's my hope that the two lords understand the position they'd be placing you in, and decide against enacting the terms of your alliances."

"And if they don't?"

"If they don't..." He turned away from her as his gaze grew distant and hazy. "If they don't, you'll be forced to choose a side, and your remaining allies will dissolve your contracts. At the least, they won't declare war on Akkinor. I suppose we have Halvor to thank for that."

Aurelia attempted to smile, but it was less than convincing. Though her uncle was only trying to be helpful, he reminded her of something she wished she hadn't pushed to the back of her mind: her only true sources of power came from her alliances and her dragon. Without her allies, she was exactly the same as every other ruler who'd come before her. Without Halvor, the only thing protecting Akkinor (and Aurelia, by default) from an invasion was its enormous population. On her own, Aurelia was nothing to fear.

But fear, as she knew, wasn't how she'd earned her allies' support or her people's obedience. The merciful, strange, and often unorthodox methods she'd used to inspire Carthinians and Akkinorians alike were rooted in the need for peace rather than in the use of force.

It was, after all, the very reason Aurelia's sobs had since transformed into tears of gold.

***

Doryn Vellas was not a great man.

He was neither a lord nor a duke. He was neither a soldier nor an honored knight. He wasn't a priest in service of the gods, a respected scholar loyal to knowledge, or a physician dedicated to healing the sick and injured. No, he was far more menial than that: as the penniless apprentice of an elderly cobbler, Doryn was perhaps one desperate measure away from joining the criminals in the Kanish dungeons.

The only thing he had was magic, and he could hardly use his powers as it was. A man born to be nothing didn't find himself being trained by the kingdom's greatest mages when his pockets were eternally empty—so empty that one might assume they were riddled with holes.

He wasn't a great man, or a strong one, or even a smart one; so how, he wondered, had he found himself breaking bread with the most powerful man in Kanibar?

The king, a somewhat young man who'd been ruling since Doryn was in leading strings, seemed to read the apprentice's mind as he sipped wine and asked, "Do you know why I've summoned you here today?"

"No." When Doryn's reply sounded more like a squeak than speech, he cleared his throat and tried again: "No, Your Majesty."

The king's lips curled into a smile. "I thought as much. You see, I've found myself wanting for a faction of men—decent, honest, regular men— capable of carrying out the plans that I myself cannot. Nobody would bat an eye at a poor cobbler lurking about where he doesn't belong, but a knight or a veteran mage?" He clicked his tongue and shook his head. "It wouldn't do. I'd find myself burying some of the greatest men in my charge."

"F-Forgive me, my liege, but I don't under—"

"As you know, our neighbors have experienced a significant rise in power over the last few years. Do you know why?" The king's eyes gleamed when he saw Doryn glance down at an open book on the tea table between them. The illustration of a dragon on the right hand page was impossible to miss. "That's it. Akkinor and its queen have changed the way of life here in Carthe. I believe it's time for Kanibar to respond before we're left behind. While those associated with Akkinor and the queen prosper, we remain at a terrible disadvantage."

Suddenly feeling brave, Doryn said, "What does this have to do with me, Your Majesty?"

The king grinned. "You're one of several men I'm tasking with paying a visit to Akkinor. I'll provide you with enough coin for lodgings and food when you arrive, in addition to twenty gold upon your return to Kanibar."

Doryn's jaw nearly fell to the floor. *Twenty gold?* Such coin would make him rich enough to do anything, to go anywhere, to survive comfortably for *years*. No person of his station had seen twenty gold even once in their lifetimes.

"Your visit will be limited to the Folly, I'm afraid." The king took another sip of wine, staining his teeth purple. "The queen has cobblers in her employment—some tasked with servicing the royal family and her court, and others with servicing her staff. Use your skills to earn a place in the palace."

"And if I fail?" Doryn tugged at the collar of his tunic, already damp with nervous sweats.

"That's not an option," the king replied. "But there are others in the Folly with knowledge of the happenings of the palace and the royal family, too. Become acquainted with them. Learn from them. Gossip is a powerful asset, and it spreads like wildfire in Akkinor."

Doryn nodded. "What information will I be seeking?"

"Anything regarding the queen, her beast, her plans, her family—whatever you can scrounge up that may highlight her weaknesses."

"Forgive me," Doryn said quickly, wiping his clammy hands on his trousers, "but I don't understand why we aren't attempting to form friendly relations with Akkinor. I assumed you'd wish for an alliance like our neighbors."

"Bah." The king waved a dismissive hand and grimaced. "Our neighbors are weak. They have but a taste of magic, wealth, and knowledge between them—*nothing* compared to what Kanibar has. They know nothing of our assets or our power, and even if we chose to boast about it all these years...They're too self-absorbed to care, frankly. They look down on us, calling us uncivilized, when they're the ones who fight their own kin." He leaned forward, setting his now-empty chalice on the tea table, and looked fiercely into Doryn's eyes. "What do you know of the *odirasen?*"

Doryn swallowed the lump in his throat. "It's the word used to describe the act of prophesizing."

"Precisely. The ways of the *odirasen* have all but gone extinct across the realm, but oracles have always existed in Kanibar. One such individual has spoken of a time yet to come in the near future—a time that may change the realm as we know it."

The king reached into his pocket and produced a folded piece of parchment before handing it to Doryn. The apprentice hesitated, unsure if he was prepared to bear whatever knowledge the message contained, but accepted the paper when he saw the urgency in the king's emerald eyes. He cleared his throat, averting his gaze from the king's as he unraveled the parchment, and read the message.

An era of uncertainty shall come to an end when, in the east, water runs thicker than blood. A period of peace and promise shall follow for five cycles, only to be broken when the sun burns hottest across the realm. Chaos and carnage shall return, demanding that a hero of western blood emerges from the shadows of men to restore the realm to glory. In the wake of such turmoil, the voice of the divine shall be heard across the realm once again through the falling of stars.

The king leaned back in his seat, smiling, when Doryn finished reading. "Do you understand?"

The apprentice's face burned with shame. "No, Your Majesty."

"Five years after a war between kin in the east," the king said slowly, "the summer season will unlock the door leading us to our salvation. A western ruler—more god than man—will rise to the occasion, doing what he must to transform his kingdom into a domain worthy of the gods. If he succeeds, the gods will return, and suffering will come to an end."

Goosebumps peppered Doryn's skin. "Is this...Is this true?"

"It's the truest thing I've ever known, good man, and you will contribute to making it a reality." The king raised a bushy, mahogany eyebrow. "Will you assist me in restoring the realm to its former glory, or will you return to a life of holding a lantern over an old man's head while he fixes shoes in the darkness?"

Doryn didn't answer, but he didn't have to—both he and the king already knew his answer. The offer of twenty gold was one Doryn couldn't pass up, but even if he wanted to...the realm depended on his contribution.

He could continue living as a poor cobbler, or he could work to find himself worshipped in the streets as a man who helped bring the gods back to the realm.

Now, the only thing Doryn could do was hope and pray that the king's interpretation of the prophecy was the right one.

VII

Later that evening, when the near entirety of Akkinor joined the sun in slumber, Aurelia made her way to her study rather than to her bedchamber. She slipped inside (with two soldiers immediately assuming their positions outside of the door) and collapsed on the sofa. Other than a sliver of moonlight peeking out from behind the curtains, the room was blanketed in darkness. She didn't bother lighting a candle or calling for a servant to light a fire in the hearth; she was prepared to fall asleep right there, still wearing her day clothes, with her hair pinned up and a tiara planted on her head.

"I've never seen you so quiet, Your Grace."

A strangled gasp escaped her throat as she leapt to her feet and produced a concealed blade from the garter beneath her skirt. Since her time in Carthe, she'd grown accustomed to being armed at all times—apparently, for good reason.

The shadowy figure lurking in the corner of the room—cleverly planted behind the door—stepped forward. The moon cast a dull ray of light over his face, allowing her to recognize his sallow skin and vibrant blue eyes, but his identity did little to calm her nerves. Lord Zhoqa may not have been a stranger to her, but of everyone she knew, he was perhaps the last person she wished to be alone with.

"M-My lord." She paused to allow her racing heart the chance to steady. "Have you no sense? If you wished for a private audience, you could've asked. There's no need to sneak about like a common criminal. This is vastly inappropriate—my dragon has eaten people for less."

He winced and sunk into the armchair across from her. "You shall have to forgive me. I didn't intend to startle you."

"I've had to forgive you for quite a bit lately." Aurelia sighed and returned the blade to her garter. "What do you want?"

75

Knowing it'd be quite some time before she was allowed to rest, she rose from the sofa to light a series of candles on her desk. As she did so, Lord Zhoqa approached the table lined up against a wall to her left and poured each of them a glass of wine. She decided against berating him for serving himself without asking for permission, as the wine was over a week old and had since lost its decadency. Drinking stale Myran wine was akin to swallowing an entire jug of rum when one thought it was goat's milk.

"There's something I'd like to discuss with you, and certain circumstances prevent me from mentioning it while the others are present." He sipped from the bronze chalice, made a face, and moved to set it aside. When he realized she must've anticipated his reaction, he instead kept the stem of the chalice nestled between his fingers as he balanced it on his knee. "As you know, Lord Zoma of Iseppa and Lord Xada of Tucana declined to meet with you five years ago regarding potential alliances with Akkinor. They've since changed their minds."

Aurelia's heart skipped a beat. "What?"

The satisfaction in his eyes made her want to strangle him. "That was a bit of an exaggeration. The truth is that they've decided to *consider* an alliance with Akkinor—if you agree to their terms, of course."

She eyed him suspiciously as she lowered herself onto the sofa. "Explain this to me precisely."

"Whatever happens with Kanibar is irrelevant. Queen Reyna has expressed interest in seizing Dofell, but her alliances with Kazamir and Orestes have made her weak. She'd rather preserve our alliances by sharing Dofell with Bozar than seize the kingdom for herself. Iseppa and Tucana are firmly against the idea of sharing Dofell with anyone but the Bozari. When the time comes to seize Dofell, Lord Zhaaran and I will stand behind our Bozari kin—it'd be a shame and a sin if we turned our backs on our fellow lords to preserve an outside alliance."

Aurelia nodded. She'd expected that much. "What does this have to do with me?"

"We Four Lords have a proposition for you: defend Bozar's claim over Dofell by standing beside us on the battlefield, and Akkinor will have secured alliances with all four Bozari territories."

Her back stiffened. "My lord—"

"We understand that this decision would place you in an unfavorable position with Taundosa and Runeia. Either way, Your Grace, you shall have to choose between your allies eventually. But only one of us is offering you an incentive."

"Lord Zhaaran is aware of this?"

"Indeed." He paused to take a smoking pipe from the inside pocket of his suit coat, then rose from his seat just enough to light it with the flame of a candle. "He may express this to you in the future, but for now, he's only concerned with maintaining peace." A snort rattled his nostrils. "The old man's gone soft."

Aurelia stared at him, overwhelmed by his proposition, as he encased the study in plumes of earthy-smelling smoke. She knew she had to respond quickly, but she couldn't decide between honesty and peace. Whichever path she chose, though, wouldn't bring Lord Zhoqa the satisfaction he craved.

"That's a generous offer, but I can't give you a proper answer until I've given it more thought. The Assembly will need to voice their opinions on the matter, too." She hesitated as he exhaled another cloud of smoke. "May I ask you something?"

"Certainly."

"What do you suppose might happen if I neglect to support any of you in the battle to come?"

That seemed to capture his attention, as he set the pipe aside while glowing embers and ash trickled onto the floor. "The terms of your alliances state that you must offer your swords to your allies during our times of need. The terms mention nothing about what's expected of you if your allies go to war with one another."

She blinked at him. "I must admit, I wasn't expecting such an objective response."

"I have my moments." He collected the pipe again but didn't take a drag. It dangled from his hand as he narrowed his eyes at her—not in a threatening or demeaning way, but as if he were trying to see through her and into her soul. "Technically speaking, none of us can dissolve our alliances with Akkinor if you fail to fight beside us while we're at war with one another. Technicalities, however, can only reach so far."

She knew that much, too. Legality might save her from losing her alliances, but her allies wouldn't forget her lack of support.

"I shall take this into consideration, then." She rose from the sofa to open the door for him, despite Lord Zhoqa appearing to have no intention of leaving so soon. He knew his time was up when the soldiers outside of the door spotted him, though. "Have a pleasant evening, my lord. You've given me so much to think about."

He offered her a halfhearted, somewhat mocking bow. "My pleasure."

When he disappeared around a corner, she assured the guards that they weren't to blame for his sneakiness, then closed the door and returned to the sofa. The study still smelled like whatever Lord Zhoqa had been smoking. Desperate for a new aroma, she found a tin of peppermint hand salve—her father's—in a drawer in her desk. She massaged the salve onto her hands, admired the remnants of wax on the tin from where her father had dripped the hot liquid while sealing correspondences, and smiled as she ran her fingers over the hardened purple lumps.

"If only you were here to show me the way," she whispered.

***

"And then what happened?"

"And then," Arian mused, "as I pulled your grandfather from the river, one wicked trout swam beneath the collar of his shirt! I could hear it flopping against his chest as it fought with the strength of a thousand men to return to the water. He was howling like a newborn babe until the poor creature finally made its escape." Aurelia's lips curled into a smile at the sound of her children's laughter. "Your grandfather never forgave me for it. I suppose I shouldn't have tossed him into the river—it wasn't a very respectable thing to do. We were only boys then, though, and boys have a way of getting themselves into trouble."

"I'm pleased to be a girl," Halle replied. Not a second later, she yelped like she'd just been bitten in the leg by a ravenous hound. "He licked me!"

Arian made a *tsk* sound with his tongue. "Now, is that any way for a prince to behave?"

Henry sniffled. "No."

"Apologize to your sister, please."

"Sorry, Hal."

The princess sniffled. "It's all right."

Still grinning, Aurelia peeled her back from the exterior wall of the nursery and poked her head into the doorway. Normally at this time of the day, the governesses were preparing the Brentwood children for their midday nap. Their daily schedule never applied when Arian visited, though. They'd do whatever it took to remain in his presence for as long as possible before his visit came to an end.

"All right." Aurelia announced her presence and took a few steps towards them. Both Halle and Henry were tucked under either of Arian's arms as he lay on Henry's bed, while baby Halyna snoozed in her bassinet to their left. Hyacinth, who wasn't particularly fond of snuggling, lay on her stomach on her bed beside them, elbows digging into the mattress as she propped her sleepy head up on her palms. "It's time to sleep, little ones. I need to borrow your uncle."

Halle's wide eyes enlarged. "But—"

78

"Your mother is quite right." Arian, with all the gentleness of a butterfly, detached the children's limbs from his body and climbed out of bed. While Halle continued to pout, he scooped her up and placed her on her own bed. He didn't join Aurelia in the doorway until he'd kissed all four children on the forehead. "Don't fret, my darlings—I'll be here when you wake."

Despite their desperate desire to keep Arian in their clutches, the children quickly fell victim to exhaustion, as they yawned in unison and crawled beneath their bed sheets. Aurelia and Arian uttered a final goodbye before leaving them, though the latter hesitated with his hand on the doorknob for just a moment too long when the door was closed between them.

Aurelia couldn't help but smile. "They'll be here when we're finished, you know."

"I know." He released the doorknob, mirrored her smile, and offered her his arm. "Queen Reyna plans to depart tomorrow evening, but she's given me permission to stay for the Changling. I don't suppose I'd be a good Hand if I didn't return home with her, though."

Now her smile was forced, and so was his. "I understand. As much as I'd like for you to stay, Reyna needs you more than I do. Are the two lords leaving with you, too?"

"They'll set out tonight. Both are leaving emissaries behind to represent them here in Akkinor while we're gone."

As they walked to meet their allies, they were joined by both Ansyl and Jack. Upon their arrival in the morning room, all four of them were brought to a screeching halt when they found the three Carthinian nobles on their feet, red-faced, and hollering.

"My word! What's the meaning of this?" Arian released Aurelia and stood in the center of the meeting area, dividing the leaders. "Has something happened?"

Reyna's eyes blazed as she looked between Aurelia and the Bozari lords. "Would you like to tell him, or should I?"

Lord Zhaaran sighed. "Her Majesty overheard what was meant to be a private conversation between myself and Lord Zhoqa. Our fellow lords wish to ally the entirety of Bozar with Akkinor, but only if Akkinor promises to support Bozar and only Bozar in seizing Dofell."

Arian paused, miffed, before turning his gaze to Aurelia. "You knew of this?"

"Yes." Her face burned with shame as both Arian and Jack stared at her, flabbergasted. "Lord Zhoqa informed me last night. No decision has been made thus far—in truth, I haven't thought much of it at all."

Lord Zhoqa snorted. "Naturally."

Reyna was still fuming. "We're meant to proceed as allies until the last possible moment, yet the two of you are already plotting against me. Have you no sense?"

"Enough," Arian intervened. "Let's all have a seat." Hot, thick tension nearly suffocated the group as they settled. "Now, the most important item on our engagement diary—for now—is Kanibar."

"We must send word to the king." The color in Reyna's cheeks faded as her temper subsided. Even as she calmed, she refused to look any of her allies in the eye. "He knows about our alliances with Akkinor *and* about the dragon. He also knows that we may be forced to battle each other, as well as Kanibar, for Dofell. He needs reminding that regardless of what happens between Taundosa and Bozar, Akkinor will fight against Kanibar."

Ansyl, who'd been standing behind Aurelia's armchair beside Jack, cleared his throat. "If I may, I don't think it wise to deliver the news by raven. King Willem is said to be the personable sort—he makes no promises or arrangements with anyone without looking them in the eye. He needs to hear this directly from—"

"—from whom? One of us?" Lord Zhoqa scoffed. "We'd be walking into the lion's den. Even sending a diplomat to his doorstep would leave the poor soul at his mercy."

The barest hint of a smile formed on Ansyl's lips. "Man cannot imprison a dragon, my lord."

That made Aurelia smile, too. "He's right. I'm Akkinor's queen—if my country is going to war with Kanibar, he should hear it from me. It's impossible for him to hold me in Kanibar if I arrive on dragonback, too. Only one question remains: what am I meant to say to him?"

Lord Zhaaran ran a hand through his shoulder-length gray hair. "If he's adamant about his plans, he'll face Akkinor, Bozar, and Taundosa on the battlefield—maybe even Krotis, too. He may surrender before the bloodshed begins, and if he refuses, he and his people will find themselves entirely at our mercy. If he accepts, no harm will come to Kanibar."

Aurelia shifted in her chair. "My largest concern happens to be the same thing each of you wishes to delay until the last possible moment. Since it's already led you to quarrel with one another today, I see no point in delaying it further. We *must* decide what to do with Dofell when the time comes. Waiting until we're forced to turn on one another is a fool's gambit."

A deafening silence flooded through the morning room. Arian merely lowered his head in response as the muscles of his jaw tightened. Reyna and the two Bozari lords stared at Aurelia, unsure of how to respond, as their bodies tensed to the point of near calcification.

At their silence, Aurelia was persuaded to continue: "Bozar has promised to ally with Akkinor entirely if I support them in seizing Dofell. Such a thing would fracture both of our alliances with Taundosa and possibly Runeia, too. The last thing any of us wants is to lose what's become a crucial bond between our nations. The only solution I can think of, other than dividing Dofell, is appointing a new leader. And surely, the natives will want a Dofelli on the throne."

"The Dofelli race will be exterminated," Lord Zhoqa said matter-of-factly. "If not by us, then by Kanibar. What they prefer means nothing to us."

Aurelia scowled. "What's the matter with you? Have you always been this despicable, or did you lose your compassion when you gained your throne? Then again, it's not really a throne, is it? You're no king." He opened his mouth to protest, fuming, but she didn't give him the chance. "What a horrific thing to say, especially given the fact that we're here because the people of Dofell need a better future. We are here to protect them, not conquer them. I won't take part in a genocide, and I urge you all to think about the message we'd send to the masses if we allow such an atrocity to take place—that we, as leaders, only care about power."

"'We.'" Lord Zhoqa came as close to sneering as he could without directly insulting her. "You have no right to count yourself as a Carthinian leader."

"So long as you demand her support in the fights to come, she has every right to count herself among you. Respectfully, my lord," Arian retorted. Aurelia flashed him a small, grateful smile. "Her Grace is correct: by proceeding with our plans for Dofell, we're answering the people's pleas for help. We must take the Dofelli's opinions into consideration when choosing their new leader. What worries me, however, is who they'd choose."

All eyes turned to Aurelia. She froze, sucked in a sharp breath, and prayed to the gods that her allies hadn't heard the gasp lodged in her throat. As far as she knew, only Jack had heard the strangled noise, as he set a hulking hand on her shoulder to calm her.

"Me?" She looked between her four guests as they stared at her: Arian and Lord Zhaaran with a sense of understanding, and Reyna and Lord Zhoqa with pure displeasure. "Why would they want *me* to claim Dofell?"

Lord Zhoqa's skin folded as he aggressively massaged his temples. "Need I remind you that your actions are what instigated this disaster?"

"No, but—"

"The people believe the gods have chosen you to improve the realm." Lord Zhaaran's attempt at offering her a consoling smile failed, as the aggravation etched onto his face overpowered the expression. "You've proven that your heart lies with the betterment of humankind. In the eyes of those who've lost all hope in salvation, the only person capable of rising Dofell from the ashes of poverty and despair is you. You've offered them more promise than anyone in the realm, Your Grace, simply by reminding them of what the gods intended our world would be—even if they've simply chosen to believe that you're Forged in Gold. Such an individual has never been named in our history, but belief in their existence promotes faith in divine intervention, anyway."

"Those Forged in Gold exist as legends meant to inspire humanity to be good and just," Reyna added. "When the realm is at its lowest, good-natured individuals attempt to improve it, and those who witness their attempts are inspired to do the same. Believing in the legend makes a difference for a time, but soon enough, the masses will come to know the Ones Forged in Gold as just that—legends. They'll lose their hope and their drive to improve the realm as they always do, and those of us responsible for maintaining structure and balance will have to respond. Such responses almost always become battles for power."

Jack's hand on Aurelia's shoulder squeezed on instinct. She turned just enough to look into his eyes, and knew exactly what he was advising her to do. The two of them had kept her secret from their friends and allies for over five years by then, and now the time had finally come to share it.

Aurelia stood from the chair and crossed the room to pour herself a glass of wine. "Not long after my return to Akkinor, I was forced to order my brother's beheading. After the execution, I prayed to the gods and thanked them for what his string of evil deeds allowed me—allowed us— to achieve. I find myself simultaneously mourning and praying quite often. You see, no eternal curse is worse than knowing that one's greatest achievements were a direct result of losing one's family. At first, I wondered if the constant reminder was punishment for allowing my brother to be executed. The gods themselves showed me that I was wrong."

As she stared at the wall in front of her—still holding a jug of Myran wine in one hand and a half-filled chalice in the other—she visualized the day of Archie's execution. She remembered the smell of rotting fruit as peasants hurled buckets of waste at the prisoners on death row, the sight of the nooses as they swayed and whistled in the breeze, and the sound of shackles clanging against the wooden scaffolding. She remembered watching her brother, only two-and-twenty years of age, placing his head on the chopping block after uttering his last words: *long live the queen*. She heard the whoosh of the executioner's sword as it swung through the air, and the *tap-tapping* of Archie's blood dripping onto the floor. She remembered the exact moment the sword met his neck—the exact moment she'd chosen her throne over her family.

As intended, her memories quickly flooded her eyes with tears. Sniffling, she snatched a clean, white linen napkin from the serving table and dabbed at the corners of her eyes before the tears leaked down her cheeks and puffed her face. Upon spotting what appeared to be glittering gold paint slathered over the napkin, she turned to face her allies, all of whom had been waiting expectantly for whatever she had in store.

The first person she approached was Reyna. As the Golden Queen stared blankly at her, Aurelia pressed the napkin against Reyna's palm.

Aurelia smiled. "Some stories, Your Grace, were never written as legends. Some were written as prophecies."

As she returned to her seat, Reyna unraveled the napkin and gasped. Lord Zhoqa, impatient as ever, stood from his chair to peer over Arian at the napkin in Reyna's shaking grasp. Upon seeing it, he collapsed into his chair again, slack-jawed and beyond belief. Only Lord Zhaaran appeared disinterested in seeing the evidence for himself—he seemed to know exactly what it was.

Jack lifted a hand to Aurelia's face. The sudden movement captured the attention of everyone in the room as their eyes turned to the couple. He smiled as he used the pad of his index finger to brush something from Aurelia's cheek: a lone golden tear, having escaped its confinement in her eyes.

"Gods be good." Lord Zhoqa's sepia skin turned gray. "That's...*impossible.*"

"As you can see," Aurelia mused, "I have no intention of decimating the entirety of Dofell—not for Taundosa, not for Bozar, and certainly not for Akkinor. I have a duty to the realm to bring peace to its inhabitants, not violence and genocide. Each of us in this room is well aware of what would happen if Akkinor claimed a Carthinian kingdom. We must proceed in the best interests of all—not in what would allow any one of us to seize power over a kingdom desperately in need of help."

Reyna's hands trembled as she stared at the napkin. "I-I—"

"I'll fight alongside you if Kanibar refuses to abandon its plans for Dofell," Aurelia continued. "I won't, however, stand beside any of you if you choose to lay siege to Dofell. That isn't what I was made for."

"No." The twinkle in Lord Zhaaran's eyes mirrored his smile. "No, it isn't."

VIII

Only a few hours after revealing her destiny to her allies, Aurelia watched from the front steps of the palace as the Bozari lords' carriage rolled out of the bailey and through the gates. Two blue-eyed, brown-skinned Bozari soldiers stood at her side: Ser Balor Yassine of Orestes and Ser Bonta Zarros of Kazamir. While their lords returned to Bozar, the soldiers would remain in Akkinor for as long as the nobles deemed fit. The lords had each left a ship behind, too, for the emissaries to take home when their time in Akkinor was finished.

Of course, both ships had full crews and a handful of soldiers aboard, too, in case the emissaries needed their swords. Aurelia would've done the same thing if roles were reversed, but that didn't mean she had to like it.

The two soldiers followed Aurelia into the palace after the carriage disappeared from view. She brought them to an empty room at the rear of the eastern corridor, where the stewardess had organized a study for them to utilize throughout their stay. After leaving them, Aurelia instructed two of her soldiers to stand guard outside of the study and to keep their ears sharp; if her Bozari allies had any intention of betraying her or sneaking around behind her back, she wanted to know about it.

The allies came to an agreement that day, and while it was subject to change—particularly if Odeya Swann, Lady of Runeia in Krotis, sought assistance from her Akkinorian ally—Aurelia felt confident in their plan. It was perhaps the only strategy they might've invented that appeased everyone; for now.

If Kanibar succeeded in seizing Dofell, the negative effects of the conquest wouldn't be limited to economic decline in the south. Other than the two kingdoms themselves, northern Carthe consisted of the Violet Forest and the port province of Caedia: both ungoverned and unclaimed. It would be neither an easy nor a quick task, but Kanibar's power would rise to astronomical levels if the king decided to seize both territories. If that happened, Kanibar would span the entire northern half of Carthe, and the Kanish would control every single thing that happened from the northernmost point of Caedia to the border of the Ngora Valley.

Perhaps the Kanish wouldn't stop there, either. Perhaps they'd try to claim the desert as their own, too. If they managed to seize the majority of Carthinian territories and terrains, the three remaining kingdoms in the south—Taundosa, Bozar, and Krotis—would be at risk of invasion, too.

King Willem would be viewed by the entire realm as the second coming of Robert Cherrane: the unifier—or conqueror, depending on one's preference—of Akkinor. The old days often felt like they were a world away, but situations such as these were a fierce reminder that not much had changed since then. Akkinor had once been composed of numerous independent kingdoms: so what was stopping Carthe from meeting the same fate?

With that in mind, the allies had agreed to proceed as such—allies—until the last possible moment. They'd stand beside one another to defeat Kanibar, and only after they succeeded would they finally address what would become of Dofell. There was no way for anyone to know for certain if the allies would end up as enemies, but for the time being, they had no choice but to rely on one another.

That plan, however, was entirely dependent on what happened during Aurelia's audience with King Willem. She'd encourage him to surrender by brandishing her dragon and her allies' decision to stand beside one another. If he agreed to surrender, the allies wouldn't have long to think of a solution for Dofell. They'd have to move quickly before Carthe's commonfolk decided to act for themselves.

Her allies wished for her to leave for Carthe alongside them, though Aurelia had no choice but to disappoint them. For one, she couldn't risk missing the fast-approaching Changling if the trip took longer than expected. For another, she had more than enough domestic issues to resolve before she committed herself fully to the problems in Carthe.

She'd known from the moment she secured her alliances that she'd always have a responsibility to Carthe. Not only had she promised her soldiers and her goods to her allies, but she'd promised herself, too. They'd do for her exactly what she'd do for them, of course, but her time of need had come to an end, and theirs had just begun. She'd be at their mercy— like a prized family sword shared between siblings—until the matter was dealt with.

But she'd promised herself to others, too: the people of Akkinor. If she failed to prioritize her people, the petty issues arising across Akkinor would snowball into problems she wasn't equipped to defeat. The people—already upset because of her closeness with Carthe—would lose faith in her as their ruler. The only thing that might've kept them from rebelling against her was Halvor, and using her dragon as her only defense would turn her into the kind of ruler her brother had been.

As Aurelia strolled to her study, she passed Thea and Mycah, Ansyl's younger siblings, walking toward the foyer. Both were wearing riding clothes and had their bows and sheaths slung over their shoulders. She stopped them briefly to make sure both their brother and their tutors knew where they were going; not unlike their late sister, they had a knack for doing whatever they pleased, whenever they pleased.

Mycah, a surprisingly wise boy of fifteen years, told her, "Master Orien isn't feeling himself today, so we thought we'd train for a bit. His Royal Highness promised to teach us how to shoot on horseback."

Aurelia flicked her eyes over to thirteen-year-old Thea. "Your brother—"

"My brother would have us confined to the classroom with nothing but old texts for company," she replied. "He doesn't see the need for us to train."

"That's where he and I disagree," Aurelia said. The siblings exchanged surprised looks before turning back to her and smiling. "It's crucial that all young people be trained in combat, even if you never see battle. You mustn't be cross with your brother, though. He only wishes to keep you safe." She glanced around to search for potential eavesdroppers before lowering her voice. "I won't tell him I've seen you, but I can't speak for others. You shall have to remind Jack to keep mum, too—he's quite the talker, as you know, and he'll want to tell Ansyl all about his day with you if he's not instructed to keep his mouth shut."

Mycah grinned. "Thank you, Your Grace."

She tipped her head in both response and farewell. Familiar with Aurelia's distaste for formalities, the siblings didn't bother bowing or curtsying before returning to their path. Aurelia hoped they finished training before Ansyl returned home from his trip to the Follian city of Elderhost: he was rather protective over his siblings, and after so many years of serving as their father-figure, he didn't take well to their disobedience.

While she understood where Ansyl was coming from, she didn't entirely agree with him. He valued their education above all else—a consequence of the children being pulled from school to support the family while they lived in Kanibar. Ansyl didn't wish for them to take their privileges for granted, nor did he wish for them to train in the same thing that led to Kaia's death. She'd been a skilled fighter, even on horseback, which was partly the reason she'd traveled the Violet Forest alone so often. In his eyes, the best way to keep his siblings safe was to focus their energies on mental strengths, not physical.

She was relieved that Ansyl had left to spend the day in Elderhost. As much as she needed her Lord Hand, she knew it'd be difficult to lie to him about his siblings' activities while he sat in front of her. She could keep quiet so long as he didn't bring them up, but if he did...She didn't wish to break the children's trust, but she didn't want to risk breaking his, either.

For a split second as she slipped into her study, she heard a teenage Archie's voice echoing in her head: *See what becomes of you if you try to please everyone. You'll end up as one of two things: a martyr or a mockery.*

A shiver traced her spine. It'd been over five years since Archie's betrayal, and still, memories were constantly emerging from the darkest corners of her mind—memories that, looking back, should have been warning signs. The memories even went as far as to prove that Archie was much cleverer than she'd given him credit for. She'd spent so many years viewing him as a selfish, silly child that she hadn't noticed when he started acting like a man.

A cruel and greedy man, but a man, nonetheless.

Aurelia sunk into the chair at her desk and turned her attention to the mountain of paperwork stacked on the wooden surface. She started by completing the task she normally left to Ansyl: separating the work by subject, and by most-to-least important. Certain matters demanded her immediate attention, but others—like marriage proposals for her children, even if the young royals were all under the age of six—were nothing more than distractions.

So many fresh concerns, plus the violence against mages and the assassins training in secret. Aurelia had enough on her plate as it was, and yet, she'd have to take a step back from everything to keep her alliances intact. But there would always be some sort of problem in Akkinor for her to solve, so even if she didn't wish to, she knew she had to prioritize the impending war in Carthe.

A soft knock interrupted her thoughts. After she gave permission for the knocker to enter, the door opened to reveal Jack on the other side.

Aurelia frowned. "I thought you were training with Thea and Mycah."

He winced and ran a hand through his wind-tousled hair. "We managed ten minutes before hollering interrupted us. Ansyl returned early from his trip to Elderhost—he wasn't pleased with us. He's sent the children to attend to their studies, but I promised to resume their lessons tomorrow when he's locked in the Assembly meeting."

"Good. I may speak to him about this when I get a spare moment, but I don't know how well he'll take it."

"Fair enough."

When he lingered by the hearth like he didn't know what he was meant to be doing, she raised an eyebrow. "Are you going to greet your queen properly, or must I command you to do so?"

"Oh, I like the sound of *that*."

Aurelia rolled her eyes, mirrored his grin, and beckoned him with her finger. He joined her behind the desk, making her yelp when he pulled her to her feet by her wrists. He grasped her jaw between his thumb and index finger, pressing his lips to hers, and forced her to step backwards against the wall when the weight of his body pressing up to hers nearly knocked her over. He deepened the kiss as his tongue explored the hollows of her mouth, and only when he stepped on her toes did they finally spring apart, both laughing and blushing like a pair of school-age lovers.

He brushed a lock of hair from her eyes and smiled. "Even twenty minutes apart from you feels like an eternity. It always has."

She blushed at the hunger in his eyes. "Stop looking at me like that, Jack."

"Like what?"

"Like you wish for us to make a fifth child."

He boomed with laughter, making both of their bodies tremble from the force of it. "Maybe in a few years. For now, I'd just like to practice."

"Good. Say—where are the babes? Arian will be itching to see them when he wakes from his nap."

"Heavens if I know. Let's search."

She gnawed on her lip as her eyes found the paperwork on her desk. "But—"

"Work isn't going anywhere, my love. You have my word that I shall deliver you back here before day's end to pick up where you left off."

She couldn't help but smile at that. "All right."

After a few minutes of searching the palace for their children, Aurelia and Jack soon found themselves standing in the doorway of the morning room. Halle and Henry were playing a game of their own creation on the floor, Celesse was reading a story to an already-sleeping Halyna, and Hyacinth was busying herself with a new toy Arian brought from Taundosa—yet another puzzle box.

"You're cheating, Henry!" Halle howled.

He crossed his arms over his chest and huffed. "Am not."

"You are! *Celesse!*"

The governess sighed. "Henry, stop your cheating this instant. Halle, quiet your whining. Even baby Lena doesn't whine like you."

As Aurelia and Jack swallowed their laughter, Henry huffed again. "I want to play with Sisi."

"She's busy, and she doesn't like playing with you," Halle retorted.

"*Why?*"

"Because you're a cheater," Hyacinth said. "I don't like cheaters."

Celesse exhaled loudly when the siblings started to bicker again. "Come here, my little loves. Your sister is losing interest in the story, and I'd like to finish it. Will you be my audience?"

Reluctant yet intrigued, Halle and Henry abandoned their game to sit at Celesse's feet. Hyacinth didn't appear interested at first, but soon set the puzzle box aside to join them. Henry scooched away when he felt Halle's knee touching his, but soon enough, he inched closer to her and rested his head on her shoulder. She put her arm around his back as if to protect him, then leaned her head against his while they listened to Celesse's story. On Henry's other side, Hyacinth reached her right hand over her lap to hold Henry's, and her left behind his back—directly on top of Halle's.

Aurelia's eyes welled with tears as Jack set a hand on her back. "They're occupied for now. Shall *we* occupy ourselves elsewhere before Arian and Reyna come searching for us?"

A shiver traced her spine at the feel of his hot breath on her ear. "Occupy ourselves how, exactly?"

His oceanic eyes danced wickedly. "I have some ideas."

She raised an eyebrow. "Shall we race?"

When his eyes glowed even brighter, she stepped out of her shoes, collected them from the floor, and wiggled her eyebrows for half a second before bolting into the hallway. He ran after her, hooting with laughter, and caught up with her in under a minute—an advantage of birth on his part, as his legs were nearly double the size of hers.

While nearby servants pretended not to observe the childish antics of their queen and her husband, Jack grabbed her by the waist and tossed her over his shoulder. He dashed up the stairs—taking the steps two at a time—while she squirmed and hollered, and before she knew it, the door to their bedchamber was swinging open and slamming against the wall. He kicked it shut, tossed her on the bed like she was a ragdoll, and immediately started working on the buttons of his trousers while keeping his eyes trained on hers.

Despite being carried for most of the journey, Aurelia struggled to catch her breath. "I take it we tied, then?"

"The race isn't over yet, my love."

She chewed on her lower lip when his trousers fell to his ankles. "You scoundrel."

"Only for you." He climbed on top of her, bringing her skirts to her hips as he did so, and buried his hands in her hair as his elbows dug into the mattress on either side of her head. His voice deepened when he whispered in her ear: "Don't think for a second that I'll let you win this one."

Her entire being—body, heart, and soul—warmed when he touched his lips to her neck. "I wouldn't dream of it."

IX

Just a few weeks after her Carthinian allies left Akkinor—Arian and Reyna having departed not long after the Bozari lords—the first day of the Changling, marking the shift from spring to summertime in the Folly, arrived.

Highborn from across Akkinor arrived in the days leading up to the five-day celebration, filling the palace with constant noise, laughter, and chaos. Most of them would reside in the palace for the duration of the Changling, as always, but others claimed vast estates across the kingdom for a bit more privacy. Additionally, any lowborn from other kingdoms who'd managed to attend filled every single inn and hostel in the Folly. There were so many civilian attendees that some Follians had turned to renting out rooms in their homes.

Most of the Changling's events took place in or around Robert's Arena—a stadium located near Oleander's Valley, a historical battlefield where most public executions occurred. Every village, town, and field between the palace and the valley had been transformed for the Changling: the calm residential areas were now accompanied by hundreds upon hundreds of tents for entertainers, traveling markets, and the like.

From sunrise to sunset on all five days, people from all corners of the country sold goods at the little stands, shops, and shacks they erected. During the winter Changling, people sold things like tea or hot chocolate, stews, blankets, furs, and so on. The summer Changling, however, saw merchants selling things like lemonade, fresh fruit, flowers, fans, wind chimes, and more to highborn and lowborn alike.

The Changling, it seemed, was a universal time of leisure across Akkinor—a few days each year when the only things that mattered were which families' knights won the jousting competitions, and which emotional ballads the opera singers performed.

FORGED IN ASHES

Early in the morning on the first day, spectators and performers alike filled the seats at Robert's Arena for a jousting tournament. Before the opening ceremony began, Aurelia stood from her seat in the royal viewing box—accompanied by her extended family, her closest advisors, and about two dozen soldiers—and approached the railing to deliver her speech. The entire arena had been watching her in anticipation for the event to begin, so every soul quieted when they saw her at the railing.

Aurelia smiled and gazed at the crowd. "Welcome, all! The time has come, once again, for our country to celebrate yet another marvelous season. Today marks the end of springtime this year, and the start of what appears to be the hottest summer of my lifetime. Let us celebrate the prosperity this spring has brought in the name of Almighty Buen." The crowd cheered, whooped, and whistled. "Now, while the next five days are meant to honor the changing of the seasons, they're also an opportunity for us to celebrate not only our good fortune, but our community. Whether those sitting beside you came from near or far, they're still your neighbors: honor them in friendship and kindness, and embrace the differences between you rather than letting them divide you."

When she nodded to the knights positioned on either side of an iron gate within the arena—several feet below where the spectators sat—they opened the gate, and a group of soldiers emerged while pushing an enormous pyre planted on a wagon. They brought the pyre to the center of the arena, hefted it from the wagon, and positioned it precisely before bringing the wagon back to the gate.

Aurelia cleared her throat. "It's my pleasure to welcome each of you to the first day of the Changling! May the Almighty bring you the prosperity you've earned, the fortune you deserve, and the success you desire."

Right on cue, a bellowing screech echoed from one side of the Folly to the other, rattling the woodlands surrounding the arena and shooing flocks of birds into the sky. Spectators gasped in awe when Halvor circled overhead before landing on the open roof above. He shrieked again, then turned his mouth toward the pyre and released a powerful stream of fire. The flames ignited the pyramid-shaped stack of wood instantly, prompting Halvor to bellow with pride before lifting off into the sky again.

As the pyre smoldered, the jousters emerged from the doorways beneath the many rows of spectator seats. Each knight wore the colors and sigils of whichever noble family they served, from the lowest-ranking highborn in Akkinor to the queen herself. They stood adjacent to each other on one side of the tilt barrier, their horses positioned behind them, while an equal number of individuals lined up on the other side of the barrier: women.

The practice wasn't a favorite of Aurelia's, but as she had been advised, tradition was tradition.

The women, all highborn, held a favor of their own creation in their hands: lengths of cloth or silk from their gowns, wreaths made of flowers and vines, ribbons, scarves, and handkerchiefs. One by one, the knights stepped forward to choose a woman, who then granted him her favor before curtsying, kissing his knuckles, and wishing him good fortune. After claiming their favor, the knights crossed the arena and tossed their gift into the fire, then took a knee to pray to Buen. When the prayer was complete, the knight mounted his steed and awaited his turn to joust.

There was one less woman than there were knights. The knight without a favor was representing the Brentwood family—Aurelia hadn't chosen him herself, so she didn't even know his name. He approached the royal viewing box, removed his helmet and tucked it under his arm, and took a knee before the queen.

"Your Grace." He bowed his head before meeting her gaze. "May I have the honor of your favor?"

She beamed. "You may."

She took the favor from Ansyl—a wreath she and the children had fashioned together—and tossed it onto his lance. He thanked her and stood, but before she could ask for his name, he made his way toward the pyre to conclude the opening ceremony.

As she returned to her seat, she summoned Marilla Page, the Assembly member who'd chosen the knight. "What's his name?"

"Ser Rayan, Your Grace. He's Holosi-born, but he was knighted into the Royal Army about a year prior to the uprising. It was he who found and apprehended Lord Bradley Reilly on the battlefield."

"I see. Thank you."

The first jousters—representing the Leightons of Omara and the Steels of Holos—took their positions. When the Leighton knight struck his opponent in the sternum, sending him flying backwards onto the dirt, the Steel knight immediately howled in pain and begged his squire for assistance.

Jack wanted to take the children to the tourney, but Aurelia forbade it after remembering how grotesque jousting could be. She was grateful for her decision when a knight representing the Silios of Sadia accused a knight representing the Stones of Laynoa of cheating, prompting the two to draw their swords until the Silio knight was killed by a blade through the eye.

Halfway through the tournament, the spectators began to boo when a knight representing the Crowlands of Myra took his place at the tilt barrier. The knight had been chosen not by Lord Crowland, but by his heir's husband, Erastus Swann of Krotis. Erastus brought several Runeian soldiers with him when he settled in Myra, and one of them—the jouster—chose to revoke his Kroti citizenship to become an Akkinorian knight. The Akkinorian people hadn't been pleased to have a foreigner amongst the country's most prestigious military organization, but the jouster didn't seem to mind their disapproval: even with the crowd booing him, he emerged victorious.

Jack, an avid fan of jousting, abandoned his seat beside Aurelia to cling to the railing while watching the Ashford family's chosen champion. He whooped and hollered in delight when the Ashford knight reigned supreme, while the other Ashfords in the viewing box groaned in displeasure. Tourney or not, most Omarans weren't fond of violence of any kind—excluding Jack, who'd never really fit in among his kin.

When Ser Rayan, the Brentwood knight, took his place against the knight representing the Normindies of Sadia, Aurelia turned around to observe her mother's family. Only a few of Cressida's siblings and their families—Andren, Rien, and Selsa—were seated in the viewing box with the queen's court.

Rien grinned at her. "I hope the odds are in your favor, Your Grace."

She snorted. "No, you don't."

"No, I don't."

Aurelia laughed. It was no wonder her mother was so forthcoming about claiming Rien as her favorite brother. Of all the Normindies and Brentwoods still alive, Rien was Aurelia's favorite of them, too.

Both Rien and Andren shouted in protest when Ser Rayan knocked the Normindi knight from his horse, winning the joust. Aurelia clapped and whistled—improper behavior for the queen, according to her advisors—as Ser Rayan led his steed to the viewing box.

"I claim my victory in your name, Your Grace," he said breathlessly.

She met him by the railing and smiled. "You were most impressive. I shall offer you ten gold in honor of your valiant representation of the Brentwood family." She tipped her head. "Forward, good man, ever forward."

He bowed as well as he could while on horseback before retreating to stand with the other jousters. Before returning to her seat, Aurelia approached Lady Page once more. The noblewoman started to stand so she could curtsy, but Aurelia allowed her to remain seated by setting a kind hand on her shoulder.

"I should like to know Ser Rayan's family name," Aurelia said. "I need to be able to find him so I can invite him to the palace—ten gold is a fair

94

prize, but I'd like to reward his valor with something more. Perhaps we might treat him to a royal feast."

She nodded. "It's Haze, I believe. Ser Rayan Haze."

Aurelia froze, and from the corner of her eye, she saw Jack release the railing and turn to face her. She met his bewildered gaze with an identical expression. She knew the name *Haze*: not because she'd worked or been acquainted with a member of Ser Rayan's family in the past, but because it was her birth father's surname.

She waved her hand dismissively at Jack, who only sighed and returned to the tourney. It was an interesting turn of events, to be certain, but Aurelia knew better than anyone that families grew like weeds: Ser Rayan was probably just a third cousin twice removed, or something else of the sort.

Even so, when she saw him remove his helmet from across the arena—revealing a head of auburn hair strikingly similar to her son's—she couldn't shake the uneasiness threatening to swallow her whole.

***

The first day of the Changling was dedicated only to jousting, and the second saw only plays and theatrical performances. Jesters took to the stage between each play, briefly interrupting somewhat tragic stories with satirical performances.

The third day was reserved for racing. From morning until midday, spectators gathered around the track beside Robert's Arena to watch the racehorses, and most highborn tended to bet on one horse in particular. The rest of the day saw other kinds of races: donkeys, pigs, hounds, and more. The betting wasn't as intense when it came to the other animals, whose races mostly existed simply to entertain observers.

The fourth day saw a combination of entertainers showing off their talents: acrobats, jugglers, and those who trained animals to perform tricks. Spectators particularly enjoyed contests, in which the participants spent weeks and even seasons training to bob for apples, shoot flaming arrows, mud wrestle, and even play board games.

Of course, the fifth and final day of the Changling was something of a celebration of the best acts and the victors of each event, as they returned for one last show. The evening was the best part, as it concluded the celebration with concerts, a massive feast, and a party that usually lasted until dawn the next morning.

While the lowborn celebrated from the streets, Aurelia hosted the highborn at the palace for the feast and the concluding celebration.

Numerous long tables had been placed in the dining hall to account for the many faces in attendance, so it was difficult to move even an inch without bumping into someone. When the feast came to an end, everyone would migrate to the ballroom to drink and dance through the night.

Aurelia, exhausted from the last five days, decided against attending the party. She'd addressed the highborn during the feast to thank them for attending, but she excused herself not long after to avoid getting lost in the crowd of drunken nobles.

While crossing the foyer to reach the grand staircase, Aurelia just barely heard a voice penetrating the ever-increasing octaves and booming laughter of her guests. She turned before climbing the first step and saw Ser Rayan Haze lingering by the doorway.

He bowed as she approached him. "Your Grace. I-I was told by Lady Page to meet her here ten minutes ago, but—"

"—but the wine has already led her to forget how to walk, so we can assume she forgot about you, too," Aurelia finished. "That's all right. In fact, I asked her to summon you. I'd like to invite you to the palace for dinner in the near future—I'm pleased with how valiantly you represented my family at the tourney, and I'd like to offer you more than coin to express my pride in your skills."

His crystalline blue eyes widened as he took a knee. "I-I thank you humbly, Your Grace, but I fear I'm unworthy of a seat at your table."

"Nonsense. Anyone is welcome to a seat at my table, as long as they earn it—and you have."

Even with the noise, she heard his breath catch. "I'd be most honored, Your Grace."

She motioned for him to rise. "Where do you live, Ser Rayan?"

"I currently live in Rockmaw here in the Folly, but I was born in Holos."

"Where?"

"Satin Valley, Your Grace. Just on the Laynoan border."

Her heart hammered. "What brought you to the Folly?"

His eyes darkened, but with sadness instead of irritation. "My home burned down when I was a boy. We thought my father was killed somehow when he didn't come looking for us—he was a soldier—so my mother took my sister and I to the Folly so we could begin anew."

It took everything she had to stop herself from reacting in any way. Arian had once shared with her a theory regarding her birth father's reason for abandoning a pregnant Katryna: he'd left a family behind in Akkinor and returned to be with them. That was the most either of them knew about Eric Haze's departure from Taundosa, but apparently, there was more to the story.

She cleared her throat. "You *thought* your father was killed?"

"Indeed. He found us several years later—he thought the three of us died in the fire, and left to begin a new life elsewhere."

"Are your parents still alive? And your sister?"

"My sister moved back to Satin Valley last autumn. My mother died of the fever many years ago—almost fifteen now. My father lives next door to me."

She prayed he didn't notice when she gasped. "Is he...Is he well? Your father?"

He furrowed his eyebrows. "Yes, he is."

"That's...That's nice to hear, Ser Rayan. I'm pleased you have such a lovely family supporting you, and do accept my sympathies over the loss of your mother."

Rayan's cheeks turned pink. "Thank you, Your Grace."

"I shall send word to Rockmaw tomorrow so we can plan a feast. Thank you for your participation this Changling, and may the Almighty bless you."

He bowed. "Thank you, Your Grace. And you."

She forced a smile before turning on her heel and climbing the stairs. When she reached the top, Rayan was gone, and she was left feeling breathless—not because of the climb, but because she now knew for certain that her birth father had been one of her subjects from the moment she was brought home to Akkinor as heir to the throne.

And Eric, wherever he was, had no idea that his queen was his daughter.

X

A week after the Changling, Aurelia found herself preparing for her fast-approaching trip to Kanibar. The moment the highborn left the palace and the lowborn visitors packed their things—instantly returning the Folly to its normal, quiet state—the matters across Akkinor and Carthe, once again, demanded the queen's attention.

Fortunately, the domestic issues had been put on hold because of the Changling, and if she knew her nobility at all, she was fairly certain they wouldn't be bombarding her with unexpected visits or letters of complaint for another few weeks: they tended to overindulge every season, so it normally took them some time to recover before they turned to their grievances again.

After learning about her relationship to Ser Rayan Haze, she wanted nothing more than to bring him to the palace as soon as possible. He deserved to be honored with a royal feast held in his name after his exceptional performance, but it'd be an opportunity for Aurelia to squeeze information out of him, too. And maybe—just maybe—he'd bring his father along with him.

Their father.

She had to put that on hold, though. Only a week had passed since the end of the celebration, but she was due to leave for Kanibar the following day. Instead of focusing her energy on the father and half-brother she didn't know, she spent her last peaceful day before the journey with her children. She was fairly certain the audience with King Willem wouldn't end poorly, but gods forbid something went awry, she wanted to be sure she'd spent as much time with her little loves as possible.

While Jack was off training Ansyl's siblings somewhere in the Follian woodlands, Aurelia took their children into the gardens for a midday picnic. They dined on tiny sandwiches, slices of pear, chocolate biscuits, and fresh lemonade beneath the same tree Aurelia and Linden used to play in when they were young.

The children brought toys with them, as always, and were eager to finish eating so they could resume their playing. It wasn't long before Halle and Henry started bickering over their toys, disturbing Halyna while she napped and irritating Hyacinth as she counted every dandelion in her vicinity.

Aurelia scowled at them. "What are you quarreling over now?"

"I want that one!" Henry pointed to the object clutched in Halle's fist. "Mine is ugly."

Aurelia examined the toy box they'd brought and sighed. The handheld wooden chest contained figurines of each animal symbolic to Akkinor: a falcon for the Brentwood family, a horse for the Ashfords, a snow leopard for the Normindies, et cetera. Different versions of the toy box existed across the country—solid gold pieces for the highborn, and wooden pieces for the lowborn. This chest in particular had been Archie's when he was a boy, and after he lost half of the pieces, Edmund had replaced them with wooden ones; not as punishment, but as encouragement for Archie to take more care with his belongings.

She held out her hand, prompting both children to place their respective figurine on her palm. Halle's golden stag (symbolic of the Tarre family) was pristine, but Henry's wooden one was cracked along the gut and missing an antler.

Henry folded his arms over his chest. "I want the shiny one."

She sighed again. "Come here. All of you." While Halyna snoozed on a blanket beside her, the elder three children gathered in front of her and mimicked her crossed legs. "I'm going to tell you a story—one I heard from my father, who heard it from his father, and so on. The tale begins with an ancient king locked in the dungeon. He wasn't a good king, so his own men locked him away to protect the people from his cruelty. But some believed he deserved a second chance, so a trio of merciful men visited him in his cell and offered him an opportunity. They told him that if he could dig himself out of his cell in three days' time using nothing but a spoon, he'd earn his freedom. They gave him a choice between two spoons: one silver and one iron."

Hyacinth's wide eyes grew even larger with curiosity. "Which did he choose?"

Aurelia smiled. "Silver. He was a king, of course, and he believed a king should always choose the finer option."

"Did he escape?"

"No, my love. He didn't. When three days passed and the men returned to the dungeon, they found the king weeping in his cell with the broken spoon sitting beside him. You see, the silver spoon wasn't strong enough—it snapped in half as soon as he began to dig."

Halle frowned. "That's a sad story."

"It is, but that's not how it ends. There was another prisoner in the dungeon, too: a poor fishmonger jailed for theft. The trio of men gave the fishmonger the same choice they'd given the king. Do you know which spoon he chose?"

"Iron?"

"That's right. When three days passed and the men returned to the dungeon, they found a hole in the fishmonger's cell that led directly onto the streets. They never saw the fishmonger again."

Halle chewed on her nails. "What happened to the king?"

"Nothing good." Aurelia raised an eyebrow at them. "Do you understand why I told you this story?"

Henry shook his head. "No, Mama."

"Sometimes, the finest, prettiest things in the world aren't as valuable as they look," she murmured. "We mustn't make decisions based on what we believe makes us look more powerful than others. What if I wore my crown to battle instead of my helmet? A crown certainly looks grander, but it won't protect me from harm like a helmet might." She gently took Henry's chin between her fingers and smiled. "Don't be fooled by appearances, little one. Just because something appears more regal than another doesn't always mean it's the better option."

While Halle and Henry muttered in understanding, Hyacinth sat in contemplative silence for a moment before asking, "What about a third spoon?"

Aurelia stared at her, miffed. "What do you mean?"

"What if there was a bronze spoon, Mama?"

"Sisi..." Aurelia trailed off, baffled by her daughter's intelligence, and cleared her throat. "Akkinorian bronze is as beautiful and regal as silver or gold, and it's stronger even than iron or steel. I suppose there wouldn't be any moral to this story if Akkinorian bronze was an option. It serves both purposes." She frowned. "Where did you think of such a question?"

Hyacinth shrugged. "I don't know."

Aurelia forced a smile. "All right. You may resume your playing, but I don't wish to hear another word of your bickering."

While Halle and Henry returned to the toy box—with Henry proudly claiming the wooden stag—Hyacinth stood from the picnic blanket to admire the tree. Aurelia observed her as she appeared to consider climbing the trunk, but decided against it. Instead, she took a few steps backwards to study it in its entirety, cocking her head to the side and planting her hands on her hips.

"What are you doing, Sisi?" Halle asked.

Hyacinth turned and locked her eyes on her mother's. "I had a dream about this tree, Mama. You were there, but you were small."

"Oh? What was I doing?"

"Sitting. A boy was with you. He had dark skin like Irina. You were eating raspberry tarts." She paused. "May I have a raspberry tart for dessert tonight?"

Aurelia's heart leapt to her throat. "Of course. But the boy in your dream—do you know his name?"

"No, but he had kind eyes."

Yes, he did, Aurelia thought. "Were we talking to one another?"

"Yes, Mama. You were talking about me and how you had to find me in the village." The princess gasped and pointed to something in the nearby bushes. "There's a bunny, Mama! May I see it?"

Aurelia didn't answer, and even if she wanted to, she didn't get the chance: all three children bolted toward the bushes immediately. All Aurelia could do was stare at the tree—at the tallies carved into the bark, marking the number of hours she and Linden hid there before they were discovered—as a forgotten childhood memory returned to her.

She'd been nine or ten at the time, and she and Linden were sitting in the branches of their favorite tree, munching on raspberry tarts they'd stolen from the kitchens. She'd been learning about poetry during her lessons that season, and while she couldn't grasp it for the life of her, Linden was marvelous at both understanding and creating it. He'd offered to help her while they lounged in the tree by making a game out of it, as they always did: they were only allowed to speak to each other in poems, and if they failed, they'd have to give up one of their tarts.

Somehow, their conversation led to Linden asking if she'd like to accompany him to the village of Mistcairn so he could gather a bouquet of hyacinths for Cicely. Because he was speaking like a poet, he'd referenced the flowers as if talking about a person:

Hyacinth is lovely and fair,
with pretty pink stars for hair.
Hyacinth brings a sweet smell to the air,
and lives in the village just over there.
Hyacinth is a treasure for my beloved to bear,
so we must hurry to find her in the square!

Aurelia knew her daughter was intelligent beyond her years, but intelligence didn't give a five-year-old girl the power to see scenes from the past in her dreams.

As she watched the children chase a bunny around the gardens, giggling and running about like headless chickens, she wondered if there was something other than Hyacinth's parentage that made her different from her siblings—something beneath the surface.

There was no time to dwell on the possibilities now, though. Aurelia would have to wait until the matter in Carthe was dealt with to dive deeper into whatever her brother's daughter was capable of.

Aurelia cursed herself immediately when her own thoughts echoed in her head. It was the first time in five years that she'd thought of Hyacinth as *Archie's* daughter, not hers.

She didn't like it one bit.

***

After dinner the following evening, Aurelia said goodbye to Jack and the children, and mounted Halvor for their flight to Kanibar—alone.

Jack and Ansyl both insisted that at least one person accompany her, but she wouldn't have it. Ansyl was needed in Akkinor to rule on her behalf, and she wanted Jack to stay home with the children. The possibility of Aurelia being killed on her mission was slim to nothing while Halvor accompanied her, but it was a possibility, nonetheless—she wouldn't risk her children becoming orphans by bringing Jack along, too. She didn't wish for any soldiers to join her, either. Of her many options, only Jack had ridden on dragonback before (reluctantly, and he'd yelped like a frightened pup the entire time), and she didn't wish to force her men into doing something that made them shake in their boots.

Before she and Halvor lifted off into the sky, two people—husband and wife, both infamous Follian inventors—presented Aurelia with a new development they'd been working on: a means of tethering Aurelia to Halvor in the event that she fell from his back. Akkinorian bronze rings were placed around the joints connecting Halvor's wings to his body, and sturdy lengths of leather connected them to another set of rings attached to Aurelia's girdle. It wasn't the most practical solution in the world, but it was just for precautionary measure, anyway. Even the worst scenario— falling and dangling from the tethers until Halvor was able to land—was a much better alternative to her catapulting from the sky.

By sea, the journey from Akkinor to Carthe took anywhere from two weeks to five, depending on the weather and possible pirate interference.

By flight, it could take between one and three days, depending on how often Aurelia stopped to rest. There was a small, uninhabited island in the middle of the Alkamura, so Aurelia and Halvor spent one night there to eat and sleep before setting out again.

As she and Halvor coasted over the Alkamura, Aurelia distracted herself by rehearsing what she'd say to King Willem. She'd hardly stopped thinking about it since she decided to meet with him herself, and yet, she still couldn't decide on one method of persuasion. Of all the Carthinian territories, she was the least familiar with Kanibar—and even less familiar with its leader. She'd have to wait until she met him face-to-face to decide how to proceed.

On the bright side, Willem Trevas was only a piece of the puzzle. Perhaps his soldiers would see a dragon of old for the first time and be frightened into laying down their swords. Loyalty and duty only went so far in the face of true terror. For a solider, the only fate worse than being killed in battle by a sword was being eaten alive—or burned alive—by a dragon. If enough Kanish soldiers refused to fight for fear of being killed by Halvor, King Willem wouldn't stand a chance against Aurelia's allies.

Having spent most of the flight above the clouds, Halvor descended by a few dozen feet when the shadows of land came into view. A plethora of ships—Carthinian, Akkinorian, and Esposi alike—were either sailing beneath them or docked around the coast of Khaba. As Halvor inched closer to the southern port province, the small shadows of land transformed into a massive continent. Aurelia could just barely hear people shouting over the sounds of Halvor's wings flapping and wind whipping against her ears, so she knew they'd been spotted.

Most of Carthe had heard about the situation in Dofell by then, but Aurelia's involvement hadn't been announced yet. Whoever was in Khaba that day to see the Queen of Akkinor and her dragon arrive in Carthe....They'd put two and two together rather quickly, and word would spread across the continent. Any Runeians of Krotis would report their observation to Lady Swann, and Aurelia's third and final Carthinian ally would certainly contact her about what Aurelia's involvement meant for their alliance—especially if the old woman was swayed into fighting for Dofell, too.

After flying over midland Bozar and northern Taundosa, Aurelia instructed Halvor to descend even lower as they passed over Dofell. He slowed his pace at her command, allowing her to observe what little she could from such a height. Not to her surprise, the streets were barren, leaving nobody to spot Halvor and holler about a dragon infiltrating Dofelli skies. If anyone *had* seen them, nobody made a fuss about it—

almost like the sight was as normal to them as spotting a rabbit in the woods.

At the least, she didn't notice any scouts or suspicious activity. The mobs Arian and Reyna spoke of were gone, and the soldiers who'd been guarding the perimeter of the Phyre family palace had retreated inside. She hadn't expected to see much in Dofell, but she'd certainly expected a handful of soldiers prowling the streets to protect their people against the threat to the west. That left one of two conclusions: either the monarchy didn't care enough about its people to offer them protection from Kanibar, or it had neither the resources nor the manpower needed for defense.

A chill traced Aurelia's spine the moment Halvor soared over the tall stone walls that encased Dofell. Only a small stretch of forest separated Dofell from Kanibar, and the latter—unlike its neighboring kingdom—had no walls or gates encircling its territory. If one weren't aware of the borders, they wouldn't know they'd left the Violet Forest behind for Kanibar.

As they coasted in search of the palace, Aurelia was well-aware of the many Kanish citizens—highborn and lowborn alike, judging by her quick glimpses of them—watching, pointing, shouting, and marveling. Some fainted at the sight of Halvor, others reached for anything that could be used as a weapon, and the rest merely screamed like they couldn't think of a better response. Fortunately, nobody shot at them or attempted to bring them down.

Aurelia took their last few moments of flight to appreciate the beauty of Kanibar. It was exactly as Kaia (and her siblings, on occasion) described it. Aurelia once told Kaia of her desire to visit Kanibar one day; she wished Kaia were alive to see her fulfill that desire, just as she wished the circumstances of her visit were different.

While distracted by a field of hyacinths in every shade of blue and purple known to man, Aurelia felt a buzzing by her ear and brushed it away with her hand. She wasn't fond of insects, and unfortunately, being accompanied by bugs of all kinds was a condition of riding on dragonback—she often returned from rides with bees or cicadas tangled in her hair. She thought it was just another pesky insect irking her that day until the 'insect' in question perched on Halvor's neck just a few feet in front of her, mirroring her position with its legs spread to either side and its arms wrapped around one of Halvor's spikes.

A gasp lodged in her throat. A faint glow surrounded the palm-sized creature, and for a brief moment when Halvor's wings stilled and the wind ceased to shriek, Aurelia heard giggling. She gasped again, and the sound was enough to capture the creature's attention. It looked over its shoulder, its enormous brown eyes locked on her blue ones, and stared at her in a way that made her feel like *it* was Halvor's master—not her.

It was gone when she blinked. She didn't know where it went, but she was certain it was a sprite: based on what she'd been told, most sprites in Kanibar served as spies for the monarchy. If King Willem hadn't already been alerted of her arrival by those who'd spotted Halvor, he'd probably know within mere seconds.

Before she could think about what the sprite was reporting to its master, Halvor parted a large white cloud with his snout, and their first glimpse of the Palace of Kanibar came into view. While looking for a spot large enough for Halvor to land, Aurelia felt a sharp, piercing sensation behind her eyes. The feeling compelled her to look directly below them at the front doors of the white limestone palace. There, a man wearing a crown stood with his hands clasped behind his back and his neck craned towards the sky. He was smiling.

XI

Halvor landed on a grassy field behind the palace, dividing the king's estate from a nearby town. Aurelia heard people screaming, as they always did, but she paid them no heed—she was too focused on detaching herself from the tethers that'd been keeping her secured to Halvor. The Follian inventors showed her how, but it was her first time doing so in front of anyone (particularly foreigners she was meant to intimidate), and she didn't wish to look a fool before she'd even met the king.

Her efforts proved to be in vain when she removed her gloves prematurely. As she turned to ready herself for the dismount, she grabbed one of Halvor's spikes for stability, and the sharp tip pierced her palm. She gasped and quickly pressed one of her gloves to the bleeding wound to ensure it went unnoticed.

Halvor lowered his shoulder blade for her to dismount. As she was sliding down his wing, a group of people—civilians, by the looks of them—approached from a distance, clearly wanting to see him up close. Protective as ever, Halvor turned his neck and bellowed at them. They scampered off, screaming, as Halvor turned to the Trevas family soldiers approaching Aurelia from his other side. He snorted, small plumes of smoke expelling from his nostrils, and the visibly frightened soldiers took a few steps backwards.

Aurelia smiled, rubbed his snout both for comfort and good luck, and turned to face the soldiers. Halvor took a few steps forward as if to follow her, warning the soldiers that if anyone raised a threatening hand to his mistress, he'd be filling his belly not with Kanish sheep, but with Kanish men.

As she inched closer to a troop of about four dozen soldiers, the sea of armored men parted to make way for their leader. Both she and Willem halted when they were only feet apart from one another. He was still flanked by soldiers on either side, while Aurelia's only defense was a dragon who, when standing, towered over the king's palace.

Willem Trevas wasn't what she'd expected. He was fairly young, maybe ten years older than Aurelia herself, and while his fawny brown skin and facial features—a broad nose, prominent jawline, and feline eyes—were distinctly Kanish, nothing else about him resembled the average traits of his people. His hair, shoulder-length and straight, was the color of mahogany rather than an inky black. His eyes weren't dark or golden brown as she'd imagined, but rather green and flecked with amber. He was shorter than she'd expected, too, but strong and muscular.

He wasn't dressed like a highborn, either. In fact, his attire reminded her of what Jack liked to wear when he was training or lounging about: a loose white tunic, brown breeches rolled up to the knees, and a pair of brown loafers. If not for his crown and the family ring on his left index finger, Aurelia might not have known he was the King of Kanibar.

"Your Grace." His accent, not unlike Ansyl's, was thick, yet easily decipherable thanks to Aurelia's years with the Bolas siblings. "I wasn't expecting you."

She smiled as Halvor growled from behind her. If she blinked, she would've missed the way Willem's frightened eyes flicked over to Halvor before landing on hers again.

"You shall have to forgive me," she said. "I thought it pointless to send a raven when my dragon tends to be more effective."

His jaw clenched, but he was smiling. "A clever conclusion. I presume to know what you've come for, and it isn't a conversation to have here in the open. Will your beast behave himself?"

"He won't touch a hair on anyone's head, so long as no harm comes to me." She raised an eyebrow. "Can you assure my safety here, Your Majesty, or shall we converse under his watchful eye?"

"We don't harm our guests in Kanibar, Your Grace. You will be protected and treated with the utmost respect while you breathe our air." Smiling still, he unclasped his hands to gesture toward the palace. "Shall we?"

Aurelia tossed one last glance over her shoulder at Halvor before following the king to the palace. She trailed a few paces behind him at first, but her hopes of keeping a safe distance between them were tarnished when he slowed to walk beside her. He was looking at her in a way that reminded her hauntingly of Lord Zhoqa, but it was...different. He wasn't quite ogling her, but rather *admiring* her. If Lord Zhoqa looked at her like a green lad choosing his first courtesan, King Willem looked at her like a suitor selecting a bride.

Both made her want to strike them.

"You have a lovely home." She wasn't fond of awkward silences, even if she hadn't come to exchange pleasantries. "I once had a dear friend from Kanibar who spoke often of your kingdom's many beauties. Her stories didn't stray far from reality."

"You must've heard stories from your Lord Hand, too. Bolas, isn't it?" He looked over at her with a ghost of a smile playing on his lips. She only stared at him, surprised, which made him chuckle. "Oh, yes. I know one of my former soldiers was sought out by Lord Cristos to replace your late Hand. How is he faring in Akkinor? Is your country everything he hoped it would be?"

She gritted her teeth. He was baiting her, and she knew it. "The Lord Hand is well, thank you."

His smile widened to a grin as the front doors of the palace were opened for them. Her breath caught in her throat when they stepped into the foyer. Even such a small portion of the palace revealed its similarities to the Palace of Akkinor. From the pedestals bearing ancient artwork, to the style of the wallpaper, to the shiny marble floors, it looked like she'd walked into an alternate version of her home. The only difference between them was the absence of Brentwood purple and bronze, and the plethora of Trevas green and gold.

Rather than taking her to the throne room or a meeting room, as expected, Willem brought her to his personal study, where he sent his guards away almost immediately. He told her to have a seat in one of two armchairs placed before the hearth, poured each of them a glass of wine, and handed one chalice to Aurelia as he lowered himself into her chair's twin. She made sure to accept it with her non-injured hand as he crossed one leg over the other, casually leaned back in his seat, and took a large gulp of wine—all without taking his eyes from her.

"Your Majesty—" she started.

"I'll be frank with you: I don't know much about Akkinor's queen," he interrupted. "I know who your father was, and I know what you did five years ago when your brother tried to take your head. I know about your alliances, too, and that somehow, you've managed to bring a dragon of old to the modern world. Tell me—how did the first Queen of Akkinor since Alora the Abysmal manage to acquire a dragon?"

"That's none of your concern."

He laughed, infuriating her, and shook his head. "I expected that. Now, you and I are both aware of the reason for your visit. I don't care to hear whatever nonsense your allies have prepared for you. Take no offense, Your Grace, but I have no interest in negotiating with my enemies' favorite plaything." When she started to protest, he talked over her. "Don't bother denying it. You're here because you have a power the rest of us have only dreamed of—the most coveted good in the realm. Without your beast, you never would've come."

"This isn't about me or my dragon." Aurelia set her still-full chalice on the table beside her as he stared at her in a way that made her feel like both a prize and a piece of meat. "You're right—my allies know that their chances of victory are higher with me at their side. They also know that I won't choose between them if and when the time comes for it. None of them need to fear death by dragon fire, Your Majesty. Only you must fear it, because I swore no oath to defend and protect *you*. I think you'll find that negotiating with me is worthwhile: not because my power bonds my allies, but because my power is the only one strong enough to assure your destruction."

He kept staring at her, but she couldn't quite place the look on his face. She only hoped he hadn't realized she was bluffing: despite what she and Halvor were capable of, she wouldn't lay siege to an entire kingdom simply to protect her alliances. If the king knew she was only trying to frighten him, he didn't show it.

"I see." He swept a hand through his thin, glossy hair and cracked a smile. "I appreciate your honesty, even if our opinions differ on certain matters. You must've inherited that trait from your father—I hear he was one of the most honorable men to ever live. My father was king during a small fraction of your father's reign, and though the pair never exchanged words, he had a certain admiration for King Edmund. Your father's reputation proceeded him, even here in Carthe."

A sudden warmth flooded through Aurelia's body and evaporated the tension from her being. Talking about her father never failed to bring her a sense of ease, even while she mourned him.

"My father was a wonderful man," she said, her tone softening, "and an even greater king. I've made it my duty to lead by his example throughout my own reign. My life as it is today wouldn't exist if I hadn't chosen to do so when I took the throne."

Willem nodded in understanding and refilled his chalice. "You've been terribly unlucky in some ways, and blessed by Vyena herself in others." He paused to refill her chalice, too, but she covered it with her hand and thanked him to let him know she'd had enough. "Finding and bonding with a dragon of old, forging alliances across the sea—even marrying by your own will. I was lucky enough to accomplish that last bit, too, but it didn't last."

"Few things do." She eyed him as he stared off into nothingness, seemingly locked in a corner within his own mind, before she added, "I've never heard anything about the Queen of Kanibar. What's she like?"

"She was lovely." He snapped out of his daze to stare down at the wine in his chalice. Aurelia exhaled when she realized he'd spoken of his wife in the past tense, and she didn't blame him for looking away from her—no ruler liked to show pain of any kind while in the presence of another. "She's been gone for many seasons now, but I still think of her quite often. I wonder about the family we might've had, the life we might've built for ourselves, the kingdom we might've ruled together—but you don't want to hear about such tragedy. That's not why you've come."

Aurelia offered him a small, cordial smile. "I'm sorry for your loss, Your Majesty, but you're right—I'm not here to trade stories with you. Perhaps we may do so in the future, but only if you agree to abandon your plans for Dofell. We can never be friends or make pleasant small talk with one another if you bring my allies to war."

"I'm doing nothing of the sort. I never had any intention of declaring war on *them*—only Dofell. They've chosen to involve themselves, and I have no choice but to respond to the threat."

He has you there, she told herself. Clearing her throat, she tried again: "You didn't leave them much of a choice in the matter, either. You're well aware of the chaos you'd inflict upon the entirety of Carthe by seizing Dofell, and my allies will do what they must to keep the balance of power equal throughout the continent. You can choose to assist them in finding a solution to the Dofelli problem, or you can proceed with your plans and lead the continent to war. It's that simple."

Willem sighed. "A solution that may appeal to all will never be found. If it existed, it'd be in Dofell, and there's nothing of value left in that kingdom nowadays. The only solution we're capable of providing is for Dofell to unite with a stronger, healthier kingdom. The others never showed an interest in Dofell until I did, and I only decided to act because the people of Carthe have grown restless. They're demanding action, and I can't be blamed if I'm the only Carthinian leader willing to listen to them. It's easier to let me proceed: the people will be appeased, Dofell will be salvaged, and my neighbors will continue on their merry way as they always have."

"Not if you claim the entire midsection of Carthe. You'd control everything traveling between the northern and southern halves of the continent—the others won't stand for that. The people won't, either, when they realize what that means. It'd give you the perfect opportunity to seize all of northern Carthe, too, if your new borders prevent my allies from passing through Kanibar and Dofell."

He waved a dismissive hand. "I have no interest in the forest or the valley. If I wanted tens of thousands of people complaining to me about being harassed by the tribes, I would've taken those territories ages ago. It'd be a waste of manpower and resources."

Her heart pounded. "And what of Caedia?"

"I don't care about Caedia, but if I did, do you really think I'd tell you?"

Aurelia clenched her jaw. "You're not being very cooperative."

"Neither are you," he said, chuckling. "While speaking to a beautiful woman often leads me to swallow my own tongue, it's never been enough to turn me into a lapdog. Save your breath, Aurelia of Akkinor. I've told you enough as it is."

He leaned forwards, resting his elbows on his knees, and brought his face so close to hers that she could smell the wine on his lips. "Regardless of my plans, your allies will find themselves at war. It doesn't matter if I turn my back on Dofell. Now that I've shown interest in the Great City, your friends won't sit idly by while the Phyres destroy whatever's left of it. My plans have given them a taste of conquest. Even if I remove myself, they'll tell you they've lost interest, and they'll plot to take it behind your back. By the time you learn of it, your allies will have slaughtered each other, and the victor of Dofell will be your only remaining friend in Carthe."

A shiver traced her spine, but she refused to let him sense her fear. "If you proceed with Dofell as intended, Taundosa and Bozar—and possibly a Kroti province or two—will meet you in battle. I'm sworn to fight for them. You'll lose, and if you're fortunate, my allies will let you live. What happens between my allies after you've been dealt with doesn't concern you. You need to decide if your plans are worth potentially losing your life, your crown, and your kingdom. I alone am more than capable of taking each of those things from you."

His grin was as charismatic as it'd been when he greeted her, but now, she felt taunted by it. "You let thousands of men die during the battle with your brother, all because you refused to use your beast as a weapon. You didn't set him loose to seize your own country. I find it highly unlikely that you'll use him to help your allies seize a place like Dofell—a place you'll never have a claim to. Brandish your strengths as you please, Your Grace, but don't do me the dishonor of pretending like you'll actually use them."

"You don't know me."

"No," he agreed, "but I know *of* you, and that's enough. This will be a war fought between men, Your Grace, not between man and dragon. I'm not frightened of men—or women, for that matter."

She exhaled. "I'm afraid my mission today has failed, then. Is there nothing I can say that might sway you into stepping aside?"

Willem pondered that for a moment. "Dofell needs better leadership. It needs a new beginning. At least three kingdoms will battle one another for it, and when all of this is over, the lone victor will decide what to do with it. Regardless of what happens, the reign of the Phyre family has come to an end. I won't step aside just to watch the southerners slaughter each other for it. We'll all have the same chance." He stood, prompting her to do the same. "Remember what I said, Your Grace. Take whatever your allies tell you with a grain of salt, and don't be surprised if they start fighting against each other—*and* Kanibar—on the battlefield."

Aurelia shivered again, swallowed the lump in her throat, and followed him out of the study as he escorted her back to Halvor. She felt there was more to be said before her departure, but the king was through with her—that, and she'd completely run out of strategies. She'd tried her hardest, and it hadn't been enough.

The trip wasn't entirely pointless, though. She hadn't considered a possibility until the king mentioned it: perhaps her allies would prematurely betray one another for Dofell. It was entirely plausible that they'd arrive on the battlefield to defeat Kanibar as one unit, only to take up arms against each other as soon as the fighting turned in their favor. If that happened, Aurelia would have mere minutes to decide whose claim to Dofell she was defending.

As they strolled through the halls, a sudden thought popped into Aurelia's head: "Answer this for me, Your Majesty: why confirm to Bozar that you intend on conquering Dofell? This mess might've been avoided if you'd kept it to yourself. You could've taken Dofell unchallenged."

"But the challenge would come eventually, wouldn't it?" he inquired. Her lips parted as she offered a reluctant nod. "They'll never let me proceed without a fight, and it doesn't matter if that fight happens before or after I claim Dofell. I'd rather do my fellow leaders the honor of being prepared for war than blindside them with an unexpected conquest. It's like I said: we'll all have the same chance. But while they fight to stop me out of fear of something I don't intend to do, I fight to repair the weak link that's hindered Carthe's evolution for centuries. Tell me, Your Grace—which would your father view as the more honorable motive?"

Dumbfounded, Aurelia's parted lips drifted even further apart while she stared at him. He only gazed at the path ahead, expressionless, and showed no interest in her reaction to his words.

He had a point: Aurelia's allies only *suspected* that he'd use his claim over Dofelli territory to control the continent. He hadn't stated that he wanted to do so, yet he'd been honest about his plans for Dofell—so maybe, just maybe, he was telling the truth about his lack of interest in the northern territories. If he *was* being honest, then the only threat to the allies—and all of Carthe—would be an uneven balance of power between the continent's rulers and their territories.

Was that enough for them to proceed with their plans to meet Willem in battle, or would they put their pride aside to trust that he'd do what was needed to repair Dofell? Even if Willem couldn't be trusted, wording his plans the way he did made it seem like Aurelia's allies were threatening Dofell's only hope of restoration. The Carthinian masses wouldn't like that, and they'd like it even less when the allies failed to agree on a better solution for Dofell.

Aurelia managed to find her voice again when they exited the palace. "I don't know *what* my father would think of all of this—particularly since I'm the one who inadvertently encouraged the masses to demand action be taken in Dofell."

"Bah." Willem waved a dismissive hand. "The only thing you did was give them a sense of privilege."

She furrowed her brows. "Privilege?"

"Of course." He offered her his hand as they exited the palace and descended the uneven front steps. "Persuading the Lord of Kazamir to better life for his people prompted other leaders to do the same. The improvements made to life around Carthe have been kept quiet, because nobody wants the realm to know about the tragedies they allowed to befall their subjects. Dofell's been a disaster for centuries, but nobody's given it a second thought until now because they couldn't. The lowborn weren't privileged enough to consider the hardships of others while they, too, were suffering. It just wasn't an option. Now that life is better for them, they can finally think of their neighbors again. You didn't instigate an unnecessary war, Your Grace—you only reminded Carthe of what it means to be selfless."

A warm, fluttering feeling erupted in her gut, making her smile. "I hadn't thought of it that way. That's...That's a very nice perspective."

"I do try. I'm not the beast I'm made out to be, you know." He clasped his hands behind his back while she trailed beside him, silent. As they crossed the field to meet Halvor, he nodded toward the dragon with his chin. "What's his preferred method of destruction? Fire, teeth, or claws?"

"All three."

He stifled a laugh. "Undoubtedly. Does he have a warring spirit?"

"His intentions change as mine do."

"A terrifying thought."

"You said you aren't frightened of women, Your Majesty."

His eyes snapped over to her, startling her. "You're no woman, Aurelia Brentwood. Your soul belongs to the dragon." She opened her mouth to respond, but no sound emerged. At her silence, he bowed to her and offered a friendly, sincere smile. "It was a pleasure to make your acquaintance. I'm grateful for your conversation. Do write to me when you've arrived home safely—I'm eager to know what your allies think of our discussion today."

"You know I can't do that."

"You can, but you won't."

He took her hand, kissed her knuckles, and turned her hand over to see her palm. Her face burned when he ran the pad of his thumb over her still-bleeding cut. She retracted her hand immediately, blood smeared over her skin, as he locked his eyes on hers and smudged the blood between his thumb and index finger.

"The blood of the rider is the blood of the dragon." A crimson droplet fell from his finger to the grass as he smiled at her. "So the stories say, anyway."

Unsure of how to reply, she merely shook his hand. "I imagine I'll see you in Dofell, Your Majesty."

"I'll be counting the days, Your Grace."

With that, she turned on her heel and slipped her fingers into her gloves before mounting Halvor. She plucked the tethers from his back, latched the clips to the rings on her girdle, and tapped his scales to signal departure. Before he broke out into a run to gain momentum for liftoff, she tossed one final glance at Willem to her left. His body was facing her, but his head was tilted downwards and to the side. A small, dim ball of light appeared to be perched on his shoulder. He nodded once, face contorted with stress, as the ball of light—a sprite—disappeared in the blink of an eye.

Disappointed but not disheartened by the audience, Aurelia urged Halvor forwards. They lifted off into the sky, leaving Willem and Kanibar behind, and spent the next hour trying to shake a pesky sprite that seemed intent on following the Queen of Akkinor home.

XII

A day later, Aurelia and Halvor left the uninhabited island where they'd rested for the evening and set out for Akkinor once again. Even after a full night of contemplation, she still hadn't decided what she'd report to her allies.

A part of her wanted to know if Willem was right—if Bozar would turn against Taundosa at the last moment, and vice versa. Her allies would never freely admit that to her, but she wasn't sure they could lie about it, either. She was their strongest ally, and the last thing they wanted was to betray her trust by lying to her.

She knew Reyna would be loyal until the very end. Even so, Reyna was a wise and clever ruler, and she knew her allies better than Aurelia did. If she had even the slightest concern that the Bozari lords would turn against her during the battle with Kanibar, she'd prepare her men for that possibility before marching to Dofell. The only thing Aurelia couldn't be certain of, however, was if Reyna would share her foresight with her Akkinorian ally.

Then, of course, there was the matter of Krotis. Like Bozar, and even Akkinor, the kingdom was composed of multiple smaller territories each ruled by one supreme noble family. The five districts worked together when necessary, but they were vastly independent of one another, each with their own alliances. That meant one thing: if Krotis decided to join the fight, all five of its provinces would have divided loyalties; or, if the gods decided to test the realm's rulers even further, the provinces of Krotis would unite to battle every other Carthinian kingdom for Dofell. If that happened, the entire continent would be embroiled in war.

Then, of course, there was the matter of something else Willem had mentioned: his reason for conquering Dofell versus the allies' reason for battling him for it. She didn't trust him after only one conversation, and she certainly didn't trust him as much as she trusted her allies—even that vile Lord Zhoqa. If they honestly believed that Willem intended on expanding his reach beyond Dofell, then she had to believe it, too. That still didn't bring her an ounce of solace, though: gods forbid Willem was telling the truth, and they went to war for nothing...Then Aurelia would find herself allied with the people who prevented Dofell from receiving its fresh start, only to create an even larger mess when they battled each other for it.

Aurelia, having been distracted by her thoughts, failed to notice the way the sky darkened as she and Halvor neared the coast of Akkinor. By the time she snapped out of her daze, gray thunderclouds had rolled in, and the seas below had grown restless. It was nearing nightfall, but the thunderclouds were so thick and numerous that Aurelia didn't see the moon replace the sun.

She urged Halvor to fly above the clouds, but it was too late. They were showered in a rain so heavy that neither could tell where the clouds began and ended. She couldn't see the ocean below anymore, either. Flashes of lightning illuminated the sky for a few seconds at a time, but even with those bursts of light, she could barely see her hands in front of her face.

Thunder boomed so loudly that she couldn't trace the direction it'd come from—it was all around, encircling them like a ring of fire. She instructed Halvor to descend towards the sea, far from the angry clouds, but even then, her vision didn't improve. She didn't let herself panic yet, though. This wasn't the first storm she and Halvor had been caught in, and it certainly wouldn't be the last.

Then a deafening groan rattled her bones, and when she turned away from the sky to look at the raging seas directly in front of her, a shriek crawled up to her throat. An enormous ship—Esposi, judging by the tattered remains of scarlet sails—towered over them, risen several dozen feet into the air by the largest wave she'd ever seen. The ship was already on its side and cracked in half. As its weight succumbed to gravity, slipping downwards, Halvor curled to the side and shot up, saving both he and his mistress from being crushed with only seconds to spare.

Aurelia refused to watch the ship plummet into the ocean. She'd spent the better portion of the last ten years imagining her parents' last moments, and if their shipwreck had been anything like this one...She didn't want to see her nightmares play out in real life.

Thoughts of her parents distracted her from seeing the ship lurch in her direction one last time, but Halvor managed to avoid the vessel with such sharp movements that Aurelia rolled from his back. She yelped, feeling her stomach rise up to her throat, as her body fell before abruptly stopping.

When the fear of falling subsided, she looked down at her feet and saw them dangling several hundred yards above the angry seas. Broken planks of wood and scraps of red sails were being swallowed by a massive whirlpool directly beneath her.

Forcing herself to remain calm, she curled her hands around the leather tethers connecting her girdle to Halvor's wings. He was screeching, having sensed her fall, but he couldn't stop or slow down while caught in a storm at sea. She'd have to pull herself up by climbing the twelve-foot-long leather straps, and she wasn't so sure she could manage it on her own.

As she blinked rainwater from her eyes and willed herself to see through the darkness, she spotted something on Halvor's underside: a faint, golden glow that reminded her of a flickering candle.

A sprite.

She thought she'd shaken the pesky creature that'd latched itself to Halvor's belly, but apparently, it was more strong-willed than she'd given it credit for. Perhaps the sprite had merely lost control of its illumination while fighting to hang on, or perhaps it was attempting to light her path— either way, she knew she couldn't leave it there to struggle. She'd have to help it somehow, but not before securing herself first.

As the sprite's fading glow revealed just how far she'd have to climb to reclaim her seat, she heard the familiar sound of Halvor's tail whipping through the air. She watched his iridescent scales reflect the white glow from short, sparse flashes of lightning. She was close enough to his long, snake-like tail that she could grab it when it flicked in her direction—but only if she could see it.

She forced herself to recall her lessons from her schooling years. One of her tutors, Barrien, once taught her about weather predictions. It wasn't a lesson the Crown Princess was expected to learn, but an interest of Barrien's that he'd wished to share with her. She'd been annoyed by the lesson as a girl, but now, she'd be thanking Barrien in her nightly prayers for the next fortnight if she survived.

Lightning strikes when the god of storms cracks his whip, Barrien had told her. *When you hear the crack, lightning will follow within seconds. What happens after lightning strikes—thunder—is the sound of Vynas's whip meeting its mark.*

Aurelia closed her eyes, steadied her breathing, and listened. When she heard the crack—a sound like a hundred tree branches being snapped—she opened her eyes, and seconds later, a flash of lightning illuminated Halvor's scales. She held her arms out as if wanting an embrace, just in time for Halvor's spiked tail to beat against her chest. The air was ripped from her lungs, but even as she struggled to breathe, she wrapped her arms and legs around Halvor's tail.

Gritting her teeth, Aurelia nestled her feet between spikes and grabbed another two with her hands. She pulled herself up as if climbing a ladder, careful not to let her feet slide against Halvor's slippery scales, until she was safely perched on his back again. Remembering the sprite, she cautiously crawled closer to Halvor's side, using one hand to grasp a spike on his back while extending her other arm to his side. It felt like her body was being ripped in half, but luckily, her efforts weren't in vain. She felt something grazing her fingertips before it latched on—like a newborn babe sucking on a finger. She retracted her arm and secured her position on Halvor's back, just barely noticing the tiny creature as it burrowed beneath her leg.

Believing the worst had come to an end, Aurelia tried to relax. It wouldn't be long now before the coast of Akkinor came into view. She should've known better, though. A queen—never mind a queen with a dragon—sacrificed her right to feel at ease the moment the crown was placed on her head.

Another crack echoed in Aurelia's ears. She didn't think anything of it until the sky lit up once again—only this time, the god of storms aimed a bolt of lightning directly at Halvor. The dragon screeched as the shock and electricity coursed not only through his body, but through Aurelia's.

The last thing she saw before unconsciousness overcame her was land. Halvor's wings curled inwards, encircling her completely, as he barreled snout-first towards the ground, unable to stop or slow down while charred scales enveloped both dragon and mistress in a smoky haze.

***

Aurelia found herself trapped in a memory from her tenth name day: a memory of her sneaking out of the palace with Linden and Cicely at her side, the three children having felt a particularly strong urge to get into trouble that day.

They'd gone for a swim in the River Gilsad after the sun set, failing to recall the last time they'd done so unsupervised, when Aurelia had saved Linden from drowning. They'd spent over an hour splashing each other, floating along with the current, and teasing each other by slipping squirming, slimy fish down the backs of their shirts. It'd been a great evening until Aurelia got tangled up in a fisherman's net, undetectable in the darkness, that'd been left behind in the water.

Panic had led her to thrash, which only made the net constrict her more, and she quickly found herself unable to swim. At one point, her head disappeared below the surface for so long that she'd convinced herself she was going to die that night. She could feel the water filling her lungs, more and more by the second, making her so weak that she couldn't have swum back to the surface even if she'd found a way to escape the net.

She still felt it as she struggled to return to her present reality: the water replacing the air in her lungs, burning her nostrils, and sliding down her throat while she screamed for help. Her survival had come down to a single moment, and she could see it hanging on by a thread as her vision faded to black.

She gasped and sputtered as she choked, but the water filling her mouth wasn't sweet like the water of the River Gilsad—it was salty.

Dazed, aching, and still struggling to breathe, Aurelia managed to lift her head. She realized she wasn't submerged after she did so, but rather lying face-down on the sand while ocean water lapped over her. She groaned, pushing herself onto her knees, and blinked the salt from her eyes as she tried to observe her surroundings through torrential rainfall and black clouds.

She wasn't ten years old anymore, and she hadn't nearly drowned in the River Gilsad, only to be rescued by Linden and Cicely when they finally reached her. She was thirty now, her destination unknown, and nobody was coming to save her.

She knelt on the shore for a moment, staring at the stormy sky, unable to remember what she'd been doing before this or how she'd ended up here. She willed her body to stand, and before she realized what she was doing, she was walking toward a nearby cluster of rocks. Her legs gave out when she got there, and her fingers burned as she scraped her nails against a jagged rock while trying to steady herself. She managed to pull herself onto the rock using her upper body, and when she was perched a few feet above the flat beach, she knelt on the stone with her hands on her thighs. She stared into the distance again, imagining she could see her palace on the horizon line—like home was within arm's reach.

Weakness and exhaustion overcame her as she stared at the silhouette of a palace that wasn't really there. When black spots started clouding her vision, she managed to lay down on the rock and close her eyes, unable to move any further as her scarred cheek nuzzled into the damp stone.

***

Jack stared through the balcony doors as the pitter-patter of rainfall obstructed his view of the palace bailey. Working men were trying to unload a shipment of goods that'd just arrived from Holos, but they couldn't see a thing beneath the dark thunderclouds, and the torrential rain made the use of torches impossible. The thunder wasn't loud enough to drown out the men's hollering voices, though.

The storm had been raging for seven straight days by then. A day earlier, the palace received word that three Akkinorian vessels had been wrecked at sea after sailing into the eye of the storm. The entire eastern coast of Akkinor had been suffering through heavy rainfall, flooding, and constant thunder since the day the country's queen left to meet with the King of Kanibar.

After the flooding subsided and a few fallen trees were removed from the streets, it'd look and feel like the storm never came. The effects of such a storm, however, meant little to Jack when, after seven days, his wife still hadn't returned home from her three-day quest.

Aurelia and Halvor would've been flying home when the storm began in Akkinor—unless, of course, she'd decided to spend a night in Kanibar to rest before taking to the skies again. He hoped she'd spotted the storm and turned back to wait it out from the safety of land. That would explain the reason for her delayed return. The only other explanation was not one he wished to entertain.

Regardless, nobody had heard from the queen in seven days. Everyone in the Folly had taken note of her prolonged absence—if she didn't return soon, chaos would ensue not only across Akkinor, but across Carthe, too.

"Papa?"

Jack snapped out of his daze and looked down to his right. Hyacinth stared up at him with those wide, alert eyes of hers, urging him to lift her from the ground. She wrapped her arms around his neck and buried her face in his shoulder as he held her close. After a moment, she lifted her head to follow his gaze as if she, too, was searching for her mother among the thunder clouds.

"When is Mama coming home?"

Jack sighed. "Soon."

"She's going to see the moon."

He stilled, frowning. "Whatever do you mean? We always see the moon."

"Not *that* moon."

"*Sisi!*" From behind Jack, Henry abandoned the game he'd been playing on the floor with Halle and ran up to his other sister. "Come play with us, Sisi."

Hyacinth shook her head. "I'm waiting for Mama."

"Mama is *slow*." He pouted his lower lip at her. "*Please* play with us?"

She sighed like a woman five times her age and wiggled in Jack's arms until he set her down. She took Henry's outstretched hand, making Jack smile as the siblings scampered over to join Halle.

Seeking a distraction, Jack sat on the floor with the children and tried to make sense of their made-up game, to no avail. After a few moments, the parlor door opened, revealing Ansyl on the other side. The Lord Hand sat on the couch beside Jack and the children, silent, as worry etched itself into the lines of his face.

Jack's heart hammered. "Aurelia?"

Ansyl opened his mouth to respond, but it was Hyacinth who answered: "She found the moon."

Jack and Ansyl stared at her for a moment, then at each other, then at the princess again. Neither knew what she was talking about, but both noticed the way a sudden breeze extinguished the fire in the hearth when she said it.

***

Aurelia woke up expelling ash and seawater from her lungs. When her coughing fit subsided, her blurry vision slowly began to clear, and the ringing in her ears started to fade into silence. She'd been laying on her side, so she used one hand—the injured one, naturally—to push herself upright. A curse escaped her when the cut on her palm was angered by what felt like tiny pieces of glass. Only then did she realize she was laying on a series of rocks, angering her cut by flooding it with tiny stone granules and sea salt.

Her hair was sopping wet, now from sweat rather than water, and the ends were singed and frayed from the lightning strike. Her girdle felt like it was suctioned to her being, so she removed it from her midriff as quickly as she could. Upon studying it, she noticed the rings attached to the metal—the rings tethering her to Halvor—had been completely torn off. The leather tethers were nowhere to be seen, and neither was Halvor.

Halvor.

She scrambled to her feet and teetered for a moment as she caught her balance. Dazed, she studied her surroundings and realized she was on a beach. The ocean—still restless, but no longer raging from the storm—sat a few feet to her left. She vaguely remembered waking up on the sand, so she must've crawled to the rocks before she lost consciousness again. She carefully navigated the slippery rocks as she climbed down, her boots leaving deep imprints on the wet sand while she walked toward the jungle to her right. Half of the palm trees had been flattened and leveled by something enormous. When she noticed the smoke enveloping the trees, she broke out into a spring in search of her companion.

It didn't take long for her to find him—after all, he was bluer than sapphire and taller than some castles. He was curled up atop the crushed palm trees, unable to move because his legs, wings, and neck were tangled in vines. He released a small, quiet whimper when he saw her and tried to lift his head in greeting, but the vines, like shackles around his neck, made it difficult. After examining his body for injuries and finding none, she took her dagger from her boot and cut every vine until Halvor was able to break free.

He was exhausted and hungry, but otherwise unharmed. She was surprised the lightning strike hadn't hurt him, but then again, his scales were an almost indestructible type of armor. The lightning probably frightened him and cooked the dead scales he was in the process of shedding. After a bit of rest and something to eat, he'd be strong enough to see them home. The only problem was this: where was home from here?

They'd clearly landed on an island—she could see the shoreline on the other side—but *which* island? Halvor followed her, trampling trees with his massive feet, as she explored the landmass for both food and knowledge. She didn't find either. Luckily, Halvor was no stranger to hunting for prey, so he lifted off to circle the island in search of food and potential threats.

After finding a fallen coconut on the ground, Aurelia opened it with her dagger and drank its water in two gulps. She heard a faint, familiar buzzing sound as she wiped the dribbling liquid from her mouth. Before she could look around for the source, a soft voice whispered in her ear:

"It's the Grin."

Yelping, she dove onto the sand and scurried backwards. Nobody was there. As her chest heaved with panic, she remembered the straggler who'd attached itself to Halvor's underside on their flight, and her panic morphed into relief.

"I'm sorry." She stood from the sand, wiping her hands on her trousers, and looked around for the creature. "I didn't mean to frighten you. It's all right. You can come out."

A tiny flash of light caught her eye. She smiled a bit when she spotted the sprite sitting on the trunk of a palm tree leveled by Halvor. Its feet dangled, and its hands were placed on either side of its hips. The sprite's golden glow faded as Aurelia approached and sat cross-legged in front of it.

The creature looked like a human, though its head and eyes were fairly large while its limbs were skinny and flimsy. Its eyes were brown, and its auburn hair was long and shaggy. It wore a tunic and breeches, both in shades of brown and green, and the garments appeared to be made out of leaves.

"The Grin." Aurelia gulped when the sprite's wide, bugging eyes refused to blink. "You mean Tullweine, don't you?"

It nodded, prompting a sigh of relief to escape her lips. Tullweine was an uninhabited island off the western coast of Quapebet, just an hour's journey by flight from Akkinor. Tullweine earned its nickname, *the Grin*, because of three ponds on the lower half of the island that resembled a smiling face.

When the creature continued to stare at her in silence, she asked, "Do you have a name?" The sprite shook its head. "I see. My name's Aurelia, but I'm sure you already know that. Tell me—why did you follow me from Kanibar? We have none of your kind in Akkinor, so I have to assume you've come to spy on me on behalf of your king."

"No. I wanted to fly."

That was innocent enough, but she minded Arian's voice in her head anyhow: *Not unlike your connection with Halvor, they latch themselves onto an individual or a family line, and they're sworn to tell the truth to their masters or mistresses. They speak nothing but lies to everyone else.*

"I'm afraid you're stuck with me, then," she told it. "I don't believe sprites can swim or fly, and I don't plan on visiting Kanibar again in the near future. Even if you *have* come to spy on me, you have no way of returning home unless I bring you back myself. We shall have to be friends."

"Friends." The sprite nodded. "All right."

"I suspect we'll depart for Akkinor as soon as my dragon fills his belly. We haven't much to do in the meantime, but I'm rather starved, so perhaps—"

Aurelia gasped when, in the time it took her to blink, the sprite abandoned its seat on the trunk to perch on her knee. It was so close now that she could see things she hadn't noticed before, like the translucency of its skin and the long, needlelike claws protruding from its fingers. Its teeth looked like they'd been filed down by razor blades, and its sunken eyes were even larger than they'd appeared from a distance.

"Your brother is here," it whispered. "He lies with the moon."

XIII

While the sprite instructed Aurelia to follow it, she tried to explain that her brother was dead and buried in Akkinor, but the creature wouldn't have it. At a certain point as they walked in circles around the island, she gave up on her explanation and instead tried to uncover what the sprite was looking for. Eventually, it stopped on a large patch of sand just a stone's throw from where Halvor had crash-landed.

"Here," it told her. "He awaits you."

She stared at it, puzzled. "What are you talking about?"

"Dig."

"Why?"

Again, the sprite did nothing but fix its abnormally large eyes on hers. Knowing it wouldn't give up until she did what it asked of her—and knowing her curiosity would get the best of her eventually, too—she knelt on the sand beside the creature and used her hands to dig.

She was breathless and sweating in minutes. "This is pointless. I'll be here for the next year without a shovel or—oh." She blushed when her nails scraped something metallic. "I suppose I spoke too soon."

The sprite didn't reply. Aurelia kept digging, her back still aching from falling off Halvor, until the metallic object in question—an iron ring—revealed itself. The ring was attached to rotting pieces of wood all nailed together, and after another few minutes of digging, she realized it was a crate.

Excited at the prospect of finding food or water in the crate, she felt around the edges until her fingers curled around the lid. It was stiff after so many years of being buried in the sand, but after a bit of force, she was able to pry it off. Immediately, the faint scent of decay wafted through her nostrils, forcing her to stagger backwards and block her nose with her hand. Her gut churned when she peered into the crate and saw the mummified remains of a man curled up inside.

She looked over at the sprite, who was also peering into the crate. "That's not my brother. I'd say this man has been dead for several centuries."

The sprite only stared at her. Curious, she examined the body with a closer eye, still covering her nose as the smell of rotting flesh corrupted her senses. She narrowed her eyes and crept closer when she saw something strange on the mummy's face: what appeared to be gold paint slathered over his cheeks, just beneath his eyes.

Her heart skipped a beat. "Oh."

It was no wonder the sprite referred to the body as Aurelia's brother. The man in the box, whoever he'd been in life, had sobbed tears of gold at the time of his death. He, like Aurelia herself, was Forged in Gold.

Despite her brain screaming at her to leave it alone, Aurelia sucked in a deep breath and carefully lowered herself into the crate. The scent worsened when she was standing only a foot from the corpse, but she managed to ignore it when her eyes found a handful of books scattered by the remains.

There were about five inches of sand at the bottom of the crate. She saw a piece of cloth tucked into a tiny hole on the side, so she took a guess at what had happened: the man was buried alive, but rather than dying by inhaling sand as it filled the crate, he'd stuffed the hole to die by lack of oxygen instead. He chose to die on his own terms, instead of his captives'.

Though the books were covered in sand and dust, lack of exposure to water and sunlight left them well-preserved, and Aurelia was able to read the titles. Each book was written in Old Carthinian, and while she couldn't translate every word, she deduced that all of them were tales—real or fictious—from Bozar, judging by their many references to Almighty Dhylo and the power of knowledge.

She looked up at the sprite, who was watching her from the sand above. "Who is he?"

"The Last King."

Aurelia froze. "This...is Iago Zanaki?"

The sprite nodded as a chill traced Aurelia's spine. Everyone in the world knew about Iago Zanaki, Third of His Name, the Last King of Bozar. In the eight-hundredth century, the once decent and honorable king was said to have been corrupted by darkness and evil. He inflicted unspeakable travesties upon his people until four Bozari noblemen rose up against him. The entire Zanaki family was annihilated, and the noblemen each claimed one of Bozar's four districts, thus transforming it from a monarchy to a feudal system. It was one of the worst tragedies to ever occur on Carthinian soil, but also one of the most mysterious. Nobody knew why a man known as *Iago the Gentle* had suddenly become a war criminal.

Before climbing out of the crate, Aurelia spotted something nestled in the king's hand. Begging forgiveness from the gods and swallowing bile as she did so, Aurelia unraveled the mummy's calcified fingers (snapping one off in the process) and took the object from his palm. It was a diamond-shaped slab of iron with a whitish rock fused to the center, and while tarnished and covered in sand, it looked like a simple, ancient relic.

She didn't get the chance to question the creature, as a shadow rolled in overhead. She looked up as Halvor circled her with a seal dangling from his jaw. He swallowed the animal before landing a few feet to her right.

Aurelia climbed out of the crate, still clutching the object, and turned to the sprite. "You aren't going to tell me what this is, are you?" It only stared again, silent. "Fine, then. I'll figure it out for myself when we get home."

The sprite glowed brighter. "Home?"

"My home." She paused. "It can be your home, too, if you do right by me. We have no room for dishonor in Akkinor—if you wish to stay, you mustn't betray me. Understand?"

The sprite contemplated for a moment before nodding. "Understand."

"Good. Say—do you know how long I was unconscious for?"

"I saw the sunrise four times."

"Four times—" Aurelia winced. She'd told Jack and Ansyl that her quest would take two days at most, and now it'd been over a week. "Good gods. Let's go before my family assumes the worst."

The sprite, apparently sharing Aurelia's excitement, scurried from the sand to perch itself on her shoulder. She was startled at first, and while she wouldn't forget the trickster nature of its kind, she couldn't deny how adorable it was—particularly when it held onto a lock of her hair to keep itself from falling.

Aurelia climbed onto Halvor's back, leaving her the Follian inventors' short-lived creation on the beach. As he ran towards the shore to build momentum before lifting off, she looked down at the crate in the sand and murmured a quiet prayer for the late king.

There was no doubting that Iago Zanaki had been Forged in Gold, but how could a person destined to save humanity commit such atrocities against his own people? How did a champion of the gods wind up overthrown, buried alive on an uninhabited island across the ocean, and left to die alone in an unmarked grave?

Aurelia's unplanned excursion to Tullweine proved something she hadn't considered over the last five years: even those handpicked by the divine to better mankind, with the golden blood of the gods coursing through their veins, did not always make the right choices.

She would be better than that.

***

Three days after his return from Akkinor, Jalhor Zhaaran was awoken in the middle of the night by a feeling he could only describe as existential dread. He sprung up in his bed, panting and sweating profusely, and set a weary hand over his breast to steady his racing heart.

"Husband?" His wife, Aida, opened her eyes and set a worried hand on his forearm. "Are you well?"

"I...I..."

"Jalhor." She sat up, removed his hand from his chest, and replaced it with her own. A gasp escaped her lips. "Good heavens! Something isn't right, my love. Shall I summon the healer?"

"No, no..." He closed his eyes and took a long, deep breath. "I'm sure it's nothing. Just a poor dream, I imagine."

Aida climbed out of bed and poured him a glass of wine from a jug across their bedchamber. She ordered him to drink and refused to return to bed until the chalice was empty. Even as she poured him another, his heart continued to beat like he'd just stared death in the face, and he couldn't shake the feeling that something terrible was on its way.

He knew he wouldn't be getting back to sleep any time soon, so he kissed his wife between the eyes, assured her of his good health, and instructed her to go back to sleep. The Lord of Orestes, on the other hand, threw his dressing robe over his shoulders and lit a candle to illuminate his path as he journeyed to his study.

Upon reaching the end of the corridor, he stopped in front of a guard. "Send word to my four elder children at once, good man. Ensure everything is right with them, and report back to me as soon as you've heard."

The soldier bowed. "At once, my liege."

While the candelabra trembled in his faltering grip, Jalhor took a left turn and, one by one, poked his head into four of the bedchambers in the corridor. After ensuring that his youngest children were alive and well, he made his way to his study, where he sat at his desk for an hour staring into nothingness, still unable to shake this suffocating uneasiness. By then, the guard had returned with reports on the elder four Zhaaran children, who lived in estates of their own. He was relieved that his anxiety wasn't tied to the well-being of his children, but troubled that he still hadn't deduced the reason for his worries.

To his surprise, a knock came at the door. It wasn't a Zhaaran family soldier or even his wife who'd come to see him, as he might've expected, but a High Priest by the name of Doku. Trained exclusively and extensively at the Holy Library of Iseppa, the realm's most esteemed religious institution, Doku had served as the Elder Priest of Orestes for as long as Jalhor had reigned.

"My lord." Doku bowed and closed the door behind him. Even with one candle lighting the study, Jalhor saw how gray the priest's face had become. "There's been an incident."

Jalhor stiffened. "What is it?"

"I sensed a disturbance not an hour ago. I thought I was mistaken, but I can't be. I was trained for this, just as my predecessors were. This torch has been passed down from Elder to Elder of Orestes for over a thousand years. I can't be wrong."

Jalhor knew exactly what'd happened by that point, but he needed to hear it spoken from Doku's lips. "It's finally happened, then?"

"Indeed." The priest grimaced. "Someone has found him—and it. Everything our predecessors feared has finally come to pass, my lord. The Lunar Staff has been claimed once more."

Jalhor brought a hand to his breast again as his heart lurched. "Good gods."

"We shall have to send word to every religious institution in the realm. The other priests will recognize what threat this poses, and they'll be diligent in helping us reclaim it. I'll send ravens to every—"

"There's no need." Jalhor flickered his gaze to the lone candle to his right. In the flame, he saw the same thing he'd seen in his nightmare: a future marked by destruction, and a world reduced to ash and blood. "I know exactly where it is."

"My lord?"

"Tell me—what's the quickest way to deliver a message to Akkinor? No ravens. We mustn't risk interception."

Doku pondered for a moment. "The Athys."

Jalhor raised an eyebrow. "The Athys hasn't been used in my lifetime."

"I'm well aware, my lord, but it's perhaps the only direct line of communication we have to Akkinor that exists beyond the constraints of time. It's our best option."

Jalhor chewed on the insides of his cheeks, contemplating. The Athys— once an ordinary, handheld mirror from the earliest days of the realm—

had been transformed into a magical object by Ceruleus, the Elemental of air. Ceruleus and Glacia, the Elemental of water, were hopelessly in love, despite their duties to the realm forcing them apart for the majority of their lifetimes. To maintain communication as they embarked on adventure after adventure, Ceruleus broke the looking glass in two, and each claimed one half.

Not only did the Athys allow each wielder to see the other in real time, but it also allowed them to speak to one another: the powers of Ceruleus made it possible for the wielders' voices to travel great distances at an incredible speed. This means of communication, however, only worked if one of the wielders was a mage specializing in air magic.

Glacia had incorporated her own magical properties onto the Athys, too. If one of the wielders was a water mage, both halves of the glass could momentarily transform into water, allowing either individual to deliver an object to the other. Of all the elements, water was most strongly associated with transportation: as long as an object could fit within each half of the Athys, it could be sent through one piece and retrieved through the other.

After the Elementals went extinct, Elder Priests from across Carthe collected both halves of the Athys so they'd be protected from misuse. The Athys was hidden away in the Holy Library of Iseppa for many years, until the priests decided to deliver one piece of it to the Monastery of Dhylo in Akkinor. The Athys wasn't split in two so the pieces could stay together and collect dust. It was only right that they be used for their intended purpose: bridging the gap between both sides of the world.

"All right." Jalhor scratched at his bushy beard, weary and exhausted, and nodded to Doku. "We shall visit Iseppa in the morning to send word to Akkinor. Even the two of us will be forbidden from using the Athys without some sort of sacrifice, though. Magic always has a price, even if we'd like to believe otherwise. Have you anything in mind?"

Doku grimaced. "Blood has always done the trick, my lord."

The Lord of Orestes sighed. "I thought you might say that."

XIV

Nobody was present to greet Aurelia when she and Halvor landed in the gardens at the Palace of Akkinor. As she crossed the gardens to enter the palace through the rear doors, she felt a gentle tug on a lock of her hair and stopped walking.

The sprite, perched on her shoulder and hidden behind her thick hair, whispered, "We are being watched."

A shiver traced her spine. She looked up at the massive estate before her and searched for proof of the sprite's claim. Within minutes, she spotted the two Bozari emissaries staring at her from a window on the second floor. As soon as they realized they'd been seen, they closed the curtains and disappeared.

"You'll have to stay in my pocket for the time being," she murmured. "I don't know how my people will take to you—we must give it time."

No reply. She didn't hear or see the creature move, but a second later, she felt a gentle weight against her left thigh. The sprite's telltale glow had faded, too.

She was halfway through the palace on her trek to the grand staircase when a voice called after her. She turned and smiled upon seeing both Jack and Ansyl hurrying toward her. She took a few steps forward to meet them, holding out her arms for an embrace from her husband, but dropped her limbs to her side when Jack folded his arms over his chest.

"You were supposed to be home four days ago," he accused. "I was nearly sick with worry."

She sighed. "I know. I'm sorry. We flew into a storm and crashed on—"

"Tullweine," Ansyl finished. She blinked at him, surprised. "Quenosi sailors spotted Halvor circling the island and sent a raven immediately. They wished to come to your aid, but they were too fearful of Halvor—I suppose they wanted me to tell them if they'd become dragon feed by approaching you while in distress."

Jack, softening, cupped her cheek in his massive hand. "Are you all right?"

She smiled and covered his hand with hers. "Just fine. Halvor was struck by lightning while we were caught in a storm at sea—it took us both a few days to regain consciousness after that, but we're both perfectly well now. Did I miss anything during my absence?"

The men flanked either side of her as they climbed the staircase. "The storm ravaged the Folly, too, which halted both imports and exports. We've managed to get everything back on track, though," Ansyl told her. "Nothing new has occurred in regard to the issues of mages and assassins, but we have several other matters that require your attention. Most importantly, though, is the matter of Kanibar. The Bozari emissaries are most eager to hear what you've learned."

"I shall inform them after I've bathed and rested."

Jack raised an eyebrow. "Good or bad news?"

"A bit of both. King Willem believes the southern rulers will seek to claim Dofell anyhow, and he doesn't wish to be the only Carthinian leader who neglects to fight for it. He claims he has no interest in the northern territories, and that he only wishes to appease the people by salvaging Dofell. He seems to think that our allies are too concerned about what he might do, and not concerned enough about Dofell's future. I don't trust his word, but it's still something to consider. Either way, he has no intention of backing off."

Jack sighed. "So we must prepare for war, then. Officially."

She nodded. "Officially."

"Well, I suppose—"

"Mama!"

The trio halted when the three elder Brentwood children raced down the hallway, being chased and hollered after by their governesses, and crashed into Aurelia's legs. She was glad they were still so small: if any of them had been even an inch taller, they would've crushed the poor sprite hiding in their mother's pocket.

She knelt down to greet them all properly, showering them with kisses and wrapping them in her warm embrace, as they talked a mile a minute about everything she'd missed in the last week. They followed her, Jack, and Ansyl to her bedchamber, refusing to take even a moment to breathe between stories. By the time they calmed down, Jack was massaging his temples to relieve a migraine, and Aurelia had already forgotten what she was talking about before the interruption.

The children begged her to visit the nursery with them so she could see their new toys, and Aurelia obliged, despite her desperate desire for a bath and a nap in her own bed. As they walked to the nursery, Aurelia glanced down at Hyacinth, who was holding her mother's right hand and staring at Aurelia's trousers.

"Sisi?" Aurelia released her daughter's hand to play with Hyacinth's hair. "Is something wrong?"

Hyacinth, still staring at the pocket containing the sprite, blinked as if she'd just emerged from a trance before meeting Aurelia's gaze. "Nothing."

"Are you sure?"

She pondered that for a moment. "Did you find the moon, Mama?"

Aurelia stopped walking so quickly that the upper half of her body lurched forwards as if her feet had gotten stuck in quicksand. The others stopped, too. When she tore her eyes away from Hyacinth to look up at Jack and Ansyl, they both responded with the same expression.

"Hyacinth—"

Aurelia stopped short when a face appeared at the other end of the hallway, just a few doors down from the nursery. The tall, scrawny elderly man wore the royal blue robes and golden waist chains adorned by all priests at the Monastery of Dhylo in Omara. The governesses, who'd been trailing several paces behind the queen and her family, quickly ushered the children into the nursery—much to their dismay—upon spotting the priest.

"Master Barrien." Aurelia beamed with delight when the familiar face bowed to her. "How wonderful it is to see you! What brings you to the palace?"

Barrien, one of Aurelia's former tutors—and Cressida's paternal uncle—forced a smile. "Good day, Your Grace. I come bearing urgent news from the monastery. Your presence is required immediately."

She frowned. "What's happened?"

"I know very little, Your Grace—only that someone at the Holy Library of Iseppa wishes to make contact with you through the Athys."

"The Athys?" She stared at him, puzzled. "I don't recall the last time the Athys was used. I was told—by you, actually—that it demands a high price from its users."

"Indeed it does. The price, to my understanding, has already been paid. All that remains is for you to answer the call."

She met Jack's eyes and smiled tiredly. "It looks like I'm off again, then."

***

Despite their exhaustion, Aurelia and Halvor departed the palace only hours after their return from Kanibar to make way for Omara. Jack insisted upon accompanying them, refusing to let her out of his sight after her near-death experience on Tullweine, while Ansyl remained at the palace to mind Aurelia's duties.

Aurelia offered to bring Barrien back to the monastery on dragonback, too, but the poor man shook in his boots at the mere sight of Halvor.

Before the reign of Oleander the Great, Omara was an independent nation protected by Dhylo, god of knowledge. Stories claimed that Dhylo had commanded the construction of a holy institution for knowledge, religion, and the arts during the old days. He cast a blessing over the structure and the entirety of Omara, ensuring that no human could ever lay waste to what he'd commissioned. It was his word that convinced the ancient leaders of Omara to join Akkinor as its sixth kingdom, but even after the unification, it was the only divinely protected Akkinorian territory.

The monastery itself was the source of Dhylo's blessing. So long as it existed, no man or woman could bring harm or evil to Omaran soil.

Most highborn and noble children attended the university after completing their private lessons. Mages, too—those who'd been in hiding over the centuries—trained and educated themselves on all things magic there, as the priests were sworn to protect their identities. Some priests and priestesses were mages, too, but most were mortals. The younger ones trained at the monastery for one of three possible futures: to service a highborn family at their estate; to educate mages or the next generation of religious leaders; or to service those who visited the monastery in pursuit of knowledge. Only a handful of them achieved the high status of Elder— which, in the old days, would've allowed them to commune with the gods. In the modern day, with the gods having gone silent, the Elders had little to do other than guide their subordinates and ensure the welfare of the monastery's ancient texts, relics, and the like.

When they arrived, Halvor landed a few feet from the monastery's entrance to drop them off, then flew to one of the structure's massive stone towers to wait for them. By then, every person in the monastery was aware of who'd arrived. The guards had already ushered most of the students and employees into private rooms as a precautionary measure, so when Aurelia and Jack walked into the foyer, the only person present to greet them was High Priest Octavien, who'd once tutored Aurelia.

"Your Grace. Your Royal Highness." He bowed in greeting, but the grave look on his face when he straightened made Aurelia's stomach churn. "You have a caller."

Aurelia raised an eyebrow as they followed Octavien through the long, empty halls. "Who is it?"

"The Lord of Orestes, Your Grace."

She met Jack's eyes and frowned. "It must be important if he's using the Athys instead of a raven. Do you suppose it's regarding what the Four Lords proposed?"

Her husband shrugged. "I can't think of anything else that would warrant this."

Octavien stopped them outside of a set of heavy, wooden double doors. "Please forgive me," he said, directing his words to Jack. "His Lordship was rather persistent in his instructions: he wishes to speak only to Her Grace."

"Of course." Jack nodded and gave his wife a kiss for good luck. "I'll mind the doors."

Octavien opened the doors, willing Aurelia to follow, but didn't close them once the pair was inside—a sign that he, too, wasn't welcome to overhear the conversation.

The room was roughly the same size as a classroom: large enough to fit a few dozen people, but small enough to provide a more intimate setting. The plain, curved white limestone walls slanted inwards to form a dome-shaped ceiling with a single, circular window at the center. One beam of sunlight cast down from the window onto a large stone slab in the middle of the room. Wooden tables lined the walls, each surface covered in thick layers of white wax from hundreds of candles that never seemed to stop burning.

A waist-high Akkinorian bronze fence encircled the slab, with a gate facing the doors. As Aurelia stepped closer to it, wrapping her thin fingers around the bronze structure, she saw words carved into the stone: hymns, prophecies, or stories, she couldn't be sure, as everything was written in an ancient tongue she couldn't decipher. Upon closer inspection, she noticed lingering traces of brown and crimson within the etchings—as if the words had been carved with fingernails.

One lone shard of glass—larger than she expected, and about the size of Jack's massive palm—rested atop the stone, directly beneath the beam of sunlight. From her angle, it was cloudy and spotted, reflecting nothing but the light and the ceiling above. It was by no means impressive, but it seemed to hum with an ancient power.

Aurelia released the breath she hadn't realized she'd been holding. "What must I do?"

"You need only wield it, Your Grace." Octavien bowed. "I shall await you with His Royal Highness."

She was so entranced by the Athys that she barely heard him leave. When the door clicked behind her, she snapped out of her daze and took a long, deep breath. She opened the gate to cross the threshold, and immediately, a sudden breeze—lacking a source—blew through the air, testing the candles' integrity and sending a chill down Aurelia's spine.

A cushion was placed at the base of the slab, so she knelt on it and set her hands on the edge of the stone. It was cold and rough beneath her palms, as expected, and another shiver wracked her body when her nails scraped the etchings. She inhaled again, then lifted her shaking hands to grasp the Athys.

For a moment, the only thing she saw was her own reflection and the orange glow of candlelight behind her. Then the queen's face disappeared, and one purple eye and half of a gray beard took its place. She gasped, startled, until Lord Jalhor Zhaaran of Orestes revealed himself completely.

"M-My lord." She willed her hands to stop trembling, to no avail. "I must say, I wasn't expecting our next meeting to look quite like this."

He chuckled with little humor, but the sound didn't come from the Athys—it came from all around her, encircling her from every direction, carried to her ears from Bozar by Ceruleus's enchanted winds.

"Apologies, Your Grace. An urgent matter was brought to my attention, and this is both the quickest and most effective way for us to discuss it." He hesitated for a moment, one eyebrow raised, before adding, "You're not alone, are you?"

"I—"

"I can hear it whispering." He paused again, and when he did, Aurelia heard the sprite hissing from her trousers. She was surprised the elderly lord had heard the creature when she hadn't, but the surprise faded quickly when she remembered how powerful a mage he was. "Never the matter. Your Grace, it's come to my attention that a strange object recently fell into your possession. Do you know what I'm referring to?" Aurelia felt her cheeks warm as she nodded. "The Elder of Orestes sensed that you'd taken it and alerted me immediately. I must ask that you refrain from keeping it."

"Why? What is it?"

He cleared his throat. "Do you know who you found on the island?"

"I do."

"Then you know what he did to earn his place there," he continued. She nodded. "Iago the Gentle reigned peacefully for many years until enacting a reign of terror on Bozar. After he was usurped by the first Four Lords, only one of them—the Lord of Orestes—uncovered the reason for his sudden transformation. My ancestor swore to the gods that he and his descendants would ensure the same fate would never befall another." He cleared his throat again. "What do you know about the Lunar Staff?"

"The Lunar Staff?" She paused for a moment, surprised. "It was a scepter wielded by the moon goddess, Edea. Not long after the First Mortals were created, a piece of moonrock came crashing down from the heavens, and Edea used the staff to prevent it from destroying the realm. To immortalize what she did for the First Mortals, she collected one piece of the shattered moonrock from the earth and fused it to the topper of her staff."

As soon as she finished speaking, she froze. Lord Zhaaran raised an eyebrow again as she reached into her left pocket to produce the object she'd taken from the crate. Only then did she remember an illustration of the Lunar Staff from a book she'd read as a youth. The topper of the scepter was almost identical to the object: diamond-shaped, iron, and beholding a piece of moonrock in the center. The original staff was encrusted with gemstones, which had apparently separated from the topper over time.

"This..." She trailed off when her voice cracked. "This is the Lunar Staff?"

"What's left of it. The piece you hold in your hands was discovered many years after the gods disappeared. It's said that Edea has been longing for it since the day she lost it, and anyone who wields it—anyone other than the moon goddess herself—is cursed with misfortune. Many have attempted to destroy it or hide it, but it has always prevailed. Men have sought it out for generations."

She frowned. "If it's cursed, why have so many people tried to find it?"

"It bears the power of the divine, Your Grace. Every magical artifact is connected to the deity who created it. Edea is said to be a mistress of compulsion—one cannot deny her, even if it usurps their free will. Wielders of the staff have been granted with that same power: the ability to convince anyone, king or peasant, Akkinorian or Carthinian, to do anything they desire."

Aurelia glanced down at the amulet as ice filled her veins. "Did you know that Iago Zanaki was Forged in Gold?"

Surprise flickered in his violet eyes. "There were rumors, but it was never confirmed. How do you know?"

"Tears of gold stain his corpse's cheeks to this day."

"I see."

"This feels wrong, my lord. If he was Forged in Gold, how could he fall victim to the curse? He was destined to better the realm, and instead, he nearly destroyed his own kingdom. It feels to me like the will of the Twelve should've overpowered the effects of one deity."

Lord Zhaaran sighed. "During Iago's shift from just to cruel, Bozar was suffering—not because of him, but because of things he couldn't control. People were starving and dying by the thousands. When he found the amulet, he thought he could use it to persuade his only ally—the King of Taundosa—into giving Bozar the resources it needed, free of charge. One use of the amulet's power blackened his heart, even if such darkness was no larger than a pinpoint. *It* ended up compelling *him* to use it. With each use, that pinpoint of blackness grew larger until it overcame him."

"But if he was Forged in Gold, he should've been able to fight it. Right?"

"Not exactly. Those Forged in Gold may be chosen by the gods to better humanity, but you were never meant to bear godly power. No human was meant to do that. The amulet brought Iago as close to the gods as possible, but even their golden blood in his veins couldn't protect him from its effects." He shook his head and clenched his jaw worriedly. "I don't know how you managed to find it, but you're the only person ever to have done so since Iago himself."

She looked down at her pocket and smiled sheepishly. "I didn't find it on my own, exactly."

"I'm not surprised. Sprites have always had a knack for treasure hunting—particularly if it means stirring up mischief." He sighed. "You have a sprite in one pocket and a curse in the other. It'd be wise to dispose of them both. Now that the Last King has been discovered, the amulet is no longer safe with him. I think it best if I take it so it can be locked away here at the Holy Library."

Aurelia raised an eyebrow, suspicious. "You wish for me to bring it to Bozar? It'd be just as safe here at the monastery. I'm certain my Elders would know what it is and why it must be protected."

"They would," he agreed, "but remember what I said, Your Grace: my ancestor swore that the Zhaaran line would claim responsibility for the amulet. It's my burden to bear." He cleared his throat. "There's a quicker way than hand-delivering it to Bozar. I myself am an air mage—hence the reason we're able to communicate through the Athys—but my Elder is a water mage. The amulet can be delivered to me right now through the Athys."

He turned to summon the Elder, who Aurelia couldn't see in the glass, and quieted as the priest tapped into the power of Glacia embedded in the Athys. Another gasp escaped Aurelia's lips when the solid glass surface liquified, now resembling the surface of a calm stream rather than a broken mirror.

Her heart leapt to her throat when the surface trembled and glowed. Not a second later, a white rose—a token of peace—emerged from the water and fell directly onto her lap. She stared at it, awestruck, before returning her attention to Lord Zhaaran's rippled reflection.

"You needn't worry, Your Grace," he assured her. "Nobody will ever see it again."

She glanced down at the amulet, then at the sprite, which was now perched on her knee and staring up at her with its enormous eyes. When she met its gaze, the sprite shook its head.

An object with the divine power to convince anyone to do anything....It wasn't an ability Aurelia had ever desired, but with everything happening around the world as of late, it could come in handy. The crown gave her authority, and Halvor gave her strength, but neither assured peace nor loyalty. The amulet, on the other hand, promised everything she had and everything she needed.

She didn't necessarily believe the lore surrounding the amulet. Iago Zanaki had succumbed to darkness because of the way in which he'd used the amulet: to dishonorably acquire what he wanted by betraying the legal system, even if his goal was to put an end to famine and poverty across Bozar. Aurelia could use it to end the squabbling in Carthe by convincing its leaders to unite to choose Dofell's new monarch. She could use it to restore peace between mages in mortals in Akkinor, too. She wouldn't be doing anything dishonorable, illegal, or unjust—not by her standards, and not by the gods' standards, either. It wasn't the most ideal means of solving the realm's problems, but it would prevent the loss of thousands of lives, the decimation of Dofelli culture, and the second coming of the magical persecution.

She didn't realize what she was doing until she felt a cool wave sweep over her fingers. Half of her hand and a portion of the amulet were already partway through the Athys's magical pool—technically on Bozari soil—when she abruptly yanked her hand back, taking the amulet with her.

Lord Zhaaran frowned, visibly confused. "Your Grace—"

"I think I'll hold onto it for a bit longer," she said. He started to protest, but she talked over him. "I've heard your concerns, but I think the amulet may be just what we need to end this war before it's begun."

He glowered in a way she'd never seen from him before. "You know the stories. You know what travesties Iago Zanaki committed while the amulet was in his possession—Forged in Gold or not. You'd be signing your own death warrant by keeping it."

"I'm not Iago Zanaki, my lord."

"Don't allow your pride to obstruct your senses. The two of you may be different, but the curse comes for every man and woman in the same manner. You're no exception."

Aurelia's eyes darkened. "There are exceptions to all things, Lord Zhaaran. Have faith."

Without another word, she set the Athys down on the slab and walked away.

XV

urelia didn't say a word about her conversation with Lord Zhaaran when she and Jack left the monastery. It was nearly impossible to have a real discussion while on dragonback, so she took advantage of the forced silence to replay what had happened, over and over again, until it felt like her brain might explode.

She knew it wasn't the wisest decision. Lord Zhaaran had been more supportive of her than some of her own subjects since their first meeting in Taundosa, yet she'd denied his rather desperate request—and betrayed his trust in the process. She hoped he understood that she only meant to do what she thought was best for the realm; after all, the amulet might be their best and only chance to prevent bloodshed before the entirety of Carthe was engrossed in war.

He wouldn't see it that way, though. He came from one of the oldest families in the realm (and was descended from mankind's first sinners, for that matter), and when it came to magic, his reputation proceeded him. He thought it was his duty to manage what little magic remained in the world—good and bad. Aurelia may not have fully believed in the amulet's curse, but Lord Zhaaran certainly did.

Aurelia wasn't concerned about the amulet's curse. She wasn't Iago Zanaki, for one: they may have shared similarities, but their situations were different. Iago hadn't given enough thought to other ways he might've been able to help his kingdom, so he'd trusted divine power more than he'd trusted himself to ease his people's woes. Aurelia, on the other hand, knew there wasn't much she could do to stop a continental war that could impact the entire realm—for her, the amulet wasn't a simple way to solve a problem, but a necessary risk that could save countless lives. For another, she had no intention of keeping the amulet after certain matters were dealt with—if she even used it at all. As soon as the realm was at peace again, she'd bring it right back to the mummified remains of the Last King.

By the time they returned to the palace, nighttime had long since settled in, and the only people still awake were the soldiers guarding the premises. Aurelia hurried for her study, hoping to lock the amulet in her safe for the time being, and shot an annoyed expression at Jack when he scampered after her.

He closed the door behind them when they were alone in the study, demanding to know what had happened. She poured each of them a glass of wine, instructed him to sit on the sofa, and lounged beside him as the amulet weighed her pocket down like a ton of bricks.

"I'll preface by saying that I think I know what Sisi was talking about," she murmured. "I *did* find the moon—a piece of it, anyway."

He opened his mouth to reply, but he didn't get the chance. The sprite, tired of its confinement, sprung from her pocket and zipped around the room at the speed of light. Trinkets fell from her desk and the bookshelves, pages from opened books whipped from one side to the other, and smoking friction marks marred the walls, floors, and surfaces like streaks of charcoal.

Aurelia sighed. She'd have to find a way to explain *that* when the servants arrived to clean.

Jack's eyes widened when the sprite's golden glow beamed from behind the desk. "What in the name of the Almighty is *that?*"

"A sprite. It followed me home from Kanibar."

He gave her a look. "And you didn't think to leave it on Tullweine? It's probably a spy for King Willem. No sprite would leave the rest of its kind behind for a tour of Akkinor."

"It has no way of returning to Kanibar unless I myself return it, which I won't be doing. It's fine here for the time being." She turned and raised an eyebrow at the creature. "Aren't you?" She couldn't hear what it said— its voice was muffled, as if it were eating something—so she turned back to Jack and smiled tiredly. "I suppose the sprite is partly the reason for my conversation with Lord Zhaaran. It helped me find what Hyacinth spoke of."

She took the amulet from her pocket and held it out for him, but refused to let him take it when he tried to pluck it from her grasp. He didn't seem to recognize it. She told him the story exactly as it'd happened, from the moment the sprite told her to dig for her brother to the moment she left the Athys.

The only expression he wore during her tale was surprise when she spoke of what she found on Tullweine. His face was slack and blank for the rest of it as he tried to put the pieces together. When she finished speaking, he stood up from the sofa and turned his back on her, bringing his hands to his face and bowing his head. His name was brewing on her lips when he turned to look at her again, and she immediately swallowed whatever she'd wanted to say as soon as she recognized the frustration etched onto his face.

"I say this because I love you: that was perhaps the most foolish thing you've ever done in your life."

She frowned. "Jack—"

"Iago Zanaki was said to be the greatest ruler in Bozari history. Now, his legacy is eternally tied to what could've been the kingdom's downfall, had the first Four Lords not intervened. He was supposed to be a saint, and yet, he became a monster." He started pacing as he often did when he was distressed, and when she stood in an effort to calm him, he ignored her. "Not only do we know exactly why the Last King became such a beast, but you have the instrument in your possession, and you refused the opportunity to dispose of it before it corrupts you, too. There are dozens of ways to prevent war, Aurelia. *Dozens.* This isn't one of them."

"You must see things objectively, Jack," she pressed, setting the amulet down on the tea table. "There aren't dozens of ways to prevent war when it's fought between an entire continent's worth of kingdoms—two if we count Akkinor. We can't please everyone, so regardless of our efforts, blood will be shed, and thousands of lives will be lost. The amulet is the only way to prevent that."

"It's not worth the risk."

"Everyone seems to claim that Dofell isn't worth the effort or the anticipated losses, and yet, the Carthinians are at each other's throats over it."

"For gods' sakes, Aurelia!" Jack bellowed. She staggered backwards, startled, as his hands balled into fists at his sides. He'd never yelled at her like that before. "You're so concerned with being the peacemaker that you fail to consider the realities of our world. Ancient magic is rare nowadays, and there are only a handful of people in the realm who understand it— Lord Zhaaran among them. You may trust yourself and your ability to stay in control when threatened by evil, but that means nothing in the face of divine power. Every fool who has ever picked up the amulet has thought that way, and look where they are now. Why do you think they cast Iago out to Tullweine?"

He paused, collecting himself.

"You can't bring about peace if you willingly allow a goddess's curse to darken your heart. You're not strong enough to prevent that—nobody is.

Even if you use the amulet with just intentions, it'll eat away at everything that makes you who you are, and you'll be a blackened, rotting shell of the person you are now."

She surged backwards, hurt. "That was ugly of you."

"It's the truth." He shook his head again. "I expected *you* of all people to heed Lord Zhaaran's warnings. I never would've thought you'd do something so rash. If the stories are true, then Iago Zanaki used the amulet because he was too lazy—or stupid—to find a solution to Bozar's woes. Or, he was naive, believing his golden tears would save him. You're none of those things. Why put your faith in a curse when you've already proven how capable you are alone?"

Her eyes darkened as she folded her arms over her chest. "I didn't keep it because I'm incapable of finding solutions elsewhere. I kept it because it might be the most foolproof way of avoiding conflict—both here and in Carthe. Our subjects will thrive if mages and mortals cease being afraid of one another. The people of Dofell will have the chance to rise from the ashes instead of being victims of genocide. Our allies will grow stronger instead of turning on one another, and innocent lives won't be lost over a battle for power. The people need this, Jack. They need me to do what no other ruler has the courage to attempt in today's world."

"It doesn't matter if today's people are grateful for what you do for them," he retorted. "What matters is how this impacts future generations, both here and in Carthe. How history chooses to remember you. I know you know this, Aurelia."

He scrubbed a hand down his face, locked in contemplation, before holding out a hand in her direction, an attempt to broker a truce. "Consider the Butcher King, Reginald Cherrane: we know him as the man who reigned over Akkinor during the worst years of the persecution. Every mage, dragon, and sprite in Akkinor was slaughtered on his word. The last of the goblins lived in Akkinor at the time, and he had them fed to his hounds. The realm will never see another goblin again because of him. Do you know what most of the stories fail to mention? His subjects *adored* him. Every Akkinorian mortal who lived under his reign worshipped the ground he walked on. He was their hero—but look what's become of his memory since then. What they were blind to. What *he* was blind to."

Aurelia forced a wobbling smile. "I see you finally got around to reading the stories I recommended."

He ran a hand through his midnight-black curls, softening. "I did, but don't change the subject." She winced, but he continued. "The world may not know that you've used the power of compulsion on them—I imagine that's how it works—but some people certainly will. Arian, Lord Zhaaran,

Lady Swann...They're all mages, so I assume that gives them an awareness of the effects of magic. How do you suppose they'll feel when they find out you corrupted their free will? They'd have no choice but to obey you, but they'd spend the rest of their lives resenting you for it. Is that really how you want to be remembered?"

"I haven't decided if I wish to use it yet. I only kept it so we might *consider* the possibility," she argued. "I've already explained myself to you. The only dilemma we might face because of it is the risk of my soul succumbing to its curse. I'm only one person, Jack. The risk is worth it if it means securing a better future for the realm."

He clenched his jaw in disapproval. "You're the Queen of Akkinor—a fact you seem to have forgotten—and so long as that remains true, you're not just one person. You're responsible for every single Akkinorian who depends on you to lead, protect, and inspire them. The curse would threaten all of us: our subjects, our allies, and even our family. I'd lose my wife, our children would lose their mother, and Halvor would lose his mistress. Even if the curse didn't kill you, your mind and your soul would be lost to us all."

"That's not true. It wouldn't get to that point."

"How do you know that?"

"I feel it."

"You *feel* it." He laughed with no humor, enraging her. He hadn't spoken to her like this since almost six years earlier, when he found out she was Queen Aurelia Brentwood, not a peasant girl named Lily Linden. "Feelings can't always be trusted."

She folded her arms over her chest. "I felt I was right to trust the guard at the Palace of Taundosa when we were awaiting entry to meet Arian, and I was. I felt Captain Lukos would be true to his word when I convinced him to let us cross the Alka safely, and he was. I felt I knew where my brother was when he fled the battle, and I found him exactly where I'd expected to. You may not have been raised to rely on your instincts to guide you, but I certainly was."

His face darkened like she'd just slapped him. "That's not fair."

"Isn't it?"

"I wouldn't have survived five years in Carthe without my instincts," he retorted. "My intuition may be different than yours, but I'm perfectly capable of trusting my gut, too."

Aurelia bit her lip, choosing silence over retaliation, as Jack shook his head and sighed before sinking into the sofa with his elbows on his knees. When she only stared at him, he patted the cushion beside him, prompting her to sit. She set her hands on her knees, silent, until he reached over to place his massive palm over her left hand. His face was still taut with tension, but the combative glint in his eyes had disappeared.

"I'm sorry."

She smiled, but it felt twisted and unnatural. "I am, too."

"I still don't think this was a wise decision. Lord Zhaaran will be cross with you, and if anyone in Akkinor finds out..."

"They won't."

"How can you be sure?" He snorted into a laugh when he saw the smirk playing on her lips. "You feel it. Of course you do."

She squeezed his hand before pressing herself against his side and resting her head on his shoulder. She could feel the tension leaving his body like steam escaping a kettle, but she knew her husband, and she was certain he'd be worrying over this for the next fortnight. She didn't blame him: if their roles were reversed, she probably would've felt the same way.

But alas, the crown was on her head, and she couldn't afford to doubt herself now.

"If the time comes for me to use it," she murmured, "I shall do what needs to be done, and then I shall give it to Lord Zhaaran to do as he pleases with it. I won't let it continue to corrupt me as the Last King did—and if I do, I'll have you to keep me steady."

He shrugged her from his shoulder so he could meet her eyes. "And if I fail?"

She furrowed her eyebrows, confused. "How do you mean?"

"What if you refuse to listen? What if the curse compels you to send Halvor after me instead?"

"Jack..." She trailed off and pressed her lips together. "You think I'm capable of such a thing? Curse or not, I'd never—"

"Mortals were never meant to trifle with the power of the gods. You have absolutely no idea what might become of you." While she stared at him, hurt and dumbfounded, he stood from the sofa and forced a smile. "I know nothing I might say will persuade you to see things as I do. That's one of the reasons I fell in love with you, you know: I finally met someone more stubborn than myself, and it delighted me. Now, in this moment, it fills me with dread." He bent down to kiss her on the forehead. "Goodnight."

She barely registered when he left. She was still staring at the empty space where his face had been only seconds earlier, a response to his statements pursed on her lips as his words melted into her brain and crushed her heart. The Jack she'd met in Carthe didn't fully believe in religious tales, but the King Consort of Akkinor did, and she wasn't entirely certain of what had happened to change his mind.

Only when the sprite appeared on the tea table before her did Aurelia snap out of her daze. The creature sat on the wooden surface, legs dangling over the edge, and watched her in silence with the amulet gleaming behind it.

She raised an eyebrow. "You knew where it was. How?"

It shrugged. "We know everything."

"Naturally." She'd almost forgotten what she'd been told about sprites: they were the most notorious spies in the realm, capable of observing and overhearing anything they desired—even in the most well-defensed places in the realm. "Why did you want me to find it?"

The sprite shook its head. "Not *it*. Him."

"Oh. Why did you want me to find *him*, then?"

It lowered its head and sighed. "To say goodbye. He was a friend."

She frowned. "How is that possible? You'd have to be over a thousand years old."

"Yes. I knew Iago when I was first born."

"That can't be right."

It hissed as if displeased by her lack of understanding. "We slept. Many of us, for many years. We had to be woken."

As she struggled to process his claims, she recalled her schooling years when she was taught about magic; or, more specifically, the persecution. Some records from those terrible decades were written by scholars and priests who, like many others across the realm, believed a large number of magical creatures went into hiding to escape slaughter. The more common (and more widely accepted) records suggested that *all* magical creatures were decimated, so that's what the realm chose to believe.

Aurelia knew the common records weren't entirely accurate. Halvor proved that much. Kaia had once told her that mermaids fled to the ocean west of Carthe that no manmade vessel could access—common knowledge for most Kanish, despite the rest of the realm believing mermaids were extinct. There were even rumors that sirens had survived the persecution, too, with the help of the Isalders, who offered them refuge in exchange for protection against enemy sailors.

Mermaids, sirens, and even the tiny, mutated dragons (amongst other species) prevailed over the centuries, but some were still unaccounted for. She knew sprites were active in Kanibar, but had they always been that way? Or had they disappeared during the persecution to hibernate until it was safe for them to return, as the creature suggested? And if that were true for the sprites, did that mean it was true for other species, too?

Aurelia leaned in closer to the sprite and narrowed her eyes. "How many of you went to sleep all those years ago?"

The creature yawned. "There are more of us than there are of you."

She didn't know what it meant—and the thought terrified her—but she didn't get the chance to ask anything else before the sprite curled up on the table and began to snore.

Sighing, she crossed the study to sit at her desk and opened a drawer on the left side. After clearing it out, she took a blanket from the sofa and shoved it into the drawer, arranging the layers of sage-green cashmere until something resembling a bed appeared. She gently collected the sprite from the table, shushing it when it hissed at her in its sleep, and set it atop the blanket while it snoozed.

"Poor little soul," she whispered. "You've lived a troubled life, haven't you?"

Rather than watching it as it slept, she merely sighed again, snatched the amulet from the tea table, and slipped it into her pocket as she quietly padded out of the study. She closed and locked the door to ensure the sprite was exactly where she'd left it when she returned the next morning. It probably wouldn't be happy when it woke up to find itself locked alone in a room, but she'd rather face a tiny sprite's irritation than a palace full of people hollering about a pesky creature pulling their hair.

They'd find out about it soon enough, but not yet—they had enough to get used to as it was.

XVI

urelia didn't make it into her bedchamber that night. When she found herself standing outside of her door, as Jack's snoring penetrated the walls, she couldn't bring herself to open it. He'd wake up when he felt her slip into bed beside him, as he always did, and it would break her heart if he turned around instead of snuggling her.

Instead, she decided to pay a visit to the gardens. It was late in the night by then, closer to dawn than dusk, but the air wasn't chilly or breezy like she'd expected. It was a humid night, hot and balmy, and despite her hair frizzing up the moment she stepped outside, she was glad for it: the weather reminded her of Taundosa, the home of her ancestors.

She fetched a lantern on her way out and nodded her head in greeting to the four soldiers positioned at the rear doors of the palace. They both straightened when she passed them, their armor clinking as one as they moved in sync, and didn't mutter so much as a hello when she bid them good evening.

She expected to find Halvor at the rear of the gardens, as always, where a large chunk of the lawn was reserved only for him. Instead of following the path to Halvor's sanctuary—she didn't wish to disturb his slumber—she decided to take a more scenic route through a different part of the lawn, where dozens upon dozens of trees had been planted to mimic the look of a real forest. It wasn't a large area when compared to actual woodlands, but it took up a fair chunk of the gardens, anyhow.

Careful not to squish the flowerbeds and berry bushes woven through the trees, she followed the narrow stone path until she found a decent spot for contemplation. She was surrounded by foliage on all sides—so thick that she couldn't see anything beyond the leaves and trunks—but she was completely and utterly alone, too.

Exactly how she liked it.

She lowered herself onto the ground with her back against a tree trunk, nestled between purple snapdragons, and closed her eyes as she buried her fingers in the soil below. She leaned her head back against the bark, soaking in the sound of fireflies humming nearby, and winced when one small movement—a readjusting of her leg—caused the amulet to fall from her pocket and onto the ground.

Muttering a curse under her breath, she collected it and weighed it in her hand. She couldn't see it very well, even with the light from the lantern beside her, but she was still in awe of its beauty. Nothing like it existed in the world anymore: the last piece of a weapon wielded by a deity.

From what she could recall, the moon goddess was associated with a few things: darkness, dusk, cold, and misfortune. She wasn't known for having a poor temperament like other deities were, but when Edea was involved, everything seemed to go awry. The ancient people who'd interacted with her were always met with bad luck, even if she favored them. It was an unfortunate trait, to be certain, but it didn't seem like one she was capable of controlling, either.

Perhaps Lord Zhaaran was right, and the amulet's curse prevailed because Edea longed for her possession to be returned to her. Then maybe, just maybe, Aurelia could escape the consequences of using the amulet by returning it somehow. The amulet certainly didn't belong with the corpse of Iago Zanaki, and it didn't belong in a locked chest hidden away in the Holy Library, either. It belonged with the goddess who'd created it and wielded it expertly for centuries.

But how could Aurelia return the amulet when the deity hadn't presented herself to the realm in well over a thousand years?

Excited by the idea, Aurelia stood and returned the amulet to her pocket, intending to visit the palace library so she could research anything that might point her in the right direction. She was so distracted by her thoughts that she hadn't realized she'd drifted from the stone path, and was now trekking through the dirt and flowers scattered between the trees. The realization finally struck her when the garden wall came into view at the very edge of the tiny forest. As she got closer, she thought she saw a few of her soldiers leaning up against the wall. Had they followed her to keep an eye on her?

"Good evening, gentlemen," she called out. "I appreciate your diligence, but I assure you, I'm quite all right. Return to your posts—I'm perfectly capable of finding my way inside."

No reply. Frowning, she took a few steps closer to the wall, wondering why they hadn't seemed to hear her. Maybe they *hadn't* followed her, and they'd simply wanted to share a flask beneath the shadows cast by the wall, where nobody could see that they'd abandoned their posts and fallen into a drunken slumber.

She opened her mouth to speak again—this time to scold them—but the words got lodged in her throat when she got closer to the bodies. That's what they were: the dead bodies of four Akkinorian soldiers, piled atop one another and stacked against the wall like scarecrows.

She sucked in a sharp breath, but before she could call out for help, a clammy hand covered her mouth while an arm wrapped around her midriff and pulled her backwards. Her feet skidded along the dirt as her screams were muffled by the hand, and she felt her back pressed firmly against an armor-clad stomach.

While thrashing and kicking in an attempt to break free, three additional assailants appeared before her. One brandished his sword and pointed it at her stomach, then pressed his index finger to his lips. She struggled to calm her heavy breathing as she stopped fighting, knowing silence and submission were, at this moment, her greatest allies.

She didn't recognize the man jabbing her gut with the tip of his sword. When the two beside him removed their helmets, she didn't recognize them, either. The reason became clear when they shifted so the light from her lantern illuminated their faces: they were undoubtedly Bozari with their sepia skin, short yet stocky builds, and intense blue eyes.

Everything made sense to her now. The bodies at the wall were the Akkinorian soldiers normally tasked with guarding the palace's real entrance, and the men she'd passed on her way outside weren't *her* men at all. They'd been lying in wait for her, likely planning on sneaking into the palace until her late-night walk gave them a better opportunity.

"Forgive us, Your Grace." The man wielding his sword smiled at her while his comrades laughed. "We were given an order, and we must follow through." He lowered his sword, so the tip was jabbing her thigh. "Give it here. You know what I'm talking about."

She tried to step backwards, but the stout, pudgy man holding her refused to budge. "No."

"Come on, now. It's simple. Hand the object over, and we'll be on our way. You can go back to doing whatever queens do in the gardens in the middle of the night."

One of the men beside him, the tallest of the quartet, slammed his boot onto the lantern, extinguishing the flame. Aurelia winced at the sound of shattering glass and began to thrash again when the third man—with a face covered in nasty scars—approached her.

He looked her up and down, a smirk forming on his lips. He seemed less intent on retrieving the amulet than he did on getting his hands on the queen: his hand found its way to the base of her neck before sliding down to her breast, prompting him to knead her flesh with his fingers.

Aurelia spat in his face. "Touch me again, and it'll be the last time you touch anything."

He grinned and wiped her saliva from his cheek. "We're not afraid of you, Your Grace. We fear nothing but the wrath of the gods."

"Oh, shut *up*," the sword-wielding soldier snapped. "Take the damn thing so we can be done with this."

The scarred man tried reaching into her pocket, but she stopped him by jerking her knee upwards until it slammed into his groin. He groaned and stumbled backwards, and the heavyset man restraining her responded by shoving her onto the ground. She fell face-first, swallowing dirt and perhaps a spider or two, and managed to release one cough before the man with the sword dragged her over to him by her ankles. She rolled over and brought herself to a sitting position just in time for the tip of his sword to graze her throat.

By then, all four men had regained their composure and were staring down at her from all sides: the scarred soldier seething and cupping his groin, the pudgy man cracking his knuckles, the tall one drawing his dagger in case she tried to fight again, and the man with the sword grinning from ear to ear, like the Queen of Akkinor was his personal jester.

"It's been fun, but we really must be going," the sword-wielding soldier said. "This is the last time I ask you nicely, Your Grace. Hand it over."

She glared at him and gritted her teeth, wondering if keeping the amulet was worth trying to fight her way out of this. Maybe if she threw a handful of dirt into their eyes, she'd have time to run, and any Akkinorian soldiers posted nearby would come to her aid.

Just then, the world around them went silent, bringing the quartet to a halt as they observed their surroundings. The cicadas stopped buzzing, the owls stopped hooting, and the bats stopped chirping. For a moment, the only sound to be heard was the soft rustling of leaves as a calm breeze blew by, and the only sight to be seen was the twinkling of stars against the midnight sky.

Now it was Aurelia's turn to smirk at her captors.

The earth beneath their feet began to shake, the trees swayed before falling flat to the ground, and a low, eerie rumble—a cross between a moan and a growl—echoed from the darkness within the foliage. When Aurelia inhaled shakily, a sliver of moonlight pierced through the shadows in the trees to reflect against one angry, glowing golden eye.

In a split second, whatever trees remained in Halvor's path were squashed under his massive feet as he hurried toward his mistress, and all four men howled in terror before running off. One—the man with the scarred face—tripped over a fallen branch and fell face-first onto the grass. Halvor grabbed the man by the ankles with his teeth, tossed him into the air as he screamed, and swallowed him in one gulp.

Aurelia rushed to her feet and followed Halvor as he left the tiny forest behind to chase his prey. Upon spotting two of the men running for the garden wall—likely hoping to climb the hanging ivy and escape from the other side—Halvor whipped his tail across the lawn, knocking them both on their backs. As they gasped for air, writhing on the ground, Halvor turned his attention to the fourth man—the plumpest one, who'd restrained her earlier—who'd foolishly taken shelter behind a marble water fountain. The man scrambled to his feet and tried darting for the greenhouse across the way, but as soon as he stood, Halvor batted him onto the ground and pinned him down like a cat might do to a mouse.

Feasting on one man was apparently enough to satisfy him; instead of eating the man squirming beneath his foot, Halvor merely lowered his head and bellowed in the man's face. Aurelia winced when long, thick gobs of saliva—and pieces of the garments the scarred man had been wearing— fell onto the soldier's face as Halvor snarled at him.

Halvor craned his neck back, shrieked, and sent an enormous ball of fire sailing through the clouds above. Not a minute later, the dark windows in the palace were illuminated, and shouting rattled Aurelia's eardrums as a handful of Akkinorian soldiers flooded into the gardens from the rear doors.

One of her men appeared at her side and touched her elbow. "Are you all right, Your Grace? What's happened?"

She said nothing as her soldiers stripped the three surviving Bozari of their stolen armor and bound them with bronze shackles. Beneath the armor, the trio wore plain brown breeches and white tunics, and the latter had the sigil of Kazamir stitched over the left breast in blue thread. Kazamir: her ally. Not Tucana or Iseppa, or even Orestes, whose lord she'd recently offended.

"Bring them to the dungeon," Aurelia instructed, "and have the two Bozari emissaries imprisoned, too. They can earn their freedom once they've given me a proper explanation." She sighed and pressed her lips together as Halvor nuzzled her shoulder from behind, ensuring she was all right. "It seems we'll need to revisit the terms of our alliance with Kazamir."

***

"Speak."

Ser Bonta Zarros, a knight and emissary of Kazamir, gulped as he knelt on the floor of his cell in the dungeon with his arms bound behind his back. "Y-Your Grace—"

"Oh, spare me your pleasantries," Aurelia snapped. "I was attacked by four men wearing the sigil of Kazamir on their breasts. If you didn't wish for me to trace them back to you, you should've warned them against flaunting their loyalties for all to see." She narrowed her eyes. "You, ser, are Lord Zhoqa's voice in Akkinor. Speak, or I shall send you home to him without your tongue."

Beside her, Jack leaned against the stone wall like this was a casual conversation instead of an interrogation. One hand was in his pocket, the other spinning a palm-sized dagger around his hand. The blade itself wasn't threatening, but when wielded by Jack—whose confidence and skill prevented him from slicing himself while he toyed with it—the weapon was as dangerous as dragonfire.

The knight seemed to know this, too. "All right, all right!" His frantic tone made his wide, azurite eyes appear even wilder. "W-We received a raven when you returned from the monastery. A priest sent word on behalf of the Four Lords, who gave him the note through the Athys. They gave us orders to collect the object in your possession."

"What of your counterpart?" she demanded. "Ser Yassine, wasn't it?"

He grimaced. "I misspoke. Lord *Zhoqa* commanded us to collect the object. Lord Zhaaran merely instructed us to observe you and report our findings. Yassine fled for Seaport when he heard what Lord Zhoqa suggested. He didn't wish to be involved."

"What was suggested?" When the emissary bowed his head in silence, Jack scowled and took a step closer to him, weighing the dagger in his grip. "Answer me."

He didn't lift his eyes from the ground. "He instructed us—*me*—to summon my brothers-in-arms from our ship at Seaport. He told me to select the four strongest men among them and order them to take the object from you by any means necessary."

A chill traced Aurelia's spine. "Why not have *you* retrieve the object instead? What with you staying in the palace as my guest, you had better access to me and my possessions than your associates."

Ser Zarros squared his shoulders as well as he could. "His Lordship didn't wish for me to sully my knighthood with such a dishonorable act."

At least he has some decency, she thought. "And then?"

"I was able to sneak them onto the grounds through the servant's entrance when the guards left to switch shifts. I knew they'd be spotted and recognized in the main corridors, so I told them to make way for the greenhouse until an opportune moment arrived. The plan was for them to kill the guards at the back door before sunrise and sneak into the palace from there, where they'd find you alone in your study before breakfast—as you are every morning. I...I didn't anticipate much of a struggle."

"It would appear that neither you nor His Lordship thought this through," she said. "Did you really think they'd be able to leave the grounds with my possession? Even if they'd managed to take it from me, they wouldn't make it halfway to the gates before they were stopped. It's a fool's gambit to steal from a queen in her own palace."

His cheeks burned crimson. "I was only doing as my lord commanded, Your Grace."

She narrowed her eyes, then turned to a guard nearby and nodded her head. "I won't punish you for doing your duty," she told the emissary as the guard unlocked his shackles. He stared at her, surprised, before the guard hefted him to his feet. "I cannot, however, allow you to remain in the palace. You'll be escorted to your ship at Seaport when I leave you, and you may never set foot in my home again."

She resisted the urge to roll her eyes when he dramatized his gratitude by falling at her feet and weeping. He knew as well as she did that she could've had him hanged for what he did. The men he'd hired could've done whatever they pleased to her (one of them already had) while collecting the amulet. It didn't matter that she was allied with their lord: he'd given the order, after all.

"Still, there's a price to be paid for what I endured tonight," she continued. He stopped weeping—like he could turn it on and off at will—and stared at her. "One of the four men was eaten by my dragon. The other three are here in the dungeon with you. I'll offer you a choice: you may take one home to Kazamir with you, and the other two will hang."

His lips parted like a fish. "Y-Your Grace—"

"The queen has given an order. Make your decision, or all four of you will hang. I'll personally see to that." Jack folded his arms over his chest while still pointing the tip of his dagger at the knight's chest. *"Choose."*

It took him a few minutes, but he did. When the sun rose about an hour later, two Bozari soldiers—the plump one and the one who'd pointed his sword at her—were loaded into a wagon to be brought to the gallows at

Oleander's Valley. The third, the tallest of the quartet, joined Ser Zarros in his carriage as they departed the palace for Seaport.

Aurelia and Jack watched the carriages depart from one of the palace's balconies. "I think we need to pay a visit to Lord Zhoqa," Jack muttered. "Your conversation with King Willem can be relayed via raven, but after what happened today...That oaf needs to look you in the eye while you remind him that you can dissolve your alliance with Kazamir, if you so desire."

She nodded in agreement. "I suppose I can say goodbye to having a day to rest."

"You can sleep on the way there. I'm sure Halvor won't mind."

She cracked a smile and took his hands. "Are you still angry with me about the amulet? Especially after what's just happened?"

Jack winced, but he squeezed her hands and mirrored her smile. "I'm not angry with you, though I still wish you'd given it to Lord Zhaaran when he asked. And I...I trust you, Aurelia. I trust that you're doing what you believe is right, even if I don't entirely agree with you. It's not like you set out to find the amulet, either. In a way, *it* found *you*. That has to count for something."

Aurelia's eyes stung with emotion, leaving her grappling for the right words. Instead of replying, she leaned up on her toes and draped her arms around Jack's neck, pressing the entire length of her body against his. He settled his hands on her waist immediately as he bent down to kiss her, parting her lips with his tongue. She giggled when she felt him grinning against her—the same innocent, yet wicked grin she'd fallen in love with five years earlier.

That much hadn't changed at all.

XVII

The last time Aurelia had traveled so consistently was during her first trip to Carthe, when she was forced to journey across the entire length of the continent to find Arian in Taundosa.

She'd moved around so much that she'd forgotten what it was to be stagnant. She was always at least half-awake, as nobody with their wits about them could sleep well while the dangers of Carthe surrounded them on all sides. Her body had begun molding to the shape of her horse's, binding them as one, and she'd worn down the soles of her shoes so badly that she could feel every stone and every blade of grass she stepped on.

Though Lily Linden and her adventures felt like a lifetime ago, recent weeks had proven that the time for quests wasn't over yet. The only difference was that nowadays, she wasn't fighting for survival or spending sixteen hours every day on horseback—she was fighting for peace. And while she missed her beloved horse, Scotch—who'd been killed in the battle against her brother—this time around, she was traveling with the most fearsome creature in the realm.

Aurelia had thought about taking the sprite along when she, Jack, and Halvor left the day after the attack, but if the creature really was a spy for Kanibar, she couldn't risk delivering it back to Carthe. It would be so easy for it to sneak off and find its way back to King Willem, and Aurelia would be none the wiser. Though she trusted what the creature told her, she couldn't take any chances. She'd left it in her study with a plate of sweets and a chalice of water, and she'd made it promise to stay put until she returned.

Despite her exhaustion from the events of the last few days, Aurelia didn't instruct Halvor to stop on the small island in the Alkamura where they normally rested midflight. She wanted to keep the trip as short as possible, even if that meant sacrificing another night's rest.

They landed in Kazamir, the southern Bozari quadrant nestled between eastern Taundosa and western Khaba. It was the same place where she'd inadvertently incited a revolution over five years earlier. Lord Zhoqa's palace, Kaerndal, stood by its lonesome atop a massive hill, leaving no room for Halvor to land in its immediate vicinity. Aurelia and Jack had no choice but to walk up a steep, winding dirt path to reach the front doors, where a Zhoqa family attendant was waiting to greet them.

The walk wasn't all bad, though: it gave Jack plenty of time to recover from his flight sickness—a horrible affliction he hadn't managed to overcome, even five years after the first time he joined Aurelia on dragonback.

"Your Grace. Your Highness." The male attendant, short and thin with curly dark hair only on the top of his head, bowed to them. "I'm afraid His Lordship isn't home. We weren't expecting you."

She sighed. "Where is he?"

"The Nexus, Your Grace. Orestes."

"We shall find our way. Thank you, sir." As she turned, he took a step forward and opened his mouth, like there was something else he wanted to say. She raised an eyebrow as a warm gust of wind lifted her hair from her shoulders. "Was there something more?"

"You...You can't visit the Nexus, Your Grace. Your husband can, but not you."

"Why not?"

He swallowed. "Women are not allowed inside the Nexus."

She couldn't help but smile. "And what do you suppose might happen if I visit? Will the building explode? Will the dead rise from the catacombs beneath the kingdom? Will the gods rain hellfire down upon us all?" He pressed his lips together, cheeks reddening, and only bowed his head in response while Jack stifled laughter. "I thought as much. I respect Bozar's customs, sir, but to my understanding, there are no laws—divine or mortal—preventing a woman from entering a meeting place of any kind. It's a matter of preference for the Four Lords, isn't it? I imagine so, and after what your liege lord put me through last night, I'm certainly not in the mood to consider what he prefers."

No reply. Satisfied with her response, Aurelia turned and descended the hill to meet Halvor on the field below, Jack hot on her heels. She felt the man's eyes on her even as they lifted into the sky, and she hoped he wasn't punished by Lord Zhoqa when the latter returned home from the Nexus. The poor man couldn't have stopped them from going if he'd tried with all his might.

It wasn't difficult to spot the Nexus in southern Orestes. She'd seen illustrations of it in books before: a two-story building resembling a ring, with an enormous, rounded courtyard in the center. Five flags—one representing the whole of Bozar, and four representing its individual districts—waved from posts so tall, they nearly disappeared into the clouds. The structure was slowly crumbling, as it had been for centuries, as time and erosion left their mark on the sandstone bricks. It was one of many ancient Bozari buildings desperately in need of repair, but it would never be restored: each of the Four Lords would need to contribute an equal amount of coin, and every generation failed to agree on how much they'd put towards the Nexus.

Because the building was located in such a busy part of Orestes, the walls surrounding the Nexus were practically kissing the borders of neighboring towns and cities. Everyone in the vicinity caught a glimpse of Halvor as he landed atop a section of the stone walls, bellowing for dramatic effect as he announced his presence to the nearby Oresteans. There wasn't enough empty space between the Nexus and its perimeter for him to land on the ground, so he lowered his wing to the grass as much as he could, allowing Aurelia and Jack to dismount by sliding down his slippery, scaly appendage.

She patted her pocket to ensure the amulet was still there as they strolled toward one of the many entrances to the circular building. Guards were posted along the entire perimeter, exactly two feet apart from one another, and an additional guard stood within each entryway. There were no doors and therefore no locks, so the guards, in effect, were using their own bodies as barriers.

None of the guards forming the perimeter moved an inch or uttered a word when they approached one of the entrances. She couldn't see any of their faces because of their helmets, but she saw one or two swallow nervously as their eyes flickered over to Halvor, and some had grown so clammy with nerves that their hands slid down the handles of their swords.

The guard posted in the entryway, however, wasn't so intimidated. "I must ask that you leave the premises at once. Women are forbidden from entry to the Nexus."

"By what law?" Jack demanded.

He stiffened. "There is no law."

"Then I can't see why you'd deny a queen her desires."

"The Four Lords have already begun their meeting. They mustn't be disturbed."

"The Lord of Kazamir has threatened our alliance," Aurelia retorted. "This is a matter of the utmost importance—it can't wait." She cocked her head to the side, smiling. "Of course, we can find our own means of gaining entry, but I don't suppose your lords would be pleased with our methods."

His eyes flashed over to Halvor, then to the massive sword at Jack's side, before landing on Aurelia again. "Very well."

She thanked him politely as he stepped aside, ignoring the other guards as they stared in utter bewilderment. She cast a final glance at Halvor before moving forward, prompting the dragon to lift off from the wall and circle the Nexus overhead. Normally, he might've flown away in search of a meal or simply to explore, but he seemed to sense that Aurelia needed her greatest weapon nearby.

The interior of the Nexus was surprisingly empty, with few decorations other than a painting or two on the stone walls. Statues, sculptures, and artifacts rested in straw-filled wooden crates on the floor— either because they were yet to be displayed properly, or because they were being packed away, so they'd be protected from the leaking, crumbling ceiling above.

The emptiness and silence of the Nexus left Aurelia feeling harrowed, but fortunately, she came across the only other person casually walking the halls. The male servant froze when he saw her, white-faced and slack-jawed, and took just a bit too long to answer when she inquired after where she and Jack might find the Four Lords. He raised an arm and pointed a shaking finger to the staircase nearby, then scurried away like a scolded hound.

On the second floor, Aurelia spotted a few other servants—all men— doing this and that, but every last one of them turned on their heel and walked away when they saw her. She'd have to find the meeting place herself, but fortunately, it wasn't difficult: the moment she heard Lord Zhoqa's booming voice from down the hall, she knew exactly where she was going.

Like the rest of the Nexus, both inside and out, the entryway was void of a door. The meeting room was curved on account of the estate's circular shape, and other than the hearth, a few crates and boxes, and the much-too-big conference table, it was empty. The Four Lords were seated in their respective chairs around the table, leagues away from one another, as servants and guards for each nobleman lined the back wall.

For a moment, nobody saw Aurelia and Jack lingering in the entryway. Then a young servant—wearing the colors of Iseppa—flicked his gaze to them, and the loud gasp that escaped his lips was enough to render the lords silent as they followed his eyes. Immediately, all four of them rose from their seats like the Nexus had been set ablaze.

In a way, it had.

"Gods above." Lord Xada of Tucana, whom she recognized based on the sigil sewn onto his tunic, was flushed with anger in seconds. "You shouldn't be here. The Nexus—"

"—is forbidden to women. I know." Aurelia smiled as she took a few steps forward, with Jack ever at her side. "I'm perfectly aware of how the Bozari treat their women, and I must say, I find it rather displeasing. I speak from experience, too, after I was recently assaulted by some of your men." Lord Zhoqa's eyes flashed when their gazes met. "You will grant me leniency so we can discuss what happened, or we will take this discussion outside instead. I shall have to warn you, though: my dragon has since grown distrustful of Bozari men, and I can't promise that he won't attempt to disgrace you as you have disgraced me. What do you suppose your soldiers would think of you if they saw you running away in terror like cowering animals?"

"*If* they mustered the strength to run. They'd probably fall to the ground and crawl away like babes—oh, do forgive me. That's an insult to *our* children." Jack directed the words at Aurelia, but he was looking at the Four Lords when he said them. His hand was still nestled on the hilt of his sword. "Halvor would get quite the thrill out of it. He's always enjoyed a decent game of cat-and-mouse."

Lord Zoma of Iseppa gritted his teeth. "How dare you threaten us in our own estate? On our own *land?*"

Aurelia laughed humorlessly. "Your hypocrisy is outstanding, my lord, truly. That's the very reason I'm here—because Bozari men threatened me on my own property. On my own *land.*"

He ignored her. "The nerve of a foreign woman to—"

"Enough." Lord Zhaaran, careful to avoid meeting Aurelia's eyes, managed to silence his fellow nobleman with a single word. His timing was excellent—Jack's wild eyes suggested he wouldn't have let Lord Zoma finish his sentence. "She's already here. There's no point in arguing it any further."

When nobody spoke, Aurelia set her gaze on Lord Zhoqa once more. "*You.*" She marched up to him, fury blazing in her eyes, as he casually lowered himself onto his seat. "Ser Zarros is currently voyaging home from Akkinor. I'm sure he'll be eager to share his side of things, but I have a few words of my own for you." She turned to glance at Lord Zhaaran beside him. "You knew about the order he gave, too, and you didn't attempt to stop him."

The old man didn't reply.

"Desperate times, Your Grace," Lord Zhoqa purred. He didn't look as apologetic as he should've, given the rash measures he'd taken to collect the amulet—but he *did* look concerned when he saw the way Jack seethed at him. "You were asked to hand it over, and you refused. There are only so many times one can ask nicely before one must turn to other means."

"Your soldiers could've killed me."

"They wouldn't have killed you."

"I believe you told them to get the amulet, and I quote, 'by any means necessary.' They could've beaten me, raped me—any number of things, really. In fact, one of them *did* lay a hand on me. Halvor ate him."

That didn't seem to bother him. "Your soldiers would've treated me the same way if roles were reversed."

"That might've been true while my brother still lived, but not anymore. Not since we swore to defend and protect one another almost six years ago," she retorted. "You want something in my possession—that doesn't give you the right to betray the promises you made by sending your men to ambush me." She shook her head and chuckled humorlessly. "If you think I'm going to fight under your banners after such disrespect, then you're a madman. This is more than enough to warrant the dissolution of our alliance. If your people weren't so dependent on Akkinorian goods, I'd be swayed to sever all ties to Kazamir. I hope you're pleased: even if I *was* considering an alliance with all Four Lords, I'm certainly not thinking about it anymore."

His eyes blazed. "How dare—"

"Never the matter. I shouldn't like to be associated with you while your soul succumbs to evil, anyway." Lord Zoma checked the time on the grandfather clock in the corner of the room. "We've discussed all we needed to today. I ought to get home before my wives slaughter me."

"Me too." Lord Xada's eyes darted between Aurelia and Lord Zhoqa. "Seeing as I had no part in this, I don't wish to be present for the discussion. Good day, gentlemen. Your Grace."

When both lords started for the exit, the servants and soldiers broke from their lineup in the back of the room to follow. They weren't halfway out of the room before Lord Zhaaran, too, gestured toward his men to prepare for departure.

"I have nothing to say to you." He spoke to Aurelia, but he still refused to look at her. "The two of us are meant to visit Taundosa tomorrow. I shall send word to Her Majesty about your presence in Carthe—I'm certain she'd like you to attend our audience, too. Perhaps she can talk some sense into you."

Lord Zhaaran paused for a moment longer, ignoring the way Jack glowered at him, before disappearing into the hallway. When he was gone, Aurelia squeezed Jack's hand and nodded her head toward the door. He hesitated, eyeing the Lord of Kazamir in a way that made even his wife shudder in fear, and lingered for only another minute before excusing himself so the pair could speak privately.

Neither Aurelia nor Lord Zhoqa spoke as they sat across from one another, burning holes into the other's skull with their eyes. A part of her wished she hadn't dismissed Jack, but at the same time, she needed her ally to respect her without her frightening husband—or Halvor, for that matter—breathing down his neck. He didn't fear her without them, but she could live with that if there was a chance he'd treat her like an equal.

"For the record, I told Ser Zarros to ensure the soldiers were decent toward you," he shared, breaking the silence. "They were firmly instructed against harming you."

"If that were true, you would've omitted the 'by any means necessary' part."

He snorted. "That still applies to non-violent activities, you know."

"It doesn't matter. You placed me in a dangerous position, my lord. If it had gone any differently—if my dragon hadn't intervened—Kazamir might've found itself at war with Akkinor. It was a foolish command to give."

"Maybe, but I couldn't see a better option."

She paused. "You were there for my conversation with Lord Zhaaran through the Athys, weren't you?"

"All Four Lords were present."

Aurelia scowled. "I was forbidden from bringing anyone along, yet Lord Zhaaran allowed the three of you to listen in? If Bozar hadn't already breached my trust, I might be more surprised than I am."

"The fewer people who know about the amulet, the better. Orestes may claim responsibility over the amulet, but all four of us are aware of what it is and what it does. The atrocities committed by the Last King affected the entirety of Bozar, remember? All of our ancestors fell victim to the amulet's curse. It concerns each of us."

"I never thought you'd be the type to—"

"—believe in ancient curses?" he finished. She only watched him, unsure if that was how her sentence was going to end. "In truth, I don't. Never did. I knew about the amulet because my father told me about it while training me to inherit Kazamir. I didn't think twice about it after my lessons."

"So why go through such trouble and risk our alliance to retrieve it?"

He sighed. "I saw what measures Jalhor took to speak with you about it. He wouldn't have done any of that unless he's afraid, and I've never known the old man to be afraid of anything. That alone terrified me, and I don't enjoy feeling like a cowering pup."

"What did he do?"

"You don't know?"

"I wouldn't be asking if I knew."

He chuckled, but the sound was bitter. "The Athys, as I'm sure you know, demands a price be paid before it can be used. The price is blood, Your Grace. Sacrifice. It can't be just anyone, either. Plucking a servant or a peasant from their bed and cutting their throat as a gift to the gods is insulting—no deity with any ounce of self-respect would take kindly to a lowborn sacrifice."

Goosebumps peppered every inch of her skin. "Who?"

Lord Zhoqa grimaced. "His brother. The killer must be the person using the Athys, too—Jalhor had to cut his own brother's throat in the holiest place in the realm, all for the chance to speak with you about returning the amulet to its grave."

Aurelia sucked in a sharp breath and prayed he didn't notice, but when his eyes flashed as he took another sip of wine, she knew he had.

It was no wonder Lord Zhaaran was so cross with her. She hadn't just betrayed his trust by refusing to give him the amulet: she'd made his brother's sacrifice meaningless.

The amulet hadn't felt like a curse before, but it certainly did now.

XVIII

Aurelia's conversation with Lord Zhoqa hadn't lasted much longer. He didn't apologize for giving the command, but she hadn't expected him to. All she'd really wanted was to know what pushed him to do it, and now that she did, she was less angry at him and more disappointed by her lack of knowledge.

That was a consequence of dealing with the Bozari: they knew everything there was to know regarding the ancient history of the realm, making the rest of the world feel—and appear—ignorant. Had Aurelia properly researched the Athys before her conversation with Lord Zhaaran, she would've known the price of using it, and it might've swayed her into heeding the old man's words.

Lord Zhoqa offered her and Jack seats in his carriage for the trip to Taundosa, but she didn't wish to be near him for longer than necessary. Instead, the couple returned to Halvor after sending a raven to Akkinor, so Ansyl knew what was happening. She'd likely arrive at the palace within moments of Reyna receiving Lord Zhaaran's raven about Aurelia and Jack's trip to Carthe. The two Bozari lords, on the other hand, wouldn't make it to the Palace of Taundosa until the following evening—a consequence of their antiquated mode of travel.

As Aurelia, Jack, and Halvor departed for the City of Gold, a sense of relief flooded the queen's veins. She was glad to be visiting Arian and Reyna before the Bozari lords arrived. She didn't know if the Taundosans were aware of the newfound tension between Aurelia and the noblemen, but either way, she wanted their opinion on the matter. Jack was right: none of her allies would be pleased if they found out she'd used the amulet to obstruct their free will, so involving as many of them as possible before she had the chance to use it—*if* she used it—was crucial for maintaining good faith between them.

A part of her wished Lady Swann would be there, too. Nobody had heard a peep from the Lady of Runeia—or any of the five reigning nobles of Krotis—since King Willem affirmed his plans for Dofell. Aurelia had a strong feeling that Lady Swann would've agreed with her, but unless the old woman chose to get involved, Aurelia was missing a crucial ally.

For a moment as they coasted over Taundosa, she forgot about everything plaguing her mind as she relished the ethereal feeling of being back in the City of Gold. It was a breath of fresh air compared to Akkinor, and it filled her with the strength she'd been lacking lately—strength born from the memories of every Cristos who'd come before her.

Halvor landed atop the massive, circular wall encasing the gardens at Reyna's palace. His claws scraped against the stone for traction as he carefully tilted his body to the left, imbedding his talon-tipped wing in the dirt so Aurelia and Jack could dismount without having to climb down the wall. When her feet touched the ground, he lowered his snout to her stomach to nudge her—both out of affection and for good luck—before lifting into the air and disappearing behind the clouds.

As they walked toward the frosted glass doors leading into the palace, she spotted a familiar face awaiting them, alongside a handful of Goldmen—Taundosa's most esteemed military branch. She grinned at her uncle and hurried her pace to meet him, not at all surprised that he'd prepared for her arrival so quickly.

"Hello, my dear. Mister Ashford." Arian greeted her with a warm hug and a kiss on the cheek, and Jack with a firm handshake, as always. "We just received Lord Zhaaran's message. You arrived just on time, though I imagine our Bozari friends are a ways behind you."

"Yes, well..." She trailed off and sighed as they glided through the doors and into the palace. "Lord Zhoqa wished for us to ride with him, but I couldn't bear the thought of it. He's shameless, for one, and for another..." She paused, clenching her jaw, and looked up at him like her children often looked at her. "I have something to tell you."

Hearing the urgency in her voice, Arian pulled them aside to a corner in the corridor, far away from gossip-deprived servants and loose-lipped soldiers. When they were certain that nobody was around to overhear, she and Jack told him everything about the amulet, Iago Zanaki, the Athys, and her displeasure with Lord Zhoqa.

Arian didn't say anything for a moment when they finished speaking. His lips were pursed in contemplation, and his eyes were trained on the floor. To Aurelia's surprise, he didn't seem upset—and in the nearly six years since they'd entered each other's lives, she'd never known him to hide his true feelings from her.

Still, his silence worried her. "Uncle? What do you think?"

He glanced down at her pocket and sighed. "I think Bozar believes too greatly in curses, and too little in the power of circumstances."

"How do you mean?" Jack pressed.

"Iago Zanaki ruled during the first blight of the Silent Death. One in four of every Bozari sheep, cow, horse, pig, and goat was infected by it, and anyone who touched or consumed their meat fell victim to the plague, too. He spent half of Bozar's funds on medicines and other remedies, to no avail, and the other half on livestock from Taundosa and Kanibar. It still wasn't enough to replace what he'd lost or to feed his subjects. He couldn't afford more livestock, nor did he have anything to offer his neighbors in trade, so he compelled Taundosa to give him what he needed.

"The amulet was a simple way for him to regain what was lost to the plague, but it wasn't the only way. The gods likely disapproved of him using divine power for theft, even if it's not the kind of theft we're accustomed to. The reasons you—or any of us, for that matter—have for potentially using the amulet don't involve taking from one to give to another. You wouldn't be disturbing the balance between peoples, but rather restoring it. The gods can't fault you for that."

"Lord Zhaaran seems to think the curse stems from Edea's longing for the staff," Aurelia murmured, biting her lower lip. "It's punishment for mortals toying with something that doesn't belong to us."

Her uncle grimaced. "Edea isn't known for mercy or kindness, but she isn't known for being a tyrant or a punisher, either. She may bring misfortune, but she has no say in how we respond to it."

She hesitated for a moment. "So you aren't angry with me?"

"Angry with you? No. Never." His eyes flickered toward something behind her as a smile graced his lips. "I'll share this with Her Majesty— I'm certain she'll appreciate being informed on what's happening between her allies before the lot of us are reunited. In the meantime, there's someone here who'd like to see you. I sent word to Agotia as soon as Her Majesty received Lord Zhaaran's letter about your arrival."

Frowning, Aurelia looked over her shoulder to follow his gaze, and an enormous grin spread over her lips when she saw who was approaching from the other end of the corridor.

Before she knew what she was doing, she was wrapped in Estylle's arms as her former governess wept onto the queen's hair. She drew her attention away from Estylle for a moment to look for Arian and Jack, who were nowhere to be found—likely having set off on an excursion to the armory, as Arian knew that Jack would admire Taundosa's new weaponry long enough for Aurelia to catch up with Estylle.

That was very well. She'd had more than enough of politics and uncomfortable conversations for one day, anyway. Until the Bozari lords arrived on the morrow, the only thing Aurelia had to do in the meantime was talk to Estylle—the only person alive who'd stood by Aurelia's side nearly every day since the moment she was born.

After the war with Archie, Estylle made the difficult decision to return to Taundosa. She missed her home, and she claimed Akkinor didn't feel like home anymore without Archie—despite what became of him. Now that Aurelia was back in Taundosa, it was the first time that both Aurelia and Estylle were standing in their native kingdom, together, since the day they followed the King and Queen of Akkinor home.

***

"And what of your dear husband? How is he faring? I didn't get to so much as say hello to him before Arian whisked him away. I do hope the radicals haven't given him much trouble."

Aurelia waved a dismissive hand. "Not in the slightest. He doesn't travel without a troop at his side for precautionary measures, but I suspect the radicals have given up their pursuit of him now that he's King Consort. There's little to no immunity for those who raise a sword against the royal family. He's very pleased to be free to travel the country without fearing for his life."

Not long before Aurelia ascended the throne, Jack and his men were targeted by radicals while traveling on the Templar's Road from Omara to Sadia. The radicals, free to worship whomever they pleased, however they pleased—an assurance made by Oleander the Great's promise of religious freedom—needed human sacrifices to perform a certain ritual, and one of those sacrifices had to have highborn blood. Jack managed to escape and flee to Carthe, leaving Akkinor to believe he'd been slaughtered alongside his men, but he never returned home for fear that the radicals would target him again to finish their ritual. His love for Aurelia convinced him to follow her home, but there'd been no way to know for certain if the radicals would try to find and kill him after hearing about his return.

Fortunately, the radicals hadn't made any efforts to do so. In fact, they'd barely been spotted since Aurelia defeated Archie. The radicals, all lowborn, blended in with the other civilians in their villages, but often prowled the woodlands to perform rituals and stalk, hunt, and butcher their intended sacrifices—both human and animal. There'd been few reports of any corpses or remnants of rituals found in the Akkinorian woods over the last few years, but nobody knew why the radicals had suddenly gone quiet.

It was just another pesky issue burning in the back of Aurelia's brain, but one she had neither the time nor the energy to face for the time being.

Estylle smiled. "I should hope so. Is he still treating you well, though? I know I needn't ask—your mother's ghost would torment him if he did wrong by you—but I feel I must, just to be safe."

"Of course he is. I daresay he's incapable of treating *anyone* poorly when it isn't warranted. I was certainly lucky to have found him when I did."

Estylle beamed, satisfied with Aurelia's response, before going on a tangent about how the radicals who'd once tried to sacrifice Jack probably chose him because of how handsome he was—a type of handsomeness one might expect from the gods, but certainly not from a mere mortal. Aurelia had to laugh at that, but Estylle wasn't entirely wrong, either.

Moments later, as Estylle was rambling about Jack (in a way that made the queen wonder if her middle-aged former governess was smitten with Aurelia's husband), Arian arrived in the doorway of Aurelia's bedchamber to announce the arrival of their Bozari allies. The trio made their way to the palace foyer, where she and Estylle exchanged painful farewells before the latter took a carriage back home to Ardiham Castle in Agotia.

Jack, having just returned from a horseback ride, found Aurelia and Arian while they strolled toward one of the palace's many parlors. As they walked, Aurelia asked Arian if he'd informed Reyna about the amulet and everything else that'd happened with the Bozari lords. He confirmed that he had, but he didn't say anything about what Reyna thought of it. That didn't matter much; Aurelia would find out for herself momentarily.

When they reached the parlor, Arian set his hand on the doorknob and raised an eyebrow. "Ready?"

She nodded and took a deep breath as he opened it. As expected, three faces awaited her in the parlor: Reyna, Lord Zhoqa, and Lord Zhaaran. Reyna rose to greet them, as customary, but the lords didn't budge.

"Your Grace. Your Royal Highness." Reyna smiled and motioned for Aurelia and Jack to sit on the couch beside her chair, directly across from the Bozari lords. Arian opted to stand between the two queens, hands clasped behind his back and eyebrows set in a thin, furrowed line. "It's a pleasure to have you back at the palace. Our allies were just telling me about your recent visit to the Nexus. I must commend you for it—I've been itching to visit myself over the years, and I've always been denied."

Lord Zhoqa grunted. "You should acquire a dragon, then."

Reyna ignored him. "I've been informed of the newfound hostility between Akkinor and Bozar, too. While I see both sides of this disagreement, I have to remain neutral. The concerns as we know them exist in the context of ancient knowledge—most of which may not apply to the modern age. The benefits of using the amulet, on the other hand, should not be diminished, as it may serve us well if we can agree on how to use it. That being said, we have more pressing matters to discuss. For now, there's no harm in the amulet resting in someone's pocket. "

Arian raised an eyebrow at his niece. "What happened during your visit to Kanibar?"

Aurelia told the story exactly as it happened, from the moment she and Halvor landed at Willem's palace to the moment they crash-landed on Tullweine. The nobles weren't surprised to hear that Willem had refused to back down, but they didn't care for the other things he'd said—and the way he'd said them.

"Clearly, you doubt our motives." Lord Zhoqa picked at his nails with his dagger, refusing to look at Aurelia as she scowled at him. "We aren't fools. Willem might tell you and anyone else who'll listen that he's doing all of this for a just cause—and that we're standing in his way because of our own quests for power—but there's no truth in that. There can't be."

"Don't fault her for being doubtful. I hear Willem's rather persuasive," Arian muttered. He turned his gaze to Aurelia and grimaced. "Balor isn't wrong, though. Willem will require an exceptional amount of coin to repair Dofell, and he barely has enough to keep Kanibar afloat. He knows we won't loan him a single piece of bronze if he succeeds, so he'll have to look elsewhere. The best way for him to pay for the repairs—if he even intends to do so—would be to tax travelers who pass through Kanibar and Dofell on their way to the north or the south. The wealthier the kingdom, the higher the tax, even if the travelers are lowborn. It'd cost us triple the amount it does now to trade in the north. We need Caedia for imports and exports, but to get there, we'd probably have to pay as much as we do for our goods. Nobody can afford that."

Aurelia nodded in understanding. "I could assume as much. Receiving so much coin so consistently would surely increase his greed, too. That's all the more reason for him to seize Caedia. Imagine how rich he'd be if he demanded you pay him to trade in Caedia."

"There'd be nothing left of the south. We'd be as penniless and desolate as Dofell, in time." Lord Zhoqa winced as his eyes flickered over to Aurelia. "In that regard, I suppose I can understand why you wish to keep the amulet. Using it to stop Willem from accomplishing such a feat—and to show Kanibar his true motives—might save us from ruin."

"That's what I've been trying to tell you," Aurelia retorted. She stuck up her nose at him when he scoffed. "You took the risk of breaking our alliance without a moment's hesitation, and you refused to consider my explanations until you realized the amulet may benefit you. So, yes—I do doubt you, my lord. Perhaps I didn't doubt you before, but after you broke my trust..."

He lowered his gaze, and for a split second, she could've sworn she saw a new expression pass over his face: shame. He certainly wasn't ashamed of what he'd done, but at the very least, he was ashamed at his failure to be clever enough—a trait the Bozari prided themselves for—to understand why she chose to keep the amulet.

Reyna sighed and turned to Aurelia. "There's a lesson to be learned from this: though he only managed to make you doubt us for a moment, he still did it. You're our ally, so imagine what others might believe if he said the same things to them—lowborn and highborn alike who don't trust us or know us personally. He'll have no trouble gaining support. I expected as much, and I knew he wouldn't yield, so I took the liberty of writing to King Elrin of Dofell several days ago to request an audience. He's agreed to host us at the palace in two days' time."

Aurelia chewed on her lower lip. "Why bother with King Elrin? He knows Kanibar wants Dofell, and he knows each of you will fight for it somehow, too. That makes you his enemies. We don't need what little manpower he has to defeat Kanibar, either. Not with Halvor and my troops at your disposal. Why would he want to meet with you when he knows you'll contribute to his destruction?"

Lord Zhoqa sighed irritably. "Whatever happens, Dofell will see battle. You're right—we don't need his men to defeat Kanibar. What we need is a solution to the problem that'll emerge after Kanibar has been dealt with: what to do with Dofell. He knows the continent won't stand to see him on the throne in the future. We'll let him keep his head after Kanibar is defeated, and in exchange, he'll provide us with a solution that won't see us slaughtering one another."

Jack raised an eyebrow. "I must admit, I'm surprised. I didn't think any of you would be so quick to abandon your claims."

"As much as we'd all like to expand our reach," Reyna said, "it isn't practical. We'd be subjecting ourselves to more loss than we can afford. It isn't worth potentially confirming what Willem may be telling the continent about us, either."

"There's a reason Dofell hasn't attempted to repair itself, and whatever it is—rumors and speculations aside—the king hasn't shared it with the world," Lord Zhaaran added. He still wouldn't look Aurelia in the eye. "We need to persuade him to tell us. Most people believe that Dofell's financial state is beyond repair. If that's the case, we can offer coin to assist the new ruler in restoring the kingdom's economy. Some believe what I myself have theorized for years: a curse was placed upon the Phyre family. If that's true, we can't allow another Phyre to rule in King Elrin's stead. The curse would prevail. Dofell's next ruler can't have a drop of Phyre blood in their veins."

Arian's voice echoed in Aurelia's head: *Bozar believes too greatly in curses, and too little in the power of circumstances.*

"The civilians will want another Dofelli on the throne," Arian added. "If any other Carthinian leader tries to take it, the people will protest. They want one of their own ruling over them. If the king knows of someone fit for the role, he'll have to share it. That name will be the only thing that saves the king's life, in the end."

Reyna's hawklike eyes found Aurelia. "King Elrin wishes for you to attend, too."

"*Me?* Why?"

"Carthinians have lost patience with him, and you're not Carthinian. He must think you'll be more merciful towards him than the rest of us."

Aurelia frowned. "You're already offering to spare his life in exchange for his knowledge. That's as merciful as it gets."

Reyna's gaze ever-so-slightly flickered over to the Bozari lords before landing on the floor at her feet. That was the only response Aurelia needed: the Bozari weren't always honest, which was no secret to the realm. The king probably didn't believe that Bozar—and Taundosa, if Reyna was convinced to follow their lead—would be true to their word. He needed to hear that his life would be spared from the only person he knew of with a reputation for mercy: Aurelia.

But what could be less merciful, Aurelia thought, *than sentencing one's own brother to death?* King Elrin might've known about the mercy Aurelia had shown to others, but were those virtuous deeds enough to make him forget how she'd chosen to punish her brother for his betrayal?

"If all goes well, and King Elrin agrees to help us appoint a new Dofelli monarch," Reyna continued, "the rest of us can leave it alone. We'd be saved from battling one another, and the only matter left for us to concern ourselves with would be Kanibar. I suppose that's where the amulet comes into play. If it's used to stop Kanibar from infiltrating Dofell—"

"—then perhaps Kanibar will turn their attention toward seizing Caedia instead, usurping the continent's largest and busiest trading port," Lord Zhaaran finished. "The amulet would have to be used again to prevent that, too, if we wish to avoid bloodshed. One use is bad enough, but two..." His violet eyes finally met Aurelia's blue ones. A shiver traced her spine when he looked at her not as a friend, but as an unwilling accomplice. "I assume you'd like to use it to solve Akkinor's current problems, too. I'm well aware of the animosity between mages and mortals in your country, so I'm certain you'd prefer to do something about it sooner rather than later. That's *three* uses. You'd be asking the gods to drive Akkinor into the ground by that point."

She narrowed her eyes. "I disagree."

"At your peril."

"I beg—"

"Finding common ground on this matter is close to impossible," Arian interrupted. "Fortunately, we needn't worry about the amulet until after the audience with Elrin."

Lord Zhaaran shook his head. "That is insufficient. What if Her Grace decides to use it when she returns to Akkinor? She'd return to Carthe to fight for us with a blackened soul. The consequences would be catastrophic for all of us."

Jack's eyes darkened. "Careful, my lord."

"Everything we know about the amulet and the supposed curse comes from the old days. Pre-persecution," Reyna said gently. "Times have changed. *Magic* has changed. I understand your concerns and the responsibility your ancestor claimed, but we can't ignore the prospect of such incredible power because we fear a curse that may or may not exist."

Clenching his jaw, the nobleman stood from his chair and clasped his hands behind his back. "I think I'll retire early today."

Nobody said a word when he left. Aurelia stared at the door after he was gone, face warming with embarrassment—why, she didn't know—before Reyna, too, announced her departure so she could attend yet another meeting. Lord Zhoqa quickly followed suit, likely hoping to find better entertainment than Arian and two Akkinorians, as he muttered something about a brothel and an old connection.

Jack glanced between uncle and niece. "I'll let the two of you catch up for a bit. I'll ensure Halvor hasn't upset any Taundosan shepherds by feasting on their flocks."

"Thank you." Arian offered Jack a weary smile before holding his hand out for Aurelia to take. "You look like you could use a walk."

She sighed, mirrored his smile, and accepted his hand. "Lead the way."

XIX

After strolling the halls for a bit, Aurelia and Arian soon found themselves standing on a balcony on the third floor of the palace, clutching the railing as they watched Halvor part the clouds above the city. The people of Taundosa shrieked and hollered with joy at the sight of the dragon overhead, like the people of Akkinor often did now that they'd gotten used to him. Men held small children on their shoulders to offer them a better look, elders dragged chairs onto the streets as if watching a theater performance, and people of all ages sat in the open windows of their homes in tall buildings, clapping for Halvor and waving their arms to catch his attention.

"Your mother would've loved this," Arian murmured. "She always dreamed of the day when Halvor would be free to explore the realm again. It broke her heart to return him to the locket whenever she released him. She thought about letting him go, consequences be damned, but our father wouldn't allow it. I think it was the only time he ever said no to her." That made him chuckle. "I can't say I envied how much he doted on her, though. Our mother rarely said no to me, either—shocking, since I wasn't her trueborn son. She never treated me any differently than my sisters. You're a lot like her in that way."

Aurelia stiffened, knowing he was referencing her relationship with Hyacinth, and took this opportunity to share her concerns about her daughter. She hadn't felt right about bringing it up any sooner, especially with Jack nearby; she didn't wish to worry him unless her suspicions were correct.

"If we're talking about Hyacinth now..." She cleared her throat and ran a nervous hand through her curls. "You know how intelligent she is— that's no secret—but lately...lately she's been saying things that can't be explained with logic or reason." She shared Hyacinth's dream about a young Aurelia and Linden in the gardens, and the strange, yet accurate, comments she'd made about Aurelia finding the moon. When she finished, she brought a hand to her breast to toy with her empty locket. "What do you suppose all of this means?"

Arian pondered for a moment. "Is it possible that her birth mother was a mage?"

"A mage?" Aurelia blinked at him. "I wouldn't think so. What happened to her...It might've been avoided if she'd had magic."

He winced. "Maybe, but mages were even less prevalent in Akkinor five years ago than they are today. Your brother, from what I understand, had a particularly unkind perspective when it came to magic. He probably would've had her killed if she'd shown any signs of having powers." He sighed and scratched at his gray beard. "It sounds like Hyacinth has foresight: the ability to see things right before or as they happen. It's a common sign of magic in children. She must have a rare form of it, though—most people with foresight can't see so far into the past, and they normally can't see into the future at all. The name is misleading in that way."

A chill wracked Aurelia's body. "And what does this mean for Sisi?"

"That's entirely up to you. You can do what your parents did, for one: neglect to have her trained, and hide her abilities as best you can until they disappear when she comes of age. The other option is to have her trained so she can grow into the full extent of her power. That, naturally, comes with significant risks. She'd have to hide her magic so the realm doesn't find out she's not your natural born daughter. If she doesn't wish for that, then both of you must prepare to answer when the realm demands an explanation. It'll be no secret that she isn't your trueborn daughter."

She swallowed the hot, thick lump in her throat and only nodded in response, unable to conjure a real reply. She was facing the exact same problem her parents had dealt with when she was a little girl: forced to consider sacrificing her child's incredible gift to prevent the realm from uncovering the truth of her birth.

It was hauntingly poetic.

***

Willem Trevas, with his hands clasped behind his back, stood on the tallest balcony at the Palace of Kanibar overlooking the courtyard below, where the kingdom's greatest blacksmiths and armorers labored beneath the blazing summer sun. He smiled as the smiths loaded Kanibar's arsenal—swords, daggers, arrows, spears, and shields—into wagons and carts to be distributed amongst the king's troops.

The sound of nervous breathing from behind stole Willem's attention from the courtyard, reminding him of the conversation he was participating in. He looked to the side, chin grazing his shoulder, and caught the faintest glimpse of his visitor: a young man whose body, face, and hair were covered by a large, woolen shawl.

The shawl was stained with sweat, and salty droplets made a tick-ticking noise as they slid from the man's nose and plopped onto the floor below. Discomfort and potential heatstroke were apparently small prices to pay for discretion—that, or it was anxiety making the poor fool sweat like a pig awaiting slaughter.

Willem turned his gaze back to the courtyard. "What more have you heard?"

The man gulped audibly. "She's facing pressure from the masses to hold herself accountable for the violence between mages and mortals as of late. Word is spreading across Akkinor of the war stirring here in Carthe, and the people aren't pleased. They wish for their queen to show more concern for her own country than for others."

A smile danced on Willem's lips. "I know this. I didn't ask you to tell me about the queen's weak spots—I asked you to tell me about the *woman's* weaknesses."

A pause. "I told you previously about the whispers regarding one of her children. Doryn seems to be rather convinced that something is amiss with the girl."

Willem nodded and envisioned the contents of a gift he'd sent earlier in the day. "I could've assumed as much. And what of the dragon?"

"Y-Your Grace? What of it?"

"His weaknesses are her weaknesses, good man. We can't let them surprise us."

He paused again. "Uncertain, my king. The most I was told is that the beast has upset a few shepherds and cattlemen by consuming their livestock. He doesn't appear to have any weaknesses other than the amount of food he requires, and his primal—if not divine—instinct to protect his mistress. He'd sooner take a spear to the throat than prioritize his own survival when she's being threatened."

"Does it fear anything?"

"The gods, I imagine, but—"

"Anything tangible?"

"Not that I'm aware of."

Willem sighed and turned from the courtyard to face his guest. "Any hope I have at claiming Dofell—and the entire north, for that matter—will be crushed if the queen and her dragon stand behind my enemies on the battlefield. She won't betray them to fight for me, and she won't remain neutral because of the promises she made to her allies. That leaves me with one option: find a way to eliminate a threat no man has defeated in over one-thousand years. I can't produce a strategy without more information, though. I need you to write to our spies and request more intel. They can acquire more information from the source—I'm certain of it."

"The source has already proven difficult to work with, Your Grace. I'm uncertain of how much more he'll be willing to divulge."

"Then have the spies remind him of the consequences of disobeying me. He hasn't another choice."

The man bowed. "O-Of course, my king. I'll relay the message."

When the man left, Willem turned to face the courtyard once more. His lips curled into a smile when a caravan of wagons and carts—all filled to the brim with weaponry and armor—were pulled out of the courtyard and onto the streets, where they'd journey to the Kanish army's training compound. With any luck, even those who could hardly lift a sword today would be masters of the craft by the time they were needed in Dofell.

Humming with contentment, Willem took a seat at his writing desk to craft a letter, believing a bit of encouragement from the king himself would persuade the source to offer more. He cursed when he realized his inkwell was empty, then searched every drawer in his desk for another. He froze, forgetting his reason for being at the desk, when he opened a stiff drawer and spotted something resting atop piles of old letters: a handheld portrait of a raven-haired, amber-eyed woman with warm skin and a smile that could've brought down the entire continent.

His jaw clenched as he plucked the portrait and ran the pad of his thumb over the small canvas. "We could've been so happy, Rae," he murmured. "I'm sorry I was too late."

He sighed as a bitter taste filled his mouth, then set the portrait on the surface of his desk beside another that was nearly identical to it—only *this* portrait depicted a woman with fairer skin, eyes like the cloudless sky, and curly golden hair that almost appeared reddish, if the lighting was right.

As he stared at the two beautiful faces beaming back at him, a grin played on his lips. "I suppose things were meant to happen as they did, my love," he told Rae. "If not for your loss, I wouldn't have the opportunity to seize the kind of fame and glory Carthe hasn't known in centuries. That is, of course, if all goes according to plan."

As Willem stood and turned from the desk, entirely forgetting about the letter he was meant to write, he heard a slight thud. He looked over his shoulder, lips pursed, and saw that Rae's portrait had fallen and was now lying face-down on the surface of the desk.

"I take it you've given me permission to proceed, then." A gurgling laugh escaped him as he exited the room. "Not that it was ever needed. She'll be filling your shoes soon enough, anyway."

***

"Have you any messages, my lord?"

"Indeed I do." Arian reached into the inside pocket of his suitcoat and produced a scroll sealed with the Taundosan sigil. "Ensure this is delivered to the Palace of Akkinor by midday, please."

The young male servant nodded, accepted the scroll, and bowed before leaving the parlor. As he bounded off, Aurelia watched him slip the scroll into a small linen bag dangling from his belt. She hoped Arian's message didn't get lost amongst the others—a message informing Ansyl of Jack and Aurelia's whereabouts. She hadn't known about Reyna's plans to meet with King Elrin when she left to have a word with Lord Zhoqa, and while the audience was still a few days away, she had to make sure her advisors knew where she was and what she was doing.

As the servant left, another young messenger boy passed him on his way into the parlor. He carried a large package that rivaled the width of his body, wrapped in pretty green paper with a golden bow tied on top. To Aurelia's surprise, he approached her instead of Arian, struggling to bow while balancing the package.

"This came for you this morning, Your Grace."

Aurelia frowned when the servant set the package on the tea table before her. Across from her, Arian abandoned his teacup to inspect the package for any signs of foul play. When it was deemed suitable for her hands, she pushed her refreshments aside to make room for the package.

"A gift from your husband?" Arian teased. He shook his head while she snorted in response. "No. I imagine he's more creative than this when it comes to showering his beloved with gifts."

Aurelia laughed. "He certainly is. Not that he'll be gifting me with anything while we're here in Taundosa, though—he's too preoccupied with riding across the kingdom and feeling the wind in his hair. He's soaking up every moment of our time here while it lasts. Do you think he misses Carthe?"

He chuckled at her joke and gestured to the package, still grinning. "There's a note."

She plucked a small, folded piece of parchment from beneath the bow and read it aloud: "'For Her Grace, the Dragon of Akkinor: I haven't stopped thinking about our conversation. Your wonderings about my late wife forced me to reflect on my life. I envy your happy marriage and your beautiful family, and I hope I might soon find a woman like you to further my line and find comfort in my arms. I hope your husband values you as much as I would, if I were ever fortunate enough to know you as he does. Perhaps if things had been different five years ago, I might've been among those who sent horrible love poems to your desk. What a thing it would be if the two of us together dominated each side of the world! Alas, a man can only dream. Please accept this token of my good favor, and remember what we discussed. I certainly haven't forgotten it.'" She looked up at her uncle with raised eyebrows. "There's no signature, but this has to be from Willem. Right?"

"Possibly." He frowned. "Let's open it."

She unraveled the ribbons before tearing the wrapping paper at the corners and moving it aside to reveal a plain white box. A gasp escaped her when she opened the lid to find a bouquet of hyacinths inside: one of every color imaginable, clustered together to form a beautiful—and chaotic— arrangement.

She swallowed the lump in her throat. "I know Katryna was as fond of hyacinths as I am, but I haven't seen any here in Taundosa. Are they native to the City of Gold, or somewhere else?"

His lips curled into a grimace. "Kanibar."

Her heart thumped wildly against her ribcage as she removed the bouquet from the box. The flowers were nestled in shallow, round pot larger than Aurelia's head, and the short, remaining portion of their stems were imbedded in some type of moss meant to fill the pot in place of soil. When she leaned over to smell them, she wasn't met with the strong, sweet aroma she knew and loved, but a scent that resembled charred nutmeg and citrus fruits: the smell of magic.

Arian seemed to smell it, too. "Someone has enchanted them," he murmured, touching the star-shaped petals of a violet hyacinth. "They've been given the gift of eternal life."

"The king definitely sent this," she deduced. "I don't know anybody else in Kanibar, and the things he wrote...We *did* talk about his late wife, but only for a moment."

"How did he know where to find you?"

178

"He must have spies posted nearby who spotted Halvor." She chewed on her lower lip as she stared at the arrangement. "What troubles me is how he knew to send hyacinths. Of all the flowers accessible to a king, he just so happened to choose my favorite?" She shook her head. "No. He must know of my love for them. But how?"

Arian's brown skin turned pale and gray. "You don't think—?"

"He must have spies in Akkinor, too. That, or he's in communication with someone who knows me well enough to divulge this kind of information. He certainly didn't know much about me at the time of our audience last week, so I have to assume he's been conducting research since I left."

He studied the flowers, frowning, and grazed the petals with his fingertips again. "He wouldn't send a bouquet of your favorite flower for no rhyme or reason, and wanting you to think about the conversation you had with him isn't reason enough. Not during a time like this. There has to be more to it."

A sudden lurching sensation upset her stomach. "It's probably exactly what it appears to be—my favorite flower, able to bloom for eternity—but he wants me to drive myself mad looking for an ulterior motive that isn't there. He's likely trying to stay in my good graces, too, by flattering me so I'm less inclined to incinerate him in battle."

"Either way, he knows more about you now than he did a week ago," her uncle muttered. "You shall have to be even more mindful now about who you trust in your court."

She flickered her gaze back to the flowers and combatted an angry, violent chill. Whether it be a sneaky servant with an affinity for eavesdropping, or a conniving highborn who'd weaseled their way into a place on Aurelia's court, someone in the Folly (or multiple people) had turned to doing Willem's bidding—either because of threats, extortion, or the promise of reward. Her favorite flower couldn't be the only piece of knowledge Willem learned from his spies, either. Whoever the rat was, they'd be telling Willem anything and everything he might need to diffuse the greatest threat to his quest for power.

Tomorrow, Aurelia and her allies would meet with King Elrin Phyre III to discuss the fate of Dofell. If he proved uncooperative, there'd be absolutely nothing—other than the amulet, of course—standing between Kanibar and its enemies on the battlefield. But the longer it took for a strategy to be developed, the better Willem's odds were at finding a way to force Aurelia onto her knees.

XX

Two days after receiving Willem's gift, Aurelia and her allies left the Palace of Taundosa for their audience with King Elrin. It was the first time she'd ever taken more than one person on dragonback at a time: Reyna and the two Bozari lords joined her and Halvor for the journey to Dofell, and none of them failed to yelp, scream, or vomit during the flight.

She'd never longed for Jack or Arian more than she did during that flight. They were the only other people who'd ridden on dragonback before, so they might've been able to help her direct and calm the others. Unfortunately, King Elrin had explicitly stated that only the four allies were invited to the audience—no advisors, no partners, no mages. For whatever reason, Elrin didn't seem interested in conversing with anyone who didn't sit on a throne.

He'd given them permission to take soldiers along with them, but that much was impossible because of the massive stone walls surrounding Dofell. The quickest route was to cross the desert, but that would've taken weeks, and they certainly didn't have time for that. The allies were relying solely on Halvor—and King Elrin's offering of peace—to protect them while in Dofell.

Halvor landed about halfway between the palace and the Dofelli coast on an empty field of dry, brown grass. When his riders dismounted, only Aurelia walked away unscathed: a white-faced Reyna dizzily wobbled over to Aurelia and clutched her arm for support as she readjusted to being on the ground again; Lord Zhaaran stumbled a bit (while refusing Aurelia's offer of assistance) and audibly swallowed the vomit that'd risen up in his throat; and Lord Zhoqa, for all his pride, fell to his knees almost immediately as he puked for the second time—the first being during takeoff, which resulted in a puddle of half-digested food landing directly on a Taundosan commoner's front steps.

Halvor followed Aurelia's nonverbal command after her allies recovered from the flight, by walking behind them on their trek to the palace. It wasn't a far walk, but it was certainly a scenic one—just not in the way one might expect.

There hadn't been any signs of life on the field where they'd landed. There were a few dead trees, and the ruins of abandoned hovels scattered around, but no villages, estates, people, or wildlife. The group followed an empty dirt road into the heart of the kingdom, and as they inched closer to their destination, signs of civilization began to emerge: small villages and towns in the near distance flanking either side of the road, dried up wells here and there, and the festering remains of old farms.

Aurelia spotted only one highborn estate in the distance: a damp, dark structure about one-fourth the size of Aurelia's palace, barely able to stand upright from its position on a muddy, slanted hill. There were no walls or gates separating the estate from civilian territories; no intricate, ancient decor on the premises, and no soldiers guarding it from the outside world. Without the flag blowing from one of the castle's towers, Aurelia might not have known it was home to a highborn family. In fact, she hadn't been entirely sure that any highborn families still existed in Dofell.

The palace ahead looked exactly how Aurelia remembered it from her brief visit to Dofell five years earlier. It was an incredibly large, ornate structure made of white limestone that rivaled the size of Aurelia's own home. She could only see what was above the second story, though—everything below it was concealed by thick, tall golden gates.

A troop of Dofelli soldiers met the allies when they were still a ways away from the palace. After greeting them, the soldiers announced that they'd be escorting their guests to the king's private garden—far from the palace itself—for the audience.

"We aren't meeting inside the palace?" Aurelia questioned.

A Dofelli soldier shook his head. "Only Dofelli natives are permitted within the Great Walls."

"Oh. Is there a reason for that?"

The soldier only stared at her before turning his gaze to the path ahead. As she glanced at the palace to her left, she studied the thirty-foot-tall gates surrounding the premises and frowned. It was dangerous for highborn to meet beyond the safety of castle walls—so why on earth did the king forbid his guests from stepping foot inside his home?

Now that they were headed for a smaller space, Aurelia sent Halvor back to the skies, where he'd circle the premises until she called him back to take them home to Taundosa. If the king or his men had any intention of breaking their promise of peace, though, it wouldn't take much for Halvor to intervene.

Aurelia hoped they were true to their word—for their sake, if not for hers.

She thought the palace was the only beautiful sight in Dofell until they arrived in the garden. Located about two hundred feet from the palace at the bottom of a hill, the garden was surrounded by golden gates and secured with three hefty padlocks. A rush of fresh, sweet-smelling air smacked Aurelia in the face as soon as she crossed the threshold. It was so lush and blooming with trees, flowers, and bushes that it was almost difficult to move without walking into a leafy branch or crushing petals beneath her shoe.

The soldiers brought them to the center of the garden, still surrounded by greenery on all sides, where four crimson velvet cushions sat adjacent to one another on the grass. One soldier urged the allies to sit while a servant manifested in the garden carrying a tray of scones and tea. As Aurelia and her allies sunk onto the cushions and accepted the refreshments, the soldier kindly asked them to wait just a few moments longer for the king.

The Dofelli soldiers stood along the entire perimeter, still and silent. Nobody spoke as they waited, so the only sounds to be heard were the eerie creaking of the gates and the dribbling of rum from Lord Zhoqa's flask to his teacup.

Aurelia leaned to her left to whisper in Reyna's ear. "How is the garden so...?"

"Lovely?" Her arched eyebrows furrowed. "Magic. It keeps this place pristine while the rest of the kingdom is left to suffer. His Majesty's ancestor had a mage on his court who placed an enchantment over the garden—similar to the oasis in the Ngora Valley. One can't see or enter the garden unless one has been invited by its host."

That made sense when she recalled her first visit to Dofell. She and Jack had passed the palace on their way to the Ngora Valley, and she hadn't seen the garden or even a path that led to it. On the other hand, she remembered the impoverished streets and the muddy hills of waste and excrement all too well.

She opened her mouth to respond, but she didn't get the chance. Two heralds descended the hill from the garden gates and stood on either side of the narrow dirt path to the left of where the allies were seated. Aurelia winced when they blew their trumpets, rattling and threatening to burst her eardrums.

Only one of them spoke: "All rise for the Great King, Elrin Ophelos Phyre, Third of His Name, King of Dofell!"

Mimicking her allies, Aurelia rose to her feet and turned her gaze to the top of the hill they'd come from. Not a minute later, she spotted four strong, burly men carrying metal poles on either of their shoulders. As they inched closer, she saw what they were carrying: an ornate golden palanquin, in which the King of Dofell sat nestled atop piles of cushions and blankets. At the rear of the palanquin, another four men carried it from the back.

Aurelia had only ever seen a palanquin used in illustrations in ancient texts or storybooks. In every depiction she remembered, a total of four bearers carried the litter—*four*, not eight. The reason the number of bearers had doubled became clear as the palanquin cautiously descended the hill, giving Aurelia a better glimpse of her host.

Elrin Phyre was perhaps the largest and stoutest man she'd ever seen. Like all native Dofelli, he had dark eyes, a broad nose, and a round face. His greasy black hair was mostly concealed by his enormous crown, and his facial hair consisted of sparse, thin whiskers above his lip and along his chin. His round, bulging belly strained against the fabric of his tunic, and a thick blanket draped over his lap covered his legs and feet from view.

Aurelia had often heard people theorizing that King Elrin suffered the effects of Dofell's poverty as greatly as his people did. After seeing him in the flesh, she knew those assumptions were false. Elrin clearly hadn't been affected by the lack of food in his kingdom. While his people ate nothing but potatoes and scraps, he'd been gorging himself.

Reyna leaned in close to her ear and whispered, "There's a custom here in Dofell: the king's feet may never touch the ground."

She raised an eyebrow. "What do they believe might happen if his feet *do* touch the ground?"

"Ancient tales tell of apocalyptic events, like a great flood or wildfires or endless storms. The more religious folk believe those stories, but most people...most people don't give the custom a second thought anymore. The worst has already happened here."

Aurelia swallowed. *That* much was inarguable.

The bearers set the palanquin down directly across from the allies. It had short legs like a chair or couch might, so even when placed on the ground, it sat several inches above the grass. Elrin made no move to rise from the comforts of his cushions and blankets so he could greet his guests properly; instead, he merely motioned at a servant with his hand, who quickly handed him a chalice filled with wine.

He drank the wine in one gulp and wiped the scarlet droplets from his mustache with the sleeve of his tunic. Only then did his beady brown eyes land on each of the allies, one by one, as if they were peasants who'd come to beg for assistance—not his equals.

"Your message was persistent." The king's voice, breathy and slow, echoed throughout the garden when he addressed Reyna. "Still, I don't understand why you've come. You mean to seize my kingdom from beneath me, do you not?"

Reyna squared her shoulders and held her head high. "No, we don't. The entire continent wishes for Dofell to be taken from you, Your Majesty, but only one—Willem of Kanibar—has decided to act on it. You know this. None of us should like to see the day when Kanish flags replace Dofelli flags. It would be disastrous for everyone here today if his plans come to fruition. My allies and I have agreed to defend Dofell from Kanibar, but unfortunately, our involvement can't end with combat. You know as well as we do that the continent won't give you or your family a second chance at ruling Dofell after another attempts to take it from you. For that reason, we've come to make a deal."

"A deal." His pudgy fingers tapped against the side of his chalice, which was full again—though Aurelia didn't recall seeing a servant pour more wine into the cup. "You mean to say that I'll be overthrown even after you deploy your swords to defend my kingdom. Why would I make a deal when no potential outcome will benefit me?"

"Your options are limited," Lord Zhoqa stated. "If Kanibar wins, Willem will take your head and the heads of every Phyre man, woman, and child in Dofell. If he loses, the very reason for all of this— your negligence as king—will remain unchanged, and the masses will take matters into their own hands. They may storm your palace and kill you themselves to appoint one of their own as Dofell's new leader. The rest of us would be forced to respond by whatever means necessary, depending on their choice, and we have no way of knowing where things would go from there. Either way, you won't live to see your next name day."

Elrin didn't seem worried about that. "What is your offer, then?"

"Your time as king has come to an end." When Lord Zhaaran spoke beside her, ignoring the king's inquiry, Aurelia could practically feel the tension rushing through his body. "That is no opinion of ours—it's a fact. Unless you can salvage your kingdom overnight, you *cannot* continue to rule Dofell. With that being said, we offer you the chance to explain your wrongdoings with honesty and integrity. If you do so, and we find your reasons to be viable, then you have our word that we shall come to a conclusion that won't end with your head on a spike."

When the king refused to answer, Reyna spoke instead: "Some of us have been led to believe that your Almighty placed a curse upon your family. When your ancestor used every bit of coin in the bank to build your palace, Myenar passed unfavorable judgement upon him and his entire bloodline. While a Phyre holds power, Dofell is subject to poverty, crime, and disease by the will of the Almighty as punishment for your family's greed. Is there any truth to this tale, Your Majesty, or have you another explanation to share with us?"

The king paused for a moment before looking between the servants and soldiers flanking him. With one motion of his hand and a jerking of his head, his subjects bowed and left the premises without a word.

"The rumors are true," the king admitted, looking weary, "but there is more to the story—our Almighty required more than an act of greed to damn us all. The first royal palace was located closer to the border of the forest. It was neither grand nor pleasing to the eye, and it crumbled into dust after a fire. When my ancestor began construction on a new palace, he picked perhaps the worst location he could have chosen. Did *your* Almighty happen to share that knowledge with you?"

He directed the question at the Bozari lords, prompting Lord Zhoqa to answer: "This property was once a magical forest, wasn't it?"

"Not just any magical forest. It was home to the Lyanoth," he stated. An unintentional gasp of surprise escaped Aurelia's lips, causing the king to meet her eyes for the first time. "You know of it?"

She cleared her throat. "O-Only a bit. I read about it in a book once. It was a sequoia tree—the only one of its kind in Carthe—said to serve as a portal between the mortal world and the heavens. Stories say that the first magical creatures arrived in the realm through the Lyanoth. Whether it be fact or legend, it's the only portal between worlds mentioned in ancient lore."

He nodded. "The Lyanoth stood where the palace currently stands. Of course, the palace was constructed centuries after the persecution, so by then, few recalled the legend—after all, no magical creature had emerged from the tree since the old days. It was thought to be nothing more than an ordinary tree. My ancestor ordered his men to cut it down and burn it, then constructed the palace in its place."

Lord Zhaaran's sigh was nothing short of melancholy. "Myenar didn't curse your family because of your ancestor's greed. He cursed your family because your ancestor destroyed the Lyanoth. Whatever connection remained between our two worlds was severed indefinitely."

"To the outside world, the curse is nothing more than speculation," Elrin claimed. "I wish I could tell you that the Almighty placed his curse on my family directly, informing my ancestor of the reason for it and what might be done to break it, but I cannot."

"The speculation is a consequence of the curse," Aurelia said thoughtfully. "It can't be proven to the masses, so the realm has nobody to blame for Dofell's misfortunes except for its leaders."

The king nodded as an emotion finally swept over his face: sadness. "Indeed. My family knows it to be true, but no other shall ever see proof of it."

Lord Zhoqa raised an eyebrow. "What kind of proof?"

"If I send a plea for help to my neighbors, the message is never delivered. Perhaps the scroll falls into the sea, or the raven is eaten by a larger beast, or the message simply vanishes into thin air. If I order my men to create new farmlands and plant seeds so my people can eat, disease spreads through the soil and murders anything hoping for a chance at life. If my apothecaries craft medicines to heal the sicknesses plaguing my people, the vials empty as soon as they've been filled." He sighed and bowed his head. "My cups and plates fill themselves. That's part of the curse, too: my plates are never empty. I'm forced to eat and eat until it makes me sick, and there's nothing I can do to stop it. I must gorge on my eternal meals, and my subjects must starve as I do so."

A thought popped into Aurelia's head. "Does this have anything to do with the reason foreigners aren't allowed in the palace?"

He grimaced. "Fits of madness befall those who enter the palace without Dofelli blood in their veins. My mage believes this punishment exists to prevent my family from forming connections with other leaders. We remain isolated and forgotten, unable to leave the walls of this kingdom or break bread with our neighbors from the comfort of our home."

Aurelia's heart lurched. "You...You can't leave the kingdom?"

"No, I cannot. My younger brother tried it once, and the moment he stepped foot into the Violet Forest, his blood began to boil. It flooded out of his eyes, his nose, his mouth, his ears. By the time our soldiers reached him, he was drained of blood and life."

She flicked her gaze toward Reyna, who asked exactly what she was thinking: "Why tell us this now?"

Elrin's smile was so riddled with pain and pity that Aurelia had to resist the urge to embrace him. "I have written to all of you over the years—the Golden Queen, the Four Lords, the Dragon of Akkinor—hoping to request an audience so you might assist me in solving this predicament. None of my letters were ever delivered, just as I told you. I had no choice but to wait until someone sent word to me."

Aurelia frowned. "But Her Majesty received your response to her request for an audience. How did that letter manage to reach her, but the others didn't?"

The king opened his mouth to respond, but it was Lord Zhaaran who answered: "Perhaps Myenar—or the entirety of the Twelve, for that matter—decided it's high time Dofell was given a proper chance."

XXI

Myenar offered no insight into how the curse might be broken, and the gods have been silent for centuries—it's not like we can ask them to show us the way." Lord Zhoqa tipped his flask upside-down over his teacup, then frowned when only dribbles of liquor splashed into the tea. "While your situation is most unfortunate, Your Majesty, it still leaves us without a proper strategy. There's no telling if or how your family might be freed from the curse. That places us exactly where we were upon our arrival: what to do with you."

Elrin shifted and toyed with the blanket over his lap. "Which means—?"

Reyna exhaled. "Even if the masses believe in the curse as you do—and I, in all honesty—we're still lacking a means to break it. The people will continue to suffer, and they've had quite enough of that. The rest of the continent, too, has grown tired of waiting for Dofell's poverty to stop taking its toll on Carthe. One way or another, a Phyre can't sit the throne while the curse prevails. The realm will call for your head, but we are prepared to defend your life if you agree to assist us in appointing a new ruler."

The king's lips pursed, surprised. Aurelia couldn't help but wonder if he thought his honesty regarding the curse was enough to ensure his place on the throne. Unfortunately, that honesty was all the more reason to see Elrin and the entire Phyre family removed from power.

"Your subjects will want another Dofelli on the throne," Reyna continued. "From what I can recall, your nobility has drastically shrunk in size over the years. You have but three or four reigning nobles remaining, do you not?" Elrin nodded. "I thought as much. Might any of them be suitable candidates?"

The king shook his head. "Not in the slightest. Two are seasons away from death, and their successors died years ago. The third hasn't been seen or heard from in years—there are rumors that he went mad after eating meat from an infected goat, and he no longer knows his own name. And the fourth..." He shook his head. "The fourth is my sister."

Lord Zhoqa raised an irritated eyebrow. "And you have no other suggestions?"

"As I just said, there are all but four other highborn here in Dofell, and none of them are in any condition to rule. My sister is healthy and strong, but she is a Phyre. And I should sooner like for my people to break down the palace doors and slaughter me in my own bed than appoint a lowborn as my replacement. Most of them have gone mad with starvation or sickness. I'd have no objections if a healthy, worthy lowborn successor presented himself, but such a man is nearly impossible to identify."

"We shall have to keep looking, then," Reyna murmured. "Perhaps we might find something of value at the Holy Library or the monastery. We have no other option except to find a suitable replacement—if not, our choices following the war with Kanibar will be limited."

"What she means to say," Lord Zhoqa muttered, snorting, "is that the rest of us will have to fight one another over who succeeds you. Not only will we destroy our alliances, but the balance of power across Carthe will be fractured, and the Dofelli will protest when we bring our foreign customs to their soil. Our only other option is to let Willem take Dofell, but that wouldn't end well for any of us—particularly you, Your Majesty."

Elrin waved a dismissive hand. "I don't fear the Kanish. Sheep threaten to destroy me, and a dragon promises to spare me." Aurelia's back straightened when his eyes landed on hers. Just as she'd thought, the only ruler's word he trusted was hers—but whether it be because of her merciful reputation, or because she'd never have a claim to Dofell, she didn't know. "Do you not?"

She swallowed as the amulet in her pocket seemed to vibrate. "I do. You may not have provided us with a solution—at no fault of your own, in perfect truth—but you *did* provide us with an explanation. If your claims are true, then I don't believe you're a selfish nor a negligent king. I believe you were dealt an unfair hand at life because of something that happened centuries before your birth. I see no reason for you to lose your head because of an inevitability. When a life can be spared, I shall spare it. You have my word."

The king relaxed, closing his eyes for a moment. When he opened them, Aurelia was surprised to see tears glistening on his lashes.

"I thank you humbly, Your Grace," he told her. She tipped her head, smiling. "I don't know if I'm capable of identifying my successor, but I shall make every effort. Is there any news regarding Kanibar's plans?"

Reyna shook her head at Elrin's inquiry. "Our scouts reported seeing signs of war preparation across the kingdom, but as of now, Willem's troops remain in Kanibar. We don't know when they plan to strike, but we shall write to you as soon as we learn more. How many fighting men can you spare?"

The king's pale cheeks turned red. "Two hundred at most."

"That's very well. We may not even need them—not if Her Grace's dragon is feeling particularly famished on the day of the battle."

That made the king smile. Before he could respond, his servants and soldiers appeared at the top of the hill, letting him know that it was time for the audience to end. He glanced at them and nodded, then turned back to the allies as a heavy sigh escaped his lips.

"Today's conversation has brought me great relief, all things considered," he said. "I'm not pleased to end over one thousand years of Phyre rule in Dofell, but if the Almighty demands it be done, I shall oblige for the sake of my subjects." His eyes turned to Aurelia once more. "Where would you have me and my family go after you've spared us?"

"Wherever you wish."

He thought about that for a moment. "A quiet life in the mountains would be preferable. A place where birds come to sing instead of cry. A place where I don't have to scavenge to fill my belly, but where food is scarce enough that I must always be grateful for every crumb on my plate. I've long since forgotten the handsome man I once was—I'd like to find him again, wherever he is beneath the weight of the many meals I stole from my people." A small, sad sort of smile formed on his lips. "I was among the most attractive men in northern Carthe before I took the throne. Look what's become of me since."

Aurelia mirrored his smile. "You're still handsome to me, Your Majesty."

His trace of a smile morphed into a grin that illuminated his entire face. As he tipped his head in both thanks and farewell, the bearers descended the hill and lifted the palanquin from the ground. Neither the king nor the allies said a word as the bearers carried him away and up the hill, where they'd return him to the palace no foreigner could enter, and no Phyre could leave without losing their minds.

***

After leaving Dofell—feeling better than they had before the audience, but not quite as well as they'd hoped—the allies returned to the Palace of Taundosa before going their separate ways once more. They were greeted by the smell of mutton and mint jelly wafting through the corridors, and they weren't given the chance to change into dinner clothes before servants ushered them into the dining hall.

Naturally, Jack and Arian joined the group as soon as they received word of their return. The allies filled them in as best they could, but Aurelia wished they'd been there to hear it all for themselves; their perspectives were incredibly valuable.

"I thought the audience went rather smoothly." Reyna paused to thank a servant as the first course—creamy mushroom soup—was set before her and her guests. "I must admit, I wasn't expecting the king to be so forthcoming about the curse, nor so accepting of his inevitable abdication. I found it all to be quite sad, in truth."

"If the tales regarding the Lyanoth are true," Lord Zhaaran added, "then I imagine nothing can be done to break the curse. We must wait for the gods to decide when the Phyre family's punishment has run its course, but it's unlikely we'll hear from them—they've been silent for too long now." He shook his head as his purple eyes stared down at his soup. "Destroying the only known portal between worlds...That obliterated any chance of the gods repopulating our world with magic. If they ever thought of sending more magical creatures to the realm, they certainly aren't considering it now. They can't."

"Magic was their most precious and sacred gift to humanity," Arian muttered. "The king's ancestor offended them as well as any human could. If Dofell's own Almighty was insulted enough to place the curse himself, then the entirety of the Twelve will ensure the Phyre family is punished for as long as possible."

"It's no wonder there isn't a lick of magic left in Dofell—other than that odd little garden, of course." Lord Zhoqa slurped a sip of soup from his spoon, alarming the others with his lack of propriety, before dropping the utensil into his already-empty bowl. "It was once the magical capital of the world, and now it is nothing."

"Unless we find someone capable of changing that." Aurelia swallowed a spoonful of soup before setting her spoon aside. Her appetite hadn't exactly grown after hearing Elrin's stories. "We must all research potential candidates for the king's successor. Perhaps we can reconvene on a selected date to discuss our findings and choose one from the list each of us puts forward. The individual must be Dofelli, and they must have at least a few drops of highborn blood in their veins. My only concern is how the others will take to this. The other half of the Four Lords, the Kroti, King Willem..."

"Willem sacrificed his right to help salvage Dofell when he decided to seize it," Lord Zhoqa retorted. "This plan of ours only works if we defeat him in battle—and since he refused our offer of peace, we're under no obligation to spare his life or take his opinions into consideration. Lords Zoma and Xada have no interest in Dofell unless they have claims to it, so I doubt they'll be an issue. As for the Kroti...the Four Lords haven't heard a peep from our allies in Krotis. Have either of you heard from Lady Swann?"

Both Aurelia and Reyna shook their heads. "I thought as much," he continued. "They know about Willem's plans, but they seem rather disinterested in the squabbling. Krotis never had any sort of relationship with Dofell, anyway. They haven't been affected by the kingdom's debts or broken promises. I imagine they'd like to spare their men rather than send their troops to fight a war they couldn't care less about."

"One can never know when it comes to the Kroti. They have a knack for getting involved at the last moment," Lord Zhaaran said. "Either way, Krotis as a whole has the smallest population in Carthe. It won't make much of a difference if they're involved or not. As long as Dofell has leadership of some kind, they won't protest our selection."

"Whatever happens," Reyna said, pausing as a servant replaced her soup with a beet salad, "we must all agree to be mindful of Dofell in the years to come. Its new leader will need us to guide and assist them, and we can't rest assured until they've proven their capability." A smile graced her lips when she turned to Aurelia. "That means you, too, Your Grace. A dragon is most effective when it comes to keeping people in line."

Aurelia laughed. "I'd be most obliged."

"Is that the wisest idea?" Lord Zhoqa stared at her with his arms crossed over his chest as he ignored the plate of vegetables before him. "It's true— we need your men and your beast to destroy Kanihar. Elrin seems to trust you, too. But when all of that is said and done, why should we continue treating a foreign ruler like one of us? You have no right to leadership in Carthe, Your Grace. You've already started enough problems as it is by trying to lead people who aren't your own."

Jack set his chalice down just a bit too firmly, making everyone except for Lord Zhoqa wince, while Aurelia scowled at the nobleman and snapped: "I gave *one* village under your charge a means of filling their bellies, and I encouraged you to cease wedding little girls to grown men— which, by the way, never should've happened to begin with. That seemed to be obvious to everyone but you, apparently. Power and basic human decency are two different things. If you had even a lick of the latter, your people wouldn't have turned to me for help. That doesn't mean I sought to rule over them. It only means that I answered their cries for help to the best of my ability while you, their liege lord, took pleasure in watching them beg."

He grimaced, flashing his teeth like a hungry panther, as his hands balled into fists on either side of his untouched plate. "In your efforts to put the bloodied and broken pieces of our world back together, you wrote the chapters leading to our destruction. That *thing* in your pocket is proof of that."

"So we've come back to this, then?"

"My people were encouraged to rebel against me after your trek through Kazamir. I managed to save my own skin by giving them what they asked for, but it could've ended differently. That encouraged others to demand the same things in Dofell, and look where we are because of it. The war with Kanibar is what led you to find the amulet, isn't it? You wouldn't have been in a position to crash land on Tullweine if not for Willem and his plot. Every last issue we've faced in recent years is a direct result of you meddling where you don't belong."

Aurelia bit her cheeks until she tasted blood, silent and humiliated, while her uncle valiantly came to her rescue: "Her Grace is quite right. Her desire to show your people even an ounce of decency had unintended consequences, yes, but she wouldn't have had to do so if you'd been the leader your people deserve. Have you heard even a whisper of displeasure from your people since you changed your ways, my lord?"

The bald, blue-eyed nobleman gritted his teeth. "No."

"I thought as much. Her Grace was given a destiny to fulfill by the gods themselves—we mustn't fault her for that. And the amulet...We may need it if we fail in our endeavors, whether you like it or not. Her Grace is fortunate enough to have allies at her side who will protect her from any potential ramifications. She's willing to darken her heart to restore peace and justice to the realm—so should we continue to insult her over something none of us have ever experienced in our lifetimes, or should we stand proudly at her side while she potentially sacrifices a piece of her good heart?"

Lord Zhaaran softened enough for Aurelia to catch a glimpse of the kind old man she'd first met five years earlier. He finally looked at her, and when their eyes met, he softened even more—like the glacier he'd erected around his heart had begun to melt.

"I won't tell you that I think it's a good idea to use the amulet," he murmured. "A curse placed on the average person could destroy them, but a curse placed on a queen—never mind a queen with a dragon—could destroy the world. You know this."

Aurelia nodded. "I do, and I know what measures you took to warn me of that danger. I'm sorry, my lord. Had I known, I might've proceeded differently, but I didn't." He softened, going as far as to smile and tip his head at her acknowledgment of his sacrifice. "Now we've found ourselves here, and...and if the time comes for me to use it, I trust that those closest to me will intervene before the curse consumes me—if it even exists. I know *you*, my lord, would be among the first to remind me of my destiny if I should ever lose sight of it."

He raised a bushy gray eyebrow. "If we tell you it's time to get rid of the object, will you oblige?"

"I will."

"If we tell you that we no longer recognize the person you've become, will you listen? Or will you seek to destroy those who question you?"

Aurelia squared her shoulders, defiant. "Five years ago, the faces at this table lifted me from the ashes when I was left with nothing. I won't destroy those who only aim to guide and protect me."

It was Lord Zhoqa who spoke next: "And what if you're too far gone by the time we intervene? What if there's nothing salvageable left within your blackened heart? We can't protect you after that. It's exactly what happened to Iago Zanaki."

"A woman's heart has seen more evil in this world than a man will ever know." Aurelia paused, locking eyes with Reyna. "I'll take my chances."

For a moment as the two queens smiled at one another, nobody said a word. Then Lord Zhaaran lifted his chalice into the air, tipping it toward Aurelia, before taking a sip and smiling at her. When he set it down again, she realized he was looking at her the same way he'd looked at her when he pledged his sword to her cause: as a man who believed in her.

XXII

Aurelia didn't receive the warm welcome she'd expected when she, Jack, and Halvor returned to the Folly. Only two faces awaited them at the rear doors of the palace: Ansyl and Ser Rayan Haze.

Both men bowed in greeting, but only Ansyl stepped forward to speak: "What news from Carthe? Did the trip prove itself worthwhile?"

"Somewhat. We'll update you later on." She snapped her gaze over to Ser Rayan, who stared at his feet with his head bowed. "What brings our guest to the palace today?"

Ansyl sighed. "He hadn't heard from you regarding his celebratory feast here at the palace. I was just asking him to return at a later date when we spotted Halvor approaching the premises. I assumed you'd like to speak with him yourself."

She nodded and took a few steps toward Rayan while Jack and Ansyl lingered behind her. The knight gulped when he met her eyes, and she faltered for a moment when she realized they were the *exact* color as hers. People often told her that she'd inherited her eyes from her mother, but while she stood beside her half-brother, she couldn't deny that they must've come from their father.

"Ser Rayan." She smiled as well as she could as exhaustion usurped her body. "You must forgive me for neglecting you these past weeks, but I haven't forgotten you. I'd be most pleased to host a feast in your honor when things calm down a bit. The warring kingdoms of Carthe have requested Akkinor's assistance, and until peace is restored to the west, there is little time for celebration."

He nodded in understanding. "Of course, Your Grace. Your invitation is honor enough—I wouldn't wish to impose during such trying times." He swallowed and straightened his spine. "I've come to inquire after the matter in Carthe, too. Some knights—me included—have heard whispers about a call to arms. I was nominated to receive confirmation or denial directly from the palace."

From behind her, Ansyl cleared his throat. "As I mentioned earlier, an official announcement will be made public when—"

"It's true," Aurelia interrupted. Ansyl clamped his jaw shut as Rayan merely watched her, surprised by her candor. "My recent audience with my allies has left no room for speculation. Sooner than later, we Akkinorians will find ourselves fighting in Carthe." She paused for a moment, debating between following protocol and following her gut. "In fact, your presence here poses an opportunity. Our allies don't need the full force of Akkinor's military in the fight to come—not with Halvor on our side. The best course of action is to establish our troops by requesting volunteers. Our army would be made stronger with mages at our side, but our mages have never seen battle before. I shall need someone to encourage them to volunteer. Would you do me the honor, good knight?"

He gaped at her. "Y-Your Grace—"

"I'd task you with traveling the country as my emissary to meet with each kingdom's coven. Most mages will follow their archmage without question, but the leaders will be hesitant to send their subjects to a warzone. It'd be your responsibility to convince them into urging their mages to fight. It's important to remember that you won't be commanding them to fight—only reminding them that they, like all Akkinorians, have a duty to our country. Ultimately, though, it's their choice."

"My queen..." He shifted his weight from one leg to the other, uneasy. "I humbly accept the assignment you've given me, but I feel it's my duty as your loyal subject to warn you about how this might be received. Our people care little for Carthe and its squabbles. It may not be a simple task, convincing Akkinorians to set our own worries aside to defend those who mean nothing to us."

"You must remind them of what may happen if our allies fall," she replied. "If we fail to abolish the current threat, their economies will be fractured, and ours along with them. Akkinor's war reparations are projected to be completed by the end of next year; if our allies are threatened, it'll take another five years for Akkinor to become what it was before the uprising. Our people can't afford that, nor should it be something they must worry about after what they endured throughout my brother's reign. I understand the hesitation to fight—truly, I do—but the

Carthinians fought for us during a time when all we were able to offer them were promises. They respected the terms of our alliances, while uncertain if the promises I made to them would ever come to fruition. The assurances they gave Akkinor can be seen all around us, my friend. We must do for them what they did for us."

Rayan nodded and bowed. "Yes, Your Grace."

"I appreciate your loyalty and cooperation, Ser Rayan. I shall send a messenger to your door tomorrow with further instructions," she said. After Rayan nodded once more and turned to leave the grounds, Aurelia directed her attention to Ansyl and Jack, urging them to follow her into the palace. "Summon the Assembly to the palace at once, Ansyl. I shall need them to send word to every reigning noble in Akkinor about the call-to-arms. I know they'll be displeased that I've come to this conclusion without discussing it with them first, but time is of the essence now. We can't know for certain when King Willem will strike, and we must be prepared as quickly as possible."

He nodded, hands clasped behind his back, as they strolled the halls. "Consider it done, Your Grace. I shall have them send word to our shipbuilders on the Nose and our blacksmiths in Laynoa, too. Both require advanced notice if they're to have our fleets and weapons prepared in time for departure."

"I'll write to my brother, too," Jack added. "The majority of our food comes from Omara, and while the Omarans will refuse to fight, they'll aim to assist in other ways. The sooner they start rationing and packaging meals for our soldiers, the better."

Aurelia reached for his hand and squeezed. "Clever. Now, I'd like to see the children before I return to my duties—but first, tell me what's happened in our absence, Ansyl. Anything of note?"

"We received word from Glenn Sherwood two days ago," Ansyl told her. She raised an eyebrow as the trio halted in the foyer. "He's agreed to have a priest from the monastery and a mage—chosen by the priest—train young Daisy at Sherwood Manor. And by some divine miracle, he's also found a new archmage for Myra: the sister of his late wife, who recently married his younger brother. As long as you approve, Juniper Sherwood will take her place as archmage by week's end."

An invisible weight lifted off Aurelia's shoulders as she beamed at him. "What lovely news! And how fares the duke? Any better?"

"A bit, yes, according to his letter—but we can't know for certain until we see him again."

She nodded. "Of course. Anything else?"

Eager to see her children after so many days apart, Aurelia began climbing the grand staircase, urging Jack and Ansyl to follow suit. As they hurried to meet her pace, Ansyl updated the couple on everything else they'd missed while in Carthe. Of the many things he brought to their attention, only two were of great importance: the first being that the warring earldoms in Holos had ceased their squabbling after Aurelia sent a letter of warning to their ringleader; and the second being that he'd increased security detail across the Folly in hopes of finding, apprehending, and questioning anyone under suspicion of spying for Kanibar.

By the time they reached the nursery, Aurelia hadn't heard anything that required her immediate attention (excluding Carthe, of course). The new legislations she'd created for the matter of the assassins were still standing strong; her people, however reluctantly, had accepted assistance from Carthinians to learn how to work with imported goods from the west; and the law she'd enacted to deter crimes against mages had proven effective, as there'd been no reports of any violence or assaults throughout the country.

The amulet in her pocket felt heavier than ever, but for the first time since finding it on Iago Zanaki's corpse, Aurelia didn't feel the slightest inkling toward using it to cure Akkinor's woes. Perhaps Jack had been right: she was entirely capable of solving her country's problems on her own.

That still didn't apply to the war in Carthe, though. Unless she and her allies could find someone worthy of ruling Dofell—and defeat Kanibar in the process—she'd inch closer and closer to utilizing the power she'd uncovered. She still didn't know how she'd use it if the time came for it, but so long as her allies stood by her side, she wouldn't have to figure it out alone.

"I shall resume our duties tomorrow," Aurelia said to Ansyl. "Take the rest of the day for yourself, my friend. Do whatever you'd like. I think we've all earned a break, however short it may be."

He smiled and tipped his head in gratitude. "Of course, Your Grace. Thank you."

She nodded as he turned, but before he could walk off, she added, "How many times have I told you to call me Aurelia?"

He froze, and for a moment, she could've sworn she saw him flinch. "Too many, my queen."

Then he was gone.

***

198

Two nights after her return, Aurelia found herself in her favorite room in the palace: the library.

After hours of tossing and turning (and being snapped at by her husband for her restlessness), she decided that a bit of reading might help ease her mind. She considered turning to one of her favorite books, but instead chose research over comfort. She hadn't stopped thinking about her audience with King Elrin since it happened, so she hoped a bit of studying would put her thoughts to rest.

The first promising text she found was dedicated entirely to Myenar. She hoped to find more information about the curse, but the punishment he'd placed upon the Phyre family hadn't been recorded in this book. For all she knew, it hadn't been recorded *anywhere*.

The next offered her a bit more, but it still wasn't enough to ease her wandering thoughts. It detailed the history of Dofell from the year it collapsed to 1987 Post Creation, three years after Aurelia defeated her brother. Again, it didn't mention anything about the curse, but it did list every tragedy faced by Dofell over the last few hundred years: how the soil became infertile for no apparent reason, yielding nothing but potatoes; how fresh drinking water became contaminated with toxic metals, which infected every well in the kingdom without cause; and, of course, how Dofell drove itself further into debt by erecting walls around the entire kingdom, sending a clear message to any outsiders: *Stay away*.

She was so invested in her reading that she hadn't heard the door open and close. What snatched her attention was a bang that echoed throughout the library, followed closely by a quiet string of profanities and nervous mumbling. When she looked up, she saw a servant just a few feet from the door, crouching down as he collected whatever he'd dropped.

"F-Forgive me, my-my queen," he stammered, clutching his belongings to his chest. He averted his gaze from hers as he offered her a weak, wobbling bow. "I was just, erm—"

"It's all right." She closed the book and smiled as she stood. "What do you have there?"

His face was redder than a cardinal. "I've just repaired these for Madam Hull. Have you...Have you seen her?"

Aurelia cracked a smile. "It's the middle of the night, so I imagine she's asleep." As she took a few steps closer to him, she realized he was holding a pair of leather riding boots. "You're a cobbler, then?"

"Yes, Your Grace."

"I see. Well, since Madam Hull isn't here, I'd be pleased to take them on her behalf. I'll make sure she receives them."

He didn't move an inch as she crossed the distance between them and held out her hands. Still refusing to meet her gaze, he handed her the boots, then immediately bowed and bid her goodnight before scurrying out of the room.

Aurelia brought the shoes to a cart on wheels along the back wall of the library. Madam Hull, the librarian, left the cart—filled with books, scrolls, and the like that'd recently been borrowed—in the same place every night. Each morning, the first thing she did was return those texts to the shelves. Seeing that this was the best place to leave them, Aurelia set the boots atop a stack of books, making sure to lay them on their sides so the soles wouldn't ruin the texts.

Just as she was turning away, her eyes found the text on the spine of one book in particular: *Roses of the Realm: The Triumphant, Scorned, and Forgotten Women of History.*

When she looked at the front cover, she found the title written above the name of the author—a High Priest at the monastery named *Petrien*—and the date of the book's creation. It had only been published last season.

She brought the book back to the table she'd claimed earlier and quickly thumbed through the pages. It was divided into sections, each dedicated to a different continent, and Akkinor's section came first. Her lips curled into a smile when she saw the last chapter of her country's section: it was dedicated to her. Though Petrien and his successors would have to revise the book as Aurelia—and the other female leaders currently holding power—furthered their reigns, he'd done a remarkable job at biographing her life from birth to the present day.

Before she started reading, she realized she hadn't any materials for taking notes, so she fetched a quill, an inkwell, and a piece of blank parchment from the writing desk across the library. As she walked back to the table, juggling the materials, her ears pricked when a strange sound—like whistling winds—cut through the silence in the library.

She gasped when she found the source of the noise. The book she'd claimed from the cart was exactly where she'd left it, but the pages were turning on their own. She stopped a few feet from the table, heart pounding, as the fluttering slowed down when the book appeared to find the proper page.

Aurelia glanced around, looking for anything—an open window, the sprite—that might've moved the pages, but she knew she wouldn't find what she was looking for. She'd checked on the sprite before she retired for the evening, and the creature was exactly where she'd left it in her study. However, it'd admitted to sneaking out when a servant (who'd forgotten Aurelia's instruction to leave the room undisturbed) arrived to clean. Nobody said a word about having seen it around the palace, but the children had been awfully giddy—and secretive—when Aurelia and Jack saw them after their return. She wouldn't have blamed the sprite if it visited the children, though: after all, they were the only people in the palace who wouldn't have been alarmed by its presence.

She set the writing materials on the table, placed a hand over her breast to calm her racing heart, and swallowed as she peered down at the pages the book had opened to.

The title page told her that this chapter was included in Dofell's section of the book, but the subheading mentioned a name she wasn't familiar with: *Althaia Phyre*. Even stranger was the introductory paragraph:

Regarded by some historians as The Spark of Neglect, *Althaia was the eldest child and only daughter of King Ophelos Phyre III. When her brother, Ophelos IV, was born ten months after her birth, Althaia was replaced as heir to the Dofelli throne and renounced by her family. All traces of her existence in the Phyre line were destroyed; all except for her birth record, which was salvaged and protected by an Elder of Dofell. Without it, the realm would never know that Dofell could have been spared from centuries of turmoil.*

Neither Althaia's name nor her father's were familiar to Aurelia, but she recognized the third name mentioned in the paragraph. King Ophelos Phyre IV was the very same man who'd destroyed the Lyanoth and, subsequently, cursed both his entire family and the kingdom of Dofell. If he hadn't been born—or, at the very least, if Ophelos III hadn't renounced Althaia as his heir—then perhaps the Lyanoth would have remained intact, and Dofell wouldn't have spent centuries in suffering.

The Spark of Neglect. The moniker made sense to Aurelia now: first and foremost, Althaia had been neglected by her family, cast aside once a male heir presented himself. Her family's treachery then unknowingly paved the way for the downfall of Dofell, as it became the most neglected place in the realm.

Knowing the book had shown her Althaia's story for a reason, Aurelia made herself comfortable at the table, quill at the ready, and she learned everything she could about the tragic tale of Althaia Phyre. Perhaps the most tragic detail was that her chapter was only a page long, front and back.

At one year old, Althaia was placed in the custody of the king's old friend, who raised her as his own. Only he, his wife, and the king knew the truth of her birth. She was given the name Althaia Phokion, and she spent the next eighteen years in a warm, loving home with her new parents. Her adoptive father, an esteemed knight and semi-wealthy lowborn, succeeded in organizing her union to Aratus Pharos, the future Earl of Charus. Althaia gave birth to their son, Aratus II, on her two-and-twentieth name day. One week later, the recently crowned King Ophelos IV began construction on a new palace for the royal family.

Commission costs of the palace placed nearly every noble family in extreme debt. When the civilians ran out of coin, the nobles were forced to deliver their own private funds to the king. The Pharos family of Charus was among those who collapsed at the beginning of Dofell's downfall. They were forced to abandon their home and luxuries, and when the hardships of lowborn life struck them down, the former earl and countess made the difficult choice to deliver their only son to an orphanage—the lone institutions in Dofell provided with enough funding to support their patrons, as the king believed the Almighty Myenar would frown upon him for neglecting the future of the kingdom.

Not much is known about Althaia's life after she and her husband were impoverished. Their names, lives, and legacies were lost amongst the lowborn population. Some, like me, believe the former earl and countess claimed their own lives. A highborn family stripped of their luxuries and privileges would rather live in the heavens than suffer on earth, and parents forced to lose their child would rather die than live without him. Nothing is known about what became of their son after he was delivered to the orphanage, either. Many like to believe that he was adopted, but we practical minds know he was more than likely a ward of the kingdom until he came of age. After that, when the orphanage no longer cared for him, he would've had no choice but to join society as a peasant.

It's often said that the fate of Dofell as we know it today might've been avoided, had Ophelos III named Althaia as his heir rather than renouncing her. While we may never know if that holds any substance, we can always think about what might have been as we reflect on the tragic tale of Althaia Phyre.

Aurelia leaned back in her chair, head spinning, as she struggled to absorb the information. She started to ask herself how the Phyre family had been so cruel, particularly to their own kin, but she quickly answered her own question: they were no different than the majority of highborn families across the realm, who ostracized or disposed of female heirs in favor of sons. The same thing could've happened to Aurelia if her father hadn't chosen to honor the line of succession instead of society's preference for a male heir. In a way, it had happened to her—only after she'd already been queen for five years, and on her brother's word rather than her father's.

She wondered why the text hadn't referenced the Lyanoth, either. It didn't say a word about the ancient portal, and it didn't mention anything about the curse, either—not even speculation about the curse's existence. Perhaps that was part of the Phyre family's punishment, too: they knew about the curse and what inflicted it when nobody else did, and while they were powerless to change things, the realm had nobody to blame for Dofell's misery except for the royals themselves.

Only when she blinked her burning eyes did she realize she hadn't taken a single note while reading—she'd been far too invested. She still didn't quite understand why the book had wanted her to know Althaia's story, but she could feel in her gut that the name wasn't one she could let herself forget.

Muttering an apology to the god of knowledge and anyone who might've selected Petrien's book as their next read, Aurelia tore out the page dedicated to Althaia and folded it into a square small enough to fit in her pocket. The book was too bulky to carry around with her, but that one page alone held all the power she needed—she was sure of it.

XXIII

The moment the door clicked shut behind him, Doryn Vellas pressed his back against the wall and closed his eyes while counting his breaths. He stretched his clammy fingers at his sides, sweat pouring down his back, and tried his utmost to calm his racing heart before the pounding of blood in his ears deafened him.

You're a cobbler, then? The queen's voice echoed in his head on a loop, filling him with dread and just a touch of guilt. She'd sounded so...*gentle*. He hadn't been expecting such warmth from a woman in possession of a dragon. In fact, he'd expected her to be cold and distant—particularly after being disturbed in her own library by a cobbler who had no business being there.

He didn't know she'd be there when he visited the library. When he walked in and saw her unmistakable head of golden hair hunched over a book, he thought he'd faint right then and there. It wasn't because she intimidated him, though—it was because he was only moments away from potentially destroying her life. She hadn't been suspicious of him, but her obliviousness only made him feel worse when he remembered what he was there to do.

Doryn had played the part well. Since arriving in Akkinor several weeks earlier, he'd managed to find a position at the palace as a cobbler for the queen's employees, and that alone had kept him busier than he'd ever been in Kanibar. Working so closely with the staff allowed him to learn more than enough about the queen, her family, her beast, and her plans, too. They were overly fond of gossip, and even if most of it was nothing more than hogwash, their whisperings had provided Doryn with the exact kind of intelligence King Willem had ordered him to uncover.

He wasn't even supposed to be in the library. He was meant to meet another Kanish spy, Orlys, on the palace grounds to help complete the final phase of their mission for the king. But he'd promised the librarian that he'd repair her shoes, and he didn't feel right about abandoning that promise. Orlys—and the other spies posted around Akkinor, for that matter—would've called him a fool if they knew the position he'd placed himself in that night, and he would've agreed with them.

When he calmed down enough to peel himself from the wall, Doryn took a deep breath and set out for the kitchens. The rooms were empty when he arrived, as expected, so he didn't have to interact with anyone when he slipped out through the servant's entrance. He walked along the exterior of the palace, keeping an eye out for anyone lingering nearby, as he pulled the hood of his cloak over his head. He eventually found himself in the gardens, just a few feet from the estate's rear entrance.

Another hooded figure awaited him in the shadows. "What took you so long?" Orlys snapped.

"I got lost," Doryn lied. He glanced around, frowning. "Where are the soldiers?"

"Dismissed." The spy grinned. "They were, ah, *summoned* to attend to another matter. I suspect we have about half an hour before they return, but that's time enough. The source of our intel should be here with the package at any moment."

Doryn raised an eyebrow. "What do you need from me?"

"Nothing, really." Orlys turned to face one of the dragon-shaped gargoyles flanking either side of the door. "Have you ever seen a living gargoyle, boy?"

"No." He froze as the realization struck him. "We're not flying back to Kanibar in the claws of a gods-forsaken *gargoyle*, are we?"

"It's the quickest way. If we take a ship, we won't make it far before the palace is made aware of what's happened, and they'll capture us before we've left the Crystal Sea for the Alkamura. We can't take any chances." Orlys turned away from the stone dragon and grimaced as he eyed Doryn. "That's not entirely true. *I* can't take any chances, but you...Unfortunately, you're a liability."

Doryn's blood turned to ice. "I beg—"

In the blink of an eye, Orlys lunged forward and planted his dagger in Doryn's gut. He held Doryn close for a moment, murmuring something in the cobbler's ear that Doryn couldn't make out, before dropping him to the ground while blood sputtered from his mouth. Doryn lay on the grass, convulsing and gasping, while Orlys towered over him.

"Do forgive me." Orlys wiped his dagger with his cloak, then sheathed the weapon and knelt at Doryn's side. "The king ordered me to dispose of any unessential contributors, and you...Well, you're no longer essential to the mission."

As the pain in his abdomen morphed into a cold numbness, Doryn watched with wide, unblinking eyes while Orlys hefted him by the underarms and dragged him to a nearby cluster of bushes. Not a minute later, Doryn heard footsteps approaching, briefly accompanied by the sound of a child's laughter.

Is that you, Myles? He pictured his little brother's face at the time of his death—only five years old. *Have you come to bring me home to the heavens?*

After a few moments, the laughter subsided, and Doryn heard the footsteps cease just a few paces from where he lay in the bushes. Another male voice filled Doryn's eardrums as he continued trembling, the chill of death washing over him like a tidal wave.

"...really necessary? I'll be noticed if I'm gone too long, and you've left me with a body to bury. He was harmless."

Orlys snorted. "He became a hindrance as soon as his task was completed. The king can't risk the boy getting himself caught. You'll have plenty of time to take care of him after I leave, too. And wipe that concern from your face—anyone who catches a glimpse of you will suspect something's amiss."

The man—the source, Doryn assumed—exhaled. "Fine. Just...Just be careful, all right?"

"I'm no fool. Now, give me a moment to awaken the creature, and stop chattering in my ear. It's distracting."

Doryn flashed in and out of consciousness for the next few minutes, entirely unaware of what was happening around him. Then, just as the pain subsided—a clear sign that death was fast-approaching—he heard the source's voice, louder and clearer than before. He managed to open his eyes, moaning, while a blurry figure hovered over him. Without Orlys's grating voice cutting through the silence of the gardens, Doryn knew the task had been completed: Orlys had brought the gargoyle to life after the source arrived, and the creature was now taking Orlys and the package home to Kanibar.

"I'm sorry." The source's voice sounded garbled, like both he and Doryn were underwater. "I didn't...I didn't know."

Doryn wished he could've questioned the man, but he couldn't speak. Just before the world faded to black, Doryn felt himself being lifted from the ground, likely to be brought somewhere else for burial. The same man would return after Doryn was disposed of to clean the evidence, and after that, nobody would ever know what had become of Doryn Vellas.

***

With only four hours until sunrise, Aurelia finally left the library to get some rest, her mind now at ease after the book she'd found pointed her in the right direction—so it seemed, anyway. She crawled into bed beside Jack, careful not to disturb him, then placed the page she'd torn from the book under her pillow. She set her hand over the page, taking comfort in her discovery, and quickly fell asleep to the sound of Jack's heavy breathing.

Within minutes, she realized the god of dreams had something in store for her that night.

She could tell she was dreaming: the torches in the wall sconces appeared blurry and hazy, the noises surrounding her echoed like she was underwater, and she couldn't feel the floor beneath her feet, or the wall grazing her fingertips, as she walked through the palace corridors. However, in the time it took for her to blink, everything seemed to steady, and the idea that she was floating in a dreamworld fizzled away completely.

Aurelia found herself walking toward the nursery. When she opened the door, the dwindling fire in the hearth extinguished, sending clouds of smoke cascading across the room. She knew there were candles and matches resting atop the wardrobe, so she lit a candle in its holder to illuminate her path as she checked on her children.

The first bed she examined—Halle's—was empty. So was Henry's, and so was Halyna's bassinet. Just before she turned to Hyacinth, she heard laughter from outside. When she approached the nursery windows, she saw Jack and their three children stargazing in the courtyard. She reminded herself to scold Jack later on for taking the children out after dark, but she wasn't entirely cross with him; she knew he was only giving their children as many wonderful memories as he could.

Then she heard a voice from behind her, and every muscle in her body seemed to calcify. It was a voice she recognized all too well, and one she hadn't heard in over five years. She still remembered the very last time she'd heard it—the very last thing he'd ever said:

Long live the queen.

Turning like her body was made of stone, Aurelia held her breath and took a few cautious steps forward. As she held up the candle, dizziness washed over her. She saw the back of a head of familiar, unruly blond hair as he perched on the edge of Hyacinth's bed. He stared down at the sleeping princess with his hands—his long fingers nearly identical to hers—set in his lap. His nail beds were red and raw from being bitten and picked at: likely a nervous habit she'd never noticed (or cared to notice) when he was alive.

When she said his name, it sounded more like a gasp than speech: "Archie?"

His entire body tensed as his spine straightened and his hands stilled. He didn't turn around—only tilted his head in her direction—so she took another few steps forward until she was only a pace or two away from him. Her eyes darted to Hyacinth, who slept blissfully unaware of what was happening, before landing on her brother once more.

"I should've known you'd do something like this." The sound of Archie's voice, softer than she remembered, threatened to rip her heart from her chest. "You always took everything that was meant for me."

She opened her mouth to respond, but for a moment, no sound emerged. "Y-You sent her mother away to exile. I know you, brother, and I know...I know you wouldn't have wanted the child anywhere near you unless you sired a son, and you didn't."

"I can see that. I'm not blind, Li."

A chill ran up and down her spine. She hadn't heard her childhood nickname since the last real conversation she had with Archie—the conversation in which both accepted that one was sending the other to meet the executioner. But as haunting as this was, she wasn't entirely surprised. Her brother had always had a knack for tossing his toys aside, only to come back to reclaim them after Aurelia showed an interest.

Her voice didn't sound like her own when she said, "Why are you here?"

"I wanted to see her." He turned to look down at Hyacinth again. "What did you name her?"

"Does it matter? You're gone, and you wouldn't have wanted her, anyway." She regretted the words the moment she said them—why, she didn't know. She sighed and let her eyelids flutter shut. "Her name is Hyacinth, but we call her Sisi, sometimes."

"Hyacinth." He pondered that for a moment. "I never understood your fascination with those weeds, you know."

"I know. I never understood your fascination with the piano, either."

"I know."

For a moment, a smile graced her lips. "Brother, I—"

"Will you tell her about me? About the things I did?"

Her lips parted as she opened her eyes again. She was glad he'd interrupted her—she didn't know what she was going to say—but she wasn't sure what to say *now*, either.

"It doesn't matter what I tell her. She'll hear it from others, eventually," Aurelia murmured. His body appeared to inflate and deflate again with the force of his exhale. "Answer this for me, Archie: if you'd lived long enough to meet her, would you have wanted to keep her? To raise her and love her as your own, bastard or not?"

He thought about it for a moment. "I don't know. Really, I don't. I just..." He sighed again. "I see her now, and it makes me wonder what might've become of me if I hadn't been stung by the Scorpion."

"I think about that, too. Quite often."

"What does it look like to you?"

She smiled again. "Home."

"Home?"

"Yes. Home." She closed her eyes as the smile refused to fade from her lips. "The way it was before Mother and Father died—before you saw me as your enemy, instead of your sister." A lump formed in her throat. "Archie, I...I know you'll call me a fool for saying this, but I really am sorry for what happened. I wish I could've prevented it, and I wish I could've found a way to spare your life. Despite everything, you're still my brother, and I'll always love you. We were the best of friends once, you and me. Don't you remember?"

When he didn't respond, she took another step forward and set a hand on his shoulder. A strangled cry escaped her lips when he turned, and in doing so, caused his head to fall from his shoulders. She dropped the candle as she fell to the ground, startled, while his body slumped off the side of the bed and his bloody head rolled across the floor. His pale blue eyes were wide open, and his last words were still playing on his lips.

She reached for the candle and hurriedly crawled to him, but by the time she made it there, both his body and his head were gone. She set a hand over her racing heart and turned to Hyacinth, hoping her daughter hadn't awoken to such a grisly sight, and felt her stomach drop to her knees when she saw an empty bed where the princess had been sleeping only seconds earlier.

Aurelia opened her mouth to call for her daughter, but she didn't get the chance. The next thing she knew, she was sitting upright in bed beside a sleeping Jack, sweating so profusely that her hair felt like a wet blanket stuck to her back.

After reminding herself that she'd only been dreaming, she tiptoed into the washroom and dampened a cloth with cool water. It wasn't as refreshing as she'd hoped when she placed the cloth on the back of her neck, but it calmed her nerves well enough.

As she tried to sleep again, she felt a sudden, almost primitive need to have her children beside her. Before she knew what she was doing, her hands were on Jack's back, shaking him aggressively until he woke.

"Gods above, woman," he grumbled, turning away from her. "I was having the loveliest dream."

She ignored him. "I need you to fetch the children. Bring them here. I-I wish for them to spend the night with us."

He looked over his shoulder at her and raised an eyebrow. "All of them?"

Aurelia nodded.

He exhaled tiredly. "As you wish."

She mimicked his exhale as he climbed out of bed with a groan, not bothering to put on his slippers or his dressing robe before he left their bedchamber. When he was gone, she laid flat on the bed, hugging herself as she stared at the ceiling and replayed the conversation she'd had with her brother in her dream.

A few moments later, the door swung open and slammed against the wall so violently that the entire suite trembled. She sat upright, alarmed, as a wide-eyed and gasping Jack rushed toward her from the hallway. The terrified look in his eyes was one she'd never seen from him before—one that rattled her to her very core.

"J-Jack? What's happened?"

His face was drained of color. "I can't find Hyacinth."

XXIV

By sunrise the next morning, the entire Folly was being torn apart in search of Hyacinth Brentwood, Princess of Akkinor.

At first, those summoned by Aurelia and Jack to assist in the search—Ansyl, the Assembly, and the royal knights—believed Hyacinth had simply wandered off somewhere in the palace, likely having fallen asleep wherever she'd ended up. Maybe, they said, she'd made her way to the kitchens for a cup of milk or a few of the chocolate truffles she loved so much. Maybe, she'd snuck into the gardens to sleep under the stars with Halvor. Maybe, she'd gotten curious about exploring the many rooms and corridors of the palace, and she didn't know how to find her way back to the nursery.

But Aurelia and Jack knew their daughter, and they knew every scenario conjured by their subordinates could not be true. Hyacinth wasn't always as obedient as her elder sister, but she was certainly clever: clever enough to know better than to go off on her own, and to know how to find her way back, even if she *did* get lost in the palace. She knew to ring for the servants if she desired anything at all, to never leave the palace (even to visit Halvor) without supervision, and to always ask an adult to accompany her if she wished to explore.

They checked every room, hall, crack, and crevice in the palace, but Hyacinth was nowhere to be found. They checked beneath every tree, behind every bush, and inside every structure in the gardens, too. They checked the servants' quarters, the crypt, the wardrobes—any place a five-year-old girl might hide, really. Nothing.

After clearing the grounds, every spare soldier in the palace—along with every Follian soldier sleeping in their homes—was awoken and tasked with scouring the Folly for the princess. Every torch, lantern, and hearth in the kingdom was lit as the soldiers questioned every Follian, searched every home and establishment, and even every well, river and stream, looking—gods forbid—for remains.

They didn't stop there, either. Troops scoured Seaport, too, and the woodlands surrounding both the coastal town and the kingdom. Soldiers took boats out to sea with lanterns, while Halvor scanned the world below from the sky. Scouts and messengers took horses to the neighboring kingdoms of Myra and Omara, sending word to anyone and everyone about the princess's disappearance.

The only thing they found was a freshly dug grave just outside of the palace grounds. Knights recovered the remains of a young man, seemingly Carthinian, and put him right back in the ground again when they confirmed the body wasn't Hyacinth. They came to the same conclusion anyone would: the Carthinian was a victim of an Akkinorian's bigotry. It wouldn't be the first time, and it probably wouldn't be the last.

Aurelia tried to join the search parties, but she couldn't manage it. She'd checked the nursery and some of Hyacinth's favorite rooms in the palace for herself, and after finding no trace of her daughter, she collapsed to her knees and sobbed until Anna led her away to the privacy of her study. She refused to move until Anna assured her that both governesses and ten soldiers were watching the three other Brentwood children—all of whom had slept through Hyacinth's disappearance from the nursery.

As the search was underway, Aurelia sat on the small couch in her study, staring blankly into the blazing hearth as silent tears rolled down her cheeks. Someone had wrapped her in a dressing robe amidst the chaos, and though her nerves were making her sweat like she'd just run the entire length of the Folly, she couldn't be bothered to take it off.

Jack had joined the search alongside the soldiers, but after a few hours, he joined Aurelia in her study—not because he'd given up, but because he knew his wife needed him at her side. He needed her, too. It was going to be a long night.

Jack paced back and forth across the study, hands pulling his hair then falling to his sides and back again, as tears stained his colorless cheeks. "This is impossible," he mumbled. "We have guards minding every entrance and exit on the grounds, servants prowling the halls, civilians lining the streets—so how could this have happened?"

"I don't know, Jack." Aurelia sounded more like a little girl than a queen when she replied. "I don't know."

"I should go back out there to look for her. I-I should be—"

"You've already done so. There are thousands of people still out searching for her, Jack. We need you here. If-If she's found soon, she'll want her father here to greet her. And when the children wake again..."

She swallowed the hot, thick lump in her throat. "They were petrified enough when the commotion woke them and they realized Sisi wasn't with them. They believed our lie that she left to visit your brother in Omara, but they'll want to know more as soon as they wake. I-I can't face them without you."

He softened, but in a split second, the gentle man she'd fallen in love with transformed into someone she didn't recognize. He slammed his fist into the wall, leaving a massive hole behind, before reaching for the nearest bookcase and throwing it onto the floor. She jumped in her seat, alarmed, but made no effort to scold him for his outburst—if she had the strength to stand, she might've done the same thing.

When a flash of golden light appeared behind the fallen bookcase— apparently having made its escape from its slumber atop a few books just in time—Aurelia was presented with an idea:

"Come here, sprite," she croaked. The creature appeared on the tea table before her in an instant. "You can travel at a remarkable speed, can't you? From what I've learned, you can travel the entire country in mere minutes. Do you...Do you suppose you could find her if I let you out?"

The sprite blinked at her. "Perhaps."

"Perhaps? *Perhaps?*" Jack slammed his hands down on the table, making it rock and shriek in protest, as the sprite merely turned to stare at him. The tormented look in his eyes nearly broke Aurelia's heart. "What the fuck does *that* mean?"

"Jack," Aurelia whispered.

"Our girl is missing." He stepped back from the table and ran a hand through his sweaty curls. His face crumpled, his eyes welled with tears, and his chin began to tremble. "Oh, my girl..."

It took everything Aurelia had to keep from sobbing again, too. "We shall try, anyhow," she said to the sprite. She managed to rise from the couch and cross the study, where she opened the window overlooking the courtyard. "Do what you can to find her, so long as you promise to return here as soon as you've finished searching."

The sprite nodded, and without another word, zipped out the window in a flash of golden light.

She sunk onto the couch again, hands on her knees, and buried her face in her hair. "She couldn't have wandered off. That's not like her, and she wouldn't have strayed so far away. Someone must've taken her."

"How?" Jack demanded. "Anyone would've seen someone leaving the palace with a little highborn girl. She wouldn't have gone quietly, either. I taught all three of the children to scream for help and Halvor if anyone lays a hand on them."

A thought popped into her head. "Halvor. He would've sensed if she were in danger, wouldn't he?"

Something sad and forlorn passed over his face. "I doubt it. The connection exists between him and the women of the Cristos family, and Sisi isn't a Cristos."

Her heart sank. He was right, as much as she hated to admit it. "I-I don't know, Jack. There are a number of possibilities. Someone could've sneaked her out through the servant's entrance—hidden her beneath blankets and empty potato sacks. And you know how she is, my love. If the person who took her told her he'd kill us or her siblings if she didn't cooperate, she'd obey them."

"I can't believe I'm saying this, but I wish she was more like her brother." Jack sunk into the cushion beside her as a strangled chuckle escaped her lips. He set his hand over hers on her knee and squeezed. "What if she isn't found in the next few hours? What then?"

She clutched her empty locket with her free hand. "If we can't find her, I'll do what needs to be done to ensure she's brought home safely."

His oceanic eyes flashed in understanding. "The amulet?"

She nodded.

"Aurelia—"

Just then, a whoosh of warm summer air washed over the room, threatening to extinguish the fire in the hearth and the candles on the desk. Both husband and wife straightened up when the sprite landed on the tea table, panting for air.

A few moments passed, but the sprite still hadn't finished wheezing. "Well?" Jack demanded. "Did you find anything, creature?"

The sprite glared at him before turning its gaze to Aurelia. "Your husband is an animal."

She ignored it. "Did you find her?"

It shook its head. "She is not on this land."

"That's impossible," Jack argued. "She has to be. Are you sure you looked hard enough? She's a tiny thing, and you'd be surprised at the small spaces she can fit into when she puts her mind to it. She's quite fond of puzzles, and finding her way out of any type of confinement is the greatest puzzle of all. She likes to read, too, so if she's on her own, she's probably somewhere with access to books—but only the ones with the illustrations. And she's mortified of insects, like her mother, so she wouldn't be outside if she could help it."

"She is not here," the sprite insisted. "I could not detect her. Not here, not in the mountains, not in the mines or vineyards. She has left this land."

"That's *impossible*," Jack repeated. He stood from the couch and began to pace again. "If someone took her to Seaport and fled by sea, they would've been spotted. We would've received reports of a vessel leaving the docks without permission from the harbormaster. Our soldiers are searching every ship in the harbor as we speak, too."

"If her captor was clever about it, it's possible nobody would've seen them leave Seaport." Aurelia chewed on her lower lip—salty with tears— before sighing and standing up. "I'll take Halvor out to sea in search of any ships that recently departed from Akkinor. They can't have gone far."

Jack shook his head. "Halvor is doing that as we speak. He knows her scent, too. If he picks up any trace of her, we'll know. We can't risk sending you out there alone, dragon or not. This could be a trap."

"I don't care if it's a trap. We need our daughter back."

"I know that," he snapped. "I'm only trying to think logically."

"What good is logic when our child is missing?"

"For gods' sakes, Aurelia—"

"I'm going to check on the children," she announced. "If I must be confined to the palace, I'd at least like to find some comfort in their presences. You, husband, will remain here until you've cooled down. If they wake, I shouldn't like for them to see you like this. You won't be useful to the soldiers searching for her if you're barking at them, either."

His eyes darkened. "Is that a command?"

"If need be, yes." As he grunted in disapproval, she turned her gaze to the sprite. "You must stay here, too. The last thing we need right now is for the staff to run amuck in terror at the sight of a Kanish sprite zipping through the halls. Understand?"

It nodded. "Understand."

"Good." She looked between the creature and her husband once more, then left them alone in the study—to sit in silence or verbally assault one another, she didn't know. In that moment, she didn't care.

She trekked up to the nursery, replaying everything that had happened since she went to sleep the night before, and wondered if her dream of Archie had been a warning. After all, the dream had ended with Aurelia finding Hyacinth's bed suddenly empty. A part of her wanted to believe that her brother, wherever he was in the afterlife, had sent the warning out of care for the daughter he'd never met—or wanted, as far as she knew. She'd never know for certain, though.

Five soldiers guarded the nursery from the hall, and another five were positioned inside with the governesses. When she entered, she saw Irina sleeping in the rocking chair with Halyna in her arms, and Celesse sleeping in the center of Halle's bed with the princess tucked under one arm and the prince under the other. All three children were asleep, so Aurelia didn't know for sure what had happened: either they'd woken up again, prompting Celesse to lull them back to sleep with snuggles, or the governess was simply shaken by Hyacinth's disappearance and wanted to keep the others as close to her as possible.

Careful not to disturb them, Aurelia sat on Hyacinth's bed and observed them for a moment, grateful for their peaceful slumber and their ignorance of what'd happened. When she found herself sniffling with golden tears leaking from her eyes—careless of what the soldiers thought of her while she was in such a state—she set her hand over Hyacinth's blanket and bunched it in her grasp, using every ounce of strength in her body to keep from weeping.

Worried she'd disturb the children as her tears threatened to overcome her, she carefully climbed out of Hyacinth's bed to leave the nursery. As she rose, she cast one final glance at her daughter's bed, and a sudden realization struck her: the bed was made.

Aurelia and Jack had tucked her in themselves the night before, so she knew the bed had been slept in, even if only for a few hours—so why was the bed made?

A gut feeling prompted her to pull down the covers. A strangled gasp flew from her lips when she saw something laying on the mattress where her sleeping daughter should've been: a single, delft blue hyacinth—Aurelia's favorite.

With a trembling hand, she lifted the flower and instinctively inhaled its scent. She jerked away from it, alarmed, when she wasn't met with the fragrant aroma she loved so dearly. Rather, the flower reeked of burnt nutmeg and citrus fruits.

The smell of magic.

Faster than lightning, Aurelia raced out of the nursery, flew down the stairs, and ran for her study as her legs burned in protest. Jack and the sprite—who appeared to have been conversing on the couch until her interruption—both jumped when the door opened with a bang.

"Aurelia?" Jack stood immediately and rushed towards her. "What is it? Has she been found?"

She shook her head, breathless, and set the flower on his palm. "I know where she is."

***

Aurelia stared at the lone hyacinth on the tea table, eyes burning, until Jack slipped into the study and closed the door behind him. "No sign of

216

Ansyl yet," he told her. "I've told the guards to send him here as soon as he's returned from the search party."

Aurelia shook her head. "We don't know how long he'll be gone for. We have Halvor, so we should set out at once. The sprite can tell Ansyl where we've gone. I imagine it won't take us long to find her—they wouldn't be sailing with Kanish flags. They would've taken an Akkinorian ship to reduce suspicions. There are mercantile vessels from Taundosa, Bozar, and Krotis docked in Seaport, too. They could've taken any of those. We can attempt to—"

The sprite hissed from its seat on the edge of her desk. "Foolish."

Jack raised an annoyed eyebrow. "I beg your pardon?"

"That plan is foolish. She is already across the sea."

"How do you know that?"

When the sprite refused to answer him, Aurelia approached it and crouched down so they were eye-level. "You're from Kanibar, and between the three of us, you're the only one with an advanced knowledge of magic. I have to trust that you know what you're talking about, but I can't do that unless you tell us everything you might know."

It sighed. "Gargoyles. I saw when I left to search. Has to be."

She frowned. "Gargoyles? What do you mean?"

"I can show you. We have to leave this room."

Without another word, she plucked the creature from the desk—making it hiss in protest—and placed it on her shoulder, hiding it with her hair. Jack followed as they left the study, the sprite telling Aurelia which turns to take and where to go.

After a bit of walking, they eventually found themselves at the palace's rear entrance. The sprite instructed them to walk a ways from the door before turning to face the palace. That's when she noticed something odd: of the two enormous, dragon-like gargoyles flanking either side of the entrance, only one was still there.

"I don't understand," Jack stated. "What does—"

"Oh, my." Aurelia brought a hand to her stomach when a wave of nausea overcame her. She tried to look down at the sprite on her shoulder without revealing its position to passersby. "You don't mean—?"

"Yes."

"My gods..."

"What is it?" Jack demanded. "What am I missing?"

She hushed him when a dozen pairs of anxious eyes turned in their direction at the sound of his increasing octave. After returning to the palace and confining themselves to the study once more, she told him what she knew about the sprite's theory:

"Gargoyles were magical creatures from the old days. They were made of stone—crafted, not born—and could be granted life by mages. If a mage cast a spell on a gargoyle, it would come to life for a brief time, able to mimic some of the behaviors of the creature or animal whose likeness it shared. If a gargoyle was crafted to look like a lion, it would act like a lion when brought to life, but it would be submissive to the mage who awakened it."

Jack's face paled. "And what of a gargoyle that resembles a dragon?"

She winced, wishing she hadn't replaced the Brentwood family's falcon gargoyles with statues resembling Halvor. It'd been one of her many attempts to signal a new age for Akkinor, and yet, it'd come back to bite her.

"I don't know if they can breathe fire. I've never read any stories about dragon-like gargoyles," she admitted. The sprite muttered in agreement. "I know they can fly, though. All gargoyles—even those resembling land animals, like a lion—have wings."

"You don't mean to say that a gargoyle came to life and carried Hyacinth across the sea to Kanibar by its gods-forsaken claws, do you?"

A shiver wracked her body. "I wish I wasn't."

"For gods' sake, Aurelia—"

"The person who took her had to be a mage," she continued. "Only one gargoyle is missing, which means her captor likely held her while the gargoyle carried *him*." She shook her head as tears welled in her eyes. "Our poor girl must've been terrified."

"Not if he put her to sleep," the sprite suggested. "It's a spell. Some mages can do it."

That made her feel better, but not by much. "I never truly believed the stories about gargoyles. I thought they were amongst the few creatures that existed in legend only—tales meant to make the realm feel more magical than it is. I wouldn't have commissioned the new gargoyles if I'd thought something like this could happen."

"You couldn't have known. None of us could've known," Jack assured her. "They're just silly decorations, and it's not like the majority of Akkinorians are familiar with the stories, either. Our people have long since forgotten what magic can look like." He sunk into the armchair across from where she sat on the couch, elbows on his knees and fingers kneading his temples. "King Willem wanted you to know that he's responsible for taking her. He knew you'd recognize the flower from his gift to you in Taundosa. You must've sent the bouquet back to him, then."

She nodded. "Arian had it returned to Kanibar. He wasn't certain if there was another spell cast on the bouquets, so he didn't wish to keep it nearby."

"Either that bouquet was a warning shot, or Willem doesn't enjoy having his gifts returned to him. Regardless, he must've been planning this for a while now. What I can't understand is this: why Sisi? If he wanted to threaten the future of Akkinor, he would've taken Halle, your heir— maybe even Henry, your only son. And if he wanted the most defenseless target, he would've taken Halyna. So why Hyacinth?"

Aurelia took a long, shaking breath. "I have something to tell you."

XXV

Jack watched Aurelia, his eyebrows furrowed in confusion, as she told him the theory she'd outlined about Hyacinth displaying early signs of magic. She repeated everything Arian had said about the choices that they would have to make about Hyacinth's future: mainly regarding whether it was worth letting her keep her powers, only to have the realm discover she wasn't Aurelia and Jack's trueborn daughter.

Before she finished speaking, he rose from the armchair and started to pace, but stopped when he was only a few feet from the wall. She murmured his name when he bowed his head, and for a moment, neither of them said a word.

She tried again: "Jack—"

"You didn't think to mention this before?" He turned around, eyes wild and blazing with fury, as she shrunk away from him. "Hyacinth is already different from the others as it is. Now, you tell me that she's more than likely a mage, and you've known for quite some time. You should've told me as soon as you suspected."

A scowl washed over her face. "I've had quite a bit to worry about in recent weeks, Jack. Forgive me if I failed to tell you something the instant I learned of it. As important as it is, we have years to—"

"That's not the point!" he exploded. "You've been harboring crucial knowledge about one of our children and didn't think to tell me until she vanished. It doesn't matter if we have years to spare before we're forced to make a decision about her magic. What matters is that we could've increased our efforts to protect her—and to keep her nature as quiet as possible—if you'd told me about this sooner. I probably wouldn't have suspected that Willem would target her, either, if I'd found out when you did. But at the very least, I would've recognized that what makes her different also places her in the line of fire. It didn't cross your mind until just now that she might be used to weaken you, did it?"

"Oh, Jack, *please*. It's like you said before: none of us could've known this would happen. She's only a little girl—I never imagined she'd be used as a pawn for Willem's schemes, mage or not."

"You still should've told me the moment you suspected something. Things might've been different." He clenched his jaw. "We might've figured it out together, too, if you'd been available for more than a few hours at a time."

Her face darkened. "That's an ugly thing to say. I've only been doing my duty as queen. Do you think I like being away from my family, being pulled left and right trying to keep everyone happy? You knew what you signed up for when you married me, so don't sit there and throw that in my face while our daughter is *missing*."

"I understand that, Aurelia. But your father managed to be present for you in spite of his many responsibilities, didn't he? I thought you'd show the same diligence toward spending time with our family. *I* certainly have. I sit in this palace day after day, minding our children better than the governesses because I want them to have at least one parent at their disposal at all times. I'm glad to be with them so often—truly, I am—but when you're away, I'm constantly thinking about what it was like when I had the freedom to leave whenever *I* pleased, too."

"I don't leave whenever I please. I leave because I have to." Aurelia stood, bristling, and folded her arms over her chest. She knew he was only being nasty because he was upset—and scared—but still, his accusations stung her. "Are you saying you'd rather go back to being Jack Sherbourne?"

He scoffed. "Don't put words in my mouth."

"You told me long ago that you stayed in Carthe because you knew the radicals would hunt you down if you came home. You didn't tell your family you were alive because you knew they'd risk everything to bring you home safely. Is that true, or were you telling me what you thought I wanted to hear? It seems to me that you stayed in Carthe because life was easier as Jack Sherbourne. It was a choice to abandon your kingdom and your family, not an act of necessity."

He stared at her for a moment, face twisted and contorted with disgust, before shaking his head and laughing humorlessly. "Do you know why I chose the surname *Sherbourne*?"

She shifted her weight from foot to foot, temper rising and patience thinning. "No."

"It's an Old Akkinorian word meaning *light-bringer*. It was often used by my earliest descendants—the first clans that eventually became the

Ashford family. They heard it from a prophet who foresaw the return of the gods and the restoration of the realm. It was their way of assuring one another that the best was—and is—yet to come. I personally don't believe in that, nor am I interested in the gods' return after they abandoned us, but my point is that the word means something to the Ashford name. I took it with me to Carthe because of what it means to them, to *us*. My duty has always been to my family, and I honestly believed I was doing what was best for them by staying away—so don't you dare accuse me of such dishonor, Aurelia Brentwood. It's beneath you."

Guilt flooded through her veins, but he'd already awakened her temper by then, and she knew there was no going back when her next words escaped her lips: "Say what you will about duty and family, but don't forget that your parents needed you after the shipwreck. Things might've been different if you'd stayed long enough to defend their names. Your supposed death fractured your family, and they weren't strong enough to save your parents from exile without you."

He surged back, visibly hurt and appalled, but no sound emerged when he opened his mouth to reply. She started to apologize when her temper subsided, knowing she'd overstepped her bounds, but he didn't give her the chance.

"We'll talk about this later," he said quietly, averting his gaze from hers. "Summon Halvor. We need to get our girl back."

***

Not a word was exchanged between the spouses when they met Halvor in the gardens and set out for Kanibar. Aurelia had tried suggesting that Jack stay in Akkinor—she didn't want to risk him, nor did she want the children to wake to find both their parents and their sister gone—but he ignored her.

They didn't speak during the flight to Kanibar, either. She felt him tense and heard a soft moan escape him at the beginning of the flight (he still wasn't exactly used to riding on dragonback), but that was the most he said or did for hours.

When they arrived, Aurelia half-expected to find the entire Kanish army waiting for them on the palace grounds. Instead, only a handful of soldiers were positioned around the same field where she and Halvor landed on their last trip to Kanibar.

A few of the soldiers escorted them into the palace, and as they walked up the steps to reach the front door, Aurelia noticed something that sent a chill down her spine: a stone, dragon-like gargoyle sitting still and frozen on the left side of the entrance. It didn't have a twin, so she knew it was the same creature that had taken her daughter from Akkinor.

The soldiers immediately led them to the throne room: an empty hall with a single green carpet along the center, flanked on either side by massive, ornate marble columns, which led to a short platform where King Willem sat atop a silver, emerald-encrusted throne. Soldiers stood behind the columns along either side of the hall, and one highborn man stood to the left of the king's throne.

"Where is she?" Jack demanded. "What have you done with her?"

Willem only smiled at them when he and Aurelia stopped at the base of the platform. "It's customary to kneel to the King of Kanibar in his throne room, you know."

"Is it *customary* to steal young girls from their beds and smuggle them across the continent in the middle of the night, Your Majesty?" Aurelia snapped. "Give me my daughter."

He *tsked* her. "And here I was, thinking you had a reputation for graciousness. How silly of me."

He turned and jerked his chin at the man standing to his left. The man made a motion with his hand, and as he did so, the smell of burnt nutmeg and citrus wafted through Aurelia's nostrils. She opened her mouth to protest, just to feel herself being forcibly pulled to the ground. Jack, too, was struggling to fight the mage's command. In a matter of seconds, both spouses had taken a knee before the king.

Aurelia gritted her teeth as her hands folded over her knee against her will. "You trespassed in my home and brought my daughter to your doorstep by a gods-forsaken *gargoyle,* of all things. I assure you, Your Majesty, I won't hesitate to incinerate you if you refuse to return her."

"You won't do anything of the sort while I have her. If you do, you'll never see her again. She'll burn right beside me."

Her heart lurched. "Where is she?"

Willem snapped his fingers, and in an instant, the mage reached into the inside pocket of his coat to produce a handheld mirror. He gave the mirror to Willem, who held it out so Aurelia and Jack could see the reflection. She didn't understand what he was doing until the glass shimmered and glowed. Not a second later, she saw Hyacinth's little face reflected back at her.

A strangled gasp spewed from her lips while Jack growled at her side. He was fighting the mage's spell with everything he had, but his efforts to lunge for the king were in vain. Aurelia was hardly paying attention to him, though; the only thing she could focus on was the sight of her daughter sitting on a cold stone floor, playing with wooden soldiers and humming an ancient lullaby Aurelia didn't recognize.

"Magnificent, isn't it?" the king said. "A simple spell can lead to such powerful results—yet not nearly as powerful as using something like, say, the Athys."

Aurelia's blood turned to ice. While his green eyes seemed to grin at her, she realized she didn't know how much he knew. The best scenario was that he only knew she'd used the Athys to communicate with one of her allies. The worst was that he knew *why* they'd needed to use the Athys—that he knew about the amulet.

"I won't ask you again," Aurelia warned. "Where is she?"

"Somewhere safe. For now," he added. "As you can see, I haven't touched a hair on her head. I meant what I told you several weeks ago: we don't harm our guests in Kanibar."

Jack growled again. "What do you want with her?"

"She's different from your other children, isn't she? I have friends in Akkinor who said they could smell it in her blood. Ser Dayne here, my best mage, confirmed what my friends theorized when he met her. She's a wonderful girl, you know. Very bright. I imagine you must be proud of her."

Jack struggled so ferociously that, for a moment, he appeared to rise from his kneeling position. The mage—Ser Dayne—merely nodded his head, and Jack was forced back into place again.

"As much as I'd love to have another mage on my court," Willem continued, "she's far too young. That's why I've decided to offer you a choice."

Aurelia's heart swelled with both fury and terror. "What is it?"

"It's simple, really: the girl for the dragon."

Everything around her seemed to stop. Jack ceased to struggle against his magical constraints, the torches stopped flickering, the clocks stopped ticking. Even the sound of her own heart beating in her ears seemed to fade into silence.

"Of course, this is a difficult decision to make, so I'm prepared to give you three days to decide." A grin spread over his lips. "I'm afraid I can't allow you to stay here while you think about it, though. You'll have to find other lodgings."

"We're not leaving until we see our daughter, you maniacal fool," Jack snapped. "I don't care about your silly parlor tricks—until she's in front of me, and I can see with my own eyes that she's all right, I won't believe a word you say."

Willem cocked his head to the side, studying him. "I must say, I expected more from the man who managed to bed and wed a dragon."

A guttural noise spewed from Jack's throat. "You slimy—"

"Bring her to us." Aurelia almost didn't recognize her own voice when she spoke again. "Bring her here, and let us see for ourselves that she's unharmed. When you've done so, I'll give you my answer. I don't need three days."

He blinked at her, surprised, before turning to Dayne. With one nod of his head, the mage bowed and left the throne room, the spell prevailing even in his absence.

"You must think me mad." Willem picked at his nails like he hadn't a care in the world. "Dragons are loyal to bloodlines, are they not? I know what you're thinking: it's a simple decision to trade the dragon for the girl because the beast will never be loyal to me. I'm afraid that isn't exactly true." She tensed, unintentionally revealing her curiosity, as he grinned at her reaction. "I can tell you this much: my ancestors never mated with Brentwoods. They did, however, marry into several noble families of Taundosa. You, too, have a close relationship with Taundosa—specifically, the Cristos family of Agotia. Isn't that right?"

Aurelia's breath caught in her throat. From the corner of her eye, she saw Jack watching her, his throat bobbing with anxiety as beads of sweat trickled down the sides of his face. Both knew exactly what Willem was implying: for one, he knew she wasn't a Brentwood by blood; and for another, at some point in history, his ancestors had procreated with hers. If that happened *after* Halvor's first mistress claimed him, then technically speaking, Willem bore enough Cristos blood to earn Halvor's loyalty.

She fought the urge to smile when she remembered a fact Willem clearly didn't know: Halvor was loyal to the *women* of the Cristos family, not the men. Yes, Halvor still obeyed and protected Arian, but he didn't follow Arian's commands without Aurelia's permission. She had to assume that the same logic applied to Willem.

Still, she couldn't know for sure what might happen if Willem got his hands on Halvor. Maybe Halvor would be disobedient and return to Akkinor as quickly as he could. Or maybe Willem had a plan for Halvor—a plan resembling the one Aurelia's ancestor had enacted to protect Halvor in the locket—that would make it impossible for the dragon to return to his rightful mistress.

While Aurelia gritted her teeth, staying silent to avoid taking Willem's bait, the door to the throne room opened again. She and Jack both attempted to break free of the spell to reach their daughter when she walked in alongside Willem's right-hand man. The princess gasped in delight and shouted for her parents, but when she tried to run for them, Dayne set his hand on her shoulder and pulled her back.

Other than her Kanish clothing, Hyacinth looked exactly as she had when Aurelia saw her last. She wasn't bloodied, bruised, or injured in any way. She wasn't filthy from being confined to a cell, either. She'd been washed, dressed, and styled for the day.

Jack's face was nearly purple with fury when he turned to Dayne and seethed, "Lay a hand on my daughter again, and I promise you, you'll die attempting to stuff your intestines back into your gut."

Ignoring him, Aurelia turned her teary gaze to Hyacinth and smiled. "Hi, Sisi. Are you okay?"

The princess returned her mother's smile. "I'm all right, Mama. You?"

"I'm all right, too, now that you're here."

"I've done what you asked. She's here, and she's perfectly well, as I assured you." Willem smiled cheerfully like he was hosting the Brentwoods for a celebratory feast. As Aurelia glowered at him, a paralyzing darkness cascading over her, he raised an amused eyebrow. "What say you, Your Grace?"

"I'm not in the business of making deals with people who force my submission. If you'd like me to choose, I shall only do so while standing and looking into your eyes—not while being forced to kneel so you might preserve your ego."

Something dangerous flashed in his green eyes, but it was gone as quickly as it'd come. He gestured to Dayne, who made another motion with his hand to break the spell placed on the spouses. They tried to run for Hyacinth, only to realize the spell hadn't been *entirely* broken: they were able to stand and move their arms now, but not their legs.

"Whenever you grow weary of your little spells," Jack hissed at Dayne, "I'd recommend running as fast as those puny legs can carry you. Cowardice may be the only thing capable of saving your life."

Dayne raised an amused eyebrow. "If that was meant to be a threat, it's a waste of your breath. I could kill you right now with a twitch of my nose, you blubbering buffoon."

"If you hurt him, my dragon will dedicate his existence to hunting you down. All the magic and stone walls in the realm won't be enough to protect you from him." Aurelia spoke firmly and loudly, forcing every pair of ears in the room to focus solely on her words and her words alone. "I'd like to remind you that what you've done warrants a declaration of war. My allies declared war on you when you confirmed your intentions for Dofell, but Akkinor wasn't at war with Kanibar—I was only defending my allies, as promised. Now, you've demanded that the full force of Akkinor's military respond to a direct threat on the royal family. It's bad enough that you threaten and disrespect me so proudly, but to risk a little girl in the process? My people won't show you mercy now. We defend our own in Akkinor, Your Majesty."

Willem hooted with laughter. "Tell that to your mages! So much for defending your own. You can't even call yourselves a unified nation, what with the chaos you've inflicted these last few years."

Aurelia's hand drifted into her pocket. "It's people like you who make people like them fearful of what magic can do. We wouldn't be standing here today if you'd utilized Kanibar's remaining magic to better the world instead of threatening to tear it apart." Her eyes found Dayne. "You've no right to call yourself a mage. If that were true, you wouldn't have used the incredible gift the gods granted you to assist in the kidnapping of a little girl. That alone has connected your soul to dark magic."

Dayne only glared at her. "I believe His Majesty asked for your decision."

Aurelia's fingers grazed the solid surface in her pocket as she glanced at Hyacinth, who stared curiously at her mother while she stood still and silent beside Dayne. For just a moment, Aurelia's attention faltered when she felt something else in her pocket: a folded piece of parchment. She knew it was the page she'd taken from a book in her library, but she didn't remember snatching it from beneath her pillow after Jack realized Hyacinth was gone.

"This choice you've given me is a mind game, if nothing else," the queen continued, "but on your quest to unravel me, Your Majesty, you made the unfortunate mistake of believing that my only strength is my dragon. You failed to consider that I, too, am rather fond of games."

She watched him, awaiting a response as her fingers curled around the amulet, but when a voice punctured the silence in the throne room, it wasn't Willem's.

"No." Hyacinth took a step forward, hindered from moving any further when Dayne tightened his grip on her shoulder. Her wide blue eyes met Aurelia's, frantic, as her voice lowered to a near-whisper: "Don't trust the moon yet, Mama."

Aurelia froze, lips parting in shock, as the Kanish looked between mother and daughter in search of an explanation they'd never find.

She knew it wasn't entirely rational to heed a five-year-old's warning, but Hyacinth was different from other children. That, and when Aurelia searched her daughter's gaze, she found nothing but a thousand years' worth of warnings—like Hyacinth had lived dozens of lives before this one, and each of them had banded together to deliver the same message.

Aurelia's fingers relaxed on the amulet before she knew what she was doing. She paused to think for a moment, knowing she could do nothing but follow her gut now that her only surefire escape had been thwarted.

When the answer struck her, she knew immediately that it was the right path to take—but it left her feeling sick to her stomach, anyhow.

"My daughter is going home to Akkinor," she announced. "Release her into my husband's custody at once."

Willem grinned. With one wave of his hand, Dayne released Hyacinth, and broke the spell keeping Aurelia and Jack in place. Hyacinth bolted into Jack's arms, sending him to his knees as he held her to his chest, while Aurelia kept her attention trained on the king.

"You won't be getting my dragon, either," she continued. Instantly, the soldiers lining the perimeter of the room aimed their swords at her. She ignored them to focus on Willem, who only watched her curiously. "There's no honor in a broken promise, and Akkinorians are nothing without our honor. I'll respect the deal we made, Your Majesty—but instead of Halvor, I propose myself."

Jack, still holding Hyacinth, rose from the ground and marched up to her. "What are you doing?" he hissed. His eyes burned with a fire more fearsome than even Halvor was capable of emitting. If Aurelia didn't know him, she would've been terrified of him. "Have you gone *mad*?"

She ignored him, knowing she'd break into a thousand pieces if she addressed him. "You sent me a gift recently, Your Majesty. Your note suggested that you have an interest in me—that you wish we could've united our forces when we had the chance. Akkinor will never answer to you, but..." She trailed off when discomfort thickened her throat. "But if you truly hold me in such high regard, then perhaps you and I can come to an arrangement of some sort that doesn't involve my family or my dragon."

Willem tapped his fingers on the armrest of his throne. "I must admit, you've surprised me—but it's a welcomed surprise. I've been longing for a partner, but what I need more than anything is an heir. And we all know how fertile your womb is." Aurelia's face grew hot while Jack growled profanities, but Willem ignored him to focus only on Aurelia. "My only concern, as you can imagine, is what the dragon will do to me when he realizes I've confined you here."

She swallowed. "My husband will take our daughter home on dragonback—"

"No." Jack shook his head, still clutching Hyacinth to his chest, as he shook with the fury of a sellsword forced to watch another claim his bounty. "Try again. I'm not going anywhere without you."

"—and Halvor will stay in Akkinor to protect my family." She swallowed again, her throat feeling like sandpaper, and ignored Jack's protests. "Princess Halle is next in line to claim him. He'll serve her moving forward."

"What a wonderful turn of events!" Willem stood from his throne and clapped, making her ears rattle with each thunderous sound. "Now, both of our kingdoms shall have what they've always wanted: a queen and heirs for Kanibar, and a reigning king for Akkinor. How splendid!"

"Aurelia—" Jack started, reaching for her.

"Escort the king and the child to the dragon," Willem told his soldiers. "Don't return until they're out of sight."

As the soldiers closed in, Aurelia kissed Hyacinth's cheek. "I love you, sweet girl. Mind your father." Then her eyes flickered over to Jack, who was staring at her in a way that made her want to vomit onto her shoes. "I'm sorry, Jack. Give the children my love when you return. I'll...I'll be home soon. Trust me."

Quickly and nonchalantly, she took the folded parchment from her pocket and pressed it against his palm. His fingers wrapped around it immediately as she lowered her voice and brought her lips to his ear.

"Send this to Arian and the others," she whispered. "They'll know what to do with it." She pressed her lips to the side of his face, squeezing her stinging eyes shut and willing herself to keep her emotions in check. "I love you, Jack, with everything I am and everything I'll ever be. Please trust me."

He clenched his jaw, nodded, and offered her a smile he didn't mean. "I do. Always." Then he turned to Willem, a veil of darkness contorting his face again, and spat on the floor. "My wife may have a dragon's soul, but I have a dragon's spirit—particularly when it comes to holding grudges. He and I both will hunt you for as long as it takes. Fortunately, he's rather obedient to me nowadays. I'm certain he'll let me do the honors when it comes to carving you up like the pig you are."

Willem only grinned. "Keep dreaming that impossible dream, Your Highness. It'll be the only thing that keeps you going while your woman finds warmth in my embrace every evening."

Aurelia didn't get the chance to retaliate against the threat. Jack growled and bolted—still holding Hyacinth—but immediately stumbled backwards, somehow keeping himself from falling, when Dayne sent a minor wave of power in his direction. The warning didn't mean much to Jack, but the way Hyacinth whimpered and clutched him for safety certainly did. He paused, glancing between his terrified wife and daughter, before closing his eyes and sighing.

"Ahh. Surrender." Aurelia heard the grin in Willem's voice while she stared at Jack. "As powerful as it is poetic, in my opinion."

Jack opened his eyes, gritting his teeth, and turned to Aurelia. There was so much she wanted to say to him—and he to her, by the look of him—but instead, he merely forced a smile and offered her a few parting words:

"I'll keep your seat warm, Lily dear. I...I love you eternally."

She smiled, forcing herself to maintain her composure as she mouthed those three words back to him, while he reluctantly allowed the soldiers to escort him out of the throne room. By the time the doors closed behind them, another handful of soldiers had surrounded Aurelia. One held a set of shackles in his hand.

"Just a precaution. You understand." Willem smirked as the soldier secured the restraints on her wrists. He lowered himself onto his throne again and smiled at her. "We'll have such a lovely time together, Your Grace. You'll see."

Intermission

A vibrant, pulsating ball of light—iridescent white with a deep blue center—beamed above Arian Cristos's palm. He closed his eyes, the heat from the light warming his face, and focused his energy on the task at hand.

As a mage, he could channel the souls of his blood relatives, both alive and dead, at will. Souls were intangible, of course, but they weren't summoned to be touched or toyed with: they were summoned so mages like Arian could ensure that wherever his loved ones were in the universe, they were all right.

Not at all to his surprise, he found nothing when he willed the soul to offer him some sort of insight as to where its human form was located. He hadn't found anything in over thirty years, despite checking every day, while searching for his sister.

He wondered if she ever checked on him, too. After all, Anysa Cristos was also a mage, and just as powerful as Arian. But did she still care for him? Would she even bother checking if he was still alive?

It didn't matter. Since she disappeared over three decades ago, she hadn't made any effort to return home, or send any sort of evidence to attest to her wellbeing.

Sighing, Arian waved his hand to send the ball of light away, saying goodbye to Anysa's soul as he did once every season. He pinched the bridge of his nose, heartache threatening to incapacitate him, before summoning another soul to his study: one composed of more colors than white and blue, and one belonging to the closest thing he had left to his other sister, Katryna.

Aurelia Brentwood's soul looked exactly as it did each and every time Arian checked on her. He hadn't done so since the day she arrived at the Palace of Taundosa seeking his assistance—the day she learned that she was as much a Cristos as she was a Brentwood. He summoned her soul often before that, though, but only after Edmund and Cressida were no longer around to keep her safe. While the Queen of Akkinor ruled for five years by herself, the uncle she hadn't yet met conjured her soul nearly every day for fear that her own people would try to kill her.

They *had* tried to kill her, but she had prevailed; Arian wasn't worried about that anymore. What worried him now was the destiny she was meant to fulfill on behalf of the gods, and the piece of divine power she'd since started carrying in her pocket.

Arian hadn't told her about his concerns regarding the amulet—he knew his opinion would sway her in one way or another, and she needed to make this kind of decision on her own. He didn't believe in Edea's curse as strongly as others did, but he knew what often became of those who meddled with the power of the gods. He could only hope that whatever she did, she did wisely and with just intentions.

Now, as he studied her soul, he searched every inch of the spherical light for signs that she'd used the amulet: a pinpoint of darkness, a shadow, a sudden emptiness. Relief washed over him like a tidal wave when he found nothing of the sort. She was still as good as she'd always been, and he prayed that much never changed—even if she were forced to use the amulet.

As Aurelia's soul disappeared from the study, a sudden pain struck Arian in the gut. He winced and doubled over in his chair as he brought a trembling hand to his side. The pain was so severe that he checked his hand for blood, thinking he'd been wounded somehow. There was no blood to be seen, though, so he merely chugged from a bottle of rum in his desk drawer to ease the pain.

He sunk back into his chair while the pain slowly subsided, and as he did so, knuckles rapped on the door. He wiped the rum from his mouth and called for the knocker to enter. He straightened up when Reyna Caltheos, Queen of Taundosa, glided into the study and closed the door behind her.

"Your Majesty." He furrowed his eyebrows and frowned when he saw the panicked look on her face and the absence of color in her cheeks. "Has something happened?"

"I just received urgent news from Akkinor." She swallowed and took a few steps forward so she could set an opened letter on his desk. "You need to read this."

Still frowning, Arian lifted the letter and muttered a curse when a separate piece of parchment, folded into a square no larger than a chestnut, fluttered from the letter and onto the floor. When he picked it up, he turned to Reyna and raised his brows.

"What is this?"

She shrugged and chewed on her fingernails. "It seems to be a page from a book. It's unimportant, though. Read the letter."

Obeying, Arian set the folded parchment aside and scanned the letter. The more Arian read, the worse the pain in his gut became.

For the eyes of Her Majesty, Reyna Caltheos of Taundosa, and His Lordship, Arian Cristos of Agotia:

I write to you on behalf of His Royal Highness, Jack Ashford, King Consort of Akkinor. Less than two nights ago, Princess Hyacinth was kidnapped from her bed by a Kanish spy. The spy, also a mage, delivered her to King Willem's palace after enchanting a gargoyle. Her Grace and the King Consort flew to fetch her immediately, and Her Grace was forced to offer herself as King Willem's captive to protect both Halvor and the young princess.

In response, His Royal Highness has officially declared war on Kanibar, and we are now preparing our troops for battle. We shall proceed with our efforts to uncover the spy's identity and apprehend any other Kanish spies lurking in Akkinor. Unfortunately, we have no way of reaching the queen in a timely fashion while so far away. If there's anything you can do for her, Akkinor will assist you in any way we can.

Please relay this message to our allies in Bozar and Runeia, too. It's imperative that we unite our strengths to bring our queen home.

Sincerely,

Lady Marilla Page, Advisor to Her Grace, Aurelia Brentwood, Queen of Akkinor.

Arian sunk back in his chair, chest tightening. "Gods be good."

"She'll be all right." Reyna's voice wavered just long enough for Arian to sense her doubt. "He won't harm her if he knows what's good for him. He won't make it easy for us to retrieve her, either. She may have to find her own way, and without the dragon..."

As she trailed off, he swallowed the lump in his throat and reached for the folded parchment. He scanned it quickly—it appeared to have been taken from some sort of biographical text—but Aurelia hadn't left any notes or hidden messages on either side of the page, so he struggled to understand why it'd been sent to Taundosa.

"Does the name *Althaia Pharos* mean anything to you?" he asked his queen. She shook her head. "It isn't familiar to me, either, but..." He trailed off as he reread the front and back sides of the page. "Do you suppose she could be connected to Dofell's successor?"

Reyna's eyes flashed. "It's certainly possible."

"This came from Aurelia. I'm sure of it." Arian held the page up by his head and clenched his jaw, worry eating away at him as he imagined his niece in King Willem's claws. "We need to summon the others. There's work to be done."

BOOK TWO: SACRIFICE

Waking up to find one's child missing from their bed was among the most excruciating things a parent might face. As it turns out, having to leave the woman one loved behind as a captive, by her request, was among the most excruciating things a husband might face.

Jack had experienced both of those things in just one day. Maybe in even just a few hours—he lost track. It was a miracle he hadn't unraveled from the inside out.

A million different things ran through his mind as he was escorted away from his wife and King Willem. She told him to trust that she had a plan for her escape, but how could she? Her dragon was taking him and their daughter home to Akkinor, and she wouldn't be able to roam freely throughout Kanibar in search of another means to escape. Aurelia would need a miracle to flee Willem's clutches, and that wasn't likely in Kanibar.

He didn't know what bothered him more: the fact that he'd been powerless to stop what had happened, or the fact that he'd walked away without a fight, knowing the King of Kanibar hoped to make a queen and a mother out of Jack's wife. He would've slaughtered everyone in his wake if it wasn't for his daughter. He knew if he wasn't on his best behavior, Willem's soldiers would've killed the pair of them.

Taking his anger out on the soldiers wouldn't have done much good, anyway. Jack might've been able to defeat a dozen soldiers in hand-to-hand combat, if the gods were kind, but he didn't stand a chance against Willem's mage. So long as Willem and Dayne had Aurelia under their thumbs, Jack couldn't have done a thing to save her.

As they were leaving the palace, Hyacinth had looked up at him while he carried her and asked, "Why isn't Mama coming?"

A sharp pang pierced his gut. "She'll meet us at home later, sweetheart."

If she'd known he was lying, she didn't show it. She merely asked if she could hold his hand and walk to Halvor, and he obliged. With his free hand, he examined the piece of parchment Aurelia had slipped him before they were separated, only to find that it was a page from a book. But there were no notes or underlined sentences to help him figure out why it was so important, and he wasn't particularly adept at making heads or tails out of the things he read, anyway. He memorized the title on the page—the name *Althaia Pharos*—then slipped it back into his pocket, knowing he wouldn't glance at it again until it was time to deliver the parchment to Arian.

The soldiers saw Jack and Hyacinth to Halvor, and, fortunately, they didn't pull any tricks when it was time for the duo to leave. Jack half-expected them to wrench he and Hyacinth apart before imprisoning them somewhere in Kanibar, but he assumed they were too fearful of Halvor to even attempt it. They might have been cruel and slimy, but they weren't stupid.

Only when they were firmly perched on Halvor's back did Jack realize something: he didn't know how to control the beast. He'd seen Aurelia— and Halle, for that matter—do it a thousand times before, but neither he nor Hyacinth had Cristos blood in their veins, and he wasn't so certain that Halvor would respond to them like he responded to the others.

"Damn it." He ran his free hand over Halvor's scaly back while the other held Hyacinth's abdomen. He didn't know who he was talking to— himself, his daughter, or the beast—when he added, "I don't know how to do this."

Hyacinth craned her neck to the side and smiled at him. "It's okay, Papa. I can show you."

A pit formed in his stomach when she tapped Halvor's scales, exactly as she'd seen Aurelia do time and time again. He realized then that she didn't need Cristos blood to control the dragon: she was a Cristos in every way that mattered, and Halvor knew it as well as anyone.

When they lifted into the air, Jack held Hyacinth as close to his chest as he could, trying with every ounce of strength to keep from vomiting. Hyacinth laughed and squealed in delight with every turn, dip, and dive Halvor made, and all the while, her father wiped tears from his cheeks before she could notice.

Hyacinth fell asleep eventually, but Jack certainly didn't. He was awake to hear every wail, moan, and shriek bellowing from Halvor's throat. The sounds didn't do anything to ease Jack's sorrow, but he found a bit of solace in knowing that Halvor was in as much pain as he was.

The princess woke once more on the flight, but by the time Halvor landed in the gardens at the Palace of Akkinor, she was asleep again. She'd have trouble sleeping that night, but Jack knew she needed the rest: she probably hadn't slept properly while in Kanibar, leagues away from her father's bedtime stories and the sound of her siblings' snoring.

There weren't many guards posted around the palace, as the majority of them were out scouring the country for Hyacinth. As Jack carried his sleeping daughter through the halls, he found a weary and exhausted Ansyl, who had just returned from a search party. Ansyl stared at Hyacinth, bewildered, before immediately asking for the queen.

Jack sighed. "Call the Assembly. I'll explain everything once we've gathered."

"Only three members are in the palace at present," Ansyl told him. "The others are across the country informing our nobility of the call to arms and overseeing preparations for the fight to come."

"Summon whoever you can, then."

Ansyl nodded, bowed, and rushed off to fulfill Jack's request. Jack ran a tired hand through his hair, using his other arm to keep a snoozing Hyacinth steady against him, and searched the halls for a spare soldier. When he found one, he instructed the man to spread word to everyone of the princess's safe return, and to summon them back to the palace at once. He watched the soldier scurry off, then made his way to the throne room to meet with Aurelia's advisors.

A long, cushioned bench sat against the wall outside of the throne room, so he carefully set Hyacinth down before kneeling beside her. He brushed a lock of clammy blonde hair from her forehead, feeling the urge to smile at the way she hummed in her sleep, but unable to summon the expression without crying. She may not have come from Aurelia, but even the littlest things—the humming, the darting of her eyes beneath their lids, the scrunching of her nose as she dreamt—reminded him of his wife.

Ansyl breezed by him with three members of the Assembly in tow: Lord Frederick Baylor, Lady Marilla Page, and Lady Emilia Litten. Jack sighed, kissed his daughter on the temple, and joined them inside the throne room, leaving Hyacinth to be watched over by a handmaiden.

A table had been brought to the throne room so the monarchy could study maps and plans for the upcoming war in Carthe, so Ansyl and the three advisors stood gathered around it when Jack joined them. He stood at the head of the table, ignoring the feel of their eyes burning holes through his skull, and scrubbed a nervous hand over his face. The motion was so aggressive that his spiky whiskers against his palm felt like sandpaper.

His wife would've told him it was time for a shave.

"Thank you for coming so quickly." He cleared his throat and tried again when his voice, hoarse and weak, didn't sound like his own. "As you saw moments ago, Hyacinth is safe and sound. That isn't why I've called you here. The matter in Carthe has escalated—it's time Akkinor officially declares war on Kanibar."

The advisors exchanged worried, confused expressions before Lady Litten asked, "Is that the wisest idea? Akkinor as a whole has no reason to declare war. The Carthinians have already responded to the Kanish threat, and Akkinor is only contributing to the fight because the terms of our alliances demand it. What you're proposing has major consequences for Carthe *and* for our people—who, let's not forget, have barely recovered from the last conflict."

"It isn't worth making more trouble." Lady Page shook her head. "The Kanish are stubborn enough as it is. Declaring war on them to strengthen our other alliances is a fool's gambit. As important as it is that we respect the terms of our alliances, this is more than our people can handle."

"We can't proceed with the efforts without Her Grace's word, anyway," Lord Baylor added. "The queen is solely responsible for declaring war. We may voice our opinions on the matter, but we can do nothing without her official decree. Not even you, Your Highness, can—"

"Enough!" When Jack slammed his hands on the table, all four of the advisors winced and stepped back. Knowing he'd overreacted, he paused and took a long, deep breath. "I'm sure you're all wondering where the queen is. After I tell you, you'll find that declaring war on Kanibar is the only option we have right now."

He told them the story from start to finish. As he explained the bit about what had happened with Hyacinth, they watched him curiously with a bit of disbelief in their gazes—as if they couldn't comprehend why Willem would kidnap the princess, knowing it would result in Akkinor declaring war on Kanibar. Jack didn't say anything about Hyacinth's powers, but as soon as he mentioned the bargain Willem had offered, the advisors' disbelief transformed into rage, resulting in a series of scoffs and scowls they couldn't withhold.

When Jack finally spoke of Aurelia's sacrifice, it was like the air was sucked out of the room. Some bowed their heads, defeated, while others closed their eyes, as if there was somewhere they could retreat to. By the time he stopped talking, though, half of them were trembling with rage, and the other half looked sick to their stomachs—a perfect combination of exactly what Jack was feeling.

"My word." Lady Page fanned her face with her hand, mouth twisted with disbelief. "We shall...We shall have to speak with the princess about what happened when she was taken. She may remember something about her kidnapper. There's no doubting that Kanish spies have been—and possibly still are—lurking nearby. We must have them found and apprehended before they attempt something else. Our efforts to identify them thus far have been in vain, apparently."

"I'll speak with her after she's settled in," Jack muttered. "For now, I need each of you to assist me. Lady Page, you'll write to our Carthinian allies about what's happened. Send the raven to Taundosa—they'll pass the message along to the others." He reached into his breast pocket and handed her the slip of parchment Aurelia had given him in Kanibar. "Ensure this is sent to Taundosa, too."

As Lady Page accepted the parchment, Jack turned to face the others. "Lord Baylor, you'll write to your fellow advisors and the five reigning nobles of Akkinor. Send the fastest ravens we have, both of you. And Lady Litten, I'd like you to meet with our generals and officers here in the Folly. Have them send word to our military leaders in the other kingdoms, too. We need all of our soldiers to march for the Folly immediately."

The trio nodded as Jack turned to Ansyl at his right. "As for you, my friend...I need you to send word to the monastery. I'd like the priests to select a trusted mage under their protection—lowborn or highborn, I don't give a damn. That individual will be tasked with protecting the royal children alongside our soldiers. We need every bit of protection we can get after what's happened."

Ansyl tipped his head. "Understood. What will you do in the meantime?"

Jack pinched the bridge of his nose as a migraine overwhelmed him. "I'll write up the official declaration of war and send it to Kanibar. I shall have to think of a plan for Halvor, too. He'll be restless without Aurelia, but we need him here and prepared to fly to war. He'll require a vast amount of sustenance, too, before we bring him to battle. I need to find a way to feed him that won't result in our cattlemen losing their livelihoods."

"And what of Her Grace?" Lord Baylor asked. Of everyone in the room, he'd known Aurelia the longest; Jack could see in his eyes that Lord Baylor wasn't thinking of the queen he served, but of the innocent little girl he'd met long ago. "Shouldn't we begin plotting for her rescue? We have the dragon, Your Highness. It'd be a simple feat for you to take him to Kanibar and use him to demand the queen's return."

"The king has tricks of his own—some of which I've seen, and some of which I can only imagine. Should he surprise us somehow by attempting to incapacitate Halvor, all will be lost." Jack clenched his jaw and shook his head, livid at his own incompetence at a time when his wife needed him most. "Lord Cristos and the others will have ideas for us to muddle over once they've found out. They know the king and Kanibar better than any of us—even you, Ansyl. You've been gone too long."

The Lord Hand nodded in agreement. "I served a low-ranking nobleman for several years, but I spent most of my life just fighting to see another day. Lord Cristos and the others may not have much luck in this area, either, but with their connections, their odds are better than mine ever were."

"I agree. Now, before I send you off, I'd like to discuss—"

"Papa?"

Jack stopped when a little voice echoed throughout the throne room. All five pairs of eyes turned to spot a groggy, yawning Hyacinth standing in the doorway, looking as dazed and disheveled as Jack felt.

He smiled. "Hello, my little love. I'm glad to see you've woken. I think your brother and sisters are most eager to see you."

She beamed, then offered a little wave when she saw Ansyl. "Hi, Ansyl."

He smiled. "Hi, Sisi. Welcome home."

Hyacinth giggled. "Thank you."

The handmaiden who'd been watching her scampered over to her, apparently having turned her back on the sleeping princess for a moment too long, and fumbled over an apology when she met Jack's eyes. He only nodded to the young woman, who set her hand on Hyacinth's shoulder and urged the princess to follow her. Hyacinth hesitated for a moment, clearly not wanting to leave her father, but reluctantly followed the handmaiden out of the room.

While Jack watched them go, momentarily forgetting about the advisors waiting for his next word, he realized something that made his stomach churn: he never *actually* thought he'd ever have to play the part of king. He never once imagined that something would happen to hinder Aurelia's ability to lead. To him, she was immortal, untouchable—but she wasn't, was she? Dragon or not, the current situation proved that much.

He wanted nothing more than to be with his children after what had happened, but he couldn't. Not now, when his wife, his queen, was gone, leaving him to fulfill his role as King Consort of Akkinor. He did not feel prepared in the slightest.

Guilt flooded through his veins when he recalled the harsh words he spat at her just the night before. What he was feeling right now, Aurelia must've felt every waking second of her life—every time the line of duty pulled her away from her family, every time the fate of innocent people rested on her shoulders. He'd given her hell and more, yet here he was, needing to step into her much-too-big shoes.

He'd never felt like he'd failed her before, but he certainly did now.

XXVI

W hen Willem's soldiers escorted her out of the throne room, Aurelia expected to be brought into the dungeon—certainly not a beautiful, spacious suite that rivaled her own back home in Akkinor. She had a real bed to sleep on, a writing desk, a wardrobe, and a sitting area. Even the washroom and the closet were exquisite compared to her own, and no aspect of her new lodgings suggested she was being held captive.

Though, the restraints on her wrists begged to differ.

The soldiers brought her into the room, ensured her shackles were secure, and left without a word. She knew they'd be standing outside of her door at all times, but they locked the door from the outside, anyway. Only then did she notice the bars on her windows, too.

As the reality of her situation hit her like a punch to the gut, she sat on the edge of the bed and let her head fall onto her hands. She wanted to cry, but she'd done quite enough of that since arriving in Kanibar—her tear ducts were empty.

The worst part wasn't that she'd volunteered to be in this—albeit luxurious—prison cell. No, that part had been simple: it was the only way (other than using the amulet, of course) to ensure both Hyacinth and Halvor were kept far away from Willem's clutches.

The worst of it was that she didn't know what Willem had planned for her. He'd all but stated in his letter that he was smitten with her—if not with her, then with the idea of her pumping out his heirs—but was there any truth to that? Did he plan to force her hand and further his legacy, or was that idea simply a shield for something even more nefarious? Was he planning to have his mage get inside her head, influencing her bit by bit each day, so she'd be forced to command Halvor to attack her allies instead of defend them?

Regardless of what he had in store, Aurelia didn't plan on staying long enough to find out. He'd have to let her out of the suite eventually, and when he did, she could study every possible means of escaping. She was no stranger to disguising herself and navigating through unfamiliar lands, either. She wasn't worried about what would happen after she fled the palace, particularly with allies to run to, so finding a way out of Willem's fortress had to be her top priority. The rest would fall into place when the time came.

She wasn't particularly worried about what was happening at home in her absence, either. Jack was now the acting King of Akkinor, and other than Ansyl, there was nobody she trusted more to serve as her voice. The two of them would be fine, especially with the Assembly at their disposal; but if Jack let his emotions get the best of him, nothing good would come of it. She had to trust that he'd do what was best for the country, not for her.

The door opened, startling her, as two handmaidens entered without so much as curtsying. "His Majesty has asked us to prepare you for supper," the taller of the pair told her. "He requests your presence at his table."

"As his guest or his prisoner?"

No reply. She didn't move an inch until the handmaidens took her by the elbows and pulled her up from the bed to guide her into the washroom. She wasn't particularly useful with her arms partially restrained, so she didn't feel bad for making it difficult for them when she stood still and mute as they undressed her. One set a kettle of hot water over the hearth, while the other drizzled lavender oil and sprinkled bathing salts into the half-filled copper tub. Aurelia stood covering her modesty as best she could, naked and ignored, as the handmaidens conversed like she wasn't there at all.

After adding hot water to the tub, they paused to let it cool before they helped her step inside. She spotted her discarded clothing piled on the floor, and when she remembered the amulet in her pocket, she asked the handmaidens to excuse her so she could use the chamber pot. They reluctantly left her alone in the washroom, muttering something about prudish Akkinorians as they walked away, and had the decency to close the door behind them. She retrieved the amulet and hid it in the only place she could find in the washroom: a clay pot filled with bath salts. The handmaidens had already used the salts, and even if they went back for more, the amulet was buried too deep for them to find it. She'd come back for it later and think of a better hiding spot, but for now, this would have to do.

Aurelia relieved herself after the amulet was hidden—both because she needed to secure the ruse if they happened to check the chamber pot, and because she hadn't done so since she left Akkinor—then called for the handmaidens when she finished.

When they returned, they helped her into the tub, ignoring the ear-piercing sound of the chains on her shackles clattering against the copper. She tried to insist that she was capable of bathing herself, but they wouldn't have it. They continued chatting as they each grabbed a sponge to wash her body, her face, her hair, her fingernails. They scrubbed until she was red and raw, ignoring her protests, and made faces at her as if she were a peasant covered in filth, rather than a queen caked in nothing but tears.

After washing her, the handmaidens helped Aurelia out of the tub and wrapped her in a fluffy green dressing robe. They sat her at the vanity in the washroom and immediately moved on to their next tasks: the taller one pinned up her still-sopping hair, and the shorter one slathered a cream over her body that reminded the queen of the elderly women in the Folly, who used numerous perfumes at once to mask the smell of their rotting teeth.

As the tall handmaiden slathered a much-too-dark red blush over Aurelia's cheeks, the queen stared at their reflections in the mirror and asked, "What are your names?"

The shorter one scoffed. "We're under no obligation to answer that."

"I can call you *the one with the snaggletooth* and *the one with the foul odor*, if you'd like—or you can just give me your names."

The short one brought a hand to her mouth and flushed crimson. "Eira."

"Eira. All right." Aurelia looked at the other, who smelled like she'd just been rolling around in the pigsty. "And you?"

"Nyla."

"It's lovely to meet you both."

Nyla snorted loudly. "You insult us, then you say it's lovely to meet us. That's quite an odd way to make introductions."

"I treat others as they treat me, for the most part. You're clearly incapable of showing respect for a queen, so perhaps you can show kindness to a fellow woman. Is that too much to ask?"

"You're in no position to be asking for anything."

Aurelia laughed. "All right, then. If your king wishes to make me his queen like I believe he does, then I'd expect his employees to be a bit more courteous with me. It'd be awfully uncomfortable for all of us if you were to attend to my needs in the future after how callously you've treated me thus far. Don't you think?"

The handmaidens exchanged worried looks, but they didn't say anything more as they finished preparing her for dinner. She wanted to scoff at herself when she saw her reflection in the mirror. She was certain the way they'd painted her face was meant to be a jest, not a reflection of Kanish beauty standards: her face was almost white, her cheeks and lips bright red, and her eyes adorned with heavy green shadow and thick black liner. They'd clearly exacerbated their impression of what highborn Akkinorian women looked like, but she wasn't sure if it was to make a fool out of her, or because they genuinely believed that such an appearance was commonplace in her country.

Another servant—a man—arrived holding a garment box. To her understanding, it was an outfit that the average highborn Kanish woman tended to wear: a plain white dress to wear over her underthings, then a thin, emerald gown with billowing sleeves on top of that. The gown was more like a robe, what with it being open in the front, and both sides were held together by an ornate golden belt that hugged her waist just a bit too tightly. The garment was adorned with patterns woven in golden thread, every design paying homage to an aspect of Kanish culture.

As the handmaidens helped her into a pair of much-too-high golden heels, a soldier arrived in the doorway and cleared his throat.

"The king is ready for you now."

Aurelia sighed. "Lovely."

***

"What a vision you've become!"

Aurelia heard Willem's exclamation before she saw him. When the soldier brought her to the dining hall, the first thing she saw was the massive table that took up most of the room. She barely noticed Willem standing at its head on the other side of the room, clapping for her like she was a winning racehorse he'd bet on.

She said nothing as the soldier escorted her to the king. Willem, grinning, pulled out the chair directly to his left and waited until she was seated before tucking it in. He reclaimed his chair when she was situated, leaning his elbow on the armrest and pressing his face against his hand as he admired her. One finger pushed the skin of his cheek upward towards his temple, his thumb tucked under his chin, as his middle finger sat nestled between his lips.

She did her best to ignore him as she tried to find an agreeable position for her arms. Every time she moved, her chains hit the edge of the table, causing a sharp clanging noise to rattle her eardrums. She wondered how

245

he expected her to eat and drink without causing a ruckus—all things considered, she still had a fair amount of control over her movements, but she couldn't help it if the chains shrieked against her dinnerware every time she reached for her chalice or exchanged cutlery.

He spoke again when he saw her shifting: "Comfortable?"

"Hardly."

"Hah!" He dropped his hand onto the table, making the cutlery rattle, and yelled over his shoulder, "Bring the wine!" In an instant, servants arrived to fill their cups. "Leave us until the first course is served. We wish to be alone."

Aurelia swallowed as every servant and soldier in the hall bowed and left. "This is quite the large table you have here." She raised an eyebrow. "Are you compensating for something, Your Majesty?"

He stared at her for a minute, flabbergasted, before hooting with laughter. "I must admit, I'm pleased that I accepted your offer. A dragon would've been a lovely asset, but his presence wouldn't bring me nearly as much joy as yours."

She resisted the urge to snap at him, instead choosing cordiality. "I'm glad I amuse you. This would be a terrible arrangement otherwise. Speaking of arrangements—have you already planned our nuptials? I assume I was right about your interest in me, since you've made no effort to deny it. And will you wait until we've married to force me into carrying your heirs, or will you leave your mark on me sooner? I don't believe you have the patience to wait—especially since I've lost my purity. Have you ever been with a woman who's birthed four children? I must warn you, my body is different than it was five years ago. I'd just *hate* for you to be disappointed."

"There's nothing so beautiful as the body of a woman who's brought new life into the universe. If anything, I find you more desirable now than I might've five years ago." His lips curled into a smile, leaving her disheartened that she'd failed to get under his skin. "And as much as I love to hear you speak so crassly about our happy future, I have to disappoint. Here in Kanibar, men wait for a woman's blessing before laying a finger on her. I have every intention of respecting the customs of my country. You have my word that I won't touch you—or force you to marry me—until *you* desire *me*, too."

Aurelia snorted. "You know as well as I do that your, ah, *chivalrous* offer will amount to nothing. I love my husband, and I'd never dream of replacing him with the likes of you. You may force my submission to achieve what you desire, but you will *never* part my soul from his."

"Hmm." Willem's emerald eyes sparkled. "We'll see."

Two servants entered the dining hall, and each set a bowl before Aurelia and Willem. In the time it took for her to recognize what she was being served—broth, lamb, and vegetables—the servants were gone again.

"Not hungry?" He smiled when she refused to lift her spoon. She *was* hungry, but she had no appetite for sharing a meal with Willem—nor did she want to risk seeing the pleasure in his eyes every time her restraints clanged against her bowls and plates. "Never the matter. You'll be desperate for a meal, eventually." He took a bite, chewed, and swallowed. "I want to tell you that you've raised little Sisi remarkably. She's a clever thing. Tell me—is it any different, raising a child who isn't your own?"

Aurelia stilled. "I beg your pardon?"

"You needn't be shy with me, darling. I know she isn't yours."

"I don't know what you're talking about."

"You do, but that's all right. You can act the fool until you're ready to admit the truth." He smirked and swallowed a mouthful of wine. "You know, I'm quite familiar with your country's hero, Oleander. He famously said that Akkinor will only thrive while a Brentwood sits the throne. Do you believe that?"

"Most of us do."

"Then I should hope you're prepared for the turmoil your country will face after your death—the same sort of turmoil you've already faced throughout your reign."

She raised an eyebrow, still refusing to touch her food. "How do you mean?"

"Your eldest—Halle, isn't it?—she hasn't any Brentwood blood in her veins. Not a drop of it. Her mother has more peasant blood than royal."

Her stomach dropped to her knees. The events of the day suggested he knew Aurelia's most damning secret, but now he was confirming it.

And throwing it right in her face.

"I believe you're mistaken," she said coolly.

Willem laughed. "No, I'm not. But say what you will, Your Grace. We've all the time in the world to find common ground." At her silence, he continued, "Now, I'm certain you're wondering what your life here may look like. I have no intention of keeping my future bride confined to her bedchamber at all times of the day. That's no way to start a happy life together. You're free to explore the palace as you please, but only while accompanied by your personal guard. Ser Rhys will be stuck to your side at all times like a fly to sugar. You'll meet him tomorrow."

"I imagine that freedom doesn't apply to the outdoors?"

"No, it doesn't. I do apologize—I know how fond you are of nature."
He finished his soup and his wine before calling for the servants to deliver
the next course. "I doubt you know this, so I'll do you the courtesy of
telling you. The shackles around your wrists are imbedded with *novellir*.
Do you know what that is?" She shook her head. "It's a type of metal once
found in the Dofelli mines. They haven't found an ounce of it in decades.
Kanibar has a limited supply of it, but most can find it at illegal markets
nowadays. Not like it matters much to the general population,
though: novellir contains properties that bind magic. A mage can't use
their powers while novellir touches their skin."

"I'm not a mage, Your Majesty."

"Oh, I'm aware. You see, the wonderful thing about novellir is that it
doesn't simply prevent a mage from using their powers—it restricts the
use of magic down to its very foundation. Even magical creatures, when
bound with novellir, are rendered as powerless as the average cat or dog.
Those shackles are probably the only thing keeping your dragon from
laying siege to my kingdom to rescue you. Your bond with him is
nonexistent now. He can't feel your pain, sense your presence, or respond
to your call. For all he knows, you've been lost to oblivion."

In other words, she thought, *I am completely, utterly alone here.*

The one living being with the power to rescue her, without fail, was
entirely out of reach. But that didn't worry her so much. The moment she
found a way out of the shackles—and she would—Halvor would sense that
she needed him, and he'd be descending on Kanibar before the king had
the chance to notice Aurelia's abandoned restraints.

Willem continued his attempts at small talk for the remainder of the
meal, and Aurelia responded with just enough to keep him satisfied. If she
didn't answer, he didn't care; he simply moved on to something else,
hoping to find a topic that would either rile or interest her. He didn't seem
to have a preference for how she reacted to him, so long as she was reacting
somehow. Even an unconscious twitching of her lips or fiddling of her
fingers felt like enough to excite him.

When the last course was taken away, Willem complained about eating
too much, while Aurelia ignored the sharp hunger pains in her stomach.
She'd lost her appetite after the day's events, but now that mealtime had
come and gone, she regretted not eating *something*.

"Breakfast is served exactly one hour after sunrise. I have an audience
each morning at that time, so you shall have to dine alone," the king told
her. "I've asked the servants to situate you in the morning room for
breakfast, luncheon, and teatime. We'll dine together for dinner each
night, though."

Aurelia sighed. "How invigorating."

Willem smiled. "You shall long for my company eventually, Aurelia of Akkinor. You'll see."

XXVII

At the very least, Aurelia wasn't being treated like a criminal by her captors.

Eira and Nyla may not have been the personable sort, but they looked after her exactly as her own lady's maids did. They undressed her, washed her face, unpinned her hair, and helped her into nightclothes before settling her into bed after dinner. The two women, plus the rest of the palace staff, were instructed by Willem to attend to her every need like they would for the king himself. The soldiers stationed outside of her door might've been there to keep her confined rather than to keep her safe, but their general presence wasn't so different from life at home, either.

She'd checked on the amulet in the pot of bath salts before she went to sleep. Knowing she couldn't risk being separated from it for longer than necessary, she decided she'd carry it around in her stocking during the daytime, and bury it deep within the pile of salts at nighttime. She'd have to be sneaky about slipping it into her garment so the handmaidens wouldn't catch her, but her earlier ruse seemed to do the trick. A few moments of privacy to use the chamber pot were all she needed.

Aurelia expected to be up through the night, mulling over what'd happened and wondering what was going on in Akkinor at the same time, but she actually managed a full night's sleep. She must've been more exhausted than she thought, because when the handmaidens woke her at sunrise the next morning, she felt like she could've slept for another ten hours.

Fortunately, they didn't force her to wear an extravagant gown or a face full of makeup like they had the night before. They braided her hair and pinned the ends into a bun on the back of her head, dabbed some cream over the bags under her eyes, and helped her into a dress simpler and lighter than her evening gown. There was some sort of metal hook that connected the chains to the shackles on her wrists, and while Aurelia couldn't remove the chains herself, the handmaidens managed it effortlessly when they had to free her hands to get her dressed. They reconnected the chains as soon as Aurelia was clothed, and they'd only laughed in her face when she asked if the chains could be removed for good.

Aurelia winced when Eira touched the scar on the queen's cheek. "This is ghastly," the handmaiden informed her. "You'd do well to ask one of His Majesty's mages to erase it for you."

"I had that option years ago, and I declined. I don't mind it."

Nyla snorted. "Queens aren't supposed to look like they've started a tavern brawl or two. You resemble a common forest wench."

Aurelia ignored the snickering women, knowing that she could remind them of her status until she was blue in the face, and they wouldn't care. To keep from exploding at them, she calmed herself down by choosing to believe their cruelty was rooted in something deeper. Maybe, like many Carthinians, they weren't fond of Akkinorians, and they resented Willem's decision to take an Akkinorian as his bride. Maybe they'd been victims of such cruelty before, and it was all they knew. Or maybe, just maybe, they were relishing the control they had over a queen in chains— after all, this was probably the only time they'd ever been given total power over someone else.

Deciding she didn't care to know the reason for their rudeness, she looked at her reflection in the vanity mirror and studied the blemish. The scar, now white, began at the top of her cheekbone and ended about an inch or so from the corner of her mouth. She'd gotten sliced with an arrow or a dagger—she couldn't remember—while fighting her brother's forces. She knew it was only right that she maintained that scar while her soldiers were forced to do the same.

When the handmaidens finished with her, a soldier standing outside of her door tipped his head in greeting. "Your Grace. I'm Ser Rhys, your guardian. It's a pleasure."

"I see. Charmed to meet you, ser."

"No, you're not." He smiled a bit. "But that's kind of you to say, anyway."

She ignored him. "Have you come to escort me to breakfast, then?"

"I have. I'll be at your side at all times of the day. The king says you're free to do as you please with your time, so long as you join him for dinner each night. The only place I can't take you is outside."

"Noted. Thank you."

He walked directly to her left, hands clasped behind his back, and didn't say another word as he led her downstairs to the morning room. The parlor was smaller than she thought: a futon and an armchair sat facing the hearth in the center of the room, and behind it was a piano, a table, and two chairs. Breakfast had already been brought to the table, so as soon as Aurelia sat down, a servant draped a napkin over her lap and filled her plate.

She eyed Ser Rhys standing beside her when the servant left. "Would you care to join me?"

"I've already eaten today, thank you."

"So you're just going to stand there and watch me? All day, every day?"

He squared his shoulders. "Those are my orders, Your Grace."

And that was that. She ate, and when she finished, a servant arrived with an armful of books, which he placed on the table in front of her as soon as her breakfast was cleared. He claimed the king had sent them, knowing how much she loved to read, and wished for her to have some of his favorite books in his collection. She could barely trifle through them to see the covers without her chains clanking against side of the table, so she could only imagine how cumbersome it'd be when she actually wanted to read something. The silence and peace she required while reading wouldn't be easy to come by when her restraints shrieked every time she turned a page.

As she inspected the covers, she wasn't surprised to find that she'd already read most of them, and they weren't exactly high on her list of books to reread. Most were works of fiction written for young women and girls—instructions from the male perspective on how females were meant to behave in society, cleverly disguised in entertaining stories and beautiful prose. It was no wonder Willem had selected these particular texts for her.

"I should like to see the library," she announced. "While it was gracious of the king to send me a few of his favorite stories, I've already read these. I'd like to explore other options."

Ser Rhys nodded. "Of course. Right this way."

As she followed him out of the morning room and through the halls, her eyes immediately scoured her surroundings for potential entrances and exits. The ceilings were incredibly tall, and the only windows were high out of reach—it'd take three men of Jack's height stacked atop one another just to graze the bottoms of each window. Even if she made it up there, she wouldn't be able to climb down the other side with ease. It'd be the same as trying to jump out of a window in her bedchamber, if they weren't barred: there probably wasn't anything to break her fall after plummeting over two-dozen feet to the ground.

It's not like she could attempt anything with Ser Rhys constantly at her side, anyway. If she made it out of her shackles and found a weapon of sorts, she could probably incapacitate any average soldier, but Ser Rhys was a formidable opponent: he was Jack's height, if not taller, and his enormous stature made Aurelia look like a child beside him. He resembled most Kanish men when it came to his facial features, and while his hair was inky black like Ansyl's, it was much longer. His amber eyes reminded Aurelia of molten gold, but one of them didn't move when he looked in any direction other than straight ahead.

He stopped before a set of wooden double doors with golden rings for handles. "Here we are."

She'd taken Willem for the type to gain his knowledge through spies and whispers instead of his own research—and maybe he did—but when Ser Rhys opened the doors, a gasp caught in her throat. It was the largest, most extravagant library she'd ever seen.

The room was so large that she couldn't see the other end of it from the entrance, and its width rivaled Halvor's wingspan when fully extended. The walls, about thirty or forty feet tall, united to form a dome-shaped ceiling made entirely out of glass. To her left, the wall from one end of the room to the other was covered in nothing but floor-to-ceiling bookshelves accompanied by rolling ladders. Circular windows stacked atop one another separated the bookshelves every now and then, offering glimpses into the courtyard.

To her immediate right, a spiral staircase led to the second story. As she moved deeper through the library, she saw the second story formed a sideways *T* shape across the room: it extended across the entire right side and had a bridge-like structure that stretched only halfway across the midpoint of the library. The entire perimeter of the second story was encased by a golden railing and adorned with seating areas, allowing patrons to gaze down at the rest of the room below.

The wall opposite the entrance—and the wall space on either side of the doors—were composed of niches and alcoves that housed even more books, knick-knacks, and collectibles. More seating areas were peppered throughout the library, complete with tables, chairs, candles, and writing materials. Statues and sculptures were on display, too, depicting everything from deities, to ancient kings, to long-extinct magical creatures.

"Oh, my..." Words seemed to fail her. "This is—"

"I hope it meets your standards." Ser Rhys clasped his hands behind his back. "I admit, I don't spend much time here, but I can point you to the directory if you're looking for something specific. Have you anything in mind?"

Aurelia approached one of the bookshelves to her left and ran her fingers along the spines. "I think I'd like to explore for a bit first."

She could hear the smile in his voice when he said, "Of course, Your Grace."

She wanted to hate that he knew she was pleased, but in that moment, she didn't care. The library was the only solace she'd met since arriving in Kanibar; for all she knew, it was the only solace she'd ever find with Willem.

***

After poking around the library for a bit, Aurelia retrieved a laughable number of books—stacked in Ser Rhys's hands after the pile became too heavy for her—and brought them to a sitting area to start reading. The knight stood across from her, still and wordless, as she read until her eyes felt like they were bleeding. She was so distracted that she didn't notice when the sun started to set, prompting Ser Rhys to light a few candles after Aurelia began to squint.

She focused her attention on one text in particular: a copy of an Akkinorian scroll from the old days, in which a corrupt priest outlined the many ways one might contribute to the persecution of mages and magical creatures. She didn't bother reading the majority of the text to spare herself from the horrific actions of her predecessors, but when she found a section dedicated to novellir, she absorbed every ounce of information she could on the metal binding her wrists.

Like Willem had told her, novellir prevented anyone who wielded magic from using their power. The average mage couldn't summon the element they specialized in, or cast any type of spell. For someone like Aurelia, whose only source of magic came from her soul connection to Halvor, novellir muted that connection so greatly that the two souls became like strangers to one another. Aurelia could reach out to Halvor with every ounce of strength in her body, and he wouldn't feel so much as an itch.

Willem had chosen to omit a few key details, though. Novellir only affected the kind of magic that was tethered to a person—it had no impact on the way external magic impacted the affected individual. If Dayne cast a spell on Aurelia, for example, she'd still fall victim to it, because the magic required for the spell would come from him, not her. If Aurelia decided to use the amulet, her shackles wouldn't prevent the object from working because the amulet's power came from Edea, not from Aurelia.

As she was finishing up with the text, she heard the door to the library open and close. A chill raced up and down her spine as she hid the text within the pile of books on her table, opting to replace it with something more innocent: an ancient fairytale intended for children, and one she remembered her father reading to her when she was a girl.

Ser Rhys bowed and left the room while Aurelia opened to a random page in the book and pretended to read. Her pulse throbbed in her neck as footsteps disrupted the serenity of the library, only coming to a halt when the visitor was close enough for Aurelia to hear his breathing. Before she could utter a word or lift her gaze from the book, her muscles tensed and her breath caught when Willem's lips tickled her ear from behind.

"What are you reading?" he murmured.

She leaned away and swallowed the lump in her throat. *"The Tale of Maximus and Lonus."*

He chuckled. "An old Dofelli children's story. It's about a little boy befriending an ogre, isn't it?"

"Indeed. You've read it?"

"Of course! It's a favorite of mine." He claimed the seat beside her, smiling, and gestured toward the heap of books on the table. "I take it you're enjoying yourself, then?"

"I'm only passing the time."

"Hmm." He paused, then leaned closer to her with his elbows digging into the table as he brought a hand to her face. She held her breath, remaining perfectly still, as he twisted a lock of her hair—having sprung free from the pins—around his finger. "I think you could grow to like it here, Your Grace."

A shiver traced her spine. "Appreciating a magnificent library doesn't mean I've accepted my fate."

"The fate you chose?"

"I hadn't another option."

"A clever retort for people who wish to avoid taking accountability for their own choices," he shot back. She gritted her teeth and slammed the book shut. Before she could stand, he took her arm—with surprising gentleness—and urged her to sit again. "Apologies. I didn't wish to upset you."

She held up her shackled wrists. "Oh, no. I'd never accuse you of *that.*"

Willem grinned. "Well, you'll be my wife one day. I can't contribute to your misery more than I already have." He relaxed in his chair when he was certain she wouldn't attempt to leave again. "Dinner is being prepared as we speak. I apologize for the lateness of the hour—an audience ran late. I didn't forget about you."

"I should hope not."

That made him laugh. "Fair enough. Where did you get that biting wit of yours, anyway? Was it inherited from the Cristos or Haze families, or did you adopt it from the Brentwoods or Normindies?"

At her lack of response, he laughed again and stood from the table. She couldn't see him when he walked away, but she imagined he was admiring the statue of Buen, Akkinor's Almighty, sitting directly behind her.

"I've often wondered if your brother's plot was a sign from the gods. You're no Brentwood, yet you sit the Akkinorian throne; perhaps the gods themselves paved the way for the uprising to see a true Brentwood on the throne. That would explain the frustrations you've faced in recent years. I wonder what might happen now: your daughter will more than likely be crowned while you live and reign here in Kanibar—with your husband serving as regent until she comes of age, of course—but she's no Brentwood, either. Her reign could lead Akkinor to its ruin. That could be avoided, though. Quite easily."

She shifted uncomfortably in her seat. "How do you mean?"

"Little Hyacinth has plenty of Brentwood blood. She'd be preferred as your heir. But your people wouldn't accept a mage as their leader, would they? Nor would they accept the daughter of a traitor."

Aurelia whirled around, burning with fury. "How dare—"

"There's no way to know for certain what might happen. We shall have to trust your husband's judgement—and I, for one, wasn't entirely impressed by him." Willem turned from the statue, but instead of reclaiming his seat, he leaned back against the table so his leg was touching hers. "Does it keep you up at night, Your Grace? Do you wonder what might become of one daughter while the other reaches her fullest potential? Do you consider the possibilities and the many ways in which they might end, or do you hope to ignore it until the last possible moment?"

"Why you think I'd tell you anything, I shall never know."

In the blink of an eye, his hand was cupping her cheek, his fingers were buried in her hair, and his face was mere inches from hers. Her breath caught, but she was too startled to pull away or shove him back.

"I'm perhaps the only person you know who's been entirely forthcoming with you," he murmured. She swallowed as his fingers tightened against her scalp, pulling her hair just enough that she felt it. Her shock faded enough for her to pull back, but his grip was too tight for her to break free. "Honesty is among one of those honorable traits you Akkinorians pride yourselves for, isn't it? And yet, so many people you trust have lied to you as of late, and you've had no idea—or you have, and you've chosen to ignore it because you can't risk losing them. Isn't it nice to have someone who will always tell you the truth? I may not tell you *everything* you wish to know, but I assure you, every word that spews from my lips is true."

Her chin wobbled, and when his eyes flashed, she knew he felt it. "I don't know what you mean. Nobody has lied to me."

Willem smiled. "Oh, they have. You just haven't realized it yet."

As his hand lowered from her face, he brushed his fingers over her cheek and rubbed the pad of his thumb over her lower lip—pulling it down a bit in the process—before dropping his hand to his lap.

It made her want to vomit.

A bell chimed in the distance. "That'll be dinner," he said, moving away from the table. His eyes gleamed as he offered her his arm. "Shall we?"

Despite everything in her mind telling her to rebuff him and stay as far away from him as possible, she took his arm, her chains rattling in the process, and let him lead her away.

XXVIII

On her third morning in Kanibar, Aurelia finished breakfast in the morning room—with Ser Rhys ever at her side—and visited the library to return the books she'd borrowed the day before. A few were leisurely reads, like short fables or ancient stories she remembered from her childhood, but others were for research purposes: historical texts about Kanibar and the Trevas family, the Lyanoth in Dofell, and divine curses.

She'd stayed up for most of the night reading the more important books, but she hadn't found anything to help solve even one of her many dilemmas. She'd hoped to search for more reading material that day, but when she found herself standing face-to-face with a statue of Kanibar's Almighty—Vyena, goddess of blessings—she realized the day had other plans for her.

She approached Ser Rhys, who'd been waiting for her by the doors. "I'd like to visit the temple today, if it pleases you."

He ignored her sarcasm and nodded. "Of course."

She followed him out of the library, hurrying to match his pace. He seemed to sense her struggle, as he slowed down to walk beside her rather than in front of her.

Aurelia blew a pesky lock of hair out of her eyes. "How long have you been serving His Majesty?"

"Not long, Your Grace. I was knighted just a week before your first visit to Kanibar. I was a soldier for the Duke of Chalara for several years until I earned my knighthood."

"Why did the king request that you serve the capital?"

"Knights are better equipped to defend the heart of one's kingdom than common soldiers are. Most men tasked with guarding the palace are knights."

"I see. Do you ever miss Chalara?"

"I haven't thought much of it in weeks. Time is a precious thing, and I mustn't waste it on reminiscence or longing."

She didn't intend to vocalize her thoughts when she muttered, "That sounds rehearsed."

He looked down at her, eyebrows furrowed, and met her gaze for just a moment too long before redirecting his attention to the path ahead. For a moment as she studied him, she saw a glimmer in his eyes that seemed to agree with her—as if he just realized he'd repeated the same brainwashing line that'd been used on him.

At the very least, their brief conversation gave her a bit of hope. Ser Rhys was almost as new to the palace as she was: he, too, was still growing accustomed to life under Willem's nose. Perhaps she could use his unfamiliarity to her advantage—but only if he continued to obey her. She knew he couldn't, and wouldn't, unlock her restraints or take her outside, but he seemed willing to do anything else she asked. As long as that remained true, she could find a way to make his constant, looming presence at her side worthwhile.

Ser Rhys led her across nearly the entire length of the palace and to a long, thin hallway with pillars and arch-shaped windows in place of walls. It cut directly through the courtyard, giving Aurelia a perfect view of the outside world surrounding her, but she couldn't attempt to flee through the windows even if she had the chance: Ser Rhys quickly informed her that an enchantment had been cast around the hallway, specifically intended to keep *her* from escaping.

At the end of the hallway, another narrow path—still with windows and pillars serving as walls—led to the left. A massive wooden door stood directly across from them, and when she peered through the arches as they turned the corner, she saw a large, round room with a dome-shaped ceiling attached to the door.

When Ser Rhys opened the door for her, Aurelia came to a screeching halt as her lips parted, awestruck. She'd expected the temple's interior to match its exterior and the rest of the palace: slightly modern compared to elder structures across Carthe, showered in Trevas green and gold, and incredibly bright because of the many windows the king seemed to prefer throughout his home. It wasn't anything like that at all.

Other than the stained-glass ceiling, there were no windows, leaving the entire room dependent on the dim orange glow emitted from hundreds of candles scattered about. The stone floors were covered in a thick layer of tiny granules, like patrons had tracked an incredible amount of sand into the temple after visiting the beach. The walls, also made of stone, had been carved to create shelves and niches for candles, holy texts, artifacts, figurines, and paintings. Massive stone slabs had been placed atop piles of rocks to imitate tables, with cushions surrounding them so patrons could kneel and pray at the structures.

At the very center of the room, an enormous, circular stone table—exactly the size of the dome-shaped ceiling—sat surrounded by cushions. A statue of Vyena, five-times Aurelia's height, stood on the middle of the table with her head tilted backwards, as if staring through the ceiling. The colors from the stained glass beamed down on the white marble statue, encasing the Almighty's body in various shades of red, blue, green, yellow, and purple. Offerings surrounded and even piled atop her feet, and the candles along the perimeter of the table cast a somewhat eerie amber glow on the deity from below.

It didn't look like the temples Aurelia had seen before—the ones built *after* the gods disappeared, as humanity made desperate attempts to entice the divine into returning. It looked like the inside of a cavern, as if the First Mortals had turned their first shelter into a place of worship after seeing the gods for themselves. Aurelia couldn't help but wonder if the cave had been destroyed so the palace could be built in its place, and those responsible for constructing the estate had kept the only portion of it that served a greater purpose.

Ser Rhys cleared his throat. "I shall wait here for you. I don't wish to interrupt your prayers."

Aurelia nodded, grateful for his compassion, and left him by the door as she approached the statue in the center of the temple. She craned her neck backwards to see as much of Vyena as she could, wondering how on earth mere mortals had managed to create something so massive and detailed with nothing but their hands, hammers, and chisels.

After admiring the statue for a bit, she knelt down on the cushion nearest to her—tattered and brown, with the imprints of other patrons' knees permanently disfiguring it—and set her elbows on the stone slab before folding her hands and closing her eyes. She had so much she wanted to say to the gods that she didn't know where to start; and once she did, she knew she'd probably be there for the next fortnight.

"Hello."

A strangled gasp escaped her lips when a hoarse, breathy female voice spoke to her right. She hadn't realized anyone else was in the temple when she walked in, but when she opened her eyes, she saw an elderly Kanish woman with braided white hair and green eyes standing beside her.

"May I join you?" the woman asked. Aurelia hesitated for a moment, still startled, before nodding. The woman sunk onto a cushion just a few feet away from Aurelia's. "Thank you. I don't wish to invade your space, but I feel closer to the gods when I'm near another devoted servant. The Twelve favor those who work together to better the realm, not tear it apart."

Aurelia smiled. She didn't know who this woman was, but she liked her already.

"You might ask the gods to do something about those shackles." The woman peered at Aurelia from the corner of her eye. "Being free to summon your dragon won't get you out of here, though. It's only the first step toward finding your freedom."

Aurelia stilled and let her arms fall against the table. "I beg your pardon?"

"Come closer, child."

Swallowing the nervous lump in her throat, Aurelia looked over her shoulder at Ser Rhys. He was turned to the side, admiring a figurine in a wall niche, and didn't appear concerned that Aurelia was conversing with another patron. She moved closer to the woman while he was distracted, hoping he wouldn't jump into action to spring them apart when he noticed.

"You must know that the gods placed you here for a reason," the woman murmured. "They don't wish for you to remain here for very long, though. You have a greater purpose that's yet to be fulfilled."

"How do you know this?" Aurelia demanded.

When the woman didn't answer her, Aurelia quickly figured it out for herself upon glancing at her companion's hands. They were brown and wrinkled, like the hands of all Carthinian elders, but permanently stained with dark ink. The pattern tattooed onto her flesh wrapped around her wrists like shackles, and while it was one Aurelia recognized, she'd never seen it in person before—only in ancient texts about prophets.

There were no such people in Akkinor, and as far as Aurelia knew, the number of known oracles in the realm could be counted on one hand. In the old days, however, oracles were abundant. They were often members of a royal or noble court, serving the same purpose as an advisor—only instead of giving specific advice on governance or finances, they used messages from the gods to help point their leader in the right direction. They weren't meant to tell their leader exactly what to do, but rather to offer glimpses into the outcomes of decisions their leader might've made. The gods knew how every possible scenario might unfold, of course, and they shared that knowledge with the prophets.

Some stories, particularly works of fiction, claimed that oracles were rather troublesome: cryptic, maddening, and sharing their wisdom only through tricky riddles or ambiguous phrases. Records written by scholars,

FORGED IN ASHES

on the other hand, described oracles as being vessels of knowledge who only aimed to guide their leader, their kingdom, and the realm in a direction favored by the gods. There was no reason to be entirely obscure when they were fulfilling the gods' wishes, and no reason to risk their leaders' failure by delivering half-truths and incomplete answers. In that sense, prophets were meant to guide others as much as they could without directly revealing the right path to take.

The scholars liked to say that an oracle was like a sword strapped in a soldier's sheath: they were ready to serve at any moment, and their purpose was always clear, but they were unable to control how their leader—or their wielder—applied the encouragement they offered.

"You're an oracle," Aurelia murmured. "Chosen by the gods at conception to serve as their voice in the earthly realm. Is it true that they plucked your soul from the heavens and delivered it to a human body on the day you were born?"

The woman chuckled. "You have a deep appreciation for the old stories, don't you?"

Aurelia blushed. "Maybe a bit too deep."

"That's all right. You, too, were born with a connection to the divine: you can't help but feel drawn to any mention of it. It will, and has, served you well—everything you've said about me is true." She turned away from the statue to meet Aurelia's gaze. "I've been waiting for you to come here since the day you were born, Aurelia Brentwood."

A shiver traced her spine. "You know what I am, then?"

"Oh, yes. I sensed the moment you wept golden tears for the first time."

"And you...you wish to help me escape?" Aurelia shook her head in disbelief. "It feels a little too simple. A strange woman visits the temple at the king's palace, exactly when I decide to visit it, on only the third day of my imprisonment. One might assume you're here to earn my trust, only to betray me so you can assist the king. And if you genuinely wish to help me, he'd have your head on a spike for committing treason. I can't imagine why you'd risk such a gruesome end."

The woman smiled, unbothered, and replied, "I understand your apprehension; and it's clear you have keen instincts. But my allegiance is to the realm and the gods, my dear child—not to any man or woman wearing a crown. I've been awaiting your arrival because the gods demand it of me. I must do what I can to see their wishes realized while they are incapable of doing it themselves. Isn't that exactly what you've aimed to achieve, too? To restore the realm to what the gods intended it to be while they're indisposed?"

262

"I've tried, but I've failed. It would appear that my efforts have only led to further conflicts."

"The most treacherous part of a storm always occurs just before it breaks." The woman, now facing Vyena once more, let her eyelids flutter shut. "You still have a bit of a voyage ahead before you reach the eye. The worst is yet to come—but so is the best."

A deep, empty pit formed in Aurelia's gut. "Do you mean to say that the gods have assured my future success?"

The woman laughed. "Not in the slightest. The gods communicate their desires to us by offering paths toward their desired outcome, but they have no control over what we do with that direction. Some of us may follow the path to greatness without fuss. Others stray from it, relinquishing divine guidance in favor of seizing things like power, wealth, or love. You see, when the gods created us and gave us the gift of free will, they didn't understand that we might use that power to assure our own destruction. That's exactly what we've done over the years. When they realized what we'd done to their world, they left—not simply to punish us, but to *study* us. Humanity is the greatest mystery they've ever faced, child. They may wish for your success, and they may provide you with the tools you need to achieve it, but they'll never alter the path you've chosen on your behalf."

Aurelia's brain, suddenly flashing back to the image of Iago's corpse, felt like it was melting into a pile of mush and goo. "I'm not sure I understand."

"You will." The woman turned to Aurelia, opened her eyes, and smiled. "Maybe not today, and maybe not tomorrow—but eventually, you will."

Aurelia frowned and furrowed her eyebrows as the woman blew her nose into a handkerchief. She still wasn't certain if she could trust this strange figure, but she'd found herself in a similar position once before with her own uncle five years earlier. Hope had prompted her to give the elusive Arian Cristos a chance, and her life changed for the better in ways she never could've imagined. Maybe, just maybe, she'd find something similar in the oracle.

Aurelia cleared her throat. "You know my name, but I don't know yours. What shall I call you?"

"Maysa. May, if you'd like."

"All right. You seem keen on helping me leave this place, May. I've heard you explain why, but I haven't heard anything about *how* I might accomplish that."

The candlelight reflected against Maysa's emerald eyes like flickering stars. "As I said, the gods have provided you with the tools you need to continue on your path. Everything you require is already in your possession."

Aurelia's lips parted in preparation to ask about the amulet—safely nestled in her stocking—but she stopped herself. She wanted to trust Maysa, but she knew it was unwise to tell more people than necessary about the power she bore. If Maysa ended up betraying her, Aurelia didn't want the king to know about the object tucked in her stocking.

"You said the first step towards finding my freedom is losing the shackles." Aurelia held up her wrists. "Willem won't remove them until he trusts me, and that's not a simple feat. He knows where my heart lies, and he knows how much I resent him for what he did to my daughter. But I know what he wants from me, too. The longer I refuse him, the less he'll be willing to offer me liberties. I..." She trailed off, throat thickening with disgust, and clenched her jaw. "I have to play the part, don't I? I have to make him believe that I've accepted my place at his side."

Maysa nodded. "Precisely. You see, the king is like all men: he desires what he can't have, and if he manages to acquire it, he thinks he's achieved the impossible—something only the gods themselves are capable of. When he's done that, every mortal woe disappears. His attention focuses only on maintaining the impossibility in his grasp. He'll do almost anything you ask to keep you happy, and he won't notice when you've started to retreat. He won't believe you're capable of deceiving him. Even the cleverest of men become weaklings when a woman dangles her heart and her body in their faces."

Aurelia chewed on her lower lip, contemplating. "It wouldn't be enough. He knows in his heart that I'll always choose my country and my family. Even if he's persuaded to grant me more liberties, I won't have what I need to leave this place. He'd never remove my shackles for fear of Halvor, and he'd never let me roam about unsupervised."

"Maybe not," she agreed, "but there are other ways to use his leniency to your advantage."

A shiver traced Aurelia's spine. "How does this benefit you? Why tell me such vital information—and assist in my escape—for nothing? The only thing you'll accomplish is earning ill favor with the king. He could have you killed."

"Bah." She waved a dismissive hand. "I have no fear of kings. I fear only the gods, and the gods have chosen you to fulfill their wishes for our world. I was placed in this realm to serve the divine, and as we live and breathe, you're the closest thing to the divine there is—so long as you continue to weep tears of gold, that is." She shook her head and chuckled. "A blessing and a curse, if you ask me."

Aurelia frowned. "What's that supposed to mean?"

Maysa paused. "How much do you know about your own destiny?"

"I admit, not very much. I know about those Forged in Gold from the Creation Story, but I'm afraid I haven't had the chance to further educate myself. We have very few texts in Akkinor that mention The Ones Forged in Gold at all, anyway."

"Hmph! How can you expect to achieve what the gods demand of you if you know nothing about what you are?"

"I...I don't..."

When a cloud passed overhead, momentarily restricting the sunlight to a single ray, a beam struck through the stained glass ceiling at an angle that perfectly illuminated Maysa's body with colored light. As the cloud drifted off, the sunlight refocused onto the statue of Vyena, drawing all attention away from Maysa and back to the Almighty.

"Those Forged in Gold were added to the Creation Story for one reason: hope," the prophet explained. "The Creation Story tells of great wonders and great travesties, but humanity has an unfortunate habit of focusing only on the latter. Those Forged in Gold exist in the story to remind us that with every tragedy, comes a sliver of hope in salvation, in peace, in happiness. Without them, and without the gods walking among us, we'd have nothing to believe in except destruction. But a deeper examination into those Forged in Gold, according to their earliest mentions in ancient texts, reveals a darker piece of their destiny that's been hidden from the world to maintain faith.

"You see, such tremendous power cannot exist without great danger," she continued. Her fingers clenched over the edge of the table, causing a shrieking sound when her long nails scraped against the stone. "The Ones Forged in Gold may have a piece of the divine etched into your souls, but that only makes you more susceptible to succumbing to evil. Half of you can look evil in the eye and never allow it to claim your soul. The other half—like poor Iago Zanaki—believe that your divine blood makes you untouchable. That's not true. Being chosen by the gods makes you a human with a purpose, but a human, nonetheless. They gave you a responsibility, not a seat at their table. Remember that."

Aurelia winced at Iago's name, startled to hear it from Maysa's lips after she'd been thinking about him just moments earlier. She knew she couldn't dismiss it as a coincidence when an oracle was involved—May wouldn't have uttered the name unless it meant something.

"Iago Zanaki." Aurelia rubbed her clammy palms on her thighs. "Why would you mention the Last King of Bozar?"

Maysa hooted with laughter. "My word, child! I'll say, you're fortunate the king's mages weren't trained to detect the moonstone like the priests in Orestes were. If the king knew about the power in your stocking, he'd have used it against you by now. It would've been a lot worse than you sacrificing yourself to protect your daughter and your dragon. He would've left you with absolutely no other choice except to use the object, knowing it might destroy you, and he'd use your sudden weakness to his benefit. Dofell wouldn't stand a chance after that, and neither would your friends. Carthe would become an empire conquered in Willem's name, for gods' sakes."

Aurelia's blood ran cold. She should've suspected that Maysa knew about the amulet in her possession—she was a prophet, after all—but she'd been so blinded by hope in Maysa's ignorance that she hadn't used her brain.

At least some relief came from this, though: Willem didn't know she possessed the amulet. He would've found it in her pocket that first day if he'd ordered his men to search her, but for whatever reason, he hadn't bothered. The only other way he would've found out about it was if one of his spies had told him about it, but nobody in Akkinor other than Aurelia and Jack knew that she possessed it. Even if his spies had reported the incident between Aurelia and Lord Zhoqa's men, nobody could've known what the matter was about.

"You..." Aurelia cleared her throat when her voice sounded hoarse and dry. "You know what I have, obviously, but...do you believe in its curse? Do you believe that being Forged in Gold might spare me from the curse, if it exists?"

"I refuse to believe in any curses unless I've seen them enacted with my own eyes," Maysa said sharply. "I do, however, believe in the word of the divine, and they don't seem to think that your destiny is enough to protect you."

Aurelia furrowed her eyebrows. "So the gods won't protect me if I use my destiny as justification for using the amulet?"

"Somewhat. If you believe yourself to be invincible because of the responsibility they've given you, you equate yourself to the only truly invincible force in the realm—a god. You'd diminish their power by thinking that way, and they'd scorn you for it."

"But if the curse doesn't exist, then I should have nothing to fear. Right?"

Maysa sighed, suddenly looking defeated and forlorn. "The prospect of the curse isn't the only trial you'll face. You must make every choice hereafter with caution, child. Don't think for a moment that the gods have

266

cast a hedge of protection over you simply because you shed golden tears. It's like I said: they've given you the tools you need, but that's where their involvement ends. You can't trust that anyone will protect you from darkness except for yourself."

"These choices I have to make..." Aurelia swallowed the lump lodged in her throat. "Do you foresee them leading me down the path the gods intended for me to take?"

"I've seen many possible outcomes. Every last decision you make— from what you eat for breakfast to the way you style your hair each day— contributes to a different outcome. I can't know anything with certainty until you near the end of the road." Maysa surprised Aurelia by setting a cold, wrinkled hand over the queen's. "You must protect your soul, but you must also protect your physical being. Some believe that those Forged in Gold are created to die: you mustn't prove them right."

Aurelia's breath caught. "How many of my kind have ended up as martyrs?"

"Too many. Sometimes, the price you pay for healing the world is losing your place in it."

"Have you...Have you seen it?" Aurelia's voice cracked. She wasn't sure she wanted to know the answer, but she had to ask, anyway. "My death. Have you seen it as a possible outcome in the trials to come?"

"I've seen your death happen hundreds of times in hundreds of ways." Maysa's eyes flashed with something Aurelia couldn't decipher as she stared at Vyena, like the statue would come to life and scorn the prophet for revealing too much. "Every possibility remains insufficient for now— particularly while you remain here, chained and isolated, unable to so much as lift a pinky to help salvage the realm. The moment you leave this place, everything will change."

"I'm working on it."

Maysa laughed heartily. "Be patient, child. When the time comes for you to break free, you'll know."

XXIX

Aurelia joined Willem for dinner hours after her conversation with Maysa at the temple, and other than the presence of an opened scroll beside his cutlery, nothing was different from their other dinners.

Maysa's voice in the back of her head persuaded her to change that.

"Good evening," she said cheerfully, sinking into the chair beside his. "How was your day, Your Majesty?"

He blinked at her, surprised. "And good evening to you, too. It was lovely—I managed to visit old friends in the countryside for a bit. How was your day, darling?"

"Oh, just wonderful! I scavenged the library for hours in search of an old story my father used to tell me. I was so pleased to have found it. Tell me—has your family's collection always been so vast, or have you added to it since taking the throne?"

"I haven't added a thing. We haven't any room for more books," he teased. She laughed, and judging by the way his face lit up, the sound pleased him. "I imagine you can say the same about your collection. You've always been an avid reader, haven't you?"

"Yes, I have. Ever since I was a girl. I'm afraid I have a terrible habit of collecting more than I read, though. I tend to reread my favorites time and time again instead of directing my attention to the newer ones."

"We're alike in that way, then."

He paused, arms resting on the table, and watched her curiously as the servants brought the first course of leek soup. When the servant—a young boy no older than fifteen—accidentally knocked Aurelia's spoon to the ground, Willem waved the boy off to fetch it himself. Aurelia muttered something about being able to retrieve her own spoon as she bent over to do the same. As both straightened up, Willem clutching the spoon, their faces were only inches apart from one another.

"You smell divine," he murmured. "Is that—?"

She smiled. "Lilies."

"Ah. Lilies." He resumed his original position, grinning as she mimicked him, and handed the spoon back to her while dipping his own in his soup. For all his research, he didn't seem to know that lilies were her husband's favorite flower. "A particularly perfumy flower, but I must say—I prefer the smell of hyacinths."

A chill ravaged her body, but she ignored it as best she could. "As do I. Clearly, or I wouldn't be here. Your gift made certain of that."

He laughed and nearly choked on his soup. "Oh, spare me," he said, bringing his napkin to his face. "You poke fun at a king at his own table? Terrible manners, Your Grace, just terrible. What if it came out of my nose? Why, you'd make me the laughingstock of the realm!"

It wouldn't be too hard, she thought.

Aurelia's eyes landed on the opened scroll at his side. "My father used to say that it's impolite to accept messages at the dining table. I was told that these dinners are for you and me—what could possibly be urgent enough to interrupt what little time we have together each day?"

For a moment, he only stared at her. She stared back, searching his eyes for any clue as to what he was thinking or feeling. The only thing she found was surprise, accentuated by the raising of his eyebrows and the slight pursing of his lips. Then, as the surprise faded, something resembling satisfaction took its place.

"Your uncle wrote to me," he told her. She stood perfectly still and kept her face expressionless to conceal her curiosity. "Say—how do you get away with that? I assume nobody outside of your family knows about your blood tie to Lord Cristos, but you often refer to him as your uncle, don't you?"

"He was my father's best friend. Many people honor close family friends by giving them such titles. It isn't a very difficult conclusion to come by."

"If you insist," he said, laughing.

She gritted her teeth. "Am I permitted to know what he said?"

"Why not?" Willem snatched the scroll, scanned it briefly, then bunched it up and tucked it into his pocket. "He writes on behalf of your husband, too—Kanibar isn't currently accepting any ravens from Akkinor. Not since your people declared war on us." She straightened up without intending to, making his eyes flash with delight. "It would appear that the new king quickly assumed your duties upon his return. Do you suppose the stress of it will have him faking his own death and returning to life here in Carthe? I should hope not. There are children involved now."

Aurelia resisted the urge to reach across the table and throttle him. "You've yet to tell me what Lord Cristos wrote."

"It's all rather boring, really. He threatens me with an invasion so you might be retrieved, but he knows it's a lost cause. Have you ever seen a magical shield, Your Grace?"

"Several times. They came in handy during the battle with my brother. Men turned into puddles of goo when they tried to breach the shields." As she said it, her heart sank, the realization striking her like a club to the back. "You've erected shields around Kanibar, haven't you?"

Willem grinned from ear to ear. "It was quite simple, actually. I summoned every Kanish mage with the power to create shields. They switch shifts every few hours to rest and replenish, but our borders are never left without protection. Only people with Kanish blood may cross the threshold into the kingdom, so your little rescue party would find themselves in a terrible position if they attempted it."

Her heart sank with defeat, but she refused to show it. "That's very well. It isn't their fault for wanting to be chivalrous, though. How could they know what a wonderful time I'm having here?"

His eyes darkened. "Don't patronize me."

Aurelia blinked innocently. "I wouldn't dream of it."

He stared at her, eyes still stony and cold. "I know what you're doing. You wish for me to think you've accepted your life here, so I won't suspect you of plotting your escape. It won't work, Your Grace. I know how much your country, your family, and your beast mean to you—the instant you're presented with an opportunity to return to them, you'll take it. My trust cannot be bought with your flattery. It must be earned."

"You don't know me as well as you think you do, then." She folded her hands on the table, her shackles clanging against the wood for what felt like the hundredth time, then leaned forward, practically demanding his undivided attention as her new position made her breasts strain against the neckline of her gown. "I've said this before, and as much as I despise repeating myself, I'll say it again: I promised myself to you in exchange for the return of my daughter and the welfare of my dragon. An Akkinorian who breaks a promise is no true Akkinorian. I won't toss my honor aside to return to a country that's already tried to kill me once. I miss my family, and I love them dearly, but I know they'll be better off without me. Everyone will be better off if I'm here. So please, Willem— distrust me all you wish, but don't do it because you think of me as one to break an oath."

She regretted the words as soon as she said them, despite knowing they were necessary if she wanted Willem to believe her ruse. The truth of the matter was that she wasn't lying to him—Akkinorians weren't oath breakers, and she'd made a promise to him when she decided to stay in Kanibar. It ate away at her, knowing she'd end up doing the very thing her people frowned upon more than anything else, but it couldn't be helped.

All she knew was that she needed to get the hell out of Kanibar, no matter the personal cost.

Willem kept staring at her, and for a few minutes, she couldn't tell if she'd impressed him or infuriated him. Then he covered her hands with his, leaned forward until they were only inches apart, and lifted one hand to brush a stray curl from her eyes. She swallowed, and the instant she did, his eyes flickered down to her throat before meeting her gaze once more.

"You know," he breathed, "that's the first time you've called me by my given name."

"I...I should hope it's normal for Kanish highborn to call their spouses by name, not title. If not, we have a very long road ahead of us."

The entire table rumbled when he laughed. "It's not, but I'll make an exception for you."

She shivered. The sound of his laughter reminded her of a pickaxe against ice: rough, grating, and unrelenting. It made her think about Jack's laugh—playful, hearty, and musical—and how she would've given anything to hear it now, even for just a few seconds.

They continued to make pleasant conversation as they ate, but when their dessert plates were taken away, Willem didn't immediately bid Aurelia goodnight like he usually did. Instead, he called for a servant, who walked into the dining room holding a large silver tray. To Aurelia's surprise, he set the tray—containing a bottle of liquor, two small glasses, and a knitted pouch—on the floor behind her seat.

She furrowed her brows. "What's all this?"

"I thought we might play a game tonight." Willem offered her a hand as they stood, then motioned for her to kneel on one side of the tray while he did the same on the other side. "This is how my father first introduced me to royal duties. I was terribly fond of games as a boy, and I was always playing something when I was meant to be studying. My father quickly realized that I retained more of the wisdom he shared with me while we were playing a game."

Aurelia's lips parted when he poured the contents of the pouch onto the tray. Five gold-plated knucklebones tumbled out, clattering against the metal tray, and while Aurelia snorted into a laugh, Willem poured each of them a glass of clear liquor. She knew it was gin by the smell, just as she knew she wouldn't be consuming a drop of that foul drink.

"I know your people call this *knucklebones*, but we call it *ayot onoba*. It's Old Carthinian for—"

"*Five stones. I know.*"

He grinned. "Very well. I presume you know how to play, then?" She nodded. "Good. I'm going to make it interesting for us, though. As a prize, the winner may ask the loser any question of their choosing. The loser *must* answer as honestly as possible."

"All right. Let's play."

"After you, my darling."

She resisted the urge to roll her eyes as she collected the talus bones in her fist, gave them a little shake, and dropped them on the tray. She picked one and tossed it into the air, catching it swiftly as she collected another from the tray at the same time, and repeated the steps until she held all five bones. Next, she dropped the bones again, tossed one into the air, and picked up two at once while catching the first. She nearly dropped the bone she threw when she went back for the last two, but she managed to steady herself before she dropped it.

After tossing the bones onto the tray again, she tossed one into the air and picked up three this time, still managing to collect the one she'd thrown. She repeated this step again to collect the last bone, and after that, she tossed one bone while planting the other four on the tray. She caught the flying bone, tossed it again, and collected the four on the tray—but the one she'd thrown clattered to the ground.

Aurelia cursed as Willem chuckled. "Better luck next time. My turn."

As she watched him take his turn, her eyes bugged out of her skull. He was much faster than she was, with reflexes like a cat's, and he didn't fumble even once. He completed every step, exactly as she had, before moving on to the finale: with all five bones on his palm, he flicked them into the air and caught them on the back of his hand, then flicked them again before flipping his wrist and catching them all in his palm again.

Willem grinned as Aurelia huffed. "I'll give you another chance, but first, you must answer my question."

She wanted to groan. "What is it?"

He paused to sip from his glass. "Take all the time you need to think of your response, but tell me honestly: did you actually want the throne before it was yours? You always knew it'd be yours someday, but did you actually want it? Or did you want something different for yourself?"

Aurelia blinked at him. She hadn't known what kind of question he'd ask—it could've been any number of things, all equally infernal—but she definitely wasn't expecting something like this. It was almost...*thoughtful*. But that couldn't be right.

"I..." She cleared her throat when she trailed off. She didn't want him to think he'd struck a nerve, but he certainly had. "I don't know. I suppose I never thought of it because I couldn't. I knew what my purpose was as soon as I was old enough to write my name. I never dreamed of embarking on adventures around the realm like my husband did. I just...I just wanted to be free to make my own choices without a room full of old men telling me how to act and who to be."

Willem smiled sadly. "Being a woman in power certainly places you in a difficult position. If I'm being honest, though...it doesn't make any difference that you're a woman. Everyone who wears a crown is controlled and bullied—even if we don't know it—by old men who think they know more about the world than we do." He sighed and gestured toward the tray. "Go on. Try again."

Inhaling sharply, Aurelia took her turn again, this time emerging victorious. She set the bones down, raised her eyebrows, and said, "It's my turn to ask something of you. Why is it that you've kept Kanibar so isolated from the rest of the continent? Hardly anyone knows what this kingdom is like nowadays. Is there a reason you've chosen to stand in the shadows?"

The corners of his lips quirked. "My people see the path to Kanibar's bright future as adaptation—altering our way of life to better reflect the cultures of places like Taundosa, Bozar, or even Akkinor. Instead of sharing elements of Kanish culture with our neighbors, my subjects would rather abandon our history. They look at places like Taundosa and Akkinor, countries that thrive against all odds, and think our only hope at a better future is forgetting ourselves. I'd hoped that restricting our interactions with the rest of the realm would remind my people of how important it is that we preserve our culture. If we lose sight of that for good, then the Kanibar that was blessed by the Almighty all those centuries ago will become nothing more than one chapter in our records."

For a moment, Aurelia didn't reply. She could tell by the strained look on his face and the anguish in his eyes that his answer was an honest one, and while she understood what he meant, she couldn't help but wonder why he thought that same sentiment didn't apply to Dofell. She wondered if he heard the hypocrisy in his own answer. *Probably not*, she decided. Men like him tended to mistake hypocrisy for righteousness.

At her silence, Willem collected the bones and played another round. She'd hoped he wouldn't keep the game going now that both of them had won a match, but clearly, he wasn't done with her yet.

After winning again, he set his hands on his thighs and raised an eyebrow at her. "I have another question for you."

Aurelia rolled her eyes. "No, really?"

That made him grin. "That's an awful lot of cheek for a queen."

"Just ask the question."

He chuckled a bit, then reached forward to brush another pesky lock of hair from her eyes. Instead of dropping his hand to his lap again, he cupped the side of her face and clenched his fingers against her scalp. Fear bubbled up in her gut when his grip tightened, but the look in his eyes wasn't menacing—rather, it was oddly sensual.

She would've preferred if it was menacing.

His voice was a low murmur: "Would it be all right if I kissed you?"

Aurelia didn't answer. Instead, she rose a few inches from the ground, closed the gap between them, and pressed her lips to his.

**

Later that night, after Eira and Nyla left her alone in her bedchamber, Aurelia dashed into the washroom and rinsed out her mouth. Still feeling like she could taste Willem on her tongue, she grabbed a bottle of wine from a table by the hearth and chugged until the bitter tannins overpowered her senses.

She'd tried to make it easier on herself by imagining Willem as Jack, but that hadn't done much good. The only thing that did was remind her that she'd betrayed her husband. She knew he'd forgive her—she had to play the part if she hoped to flee—but it made her stomach churn to kiss a man who wasn't her husband, and even more so when she remembered that Jack was well aware of what Willem had planned for her.

At the very least, she'd taken a great stride that night in terms of earning Willem's trust. After breaking the kiss, he'd told her, "I didn't imagine our first kiss happening quite like that. Then again, you're beyond what my mind is capable of imagining."

Then he'd kissed her cheek, licked her saliva from his lower lip, and told her he'd see her the following evening for a fete he was hosting—a fete she was meant to attend as his future bride.

The thought of sitting by his side, like a trophy, while he presented her to his subjects made her sicker than their kiss.

She tried willing herself to sleep after settling into bed, but it felt impossible. She tried everything: drinking a cup of warm milk and honey, reading a few chapters of the new book she'd found in the library, and gazing out at the stars through the bars on her windows. With everything she attempted, though, her thoughts kept racing: the guilt she felt over her kiss with Willem, how deeply she missed her husband and their children—particularly the newborn baby she'd been taken away from—and what both her country and her allies were doing in her absence.

Surely, she thought, her absence would inflict all kinds of uproar across Akkinor. She trusted Jack, Ansyl, and the Assembly to keep things in order, but they were only ten people, and Akkinor was home to millions. If her subjects fell into a panic over her absence, it'd be difficult to keep them in line—particularly while war loomed on the horizon.

And her allies...She knew they'd do everything they could to bring her home, but their options were limited. They couldn't retrieve her because of the shields surrounding Kanibar, and they were too distant from the Kanish people to find any natives willing to help Aurelia escape—even in exchange for riches. For the time being, their primary concern would be finding Elrin's replacement as Dofell's leader. It was the most they could do until Willem's troops started marching for Dofell.

She knew they were also panicking over the battle to come—how could they not? Halvor responded to Aurelia and her daughters only when given commands. He was growing more submissive to Jack as the years passed, but he'd never share the same connection to Jack that he did with Aurelia. That left two possible scenarios while Aurelia was incapacitated: either Halvor would remain in Akkinor to defend the country while the allies fought; or he'd accompany Jack to battle in Dofell, making it impossible for anyone to know for certain if he'd obey or ignore Jack's commands.

Exhausted by her thoughts, Aurelia swung her legs out of bed and headed for the door. She wasn't sure what she intended to do—maybe visit the library—but she needed to do *something* if sleep was going to continue to evade her.

As soon as she opened the door, her nose nearly kissed a plate of steel armor. She took a few steps back, having forgotten she was being monitored like a common criminal, as Ser Rhys turned to face her.

"Your Grace." A worried crease formed between his eyebrows. "Are you well?"

She cleared her throat. "I'm finding it difficult to sleep tonight. I was hoping to take a walk."

"You know I can't let you do that."

She chewed on her lower lip, contemplating. "You can if you come with me."

He pondered that for a moment. "All right."

Smiling, she closed the door behind her and began walking down the hallway as the knight strolled at her side. His clunky armor jingled with each step he took, masking the sound of her rattling chains. She almost felt sorry for him: he was tasked with guarding her at all times of the day, his only respite being a few hours of rest before dawn when another took his place. She assumed he'd been appointed as her guard because he was new to the palace—newcomers were always given the more toilsome tasks.

Discomforted by the silence, Aurelia asked, "Did you grow up in Chalara, too?"

"Yes, Your Grace. I was born there."

"What's your family like?"

"I wouldn't know. I was orphaned at a young age."

A pang pierced her heart. "I'm sorry to hear that. What happened?"

Ser Rhys clenched his jaw. "My mother died of typhus. And my father...He spent many years trying to keep the two of us alive with what little he had. He was branded a thief after he was caught stealing bread and meat from a tavern. When they caught him for the third time, the soldiers tossed him into a pit filled with venomous vipers. After the first one bit him, he was dead in seconds."

Aurelia swallowed the lump in his throat. "What a terrible way to die."

"It was the most merciful option. The Almighty blessed him with a quick and painless death."

"I hadn't seen it that way," she admitted. "Either way, I'm sorry for your losses. How old were you when your parents died?"

"Two when I lost my mother, and four when I lost my father. My aunt took me in after my father died, but I left her house and enlisted in the army as soon as I came of age. She wasn't a particularly kind woman—she didn't show the same mercy to orphans as most Kanish do. She despised the fact that she had to waste precious goods on the likes of me."

Aurelia nodded as they descended the staircase. "I once had a friend from Kanibar. She was an orphan, too. It's difficult to imagine what trials the two of you faced while I roam these halls, though. Kanibar feels like a wonderful place to live; that, and I can't imagine why His Majesty would spend so many resources on claiming Dofell if his people are still suffering." She raised an eyebrow when they stopped at the bottom of the stairs. "What do you think? Is Kanibar truly a wonderful place to live nowadays, or is the king merely making it appear that way?"

The knight paused as his lips pursed with contemplation. She worried she'd overstepped until his gaze met hers again, and she saw in his eyes that he'd genuinely considered her inquiry.

"I think Kanibar is a lovely place to live," he told her, "but I think His Majesty has been coerced into ignoring the needs of the average man, too. I daresay he isn't the only one, either. From what I've heard, many world leaders have chosen negligence and power over care and compassion in recent years. Only a select few have made efforts to change that."

She sucked in a sharp breath and started walking again, with Ser Rhys hesitating for a moment before following. Both of them knew exactly what he meant: just five short years ago, Aurelia proved to the realm's leaders that change was possible, maybe even inevitable. And now she knew that some of them were responding to her call.

XXX

*T*here is nothing so lovely as a woman sculpted from the imaginings of men.

As Nyla and Eira readied Aurelia for Willem's fete, the same line from an old text played on a loop in her head. The text was attributed to the first King of Bozar, a man notorious for his foul treatment of women, and dedicated several thousand words to the same belittling ideology: a woman was unattractive, uneducated, and unrefined until a strong man stripped her of everything she was, then forged her into what she was meant to be—for him, anyway.

In this moment, that was exactly how Aurelia felt. She'd been given no say in how she'd present herself that evening; instead, Willem gave firm instructions to her handmaidens about how they were meant to style her. Once again, her face was whiter than a sheet, her cheeks were red like rubies, and her eyes were lost in thick layers of Trevas-green pigment and black liner. Her hair had been slicked back and knotted in a tight bun on the back of her head, making her scalp throb and her face look far too severe.

She'd protested when the handmaidens presented a Trevas family tiara—it was considered treasonous for an Akkinorian ruler to wear a crown that didn't represent their country—but as Eira had so delicately phrased it, Aurelia didn't have a choice.

Her gown was similar to those she'd been forced to wear to dinner each evening, but the neckline of the underdress was lower than anything she'd ever worn, drawing attention to her cleavage, her long neck, and her clavicle. The robe-like gown was emerald green and gold, naturally, and paired with a matching sash customary of Kanish royals to wear at major events. And if that wasn't enough to show just who Aurelia belonged to, the sash was secured to the shoulder of the gown by a golden pin shaped like a swan—a symbolic animal in Kanibar worn by highborn women to display their betrothed status.

Aurelia couldn't decide which was worse: the pin, the tiara, or the fact that she didn't recognize herself when she looked in the mirror. She was exactly what Willem wanted her to be, and what she herself never wanted to become.

At the very least, Willem had ordered that her chains be removed for appearances' sake. She was still wearing the shackles, but they were hidden by her long sleeves, and they might've been mistaken for thick bangles if seen from a distance. Perhaps, if she played the part well enough at the fete, Willem would let her spend the rest of her time in Kanibar without the chains.

As Nyla and Eira adjusted her gown in front of a floor-length mirror, she thought aloud: "I spent the better portion of my life fighting for my right to choose a husband who wouldn't change me. I suppose I had to experience this eventually, as all women do at some point in time. Whether it be our husbands, our fathers, or our brothers...We all find ourselves playing a part that doesn't belong to us. It's regrettable that only a select few of us are lucky enough to find ourselves again."

In the mirror, she saw the handmaidens exchange looks, but neither of them said a word in response. When they were finished with her, Ser Rhys met her in the hallway and escorted her downstairs. He didn't say a word, either. Instead, he merely trailed behind her as they walked the halls and descended the stairs, lifting the train of her gown from the floor to prevent it from getting muddied.

Ser Rhys took her to an entrance she didn't normally use to reach the dining hall. She understood why when he opened the door for her, revealing a bolstering, frenzied display of drunkenness and dancing. The alternate entrance saw Aurelia standing behind the massive dining table, which was shifted from its normal position to stretch horizontally across the room, thus dividing the king's table from his guests.

The chairs had been removed from the room, leaving only two behind at the center of the table. Willem occupied one, and Aurelia assumed the other was reserved for her. There were no other tables and chairs, so it seemed like the fete was a rather informal one: the guests were invited to drink, dance, and chat to their hearts' content, but not to dine at the king's table.

Aurelia took a long, deep breath before approaching the empty seat beside Willem. She stared at the back of his head—wondering if the dimness of the room was making his hair appear darker—until he sensed her approaching and stood to greet her.

"My word." His eyes, colorless in the lighting, shimmered with desire as he took her in. "You look..."

She forced a smile. "My handmaidens captured your vision, then?"

"Most ardently." He took her hand and kissed her knuckles, all without tearing his eyes from hers. "You're the epitome of grace and beauty, Aurelia Brentwood. Kanibar has been enriched by your presence."

"You flatter me."

He grinned, and for a split second, the expression paralyzed her. It felt...*familiar*. She couldn't explain it, but somewhere deep in her heart, she *knew* that grin.

She shook the uneasiness from her shoulders and claimed her seat beside him. Almost immediately, two servants arrived with plates, bowls, and cutlery for her and Willem. The guests were being served finger food from golden platters, but apparently, only the king and his chosen bride were provided with full meals.

Willem leaned in closer to her and used his chalice to point at the crowd. "Most of our guests tonight are highborn from across Kanibar. A few of them are lowborn, though—they recently proved their worth by servicing the crown, so I invited them as a token of my appreciation. They'll be telling stories of this night to their children and grandchildren for as long as they live."

Aurelia's forced smile didn't falter. "How kind of you. May I ask the reason for tonight's fete?"

"My nobles tend to fall victim to sloth, so when they've proven their diligence, I reward them with a celebration. I've found that they're more inclined to do their duty to Kanibar when they know they'll be honored for it—consistently, of course."

Aurelia leaned back a bit as a servant set a bowl of tomato soup in front of her. While another servant filled her chalice, she studied the faces in the dining hall and found that more than half of the guests were men. Some were as young as thirteen, and some were too brittle to peel themselves from the walls for fear of falling. The handful of women present, she noticed, clung to their male escort's side like they'd implode if they moved even an inch in another direction.

As she and Willem feasted on one course after another, she continued observing the scene before her and concluded that neither she nor Willem were expected to partake in the festivities. Their role was to sit at the table, watch, and interact with their guests only when they were approached.

At least Aurelia was allowed the indulgence of wine if she was barred from dancing.

"Is this anything like your festivities in Akkinor?" Willem asked. "I do hope it is. You'd feel much more at home here if some of our customs reflected yours."

"It's very similar." She said it with a smile, lying through her teeth, and internally praised herself when Willem offered her a smug grin in return. "Our parties are a bit grander, though."

"But of course! Kanibar is about the size of Akkinor's smallest kingdom. I couldn't fill a ballroom with highborn like you could in Akkinor."

She raised an eyebrow as a servant placed a plate of raspberry tarts in front of her. "You shall have to forgive me. I was under the impression that Kanibar's population is quite large—too many people, and not enough space or resources for them."

"That applies to our lowborn." The king's voice had a biting edge to it now, but his face remained calm. "We're overrun by them, in truth. It's been a task in my engagement diary to appoint more nobility to assist them."

Aurelia paused. "Is that something you'd like my help with? I do have some experience in this matter, after all."

Willem guffawed as he reached for his chalice. "No. Thank you, darling, but no. The only thing I require of you is to present yourself according to the expectations of a Kanish queen."

It took everything in her power to maintain her composure. Apparently, to Willem, the only thing she was good for was sitting at his side and donning a pretty smile.

A few moments later after the pair finished eating, the doors at the main entrance opened, and the crowd parted to make way for new arrivals. Willem shifted excitedly, while the guests flanked either side of the room and the musicians ceased to play. While the noise reduced to soft murmuring before silencing completely, a group of what appeared to be thirty men gathered in the center of the room.

The first thing Aurelia noticed was that all of them were amongst the most beautiful specimen she'd ever laid eyes on. Their chiseled bodies looked like they'd been sculpted from clay, and their skin—ranging from a light, fawny brown, like Kaia's, to a darker, richer brown like Ser Rhys's—glistened like they'd been oiled from head to toe. Some had hair long enough to be tied back in a braid that reached their hips, and some had shorter hair like Willem's that dusted their jawlines. They wore nothing, not even shoes, except for skirts that reached their knees, all in shades of green or gold. One man—the only one of the group whose dark hair was streaked with white—approached the dining table while the rest of them fell into place. They stood in six rows, spaced evenly apart in every direction, with their hands clasped behind their backs and their faces expressionless.

"My king." The older man bowed. "We were honored to receive yet another invitation to the palace. Thank you for welcoming the *Voduris* into your home."

Willem smiled. "It's my pleasure. I'm most eager to introduce you all to my future bride." He took Aurelia's hand and kissed her knuckles again. "What will you be performing for us tonight?"

"The *Kelea*, Your Majesty."

"Excellent!" Willem clapped, reverberating Aurelia's eardrums, and turned to face her. "The men standing before us are members of a group known as the *Voduris*. They're your average lowborn by day, and Kanibar's greatest performers by night. They claim responsibility over keeping elements of Kanibar's ancient culture alive. Our people were once regarded as the greatest performers in the realm, you know. Anyone could identify us through our song and dance. The *Kelea* is perhaps the oldest and most profound of Kanibar's performing arts. In the old days, it was often performed as a means of protesting, or of promoting Kanish nationalism. That's one of many reasons I'm proud to have them serving in my army."

Aurelia didn't bother telling him that she already knew about the *Voduris* and the *Kelea*. Ansyl's father had been a member of the *Voduris*, and, before his death, taught all of his children the most popular and significant dances. Ansyl, Thea, and Mycah had attempted to perform the *Kelea* for Aurelia and her family once before, but it hadn't gone well—poor Mycah lost his balance and fell on top of Thea, breaking his wrist and concussing his sister.

She nodded and batted her eyelashes at Willem. "You honor me by allowing me to bear witness to such an important aspect of your culture."

He beamed, visibly pleased. "I hope you feel it as we do."

With one gesture from Willem, the man returned to his position with the other thirty men while the entire room watched in silence. After a moment, the same man began making breathy, guttural noises—a sound that reminded Aurelia of traditional Sadian throat singing, a rare practice in modern times. A few other men joined him, one at a time, all reaching different pitches and octaves to create their own music. Half of the men who weren't singing started stamping their feet so aggressively that Aurelia's chalice rattled on the table. At the same time, the remaining half began pounding their fists against their chests, forming instant, knuckle-shaped red marks on their breasts.

When the leader suddenly stopped, took a knee, and made a low, growl-like sound in his throat, the other men followed suit, moving so synchronically that they almost appeared inhuman—like gods. They turned the upper halves of their bodies to the side, banging on their chests like drums as the sound perfectly aligned with their singing.

Aurelia felt Willem's eyes on her as she watched, mesmerized, while the men performed in a way that felt like it was meant to be violent—but it wasn't. She could see it in their eyes, hear it in the sounds emerging from their throats, feel it in the way they bruised and bloodied themselves like the realm depended on it. It was perhaps one of the most beautiful things she'd ever seen, and not simply because of the dance itself: it was because the love they felt for their kingdom radiated from them in a way that made even the Akkinorian queen feel the soul of Kanibar burning in her chest.

As she watched the performance, Aurelia came to a painful realization: soon enough, the men currently expressing their undying love and patriotism for their country would be the same men laying down their lives in a fight against Aurelia's soldiers. Perhaps some of them would survive and contribute to keeping the mission of the *Voduris* alive, but for most of them, they'd never get the chance to perform again.

These men wouldn't be fighting for Dofell, or for Willem's quest for power, or for the chance to see Kanibar conquer the continent. No, these men would be fighting for something deeper and far greater: the preservation of their way of life, the immortality of Kanish culture at its roots. They didn't strike her as the kind of men to pick up their swords and risk ending the *Voduris* line because their king commanded it, or because they gave a damn about what happened to Dofell. They were fighting for something else: the fear of losing what they'd dedicated their lives to protect.

It was no secret that Kanibar's ancient culture was dwindling, so Willem had likely told them that expanding the kingdom's reach would keep their culture from dying out—even at the expense of another kingdom's way of life. They were being used as pawns, as pieces in Willem's game, all because they were willing to do whatever it took to make sure the realm didn't forget what it meant to be Kanish.

When the performance ended, the floor was coated in sweat and oil, but the men didn't struggle to catch their breath. They resumed their starting positions, hands clasped behind their backs, and merely tipped their heads as a show of respect to their king.

Before she knew what she was doing, Aurelia stood from her chair and raised her chalice. Willem, along with every other soul in the dining room, stared at her in bewilderment as soon as they heard her chair screech against the floor.

She ignored all of them.

She smiled. "What a lovely performance! I'm honored to have observed it. Kanibar is fortunate to have its culture and history represented so passionately by such esteemed men. I'm a stranger in this country, but tonight, I feel as though I've known your way for my entire life. I could hear the ancient drums, and I could feel the gods smiling down upon you." She lifted her chalice a bit higher, prompting the highborn flanking the room to follow suit. Willem didn't move a muscle. "May the Almighty bestow her blessings upon each of you. May she bring you safety, comfort, and joy in all things. May she ensure the *Voduris* always have a voice—or a stage—in our world."

A few people chuckled, encouraging her to continue: "The ancient ways of the world have been lost to most of us, but Kanibar continues to prevail. It's my sincere wish that nothing may happen to threaten the duty you have to keeping your culture alive. The gods shall always favor those who remain loyal to the vision they had for our world." Smiling, she brought the chalice to her lips. "To you."

As the crowd echoed her, she sunk back into her seat, ignoring the way Willem was staring at her. Instead, she focused on the *Voduris*. Many of them had abandoned their blank faces to adopt a new expression: the same one often wore during her first trip to Carthe while questioning everything she thought she knew.

"That was very kind." Willem's voice, low but not angry or suspicious, dragged her from her thoughts as she sipped from her chalice. "You'll make a fine queen for Kanibar."

As the musicians began to play again, Aurelia turned to the king and started to offer him a smile. The expression wiped clean from her face when the light caught Willem's eyes, which momentarily presented themselves as blue rather than green. When she blinked, his eyes were as emerald as ever.

"Aurelia?" He set a hand on her thigh and furrowed his eyebrows. "Are you all right?"

She forced a smile. "Just fine. Might we see another dance?"

***

"And how did you get to the gardens?"

Hyacinth shrugged. "I walked."

"You walked." Jack sighed and watched as she constructed a tower out of wooden blocks. "Who brought you there?"

"No one."

"Hyacinth," he warned.

She tore her eyes from the tower to glare at him. "Yes?"

"Enough of your cheek. I've asked you a dozen times now, and I expect you to answer me." When she reached for the block in his hand, he held it out of her reach, making her huff in protest. "You were taken away to a very bad place, Sisi. I need to know who took you so they can be punished."

She sniffed and swatted at her face when a blonde curl fell over her eyes. "I can't tell you, Papa."

Frustrated, Jack pinched the bridge of his nose and sighed. "Why not?"

"Because you'll be mean. Mama will be nicer than you."

He softened like he'd been punched in the gut. He never wanted his children to see that side of him—the dark, volatile side—but with Hyacinth, it couldn't be helped. For one, she'd been there in Kanibar to hear the things he'd said and the threats he'd made. For another, her foresight allowed her to see glimpses of the past, and Jack's past was riddled with carnage.

She knew exactly who her father was when it came to dealing with those who wronged him. She knew exactly who her mother was when it came to those situations, too. While Jack was always eager to swing his sword, Aurelia was always merciful—or, at the very least, she always *considered* mercy. Jack wasn't built that way.

"All right." Defeated, Jack made a motion with his hand. "Return to your lessons with Halle and Henry. We'll discuss this again later."

Hyacinth nodded, kissed her father on the cheek, and bounded across the nursery to join Irina in the doorway. As the pair left to join Celesse and the other royal children, Jack lingered and stared at a puzzle box on Hyacinth's bedside table, wondering how on earth such an intelligent little girl could be so reluctant to punish someone who'd put her in danger.

She's too much like her mother for her own good, he thought, and immediately felt his face crumple when he remembered that her mother was across the sea, trapped with that loathsome king.

When he regained his composure and left the nursery, it wasn't long before he was stopped in the hallway by Ansyl. The Lord Hand, despite being several years younger than Jack, looked more weathered than a man twice his age. His dark, goldish eyes had lost their sheen, and the lines on his face were more prominent than Jack remembered them being a few weeks earlier.

"Any luck?" Ansyl inquired. Jack only shook his head. "She'll come around, eventually. It may be the trauma that's keeping her from speaking about the kidnapping."

"No, it's not," Jack muttered. Ansyl raised a curious eyebrow, but Jack waved him off as the pair began to stroll the halls. "Are there any updates?"

"A few, but nothing good. Lord Cristos wrote to inform us that Willem has erected shields around the entirety of Kanibar—any non-Kanish natives will be killed on impact if they attempt crossing the threshold. I've already called off the rescue party you formed. We can't send them to their deaths. I'd volunteer myself to go, but I don't think Willem would let me take more than a step toward the palace before striking me down."

Jack grimaced. "I assume the shields work to prevent Halvor from entering Kanibar, too."

"I'd imagine so. If that were untrue, he might've already attempted returning to Kanibar by now."

"He's been restless—he knows exactly where she is and what he'd have to do to bring her home, but he can't act on it. He's trapped here like the rest of us." Jack sighed and shook his head, barely managing to control his temper. "Anything else?"

"We've apprehended approximately eight Carthinian individuals living throughout the Folly. I'm personally overseeing the interrogations. So far, I've only managed to identify one of them as Kanish, and he hasn't revealed a thing. None of the prisoners seem to know anything, so I'm assuming Willem's spies returned to Kanibar after the princess was taken."

Jack winced. He wasn't fond of Ansyl's method—Aurelia wouldn't be, either, if she knew her Lord Hand was arresting innocent people—but at the same time, he knew what had to be done to bring his wife home and find the person responsible for kidnapping his daughter. It may not have been the most honorable tactic in the world, and he may not have liked it, but it was necessary.

Jack's hands balled into fists at his sides. "So we have nothing to go on, then?"

"No, Your Highness. I'm sorry. I even relayed the name you gave me—Althaia Pharos—to the monastery, but the priests haven't found anything of substance. Nobody knows why Her Grace kept that page so close to her. Perhaps Lord Cristos and the others will have better luck." Ansyl cleared his throat as they descended the grand staircase, cautiously eyeing Jack's fists. "As of now, there's nothing we can do except prepare our men for battle. Our war preparations are progressing smoothly, so it shouldn't be long before we're able to deploy our troops to Carthe. Hopefully, we make it there before Willem marches for Dofell."

"Why do you suppose he hasn't done so already? He could've taken Dofell by now, for gods' sakes. His odds of success grow slimmer and slimmer by the day."

Ansyl shrugged. "Uncertain, Your Highness. Perhaps he's waiting for something."

Jack was grateful that Ansyl hadn't said it aloud, but he knew they were thinking the same thing: *He's waiting until his line of succession has been assured—waiting for Aurelia to give herself to him.*

Though he knew his wife would never do such a thing by her own free will, the thought made him want to plant his fist through the wall, anyway.

"We need to keep searching for the traitor, then. It's the best we can do," Jack muttered, desperate to change the subject. "Even if the Kanish spy who took Sisi is long gone, they couldn't have done it alone. I'm sure of it. They would've needed help from someone who knows the palace and the Folly—someone who knows *Sisi*, too. I think..."

He trailed off, eyes widening, as Ansyl gawked at him. "You think she knows her kidnapper? Or the person who assisted her kidnapper?"

Jack shook his head. "No. I know exactly who's responsible for this— or, rather, *what's* responsible."

Before either of them had the chance to say anything more, he turned on his heel and raced through the corridor like he was being chased by a pack of ravenous hounds.

After Aurelia and Jack had returned from Carthe, what felt like ages ago, they'd learned that the sprite had escaped its confinement in Aurelia's study. It didn't want to eavesdrop or cause mischief; it just wanted companionship, so it surrounded itself with the only people who weren't afraid of it: the children. Aurelia and Jack hadn't given it a second thought after observing how much the children loved the creature when they spoke of it. The delight Jack felt at seeing his children so happy had made him forget that the sprite was technically Kanish—hidden away not only because it would've given the staff a fright, but also because Aurelia wasn't sure if she could trust it yet. Apparently, she trusted it more than she thought—and so did Jack, gods help him.

Upon reaching Aurelia's study, a breathless Jack slammed the door behind him. "Come out, sprite!" he barked. "I'd like a word with you!"

His demand was met with silence. Growing more impatient by the second, Jack began tearing the study apart in search of the creature. He ripped books from the shelves, flipped cushions, scattered burnt wood in the hearth—and yet, no sign of the sprite. He checked every nook and cranny in the room, kept his eyes peeled for any flashes of golden light, and listened carefully for the sprite's irritated hissing or childlike laughter.

Nothing.

As he willed himself to calm down, Jack realized something damning: he hadn't seen the sprite since before he and Aurelia left for Kanibar. He'd been so distracted in the days that'd passed since Hyacinth's return that he hadn't realized he'd forgotten to check on the creature. He knew what that meant: somehow, the sprite had followed Aurelia and Jack to Kanibar—probably to report its findings to Willem after several weeks of spying on Akkinor.

If it was the sprite that had convinced Hyacinth to leave the palace, then Jack had no way of interrogating it; and if the creature actually *had* been spying for Willem, then Aurelia was in far more danger than she realized.

After releasing a frustrated roar, Jack ripped the door open and shouted for a servant. He was too blinded by rage to identify the person who scurried over to him, but he managed to ask for Ansyl. He waited in the hall for a few moments when the servant left, pacing back and forth in front of the door, until a breathless Ansyl appeared before him.

"I don't care what you have to do to make this happen," Jack seethed, "but tell everyone you can that we're departing for Carthe at dusk tomorrow. I'll send a raven to Taundosa so they know to expect us. We still can't rescue her if we're in Taundosa, but at least we'll be closer to her than we are now. We need our allies to help us strategize, too."

Ansyl nodded. "Consider it done. I'll send half of the Assembly along with you, and the other half will stay here with me to reign in your absence."

"No." Jack shook his head and ran a hand through his tousled hair. "You're coming, too."

Ansyl blanched. "It's the responsibility of the Lord Hand to mind the queen's duties in her absence. I can't leave if both you and Her Grace are elsewhere. I'm needed in Akkinor to lead our people."

"The Assembly has done a fine job of ruling on their own, however temporarily, in the past—they'll be fine." Softening, Jack set a hand on Ansyl's shoulder. "I...I wouldn't be able to do this if not for you, my friend. I'm no politician. I need you there as the voice of reason while we strategize with our allies. Aurelia would say the same if she were here."

Ansyl hesitated, looked between Jack's eyes, and nodded. "If that's what you wish, then it's my duty to oblige—but only if you assure me we'll be traveling by sea." He offered Jack a small, playful smile. "I couldn't manage the flight without vomiting all over you."

Jack laughed. "You and me both."

XXXI

The next morning after breakfast, Aurelia asked Ser Rhys to escort her to the temple again. Upon her arrival, she found Maysa kneeling in front of the statue of Vyena, as always. A part of Aurelia wondered why Maysa was always there, awaiting her in the very same spot, but then again, Maysa was an oracle. She probably knew exactly when Aurelia was planning on visiting her, each and every time.

When Aurelia knelt beside her and murmured a greeting, Maysa didn't acknowledge the queen. She merely kept her eyes shut and her hands folded on the stone slab, moving her lips in miniscule increments as she finished a prayer.

"Hello again, child." Maysa opened her eyes after a moment of silence and turned her gaze to Aurelia's wrists. She smiled when she saw the absence of the chains—which Willem had agreed to remove for good after the fete—but her expression quickly morphed into one of inquiry. "I see you've lost your chains, but something else is different, isn't it? With the king."

A shudder wracked Aurelia's body. "I kissed him. A few days ago."

"Ah." Maysa tipped her head, like she pitied what Aurelia had done. "It isn't enough, though. He isn't so easily tricked." Aurelia nodded as the prophet glanced over her shoulder at the door. "Your shadow is absent today."

"He agreed to remain outside."

"Hmm." She closed her eyes again and leaned her neck backwards a bit to face the ceiling. "He trusts you, you know."

"Who? Willem?"

"No. The knight."

Something warm and encouraging bubbled up in Aurelia's stomach. She still didn't know what to make of Ser Rhys: he shared more than she'd expected him to whenever she probed for details about his life, and he always spoke to her with grace and respect—like the queen she was, not the captive Willem had made her. But if Maysa was right, and she'd somehow managed to earn his trust, then the knight was someone she needed to keep close.

It wasn't as if she could distance herself from him if she wanted to, anyway.

Aurelia cleared her throat. "There's something I've been meaning to ask you. Willem's fete distracted me a bit, but—"

"You wish to know about Elrin's successor."

The queen straightened up. "Well, yes. Do you know anything that might help me?"

"Of course I do."

She scowled, annoyed. "Are you going to tell me?"

"Remember what I told you, child: the gods have already given you the tools you need to succeed, but they can't tell you how to use those tools. Think of it like this: a young farmer readying for his first harvest is given a sickle. Does he expect the sickle to work on its own, or does he learn how to use it through trial and error?"

Aurelia understood that well enough. Maysa was a tool the gods had placed on Aurelia's path, but she couldn't give Aurelia the answers to her every question so easily. If Aurelia wanted guidance, she had to ask the right questions.

"All right." The queen smoothed her skirts and cleared her throat again. "The successor must have Dofelli blood, and they must be highborn. Dofell's nobility has all but gone extinct over the decades, so our options are fairly limited. The king himself couldn't think of a worthy contender. My allies are searching for a successor, too, but it seems highly likely that each of us will be met with the same disappointment."

"What about your husband?"

"My husband?" Aurelia blinked at her, not understanding. "What about him?"

"When you first came to Carthe, you were looking for allies—powerful highborn allies, to be specific. Your husband, at that time, was neither powerful nor highborn, yet he became your closest ally."

Aurelia shook her head. "That's impossible. Dofell's next leader can't be a commoner. The continent wouldn't stand for it, even if I happen to disagree with that sentiment. It's not about what I think is right—it's about finding someone nobody can refute."

"Just because something looks ordinary doesn't mean it really is. Lily Linden and Jack Sherbourne are proof of that."

As Aurelia chewed on her lower lip, contemplating, she recalled the story she'd recently told her children—the same story she'd heard from her father many times before. An ordinary iron spoon in the hand of a poor fishmonger had meant the difference between his freedom and his eternal imprisonment: the same might be true for her.

"So, there's a commoner somewhere in Dofell with enough highborn blood to make them a worthy successor," she summarized. "They must have at least a small connection to Dofell's highborn—if not, just about anyone could fill the role, and we'd be forced to question thousands of people. But how do I go about finding this man?"

Maysa chuckled. "If you look for a man, you won't find him."

"A woman." Aurelia couldn't stop herself from smiling at that. "Where should I start looking for her, then?"

She rolled her eyes. "You and I both know you've already started."

Aurelia's lips parted. Until that moment, she'd nearly forgotten all about the book she'd found in her library—Roses of the Realm—and the way it'd opened on its own to a chapter about Althaia Pharos, the renounced daughter of King Ophelos Phyre III.

"It was you." Aurelia's voice was nothing short of a whisper. "You showed me the page about Althaia Phyre. How?"

"That isn't for you to worry about. What did you gather from that reading?"

She exhaled in aggravation. "Dofell might've been spared if Ophelos III hadn't renounced his daughter in favor of his son. By rejecting her, he put the man who cursed the kingdom on the throne."

"Is that all?"

Aurelia blinked at her. "Well, yes. That's as far as I made it. I didn't think I'd learn anything more from that story, anyway. Althaia Pharos was lost in history among the lowborn, and her only son along with her. Even if their line prevailed to the modern age...Their descendants would still have Phyre blood, and Dofell is unsalvageable while a Phyre sits the throne."

The old woman smiled in a way that chilled Aurelia's bones. "Have you considered the possibility that curses aren't tied to blood, but to family?"

A shaky gasp escaped Aurelia's throat. She knew better than anyone that family and blood didn't always go hand in hand.

Aurelia set a hand over Maysa's and squeezed. "Thank you."

She cocked her head to the side, smiling, and raised her eyebrows. "There's something else you wish to ask me, isn't there?"

Aurelia's lips parted. There was, but she'd hardly considered it until then: it'd been a minor thought in the back of her head, one she'd pushed aside to make room for more pressing matters. Now that she had Maysa's private ear, though—and her omniscience—there was no better time to give that thought the attention it deserved.

"When Willem loses the war, I can't say for certain that my allies will let him live," she said. "They certainly won't let him continue ruling Kanibar, but from what I can tell, he hasn't a successor. My allies would have to work closely with the Kanish nobility to appoint a new ruler, and I doubt the nobles will be constructive after their defeat. We've been thinking about the future of Dofell so strongly that we haven't considered the future of Kanibar: by salvaging Dofell, we'd be leaving Kanibar in a state of disarray. The gods certainly didn't place this responsibility on my shoulders so I could let one kingdom fall while saving another." She raised an eyebrow. "Do you happen to know who'd succeed Willem if he's dead or overthrown?"

"He has a nephew in Krotis. The boy's name is Harryn. The king has friends in Vrurith, so he sent the boy to ward there many years ago. Harryn's father, the king's younger brother, died many years ago. Harryn has been the king's charge ever since."

"Has the king named Harryn as his heir?"

"No. I don't think he ever will, either. He despised Harryn's father, you see, and wishes to keep the boy as far from the palace as possible."

She frowned. "Why did he hate his brother?"

Maysa sighed and patted her hand. "I've told you enough for today, child. Hurry to find your shadow before he fetches you himself."

***

Aurelia wanted to pay a visit to the library after leaving the temple, but thought better of it before she and Ser Rhys even reached the main corridor of the palace. It'd be suspicious if she ran to the library to research the Phyre family immediately after leaving the temple, and the last thing she wanted was for anyone to wonder about what she was doing in the temple.

Ser Rhys didn't seem to think anything of Aurelia's visits or her conversations with Maysa—he probably assumed the old woman was just another patron, and she'd bonded with Aurelia over their prayers. That, or he chose to swallow any suspicions he might've had to grant Aurelia just an ounce of solace while her other freedoms were limited.

Instead of researching, she decided to do what Maysa had suggested days earlier: play the part. She spent a few hours in the parlor doing this and that—embroidering, reading, taking tea—before promenading around the corridors. She even stopped the stewardess to discuss potentially changing the decor in the palace so it suited Aurelia's tastes. When she saw the aggravation on the woman's face, she knew the stewardess would report the conversation to Willem as soon as she could. Giving the king a kiss and a civil conversation at the dinner table wasn't enough to prove her loyalty to him, but if she showed interest in making his home her own, he might let his guard down.

Not long after, her handmaidens found her and requested that she follow them back to her bedchamber so they could prepare her for an outing with the king. As soon as they produced trousers and a pair of boots from her wardrobe, she knew what the king had in mind for their activity that day: a ride.

She didn't know what to make of that. It felt like a test: *give her a horse and an open road, and see what she does.*

"This is most abnormal," Eira said as she pulled the strings on Aurelia's corset. The queen grunted in protest: she'd been given a somewhat loose shirt to wear that day, and still, she was expected to wear a corset beneath it. "*Most* abnormal."

Nyla nodded in agreement while tying Aurelia's hair into a ponytail. "His Majesty continues to surprise me."

"Why?" Aurelia knew they hadn't been talking to her, but she inquired anyway.

"His Majesty isn't fond of horses," Eira told her. "Hates them, actually."

"Not to mention he's letting you outside," Nyla added. Aurelia winced when the handmaiden pulled her hair to secure it in the band. "I can't imagine why he'd wish for this. I doubt he'll give you your own horse."

"He might," Eira argued, as if Aurelia wasn't there. "It will look poor if he has her shackled *and* glued to his side, Ny."

Nyla smirked a bit as she gazed at Aurelia. "He'll want you to ride sidesaddle, anyway. You wouldn't make it far."

Aurelia's face warmed. She'd never ridden sidesaddle before in her life. Nyla was right: she wouldn't make it far if she had to reposition herself before making her escape.

"I wonder why he planned this particular activity for the two of us," she thought aloud. "I do like horses, but I'm not an avid rider. And if he despises it as much as you say he does..."

Eira shrugged. "Perhaps he thinks it would please you. He only wishes to please you, you know."

No, Aurelia thought. *He wishes only for my body and my blood.* She was willing to give him one—albeit not in the way he desired—but certainly not the other.

When she left her bedchamber, Ser Rhys escorted her downstairs to the foyer, where the king was waiting for her by the front doors. They were wide open for the first time since she arrived, offering her a tiny glimpse into the outside world after a week trapped indoors. She wanted to appreciate it, but the second she saw the world beyond, she recalled the last time she'd seen it: the panicked, blurry moment she and Jack had landed in front of the palace to retrieve their daughter from Willem's clutches.

It felt like years ago, and yet, at the same time, like it'd happened just that morning.

Willem smiled as she glided towards him. "I see you've prepared for our outing. I was uncertain of our plans for today until I recalled how fond you are of the outdoors. I feel terribly for keeping you confined to the palace, so I thought we'd take a quick trip together."

Her eyes flickered to the bailey behind him, where a pair of stable boys minded two horses: one large and blacker than night, and the other a bit smaller, with hair like chestnuts. Behind them were about half-a-dozen soldiers perched atop horses, so she knew she wouldn't be alone with the king while they rode.

"I appreciate your thoughtfulness." She tucked her arm into the crevice of his elbow, hiding a smile when she felt his body tense in response. "I appreciate your trust in me, too."

He expelled a dry, odd-sounding cough. "Of course. The soldiers will follow to protect us, but we have nothing to worry about. My subjects are rather passive."

Aurelia beamed. "We have a lovely afternoon ahead of us then, Willem."

As she turned to face the bailey, letting him guide her down the front steps, she saw a ghost of a smile grace his lips from the corner of her eye. She resisted the urge to grin at that: he was letting her know that she had him wrapped around her finger, and he had absolutely no idea.

She was forced to ride sidesaddle, which was as uncomfortable as it was humiliating. She was also instructed to keep her hands close together on the saddle and to move her arms as little as possible, so her sleeves would cover the shackles on her wrists.

When she asked Willem what his subjects knew about her presence in Kanibar, he replied, "They believe you're here willingly, in an effort to unite the realm by establishing a relationship between Akkinor and Kanibar. I told them nothing—they presume to know based on your reputation."

That didn't surprise her. It explained why Willem was so cautious about concealing her shackles, too: he claimed he always told the truth, and if his subjects noticed something untoward, he'd have a tough time explaining why his "willing" bride needed to be restrained with magical cuffs.

They didn't say much at the beginning of the ride. Willem told her they'd be traveling through the nearby villages for a bit, but quickly fell silent afterwards. She knew why when she saw the way he fidgeted with the reins and tried readjusting his position time and time again. Nyla and Eira were right: he wasn't fond of horses, and he wasn't skilled at hiding it.

His horse trotted directly beside hers, while three soldiers rode ahead of them and three trailed behind. Aurelia didn't think there was a need for so many of them: there weren't enough people on the streets to pose a threat. A few people hung clothing on drying lines outside of their homes, beggars pleaded for coin on the street corners, and peddlers walked in circles trying to sell the goods strapped to their backs. They bowed or curtsied when they saw the king, but nobody asked him for coin, tried to make conversation with him, or rushed to tell their neighbors that the king was riding through their village.

In fact, Willem's presence didn't seem to affect them at all. Nor did Aurelia's.

"Your villages are rather...sleepy," Aurelia commented. "There's hardly anyone on the streets. Why is that?"

"The villages surrounding the palace are a bit different from the others," he responded. "All able-bodied men who live in this area serve as knights and soldiers, so they're always on duty. I pay them well enough that they're the sole providers for their families. Their wives mind their homes, their children, and their elderly parents while they serve the crown. It isn't like other parts of Kanibar, where most—if not all—members of one's family must contribute to making a living."

It was no wonder Willem's army was so large—any man would serve the crown for as long as he could if it meant receiving the highest wages in Kanibar. It was almost like the monarchy had made the decision for them: *You can either die in the streets, or die serving your country.*

"I see." Aurelia craned her neck to watch an elderly peddler—probably a former soldier forced into retirement by old age—knock on door after door. "We haven't many peddlers in Akkinor, you know. I've only ever met one in the Folly. He was a seventeen-year-old boy, the same age I was at the time, forced to peddle after an accident blinded him."

Willem raised an amused eyebrow. "How on earth did the Crown Princess of Akkinor find herself acquainted with a blind peddler?"

"I'd sneaked out of the palace to find a gift for my friend in the village. He'd pointed it out a few days earlier, and I wished to retrieve it myself as a name day gift. The peddler was there at the shop, trying to trade some of his treasures for theirs."

"He didn't know who you were, did he?"

Aurelia shook her head. "I was dressed like a servant to protect my identity, anyway, but no. I told him my name was Emmy, after my middle name, Emmeline. He didn't question me. I liked it that way—one feels more human when they aren't constantly being bowed to." She paused for a moment and gazed at him, studying the genuine interest etched onto his face. "I saw him a few times after our first meeting, too. We often ate bread and jam by the river while my knight—the friend I mentioned earlier—guarded me from afar. We had some lovely conversations."

A wicked glint shimmered in the king's eyes. "Is that all you did, Your Grace? Converse over bread and jam by the riverside?"

A blush warmed her cheeks. "No, it's not."

He guffawed. "Oh, do tell!"

"There isn't much to tell. We kissed a few times, but it was difficult to do more than that. He told me he loved me on our fifth adventure together. I wasn't quite ready to say it back. A few days later, I waited by the river for our next visit, and he never came. My friend found out that the boy—Caledon, though I called him Cal—had been beaten to death by thieves on the Templar's Road." A long, heavy sigh escaped her as the tiniest twinge of grief bubbled up in her gut. "I mourned for seasons after that, but if I'm being honest, I haven't thought about him in a long time."

She'd mentioned the Follian peddler so she could persuade Willem into opening up to her, but it wasn't a tall tale. The story of her time with Caledon was authentic—anything less than a genuine memory would've made itself known, destroying any credibility she had in Willem's eyes.

"I'm sorry to hear that," he murmured. "Loss in any form is never easy."

Aurelia raised an eyebrow. "Have you ever experienced something like that? I imagine so—a handsome, powerful man such as yourself would have no shortage of love in his life."

He grimaced, but not in a way that suggested he was off put by her inquiry. "Of course. I've already told you about my late wife."

"Not in any detail." She batted her eyelashes and pouted her lower lip, just for dramatic effect. "Will you tell me about her, Willem?"

The king glanced over at her, lips parting, and observed her for a moment—searching her eyes for any sign that she had an ulterior motive. She did, but when he sighed and turned away, she knew he hadn't found what he was searching for.

"All right." He cleared his throat and focused his emerald gaze on the path ahead. "I was young when I met her—Rae Meldros, the only daughter of the Lord of Tiluth. She was sent to the palace as my potential future bride, among other young women, but the rest of them never stood a chance. She was beautiful: raven-haired, amber-eyed, and with a smile that brought a man to his knees. I was smitten with her from the moment she arrived, unable to eat or sleep while she plagued my every thought. I told my father I wished to marry her, and he said it was impossible."

Aurelia frowned. "Why? She was brought to the palace to be considered as your future wife, after all."

"My younger brother, Myron, reached my father's ear before I did." His knuckles turned white as his hands on the reins clenched into fists. "Myron had fallen in love with her, too, and she with him. My father was prepared to force her to marry me after I refused to take another bride, but she resisted. She claimed the Almighty Vyena had already blessed her union to Myron."

Aurelia sighed with genuine sympathy. "She was pregnant."

"Yes." His face contorted with anger, but his expression was smooth again when she blinked. "My father wanted us to marry, anyway. He said I'd raise Myron's child as my own, as my heir. I had a poor relationship with my brother, so his protests meant little to me, but I couldn't bear to go through with it when I saw the pain in Rae's eyes. I knew she'd resent me forever if I forced her hand. I couldn't do it."

She reached over, ignoring the jingling of her shackles, to place her hand over his. "I'm sorry, Willem. I can't imagine the pain you felt."

He smiled, but it was unconvincing. "It's all in the past now."

"But you ended up marrying her, didn't you?"

"I did." His face darkened again, but once more, he wiped the bitter look from his face as quickly as it'd come. "My brother disappeared off the face of the earth, leaving Rae and their unborn child behind. Despite my heartache, I didn't feel right about leaving her alone to raise the babe by herself. She accepted when I asked for her hand again, but our marriage didn't last as long as I'd hoped. I cared for her very much, though, despite everything." He smiled a bit. "I've put everything far behind me now. There's no use in dwelling on the past when such a bright future awaits me, is there?"

"No, there isn't." She forced herself to mirror his smile as he threaded his fingers through hers and squeezed. "How did Rae die? And what happened to the child?"

The corner of his mouth twitched as he pulled his hand away. Her heart pounded as she settled her hand on the saddle again, wondering if she'd overstepped, but Willem quickly smiled again and pointed at something up ahead.

"There's a river just over the hill. I haven't any bread or jam, but perhaps we can converse by the riverside for a bit—just like you once did with your dear Caledon."

XXXII

She appears very content, my liege."

Willem ignored Dayne and continued staring at the handheld mirror in his grasp. The mirror showed him exactly what his future bride was doing in this particular moment: strolling through the halls with her nose buried in a book, a chuckle escaping her perfect lips when she read something that amused her. Ser Rhys trailed a few paces behind her, his arms straining as he carried a stack of books that nearly towered over him.

She'd been bathed after their horseback ride, so her golden, partially dried hair now hung in a frizzy braid along her spine. Her simple, jade gown dusted the floor as she walked, and when she lifted the hem while stepping over an uneven tile, Willem saw that her feet were bare.

Aurelia came to an abrupt halt when she realized Ser Rhys was behind her, not beside her. "Come on, now," she teased, her voice echoing through the mirror. "Are the books too heavy for you?"

"Only a bit," the knight replied.

"I can take a few, if you'd like."

"No need, Your Grace. Carry on with your reading."

Frowning, she closed the book, then wrestled three larger texts from Ser Rhys's arms. He protested, but she ignored him like it was an instinct. She placed the one she'd been reading atop the others, balancing the stack between her arms and her chin, and grinned at the knight when he attempted to scold her.

Willem handed the mirror back to Dayne and raised an eyebrow. "She *does* seem rather content, doesn't she?"

"Why wouldn't she?" Danye leaned against the pillar behind him, still facing Willem as the king sat at his desk. "She has everything she could possibly want in this palace. She may still long for her children, but she'll forget about them when she has a new babe to fuss over."

"That's the hope. Have you learned anything else from her memories?"

Dayne grimaced. "It's been rather...difficult, my liege. The spell I've been using to tap into her mind has required more energy than usual to cast. It's like she has walls erected around her mind now." He winced and shook his head, disappointed. "I suppose the shock and uncertainty of everything made her more vulnerable when she first arrived. Now that her fear has subsided, she's grown stronger—even if she doesn't realize it."

Willem raised an eyebrow. "And that means—?"

"If you wish to know her thoughts and motives, you must trust your instincts and your instincts alone—if she refuses to answer your questions, of course." Dayne bowed. "My deepest apologies, Your Majesty. I'll proceed with my attempts, but I fear this method of gathering intel has run its course."

"Very well. You found more than enough to be useful, anyway." The king stood from his desk, clasped his hands behind his back, and approached the nearest window. It was a dreary day, and the thick clouds made it nearly impossible to see beyond a few miles in any direction. "I'm surprised the dragon hasn't come back for her. Even if he's incapable of flying through our shields, I expected to see him loitering along the borders—threatening us, warning us, whatever it may be."

Dayne cleared his throat. "She was true to her word, then. The dragon remains in Akkinor to protect her family."

"For now. What happens when we march to battle? The southerners know they need the beast to defeat us."

"Their wisest option is to leave him in Akkinor. Isn't that partly why you hoped she'd trade herself in his place?"

The corner of Willem's mouth twitched. He'd planted an idea in Aurelia's head after her first visit to Kanibar—the idea that he needed a wife and heirs, and she would've made the perfect candidate. She likely thought she'd come up with the idea to sacrifice herself on her own, too, which was an added bonus. But that wasn't the only reason he'd hoped she'd give herself up to him: he knew that her beast would be useless while she was trapped in Kanibar, and while it'd be nice to be known as the hero who defeated a dragon in battle, Willem still didn't want to take the risk of becoming dragon chow if he could help it.

"While she's here, the dragon only responds to a five-year-old girl," Willem muttered. "The southerners wouldn't dare bring him to battle with only her fool of a husband to command him. The beast wouldn't respond to him, and they'd risk incinerating themselves, too. We have to believe they're smart enough to leave him in Akkinor." Clearing his throat, he approached his desk again and opened a drawer. "If things don't go according to plan, though, there's something I must ask of you."

Dayne nodded. "Anything, my liege."

"This must be delivered in the event of my death in battle." Willem handed him a sealed envelope, gave him a moment to inspect the recipient's name, then reclaimed the envelope and returned it to the drawer for safekeeping. "While it's very unlikely, we must be prepared, nonetheless."

"I understand." Dayne tipped his head. "I shall appoint another to deliver the message in my place if I, too, happen to die in battle."

"Thank you, Dayne." Willem checked the time on the grandfather clock beside him. "It's almost time for dinner. If you'll excuse me, I'm off to meet my bride."

Leaving Dayne behind in his study, Willem strolled to his bedchamber to change into his evening attire, then made way to the dining hall to await Aurelia's arrival. To his surprise, she was already there, seated in the same chair she always claimed. She held a chalice of wine in one hand, and used the other to turn the pages of the book draped over her lap.

When she heard him approaching, she closed the book and set it aside, offering him the widest, most beaming smile he had seen from her. He might not have been convinced that her smile was genuine if it didn't meet her eyes, but it did—and it had been doing—as of late.

A good sign, he told himself.

As always, the pair exchanged stories about their days while the servants served each course and refilled their chalices. She'd long since stopped asking about the upcoming battle, her allies, or her family, so he didn't bother mentioning a word of anything—it was best to keep her in the dark, of course, but he knew he'd only push her away if he neglected to answer when she asked him something. So long as she remained uninterested, he didn't have to tell her a thing.

"...new lady's maids, after we're married," Aurelia was saying. He snapped out of his daze and swallowed a bite of mutton, nodding like he'd been paying attention the whole time. "They seem to dislike me, so I'd rather select my own handmaidens when the time comes. Would that be all right?"

"You may dismiss or appoint any staff members you'd like," Willem said with a smile. He knew she'd already been meddling in palace affairs, and it delighted him to know that she was trying to make his home, hers. "That's your responsibility as mistress of my estate, after all."

"I hoped you might say that." She set a cold hand on his forearm and squeezed. "Thank you."

Locked in a trance by the feel of her flesh against his—and the sight of her breasts straining against her corset—Willem cleared his throat, scooched his chair backward, and held out his arms for her.

She hesitated only briefly before rising from her chair and settling on his lap, one arm draped over her legs and the other over his shoulders. He set a hand on her lower back to keep her from falling, then held her thigh against his other palm. While her eyes bore holes into his, he was overwhelmed by the urge to explore her mouth with his tongue. He lifted his hand from her back and grasped the nape of her neck to bring her face closer to his, and the moment he did so, something unmistakable—fear—flashed across her eyes.

Willem paused for only a second, wondering if he'd imagined the expression, while her hand on her lap drifted to his leg. He resisted the urge to moan in delight when he felt her palm kneading against his flesh. By the time she lowered her head to kiss him, he'd forgotten all about that tiny flicker of doubt in his heart, and he tightened his grip on her neck while losing himself in their kiss.

"Mhm." When they separated, Willem grinned and rubbed his thumb over her lower lip, relishing the taste of her on his mouth, then threaded his fingers through hers. "You're terribly skilled at that, you know."

"I've been told. Many times, actually."

He laughed. "Jest or not, speaking of old lovers while perched on your groom's lap...Any other king might have you hanged for that."

"You're not any other king." Aurelia swung her legs to the side and stood, gently pulling her hand from his when he refused to let her go. He was hot and desperate for her now, and even more so when she taunted him by resuming dinner like nothing had happened.

Willem watched her as desire burned in his chest, rendering him silent. She took a large sip of wine and swished it around in her mouth a bit—almost like she was trying to mask the taste of him. That couldn't be true, though: not while she rubbed her shoeless feet against his calves, teasing him, and certainly not while she stared at him like a lioness might stare at her mate.

She didn't love him, but that was just fine—she didn't have to love him to desire him, and that was all he needed. As soon as their bodies united, she'd be entirely at his mercy.

***

The next morning—following a horrible dinner that'd brought her too close to the king for comfort—Aurelia visited the library once again, hoping to find some information on the descendants of Althaia Pharos. She knew her allies would be searching, too, but she had no way of knowing for sure if they'd find a connection between Althaia and Dofell's successor.

Willem's library was so organized that it didn't take her long to find what she needed. An entire section of the library was dedicated to Carthinian history, including massive books that traced the lineages of every highborn family that had ever ruled on the continent.

When she found the book dedicated to highborn Dofelli families—taller and wider than her torso, leatherbound, and caked in dust—she brought it to a sitting area and dropped it on the table. A cloud of dust enveloped her as soon as the book came in contact with the furniture, making her cough and gag as it filled her nostrils and crept down her throat.

Across the room, Ser Rhys raised an amused eyebrow. "I would've carried it for you."

She waved a dismissive hand. "I'm not lacking for strength, ser."

"I'd never dream of suggesting such a thing."

She allowed herself a small smile when she saw him smiling, too. He didn't seem curious about what she was reading or why; he merely stood with his back to a bookshelf, hands clasped behind his back, as he stared out the window across from him.

The first thing she did was search the index for the name *Pharos*. She didn't find anything she didn't already know about them. All traces of the Pharos family disappeared after Althaia and her husband were impoverished, and because the book only detailed the lives of highborn families, Althaia's son—and any of *his* descendants—weren't mentioned.

Defeated, Aurelia stood from the table to return the book to its home. A gasp escaped her when she heard a thud from behind. Ser Rhys called after her as she turned, frowning, to examine another large, leatherbound book that appeared to have flown off the shelf and landed on the floor. She waved the knight away when he appeared at her side, claiming she'd dropped the book while attempting to return it.

When he left, she knelt on the floor and examined the book's cover. It was nothing of great importance, so she didn't waste any time heaving it from the ground to put it away.

As she picked it up, she heard a buzzing by her ear and waved a hand to shoo what she *thought* was a pesky insect. Just as she was about to summon Ser Rhys to kill it, she saw a faint golden glow from the corner of her eye, and a strangled gasp caught in her throat.

There, perched on the empty slot on the shelf where the book had been, was a sprite. But it wasn't just any sprite—it was *her* sprite.

"What are you doing here?" Aurelia kept her voice low to avoid catching Ser Rhys's attention as she stood, now eye-level with the tiny creature. "How did you—?"

It smiled. "I flew."

"What?" She stared at it, dumbfounded. "You-You came to Kanibar on *Halvor?"*

"Yes. On his belly."

"Good gods." She brought the back of her hand to her forehead, overwhelmed, but quickly dropped her arm to her side when a realization struck her. "You've been here as long as I have?"

"Yes."

Aurelia gritted her teeth. "That explains it. You knew I'd fly to Kanibar to retrieve Hyacinth, and Halvor was the only way you could return to your master. You've been here all this time, telling Willem everything you overheard in Akkinor. What a rotten thing to do."

The sprite's golden glow—already dimmer than she recalled—faded. "I did not."

"And you expect me to believe you?"

"I came to help."

"If that were true, you would've come to me sooner. But it seems you've been too busy, more than likely selling my secrets to Willem." She shook her head and chuckled humorlessly. "Everyone told me not to trust a sprite, and I didn't listen."

The creature's lower lip wobbled. "I speak true."

"Then where the hell have you been?"

It shook its massive head. "May told me to wait."

"May?" She furrowed her eyebrows, softening a touch. "You know Maysa?"

"She's my friend."

"And she told you...to wait?"

The sprite nodded, still looking hurt. "She needed time."

"Oh."

Aurelia wasn't sure what to make of that. On one hand, it made sense: Maysa had been waiting for Aurelia's arrival in Kanibar, and if the sprite had helped Aurelia escape right away, she wouldn't have learned all she needed to from the oracle. On the other, sprites were tricksters loyal only to their masters, and Willem had already proven that he had spies in

Akkinor. She wanted to trust the creature—she'd grown to care for it, warnings be damned—but she'd already been betrayed before by people she trusted.

She bit her lower lip, contemplating. "All right. Here's what we're going to do: you'll come with me to see Maysa, and if she confirms your story, I'll owe you an apology. If not..." She trailed off, knowing in her heart that she'd be proven wrong. Instead of finishing her sentence, she cleared her throat and asked, "If I give you a message, can you deliver it to my uncle in Taundosa?"

"Yes."

She exhaled. "All right. We'll get to that after we speak with May."

Not a second later, the sprite zipped from the bookshelf and disappeared under her skirts. She lifted the hem of her dress and found it clinging to her ankle, sitting on her foot like the appendage was a throne. She snorted into a laugh, dropped her skirts, and told the creature to hold on tight.

After returning the fallen book to the shelf, she asked Ser Rhys to escort her to the temple. It was growing late now, almost time for dinner with Willem, so she'd have to make her visit a short one.

She left Ser Rhys to guard the temple, then found Maysa exactly where she always was. Before Aurelia could utter a word in greeting, the sprite zoomed out from beneath her skirts and presented itself to Maysa. The oracle chuckled, welcomed the creature home, and let it nestle on her shoulder as she blinked at the queen.

"I see our little friend has finally found you," she mused as Aurelia knelt beside her. "You must forgive me for keeping it from you. We needed time, you see, but that time has come to an end. You're leaving soon."

A hot, thick lump formed in Aurelia's throat as she glanced at the sprite. "I'm sorry. I should've trusted you."

It raised a thin, arched eyebrow. "Friends?"

"Friends." She mirrored the creature's smile before turning back to Maysa. "Is this really almost over? How can that be?"

"The sprite will show you the way," Maysa's eyes reflected the candlelight before her as she gazed at Vyena. "You must trust the creature, but you must trust your instincts, too. They're your greatest strength."

Aurelia nodded, but the idea of never seeing the oracle again filled her with sadness. "Will you come with me?"

The old woman laughed. "No, child. I must stay here."

"You're always here. Don't you ever leave?"

"I would if I could. I haven't seen the sunrise in years—I've been longing for it."

Aurelia frowned. "Are you confined to the temple? I never thought to ask why you're always here, day after day. I assumed you always arrived just before I did because you knew I was coming."

Maysa only smiled. "Did you learn everything you needed to?"

"I-I believe so. The king opened up to me yesterday—he told me about why he despises his brother. I imagine there's more to the story than what he shared, but I know it had something to do with his late wife."

A shudder corrupted her being when she remembered what else had happened the day earlier: a deep kiss filled with false passion on her end, and primitive desire on his. She knew she had to keep playing the part to avoid making him suspicious of her, but that didn't make her feel any better about sitting on his lap and sticking her tongue down his throat.

Thank the gods for wine, or she'd probably still be tasting the mung beans on Willem's breath.

"That's right. Rae married the king's younger brother, Myron, despite Willem's affection for her." Maysa paused to take a blueberry from her pocket, which she handed to the sprite. "Myron was a fool. He told everyone who'd listen that his son would be the next king. The people turned on Willem, pressuring him to secure the line of succession, and he blamed Myron. By that time, Myron and Rae had two sons. Willem had Myron and the boys murdered."

Aurelia's breath caught. That wasn't the story Willem had told her. "What?"

Maysa grimaced. "His pride was wounded. He wanted Rae, but Myron put her into hiding before his death. When Willem found her....He forced her to marry him, claiming she needed someone to take care of her now that Myron was dead, but he was unaware that she was carrying Myron's third son. When Rae fought back, he locked her away. He told her every day that he'd kill her after she gave birth, and he did. The infant—Harryn—is the boy Willem sent to ward in Krotis. He's only kept Harryn alive as a failsafe in case he doesn't sire children."

"My word. I...I was under the impression that Myron abandoned them." Aurelia shook her head and clenched her jaw. "He was clever about it—he told me the truth, but not the whole story. He certainly didn't tell me any of *that*."

"No, he wouldn't have." Maysa set her hand over Aurelia's and squeezed. "It was a terrible thing, but not unexpected. Unrequited love leads to disaster more often than not. Such turmoil will happen again if you stay here a day longer."

Aurelia nodded, realizing just how dangerous a game she'd been playing. "I do wish you'd come with me."

"Worry not, child. Our paths are destined to cross again in the future, years from now, but only if you prevent Willem from seizing Dofell. If he loses, there will be no shortage of blessings in the years to come."

Aurelia raised an eyebrow, sensing there was more Maysa wanted to say. "How do you mean?"

"There's a prophecy," she said slowly, "that speaks of an age of great promise in the near future. Kanibar and Dofell are at the center of it—as are you."

"What does it say?"

"A war between kin opens a door for a western hero to conquer the realm. If Willem succeeds, the realm as we know it will crumble. If he loses, the ancient way—the *right* way—will return to us. That's the most I can tell you." She shook her head and sighed. "Willem has the people believing that he's the hero, and the rest of you are threatening the restoration of our world."

A sudden realization struck Aurelia. "That's why he keeps you confined to the temple. You're the only one who knows the truth about what he is and what he desires."

For the first time since meeting her, Aurelia saw tears in Maysa's eyes. "Yes. He has wards erected at every exit so I can't leave. He claims it's a blessing: instead of locking me away in the dungeon, he keeps me here, where I'm closest to those I serve. I suppose it's the best a poor mother can hope to receive from her rotten son."

Aurelia stilled. "Willem...is your son?"

"He *was*. He hasn't been my son since the day he killed his brother."

"Oh, May..."

A strangled gasp escaped Aurelia's throat when Maysa turned to her and grabbed her wrist with a vise-like grip. Aurelia opened her mouth to question the oracle, but words failed her when she looked into Maysa's frantic, urgent eyes. Only then did Aurelia finally see that Maysa's emerald eyes were identical to Willem's.

"The king must die," the oracle whispered. "It's not enough that he loses in Dofell—he *must* die. Do you understand me?"

Aurelia swallowed. "Y-Yes. I understand."

"Good. You best be off before you're late for dinner." Maysa released Aurelia and relaxed as the queen nodded and stood. Aurelia beckoned the sprite to latch itself to her calf again, but she couldn't will herself to leave before exchanging parting words. Just as she opened her mouth, Maysa

308 FORGED IN ASHES

chuckled and added, "You needn't waste time on pleasantries. I already know what you wish to say. Go on, child. Your subjects await you."

XXXIII

To Aurelia's surprise, Willem cancelled dinner that night. When she returned to her bedchamber to prepare herself for the evening, she found a tray of dinner awaiting her, along with a note from Willem apologizing for the change of plans.

As soon as Aurelia was alone in her suite, she wrote a short letter for Arian, detailing everything she'd uncovered throughout her time in Kanibar. The sprite left to deliver the message, and it returned in minutes—before she had the chance to make a dent in her salad—with confirmation that the message had been delivered.

Another surprise came a few moments later when her handmaidens arrived to collect her dinner plates. They brought a handwritten message from Willem, who requested that she visit him in his bedchamber for an evening drink.

She was already wearing her nightdress, so she threw on a dressing robe and secured it before Ser Rhys escorted her to the king's chambers. She took a long, shaky inhale when she knocked on Willem's door, knowing how difficult it'd be to face him—and maintain her charade—after what Maysa had told her earlier.

"My darling." He beamed when he opened the door. "Come inside, please."

She swallowed the nervous lump in her throat as soon as the door closed between her and Ser Rhys. Something about the knight's presence brought her solace, and while the sprite was confined to her suite, Rhys was the closest source of comfort she'd have nearby.

"I-I missed you at dinner." She nonchalantly observed his room—plain, impersonal, and decorated in shades of brown, green, and gold—as he invited her to sit in an armchair by the hearth. "Are you well?"

"Quite. A matter was brought to my attention, but it's been handled."
Willem's back was turned to her as he filled two chalices at a nearby table.
She smiled and thanked him when he sat in the armchair beside hers and
offered her one of the chalices. "I hope I didn't worry you."

"Not at all." She drank the wine quickly, knowing she had to rely on
liquid courage if she wanted to look him in the eye. When her chalice was
empty, she stood and strolled around the room, observing. "I didn't worry,
but I did long for you. It was an awfully lonely evening."

She heard his chair creak but didn't turn to acknowledge it. Before she
knew it, his arms circled around her waist from behind, and his chin rested
on her shoulder. She resisted the urge to recoil at his touch, instead
expelling a dramatized, delighted gasp to strengthen her ruse.

"I missed you, too." His nose brushed against the side of her neck, his
lips not far behind, as his hands tightened over her midriff. "What did you
do without me?"

"Nothing, really." She shimmied out of his grip to pour herself another
glass of wine. He sat on the edge of his bed, admiring her, while his own
chalice sat untouched by the hearth. "I went back to the library for a bit. I
do love it there, you know."

"I know. You may claim it as your own, if that's what you wish."

Aurelia smiled fleetingly and swallowed a few large gulps of wine,
ignoring the sudden dizziness washing over her. He beckoned her over,
prompting her to set the chalice aside and sit beside him. He only gazed at
her for a moment, studying her, while she forced herself to set a hand on
his knee as a fog rolled in over her brain.

His fingers clasped her chin and turned her head in his direction. "May
I have the honor?"

She relaxed just enough for him to know her response. He smiled a bit,
then closed the gap between them and pressed his lips to hers. One of his
hands settled on the back of her neck, and the other clamped itself on her
thigh. She let him part her lips with his tongue and tighten his grip on her
leg, wondering why on earth she didn't hate the kiss—or his grip—as much
as she wanted to; as much as she normally did.

When he broke the kiss, both of them panting for air, she leaned away
just enough to study his face. Every part of her body that he touched was
hot and throbbing, but she couldn't focus on that while she looked into his
eyes. Something about him felt different that day, but it had nothing to do
with what she'd learned recently. It was just...*him.*

Unaware of what she was doing, she brought a hand to his head and
wove her fingers through his short, midnight black curls. She wondered
why she'd never given his hair any attention before—it was beautiful.

Then her gaze dropped to his eyes, and she sucked in a sharp breath when she could almost see waves crashing in his oceanic irises. She was entranced by him, and too marveled by his beauty to even consider resisting when he kissed her again.

Before she knew what was happening, she found herself falling backwards against the bed, the heavy mass of his body pressing down on hers. A quiet moan escaped her when his tongue explored the hollows of his mouth, his hands trailed firmly up her sides, and his hips nestled between her legs. She buried her hands in his hair, gripping his dark curls like a horse's reins, as his lips found her neck, her ears, her chest. When one of his hands slipped beneath her nightdress and crept up her leg, she pushed herself closer to him, inviting him to do whatever he pleased.

It was like she had one foot in reality while the other was lost somewhere in the universe. She could feel him, taste him, smell him—but after a few minutes, she couldn't identify the *him* in question. She forgot where she was, who she was with, and how she'd ended up on her back with a pair of warm lips on her neck. Her brain seemed to hum like a fly was buzzing around inside her head, and though she felt a certain numbness within her body, her flesh was searing with heat and desire, so she knew that whatever this was, she didn't want it to end. Perhaps it was because the *him* she could no longer identify was familiar; and while a part of her, buried deep within her soul, felt that something wasn't quite right, that sense of familiarity brought her just enough comfort to ignore the warning signs.

As his hand squeezed her thigh, he brought his mouth to her ear and expelled hot breaths of air, making her shiver with pleasure. "You like that, don't you?" he murmured. "What else do you like? Tell me, and I shall oblige. I only wish to please you, Lily dear."

Lily dear.

Those two words were enough to stop her world from spinning in the blink of an eye. Everything came flooding back to her, stripping her to the bone better than Willem's hands ever could.

It was like a fog had lifted from her brain, opening her eyes to the reality before her. It wasn't just that she'd let him take her into bed when she was meant to be fooling him. It was the realization that Willem's hair was straight, long, and mahogany instead of black, short, and curly; and that his eyes were solid and clear like raw emerald, not adventurous and unpredictable like the ocean during a storm.

In a flash, Aurelia shoved him away and stumbled off the bed. She staggered over to the opposite corner of the room while he knelt on the bed and stared at her with a dumbfounded look in his eyes—eyes that seemed to be shifting from blue to green and back again.

"What did you do?" The words sounded more like a gasp than a question. "What have you done to me?"

"Relax, darling. Everything's all right. Come back to bed."

"No." She shook her head, trembling, and pushed herself further against the wall as he took a few strides towards her. "Stay away from me. What did...What did you do?"

"I've done nothing. You seem to be having an episode." He cocked his head to the side, feigning concern. "Let's sit and discuss this calmly. Perhaps—"

She stepped away from the wall when she saw the chalices by the hearth. Hers was empty—she'd had two glasses—but *his* hadn't been touched.

"You put something in the wine," she whispered. "You—"

A strangled gasp escaped her when she caught sight of something not far from the chalices: a mirror, angled toward the side of Willem's face. She could see just enough of it to notice that the reflection showed not a young, handsome man in his late thirties, but an aging, wrinkled man whose dull mahogany hair was streaked with gray and white.

He followed her eyes to the mirror. His body tensed instinctively as he lowered his gaze to the floor, sighed, and closed his eyes without uttering a word. Then, in a matter of seconds, his demeanor shifted in a way that shook Aurelia to her core. He began to laugh—a horrible, maniacal sound—before looking up at her like she was a beast he'd dedicated his life to hunting.

"You've caught me. I'd forgotten to move that gods-forsaken mirror. *Idiot.*" Even his voice, normally smooth and charismatic, transformed into a tone riddled with cruelty. "I'm afraid I haven't been entirely forthcoming with you. Ser Dayne casts a glamour spell over me every morning, and he's done so for the last—gods, over fifteen years now. I've found that youth and attractiveness tend to be more effective when it comes to leadership and intimidation. I suppose that's why you lasted so long before your own people turned on you. Beauty is blinding, isn't it?"

Terror coursed through her veins, but she tried her utmost to conceal it from him. "That isn't the only glamour spell he placed on you."

He grinned and ran a hand through his dark hair. "Wonderful, isn't it? One look at your dear husband, and Dayne was able to replicate his appearance to near perfection. Of course, it was up to me to mimic your husband in other ways, but I daresay my performance was *excellent.* I could've taken you right there, drugged wine or not, and you would've let me."

Aurelia scowled. "If you were really starting to believe my ruse, why bother drugging me?"

"A wise man takes no chances. Whether I believed you or not, I needed to ensure we'd end up in this bed together, bound as one." A sinister smile corrupted his mouth. "It would've been perfect: nine months from now, I'd have an heir and a permanent connection to Akkinor, all because you're too frenzied over your husband to deny anything that resembles him. Of course, I'll continue tampering with your senses in the future—whether you caught me or not, it's always been part of the plan. Just a precaution to ensure that you're always willing to climb into my bed."

The more she thought about it, the more everything came together. He'd been building up to this since her arrival. He'd taken her for a ride, despite his hatred of horses, because he knew Jack loved them. Even the horses the king had chosen that day resembled the steeds she and Jack had bonded with during their time in Carthe: Willem rode a black one identical to Jack's, Sterling; and Aurelia rode a chestnut one identical to hers, Scotch.

After their first kiss, Willem had said something she didn't think twice about in the moment: *You're beyond what my mind is capable of imagining.* It was almost exactly like something Jack had said to her on their first night together: *What you are is beyond my imagination.* Somehow, Willem (or, more likely, his mage) had slithered his way into the deepest corners of her mind, extracting everything he could about Jack and their relationship.

When she felt Willem's eyes burning holes through her skull, Aurelia spat on the floor by his feet. "Try as you might, you'll never be him. You're nothing but a pathetic, groveling fraud, grasping at the last dangling thread of control you have."

She barely had time to process what happened next. One moment, she was standing a few paces away from the king, and the next, she was on the floor, hand instinctively pressed against her face, as blinding pain spread across her cheek. She didn't see him move to strike her, but she certainly felt the spot on her cheekbone where his family ring had broken her skin.

As she sat sprawled on the floor, using her other hand to prop herself up, he crouched down beside her and snatched her chin to force her into meeting his eyes. Relief coursed through her when she saw that his eyes were green again.

"I knew you were lying," he seethed. "I wanted to believe otherwise, but I couldn't. A woman like you would never leave her country behind.

The crown means too much to you." He chuckled and tightened his grip on her face, making her whimper. "Do you wish to know the worst part? I can see in your eyes that this isn't just about Akkinor, or saving Dofell, or the golden tears the gods demand you weep. This is about something far less important. Silly, even." He sneered as he leaned in closer. *"Love."*

She tried to tug away, but his grip tightened. "It's like I said," he continued. "Our countries will both have what they want if you accept your life here: Akkinor will finally have a king—permanently, if your husband names your son as heir like a wise man would—and Kanibar will finally have an heir. You know this, too. You know that your role in Kanibar wouldn't be the worst thing in the world, yet you refuse to consider it out of devotion to your traitor of a husband. There's no greater weakness."

"Love is more powerful than you give it credit for, Your Majesty. I wouldn't be alive without it—or my husband," she croaked. "I'd choose him over and over again in every lifetime, in every scenario, on every plane of existence. His love is what reminds me of my strength when I forget myself. It's what grounds me, inspires me, *ignites* me. It has nothing to do with the way he looks or the things he says, but it has *everything* to do with the kind of man he is. You could hardly even dream of becoming anything like him or loving me the way he does. I suppose that's why you needed that shameful glamour spell—because pretending is the closest you'll ever come to what I have. But truthfully, that's only one of thousands of reasons I would never stay here with you."

Aurelia cracked a smile, ignoring the throbbing on her cheek, before she continued. "You think you're the chosen one? The hero of an ancient prophecy? You couldn't even manage to secure a bride with any dignity, or even leave this gods-forsaken room without wearing a different face. Not to mention, you murdered your own wife, brother, and nephews because their very existence threatened your rise to power. Every leader has a duty to the realm to make it as wonderful as the gods imagined it would be, and the only duty *you've* ever known is serving yourself."

He stilled and loosened his grip on her face. She allowed herself a small, smug smile when she saw the rage and surprise flickering in his eyes. It was clear that up until this moment, he'd been completely unaware of her visits to the temple. She'd have to remember to thank Ser Rhys for his discretion.

"You've spoken to her." His voice, low and rumbling, frightened her more than it would if he shouted at her. "Maysa."

"Many times now. She's been ever so helpful."

He hesitated for only a moment, but as soon as he saw her wicked grin, he growled and grabbed her by the hair. She yelped and clawed at his hands as he dragged her across the room and through the door, down the hall, and into her bedchamber, where Ser Rhys was waiting outside of her door, having resumed his usual post. Willem had likely told him to leave them be after he saw Aurelia to the king's room, given the *activity* Willem had planned for the night.

Willem threw her into the room like a ragdoll. "Nobody goes in or out without my permission," he snapped at the knight. "Do you understand me?"

Ser Rhys squared his shoulders. "I understand, my liege."

"Good. And no more visits to the temple." Willem tossed one final glance at Aurelia. "I told you I'd wait until you desired me, but that much is impossible after the hysterics you've displayed tonight. Sleep well, Your Grace. Tomorrow, our life together begins."

Then he was gone.

She brought a hand to the back of her head, her scalp burning like her hair had been set ablaze, before touching the swollen welt on her cheek. She winced as her fingers trailed the five-year-old scar beneath the welt. She'd have another scar there now, exactly the size and shape of Willem's ring.

As she sniffled and bit back tears, she sensed Ser Rhys loitering in her doorway. "Go on, then," she said hoarsely. "Man your post as you always do. There's no need to stare like I'm a helpless animal."

He stiffened. "I beg forgiveness, Your Grace, but in this moment...You seem to be one, but not the other."

Despite herself, a weak smile formed on her lips. "I'm an animal, then?"

His lips twitched like he wanted to chuckle, but his face smoothed out again in the time it took her to blink. To her immense surprise, he slipped inside and closed the door. She demanded to know what he was doing when he disappeared into the washroom, but he ignored her, only to return with a damp cloth in hand.

He lowered himself onto the floor across from her. "May I?"

She nodded and watched him carefully as he brought the cloth to her cheek. She winced and hissed in pain, but only for a moment—whatever concoction he'd soaked onto the cloth worked wonders within seconds.

"Thank you," she whispered. He didn't so much as smile in response. "Where did you learn this?"

"My aunt was an apothecary."

"The wretched aunt?"

"That's the one."

"At least something good came from your time with her." She smiled when he chuckled a bit, then set her hand over his armored forearm to stop him. "You're a good man, Rhys."

The knight didn't reply. He merely sat there beside her, holding the cloth to the throbbing welt on her cheek, not uttering another word until the midnight bells chimed in the distance.

XXXIV

That's impossible," Lord Zhoqa snapped. "Do you have any idea how difficult it is to find a Kanish person willing to betray their country? Even the traitorous or desperate ones would rather die than assist an enemy of the kingdom. Word would reach Willem's ear about our attempt immediately, and he'd respond accordingly. It's not worth the risk."

"'*It.*'" Arian scoffed, exhausted by the conversation and the dozens of times he'd heard the same excuses. "The Queen of Akkinor isn't an *it*, Balor. She's the best hope we have. Mind that revolting tongue of yours."

"Why? Because she weeps tears of gold and commands a dragon?" The Lord of Kazamir shook his head. "We have an enormous army between the four of us, and almost half of our numbers include mages. We already overwhelm Willem's troops as it is. The beast would be a useful asset for keeping the bloodshed to a minimum, but wars have been fought and won *without* dragons for over a thousand years now. We don't need him to drive Willem into the ground."

Nobody replied. Arian, standing directly across from Lord Zhoqa, planted his hands on the table between them and studied the battle map spread over the wooden surface. The others—Queen Reyna, Lord Zhaaran, and the two kingdoms' most esteemed war generals—stood gathered around the table, too, strategizing as well as they could with what little information they had.

Neither Lord Zhoqa nor Lord Zhaaran had seen Bozar since word spread of Aurelia's captivity. Reyna opened the doors of the palace for them, ignoring the fact that Taundosa and Bozar were recently prepared to battle one another for Dofell, and invited them to stay as long as they required while the allies readied for war. Naturally, the planning and strategizing always came back to the same matter: plotting a way to retrieve Aurelia from Willem's clutches.

Unfortunately, a rescue mission was easier said than done. Willem had responded to Arian's threatening letter with a claim that he'd erected magical shields around the Kanish borders. Reyna suggested finding and hiring Kanish natives to carry out the rescue mission, but that foul Lord Zhoqa had a point: the Kanish were eternally loyal to their kingdom, even the worst of them, and neither coin nor glory would be enough to sway them.

"Willem's forces are stronger than he lets on." Reyna clenched her jaw as she gestured to the spider-shaped figurines—representing Kanish troops—on the battle map. "He has more mages than he would ever reveal to the rest of the continent. He has dozens of sprites at his disposal, too, though I doubt he'd send them to battle. He'd only need them to spy on us. And his troops..."

"The Kanish army is large, but weak." Lord Zhoqa added more elephants to the Kanish troops. "My scouts have reported a larger number than we previously thought. They saw the Kanish training camps, and they have reason to believe the king offered some sort of incentive for expanding his army. There are women among his troops now—hundreds of them."

"Women?" Reyna pursed her lips. "That can't be right. Kanibar has always viewed women as homemakers and mothers—nothing more. Only the poorest of them work at all. We have to assume he's desperate for manpower if he asked women to join the fight."

"I assume that's why he hasn't marched on Dofell already—he needs time to train his newest recruits, and time to find resources to provide for a larger army," Lord Zhaaran replied. "Either way, we still outnumber him. We may not need the dragon at all."

"You said it yourself many weeks ago: Halvor is the best deterrent we have," Arian retorted. "Why waste lives when we don't have to? The Kanish have never met a dragon in battle before. Half of them would probably flee on sight when they saw him, even if they knew to expect him. But Halvor isn't the only reason we have to prioritize Her Grace's safe return. She's our ally—we can't leave her at Willem's mercy. Akkinor would fall to chaos, and we along with it."

Lord Zhoqa pinched the bridge of his nose. "What do you suggest, then? I won't send my men to die while attempting to retrieve her. She—"

Just then, a golden ball of light zipped around the meeting room like a rogue star, prompting everyone to draw their weapons, hollering as they desperately attempted to spot the fast-moving creature. When the light settled on the table in front of Arian, the golden glow faded to reveal a sprite carrying a tiny scroll.

Arian held up his hands to keep the others at bay. "It's all right. The creature has brought a message."

The sprite set the scroll on the table at its feet. "From Aurelia."

"Aurelia?" Arian snatched the scroll immediately and opened it just enough to glimpse at the writing. It was, indeed, his niece's hand. He raised an eyebrow at the creature while it merely stared at him, head cocked to the side as if awaiting a reward. "You've seen her? Is she well?"

It nodded. "Yes. I have to go back now. We hope to leave soon."

"'We?'" Lord Zhoqa snorted. "Since when do Kanish sprites latch themselves to foreigners?"

The creature hissed at him, but before the nobleman could lunge across the table to throttle it, the sprite's golden glow returned, and it fled the room as quickly as it'd arrived.

Arian turned his attention back to the scroll, read the message, and sighed in relief. "She's just fine, or at least as fine as she can be. She's plotting an escape, and she's managed to uncover some helpful information." He turned to Lord Zhaaran and raised an eyebrow. "Do you happen to know a Kanish oracle by the name of Maysa?"

The elderly nobleman nodded. "She visited the Holy Library many decades ago when I was studying there. Cryptic and curious, to be certain, but as wise and knowledgeable as they come."

"Aurelia writes that Maysa is the king's mother. He has her imprisoned in the temple at the palace. There's a prophecy coming to fruition in the near future, and she believes Willem must die to ensure the most favorable outcome. Aurelia inquires after our progress regarding Elrin's successor, too, and claims we need to be searching for a woman."

The Golden Queen grimaced. "We've already sent men to Dofell in search of the potential successors we identified, but it'll take time for them to return—if they manage to find these individuals, of course. If they don't..." She clenched her jaw and exhaled. "The civilian population of Carthe helped instigate this conflict because they want Dofell reformed, not conquered. That applies to the Kanish, too. They may be loyal to Kanibar, and they may fear Willem's wrath, but neither fear nor loyalty can assure participation. If they know Dofell is being passed down to a just, worthy ruler capable of repairing the kingdom, they may not wish to sacrifice their lives for Willem's greed."

"We saw proof of that when Queen Aurelia won the war against her brother." Ser Xantos, Commander of the Goldmen, nodded in agreement. "Half of the Scorpion's troops fought for him out of fear, the other half out of loyalty. Most of them brought their swords to Her Grace's side when she gave them the choice between fighting for power and fighting for justice."

"All soldiers swear an oath to serve, defend, and protect their kingdom's leader," Lord Zhoqa said accusingly. "It doesn't matter how deeply they fear the consequences of laying down their swords. It doesn't matter if they doubt their leader's motives or if they wish to do what's best for the realm, either. An oath is an oath, regardless of the circumstances. We can't rely on the hope that Willem's troops will back off."

Lord Zhaaran sighed. "He's right. It's a possibility, but we can't be certain of anything." He paused, looking like he'd aged ten years in a matter of seconds, and bowed his head. "At least we have the amulet on our side."

Arian raised an eyebrow. "You've been against the use of the amulet since the start. What changed your mind?"

"Her Grace was as persuasive as she was logical when we last spoke of it. I haven't stopped believing in the curse, but I've certainly started believing in *her* again. I never should've stopped." Lord Zhaaran's purple eyes fluttered shut. "We must save it as a last resort option, but we can't even consider using it until she's left Kanibar. If we can't retrieve her ourselves, we must pray to the gods that she finds the answer on her own."

"She will." Arian turned to glance out the window to his left, where the sun was just starting to set on the horizon line—though not completely, of course. The sun never slept in the City of Gold, after all. "She always does. In the meantime..." He sighed and gestured to Aurelia's scroll, now clenched in Lord Zhoqa's fist. "We have a bit of studying to do, my friends. A prophecy awaits us."

***

Not at all to her surprise, sleep was impossible to come by that night. When Ser Rhys left her, Aurelia paced around the room, desperately trying to invent a plan. The time for games had come to an end; now, the only thing left to do was flee.

The sprite revealed itself as soon as the knight was gone. It didn't say much—only sat on her bed, watching her—but she felt comfort in its presence, anyway.

"I need to remove these." She held up her shackled wrists. Luckily, Willem had been too distracted by the night's events to remember to chain the shackles together again. "While I'm wearing them, my only option—if I can find a way out of the palace, anyway—is to travel north and cut through the Violet Forest so I can board an Akkinorian ship docked in Caedia. That journey would take weeks, giving Willem plenty of time to hunt me down. Halvor, on the other hand, would reach me in a day or two if he felt me calling for him." She stopped pacing and raised an eyebrow. "Can you remove them?"

"No. The locks cannot be picked."

A low, growl-like sound escaped her. "What about what May said? She told me that you can help me flee. What did she mean by that?"

"I can lead you out of Kanibar."

"How?"

"I have to show you."

"Naturally," she grumbled. "But you can't do that until the shackles are removed and I've found a way out of the palace. Any ideas?"

The sprite thought on that for a moment. "We must leave while it's dark. Fewer guards. No moon tonight."

"The moon." Aurelia practically squealed in delight as she fetched the amulet from beneath a pile of clothing in her wardrobe. She'd placed it there for safekeeping, under the sprite's watchful eye, when Willem summoned her to his bedchamber. "I can use it to flee. It'd be simple, really: all I'd have to do is use the amulet's power to compel the soldiers into letting me go. I could make them forget it ever happened, too."

The creature hissed. "No. You cannot trust the moon yet."

Aurelia stilled. "What did you say?"

"You cannot trust the moon yet."

"Hyacinth said the same thing," she murmured. "What do you mean by that?" The sprite didn't answer—only stared at her as if she was supposed to know what it meant. "Fine, then. Keep it to yourself."

Defeated, she sunk onto the floor at the foot of the bed and leaned her back against the mattress. She turned the amulet over in her hands, eyes trained on the fragment of moonrock, and wondered how on earth she was supposed to trust the moon—or the moon *goddess*, who hadn't been seen in over a thousand years.

When a droplet of glittering gold landed on the moonrock, she brought a hand to her face to wipe her tears away, unaware until then that she'd begun to cry. She slipped the amulet into her stocking, feeling the dam she'd erected in her heart upon her arrival in Kanibar beginning to break. Everything struck her like a typhoon, all at once: the deal she'd made to save her daughter and her dragon, the disarray she'd left her husband and her allies to deal with, the measures she'd taken to earn Willem's trust while plotting behind his back...It was all going to be for nothing.

She barely heard the soft knock at her door, but the sprite certainly did. It zipped under the bed and dimmed its golden glow just as Ser Rhys slipped inside. She didn't acknowledge him or even notice when he sat beside her, mimicking her position with his back against the bed.

Only when he offered her a handkerchief did she look at him. She forgot to thank him as she wiped her cheeks and nose, but she must've missed a stray tear, as he reached over to brush it from her cheek. Sniffling, she calmed enough to watch him as he smudged the golden liquid between his thumb and index finger.

"I've heard that those Forged in Gold are created to die," he murmured. "I hope that isn't always the case."

She wasn't surprised that he'd overheard one of her conversations with Maysa, but it made her feel worse. She folded her arms over her knees and tucked her head on her forearms, hiccupping with every sob, wishing for a moment that she had never met the oracle.

Then she heard a soft jingling, and felt something brush against her arms. When she lifted her head, she inhaled a sharp breath at the sight of the knight unlocking her shackles.

"Ser Rhys," she whispered. "What are—"

"Two doors down on your right, you'll find a linen closet. That's where the servants keep spare clothing if they happen to dirty their uniforms and have to change quickly," he said as he freed her wrists. Almost immediately when the shackles clattered to the floor, she felt a surge of power rush through her body. "Change your clothing, and be sure to cover your hair. There aren't any blonde women in Kanibar. Keep your head down while you walk to the kitchens. You know where the door is. The servants have all gone to sleep. so you shouldn't find anyone down there. Two guards will be stationed outside of the servant's entrance. Don't look at them, but speak these words: *hasi louor ie tobad*. They won't question you."

"*Rhys*—"

"There are no walls surrounding the grounds, as you know, so you can cross the field directly into the village of Koufor. Find a tavern called *The Yellow Gauntlet*—it has a yellow door, so it'll be difficult to miss. The barkeep is an auburn-haired woman named Sora. Tell her I sent you, and she'll look after you."

Aurelia's eyes welled with tears once more. "Why are you doing this? Willem will have you killed."

His face crumpled for a moment, but it was smooth again when she blinked. "You're the only person in this palace who's treated me with kindness and respect—like I'm your equal. You didn't have to, but you've never failed to." He brushed another tear from her cheek, smiling, and examined the gold on his finger again. "We've spent so long serving mortals that we've forgotten we're supposed to be serving the realm, the gods. Betraying my king is nothing compared to betraying my realm, and that's exactly what I've been doing by helping him restrain you. It isn't right."

Her lower lip trembled. "I can't leave you here to face his wrath. I won't."

"Kanibar may not be the most marvelous place at the moment, but it's still my home. I can't leave it behind."

She took his hands and squeezed. "Thank you, Rhys. I'm forever in your debt."

"There's no debt to be paid, Your Grace. Not while my actions service the realm." He smiled and squeezed her right back. "It's been an honor to make your acquaintance. I hope...I hope we can meet again."

"As do I." She leaned over to kiss his cheek. "Thank you."

He touched the spot where she'd kissed him, blushing, and offered her a sheepish smile. "You're welcome. Now, you go on ahead of me—I'll return to my post when you've slipped into the closet."

"What will you say when Willem asks about how I managed to escape?"

Rhys grimaced. "What would you have me say?"

She thought on that for a moment, then produced the amulet from within the folds of her skirt. "Tell him the last thing you remember is seeing me with an object that resembles moonrock. Tell him you swear you've seen it before, perhaps in a book, and that you felt a lack of control over your being when I spoke to you."

"All right." He frowned. "What is it?"

"The king will know. Trust me."

A part of her knew it wasn't wise to tell the king that she had the last piece of the Lunar Staff, but she had to believe it was the best course of action, for her and for Ser Rhys. Willem would fall into a panicked frenzy when he found out—not only because he'd lost her, but also because such a powerful tool had been hiding right beneath his nose the whole time. If he or his men happened to find Aurelia before she had the chance to flee Kanibar, she'd do what needed to be done to protect the amulet: give it to the sprite, who would deliver it to Arian for safe keeping.

As soon as she stood from the floor, she felt the sprite latch itself to her ankle. She said one final goodbye to Ser Rhys, thanked him again, and quickly slipped out of her bedchamber—all while praying to every god in the realm that she wasn't intercepted by a lurking servant.

Or worse, the king himself.

Aurelia followed Rhys's instructions to the closet and searched the shelves of clothing for garments that would fit her. She shimmied out of her slippers and nightclothes, then changed into something she'd often seen her handmaidens wear: a plain, muslin brown dress with a white apron, stockings, and brown loafers. She found a shawl, too, and secured the strings over her chest. She was lacking a ribbon or band of sorts, but she managed to tie her hair up with the belt from her dressing robe. When her hair was pulled back as tightly and securely as possible, she lifted the hood of the shawl over her head, took a deep breath, and slipped out of the closet.

Minding Rhys's voice in her head, she kept her chin down as she walked down the hall and to the first story of the palace. There were a few guards posted here and there, but most were sitting around, exchanging flasks, and sharing crass stories about their sexual conquests. None of them batted an eye at a handmaiden roaming the halls in the middle of the night.

When she made it to the kitchens, she didn't immediately run for the door. Instead, she snatched a piece of paper from a nearby table, marred with smudged black ink—a shopping list—and quickly lit a lantern with a match. She hesitated in front of the door, chest heaving with nerves, before pushing it open and taking her first steps toward freedom.

The soldiers outside, standing on either side of the door, immediately straightened up to face her. She kept her head down, brandished the list, and said, "*Hasi louor ie tobad.*"

She knew what the Old Carthinian words meant: *we live to serve.* What she *didn't* know was what the words meant specifically to the staff at the Palace of Kanibar. When the soldiers merely snorted in laughter and wished her luck, relaxing and resuming their previous conversation, she swallowed the squeal of delight inching up her throat and started walking for the village in the near distance.

The sprite hissed something at her from its new hiding place in the pocket of her apron, but she could hardly hear it over the rushing of blood in her ears. She wanted to look back at the palace, to catch one final glimpse of the place that'd imprisoned her, but she couldn't do it. She had to leave the palace—and Willem—as far behind her as she could.

The village of Koufor was fast asleep, as expected, with the only signs of life coming from taverns, inns, and brothels here and there. It was surprisingly lacking for nasty men and common criminals prowling the darkness for victims, and the lanterns lining the streets made it easy for her to find her destination: the only establishment in the entire village with a bright, sunflower-colored door.

She slipped inside, immediately relieved to find that the only patrons were drunk old men asleep at their tables. The auburn-haired woman at the counter, about a decade or so older than Aurelia, barely looked up from counting coin when she heard the door open. Only when Aurelia appeared in front of her, panting and pale, did the woman finally acknowledge her.

"Good gods," the barkeep muttered. "What do you need?"

Aurelia shook her head. "You're Sora, aren't you? Rhys sent me. He said you'd look after me."

Sora abandoned the coin and narrowed her eyes a bit. "Who are you? You're not Kanish."

"No, but Rhys—"

"Oh." Sora's eyes flickered with recognition, and her somewhat frosty exterior melted away. "I see. He wrote to me about his newest assignment, but I hadn't expected..."

"Can you help me?"

Sora stared at her for a moment, then stepped out from behind the counter. "Follow me."

Aurelia sighed in relief and followed Sora into a storage room at the back of the tavern. It was full of ale, wine, food, dishes, and cutlery—a disaster if Aurelia had ever seen one—and the mountain of crates and barrels stacked in the corner offered a perfect hiding spot for one small woman.

"You can stay here for now," Sora told her. "I'll bring a blanket so you don't catch your death. I'll find you something to eat, too." She raised an eyebrow. "When do you hope to leave Kanibar?"

"As soon as possible."

"Daylight's only a few hours away. The entire army will be out searching for you. I can't keep you here—if they find out I'm protecting you, I'll lose my head. You have to leave before sunrise."

Her heart sank. "But—"

"Here." Sora fetched a metal canister from a nearby shelf and opened it. Aurelia frowned, not understanding, when she saw nothing but coffee grounds inside. "Slather this over your hair—it'll change the color for a time. Dirty your clothing and your fingernails. Might as well muddy your face, too, just to be safe. Nobody will give you a second look if you're as filthy as the average peasant."

Aurelia nodded. "All right. Thank you."

"I'll be back in a minute or two with food and a blanket."

As Sora turned to leave, the queen said, "May I ask you something?"

"Of course."

She cleared her throat. "Why are you doing this?"

"Helping you?" Sora blinked at her. "Rhys sent you. He wouldn't take such a risk unless this means something to him. My brother has never been the type to do anything unless he believes in it."

"He didn't tell me he had a sister."

"Half-sister, and much older," she corrected, smiling. "I left home when he was a toddler. He tracked me down when he was assigned to the palace."

Aurelia returned her smile. "Your brother is a wonderful man, you know."

Sora beamed at her. "I know."

XXXV

After only three hours of sleep, Aurelia was shaken awake by Sora, who claimed sunrise was less than an hour away. As Aurelia collected herself, Sora scoured the storage room until she found what she was looking for: a tattered, faded leather satchel. She grabbed this and that—an empty canteen, a package of sugared nuts, a loaf of bread, bandages, and the like—and threw all of it into the satchel.

"One of my former patrons left this behind," Sora said, patting the bag. "I let him spend the night after his wife kicked him out. Woke up to find him face-down in a bowl of broth he'd stolen from the kitchen after I retired. He fell asleep, drunk, and drowned. His wife told me I could keep whatever he brought to the tavern—and gave me my choice of his things before she tossed them onto the street."

Aurelia cracked a smile. "I don't know whether to laugh or to pity him."

"You can laugh. He was a horrid man." Sora secured the rusting metal clasps on the satchel and set it down by Aurelia's feet. "That should be enough to see you out of Kanibar. You should dirty yourself while I hide the evidence of your stay."

Nodding, Aurelia reached for the coffee cannister and brought it over to a cracked, stained mirror hanging lopsided on the wall nearby. She took a handful of coffee grounds, added a splash of rum from a nearby jug, and slathered the muddy mixture over her hair, lock by lock, until every last strand had transformed from a coppery gold to a dark brunette.

Instead of washing her hands, she wiped them on her dress and apron, then added a bit more sludge to her face and neck. Brown speckles were imbedded in the lines on her hands and buried beneath her fingernails, but she didn't bother cleaning it.

"How do I look?" Aurelia turned to face Sora, who immediately grabbed a clean cloth and wiped coffee drippings from the back of Aurelia's neck. "Thank you."

"I wouldn't look twice at you if I were searching for a queen," Sora told her. "Just keep your hood up and your sleeves low to your wrists—you're too pale to pass as a native Kanish, so it's best if passersby can't see your skin. If anyone happens to stop you and comment on your ethnicity, tell them you immigrated to Kanibar from Espos. They never question those who come from a place with no true heritage."

She nodded. "Understood."

"You best be off, then. Breakfast at the palace is normally served right at dawn, isn't it? Your handmaidens will alert the king of your disappearance soon enough. You need to gain some distance before he sends the troops after you."

"All right. Thank you, Sora. For everything."

The barkeep smiled at her. "I left my brother behind when he needed me most. I swore I'd spend the rest of my life making it up to him, though this isn't exactly what I expected." She attempted to curtsy, but it was wobbly and much too high. "It's been a pleasure, Your Grace. Good luck."

Aurelia took the satchel and slung it over her shoulder, then touched both the pocket of her apron and the side of her stocking to ensure the sprite and the amulet, respectively, were still on her being. After pulling her hood over her head, she followed Sora out of the storage room and across the tavern to the rear entrance, where the barkeep accepted deliveries and disposed of waste.

Sora had closed the door behind Aurelia before the queen had the chance to say one final goodbye. Sighing, Aurelia wrinkled her nose and navigated muddy puddles of old ale, piles of food scraps, and what appeared to be a river of vomit trickling down the hill behind the tavern.

She'd never expected to become Lily Linden again after meeting Arian in Taundosa all those years ago, but in a way, it brought her great comfort. And it was far better than the name she was running from: Queen Consort Aurelia Trevas.

"Where should I go?" she whispered. "Which direction?"

"West," the sprite said from her pocket. "We need a horse."

"The west? But—"

She stopped talking when she remembered that she was roaming the streets of a Kanish village, surrounded by people, and she wouldn't remain unnoticed if the commoners saw a strange woman talking to herself.

Kaia had once told her all about western Kanibar. The coast was made up entirely of massive, dangerous cliffs overlooking the very edge of the

Alkamura Ocean. It was the only part of the ocean and the only body of water in the realm inaccessible to manmade vessels. There were no harbors or ports, which meant no transportation by sea. The only route she could think of was traveling northwest toward the border of the Violet Forest, where she'd have to cross the river—along with the entire forest—to reach Caedia and find passage home from there.

She'd barely made it through the Violet Forest on her own the first time she was forced to cross it. Now, she was at an even greater disadvantage: she was alone, unarmed, and had an entire army chasing her scent. She had the sprite and the amulet, of course, but neither would do much good if she happened to come across cannibalistic tribes or a band of rapists or thieves.

As the sun came up, Aurelia roamed the streets of Koufor in search of horses. The first stables she came across only sold mules for transporting goods, and the groom of the second practically chased her away when he saw her approaching. A person who looked like she did probably couldn't afford one of his steeds—and he was right. Only then, when the man shooed her away so vehemently, did she realize she didn't have any money.

Fortunately, she had the sprite.

She felt a slight tremor in her pocket after muttering something about her lack of coin, and a few seconds later, another series of tremors shook her apron, one after another. She peered into her pocket and bit back a laugh when she saw the sprite sitting atop a pile of silver coins.

She found another man selling horses and flashed him a handful of silver before he had the chance to shoo her away. She traded three pieces of silver for a sleek, deep brown horse, and another two for the saddle. She led the horse out of the clustered streets until they reached the edge of Koufor, then mounted him and set out for the west.

"Do I want to know how you acquired the coin?" she asked.

The sprite giggled. "The groom's coin pouch."

Aurelia cracked a smile. "Sneaky, but clever. I'll bet—"

Deafening horns and bells cut through the air as they echoed from the towers of the palace across the way. Shouting and clamoring followed suit almost immediately, and any soldiers lingering near the village abandoned what they were doing to run for the palace. The horns and bells blared for much longer than necessary, alerting every living soul within miles of the palace that something had gone awry.

Now, the chase would begin.

Time was of the essence, but Aurelia wouldn't increase the horse's pace until they were a safe distance from the palace. She didn't want to risk Willem's men spotting a hooded female figure galloping away during a time of crisis. She stayed calm, visibly unaffected by the chaos, and kept her eyes forward and her head down while she gained as much distance from the capital as possible.

She followed the sprite's instructions through another village—Tamur—then toward a dirt path that cut directly through the middle of woodlands. There were a few tiny cottages here and there, but nobody else was on the road. That wouldn't last long now that a search party was underway, though. Soon enough, the roads would be flooded with soldiers, and the quiet, sleepy homes would be torn apart in search of the king's escaped bride.

When they reached a part of the forest where no homes flanked either side of the road, the sprite crawled out from her apron and perched on the horn of the saddle. It began to hum as the cool breeze lifted its shaggy hair from its shoulders and rustled its leafy garments. As the wind ceased whistling through the trees, offering a moment of silence, Aurelia realized she knew the song the sprite was humming: it was the same song she and Jack often sang to their children.

"You've spent more time with the children than I thought, haven't you?"

The sprite giggled. "Yes."

"Naturally." She smiled, envisioning the delight on her children's faces when they set their sights on the creature. "I hope they were gentle with you. Henry doesn't always realize when he's being rough."

"They were very gentle."

"Did they torment you at all?"

"No, but Sisi was sad."

She smiled, wondering how such an ancient creature could be so childlike. "Why was she sad?"

"I don't have a name. She thinks I should have one."

Aurelia opened her mouth to reply, but no sound emerged. The sprite didn't seem bothered, though. It continued humming like it hadn't a care in the world, all while Aurelia bit back tears at the thought of such an intelligent, powerful little creature living hundreds of years without a proper name.

"I've decided to call this horse *Brandy*," she shared, petting the steed's neck. "It's about the same color as the liquor, and the horse I rode when I first arrived in Carthe was named Scotch. I'd like to maintain the theme." Though it wasn't looking at her, she raised an eyebrow. "I can give you a name, too, if you'd like, or you can choose your own. Sisi would be so pleased—as would I."

It didn't answer for a moment. When it did, its voice was soft and barely audible: "You can choose."

Aurelia smiled. "All right. What about *Edom?* It means *red* in the old tongue. Your hair is fairly red, isn't it?"

"Edom." She couldn't see the sprite's face, but she knew it was smiling. "Sounds nice."

She chuckled. "Yes, it does. I'm glad you like it." It didn't reply, but its humming grew louder and more melodic. As they rode in silence for a few minutes, a thought struck her that made her laugh again. "You know, I never imagined myself speaking this way to a creature no larger than my hand. I never imagined I'd have a sprite for a friend, either. I didn't even know your kind existed until recently. I've never read a story featuring sprites."

Edom turned on the horn so it was facing her, rather than the path ahead. "Do you know the other creatures?"

"Personally? No. Most are extinct now. I have Halvor, of course, and you, but I've never seen another magical creature before. Only in books and illustrations."

"Would you like to be friends with any of them?"

"I'm friends with you, aren't I?"

"Not what I asked," Edom said, but it was smiling.

"I suppose I don't really know." She paused for a moment, recalling the many stories she'd read about magical creatures in her lifetime, and reconsidered her answer. "Now that I think of it...When I was a girl, I dreamt of befriending a nymph—a tree nymph, to be specific. I've always had a fascination for trees. I used to imagine a nymph would crawl out from the trunk of the tree I was sitting in, and she'd join me in the branches to share stories and sweets. I'd ask her if we could trade places for a day, so I'd know what it was to be one with the trees." Her cheeks warmed with embarrassment. "It sounds silly."

"Not silly. Nymphs are lovely."

"Did you know any? Before the persecution, I mean."

Edom nodded, and for the next several minutes, proceeded to tell her a story about a tree nymph it once knew named Laurel. According to the sprite's tale, Laurel left her home in the Violet Forest to join her sisters in Akkinor after a wildfire devastated a vast portion of the Holosi woodlands. They managed to repair the forest, but the persecution began before Laurel could return to Carthe. Edom never saw or heard from her again, but it didn't know if she'd been killed or if she went into hiding. Aurelia didn't have the heart to tell Edom that, given the brutality of the persecution in Akkinor, Laurel probably hadn't survived.

The story seemed to upset the sprite, as it crawled back into Aurelia's pocket while claiming to need rest. Now that she had nobody to speak with, she urged Brandy into a gallop to gain as much distance as possible from the palace. Eventually, after what felt like hours of riding, she brought Brandy to a stop by a creek in the forest so the horse could rest and drink.

While Brandy drank from the creek, Aurelia walked around the forest in search of food. She had the bread and nuts from Sora's tavern, but Kaia's voice in the back of her head reminded her that she couldn't rely solely on what she had. The goods would be gone before she knew it, so if she came across any sightings of food on her journey, it was in her best interest to collect it.

She managed to find a strawberry bush, so she tore a piece of her apron to use as a pouch as she collected the berries. She tried tying the fabric up so the strawberries wouldn't make a mess of her satchel, but she dropped everything to the ground at her feet when the sprite zoomed up from her pocket, temporarily blinding her with its magnificent golden glow.

"Good *gods*, Edom—"

"We are being followed."

She couldn't see the sprite, but she could hear it, and she trusted its instincts better than her own. She abandoned the berries—but claimed the strip of fabric to avoid leaving evidence behind—and immediately mounted Brandy again. By the time she was settled, with Edom nestled in her pocket once more, she heard the unmistakable sound of hooves beating against dirt.

She urged Brandy into a gallop as the hoofbeats grew louder. Her heart pounded with nerves, but she reminded herself that the riders behind her may not have been soldiers—though it certainly sounded like they were, judging by the clanging of metal and the barking voices piercing the silence of the forest.

As they neared the edge of the forest, she looked over her shoulder and inhaled sharply at the sight of ten Kanish knights on horseback. She caught a glimpse of them just as they ascended a hill in the road, so as soon as they made it onto level ground again, they'd have a perfect view of her.

Aurelia may have looked like a common peasant girl to the untrained eye, but Willem's soldiers knew what she looked like, and even coffee grounds staining her hair and muddying her face wouldn't stop them from recognizing her pale skin and blue eyes. Even if they merely suspected she was the woman they were looking for, they'd bring her back to Willem for confirmation, and *he* certainly wouldn't be fooled by her disguise.

She was breathless now, her cheeks burning from the air whipping against her skin, and she was gripping the reins so tightly that she wondered if she'd have to peel her fingers off the leather, one by one, when it finally came time to dismount. She knew the knights had finally spotted her when they hollered and commanded her to stop by order of King Willem, which left her with two options: do as they commanded, risking that they would bring her back to the palace, or keep going, hoping to outrun them eventually.

As the soldiers closed in on her, she realized the road ahead was quickly coming to an end. It forked to the left and right, leading to towns and villages in the distance, but there was nothing directly in front of her other than grass and blue skies. She knew she couldn't flee into any of the civilizations without them following her, and it wouldn't be a simple task to hide or find refuge while she was being tracked. Cutting through the civilizations in hopes of losing the soldiers, too, would be an arduous task: she was entirely unfamiliar with the territories, and she had no idea what awaited beyond them.

"Edom," she gasped, "if you have any ideas, now would be the time to tell me!"

"Keep going!"

"*Where?*"

No reply. She glanced over her shoulder again, stomach churning when she realized the soldiers had separated to close in on her from all sides, and knew she had no choice but to obey the sprite.

That, however, became much more difficult when she saw what lay ahead.

They'd been riding on an incline, so she couldn't see anything beyond a grassy field until they reached the top of the hill—which wasn't a hill at all. It was the top of a cliff, and if she hadn't pulled Brandy's reins when she did, they would've toppled over the edge and into the ocean below.

"Mother of—" She turned Brandy to the side and peered over the edge of the cliff, swallowing when she saw the drop. "What do we do, Edom?"

She knew the answer as soon as she asked. The sprite had known all along, too, but hadn't bothered to tell her—probably because it knew she'd refuse when she heard the plan.

"We have to jump," Edom said. "No other way."

She hesitated and looked to the side at the road in the distance, where the soldiers were inching closer and closer by the second. She took a deep breath, nodded, and dismounted Brandy so she could stand at the edge of the cliff. A pit formed in her stomach when she looked down at the water, and she couldn't help herself when she took a few steps backward.

"I don't think I can."

Hollering and clanging armor drew her attention to the road again. Her breath caught in her throat when she realized the soldiers were slowing down. They were close enough now that they wanted to end the pursuit on foot—giving her mere minutes to spare.

Edom manifested on her shoulder, clutching the fabric of her shawl for support, and asked, "You trust me?"

Aurelia gulped as she looked over the edge of the cliff again. "Yes. I do."

The sprite hissed. *"Jump."*

As the soldiers ran for her, Aurelia ignored the warning bells chiming in her head and followed the creature's command, praying to every god in the realm that the ocean below was closer than it looked.

XXXVI

The closest Aurelia had ever come to jumping from a cliff was falling from Halvor's back before they crashed on Tullweine. Even then, she hadn't fallen from a great distance—the leather tethers had caught her before she could plummet into the ocean. This time, she had absolutely no idea what awaited her, besides the rocky waters of the Alkamura Ocean.

The fall felt slow—slower than she thought it should feel, at least—and while her stomach rose to her throat, she didn't experience any nausea, pain, or shortness of breath. It was almost serene, descending several hundred feet from the world above, yet everything in her brain told her to shriek in terror.

For a split second as she fell, she heard something that sounded like a woman's giggling, and she saw what she thought was a female face floating in the air beside her. The face was transparent, barely visible against the blue sky, but she could've sworn it was there: smiling, observing her, and staying nearby as she plummeted.

Wind nymph, she thought.

She hit the water gently—*too* gently, like she'd jumped into the ocean from a mere five or six feet. The water seemed to welcome her with its warm embrace as she held her breath and waited for the bubbles to subside so she could see. Even when the bubbles disappeared, the water was fairly murky, so she could only see the light from the sun above.

Aurelia was preparing to swim to the surface when something caught her eye beneath her feet: a bright golden glow. A few air bubbles escaped her lips by accident when she gasped—not only because she was surprised sprites could swim (she'd been told otherwise), but because both she and Edom were surrounded by what appeared to be a slimy green net.

Aurelia had to cover her hand with her mouth to keep from gasping again when she spotted something to her left, just a few yards from the cliffs. A stone statue of an elderly man towered over her, so massive that his nose spanned the entire length of her body. His chin rested in his hand, but she couldn't see anything below his forearm. If the statue was nestled on the sand at the bottom, then the water was much deeper than Aurelia thought.

The net and the statue weren't the only things surrounding her. Whatever air remained in her lungs escaped as air bubbles when she saw half a dozen mermaids encircling the net. The creatures worked together, laughter echoing through the sea, to pull and tighten the net before raising it toward the cliffs. The sprite didn't seem concerned, as it merely latched itself onto Aurelia's dress and grinned.

The mermaids must've known she was losing oxygen, as one of them swam through the opening in the net to Aurelia's right and pursed her lips as if to whistle. No sound emerged, but rather a large bubble of air about the size of Aurelia's head. She treaded the water, heart pounding, as the bubble floated toward her before slipping between her parted lips. She felt an instant burst of strength flow through her as her lungs filled with air, but by the time she redirected her attention to the mermaid, the creature was gone.

As the mermaids pulled the net, Aurelia began to swim, following the six scaly tails into a dark abyss. She briefly looked over her shoulder, unsurprised to find that she could no longer see the statue without the sprite's glow directly in front of it, before forcing herself to swim faster to meet the mermaids' incredible pace. She knew it didn't matter much if she swam or not, though; the net would ultimately bring her to her destination.

Kaia had once told her that mermaids still lived in this part of the Alkamura, but Aurelia never expected to see them in person—nor did she expect to find herself being rescued by them. She assumed Edom had had this planned since the moment Willem imprisoned Aurelia, as six mermaids lingering by the Cliffs of Morinna, with a Halvor-sized seaweed net, could not be a coincidence.

Just as Aurelia felt herself losing oxygen again, the sprite's glow revealed their destination: a cavern beneath the cliffs. The mermaids swam upwards now, pulling Aurelia along, until their heads breached the surface. She gasped and wheezed for air when she did the same, Edom now perched on her shoulder.

There was a narrow ledge nearby, so Aurelia heaved herself onto the path-like chunk of rock while expelling mouthfuls of seawater. Edom shook its head to dry its shaggy hair while Aurelia leaned her back against the jagged wall of the cavern. As she caught her breath, she gulped at the sight of all six mermaids sitting on the edge of the rock, staring at her.

The illustrations didn't do them justice. They were among the most beautiful women Aurelia had ever seen in her lifetime, with perfectly symmetrical faces and features that seemed unique to each of them. Their complexions ranged from pale white, like an Isalder, to fawny brown, like a northern Carthinian, to dark umber, like a Quenosi. Some had ordinary human eye colors like brown, blue, or green, but others had purple, yellow, or even red eyes. Their hair had no limitations in terms of color, texture, or length. All of their lips were pink, their cheeks were rosy, and they were void of any type of blemish.

Thick, iridescent scales in a variety of colors—that almost reminded Aurelia of chainmail armor—covered their breasts, but the scales had a gradient effect: as they crawled up toward the mermaids' necks and down toward their hips, the scales became thinner and more translucent. Their tails, about the length of Aurelia's body, were made up of scales that matched their chests. Their fins fanned outward for several feet, embellished with thin, tulle-like flesh that gave the appearance of ribbons.

Aurelia cleared her throat, knowing they were waiting for her to speak. "I-um-thank you."

A mermaid with burgundy hair and brown eyes laughed. "You're welcome."

"I didn't expect..."

"Just because you can't see us," Edom murmured, "does not mean we don't exist."

Aurelia's lips pursed. The sprite was right, of course. She couldn't imagine just how many other magical creatures were out there in the world, hiding for fear of the humans who had persecuted them.

"I'm forever in your debt," Aurelia said earnestly, glancing between the women. "Is there...Is there anything you need? Anything I can do for you?"

They exchanged looks and giggled. "Not yet."

Then they were gone.

As their fins splashed water in her face, Aurelia looked down at Edom. "You orchestrated this, didn't you?"

"Yes."

"How?"

Its enormous eyes darkened. "You have your allies. I have mine."

"Fair enough. Where do we go from here? They didn't offer directions."

Edom pointed at the darkness ahead. Aurelia couldn't see much, but she assumed it was a tunnel system beneath the cliffs and western Kanibar. A system like this one existed in Holos, too: if one were to swim beneath the Holosi cliffs, they'd find a small opening to an underwater cavern that eventually led to dry land.

"Where does it lead to?" she asked.

"One way takes you to eastern Kanibar, the other to Caedia."

A sigh of relief escaped her as she squeezed the water from her hair. "We shall set out for Caedia, then. Halvor would've felt our bond restored when Rhys removed my shackles—if he isn't already on his way, he will be soon enough. We can wait for him in Caedia, but even if he doesn't come, we can find passage to Akkinor at the harbor." She stood, but when her legs throbbed in protest after a long day of riding and swimming, she sat down again. "Perhaps we might rest for a bit. I don't anticipate anyone finding us here."

Everything Sora had given her was soaking wet, and even if she possessed the materials to start a fire, they would've been too damp to make a difference. The best she could do was curl up in the fetal position with her satchel under her head and her back against the wall of the cave, relying on her own body heat to keep her warm. Edom nestled on the ground against her chest, but it didn't bother using her clothing as a blanket.

Aurelia fell asleep to the sound of water lapping against the rock walls, refusing to close her eyes until the sprite's glow faded into slumber, bathing the cavern in darkness once more.

***

For a time, Aurelia didn't know she was dreaming.

She was sitting on the rocky ledge with her skirts drawn to her thighs as she dipped her legs in the ocean. The cavern was pitch black, silent other than the sound of lapping waves and dripping water, and while she was still damp, she didn't feel the slightest bit of cold or discomfort. She couldn't see her own hand in front of her face, but she was content, nonetheless: alone with nothing but her thoughts, all worries far away as saltwater embraced her wiggling toes.

Suddenly, a light from behind persuaded her to look over her shoulder. It wasn't the sprite's telltale golden glow, but rather a fierce white light that made her squint in pain as soon as she glanced at it. The light was coming from the bunched-up stocking she'd discarded before dipping her legs in the water—or, more specifically, from the amulet she'd been storing in the garment.

She heaved her legs out of the water and removed the amulet from the stocking, wincing when its light grew brighter—and almost blinding—when it was no longer weakened by the fabric. It wasn't the amulet itself that had begun to glow, but rather the piece of moonrock fused to the center of the iron slab.

Frowning, Aurelia ran the pad of her thumb over the rock. "What a mystery you are."

"Every mystery can be solved if one is worthy of finding the answer."

She gasped, nearly dropping the amulet, when a melodic female voice pierced the silence. A heavy, terrifying feeling settled in her chest when she saw a woman standing to her left. She scrambled to her feet, clutching the amulet to her chest, as the pale, thin woman smiled at her.

Aurelia could've sworn she'd seen the woman before, but she couldn't think of a name or even a place. The stranger reminded her of an Isalder: skin so light it was nearly translucent; pin-straight white hair, so long it dusted the floor; gray eyes that swirled like pools of molten silver; and a powerful, fierce aura that suggested she wasn't one to be trifled with. She wore a silvery gown with long, billowing sleeves that almost appeared to liquify whenever she moved.

The woman gestured toward the amulet. "Trust it. Allow it to show you the way—but only if you believe yourself to be worthy of it."

The queen's lips parted. "I thought I was, but nearly everyone I've spoken to has suggested otherwise. They're wary of the curse."

"Curses aren't placed on those who are exactly where they're meant to be. You would've felt your soul slipping away from the moment you touched the stone if you weren't meant to find it." She cocked her head to the side. "What troubles you?"

"I-I don't know." The confession spewed from Aurelia's lips before she could question the woman's inquiry. "I suppose...I suppose I don't understand what I'm meant to do. I've experienced hurdle after hurdle on my path, and yet, none have been horrible enough to justify using this power. How will I know which hurdle warrants use of the amulet above the others? And even more—how will I know for certain that using the amulet won't set me on the path toward my own destruction?"

The woman smiled, but it looked like the expression was paining her. "Sometimes, child, the hurdle becomes the path. Everything you've ever done has a greater purpose—you must simply believe that you're deserving of that purpose."

Before Aurelia could reply, a spark of white light appeared on the woman's chest. What started as a pinprick quickly grew until the light seemed to swallow her whole, forcing Aurelia to squint and turn away.

When the light began to fade, Aurelia turned back to look at where the woman had been standing, only to find a ball of white light disappearing into the cavern walls.

Then Aurelia's eyes snapped open as she woke with a gasp, still curled up in the fetal position against the side of the cavern, while Edom snoozed beside her. She sat up, careful not to disturb the sprite, and brought a hand to the back of her clammy neck. Something foreign and ethereal had overcome her, like a divine parasite, and she felt it burning in her soul from the moment she opened her eyes.

She knew now that she'd been dreaming, but it hadn't felt like a dream—it felt like a vision. There was only one being in the universe who could've activated the amulet, even in a dream, and Aurelia was certain she knew exactly who it was.

She scrambled to roll up her skirts, where a bright white glow was emitting from her stocking—exactly as it had been in her dream. She retrieved the amulet, lips parting in shock, as the moonrock glowed as brightly as the sprite often did. She swore she could feel it throbbing against her palm, too, like a beating heart.

Edom, now awake, perched on her knee as she squinted at the amulet. She ran the pad of her thumb over the rock, watching as the light dimmed and brightened again when she moved her digit, as a realization struck her: Edea—the very same individual said to bestow a curse upon those who wielded her lost artifact—hadn't seemed at all angered by Aurelia possessing the amulet. In fact, she'd been just the opposite. Perhaps, Aurelia thought, Edea was glad that she had been the one to find it, after all these years.

"Edom," she whispered, "I think it's time for me to trust the moon."

***

Whether the mysterious figure in Aurelia's dream was really Edea or just a figment of Aurelia's imagination, one thing was abundantly clear: the moon goddess approved of Aurelia wielding the last piece of her beloved staff.

Almost immediately after waking, Aurelia and Edom set out for the tunnels to make their way to Caedia. Both Edom and the amulet offered enough light for Aurelia to see the path ahead—and to avoid falling into the freezing, opaque ocean when the cavern ledge grew narrow and uneven.

Eventually, as she followed the ledge, she came across an enormous chunk of earth that blocked the ocean's path. She had to squeeze through a gap between the rock walls—sideways to avoid getting stuck—before the path widened again on the other side. She quickly found herself at a fork separated by another vast rock wall: one path leading to the left, and the other to the right.

She didn't get the chance to ask Edom for directions. The amulet's light almost faded completely when she started for the right path, but when she turned to the left, the glow nearly blinded her. She followed the amulet's guidance, hoping and praying it didn't take her back to Willem's palace.

At the very least, though, she'd gotten out of Kanibar without coming into contact with the magical shields. It was a loophole in Willem's near-perfect plan: traveling beneath the shields, underground where the magic didn't penetrate.

She had no way of knowing how long she was walking for. As tired and sore as she was, she kept moving, knowing it wasn't in her best interest to rest for longer than necessary. Fortunately, walking through underground tunnels was much quicker than walking through the land above: there were no obstacles ahead, no enemies awaiting her, and no manmade structures to navigate.

She was starving, thirsty, and still freezing after her swim, but she had nothing other than the sopping remains of whatever Sora had given her. She knew she could've asked Edom to fetch food or water (he could, after all, travel hundreds of miles within minutes), but the creature was too small to carry what she needed.

Eventually, she noticed Edom's glow beginning to fade—signaling its exhaustion—and decided to stop. They both slept for a bit until the cavern began to shake above their heads. The pair woke with a start, staring at the ceiling in silence as dust, dirt, and rubble rained down on their heads. They held their breath, in preparation for a cave-in, until the rumbling finally stopped.

The sprite hissed. "Carriages."

Aurelia raised an eyebrow. "Do you know where we are? Or, rather, what we're below?"

"The forest."

That seemed likely enough. Other than the Violet Forest, the only territory they'd be passing through was Kanibar, and she couldn't imagine why a caravan of carriages would be bolting through the Kanish streets like that. It would have also made sense if the rumbling was caused by marching troops headed for Dofell, but if that were the case, Aurelia would've spent the next few hours—not minutes—brushing debris from her shoulders as thousands of men crossed the road above.

After what felt like hours of nonstop walking, Edom hissed at her to stop. The sprite disappeared for a moment, leaving Aurelia with the amulet as her only guiding light, before reappearing on her shoulder in the time it took for her to yawn.

"A grate lies ahead."

Aurelia frowned. "A sewer?"

"Yes."

The thought made her shiver with disgust. She kept walking, and within minutes, she came upon the sewer in question. The path ahead was muddied by about three inches of filthy water, but that wasn't all: rats scurried away from the puddles in search of dry land; insects crawled along the walls, desperately seeking light; and waste of all kinds—excrement, garbage, and even lost treasures—either floated or sat half-drowned in the muck.

As much as she wanted to vomit, she couldn't—not when she had to keep pushing herself forward, and her stomach was empty enough. She craned her neck backwards to look up at the ceiling, where a few dim beams of light penetrated the sewer grate above. She couldn't see much, but a glimpse of blue skies and sunshine was all she needed to feel a little better

The tunnels must've been used often in the past, as the wall to her left had been carved out in various spots from top to bottom to form small niches. The holes were the perfect size for the toes of her shoes, and while there were no handrails, she could grip the niches above to pull herself closer to the grate—but not before returning the amulet to her stocking for safe-keeping.

She'd never been more grateful for Edom than she was when the sprite zipped through the holes in the grate, removing the mechanisms holding the iron structure in place. Aurelia wrapped her fingers around the grate as Edom loosened the last mechanism, and when she felt the weight fall heavily against her palm, she pushed it up and to the side so she could crawl through the opening. In a matter of minutes, she found herself sitting on the grass, surrounded by trees and birdsong as she stared down at the dark opening she'd emerged from.

Aurelia wiped the muck from her hands on her dress. "Well, as Jack would say, that was invigorating."

Edom only grinned.

She recognized the Violet Forest surrounding her, but she couldn't be sure where exactly she was. She had to assume she was closer to Caedia than to Dofell, but even then, that could've meant she was still miles and miles away from the port province.

After returning and securing the grate so other travelers didn't fall into the sewer, she searched her surroundings for the dirt path—not because she wished to follow it into Caedia, but because she needed to stay as far away from it as possible. Kaia had taught her that on the first day they met, and she hadn't forgotten it.

Aurelia kept her eyes peeled and her ears sharp as she navigated the thick brush and whatever remained of previous travelers' camps. She didn't see or hear any sign of civilization nearby, but she knew the natives of the forest weren't the type to make themselves seen or heard; for all she knew, they could've been surrounding her from the moment she emerged from the grate.

As she trampled twigs and leaves, her legs aching with every step, she felt a strange lurch in her chest. It was like she was being pulled to something, guided in a specific direction: but to where, she didn't know.

Just then, enormous clouds rolled in overhead, bathing the forest in darkness. She started uttering a prayer, hoping the rain would spare her that day, until a bellowing shriek interrupted her thoughts and shook the leaves from the trees. The lurch in her chest grew stronger, like she was tethered to something she couldn't see, as she turned her gaze to the sky.

The clouds above were white and transparent against the blue sky, and certainly not angry enough to darken the entire forest. No, it wasn't the clouds: it was Halvor, coasting overhead while his massive body blocked the sun.

As a grin spread over her lips, Aurelia began to laugh, and the sound seemed to summon him. Edom sat on her shoulder and clung to her hair while Halvor descended, flattening a few dozen trees as he landed—and a dozen more when his tail whipped from side to side, destroying (and warning) everything in his wake.

Aurelia rushed up to him, set her hands on either side of his snout, and pressed her forehead to the tip of his nose. She smiled when he chuffed, sending a hot gust of air blowing through her hair.

"I knew you'd come for me," she whispered.

XXXVII

Aurelia knew Halvor's flight routine better than she knew her own schedule, on most days. If the flight was a short one, he tended to coast closer to the ground; but if the flight was a long one, he always soared above the clouds, descending only when he was approaching his destination.

As soon as they left the Violet Forest, Aurelia noticed that he was flying *beneath* the clouds. She didn't think much of it at first, assuming he was merely tired after the long flight from Akkinor, but when he refused to ascend, she knew he wasn't taking her home. He didn't change course when she tried to remind him that they were going home, either. He merely kept flying, ignoring her, as she caught a glimpse of a familiar sight in the near distance: a glittering city made entirely out of gold.

He *was* taking them home—just not to the home she'd had in mind.

As Halvor descended toward the Palace of Taundosa, Aurelia spotted something odd on the streets surrounding Reyna's estate: blue and gold banners waving above a sea of bronze. At first, she thought soldiers from Agotia were guarding the perimeter of the palace, as the Cristos family colors were nearly identical. But the sigil stamped on the banners wasn't the Cristos hummingbird—it was a dragon.

A combination of excitement and confusion bubbled up in her gut when she realized what was happening. About a season before the mess in Carthe was brought to her attention, Aurelia commissioned a few changes to Akkinor's representation: the Akkinorian sigil would now be identical to the Brentwood sigil, furthering the legacy of Brentwoods on the throne; and the two old sigils—a colorful cornucopia for Akkinor, and a purple-and-bronze falcon for the Brentwood family—would both be replaced by a blue-and-gold dragon.

Aurelia's reign marked a new era in Akkinor, and she didn't think it was right to have both her family and her country represented by such menial symbolism. The entire realm associated Akkinor and the Brentwoods with Halvor nowadays, so she wanted their sigil to reflect their new power—a power nobody else in the realm had in their possession. The colors matched Halvor, of course, but they were also the colors associated with Aurelia's birth family.

The troops must've just arrived in Carthe, because as Halvor descended lower, she saw that her soldiers were unpacking goods from wagons: weapons, armor, medical supplies, food, liquor, all of it. Nobody knew when Willem would start marching for Dofell, so Aurelia's troops would have to make themselves comfortable in Taundosa for the time being.

A giddy feeling erupted in her stomach when Halvor landed atop the garden wall at the palace, and for one reason only: if her troops were here, that meant Jack was here, too.

The guards stationed at the palace's rear doors stumbled over their words when she approached, clearly still in shock that she was here and not locked in a Kanish dungeon. Even as they directed her to a meeting room, or symposium, where her allies were gathered, she caught them wrinkling their noses and holding their breath as she walked by them— clearly, she still stank of sewage and filth, and her appearance probably wasn't much better.

She practically ran through the halls, barely acknowledging the servants who bowed and curtsied to her, until she found the symposium in question. She paused outside of the closed door, absorbing every ounce of peace that flooded her veins at the sound of Arian's voice, and took a deep breath before pushing it open.

Her allies, plus Jack, Ansyl, and a handful of war generals, were gathered around a large meeting table in the center of the room. Half of them were on their feet and shouting at one another, and the other half merely sat in their chairs and massaged their temples, clearly having lost patience for the discussion. Jack was among the latter, his back facing the door, and she could ascertain just by the slumping of his shoulders that he was nearing his breaking point.

Aurelia cleared her throat. "Am I interrupting?"

Jack's head shot up immediately. "Lily?"

In the time it took for her to grin at his genuine error, Jack tore across the room like a cyclone and enveloped her in his arms. She chuckled a bit as he lifted her from the ground, burying his face in her shoulder and inhaling like she smelled of roses rather than sewage. He held her so tightly—albeit trembling like a wet dog—that she had to ask him to set her down before he crushed her ribcage.

When he did, he took her face in his hands and studied her. "What happened? Are you all right? Did he touch you?"

She barely heard a word of his dozen questions. For a moment, all she could do was smile as she gazed into his eyes. She knew then that all the magic and glamour spells in the world couldn't have turned Willem into Jack. The oceans in his eyes were fiercer and livelier than Willem's had been, filled with more passion, kindness, and wonder than the king would ever know in his lifetime.

"I'm all right," she murmured. "I'll tell you everything later. For now, there's work to be done."

"Aurelia—"

"Later." She leaned up on her toes and pressed a soft kiss to his lips. Even when they parted, she kept her eyes closed for a moment. "Mmm. I missed that."

He was grinning when she opened her eyes. "I did, too."

"Aurelia." Arian was at her side before she and Jack had the chance to release one another. He engulfed her in his arms, ignoring Jack, and cradled the back of her head like one might do to a small child. "Oh, my dear..."

"I'm all right, uncle, I assure you." She inhaled his familiar scent—sage and peppermint, like her father—and smiled at the comfort it brought her. "I'm all right."

"I know." As he pulled away to inspect her face, grimacing at the cut on her cheekbone, he chuckled and brushed hair from her shoulder. "Hello again, sprite."

She'd nearly forgotten that Edom had been perched on her shoulder since they left the Violet Forest. The sprite only stared at him, still clinging to a thick strand of her hair, as they joined the others at the meeting table. Jack was watching the sprite, looking a bit skeptical, which prompted the creature to hide behind Aurelia's hair. Aurelia only met her husband's gaze and offered him a slight nod of reassurance, and he soon relaxed. She didn't blame him for being cautious—the sprite's absence from Akkinor during Aurelia's time in captivity must've been suspicious. She'd tell him all about what the creature had done for her when they were alone, so he'd know for certain that Edom hadn't done any harm.

"Your Grace." Lord Zhaaran stood, prompting the others to follow suit. "We weren't expecting...We thought..." He trailed off and cleared his throat. "Are you well?"

"Perfectly fine. I stink of sewage and dragon, of course, but such woes are easily remedied." She smiled when the nobleman raised an eyebrow at Edom. "The sprite can be trusted. I wouldn't have escaped Kanibar with my life if the creature hadn't come for me. It was an experience, to be certain, but—"

"I'm sure we'll all be delighted to hear about your grand adventure later on," Lord Zhoqa interrupted. "For now, we have things to discuss. Will you contribute, or must you excuse yourself for a bath first?"

She glowered as Jack took a step closer to him, warning him. "It's nice to see you, too, my lord," she drawled. "I haven't the patience for your lack of manners today. If you'd like to continue behaving like a petulant ass, you can leave—we'll all be better for it, anyway." His face was nearly purple with rage as his fists trembled at his side, but he made no effort to reply. She cocked her head to the side, smiling, and added, "Gone mute, have you? About time."

"Leave him be. A hound can't help but bark." Reyna smiled as she said it, making Aurelia's smile grow wider and Lord Zhoqa's face turn even redder. "Welcome back, Your Grace. You've arrived in the midst of a debate, so your input would be most valuable—particularly after your stay in Kanibar. We can't seem to agree on when to deploy our troops to Dofell. Some of us, like Balor, believe we should send our troops now so they're at the ready whenever Willem decides to march. The rest of us, including myself, believe we should wait until we find our successor."

"Sending troops to Dofell now sends a message to Kanibar—it tells him we're ready, and we aren't." Jack crossed his arms over his chest while examining the battle map spread over the table. "He'll have spies in Dofell, so he'll know as soon as we send our soldiers. If he happens to march for Dofell before we've found our successor, then we've lost one of our greatest deterrents. The Kanish—even if it's only a portion of them—won't be convinced to drop their swords if we can't provide them with an alternative ruler for Dofell. It'll come down to us or Willem, and they'll always choose Willem."

"Willem will want to make a spectacle of things. I'm sure of it," Aurelia muttered. "I believe that, for him, it's less about seizing Dofell and more about making sure the world knows about what he may accomplish. He's a villain if he conquers a defenseless kingdom, but if he manages to defeat four armies and a dragon in the name of salvaging said kingdom? Then he's a hero."

Arian raised an eyebrow. "What are you saying?"

"He knows we have spies posted around the area, so he'll ensure his troops are seen by our men so they can report his movements back to us.

We're closer to Dofell than he is, so by the time we receive word of it, we'll be able to reach Dofell at the same time he does. It doesn't matter if we deploy a few troops now or later—he wants everything to be on his terms, so he won't care about what we do until he's ready to fight."

"He knows we'll rush to meet him as soon as we know he's coming," Jack summarized, "but *he* won't rush to meet *us* if we're the first ones to march for Dofell. We'd be sitting ducks that way, and he'd be empowered by the thought of us squirming while we wait for him."

Lord Zhoqa coughed to catch everyone's attention. "We're forgetting one very important detail. We're closer to Dofell in theory, yes, but not in practice."

Arian sighed. "The walls."

The Lord of Kazamir nodded, grimacing. "It'll take weeks for us and our troops to cross the valley into Dofell. Even if we do, the chances are high that we'd cross paths with the Kroti. That could be disastrous."

"The Kroti?" Aurelia frowned and glanced between the faces surrounding the table. Almost every single one of them either winced or averted their gazes. "What are you talking about?"

"We still haven't heard word from Lady Swann," Reyna said quickly, "but as for the rest of Krotis...Three provinces have agreed to fight for Willem. Lord Zhoqa's scouts in the Ngora Valley spotted Kroti troops marching toward Kanibar not long ago. I imagine Willem's waiting for them to arrive before he and his troops march for Dofell, but there's no telling when that might be. We all know what traveling across the valley is like."

Aurelia raised an eyebrow. "I didn't think it was possible to reach Kanibar from the valley. Everything I've heard makes it seem like the southern border of Kanibar is as inaccessible as Dofell."

"It isn't wise to travel from Kanibar to the valley, or vice versa, but it's not impossible," Jack explained. "The entirety of Kanibar's southern border is composed of cliffs. If you want to get from the valley to Kanibar, you'll have to climb a steep rock wall about six-hundred feet tall. The elevation decreases as you get closer to the Dofelli border on the east, but that's where the desert tribes tend to linger. The tribes are the only people who can climb the cliffs with ease—they've been doing it since the first of them settled in the desert—but even *they* haven't attempted it in decades. So I've heard, anyway."

A thought popped into Aurelia's head as she turned to Arian. "Willem told you he'd erected magical shields around the kingdom's borders to prevent any non-Kanish natives from entering. What if he erected them *before* I was his captive? What if they've been protecting the Kanish borders for decades?"

"It's certainly possible," he agreed. "That would explain why even the tribesmen haven't managed to reach Kanibar from the valley in so many years. He probably took the shields down each time he saw you approaching on Halvor—because he wanted you to come."

"That can't be right." Jack shook his head. "I've been to Kanibar many times. So have other foreigners I've known over the years."

"Maybe the shields are charmed to only keep certain people out," Reyna offered. "Someone only wishing to visit or pass through Kanibar is welcome there, but someone with more nefarious motives would be melted by the shields. I suppose that's how the Kroti will be allowed entry: the shields won't target the Kroti as they would us. Even so, the Kroti will still have to survive the tribesmen before they can reach Kanibar." She clenched her jaw. "Lady Swann appears to be ignoring us to protect Runeia from any potential ramifications. I can't say I blame her."

Aurelia cleared her throat. "All right. Once the Kroti arrive in Kanibar and recover, Willem will likely take them through the forest to the northern Dofelli gates. We can't take the same route without meeting them on the road, and we can't cut through the valley to reach the southern gates without losing time." She inhaled sharply when a sudden thought struck her like a club to the back. "I might have an idea, but it's mad."

"Madder than the King of Kanibar potentially conquering the continent?" Lord Zhoqa said with a snort.

She ignored him. "The Dofelli walls are our greatest obstacle. They always have been. Dofell and Taundosa share a border, yet it's impossible to travel directly from one kingdom to the other."

Lord Zhaaran pursed his lips. "You want to destroy the walls."

"Not the entire perimeter," she said quickly. "Only a section along the Taundosan border. It has to be large enough for our troops to enter Dofell swiftly, but not so large that it crumbles the entire foundation. If and when we find a successor, they can decide if the entirety of the Dofelli walls should be taken down for good. It isn't our place to destroy the whole structure."

Nobody answered for a moment. Then Lord Zhoqa shrugged and said, "It's not the worst idea. Might be the best option we have. Of course, our economies will suffer if there's no longer a need for us to supply goods to the tavern and those crossing the valley, but we can remedy that in the future. It's a necessary sacrifice at this point."

Aurelia raised an eyebrow at Reyna. "What do you think, Your Majesty? It's your border, too."

Reyna chewed on her lower lip, contemplating. "I agree—it's our best option. But Taundosa is a heavily populated kingdom, and we have civilizations built along every border. We shall have to be mindful of which section we choose to destroy."

"I'll send word to the nobility of Morvis and Brorane—those territories sit just along the Dofelli border. The lords will provide us with a location of their choosing." Arian sat down to write the letters, and when he did, an inkwell, quill, and sheets of parchment magically appeared in front of him. "We should hear back by dawn tomorrow. I doubt they'll have any—"

Just then, a servant entered the room, silencing Arian. "Forgive the interruption, my lieges, but—"

He didn't get the chance to finish before three tiny individuals bolted through the doorway on either side of him. In the brief time it took for Aurelia to recognize the intruders as her children, they were clinging to her being and tugging her down to the ground, showering her in hugs and kisses while talking a mile a minute about everything they'd seen and done throughout their stay in the City of Gold. It'd been weeks since they'd last seen their mother, yet they didn't seem to think she'd been gone for more than a few days.

She watched and listened to them in silence, barely returning their embraces, as shock paralyzed her. She managed to look over her shoulder at Jack, who only shrugged and grinned in response. When she realized she wasn't imagining them, she pulled all three of them into her arms, fighting the urge to cry while some of the realm's most powerful individuals looked on.

One of the governesses, Irina, stood in the doorway beside the servant while baby Halyna cooed in her arms. Celesse wasn't there, but somebody else was: Estylle. The same woman who'd helped raise Aurelia had come to mind Aurelia's children—the grandchildren of her late friend, Katryna Cristos. Only then did Aurelia realize that this was the first time her children were visiting their ancestors' native kingdom.

She wished the circumstances were different, but that longing didn't last for more than a few seconds. Holding her children in her arms made it possible for her to finally acknowledge that she was safe: she was free from Willem's clutches, surrounded by allies and loved ones while her dragon protected them from the skies, inhaling the same air she had when she took her first breath.

If there was anything to be grateful for during wartime, it was this.

XXXVIII

T he allies suspended war preparations after Aurelia was reunited with her family, giving her just enough time to eat, bathe, and catch up with her children before the sky darkened. Though the sun technically didn't set in Taundosa, the children were fast asleep as soon as the sun began to descend, having nodded off in the same bed their parents had shared over five years earlier.

While Halyna slept in her bassinet, the elder three children were snoozing between their parents on the bed. Aurelia propped herself up on her side to gaze down at her sleeping children, still combatting the shock of being reunited with them here in Taundosa after what she'd left behind in Kanibar.

"How has she been?" Aurelia whispered as Jack brushed hair from Hyacinth's forehead.

Jack smiled a bit. "Perfectly fine—even better since we arrived here two days ago. No signs of trauma, no nightmares, no tantrums. She's been her normal self. She hasn't said anything odd or prophet-like, either." He sighed, smile fading, as Hyacinth made a sweet little noise in her sleep. "She won't say a word about that night. She'll only speak to you about it."

Aurelia frowned. "Not a word of it?"

"Nothing. I thought the sprite might have something to do with it, but—"

"It didn't."

Jack's smile grew again. "I know. Arian told me the creature delivered a message on your behalf just before I arrived."

She turned to look over her shoulder at the open wardrobe behind her. There, nestled atop a pile of shawls and cloaks, was the sleeping sprite curled up against the amulet. She was glad the creature had proven its loyalty; she didn't wish to be parted from Edom now that they'd become friends, nor did she wish for it to be viewed as a traitor or an enemy because of its birthplace.

When she met Jack's eyes again, he jerked his head to something behind him: the hearth. Knowing what he meant, she carefully peeled herself out of bed while he did the same. They left their snoozing children to sit by the hearth—not in their twin armchairs, but on a blanket on the floor. They sat in silence for a moment, shoulder to shoulder, while the heat from the fire warmed her cheeks and the glow from the flames reflected in Jack's eyes.

Aurelia broke the silence: "Jack—"

"I know we have more than enough to catch up on," he interrupted, voice hoarse, "but I have something to say first."

She swallowed the lump in her throat. "All right."

"I'm...I'm sorry about our last conversation—the one before we left for Kanibar. It was wrong of me to be so nasty towards you. I shouldn't have let my emotions get the best of me. I'm sorry, my love."

She rested her head on his shoulder and squeezed his hand. "I'm sorry, too. I was even nastier to you—you, of all people. You're the least deserving person in the world of such ugliness."

"It's different," he insisted. "Everything you said...You weren't wrong. You had every right to say those things, but me? I was angry that you were always away, always working, and I rarely got to see you. What you told me about Sisi triggered the explosion, but it'd been building up for some time. It was terrible of me to hold such resentment over something I didn't understand. While you've been gone, and I've had to sit your throne and mind your duties..." He shook his head, grimacing. "I finally understand the stress and the pressure you feel, day after day, though I know I still have only really seen a fraction of it. You've been in this position since you were twenty years old, and you won't escape it until you die. I can't begin to imagine what that must feel like. Just a few weeks of it nearly drained me of life."

She forced a smile. "You get used to it."

Jack's body rumbled when he laughed. "So you say. I can't picture myself ever getting used to that. I suppose you were right about what you said that day, too: as much as I love my family, I think the idea of being Lord of Omara compelled me to stay in Carthe more than the threat of the radicals did. I wasn't built for leadership."

"Yes, you were. You were built to lead in every other way, Jack—just not politics, though I can already see you did a fine job of it."

Sighing, he leaned his cheek against the top of her head. "Every moment while you were gone, I imagined what you were enduring at

Willem's hands. I couldn't stop, as hard as I tried, and every scenario I imagined was worse than the last. So...So if it was as ghastly as I think it was, I don't wish for you to relive it on account of my curiosity."

Wincing, she lifted her head from his shoulder and set her hands on her lap. "It wasn't all that bad, actually. I made a few friends."

"Really?" He blinked at her, surprised. "How?"

As she was certain she'd have to do a dozen more times in the near future, she recounted her stay in Kanibar from the moment Jack left with Hyacinth to the moment Halvor rescued her in the Violet Forest. She told him everything she could about Willem, Maysa, Rhys, Sora, and the information she'd uncovered throughout her stay. When she got to the last bit, though—her final night with Willem—she slowed down, knowing she'd have to choose her words carefully.

"I-I don't know what I was thinking, exactly. I was disoriented," she murmured. "Maybe a part of me believed he was you, or at least wanted to believe he was you. Or maybe...maybe I didn't know what was happening until I realized he was trying to become you. All I know is that I snapped out of it when he gave himself away, and everything came flooding back to me."

"How did he give himself away?"

Her cheeks warmed. "He called me *Lily dear*."

No reply. Worried she'd crushed him, she lifted her eyes to his face to study him, but she didn't find anything that suggested he was hurt by what she'd done—or *almost* done—with Willem. He was just...blank.

"Jack?" She cleared her throat when her voice cracked. "Can you say something, please?"

He inhaled sharply as the corner of his mouth twitched. "I'm not upset with you, if that's what you think. I just can't believe he sought to use *me* as a means of securing you. Even if he wanted to believe your ruse, he knew you'd never choose him, so he decided to seduce you while he looked like me." He scoffed in disgust, looking like he'd just swallowed something bitter. "If his plan had worked, it would've been my body you'd laid with, not his. He tethered me to him forever by using me to hurt you. I wouldn't blame you if you never wanted to touch me or look at me again."

"It doesn't matter that he tried to look like you, Jack. I fell in love with *you*, not your looks—though being as handsome as you are certainly has its perks."

He snorted into a laugh. "Gee, thanks."

Smiling, she snaked her arm around his and threaded their fingers together. "Are you okay?"

"Grand," he said sarcastically. She chuckled as he turned to finally meet her eyes. "I'm not pleased to hear that my wife was nearly taken to bed by a corrupt king who used my likeness to seduce her, but...Do you know how difficult it is for a mortal to overcome disorienting drugs or to see through a glamour spell? Our brains aren't wired to best such things with ease. You managed it, all because he said two words that reminded you of me." He brushed hair from her face and smiled. "You must really love me."

Her eyes burned with emotion. He was mirroring something she'd once said to him when he agreed to follow her home to Akkinor, even at the risk of being executed for treason or hunted down by religious radicals.

"More than anything," she whispered. "Even if I found myself unable to leave Kanibar before Willem tethered me to him forever...My heart will belong to you until the heavens collapse, if such a thing is even possible. It's belonged to you since before I knew you existed, and it'll belong to you even when we're nothing more than two souls floating through oblivion in the world beyond."

He cupped the side of her face, tilting her head to better face him, and pressed their foreheads together as his lips brushed hers. "Our souls will never be parted from one another again. And if they are..."

"You'll find me?"

Smiling, Jack touched his lips to hers. "Yes. I'll always find you."

***

"There we are." As Ser Dayne lowered his hands from the king's face, the pale yellow glow emitting from his palms slowly faded before disappearing altogether. The mage raised an eyebrow as he wiped his clammy hands on a nearby cloth. "How do you feel?"

Like I've just been reared in the face by a horse, Willem wanted to say. He'd experienced the same pain each and every morning for years, but it still wasn't any easier to bear. It felt like his flesh was being stripped from his body and sewn back together again for one long, excruciating hour. It wasn't just his face, either, but rather any part of his body that might've shown signs of aging.

"Perfectly fine," he lied, gently touching the supple skin of his forehead, cheeks, and eyes. "You've outdone yourself yet again, Dayne."

"Only the best for you, my liege." Dayne approached a table to the left of where Willem sat at his writing desk, where a tray awaited him. After adding the contents of two vials—both pain relieving tonics—into a steaming kettle of foul-smelling tea, Dayne poured the mixture into a

354

silver cup and handed it to the king. "Here you are. Drink all of it, please, as always."

Willem didn't bother waiting for the tea to cool before chugging it. He winced at the burning sensation traveling down his throat, but the discomfort was almost immediately replaced by ease and strength.

For the most part, nobody other than he and Dayne had seen what he really looked like. Even those who knew his true age didn't suspect that he was using a glamour spell to alter his appearance—and if they did, they were smart enough to keep their mouths shut about it.

Reflective surfaces revealed his true appearance, so he avoided them as best he could while in the presence of others. He'd gotten away with it until that Akkinorian whore caught him. That was one of the many reasons he regretted accepting her offer: she'd shown him who he really was after he'd dedicated the last two decades of his life to hiding himself.

When the last bit of pain subsided, Willem got dressed and picked at the breakfast tray a servant had left outside of his door—after all, nobody was allowed inside the king's chambers until after his audience with Dayne each morning. After filling his belly with scones and grapefruit, he made his way to a part of the palace he hadn't visited in years: the temple.

Dayne trailed beside him, as always. "Are you certain about this, Your Majesty?"

Willem grimaced. "I should've gone the moment I found out she escaped. There's no point in waiting any longer." He raised an eyebrow. "Are there any updates?"

"None, my liege. Nobody has seen or heard from her since our soldiers spotted her jumping from the Cliffs of Morinna."

"So, either she's dead, or she managed to plot an escape route through the western Alkamura. Neither scenario seems likely, but if we're choosing to believe what the knight said before we apprehended him..."

Dayne made a sour face. "I doubt it. The last piece of the Lunar Staff was lost ages ago, Your Majesty. I can't imagine how the Queen of Akkinor would come to possess it, and even if she *does* have it...She won't use it. Everyone in Carthe knows the staff demands a tremendous price, and she doesn't seem like the type willing to take that risk."

"It might've been her only means of escaping with her life," Willem shot back. "She's hasty and lawless, and as foolish as it would be for her to use it, I don't believe she has the patience nor the intelligence to seek an alternate route. Returning to her throne is worth the risks associated with the staff. I'm sure of it." He inhaled sharply when they arrived at the entrance to the temple. "Wait here. I'll only be a moment."

As soon as the king entered the temple, an unexplainable aura overcame him—one riddled with a power he didn't understand, and an omniscience he didn't wish to acknowledge. He felt it inching down his throat and creeping throughout his body like a parasite, threatening to devour him from the inside out.

A trio of servants praying at the altar scurried away as soon as they saw him, but the only other person in the temple—an elderly woman with her head bowed and her hands folded in prayer—didn't so much as twitch. Willem, scowling before he realized what expression had overtaken him, marched up to her and stood at her right, folding his arms over his chest and impatiently tapping his foot as she refused to acknowledge him.

Finally, she sighed and lowered her folded hands onto the stone slab. "Despite your best efforts to appear like a young man, you're still a middle-aged fool with the temperament of a small child. It's no wonder those around you are so easily tricked by your silly spell: your immaturity secures your ruse."

Willem gritted his teeth, trying his best to keep a lid on his temper. "What did you tell her?"

"Only what she needed to know."

"That's not an answer."

Maysa laughed. "It's not the answer you desire, but it's an answer, nonetheless."

It took everything he had not to throttle her. "Where did she go?"

"Home, of course."

"By what means?"

"How should I know?"

"You know everything, witch." Willem bent over and leaned in close to her, but she refused to turn her head in his direction. "If you don't wish to tell me, I shall find out eventually. I wouldn't recommend testing my patience, though. I could easily confine you to a cell instead of the temple."

"What you do with me makes no difference in the grand scheme of things. You know that."

He scrubbed a hand down his face, already exhausted by his mother's game of cat and mouse. She hadn't changed a bit since he saw her last, but he didn't know if that would make it easier or harder for him to acquire what he needed.

"Mother," he said, lowering his voice, "you'll tell me what you know—and what *she* knows—or you'll find yourself with rats for company instead of gods. If that threat is meaningless to you, then perhaps I'll do what I should've done ages ago: have your neck fitted for the chopping block.

We've found ourselves in a bit of a dry spell as of late, so I'm certain the executioner would be pleased by his summons to the palace."

Maysa stiffened just enough for him to notice. "Do what you will, boy. It won't change anything. Besides—you know the ways of the *odirasen* as well as I do."

A low, growl-like sound emerged from his throat. *Odirasen*—the ancient word used to describe the practice of prophesizing—was, indeed, a concept familiar to the king. Even if Maysa, an oracle, was dead, the same responsibilities bestowed upon her by the gods would be transferred to another. Perhaps the person who would gain Maysa's abilities after she's gone was a child yet to be born, or perhaps they were a soul who'd already lived several decades of life, predestined to absorb the power of a dead oracle. Either way, Willem knew what that meant: the information Maysa bore wouldn't die with her, and therefore, it'd continue to haunt him for the rest of his life.

"Very well, then." Willem ran a hand through his hair and sighed. "There are others in this palace who spent quite a bit of time with the queen before her departure. With some convincing, I'm sure they'll have something of value to share with me—even if they don't know it."

Maysa's shrill laugh tormented his eardrums. "My word! Torturing your own staff into telling you things they're oblivious to...You know they'll only invent the answers you wish to hear, don't you? You'd be wasting your time, but alas—desperation demands foolishness."

"Desperate? *Me?*" Willem cackled with such malice that Maysa winced. "Oh, Mother. You seem to be mistaken. I wish for answers, but I don't depend on them. I have more than what I need to defeat my enemies, anyway—and I don't suppose they have any idea about it." When Maysa turned to him and cocked her head to the side, revealing her interest, he grinned at her. "Oh, yes. I wouldn't expect you to know any of this, either. You may be an oracle, but you're still human. And humans have a way of ignoring what's right in front of our faces while we exert our energy on trivial things—like, for you, a little girl in a crown, and a silly prophecy."

Her eyes gleamed with ferocity, but her face remained blank. "What have you done?"

"Only what every ruler in my position might do in times of war: initiated a call to arms."

As Maysa's eyes fluttered shut, she lowered her head and pressed her lips together, silenced by the one thing she hadn't bothered to see on the path ahead.

"Lord Reesa of Vrurith, Lord Selle of Bruila, and Lord Quagg of Osanad are marching to Kanibar with their troops as we speak," Willem told her.

"The Reesas have the largest army in Krotis, and the Quaggs haven't seen a loss in battle since the old days. Even the Selles—while weaker and smaller in number—offer a magical advantage that puts Taundosa's covens to shame. The Kroti may be victims to their virtue, but righteousness doesn't apply during wartime. They'll be as fearsome on the battlefield as any other." His grin widened as he lowered his face to hers again, whispering directly into her ear: "I assume your precious little protege and her imbecile allies don't know a thing about *that.*"

No reply. At her silence, Willem pulled away and straightened up. "I wish I could say that it was a pleasure to see you again. I hope you enjoy your confinement."

Just as he turned away, Maysa finally looked at him, her emerald eyes a perfect reflection of his. "Even after all this time, you mistake tyranny for respect. Mind yourself, boy: sooner or later, those you've bullied into compliance will want to see your head on a spike. I pray that day comes before my return to the heavens."

Willem's body grew hot with rage, but instead of lashing out, he merely turned toward the exit and murmured, "Some mother you are."

***

When Aurelia woke the next morning, it took her a moment to remember she wasn't shackled and sleeping in a room with barred windows, or shivering against a damp cavern wall with a sprite curled up against her chest. A smile graced her lips when she opened her eyes to see her three elder children sleeping between her and Jack in a golden bed, and the sprite snoring in a wardrobe marked with the sigil of the Caltheos family.

The peace didn't last long, though. Reyna's lady's maids, footmen, and the governesses arrived within moments. The footmen opened the curtains to flood the room with sunlight, the lady's maids delivered breakfast trays, and the governesses carried the children back to the nursery as soon as Aurelia climbed out of bed.

She barely had the chance to pick at her breakfast before the lady's maids readied her for the day. She had to take another bath—traces of dirt still lingered beneath her fingernails and behind her ears—so by the time she was dressed, styled, and adorned with her crown, Jack had already been ready for almost an hour.

They were meant to meet their allies to resume war preparations, but Aurelia changed her mind when she and Jack passed a portrait in the foyer. The portrait was of Reyna as a girl, but the young Golden Queen wasn't what caught Aurelia's attention. Little Reyna had been painted holding a bouquet of pink hyacinths—strikingly similar to a portrait of Katryna on display in Ardiham Castle, the Cristos family's ancestral home.

As she admired the painted flowers, a sudden thought struck her: she still didn't know who'd betrayed her on the night her daughter was kidnapped. Whether it was a trusted member of her court or a servant whose name she hadn't yet learned, someone had helped a Kanish spy take a Princess of Akkinor from her bed, with enough time to spare that they were able to leave one of Willem's immortal hyacinths behind as a message.

She knew nothing of great importance would be discussed until luncheon when Reyna returned from a meeting with her nobility, so she visited the nursery to speak with Hyacinth. If what Jack had said was true, and Hyacinth only wished to tell her mother about that dreadful night, then now was the time to ask about it before Aurelia was pulled away to battle.

She didn't wish to discuss it in front of Halle and Henry, so she brought Hyacinth downstairs to an empty parlor. The princess immediately ran for the window so she could watch the horses on the streets, so Aurelia knelt on the floor beside her while she marveled at her father's favorite animal.

"They're so *tall*," Hyacinth remarked.

Aurelia chuckled. "Those are cavalry horses. They're larger than others."

"Papa's horse is very tall, too."

"That's because Papa is a very tall man. But Valor is actually rather short compared to Papa's old horse, Sterling."

She nodded. "Yes. Sterling was very big."

"How do you know that?"

"I've seen him."

Right, Aurelia thought. She'd have to give more attention to Hyacinth's magical symptoms—and to deciding if Hyacinth should keep her powers—but now wasn't the time for that.

"Sisi," she murmured, "there's something I'd like to ask you."

Her daughter sighed as she folded her arms on the windowsill. "About my trip?"

"Your...trip. Yes." Aurelia cleared her throat, grateful for Hyacinth's childhood naivety. "Do you remember the palace where your father and I came to fetch you? I'm wondering how you got there."

She shrugged. "I was sleeping, then I woke up, and I was there."

FORGED IN ASHES

That confirmed Edom's theory. She knew the Kanish spy who'd taken Hyacinth across the sea was a mage—they couldn't have awakened the gargoyle if they were mortal—but now she knew for certain that the person had cast some sort of sleeping spell over the princess while the gargoyle carried them to Kanibar.

"What do you remember before that?" Aurelia pressed. "Papa and I tucked you in that night when you went to bed. Did anything happen after that, or were you asleep the entire time?"

Hyacinth shook her head. "I was in the gardens. That's where I went back to sleep."

"How did you get to the gardens?"

The princess blinked like it was the silliest thing she'd ever heard. "I walked."

That's exactly what she told Jack, Aurelia thought, recalling what her husband had told her about his efforts. Hyacinth had told him that she wanted to wait until Aurelia came home to talk about the incident, knowing Aurelia would be more merciful to whoever was responsible, but clearly, she didn't have any intention of making it easy for her mother, either.

"You didn't just wake up and decide to walk to the gardens, Sisi. That's unlike you," Aurelia said pointedly, narrowing her eyes. "You went for a reason, and you weren't alone. I don't wish for you to lie to me or to continue telling me fractions of the truth. Akkinorians are honest people— you know that. I expect you to respect the values of our people by telling me the whole truth. Am I understood?"

Hyacinth's eyes hardened, making Aurelia frown. "You can't be mean to him, Mama."

Him, Aurelia thought. *We're getting somewhere.*

Aurelia sighed. "Hyacinth...I know you're too young to understand this, but there's a time and a place for mercy. Anyone should be punished for taking a little girl from her bed, whether the child is a princess or a commoner. I'll do my best to offer grace to whoever did this, but the way I choose to punish them depends on who they are and why they did this." Sensing that she hadn't yet persuaded her daughter to tell the truth, she tried a different tactic: "What if this person had taken baby Lena instead of you? How would you feel then?"

Hyacinth's eyes widened. "But he didn't."

"He could've."

The princess paused, chewing on her lower lip. "I would be very upset with him."

360

"That's how Halle and Henry feel about what happened to you. They were scared when they woke up and you weren't there. I'm sure they're still scared that whoever did this might come back for them, too. Your father and I have the same fear—we want to make sure the person responsible can't get to you or your siblings ever again. We can't do that unless you tell us what happened that night." Aurelia paused and brushed a lock of hair from her daughter's face. "You left your room and went to the gardens. Why?"

Hyacinth bowed her head. "Ansyl brought me there. He wanted to look at the stars. I like the stars, too."

Aurelia's blood turned to ice in her veins. "*Ansyl* took you into the gardens?"

"Yes, Mama. He carried me 'cause I wasn't wearing shoes. My toes were cold. He said to look up at the stars, and I did, and then I fell asleep, and then I woke up in the other place!"

She didn't want to believe it. "Are you sure it was Ansyl?"

"Yes, Mama."

Of course she's sure, Aurelia thought. *She's known him since the day she was born.*

It all came together now. It was no wonder the soldiers guarding the rear entrance to the palace hadn't seen or heard anything: Ansyl knew their rotation schedule, so he could've stalled them somehow when the second round of watchmen prepared to take their positions. They would've lingered with him for as long as he needed, too, because they wouldn't do anything to disobey or disrespect the queen's second-in-command. They'd never think that he had anything to do with Hyacinth's kidnapping, either, so they probably hadn't even thought to tell anyone about their interaction with Ansyl that night.

Hyacinth would've gone anywhere with him willingly and quietly, and even if any servants had been awake at that hour to see them together, Ansyl knew how to navigate the palace without being spotted. He knew which halls and corridors were almost always empty, which entrances and exits saw the most foot traffic, and which parts of the palace were more heavily guarded than others.

Not to mention the most damning factor of them all: Ansyl was Kanish.

XXXIX

For the first time since making his acquaintance, Aurelia didn't return Ansyl's smile when he arrived in her temporary study—a spare room offered by Reyna. Jack didn't greet the Lord Hand with any kindness, either: he merely stood at Aurelia's side behind the desk, arms folded over his chest, while watching Ansyl with a look in his eyes that was nothing short of murderous.

"Your Grace. Your Highness." Ansyl bowed in greeting, as always, before clasping his hands behind his back. "If it's all the same to you, our audience must be a quick one. Our mages are rather directionless without their archmages to guide them, and they're having some difficulty answering to the Taundosan coven. I've had to play the part of peacemaker thus far, but it hasn't taken just yet."

Aurelia didn't bat an eye. "Sit down, Ansyl."

Furrowing his eyebrows in confusion, Ansyl obeyed and claimed the seat on the other side of the desk. She studied him for a moment, searching for any signs of deception, but found nothing except for the kind eyes and gentle smile that reminded her so much of Kaia.

"A matter has been brought to my attention," she said, "and I wish to hear your side of it, too. Tell me, my Lord Hand—do you know why Hyacinth named *you* as the person who took her from her bed on the night she was kidnapped?"

In the time it took for her to blink, Ansyl's fawny skin had turned gray, and beads of sweat had already begun forming around his hairline. His hands on his lap clenched into fists, too—a nervous habit she'd noticed within her first few weeks of knowing him.

"Y-Your Grace, I haven't the slightest—"

"Oh, please," Jack snapped. "Don't bother denying it. The only reason it's taken us this long to learn the truth is because our daughter loves you so much that she tried to protect you. How dare you disrespect her, yet again?" He scoffed and shook his head, seething. "All this time, I trusted you with finding and apprehending the person responsible for putting Hyacinth in harm's way. You told me you were personally overseeing the interrogations. You never went through with any of it, did you? You took advantage of my trust to protect yourself and your kin, and you accused innocent people of being criminals to cover your tracks. I even brought you here because I trusted you to guide me—not as Lord Hand, but as a friend. How could you do this to us?"

Ansyl's golden eyes welled with tears as he met Aurelia's gaze. "Your Grace—"

"I don't want to believe it," she interrupted. "It makes perfect sense, yet I still struggle to accept it. How can it be that the person I chose to rule by my side—and in my place, when necessary—is the same person who helped deliver my child to my enemy? How can it be that the person I've trusted most for the last five years is the same person who left my daughter at the mercy of an evil man across the sea?" She shook her head, chuckling without humor. "You know, the Assembly and the nobility warned me when I made you my Hand. I was meant to choose a native Akkinorian, but instead, I chose a foreign man with the same blood as the friend I'd trusted with my life. Do you suppose Kaia would be pleased that you've betrayed me like this?"

"You betrayed her first." Ansyl's voice cut through the air like a knife, churning Aurelia's stomach and making her lips part in shock. The guilt had momentarily disappeared from his eyes, now replaced by hatred. "I don't know what exactly happened while you were acquainted with my sister, but I do know that she did just fine on her own for years until she met you. A few weeks with you, and she winds up dead."

"Is that what this is about?" Jack seethed. Aurelia was glad for his intervention—she didn't know what to say. All she could do was listen to the sound of Kaia's laughter as it echoed in her head. "Good *gods*, man. I never met your sister, but I know her through stories from Aurelia, you, and your siblings. She was the kind of person who helped someone in need without a second thought, wasn't she?" Ansyl lowered his gaze, face turning crimson, and clenched his jaw. "I thought so. Aurelia didn't ask Kaia to accompany her on a dangerous journey. She didn't shoot Kaia with a poison arrow. She accepted Kaia's help when it was offered, and she mourned for her friend after a terrible accident took Kaia from the realm. There was no betrayal, and there's no reason to blame Aurelia for something only the gods could've seen coming."

Aurelia took a moment longer to compose herself. She didn't believe Ansyl had been working for Willem since the day he and his siblings arrived in Akkinor, but now, she certainly believed he'd been harboring resentment toward her all these years. He never showed it, but behind closed doors, he blamed her for his sister's death—and he'd never once asked her to tell him exactly how Kaia had gotten shot with a poisoned arrow. Aurelia had spent years convincing herself of the very same things Jack had just said, working tirelessly to combat the guilt she felt at something she couldn't control; and until today, her efforts had worked.

"I only knew Kaia for a short time, and she became one of the best friends I've ever had." Aurelia's voice, though hoarse and dry, was powerful enough to make Ansyl flinch. "I tried as hard as I could to save her. I replay her last few days in my head all the time, wondering if I could've done things differently, but I know I couldn't have. I'm sorry that you lost Kaia, I really am, and I understand why you might still blame me. But to take your anger out on my daughter? That's the most despicable response I could ever imagine."

"You lost a friend, but I lost a sister. Even so, it wasn't just because of Kaia." When Ansyl blinked, the tears glistening in his eyes rolled down his cheeks. He'd dropped the scorned brother act, only to replace it, once again, with cowardice. "I'm truly sorry for what I did, but you don't understand. Willem...He-He sent me a letter not long before your first visit to Kanibar. He knows Thea and Mycah's daily routines from the moment they wake to the moment they go to sleep, and he implied that he's had spies watching them for years now. He threatened to have them killed or kidnapped and brought back to Kanibar to be used for slave labor unless I cooperated with him. I had no choice but to comply."

"What kind of excuse is that?" Jack set his hands on the desk for support, leaning forward and glowering at Ansyl in a way that made even Aurelia wince. "If you'd come to us for help, we could've found a solution together. Thea and Mycah could've stayed in Omara with my family— you know Bryan would've protected them like his own children."

Ansyl shook his head frantically. "The spies—and the king—would've known if I'd come to you. They would've found a way to strike my siblings down before Thea and Mycah caught a glimpse of Omara. You, Your Highness, know from experience that even highborn protection detail doesn't guarantee one's safety on the Templar's Road."

"You dare to use my own experiences against me?" Jack's chuckle sounded more like a growl, making Ansyl shrink further into his chair. "What happened to me ten years ago is a rare occurrence nowadays, and you know it. Stop trying to justify your reason for aiding in Hyacinth's kidnapping. It only makes you look more pathetic than you are."

"There were other ways, too," Aurelia added. "You know I would've done everything in my power to protect your family. I owe that much to Kaia, and even if I didn't...I'd try my hardest, anyway, because the three of you are my family, too."

Ansyl's lower lip trembled. "Your Grace, I..."

"You *what?* Hmm?" Aurelia's temper threatened to explode, but fortunately, Jack's hand on her shoulder kept her steady. "As much as I understand the need to protect your family, you had other options at your disposal. Spying for Willem is one thing, but to bring my *children* into this? They trust you with their lives, Ansyl. They trust you to protect them as much as your siblings do. And they love you. How can I ever ask them to trust anyone again after what you did?"

"I'm sorry. I'm so sorry." He was crying in earnest now, something Aurelia had never witnessed from him before. "I-I didn't intend for this. I made the others swear not to harm her. I even convinced them to give her the dreamer's draught instead of casting a sleeping spell over her—I knew she's taken it before, and the same amount, so I knew she'd be all right."

Aurelia frowned. Dreamer's draught was an herbal concoction meant to induce a deep sleep for a full day. Hyacinth had needed it once two years ago when she'd fallen ill. Offering a more trusted means of putting Hyacinth to sleep, however, didn't excuse the fact that he'd hand-delivered her to the enemy.

Ansyl gulped. "I swear, Your Grace, I wouldn't have let her go if—"

"—if they didn't make that promise?" Jack scoffed. "How foolish can you be, trusting the word of a man who was ready to kill your own blood? You're certainly lucky that they were true to their word. If they'd harmed even a hair on her head, I can promise—"

"Enough." Aurelia set her hand over his as his fingers clenched on her shoulder. "It's not just about Hyacinth. Now we also know how Willem came to possess the crucial information he needed to force my hand. You told him everything he might need to destroy me: the truth of my birth, Hyacinth's adoption, her signs of magic—*everything*."

She paused, feeling a bit ill. "Combined, every last thing you've done warrants execution."

If possible, his face turned even paler. "Y-Your Grace, I beg you—"

"You already know that the punishment for treason is death by hanging—or, in your case, as a member of my court, beheading." The words were difficult to utter aloud, sticking in her throat like tar, but she forced them out. "I bestowed upon you the highest honor one might hope to achieve in Akkinor, and you used that power to assist in my destruction. Nobody will say a word against it if I summon the executioner...but I won't."

Ansyl stopped crying long enough to gape at her. "Your-Your Grace?"

Beside her, Jack appeared equally as miffed. "Aurelia?"

"Everything in my soul is telling me to do exactly that, but everything I believe in is telling me to spare you, gods help me." She cleared her throat and smoothed her skirts. "Hyacinth was right to wait until my return to share what happened that night. I'll let you live, but only for the sake of your siblings. They've already lost Kaia, and I don't wish for them to lose you forever, too. They don't deserve that. Instead of sentencing you to death, your punishment is exile from Akkinor. If you ever attempt to return, you'll be executed on sight."

"Aurelia," Jack hissed in her ear, "you can't possibly—"

"I wouldn't be alive today without Kaia." She swallowed the lump in her throat as she stared at Ansyl, who only gazed down at his hands in his lap. "I wouldn't have met you, either, Jack. Subsequently, we wouldn't have our children. Kaia is the root of all things I've grown to love and appreciate in my life, so I shall repay her friendship by letting you live. Not for you—for her."

She nodded her head at Jack, who glared at Ansyl before crossing the room and disappearing into the hallway. When he was gone, she asked Ansyl to look at her. It took him a moment to lift his eyes from his lap, and when he did, she struggled to see beyond the mask of the friend she cared for.

"I understand why you did it," she murmured, "Really, I do, and you were in a situation no one should ever have to find themselves in. But you took the path that felt easiest for you, instead of trusting me to help you. And to be perfectly honest...I would've considered forgiving you for serving as Willem's spy. What I can't forgive is that you put my daughter in danger—and broke her trust in the process. My daughter, who adores you and looks up to you like an elder brother. Who would do anything you asked if it meant seeing you smile because she loves you with everything in her heart. The little girl who went to see the stars with you in the middle of the night, without a single worry. *That*, Ansyl, is beyond what I'm capable of forgiving."

Ansyl's chin wobbled as his eyes welled with tears again, but he didn't get the chance to respond before Jack returned with two knights. The taller of the knights had a pair of Akkinorian bronze shackles dangling from his fingertips.

"Ser Gerald and Ser Francis will escort you to the dungeon," Aurelia continued, standing. As she spoke, Ser Francis hefted Ansyl from his seat by his underarms while Ser Gerald bound Ansyl's hands behind his back. "When all of this is over, you'll be exiled at the border of Quapebet, as tradition. I'd considered exiling you here in Carthe, but quite frankly, I don't think you should be anywhere near my allies after you betrayed their trust, too. If you find your way back here from Quapebet, so be it—but I won't be the one to send you home. Thea and Mycah deserve the opportunity to say goodbye to you, too."

"Aurelia has kindly asked the guards in the dungeon to refrain from treating you like a common criminal." Jack's face was still contorted with loathing, but he managed to keep his voice calm and professional. "You'll have no shortage of luxuries. Proper food, clothing, and anything else you might need will be provided to you. I personally find you unworthy of such kindness, but my wife is a better person than I am."

Ansyl sniffled as the tears in his eyes finally began to dry. "Thank you, Your Grace. I don't deserve your generosity or your mercy."

"No, you don't. But I cared for you once, and my children still do—that's worth more than letting you rot." Aurelia raised an eyebrow. "Have you anything more to say?"

He swallowed as both knights gripped him by either arm. "For what it's worth, I'm sorry for what I've done. And...And I do love the children, Your Grace. Very much. I regret that my efforts to protect my siblings meant putting those beautiful souls in harm's way. They deserve better than that." He paused for a moment, face crumpling with emotion, before meeting her eyes. "Will you...Will you tell them goodbye for me? And will you tell Sisi that I'm sorry for what I did?"

Aurelia didn't reply—mainly because she didn't know what to say. With that, Ansyl sighed and bowed his head while Aurelia nodded to the knights. The pair turned Ansyl toward the door, and as they disappeared into the hallway, Aurelia studied her former Lord Hand for what would be the second to last time.

When they were gone, Aurelia slumped into her seat again as Jack closed the door. She leaned back in her chair, chewing on her fingernails and fighting tears, as Jack knelt by her side and set his hands on her arm.

"Are you all right?" he asked.

Her eyelids fluttered shut. "I've been better."

"You did the right thing. In fact, you did the right thing a bit too well. I would've had him beheaded as soon as he admitted to it."

"A ruler can't behead every person who wrongs them, Jack. That's when they become a tyrant." She sighed and massaged her aching temples.

"I know I should've sentenced him to death, but I meant what I said. Letting him live isn't a favor to him, but to his siblings—all of them. I just still can't believe..."

When she trailed off, Jack exhaled and shook his head. "Neither can I. He played the part far too well."

"I don't think he was playing a part," she said softly. "I think he was true to everything until Willem forced his hand. That doesn't excuse what he did, but at the very least, we can rest easy knowing that he wasn't deceiving us from the moment he arrived in Akkinor."

"Maybe."

She dropped her hands to her lap and turned to face him. "The children will be asking for him, you know."

"I know. What will we tell them?"

"That he had to move away. That's the most they'll be capable of understanding, anyway."

"And Thea and Mycah?"

Aurelia flinched. "They're old enough now to understand exactly what he did and why he has to be punished for it. They won't be pleased, of course, but they know that actions have consequences—even for nobles and royals."

"I know you don't want to hear this, but the people will want to see Thea and Mycah exiled, too. Our subjects won't trust any Kanish person in court—or in Akkinor as a whole—after word spreads of Ansyl's betrayal."

Aurelia scowled. "How would that help ease the tension between Akkinor and Carthe that already exists? Even if we aren't friendly with Kanibar, it isn't right to alienate and belittle an entire country because of the misdeeds of a select few. They wanted me to execute and imprison the entirety of the Reilly family after the war with my brother, remember? Even those who had nothing to do with it, like the children. There's no honor in that, even if our people like to believe otherwise."

Jack smiled and brushed a lock of hair from her eyes. "All right."

She looked away from him for a moment, staring at the empty chair Ansyl had warmed only a few minutes earlier, until a sudden realization struck her. When it did, she glanced down at Jack again while Ansyl's voice echoed in her head.

"I suppose I should've seen that there was a growing distance between Ansyl and I. A wall he put up when I tried to get too close."

"How do you mean?" Jack asked.

Aurelia smiled, but it was forced and unconvincing. "He never called me by name. Not even once."

***

"How is he?"

Jack shot Aurelia an annoyed look, but then clamped his jaw shut when he saw the stern, unwavering expression on her face. "He's fine. The guards are treating him kindly, and I promise, I refrained from ripping him to shreds when I inspected the quality of his cell. He did give me something that he'd like you to have, though."

Frowning, Aurelia accepted a folded piece of parchment when he held it out to her, ignoring the stabbing sensation in her gut when her eyes found Ansyl's handwriting. She hadn't seen or spoken to him in three days, but she'd sent Jack to ensure that the conditions of Ansyl's cell weren't too atrocious. She certainly hadn't expected Ansyl to send her a message, though.

She sighed when she finished reading it. "He's compiled a list of his potential replacements—anyone he believes might be suitable as my Hand."

"He's trying to get back into your good graces, then. Maybe he hopes you'll change your mind."

"No." She shook her head and handed the note back to him for safekeeping. "He just wants to remind me that he's still a good man at heart, circumstances be damned." She sighed again. "It doesn't matter. Let's meet the others before they start without us."

Shaking Ansyl from her thoughts, she took Jack's arm as the pair strolled to the symposium, where their allies awaited them. As always, the group was gathered around the meeting table and brooding over a battle map, looking disheartened by whatever they were discussing.

"What have we missed?" Aurelia asked, positioning herself between Arian and Jack.

"Nothing of substance," Lord Zhoqa replied. "Even with your covens and your dragon, we're still at a terrible disadvantage when it comes to magic. We can't seem to think of a tactic that might weaken Willem's mages—they're exceptionally skilled, from what our scouts have reported." He paused when something whooshed through the air in a flash of golden light. Aurelia smiled when Edom perched on her shoulder, but Lord Zhoqa only snorted and said, "Have you any suggestions, sprite?"

Edom shook its head. "No."

The nobleman rolled his eyes. "We have a humanoid magical creature on our side, yet it offers us no insight into our magical conundrum. Why are you even here?"

"Leave it be," Jack snapped at him. "It's been nothing but helpful thus far. Don't make it think it's chosen the wrong side."

Edom sniffled. "Thank you, Highness."

Aurelia cleared her throat, resisting the urge to smile—she knew Jack was fonder of Edom than he'd let on. "This isn't worth exerting ourselves over. There's nothing we can do about Willem's advantage when it comes to mages. Let's discuss the other matter: King Elrin's successor. Have you found her? If we have her on our side when the battle begins, some of Willem's soldiers might be swayed into dropping their swords. After all, he's been telling them that Dofell's restoration is the key to fulfilling the prophecy, and his involvement won't be necessary if the kingdom has a new, capable ruler free of the curse."

"We found three possible options with the information you provided on Althaia Pharos," Lord Zhaaran replied. "The first died two seasons ago, but he was a man, anyway. We found the second and invited her to the palace, but..."

Lord Zhoqa snorted. "She was madder than anyone I've ever met, like a toddler trapped in the body of a middle-aged woman. When we had to remind her of her name for the third time, we sent her back to Dofell."

"We identified a third candidate, too, but we haven't managed to locate her," Arian added. "We deployed a few trusted soldiers to find her. We haven't received so much of a letter regarding their progress, though."

"Our only option now is to hope and pray that she's found—and that she's sane," Reyna muttered. "If we can't find her..."

She didn't need to finish. Everyone in the room knew the stakes: if a successor couldn't be found, the allies would remain as such—allies—just long enough to see Willem defeated. After that, they'd have no choice but to battle one another for control of Dofell, exactly as they'd feared from the start.

As thoughts and hopes of Willem's defeat ran rampant in her brain, Aurelia remembered a conversation she'd had with Maysa and immediately asked a servant to fetch writing materials. Nobody said a word as she sat down at the table, crafted a short message, and folded the parchment into a square small enough for the sprite's hands. On the blank front side of the parchment, she wrote the word *Krotis*, then signed it with a gods-awful illustration of a dragon.

The sprite had been watching her write from its position on her shoulder, so it knew exactly where to deliver the letter. When she finished signing the parchment, Edom jumped to the table before her with its hands outstretched.

"You know what to do," she said. "Hurry back."

Edom nodded, took the letter, and disappeared from the room in a flash of golden light.

Jack raised an eyebrow. "You're writing to Krotis? Why? It would appear that Lady Swann has made her stance clear on the matter. It isn't worth sending a plea for help, as much as we need Runeia."

Aurelia smiled. "Trust me."

"I don't believe I wish to know what you're plotting." Lord Zhoqa pinched the bridge of his nose and exhaled. "There's something else we have to discuss, too: the battlefield. Willem hasn't let anything slip about where he plans to incite the battle, and there are too many barren spaces in Dofell for us to choose from. If we set out for the wrong place, he'll storm the palace and slaughter the Phyres, all while the rest of us scour the kingdom with our tails between our legs. Even if we find a successor, he will have already claimed the Dofelli crown for himself."

"He can't enter the palace without going mad. You heard King Elrin," Reyna reminded him. "He must know that, too. He'd have to lure the Phyres out somehow, and that could take ages. Elrin won't give himself and his family up to Willem until he knows he's out of options—until we've been defeated. Willem has no choice but to take care of us first if he stands a chance at reaching the Phyres."

"He'll probably meet us wherever we are," Jack offered. "So maybe we should just choose?"

Aurelia chewed on her lower lip, contemplating. "I might have an idea, and I think Willem would have the same one, but—"

The rest of her sentence fizzled away when the door to the symposium creaked open. Every pair of eyes turned to the door, where a servant was bowing to them and trying his utmost to avoid meeting their gazes.

"Forgive the interruption, my queen. You have a visitor."

Reyna sighed. "Have them situated in the morning room. I'll be with them momentarily."

The mousy-looking man cleared his throat. "I-I believe you'll wish to take the audience now, Your Majesty."

Reyna furrowed her eyebrows, frowning, and nodded in approval. The servant disappeared into the hallway, and a moment later, a woman took his place.

The first thing Aurelia noticed about the woman was her scent: a combination of filth, manure, and sour milk. The woman's features—fiercely dark eyes, tanned skin, and long black hair—were distinctly Dofelli. Her tattered, stained clothing, paired with the dirt staining her skin and the gauntness of her entire being, confirmed that she was a Dofelli peasant.

Trembling, the woman lowered herself into a lopsided curtsy. "Y-Your Majesty."

"Rise." On Reyna's cue, the woman straightened up and nearly lost her balance. Nobody spoke as the Golden Queen studied her visitor. "What's your name?"

"Diantha Pharos, Your Majesty."

Aurelia gasped before she could stop herself. *"Pharos?"*

XL

For a long while after Diantha arrived, the allies were silent. The only person who spoke was Reyna, and she only did so to inquire after what type of refreshments Diantha preferred. The others stood around the meeting table, silent, and watched as Diantha sipped from a steaming mug while sitting rigidly in a chair much too large for her wiry body.

Finally, Arian cleared his throat. "Do you know why we asked you here today, madam?"

She only stared down at the mug between her hands. "No, my lord."

"We'd like to ask you a few questions about your bloodline." Lord Zhoqa ignored Aurelia when she glared at him. He didn't seem to believe in the idea of breaking news gently. "Are you aware that one of your direct ancestors was the biological daughter of King Ophelos III?"

Diantha's head shot up, eyes widening, as her lips parted in shock. "I-um-no, my lord."

"You've been summoned here today because you're the last living member of the Phyre family—excluding the current royal family," Reyna told her. "You may be a distant relative, but you have enough royal blood in your veins to be of use to us. Dofell's only hope is to appoint new leadership as quickly as possible. King Elrin himself has already agreed to abdicate the throne. When he and his immediate family are removed from power, and a new monarch takes his place, the misfortune Dofell has experienced over the centuries will transform into prosperity. The curse Myenar placed on the kingdom will be broken."

"It's our understanding that King Elrin's successor must be a Dofelli commoner descended from the Phyre family," Lord Zhaaran said carefully. "You, madam, are our only option."

Diantha's waxen cheeks turned gray as she slid her hands onto her lap. "Y-You must be mistaken. I have no qualifications for—"

"We didn't expect you to be qualified for leadership," Lord Zhoqa interrupted, snorting at her. "We're well aware that commoners aren't trained like kings and queens, but apparently, only a lowborn can lead Dofell to salvation. It's what needs to be done to ensure the curse is broken."

"What His Lordship means," Aurelia said gently, glowering at him, "is that those of us in this room are prepared to guide you in every way. We'll teach you the ways of a monarch as best we can, and we will not leave you high and dry after the crown is placed on your head."

Diantha shook her head. "I-I scrub the floors at the Dofelli bank. I polish the doorknobs. I chase mice out of the walls and onto the streets. That's what I've done for my entire life. I-I couldn't even think of—"

"—doing anything else?" Lord Zhoqa chuckled humorlessly. "Forgive my brashness, but you haven't another choice. If you refuse, whatever remains of Dofell and its culture will be destroyed by Kanibar. King Willem may commit genocide against your people to fill Dofelli lands with the Kanish. Do you have children?"

"Yes."

"Then you should know that you and your children will be dead by the end of this if you walk away from us."

"Balor!" Lord Zhaaran snapped. *"Enough.* That's no way to speak to someone whose trust we must earn. Have some compassion."

Lord Zhoqa softened, but not by much. "Even if you refuse, and we manage to prevent Willem from seizing your home, somebody else will have to rule in Elrin's stead. The curse can't be broken while a legitimate member of the Phyre family sits the throne, and Dofell will continue to fall until it's beyond repair. Each of us in this room will find ourselves pitted against one another to provide Dofell with new leadership. The continent will be embroiled in a bitter civil war, and the entire realm will suffer for it. Is that what you wish?"

Diantha's face turned crimson. "N-No, my lord, but—"

"I'm afraid we're beyond *buts.*" Reyna offered her a small, sad sort of smile. "I know we've given you quite a bit to consider, but it's best if you provide us with an answer quickly. Our plans for the future depend on you."

"It seems like everything depends on me." She shook her head again, clenching her jaw, before looking between the highborn as they stared at her. "My only qualification is my lineage. I have nothing else to offer."

Lord Zhoqa scoffed and pointed at her while facing his allies. "This is ridiculous. I knew it when the sprite delivered Her Grace's message from Kanibar, and I knew it the moment this woman walked into the room. Look at her, for gods' sakes. If she can't manage to keep louse from her hair, how can she manage to govern a nation, even one as pitiful as Dofell? The kingdom needs strength and security, and she isn't capable of providing either."

Nobody replied. Aurelia couldn't ascertain exactly what the others were thinking—if they agreed with him or if they were merely constructing a rebuttal—but she heard Maysa's voice echoing in her head, reminding her that Diantha was the star Dofell needed to follow to greatness. Maysa was one of only a few people left in the world whom the gods had chosen as their voice on earth, and Aurelia trusted their word more than Lord Zhoqa's ignorance.

As she studied Diantha, her own voice replaced Maysa's in her head. The story of the king and the fishmonger with the two spoons came flooding back to her as she observed the rags covering Diantha's frail body, the thick layers of dirt under her fingernails, and the buildup of oil and filth corrupting her sleek black hair. As much as Diantha *looked* like a common peasant, something about her demeanor suggested otherwise. She didn't tremble out of fear or intimidation, particularly for one standing in a room with four world leaders. She kept her shoulders squared and taut as if she were the only highborn in the room, and the *others* were the commonfolk. She held her chin high—out of defiance or strength, Aurelia couldn't be sure—and hadn't let Lord Zhoqa's mention of her children upset her.

It almost looked like she wore the signs of peasantry like a badge of honor; like highborn life was beneath her, and like it was the realm's most desolate individuals who held all the cards—because they did.

Aurelia recalled the lesson she'd relayed to her children when she told them the story: *Just because something appears more regal than another doesn't always mean it's the better option.* When she heard the story from her father, he'd said something that sounded similar, but the message was quite different:

"'Just because something appears ordinary doesn't mean it's incapable of greatness,'" she said aloud. From the corner of her eye, she saw Arian erupt in a grin, and she knew he'd heard the same line from Edmund at least once before. The others turned to her wearing puzzled expressions, but Diantha regarded her curiously—and a bit skeptically, too.

She paused for a moment to consider her next words. "The Book of Desmor. Has anyone heard of it?"

"But of course," Lord Zhaaran replied. When both Diantha and Jack shook their heads, he added, "Desmor was the last Elder in the realm to commune with the gods before they disappeared. He's largely regarded as the holiest mortal who ever lived. Many priests achieve the status of Elder in their lifetimes, but Desmor was the only *High* Elder in history. The Book of Desmor is a series of texts attributed to the High Elder throughout his lifetime. It discusses everything from the messages he received from the gods, to dissections of the realm's history, to his predictions for the future of our world. Bozar considers it to be the most important text ever written."

Aurelia nodded. "There's a section in the Book of Desmor dedicated to divine curses. One particular line comes to mind: *'Most curses can be broken by one who cares more for hearth than home.'* What do hearth and home represent?"

"*Hearth* is community, family. Gathering around the fire, welcoming your neighbors, lending a helping hand to those around you," Jack offered. "*Home* refers to the more material aspects of life—shelter, food, and so on. All the basic necessities one needs to survive."

"That line is often interpreted as promoting selflessness," Aurelia said. "One must proceed in the best interests of the whole, not the individual—even if they suffer for it."

She hadn't realized she'd been walking until she found herself standing directly beside Diantha. She grazed her fingers over the edge of the table as she looked down at Diantha, who was distracted by Halvor shrieking outside the window across from her.

"That's why I think we're right about how the curse can be broken," Aurelia continued. "A commoner may not always be assured home, but they can always rely on hearth. Someone raised in a highborn household can't understand the difference between them—or the importance of hearth over home—because we've never had to. The kingdom's only chance is someone who will do what needs to be done for the sake of the whole, not themselves."

Diantha's eyes narrowed a bit. "You speak of a commoner's ability to provide the kingdom with what it needs, Your Grace, but none of you know anything about Dofell or its people—especially we lowborn. You only know what you see, and you only see what lines the streets of my kingdom while you cross from one side to the other."

Aurelia blinked at her and surged backwards a bit. "Madam, I—"

"*Home* doesn't exist anymore for most of us. *Hearth* continues to crumble by the day." She was clasping the edge of the table with such an iron grip that her nails began to splinter the wood. "We have nothing to

376

rely on, nothing to believe in, nothing to fight for. Anyone who might've invited me to sit by their hearth has nothing to offer other than pity and resentment, let alone tea and conversation. The whole has been broken beyond repair, Your Grace."

"For now." Arian manifested at Aurelia's side and smiled down at Diantha in a way that made her soften, like she couldn't help herself. Aurelia knew the feeling—Arian had that effect on people. "You have the opportunity to change that, madam. Four of the realm's most powerful rulers are here today to assure you that they'll assist you in that transformation. Dofell has been neglected and forgotten for far too long, and we have no intention of letting the kingdom and its people continue to suffer."

As Diantha appeared to contemplate his words, Aurelia cleared her throat. "You're right. We know little about what life is really like for you and your people. I think I speak for all of us when I say we're too frightened of what we might find to look beyond the trail leading from one set of gates to another. But you know everything about it, don't you? Far more than any of us in this room could imagine. That's why you're here: because only you have the power to heal your kingdom before it's lost forever."

Diantha snapped her gaze up to meet Aurelia's, and for a moment, deafening silence struck the room as the pair stared at one another, neither of them so much as twitching or blinking. But when Diantha sighed and dropped her gaze to her lap again, offering the slightest nod Aurelia had ever witnessed, the Queen of Akkinor felt an invisible weight lifted from her shoulders.

***

"We must send word to the others immediately." Lord Zhaaran planted his hands on the table on either side of his hips while gazing at the battle map. "Lords Xada and Zoma must be informed—they've decided against fighting beside us, the cowardly oafs, but we can't keep them in the dark. Lady Swann should know this, too."

"I'll have our messengers send ravens at once," Arian replied. "King Elrin, of course, must know everything, too. We don't need his approval, but it's the decent thing to do."

Reyna nodded before turning to Diantha. "I shall have my staff prepare a room for you here in the palace. My men will locate your family and have them brought here, too. They'll be under my protection until the matter with Kanibar is dealt with. Where can we find them?"

"Thank you, Your Majesty. My husband's name is Aerodos Pytheon—you'll find him and our children in the village of Dilogne. We live in an abandoned stable on the northeast side of the village, directly beside the old tanning shop." Diantha, now standing by the window while watching Halvor circle the City of Gold in the near distance, didn't turn to acknowledge her host. "When will I be crowned?"

Lord Zhaaran grimaced a bit. "I can't say for certain just yet. We may not have time for a legitimate ceremony before the Kanish arrive in Dofell. We shall need you present on the battlefield—momentarily, of course—in the event that any of King Willem's soldiers are deterred from fighting. Most of them are under the impression that Willem wishes to salvage Dofell, but if we show them that we've found new leadership, they may not see a reason to fight anymore. It may affect Willem's leadership, too, if he sees with his own eyes that his claim has been weakened."

"Either way, you're Dofell's new queen." Lord Zhoqa looked like it was taking every ounce of strength in his body to get the words out. "We don't need a legitimate ceremony to make that true. There will be time enough to crown you before the masses after we've defeated Kanibar. For now, your very existence is all we need."

Diantha exhaled. "All right."

Aurelia's hand accidentally drifted to her trousers, where the weight of the amulet strained against her pocket. She recalled her dream from the cavern beneath Kanibar of who she believed to be Edea, goddess of the moon. Her gut was telling her that she'd found the amulet for a reason—a reason other than needing it to help her find a way out of the cavern system and back home to Akkinor.

"Myenar," she blurted.

All eyes turned to her, but only Lord Zhoqa replied as he raised an amused eyebrow. "Having an episode of hysterics, Your Grace?"

Jack took a step forward, warning him, as Aurelia narrowed her eyes. "You'd like that, wouldn't you?" she snapped, shaking her head at him. He rolled his eyes at her as she turned to face the others. "I've just had a thought. When Edea came to me in a dream—"

"She did?" Lord Zhaaran's lips parted in shock. "You didn't share that with us."

"I was a bit distracted after running for my life," she reminded him. He nodded in understanding. "She visited me in a dream after I fled Kanibar. I told her of our concerns about using the amulet, and she assured me that I'd be spared from its curse. But I don't believe that's why I found it. I don't think I was ever meant to use it, curse or not. I think Edea—or the entirety of the Twelve, for that matter—was sending me a message. Pointing me toward the right path, so to speak."

Arian's eyes shimmered with childlike excitement, as always. "And what path would that be?"

She glanced down at the battle map—specifically, at Dofell. "Myenar was chosen to be the patron god of Dofell centuries ago because their culture depended on order and justice, and neither of those things can exist without judgment. It was the only civilization in the world where crime was close to being nonexistent. One couldn't find such effortless harmony anywhere else in the realm. The ancient people believed Myenar would ensure that peace in perpetuity, but instead...With his curse, he's done exactly the opposite of what the ancient Dofelli believed he would. He's betrayed them."

Reyna shivered. "Careful, Your Grace."

Aurelia ignored her. She had no fear of a god who'd turned his back on the people he was meant to protect—not while another deity seemed to agree with her.

"If we truly want Dofell to see a brighter future," she continued, "we can't allow their patron deity to be one who's already damned them in more ways than one. Whether or not his curse was warranted, Myenar chose to let an entire kingdom suffer for centuries. I think...I think Edea has been trying to tell me that Dofell needs a new beginning. A new representative."

"Edea herself." Arian sunk into the chair closest to him while clutching his breast. "My gods."

For some reason, as silence swept the room, Aurelia's eyes flicked over to Lord Zhaaran. His eyes were lowered, and his jaw was clenched, but in contemplation rather than disapproval. When he sensed her watching him, he lifted his violet eyes to meet hers, and a ghost of a smile formed on his lips.

"It almost feels like naming a new Almighty is a consequence of naming a new reigning family. Some say a god latches not onto a kingdom, but onto a family—much like a dragon." His weak smile transformed into a full-fledged grin. "Mortals weren't meant to trifle with the power of the gods, but your dragon is the greatest example of divinity we've seen in the modern age. You manage to control him, Your Grace—I should've trusted you to control the amulet. I should've trusted that you'd know what to do with it."

Aurelia cracked a smile. "Apology accepted."

While he laughed, Lord Zhoqa shook his head. "It's madness. We risk offending Myenar in a way no mortal has ever even dreamed of. I'm not overly fond of the idea of playing victim to his wrath."

"Edea herself believes this is the right path," Arian retorted. "She'll protect those who see her become Dofell's Almighty. I'm sure of it. But this decision isn't ours to make anymore, my friends."

All eyes turned to Diantha, who paled and hugged herself for comfort. "I-I admit to knowing little about Edea and even the Almighty himself. I wasn't privileged enough to receive a proper education. But..." She closed her eyes and sighed. "But I've been one with the moon for as long as I can remember. More active at nighttime than I am during the day. When I was a girl, I used to talk to the moon like it was an old friend. I could've sworn it talked back."

Aurelia smiled. "Maybe it did. Maybe *she* did. You may have rationalized it as you grew older, telling yourself it was impossible, but maybe it was exactly as you thought it was. After all, Edea would've known your destiny from the moment your soul inhabited a human body."

Diantha's eyes flashed with understanding. "I think you may be right."

"So?" Lord Zhoqa tapped an impatient foot against the floor. "What say you, Your Majesty?"

Diantha flinched but quickly masked it by shifting her weight. "I think it's worth trying. I don't know what you mean about an amulet or a dream, but I know what I feel, and everything in my soul is telling me to trust the moon."

You can't trust the moon yet, Mama.

A gasp escaped Aurelia's throat at the exact moment Jack said, "Mother of Buen."

"What?" Lord Zhoqa demanded.

"Nothing, nothing..." Aurelia laughed a bit as Jack scrubbed a hand over his face, dumbfounded. "Someone close to us has used almost that exact phrase on numerous occasions. I'd say that's a sign, wouldn't you?"

"That's it, then," Lord Zhaaran murmured. "Upon the coronation of Diantha Pharos, Queen of Dofell, the kingdom's Almighty will become Edea rather than Myenar. The people probably won't find it difficult to align their values with Edea's after Myenar's have led them astray. It's a mad thought, but the last five years have been nothing short of madness, anyway. I expect—"

Just then, a flash of golden light whipped across the room, and a breathless Edom appeared on the table before Aurelia. While Reyna assured a flabbergasted Diantha that the sprite was an ally of theirs, Aurelia lowered her face so she was eye-level with the creature. She knew just by observing it that it wasn't exhausted from its journey, but frightened of something.

"Edom?" A worried crease formed between her eyebrows. "Are you well?"

The sprite wheezed and gasped for a moment before whimpering, "The king."

A jolt of panic corrupted her body. "What about him?"

"He marches for Dofell."

"Gods above." Lord Zhoqa cursed and ran a hand over his bald head. "I thought we'd have more time."

Reyna shook her head, forlorn, and said, "We'll have to depart for the border tomorrow, then. We won't arrive in time if we wait a moment longer. We must inform our troops immediately—and our nobility at the Dofelli border. It's getting late now, but we shall reconvene at dawn to finalize our strategy." She turned to Diantha and forced a smile just as the door to the meeting room opened, revealing a pudgy middle-aged woman standing in the hallway. "Madam Torkos will escort you to your bedchamber," she told Diantha. "She'll attend to your needs. Please don't hesitate to make her aware of anything you might require. We'll work on getting your family out of Dofell as quickly as possible. I promise."

Diantha nodded. "Thank you."

As she passed the others on her way to the door, Halvor released a bellowing shriek, bringing her to a halt as she looked over her shoulder at the window. Aurelia turned to the window, too, and smiled a bit as she admired her dear friend. When she turned her eyes back to Diantha, her smile faded into a frown at the sight of Diantha's sour expression and the disapproving look in her dark eyes.

"It sounds like he's hungry, Your Grace," she said.

Then she was gone.

XLI

Why the moon? Why Edea?"

Aurelia sighed. "I don't know. Perhaps it's because Edea has always been regarded as the most insignificant of the Twelve, and Dofell has become the most insignificant civilization in the realm. They're two sides of the same coin."

Jack emerged from the washroom attached to their suite at the Palace of Taundosa, wearing nothing but brown breeches while he dried his hands with a white towel. Aurelia, momentarily distracted by his chiseled form, blinked and asked him to repeat himself when she realized she hadn't heard his response.

He grinned. "Cat got your tongue?"

She blushed and looked away from him. "Something like that."

"Naturally." He tossed the towel aside and perched on the armchair adjacent to hers. All traces of humor disappeared from his face as he turned his gaze to the crackling hearth in front of them. "There has to be another reason. Edea wouldn't risk tension with Myenar simply because she feels connected to Dofell."

"The gods work in mysterious ways, my love. We may never know the real reason—it's beyond what our mortal minds are capable of understanding."

He shook his head and pressed his lips together, frustrated. "It's going to eat at me, you know. If she hinted to you that she wishes to be Dofell's Almighty, shouldn't she have provided a reason?"

Aurelia smiled sadly. "That isn't how things are meant to be, Jack. The gods aren't required to explain themselves to us. They provide us with the tools we need to serve them, and it isn't our place to question them—only to obey."

"Hence the reason I've never been one to focus my energy on religion," he said with a shrug. "I don't wish to obey something I can't see with my own eyes."

"I know."

Jack merely sighed as he stared at the hearth, with the flames flickering against the oceans in his eyes. It had taken years for Jack to approach religion with any degree of sincerity, and Aurelia knew she couldn't push him to believe the way she did. He had to find the path to faith all on his own, if he did at all.

Aurelia's gaze found the left side of the hearth, where the couple's weapons were resting against the wall. She'd forgotten her bow and sheath at home, but Arian was kind enough to gift her with the same ones Katryna had used before her death. Her sword was somewhat new, too—it was gifted to her on her thirtieth name day by Linden's sister, Lady Gemma Stone of Laynoa, and made of Akkinorian bronze freshly acquired from the Laynoan mines. Jack's sword, on the other hand, was the same one he'd carried when Aurelia first met him in the Violet Forest.

Aurelia couldn't help but wince at the sight of it. "A part of me wishes you'd stayed home," she admitted.

He scoffed at her. "Gee, thanks."

"That's not how I meant it. It's just...I have a bad feeling about this, Jack. Something in my gut is telling me that we're in way over our heads. Gods forbid something happens to both of us...Our poor children are too young now to remember us when they're older. I don't know how we're meant to say goodbye to them tomorrow when it's possible we might never see them again."

The corner of his mouth twitched—an indication that he shared the same fear—but he chose his next words carefully: "Nothing will happen to us. We've been through so much together, you and I, and our story does not stop here. And even if I'm wrong...They may not remember us, but they'll grow up hearing stories of us. They'll know we died for something larger than ourselves. That has to count for something."

"I suppose." Her eyes flicked over to his sword again. "I still wish you'd stayed home, even if your sword bears the power of ten."

That made him smile, but it was wobbly and unconvincing. "I'm not here because I'm an excellent swordsman, Aurelia. I'm here because I refuse to let you march into battle without me at your side. Everyone else will protect you out of duty, and while that brings me some comfort, I feel better knowing I'll be there to protect you because I can't imagine a world where you don't exist."

She sighed. "Jack..."

"Don't fret, Lily dear." He slithered out of his seat to sit at her feet, resting his head on her lap while snaking an arm around her calf. "We'll be all right, the two of us. We've always worked so well together. Even those days when you thought I was a nuisance, and I thought you were impossible, like one of Sisi's puzzle boxes."

That made her laugh. "Have you solved this particular puzzle yet, Jack?"

"I'm still working on it, but I daresay I've gotten pretty damn close. Though I do enjoy learning something new, each and every day."

She buried her fingers in his dark curls, smiling. "Is that what you tell yourself when you're cross with me?"

"I'm rarely cross with you," he reminded her, "but no. That's not it. I tell myself that you gave me my second chance at life—a real life, one with purpose—just as you've done for nearly everyone you come across. I don't like that we've found ourselves at war again, but if we weren't here, it would mean you'd stopped wanting to give the realm the same chance you gave me. Our world can't afford to lose someone like you. I suppose that's another reason I couldn't just sit at home and wait for your return from battle: I want to be there tomorrow while you offer a better future to those who need it most. You're the heart of everything, Aurelia, even if some people choose to believe otherwise."

Pride and passion gurgled up in her gut. "Like whom?"

"Anyone, really. Even your allies believe they're at the center of this, what with you being a foreigner and this being their land, but we wouldn't be here if not for you. I'm not blaming you, either—I'm merely reminding you that Dofell has a second chance because of you, even if it's not what you intended."

She paused for a moment. "And what if we lose?"

Jack hesitated briefly before murmuring, "If we lose, then I pity the poor souls who stand in your way while you attempt to make things right again."

She opened her mouth—to say what, she didn't know—and quickly clamped it shut again when a thick, hot lump lodged itself in her throat. Instead of replying, she relaxed in her seat while still playing with Jack's hair, knowing she couldn't breathe life into her fears by continuing to talk about them. The more she worried about losing the battle, the chances of it actually happening increased tenfold.

Tomorrow when the sun rose over the horizon line, Aurelia and her allies would march to the border of Taundosa and Dofell to meet Willem's troops in battle. They'd spent the entire day—and the previous night, for that matter—strategizing and finalizing their plan, so the only thing left to do now was fight.

What worried her most was Willem himself. Her brief stay in Kanibar exposed her to a side of him that nobody else (other than Maysa, of course) seemed to know about. He was perhaps the cleverest adversary she had ever faced, with a particular aptitude for keeping secrets—and keeping them well. Even the most powerful people in Carthe didn't know what power he kept hidden within the Kanish borders. As much as she hated to admit it, she knew that she and her allies would be facing more than one shock when they met him on the battlefield. They could plot and strategize until they were blue in the face, and it wouldn't be enough to prepare them for whatever surprises Willem had in store.

Kanibar and Dofell were alike in more ways than she realized. Both had been largely ignored by the realm, as the masses only really seemed to care about the magnificent City of Gold or the holy kingdom of Bozar. Even the treachery of the Violet Forest and the Ngora Valley received more attention than either Kanibar or Dofell. Nobody bothered to learn what happened within the borders of each kingdom, and now, both Kanibar and Dofell were at the center of Carthe's first-ever continental war.

And of course, so was Aurelia.

***

The last time Aurelia found herself marching to war, it'd been at home, and she had to prepare to put at least one person she cared for—her own brother—to the sword. She had the greatest power in the realm tucked in a locket dangling from her neck, but up until Archie killed Linden, she hadn't known for sure if she was going to release Halvor into the world. In fact, she hadn't known *anything* for sure.

A similar feeling idled in her gut as she and her allies marched from Reyna's palace to the border separating Dofell from the Taundosan district of Morvis. The feeling was worse now than it'd been before, knowing she might not have any more tricks up her sleeve. At least she and Jack had gotten the chance to see their children before they left—only Reyna had been given the same luxury. The two Bozari lords merely sent letters to their families, while Diantha had left a note behind at the Palace of Taundosa. Goldmen were retrieving her husband and children while the allies marched to battle, and if they were lucky, they'd manage to sneak away into Taundosa without running into the warring parties. If not, the Goldmen would have to bring the family somewhere safe in Dofell until the battle ended.

Aurelia, Jack, and her allies rode adjacent to one another on white horses, as it was a Taundosan custom for highborn to ride into battle on snow-colored steeds. That way, everyone—spectator or soldier, friend or enemy—would know exactly who they were. The only ally not riding a horse was Diantha. They needed to keep her as safe as possible, so she rode by her lonesome in a carriage behind the white horses. Lord Zhaaran had even enchanted the exterior of the carriage so that any arrows, spears, or stones launched at it would disintegrate on contact.

Aurelia woke before sunrise that morning to send Halvor to northern Orestes so he could feast before the battle. It'd been Lord Zhaaran's suggestion, as he knew flocks of wild sheep tended to roam the area. Aurelia had offered to compensate him for the loss—she knew Halvor would devour at least five of them—but he refused. Instead, he advised her to start importing wild sheep to Akkinor and letting them roam in quiet areas, where Halvor could hunt and fill his belly without upsetting any shepherds like the poor old man in Horscola.

Halvor would make his grand entrance, as always, but not too soon. Willem expected to meet Halvor on the battlefield, but he had no way of knowing how Aurelia would use her greatest weapon. She'd keep him on his toes until the precise moment arrived, making sure the king and his troops spent plenty of time shaking in their boots. Willem loved to be in control, and the best way to terrorize him was to remind him that he couldn't control a dragon for the life of him.

As they approached the wall, Jack turned to her and raised an eyebrow. "Are you nervous?"

"A bit," she admitted. "I'd be a madwoman to feel otherwise." She mimicked his expression. "Are you?"

"Quite." He adjusted his armor with one hand while clutching his horse's reins with the other. "It's oddly comforting, though."

"What is?"

"Knowing we've done this before, and we emerged victorious."

Aurelia sighed. "That victory didn't come without pain and suffering, Jack. We lost many good and honorable people because of it. We'll lose more today."

Her husband winced and turned his eyes back to the path ahead. Instead of pressing him for conversation, she looked over at Reyna. Wearing golden armor from head to toe, Reyna held her head high and kept her shoulders squared, offering a picture of complete and utter confidence. Her face, though, revealed a kind of fear Aurelia had never seen from her before.

Only then did Aurelia remember that Reyna had never seen battle before. The Bozari lords—the two present ones, anyway—certainly had, but their combat experience was limited to petty squabbles between their own people. While they'd sent their men to fight for Aurelia five years earlier, they hadn't been there to watch men run around screaming, set ablaze by dragonfire, before being swallowed by Halvor.

The battle to come was nothing like the ones they knew and lived through. Today's events would mirror the ones they'd read about in tales of old for their entire lives, where it was difficult to find a Carthinian battle where dragons didn't fight men—and other dragons.

Somehow, Aurelia and Jack—the only foreigners among the group— were the ones with the most accurate expectations of what was to come.

"Let's not forget," Lord Zhaaran muttered as they approached the wall, "that Willem and Dayne are the key to ending this. The mages answer to Dayne, and the entirety of Kanibar answers to Willem. Even the Kroti— if the rumors are true—will be answering to Willem. If we kill them, there's nobody left for the troops to fight for. They're doing this because they believe Willem is a prophesized hero, so if he's gone, they have nobody to lift up like a god. The Kroti will lose their promised gold, and the Kanish will lose the only thing they believe in nowadays. We *have* to take that from them."

Reyna sighed. "We take their hope, then."

"No." Aurelia shook her head. "We give it back. They may not understand today, or tomorrow, but eventually, they will."

Jack turned to her, beaming. "I love you."

She rolled her eyes, smiling, and joked, "Must you say that every time we're marching to our deaths?"

"Oh, for the love of the gods, *shut up*," Lord Zhoqa snapped. "We have more important things to discuss than your nauseating love for one another. What if we fail to kill the mage? Then what?"

"We can't afford to fail. Willem relies on Dayne far too much, so it's possible that for him, losing Dayne is worse than losing the battle," Aurelia pointed out. Her allies nodded, likely recalling what she'd told them about the glamour spells. "Dayne is probably the only person who knows what Willem wishes for in the event of his death, too. We can't say for certain if Willem even *has* a plan for Kanibar if he happens to die, but if he does, Dayne will know about it, and he'll carry it out."

Jack raised an annoyed eyebrow. "How can you be sure? I wasn't aware that Dayne fulfills the role of Willem's Hand, too."

"Monarchs don't have Hands in Kanibar," Arian replied. "The kingdom's magic has become Willem's greatest strength—perhaps his *only* strength. Even if technicalities prevent him from giving Dayne the title of Lord Hand, he needs a mage as his second-in-command to control Kanibar's magic. Based on what Her Grace knows about Dayne's involvement in Willem's personal affairs, we have to assume he's fully aware of Willem's political schemes, too."

Aurelia clenched her jaw and kept silent. In truth, she didn't know much about Ser Dayne (other than the fact that he resembled a sorcerer more than a mage), but there was one more thing she recalled that worried her. Dayne had been the one to get inside of Aurelia's head and confirm some of her darkest secrets to Willem, and it was entirely possible that Willem's final move, even posthumously, would be to have Dayne expose Aurelia to the realm in more ways than one. Willem hadn't done it yet, so Aurelia couldn't help but wonder if he was using her secrets as a backup plan for her destruction if she defeated him in battle.

When they reached the wall dividing Dofell from Taundosa, Arian dismounted his horse to converse with the Lord of Morvis, who lingered nearby while he and his men watched the troops roll in. Aurelia watched the nobleman give a few curt nods and mutter a response to her uncle before walking away and urging his men to follow.

Arian gave the cue to the people leading the troops, just ahead of the highborn: twelve mages from Taundosa's coven. They faced the wall in a single-file line, held their hands up in unison, and waited for their leader's booming voice to command them before igniting their palms with flames. Each time their leader shouted a word Aurelia couldn't hear, balls of fire soared towards the wall, charring the stone blocks and sending plumes of smoke wafting into the sky.

As the heat from the flames warmed her face, Aurelia turned to her left, where a group of men were approaching. They took the mages' place at the frontlines while carrying an enormous battering ram made of Akkinorian bronze—ten men on either side of it. They brought one end close to the scorched, smoldering portion of the wall, then struck it again and again until chunks of stone rained onto the ground. Soon enough, the first window into Dofell emerged.

A soldier on horseback slithered his way between Aurelia and Arian from behind, but she was too distracted by the wall to pay him any heed until he spoke to her:

"Good day, Your Grace." Ser Rayan offered her a fleeting sort of smile as she greeted him. "My commander received a note from you requesting that I meet you before the battle."

"Yes." As the wall continued to shatter, leaving piles upon piles of rubble on the ground, she looked over her shoulder at the carriage carrying

Diantha and pointed. "Do you see the carriage behind us?" He followed her eyes and nodded, prompting her to continue. "The woman inside is the new Queen of Dofell. We need to reveal her to the masses before the battle begins. She may be able to sway some of the Kanish soldiers into laying down their swords. The coachman is under orders to bring her to the lord's estate here in Morvis after we've proven that she exists. A Goldman will accompany her for her protection, of course, but...May I be frank?"

"Of course, my queen."

She swallowed the lump in her throat. "I don't trust that Willem won't send his men after her when he sees her fleeing, and one Goldman won't be enough to protect her. I'd like you and four of your best men to see her to her destination. I know you're more than capable of protecting her, should anyone follow you, and you've proven your loyalty well enough for me to trust you with this."

He nodded. "Of course, Your Grace. It would be my honor."

She offered him a small, wry smile. "Thank you. Return to your men, ser. They'll be expecting you."

He tipped his head—the closest thing to a bow he could accomplish while on horseback—and turned around to rejoin the troops. She glanced over her shoulder to watch him go as a sense of relief coursed through her. It wasn't just that she wanted Diantha protected, either. A part of her simply wanted to be certain that Rayan wouldn't be among the Akkinorian bodies she brought home in wooden caskets. Even if he didn't know the truth, she wasn't willing to lose another sibling to war.

By the time she turned her attention back to the wall, another group of mages were using their power to levitate the debris and move it out of the way to create a clear path. The hole in the wall was large enough for approximately seven horses to pass through while riding side-by-side, so while it would take some time for the entirety of the allies' forces to cross the threshold, it was better than losing dozens of men to the horrors of the Ngora Valley.

When the mages finally stepped aside to rejoin their covens, the world seemed to stand still for a moment. Everyone—the allies, mages, and mortals alike—stared at the hole in silence, leaving no sounds to be heard other than the whistling of the wind and the distant laughter of Morvian commoners. Every pair of eyes was trained on the gap, and as Aurelia observed those around her, she saw that a few of them were crying.

Arian noticed it, too. "Nobody has even thought about doing something like this since the walls were erected. I think we'd all made peace with knowing we'd never see Dofell from beyond the borders."

"It was bound to happen eventually. Carthe is a place of liberty, not confinement." Aurelia turned her gaze to the right, where Reyna was marveling at the hole like everyone else. "Your Majesty?"

The Golden Queen's azurite eyes found hers. "Yes?"

"I believe everyone's waiting for you. We march on your word."

Reyna turned back to the wall, sucked in a sharp breath, and murmured, "Forward, good man, ever forward."

XLII

They hadn't made it ten yards from the wall before a thick, balmy fog rolled in. Aurelia could hardly identify the flagbearers leading the pack in front of her, and the fog made it impossible to see the sky above.

Like most of Dofell, the land being trampled beneath boots and hooves was lifeless: brittle, colorless grass; tiny fragments of rubble from long-forgotten civilizations and conflicts; and no signs of life whatsoever—not even an anthill or animal droppings.

A modern map of Dofell referred to this area as Thurran Valley: an expansive field of nothingness on the southeastern border of Dofell, located on the opposite side of the kingdom from the palace. A map from the old days depicted Thurran as only one-third of the size it was in the modern day. Back then, the valley had been the division between the warring villages of Grisal and Sheera. After the Sheerans slaughtered the Grisali and destroyed every structure on Grisali land, the village was wiped from existence, and the empty land eventually joined Thurran Valley.

Neither Willem nor the allies had offered the other a location for the battlefield. Though Dofell had plenty of barren lands to choose from, only one sat close to the Taundosan border—close enough that it provided Kanibar with an opportunity to take the fighting into the City of Gold, weakening the allies by giving them more people and land to defend.

The night before marching to battle, Aurelia's allies were at their wit's end while trying to determine where they'd be meeting Willem's forces. Aurelia had been the one to suggest Thurran Valley as Willem's most likely choice—after all, she knew how his mind worked better than any of them, and she was fully convinced he'd choose a location that posed the greatest threat to his enemies.

"Look." Arian grimaced as he lifted an arm, still holding his horse's reins, to point at something to their right. "That'll be Sheera."

Aurelia squinted, attempting to see more clearly through the fog, and caught vague glimpses of the former civilization. What wasn't completely masked by the fog presented itself as ruins: abandoned hovels, shops, wells, and the like, all crumbling into pieces and infested by invasive species of plants and insects. When the fog faded enough for her to get a better look, she saw stray objects—a boot, a children's toy, a wagon wheel—partially buried in the dirt and strangled by weeds.

Aurelia cleared her throat. "Sheera was abandoned after an epidemic, wasn't it? The survivors believed the land itself was cursed, so they migrated elsewhere."

"That's right." It was Lord Zhaaran who answered, his violet gaze trained on the ruins. "A plague ravaged the Sheerans, sent by Myenar himself to punish them for the genocide of the Grisali. 2,695 Sheerans died over the course of one season. That was exactly the population of Grisal at the time of its annihilation. One Sheeran life for every Grisali life they claimed. Myenar passed his judgment and punished them accordingly, as he always does."

Aurelia shivered. The more she explored and learned about Dofell, the more she was convinced that the moon goddess was exactly what the kingdom needed after over one-thousand years at the mercy of a punisher.

They were approximately halfway across the valley when they spotted the first signs of battle: emerald and gold banners hanging limply from masts, as the air in Dofell was perpetually still. Just as panic bubbled up in Aurelia's gut, horns blew from across the valley, letting her and her allies know that Willem's troops had spotted them, too.

The closer they got to the enemy, the more the fog lifted. By the time they stopped moving, they were close enough that Aurelia could see the grin on Willem's face as he stood at the forefront of his troops, but far enough away that the horses would need to gallop for a bit to reach the other side. The fog disappeared almost completely by then, and Aurelia knew what that meant: Willem's mages had been causing the visual impairment.

"We were right," Lord Zhoqa muttered. "Look at the banners in the back. Krotis stands behind him."

"Not all of Krotis," Aurelia reminded him.

He snorted, but his eyes glimmered with worry. "Most of it."

Willem dismounted his horse when the allies' troops stopped moving, then took a few steps forward as Dayne trailed behind him. With one wave of Dayne's hand, a white light briefly formed within Willem's throat before it disappeared, prompting him to speak:

"I see you've taken the road less traveled. I commend you for your ingenuity—few souls in history have considered destroying the wall, and you've gone and made a doorway out of it. I shouldn't be surprised that you chose the easy route instead of weeding out the weak from the strong by crossing the valley. Krotis isn't renowned for its bravery, but they took the challenge and endured it, anyway."

When his voice echoed for what felt like miles in every direction, Aurelia realized Dayne had cast some sort of amplifier spell on Willem's voice. She opened her mouth and turned to Arian, preparing to ask him to do the same for her and the others, but she didn't get the chance. As soon as her lips parted, a sudden warmth encased her throat, like swallowing a mouthful of piping hot tea, before disappearing after a few seconds. Quick glances in either direction revealed temporary white light beaming from within her allies' throats, so she knew Arian had extended the spell to all of them.

"You left us with no other choice!" Lord Zhoqa hollered. "You've rallied your forces in the name of salvaging Dofell, but you have no intention of restoring the Great City to what it once was—only destroying whatever remains. And when you've succeeded in uprooting Dofell for your own rise to power, you'll take Carthe's unclaimed territories for yourself, and you'll squash *their* ways of life beneath your boots, too."

Willem cocked his head to the side, feigning innocence. "What an accusation! And from one of the Four Lords, no less—meant to be the wisest among us. It's a pity you haven't any magic like your counterparts. If you did, then perhaps you'd feel more fulfilled. That's why you're here, isn't it? You hope Kanibar will lose so Kazamir can seize Dofell for itself. A Bozari lord without magic is a pitiful one, but a king without magic is still a king."

Lord Zhoqa gritted his teeth so hard that Aurelia feared he'd break them. "Why, you weaselly—"

"Hello again, darling." When Willem's voice rang out again, chills traced Aurelia's spine as she snapped her eyes over to meet his. "You look well, though you've lost the glow you adopted during your time in Kanibar. I'd blame it on the circumstances of our reunion, but that can't be it. You're no stranger to war, and Dofell is nothing to you, anyway. I rather think it's because of a certain lack of satisfaction. Have you been wanting for passion while we've been apart? You look like you haven't been pleasured since, well, *me*. I certainly haven't forgotten the feel of your legs wrapped around my waist..."

Jack, with his face redder than a cardinal and his eyes blazing with fury, sneered with such hatred that Aurelia almost didn't recognize him. If the flagbearers in front of him weren't blocking his path, she knew he would've raced across the valley to gut Willem like a fish—battle protocol and his own life be damned.

Aurelia kept her composure. "Tell me, Willem, is it 'passion' if you drug me? Is it 'pleasure' if you have to alter my senses, just so I can stomach you? No wonder Kanibar has never seen a queen." Her eyes flicked over to Dayne as her lips curled into a smile. "And tell me, Ser Dayne—how long does it take you each morning to cast your glamour spell? His Majesty must've surpassed fifty years by now, so I can't imagine it's an easy task to transform those jowls and wrinkles into something resembling a young man."

Even from a distance, she saw a veil of darkness—however briefly—pass over Willem's face. "Spare us your attempts at diversion," he shot back. "We already know you're prone to hysterics. That's of course the only reason you'd leave a life of leisure and luxury behind"

Aurelia smiled sweetly. "Isn't it funny how the red-faced, finger-pointing, pompous man is always the one so concerned about 'hysterics'?" She paused, letting out a small chuckle. "Were you in a rush today, Ser Dayne? It would appear that you missed a few silver hairs. They seem to be looking more white than gray, though. His Majesty must be older than I thought."

"Oh, enough of your blabbing." The hand resting on the hilt of his sword clenched, his knuckles turning white, as Willem's eyes hardened. "Let's discuss the reason we're all here today, shall we? It's not a tale of conquest or expansion, but rather one of divine intervention. You see, an ancient prophecy speaks of a western king who will restore the realm to its former glory at this very point in time. I am the strongest of the western kings, with the greatest magic in the realm at my disposal, and a country that sits in the perfect place for me to dominate both halves of the continent. Akkinor, Taundosa, and Bozar stand in the way of the prophecy's fulfillment—and, subsequently, the restoration of the realm. And for what? Because you're unwilling to let Kanibar surpass you in territory, wealth, and infamy? Kanibar and Krotis know *you* are the selfish ones, and we're prepared to give our lives today to prevent you from letting the realm fall even further."

"The prophecy you speak of doesn't refer to a king at all." Aurelia's head whipped to the side at the sound of Lord Zhaaran's voice. Before this, he hadn't mentioned a word about knowing what the prophecy said. "You've fed your people lie after lie for decades now, reshaping the prophecy to fit the aspirations you have for yourself. And if you had paid attention to the words instead of your ego, you'd also know that Dofell is only a fraction of the story."

"Dofell's restoration is a necessary component of seeing the prophecy realized, but it was never the instigator," Reyna added. Aurelia's lips pursed in shock; apparently, the Golden Queen knew more about the prophecy than she'd let on, too. "You chose Dofell as your means of seizing power because it's a weak and easy target. You know this land is cursed, and you don't have the Dofelli blood needed to break it. As a result, myself and my allies made it our mission to find the one person alive with the power to solve this piece of the puzzle."

Aurelia glanced over her shoulder as the sea of soldiers parted in two. Riding along the path they'd created—on the back of a pure white horse—was Diantha, led by Rayan and flanked on either side by Akkinorian soldiers.

Reyna smiled. "It's my pleasure to present to you Her Majesty, Diantha Amarylla Pharos, Queen of Dofell."

Aurelia held her breath as Diantha's horse inched forward until the new Dofelli queen was positioned between Reyna and Jack. For some reason, she wasn't surprised to see Diantha sitting with her back straight, her shoulders squared, and her eyes hardened. Fear was the last emotion she exhibited, and her confidence only seemed to grow when the shocked, curious mumblings of Willem's troops became loud enough for the allies to hear from across the field.

Before departing the palace that morning, they'd made sure Diantha looked the part. She'd been bathed three times, her hair was combed and tied back in a sleek, tight bun on the back of her head, and she was dressed in a suit of golden armor identical to Reyna's. At first glance, nobody would've known she'd been taken from an actual pigsty not just days earlier.

Willem gritted his teeth. "You present us with a false queen! She looks Dofelli enough, but anyone with access to a library knows there are no highborn Dofelli women with a claim to the throne. Plucking a random woman off the streets and calling her a queen doesn't make her one."

Diantha stiffened, but not enough for Willem to notice from such a distance. "I'm descended from the Phyre family," she called out, her throat glowing as Arian's hand gestured in his lap. "Our relation is close enough that my Phyre blood can be detected, but distant enough that I'm spared from the curse placed on the king and his family by the Almighty Myenar. I'm the future of Dofell, Your Majesty—me, a native Dofelli, instead of you, a foreigner grasping at power."

A few soldiers behind Aurelia and her allies cheered, but Willem wasn't convinced. "And you expect us to believe you?" He scoffed and laughed in unison. "It really is pitiful, you know. The people standing beside you brought you here to die, you know."

Diantha didn't so much as flinch. "It doesn't matter if you believe us. By the end of this, I'll be sitting the Dofelli throne, and my people will be building their new homes out of your bones."

Aurelia could've hugged her right then and there.

"As you can see," Jack mused, "the gods themselves have chosen Diantha Pharos as the new Queen of Dofell. You're an even bigger idiot than I thought you were if you think they'll favor you for disobeying their wishes."

"Quiet your hound," Willem snapped. Aurelia glared at him when she saw him looking at her, but the moment their eyes met, his lips curled into a vicious sneer. "While the lot of you stew in the failure of your ploy to sway me and my people, I have an offer for *you*, my lioness. What with your apparent, ah, *affinity* for the lowborn, I can't help but wonder if you'd choose to save one or five hundred—and you and I have had such wonderful luck when it comes to choices, haven't we?"

She raised an eyebrow, amused. "What a silly question. I—"

"I haven't finished. The individual is one you know and care for. The other five hundred are strangers—a group of Kanish men and women who left their children behind to volunteer to fight for me today. If you choose the individual, he'll go free, and the others will risk their lives in battle. If you choose the others, they'll march home to their families, and the individual will die. You have my word."

Her words lodged in her throat when she opened her mouth to speak. Panic struck her chest like a spiked club—she knew exactly who the individual was.

Her breath caught when two soldiers dragged a man out from the troops gathered behind Willem. The man was bound with shackles around his wrists, and a potato sack had been placed over his head. The soldiers forced him to his knees beside Willem and removed the sack to reveal none other than Ser Rhys.

"Not only did you go back on your word when you fled," Willem continued, "but you also corrupted one of my best knights with your lies. Did you really think I'd believe what he told me about your escape? It only took a few minutes for Dayne to observe the traitor's memories, then we knew for certain that he aided you on his own accord, for whatever foolish reason. It must remind you of one particular knight who met a similar fate five years ago."

Jack hung his head and closed his eyes. "Gods..."

Aurelia knew they were thinking the same thing: Linden. Archie had promised to spare Linden's life if she surrendered to him, and when she refused, he slit her best friend's throat right before her eyes.

"Choose." Willem's voice grated her eardrums as he grinned at her. "One friend or five hundred strangers."

She felt Ser Rhys's eyes burning holes into her skull from across the valley. She didn't have to see or hear him to know he was pleading with her to choose him.

When the black spots clouding her vision faded, she snapped her gaze to Willem and let her entire being succumb to blind rage while he sneered at her. He already knew her answer.

"You're lying." When she found her voice again, it didn't sound like her own, but rather a muffled, garbled version of it. "If I choose him, you'll kill him anyway. If I choose the others, you won't let them leave. I know you, Willem, and I know how fond you are of mind games. You won't win this one."

She briefly glanced at the young men and women among Willem's troops—the only people wearing weak leather armor over tattered clothing, carrying thin iron swords instead of heavy steel, and with more desperation in their eyes than determination. These weren't soldiers at all, but rather normal people fighting only for their promised coin—and, therefore, their own survival.

"What kind of king wagers the lives of his own people?" she demanded. "You promise the highest wages in Kanibar to those willing to fight for you. The five hundred people you speak of are here risking their lives for the chance to receive that coin and feed their families, and yet, you dangle their hopes and dreams out of their reach. Where's the honor in that?"

"They know what they signed up for. Even if I didn't make you this offer, they'd be fighting today. You, however, are being given the chance to send them home to their families—with the wages I promised them, of course." He raised an eyebrow, unbothered. "What will it be?"

Her eyes flicked back to Rhys. He was the reason she was standing beside her allies and not locked up in Willem's palace—she owed him her life. But if she didn't save the five hundred souls Willem spoke of, any hope of swaying the Kanish and the Kroti to drop their swords would disappear. They were already skeptical of what she and her allies claimed, so proving herself as selfish wouldn't do her any good.

Just then, a dark cloud rolled in overhead—except, of course, it wasn't a cloud. Halvor circled and released a bellowing shriek, which sent some of Willem's soldiers plummeting to their knees.

At the exact moment Willem turned his head to the sky, terror blanching his face, Aurelia locked eyes with Rhys. He seemed to know exactly what she was telling him to do when he pulled himself from his knees to his feet and began to run toward the allies. Even if he didn't make it, it was better to try than to wait until Willem brought a knife to his throat.

She hadn't been able to save Linden, and that guilt ate her alive every day since the moment he collapsed on the battlefield. She owed it to his memory to do everything in her power to save another friend from the same fate.

As she prepared to yank her horse's reins, Jack reached over to stop her, the sea storm in his eyes wide with warning. "Aurelia," he murmured, "*don't.*"

She was gone before he uttered the last syllable.

As she galloped across the field to meet Rhys, Willem's men shouted, alerting him of the escaped captive. Rhys wasn't running very fast—he'd clearly been beaten and tortured, and he was already emaciated—so she knew it was up to her to get to him first.

She didn't get the chance to even lower her hand for Rhys to grab. When he was close enough that she could see the whites of his eyes—and the fear making them shine like the stars—the tip of an arrow appeared in his mouth. In an instant, the life faded from his eyes, blood sprayed in every direction, and he fell to the side like a sack of flour.

For a moment, she couldn't do anything but stare at the tail of the arrow peeking out from the back of his skull. The shock of it paralyzed her so much that she barely heard her allies hollering behind her, or Halvor shrieking from the sky, or even Willem thanking the archer with his amplified voice. All she could do was stare at Rhys's corpse while his voice echoed in her head:

It's been an honor to make your acquaintance. I hope...I hope we can meet again.

She didn't realize she was crying until she saw golden droplets on the back of her hand. She tilted her head back to look up—not at Halvor, but at the gods in the heavens—and for a moment, she forgot she was directly in between her friends and her enemies, defenseless and alone.

Then Halvor landed behind her with a thud, shaking the ground from southern to northern Dofell, and screeched at Willem's troops so fiercely that some of them staggered backwards or fell completely. Even Willem gasped and took a few steps back, bumping into the soldiers behind him while they attempted to steady him. Growling and baring his teeth, Halvor planted his front legs on either side of Aurelia while her horse trembled, paralyzed by the same fear that made every Kanish and Kroti soul on the battlefield start praying to their Almighty deities.

Halvor's hot breath lifted her hair from her shoulders as Willem yelled, "W-What kind of message are you trying to send? You claim you're here to salvage Dofell, but you threaten every inch of this kingdom with dragonfire. Forging a path to victory through ashes is no true victory!"

She cleared her throat and tore her eyes from Rhys's corpse. "He won't touch a single Dofelli brick or stone, but he *will* incinerate any Kanish or Kroti man and woman who refuses to lay down their sword and bend the knee to the rightful Queen of Dofell. They'd be meeting an excruciating death for no just cause. You've just shown them yourself that your word can't be trusted."

Willem didn't seem phased by that. "How, exactly, did I do that?"

"When you offered me a choice, you made the mistake of uttering one damning sentence: *you have my word.*" Despite the guilt and pain in her heart, she smiled. "I chose the individual, and you broke your word for all to see. Now, your own subjects know—just as I did from the start—that you wouldn't have spared them from fighting if I'd chosen them. How can they trust anything you say after you so thoughtlessly revealed the kind of man you truly are?"

The king opened his mouth to respond, but he didn't get the chance. Aurelia watched as Willem turned to observe the first phase of his downfall: his soldiers dropping their weapons at their feet, turning on their heels, and disappearing into the fog as they ran for their lives while Halvor shrieked at them.

Aurelia had expected that response. Though Willem had surely prepared his soldiers to meet Halvor, there was a difference between the idea of facing a dragon on the battlefield, and coming face-to-face with one in real time.

Halvor craned his neck lower until his head was adjacent to Aurelia's. When they turned their heads to look at one another, she could've sworn he was grinning.

XLIII

When Willem turned to face his remaining soldiers, Aurelia knew Dayne had removed the amplifier spell, as she couldn't hear what the king was saying. While he tried to excite the crowd of confused, trembling soldiers from Kanibar and Krotis, those who'd left his side ran home to Kanibar. The emerald capes they'd shed while running were now laying abandoned on the brittle grass, soon to be trampled by boots and hooves.

One of the capes fell atop Ser Rhys's legs. As she ignored urgings from Jack and her allies to return to their formation, Aurelia swallowed the lump in her throat and stared at his lifeless body, wondering what on earth she'd tell Sora when she informed the barkeep of her brother's demise.

She sniffled and turned to Halvor. "Bring him somewhere safe. I don't wish to lose him in the carnage. When all of this is over, we'll give him a proper burial."

She didn't need to say it for Halvor to know his command—he could sense it in their shared soul. In fact, he'd already begun stalking towards Rhys's corpse before she finished speaking.

A few of Willem's soldiers gasped in alarm when Halvor moved from behind Aurelia, and they watched in both confusion and disbelief as the dragon gently plucked Rhys from the ground in his front left claws. After shrieking at the enemy once more, Halvor lifted off into the sky with the knight's lifeless body dangling from his grasp, his destination entirely unknown to his mistress.

Just before she turned to rejoin her allies, Aurelia caught another glimpse of the soldiers at the forefront of Willem's formation. Even from a distance, she could see the conflict in their eyes: both she and Willem had proven their characters for all to see that day, and it was infinitely clear that only one of them had good intentions.

"...back to the carriage." Reyna was speaking to Diantha when Aurelia rejoined them. "They've seen you—that's all that matters. We need to keep you safe."

"Don't go back to the carriage. If anyone follows you, they'll be looking for it," Jack intervened. He gestured for Rayan to approach before he continued. "Find her a helmet, ser, and ensure her hair is tucked inside of it. Make her look like another soldier, and guide her out of here on horseback. Gather two groups of men—three per group will do—and have them depart Thurran alongside you. Instruct the groups to separate immediately if you think you're being followed. Willem's men won't be able to tell which one of you is Diantha, so they'll have to risk following the wrong group."

Rayan nodded. "I'll see to it, Your Highness."

Aurelia offered Diantha an encouraging smile. "Good luck."

"The same to you," she said.

Then she was gone, with Rayan and about a dozen soldiers trailing after her. Aurelia watched them go until they disappeared within the sea of bronze and gold, and for some reason, she felt no fear or worry for them. Every other aspect of this day made her green with nerves, but somehow, she knew the new Queen of Dofell would prevail—soldiers at her side or not.

"What's he doing?" Lord Zhaaran's voice drew the allies' attention. "He appears to be waiting for something."

Arian grimaced. "There hasn't been an official declaration. Until one of—"

As if on cue, blood-curdling screams rang out from behind the allies' formation. They turned, startled, and watched as soldier after soldier— Akkinorian, Taundosan, and Bozari alike—collapsed to the ground. Others backed away from them, terrified, as a mysterious affliction overcame what appeared to be one in five soldiers.

"What in the name of the Almighty is going on back there?" Lord Zhoqa demanded.

Aurelia's heart pounded as she contemplated, unable to do anything to help her own men as they fell to the ground in agony, and tried to see what became of them when they collapsed. She was too short, even on horseback, to see anything with ease, but hollering from the surviving soldiers confirmed that the fallen were either dead or dying.

"Oh, gods." All eyes flickered to Arian as his russet skin turned gray. He swallowed as he looked away from the soldiers and met Aurelia's eyes. "Do you have reason to believe that Willem's mage may be a sorcerer?"

She nodded. "I thought as much when I first met him. But now it's abundantly clear that he clearly hasn't been using his power justly as the gods intended—the only true mark of a sorcerer."

"I think you're right," he muttered. Ahead of them, the hooting and cheering of Willem's men grew louder, so Aurelia knew that anyone who was still on the fence had been swayed to stay and fight. "There's an ancient spell that, when cast over a large population, stops the hearts of those with a physical or mental affliction. It was meant to weed out the weak from the strong in hopes of creating a superior race. The spell can only be cast with the darkest magic known to the realm—I myself have never seen anything of the sort in my lifetime."

"Nor have I," Lord Zhaaran agreed. Beads of sweat trickled down the side of his wrinkled face. "They're killing us off before the fighting has even begun."

Gritting her teeth, Reyna looked over Jack and Aurelia to meet Arian's eyes. "Call them."

Wordlessly obeying, Arian flipped his right hand over, so his palm was facing the sky. A fluorescent burst of white light shot up from his hand and into the clouds, briefly illuminating the darkness for miles. At the same time, wooden catapults became visible behind Willem's troops, having been camouflaged by the fog until the precise moment arrived.

Aurelia's heart rattled as Willem's men loaded the catapults. "Uncle, I—"

She didn't know what she was going to say, but she didn't get the chance to finish speaking, anyhow. From the right side of the allies' formation, battle cries echoed throughout all of Thurran Valley, though the source remained hidden while the fog enveloped them. A few moments later, shadowy figures became visible in the haze as soldiers carrying Dofelli—and Phyre—banners rushed the center of the battlefield, directly between the opposing sides.

A sigh of relief escaped Aurelia's lips. Earlier that day, she'd sent Edom to King Elrin to inform him of their battle strategy. The king hadn't been able to spare many fighting men, but he sent every last one of them, anyway. Edom reported back to Aurelia that the Dofelli soldiers would lie in wait in the abandoned village of Sheera until they received a specific signal from the allies: the closest thing to a real sunrise Dofell had seen in centuries. She'd sent the sprite back to Dofell after that—where it was instructed to stay until the fighting ended—so Elrin could tell his men exactly what to expect.

The arrival of the Dofelli troops had silenced Willem's men, and by the time the Dofelli—and the rest of the allies—stopped whooping, there was nothing to be heard other than the final gasping breaths of the men targeted by Dayne's spell. Aurelia held her breath, waiting for her allies to commence the fighting, as Willem took a few steps forward like he was presenting himself as a trophy.

Then he held his arms out in either direction like a bird taking flight, grinning, and his mahogany hair lifted from his shoulders as his men rushed across the battlefield in a blur of green and gold.

Aurelia didn't hear Reyna make the declaration, but the next thing she knew, the allies' soldiers were rushing past their leaders and charging for the center of the battlefield. The sea of fighters grew so thick that she couldn't see anything in front of her except for armor and the backs of her soldiers' heads. The scene seemed to play out slowly, like time was halting, until flashes of colored light—magic—illuminated everything around her.

Jack tightened his grip on his horse's reins, prompting Lord Zhoqa to shoot him a look of warning. "Not yet," the nobleman said to him. "Our men need their leaders alive. We can't act too soon."

"I'm not a leader," Jack fired back. "You don't need me here."

Aurelia's smile was nothing short of painful. "Go."

He hesitated for a moment before taking her hand and kissing her knuckles. They met eyes for a split second, but it was long enough for a silent message to pass between them: *I'll find you.* As the words echoed in her head, Jack jerked the reins and disappeared into the heart of the fighting.

"That was idiotic," Lord Zhoqa told her. "He's going to get himself killed."

"No." She shook her head, smiling even as she lost Jack in the crowd. "This is where he belongs. This is who he is."

She hadn't wanted him there at all, initially, but she meant what she said: he belonged on horseback with a sword in his hand, slaying every enemy who looked in his direction and rescuing every fallen friend who needed him. This was the man she'd fallen in love with many years earlier on this very same continent—not the man she'd asked him to become when he married her.

A few minutes later, a bellowing shriek rattled her eardrums just as an enormous shadow coasted overhead. Halvor had returned, but not to lay siege to the enemy—not yet, anyway, and hopefully not at all.

403

Lord Zhoqa, the only leader other than Aurelia with a bow and sheath slung over his shoulders, raised an eyebrow at her. "Shall we?"

She nodded and mimicked him when he claimed his bow and nocked an arrow. She could feel the others watching them as they aimed at the sea of soldiers, looking for any Kanish or Kroti without armor or with exposed weak spots. Aurelia was able to kill one Kanish woman with an arrow through the throat, then a Kanish man in the same fashion, all before Lord Zhoqa claimed one victim.

She'd tease him about that later on, but now wasn't the time.

There were still a few hundred men gathered behind Aurelia and her allies, waiting until their leaders joined the fighting to follow suit, but all of them would be dead without the mages. Flaming stones were launched from Willem's catapults every so often, aimed directly at the allies and their lingering soldiers, but the mages were able to break the rocks into tiny fragments while they were airborne. Pebbles and sparks rained down on them, but the soldiers used their shields to protect their heads while other mages erected magical shields over their leaders.

"It's time," Lord Zhaaran said to the others. "They aren't showing any signs of slowing down with the catapults, so they must have a vast artillery. We'll be sitting ducks if we stay here any longer—our mages will grow weary soon enough."

Reyna nodded and took a long, deep breath. "I suppose this is it, then. Good luck, my friends. I hope to see each of you alive when this is over."

"If you can't find me," Lord Zhoqa seethed, "I'll be flaying Dayne alive somewhere out there. Filthy sorcerer."

Before they disappeared into the fighting, Aurelia allowed herself one last laugh. She hadn't expected a man like Balor Zhoqa to bear such hatred against practitioners of dark magic.

She and Lord Zhoqa stayed behind after the others left—their remaining soldiers hot on their heels—until their sheaths were empty. Rather than taking her horse into battle, she dismounted and proceeded on foot, not wanting to lose the precious mare the same way she'd lost Scotch during the battle with her brother.

Before she knew it, she was surrounded by battling men and women on all sides—some using physical weapons, like swords and spears, and others using magic. Flashes of magical light blinded her if she looked too closely, and the clanging of swords reverberated her eardrum as she swung her own time and time again, often unsure if it met its mark.

When she found herself up against a Kanish man three times her size, she knew she didn't stand a chance on the offensive. She deflected his blows as best she could until he brought his sword down on hers, forcing the edge of her own blade to inch closer and closer to her throat. He brought her down to one knee as she used every bit of strength she had to keep the sword from her neck, gritting her teeth and scowling at his dark, predatory eyes. Just as the blade kissed her throat, drawing blood, the head of a spear emerged from the assailant's forehead. He dropped to the ground, nearly collapsing on top of her, and revealed the leader of the *Voduris* standing behind him.

She accepted the leader's hand when he offered it, but she didn't get the chance to thank him. He'd disappeared into the crowd as soon as she was on her feet again.

The leader of the *Voduris* hadn't just stuck his neck out to help her—he'd killed one of his own to save her life. She'd known from her first interaction with the *Voduris* that they hadn't wanted to fight in this war out of fear for what might happen to Kanibar if Willem lost. While some of Willem's soldiers had been swayed into fleeing before the battle began, it seemed like the *Voduris* had been swayed in another direction. If their leader had chosen to leave Willem behind, Aurelia had to assume the rest of the group was following his lead, too.

To her left, she saw a young woman in the same position she'd been in not a minute earlier. She wasn't defending herself with a sword, though: she had her hands, glowing with yellow magic, hovering over either side of the Kanish man's sword. She sneered at her opponent before throwing her hands up in the air, causing his weapon to ricochet backwards and slam into his face—effectively slicing his face in two, right down the middle.

A man wearing the sigil of Vrurith, the southernmost Kroti province, charged Aurelia when he saw her standing unchallenged. He wielded long daggers in either hand and immediately attempted slashing at her face with a speed she hadn't anticipated. She managed to knee him in the groin, forcing him to drop his weapons, but that only stalled him for a moment.

When he straightened up, he grinned at her, spread his arms wide, then clapped his hands together as green sparks emitted from his palms. The next thing she knew, the earth beneath her feet gave way, and her instincts begged her to reach for the edge of the ground before she could plummet into the sinkhole he'd created.

Still grinning, her adversary lifted his foot in preparation to stamp on her fingers so she would be forced to let go. Just as she reached for his other ankle—intending to bring him down with her if she couldn't pull herself up—a flash of royal blue and gold swooped over to him. Halvor plucked the man from the ground with his teeth, threw him into the air, and caught the man in his mouth before swallowing him whole.

Aurelia lifted her arms onto the solid ground and dug her elbows into the earth until she had enough leverage to pull herself up. Her ears were ringing so loudly that every sound on the valley was muffled, her joints and muscles ached worse than they ever had before, and she quickly saw that she'd lost a boot to the sinkhole when she felt something wet seeping into her stockings. When she looked down, she realized it was blood.

The blood was seeping from the decapitated body of a Kroti soldier, and there were many of his kind laying lifelessly nearby. As she took a moment to study the corpses in her vicinity, hope sparked in her chest when she realized most of them were enemy soldiers.

That hope fizzled away as quickly as it'd come when she heard a sound she never thought she would. It came from Halvor, she knew that, but it wasn't a bellow or a battle cry. It was a whimper.

Her head jerked back to look up at the sky, just as a sharp pain pierced her heart, nearly bringing her to her knees. She gasped for air and clutched her chest, eyes widening with terror, when she saw her beloved companion in the sky. His legs, wings, neck, and tail were wrapped around his body, making him look like a twisted ball of appendages rather than the realm's most ferocious warrior, and it was clear by the way he howled that he wasn't contorting himself that way by will. Terrified flames spewed from his mouth, enveloping him, as his screeches echoed for miles. As Aurelia's eyes adjusted to the fog, she saw what looked like gold thread—or veins—entwined around his scales like ropes.

As he shrieked in pain, splitting her ears, he managed to unwind himself long enough to fly even higher. A strangled scream escaped her when he sharply barreled to the side as if being pulled by a beast five times his size. The next thing she knew, he was curled up in a fiery ball again and plummeting towards the earth, headed for a place too far away for Aurelia to see as he disappeared into the fog.

"No." It was the only thing she could say as his telltale blue and gold scales faded from view. "No."

She'd never seen him fall before. She didn't even realize there was anything in the modern world capable of taking a dragon from the sky, let alone one of Halvor's size—but somehow, Willem and his mages had found a way to incapacitate their greatest threat.

And her greatest friend.

Suddenly, hands seized her biceps, forcing her to look away from where Halvor had fallen and into the eyes of the man standing before her: Arian. He had a shallow gash over his left eyebrow, and another soldier's blood had sprayed over his cheek, but he looked otherwise unharmed. The look in his eyes was wild, frantic, but at the same time, his familiar gaze brought her the comfort she so desperately needed.

"He'll be all right!" he shouted over the clanging of swords and agonizing screams. "He'll recover! You can't stay here, Aurelia. Willem saw Halvor come to you—he'll be sending soldiers out to find you!"

She swallowed the thick, hot lump in her throat. "Uncle, I don't—"

Before she could finish speaking, something she could only describe as pure power struck them both like a tidal wave colliding with a wooden house. Aurelia, Arian, and everyone in their vicinity were lifted from the ground, sailing backwards in the air until their backs collided with the earth. Black spots clouded her vision immediately as she wheezed for air, unable to fill her lungs fast enough, while her chest heaved and her throat gurgled. When she finally managed to catch a breath, she rolled onto her side, coughing and gasping so hard she worried she'd spit blood onto the grass.

Arian had landed several feet away from her, but his eyes were closed, and he wasn't moving. Still gasping, Aurelia crawled to him on her arms and knees and grabbed him by his breastplate, shaking him and shouting his name until he released a weak, guttural groan.

Aurelia knew what had happened when she recalled something similar the Taundosan mages had done during the battle with Archie: Willem's mages had joined together to create a powerful shockwave. They didn't seem to care that they'd incapacitated some of their own fighters—but they didn't need to care. That one display was enough to show everyone that Kanish mages were far more skilled and advanced than the others.

As Arian struggled to regain consciousness, something instinctual pricked in Aurelia's ears. She didn't know what it was until she looked up, her heart plummeting to her knees when she saw half-a-dozen Kanish soldiers approaching her. They'd formed a circle and were inching closer to where she knelt by Arian, and every last one of them wore Willem's personal sigil—a bolas spider, of all things—on the shoulders of their armor.

She knew what that meant too: they were Willem's most elite military personnel, tasked with fulfilling their king's most vital commands. Yet here Aurelia was—without her sword, without her dragon, and her uncle barely holding on. She was utterly defenseless.

"Uncle," she whispered as the soldiers closed in, "we-we need to go. You need to get up."

No reply. She moved so her back was pressed against his side and covered his chest with her arm, panic rising up in her throat like a scream while the soldiers weighed their swords and taunted her, grinning and hissing profanities along their way. She kept her eyes trained on the man closest to her, telling herself that if she died that day, she'd die with dignity by looking into the eyes of her killer until her last breath.

Then, just as the soldier in front of her raised his sword, he froze. In a split second, his eyes were bugging out of his head and he was screaming, and so were the others. The screaming didn't last long, though: in the time it took for her to blink, their eyeballs exploded, sending each and every one of them hurtling to the ground as they clawed at their empty sockets and wailed like babes.

She whirled her head around to look down at Arian. His eyes were still closed, but he'd raised one arm, and blue magic sparked on his fingertips before fading completely. She was sputtering something that she herself couldn't understand, but he interrupted her by smiling and weakly opening his eyes.

"Water mage," he reminded her, his voice hoarse and dry. "Eyes are...mostly water."

Aurelia wanted to throw herself into his arms, but now wasn't the time for that. She helped him to his feet, ensured he was steady, and fetched abandoned swords from the grass for each of them. She wanted to order him to leave while he was still so weak, but she knew he wouldn't listen— just as she knew that Arian Cristos would bounce back faster than a man half his age.

"Are you all right?" she asked.

"Fine." He didn't look it, but she knew better than to argue with him. He cleared his throat and pointed his sword at the men, who were still clawing at their faces. Some of them even had long, bleeding scratches trailing from their browbones to their cheeks. "Shall we?"

She grimaced, nodded, and helped her uncle slit the throats of the six men—the men who couldn't see their deaths approaching.

XLIV

At the very least, Diantha wasn't being hunted.

Soldiers flanked her on all sides, guiding her across the Dofelli wall and into Taundosa, as every one of them—Diantha included—periodically glanced over their shoulders to ensure they weren't being followed. That's what she told herself, anyway; the wiser part of her knew that all of them were looking back because they could hear their loved ones screaming, even miles away from Thurran Valley.

As if he could read her thoughts, the knight in charge—Ser Rayan, an Akkinorian—offered her a sad sort of smile. "Don't worry, Your Majesty. Everything will be all right in the end."

She grimaced. "Do your ears fail you today?"

"I wish." He winced like he could feel the pain of his brothers-in-arms as they met their deaths. "This kind of carnage is inescapable under such circumstances, but our forces are strong. We'll prevail."

"Maybe." A Taundosan Goldman gritted his teeth. "So much suffering, all because one man wishes to climb to the heavens to sit among the gods. Only an imbecile would believe the gods would accept someone like that."

Diantha stiffened, her head cocked to the side. "There's no such thing as climbing to the heavens, ser—only flying."

The Goldman didn't seem impressed. "Unless the king sprouts wings, he's stuck here on earth with the rest of us."

"One doesn't need to sprout wings to fly. One only needs to be *chosen* to fly."

From the corner of her eye, she saw the soldiers exchanging puzzled—and somewhat amused—expressions. She knew they didn't understand her, and they never would. Only one person alive would've known what she meant, and that person was likely drawing every enemy soldier to her being by brandishing her unmistakable golden locks (and her dragon) for all to see.

As if on cue, an ear-splitting shriek rang out from what felt like every direction, making Diantha gasp in alarm. Ser Rayan and the other soldiers on horseback flattened themselves against their steeds, but those traveling on foot immediately dropped to the ground and shielded their heads with their arms. Diantha crouched against her horse, her heart throbbing against her ribcage as the shrieking continued, and glanced over her shoulder at the sky behind her.

They were miles and miles away from the battlefield by then, but Queen Aurelia's dragon was large enough that Diantha could still see his entire body as he flailed between the clouds. A hard lump formed in her throat when she saw him rolling in the air, limbs curled up in a way she could only describe as a dragon's version of the fetal position. Sputtering flames emitted from his mouth, enveloping him as he wailed, and before she knew it, a ball of fire and blue scales fell from the sky like a comet.

The portion of the Dofelli wall that hadn't been destroyed blocked her view of where the dragon had fallen, but she was still able to see a cloud of smoke, flames, and earth burst into the sky above. There'd be an enormous crater where the dragon collided with the ground, but it was better than if he'd fallen over the coastline and onto Dofell's notorious sea stacks.

"Gods be good." An Akkinorian soldier's chin trembled as he stood from the ground. "He isn't...?"

"Dead? Impossible." Ser Rayan's reply was immediate, but his eyes shone with doubt. "He'll be all right. Dragons of his kind were created to withstand things like this."

"What did that to him?" The shortest of the Akkinorians chewed on his lower lip, sweat pouring from the sides of his face. "I didn't think it was possible to incapacitate a dragon."

The Goldman grimaced. "I heard King Willem's mages are among the most skilled on the continent. He's kept mum about them all these years so we wouldn't see him as a threat. He could've formed alliances across Carthe with the promise of such power, but he didn't even consider that, did he? He's been treating the lot of us like his enemies from the start, knowing we'd end up exactly where we are today. It was a clever tactic, I'll give him that, but—"

"We have to help him," Diantha interrupted.

Nobody answered for a moment. Then Ser Rayan cleared his throat and said, "Your Majesty?"

She hesitated, momentarily forgetting he was referring to *her* when he said *Your Majesty*—that would take quite a bit of getting used to.

"The dragon." She looked over her shoulder again as a few weak plumes of smoke rose into the sky from wherever the creature had landed. "The others will be needing him, and if he's hurt or stuck, he won't make it to them in time—if at all."

Ser Rayan shook his head. "I'm afraid I can't allow that. We're under orders to bring you to safety—nothing more."

"What if he needs assistance? We can't just leave him when we know where he is."

"Dragons are unpredictable," he said firmly, blue eyes hardening. "He doesn't know us. He could lash out at us—in fear or pain, it doesn't matter. The only person capable of assisting him is Her Grace."

Diantha narrowed her eyes. "Need I remind you that I'm now the Queen of Dofell? I thought soldiers were supposed to obey a royal's decree."

"We don't take orders from you, queen or not," another Akkinorian piped up. "We only take orders from Her Grace or His Royal Highness."

She scowled. "Even if my order might save their lives? If what we've heard about Kanibar and its mages is true, then your queen and her friends are at a pitiful disadvantage without the dragon. It'd be impossible for her or anyone else to leave the battlefield to ensure his welfare, and the lot of us have nothing to do other than sit by a hearth until they return."

"All due respect, Your Majesty," Ser Rayan murmured, "but whatever did that to him may do it again if and when he returns to battle. He could become a liability. They can still win without him, but if anything happens to you...Without you, Dofell is unsalvageable. Without you—even if Kanibar loses—battles will be fought for control over your kingdom. The same people fighting beside one another will be forced to raise arms against one another instead. We can't take that risk."

She bit the insides of her cheeks, silent, as Ser Rayan urged everyone to keep moving forward into Morvis. She didn't give her horse the cue to move, though, causing the others to halt again when they realized she wasn't following them. She closed her eyes, ignoring them as they repeatedly asked why she wasn't moving, and began to hum.

As a familiar feeling of comfort and power surged through Diantha's veins, she opened her eyes to see the path ahead as her lips curled into a satisfied smile.

***

Aurelia had found herself parted from Arian just minutes after they finished off their attackers. She'd turned away from him when she spotted

411

a familiar face—Lord Kallan Tarre of Holos—take a sword to the thigh, nearly severing his limb from his body. She'd managed to stab his opponent from behind (a dishonorable kill, but a necessary one), tie a tourniquet around the nobleman's leg using a fallen Kanish cape, and prop him up against a pile of corpses so he'd be camouflaged amongst the dead until the battle ended. By the time she turned around to find her uncle again, he was gone.

She fought as she roamed the battlefield in search of familiar faces or fighters in need of assistance, and just as she sprinted toward a distressed Akkinorian mage, she tripped over what she thought was a stone or a twig. When she pulled herself up and looked back, she realized it was a human arm.

Bile didn't rise up in her throat until she saw the armless body laying nearby. The middle-aged man's green eyes were wide with fear, his mouth was open, and a dagger was still lodged in the side of his neck. The body belonged to Sylvan Halloway, a member of her Assembly. She crawled over to him, murmuring a silent prayer, and closed his eyes while fighting the urge to vomit.

Sylvan Halloway was the most decorated Akkinorian veteran of the modern age, having volunteered to fight in every battle Akkinor had seen since he turned sixteen years of age. Aurelia hadn't been particularly close to him, but every Akkinorian alive respected his service to their country. There was no greater soldier, and now even *he* was dead.

Aurelia had known from the start that Willem's forces were stronger than he let on, but she still hadn't anticipated anything of this caliber. Amidst all the chaos, she looked around at the swords clashing and bodies piling up near her—far more friends than foes. It was entirely possible that the Trevas banners would be raised in Dofell by the end of the day.

No. She shook the thought from her head immediately. They'd already come this far, and everyone who'd stood beside her earlier that day would do whatever it took to see Willem defeated. She'd made a promise to Maysa, too, that she refused to break: in one way or another, Willem was going to die that day.

Of course, that one sliver of doubt haunting her brain would've disappeared completely if she knew where Halvor was. She still didn't know what Willem's mages had done to her beloved companion, but she knew he was alive: she would've felt something if he was severely hurt, so unless he was trapped somewhere, it was only a matter of time before he made his return.

As Aurelia rushed to help a Taundosan mage to her feet, she noticed the sea of soldiers growing thinner. Only her allies stood within her immediate vicinity now, with all enemy soldiers having fled the scene. The Kanish and Kroti had seemingly evaporated, which meant only one thing: Willem had another surprise in store.

The young mage Aurelia had helped whimpered as she clung to the queen's arm. "What are they doing?" she asked.

Aurelia frowned as the soldiers nearby backed into them like they were being forced to retreat by spears. She wished Edom were there: the sprite could've gotten to the bottom of Willem's antics in seconds, and it could've helped her find the king so she could end this. At the very least, Willem hadn't sent the other Kanish sprites to battle, either. It was possible that Willem was saving the sprites for an opportune moment, but something in her gut told her that the creatures would never arrive.

Looking over a Goldman's shoulder, she saw exactly what the Kanish and Kroti were doing: forming a circular perimeter around the allies' troops. It was like they were corralling their enemies into a pigpen, leaving them with nowhere to go.

"Oh, gods." The woman covered her mouth with her hand like she was going to be sick right then and there. "They're going to kill us all, aren't they?"

Aurelia didn't answer. She looked around slowly, but she still couldn't make sense of what her enemies were doing. They were armed, but they weren't pointing their weapons at Aurelia and her allies. There was no telling if they'd use their weapons or their magic—or both—after they were done taunting their opponents by forming a perimeter with their own bodies.

Even with everyone packed so densely, Aurelia couldn't spot a familiar face for the life of her. Jack, Arian, Reyna, and the two Bozari lords were nowhere to be found. She didn't doubt that Jack and Lord Zhoqa were alive, but the others...Reyna was trained in combat, like most royals, but she'd never seen battle before. Lord Zhaaran was only a few short years away from being considered elderly, so even with his experience in combat and magic, he was vulnerable without the same speed and strength he'd known as a young man. Even Arian was a bit too old to be fighting in a war, and after the shockwave, Aurelia wasn't certain he'd be able to stand his ground.

She worried for each of them, wherever they were, and hoped they were prepared to face whatever threat Willem's soldiers posed next—she certainly wasn't.

Just then, a massive shadow rolled in overhead, blanketing the battlefield in darkness. A spark of hope glimmered in her chest, but she didn't feel the same power she normally felt when Halvor was near.

Another airborne threat had taken his place, and Aurelia had no idea whose side it was on.

Then the shadow broke through the clouds above, and a gasp escaped her lips when she saw a cluster of what appeared to be birds flying in a V-shaped formation. As they descended, she realized they weren't birds at all—they were gryphons.

The gryphon, a magical creature with the body and rear legs of a lion and the head, wings, and talons of an eagle, had supposedly gone extinct during the persecution. One had been spotted in the wild in Aurelia's lifetime, as told to her by Arian, and the poor creature had been slaughtered by hunters in the Violet Forest. In the old days, though, gryphons were the dominant magical species in one particular civilization: Krotis.

The gryphons shrieked as they broke their formation and swooped toward the battlefield. As they grew closer, Aurelia saw they were carrying massive stones in their talons. Some of the enemy soldiers surrounding Aurelia fled the circle in terror, but others held strong—that is, until the gryphons dropped the stones directly on top of them, killing them instantly.

A laugh escaped Aurelia's throat when she saw that each of the gryphons wore capes over their backs. The image of a dragonfly was stamped on each amber cape, identifying the creatures as having come from the Kroti province of Runeia.

"Krotis is attacking its own people?" The young mage stared at Aurelia, wild-eyed. "How—?"

"Runeia promised to fight for me and my allies. They couldn't send troops to fight their own kin, but they *could* send something else." Aurelia grinned from ear to ear as the soldiers around them were finally able to rush the battlefield once more. "Lady Swann continues to surprise me."

Edom had said it before: magical creatures still existed around the world, albeit in hiding, and most had survived to the modern age because of people like Aurelia and Lady Swann; people who, like their ancestors, fought to protect the creatures from extinction by concealing them. The Swann family had likely been hiding their secret arsenal for centuries, waiting for the perfect moment to reintroduce this power to the realm.

With the fighting resumed after Willem's latest plan was foiled, Aurelia bid farewell to the mage she'd rescued and scoured the battlefield for her next target. Now that both friends and enemies alike had blended together again, the gryphons had ceased dropping stones and were now contributing in any way they could: plucking enemy soldiers from the ground and tossing them aside like ragdolls; slicing through enemy chests and abdomens with their claws; and, of course, eating wounded enemies alive while they flailed on the ground. Nothing was as tasty to a gryphon as the flesh of a rotten human.

Something hard clanged against Aurelia's side, rattling her armor and sending her stumbling a few steps to the left. She whirled around just in time for her sword to kiss another wielded by a furious Kroti.

They sparred until she disarmed him, but he didn't stop there. He pulled a concealed dagger from his boot and slashed at her, narrowly missing her throat, and she gritted her teeth as she struggled to defend against his swift, almost thoughtless motions with a weapon that made her slow and sloppy in comparison. He kicked her in the chest when she prepared to strike him, sending her plummeting to the ground and wheezing for air.

He straddled her, his thighs squeezing her hips, but she managed to grab his wrists before the tip of his dagger could meet her jugular. While he hissed in her face, saliva dripping from his mouth onto her cheek, she brought her knee to his groin as hard as she could and shoved him to the side. He growled in frustration as she kicked him in the face, putting him on his stomach and forcing him to drop his dagger in the process. She climbed onto his back, pulled his head toward her by his hair, and cut his throat with his own weapon.

Aurelia brought herself to her feet on wobbly knees, wiped blood and sweat from her face, and turned just in time to fend off another attacker. This man, a burly Kanish, let her disarm him before bringing his fist to her mouth. She staggered backward but didn't fall, already feeling the blood pooling in her mouth, as the same young mage she'd helped earlier returned the favor by strangling the assailant with roots she summoned from the earth.

She smiled in gratitude, then turned her head to spit a mouthful of bloody saliva onto the ground. She was surprised a tooth hadn't fallen out, what with the excruciating throbbing of her entire jaw. Her whole body throbbed, too, as her tight armor continued to vibrate from impact after impact. The feeling of her bones trembling against her flesh—and the realization that she couldn't move very fast while being weighed down by heavy bronze—led her to shed as much of the armor as she could. She let her breastplate and the pieces on her thighs clatter to the ground, ignoring the voice in the back of her head that reminded her about what often happened when a soldier fought without proper protection.

Aurelia weighed her sword in her hand as she kept moving forward, hoping to find Willem before he attempted to flee the scene. If she couldn't find him, she'd keep looking for her allies—after all, they were looking to find and kill Willem, too. Wherever they were, Willem wouldn't be far away.

When she finally spotted the king, her heart stopped for a moment. Because of course it wasn't either of the Bozari lords, Reyna, or even Arian swinging a sword at Willem. It was Jack—the very last person she wanted to get within an inch of the king, let alone be pitted against him.

She wasn't worried that Willem was a better swordsman than Jack. One of Lady Swann's gryphons could probably handle a sword with more grace than the king. No, what worried her was that Willem's greatest weapon was his words, and he knew exactly how to get under Jack's skin. And if Jack let the king's taunts cloud his judgment, Willem would know exactly where to plunge his sword.

Even from a distance, she saw Willem's lips moving as the pair circled one another. She didn't have to hear him to know what he was saying: *Does it keep you up at night, knowing that I know what your wife tastes like? Does it plague your thoughts, knowing that I can still feel her breasts throbbing against my chest? Does it make your skin crawl, knowing that I was mere seconds away from uniting our bodies as one?*

As another assailant charged her, Aurelia's last thought before raising her sword was this: *Think like a king, Jack. Just this once, and never again.*

XLV

*D*on't be an idiot. Don't be an idiot. Don't be an idiot.

The same four words echoed in Jack's head as he and the King of Kanibar circled one another, swords raised and pointed at the other's chest, but he knew he wouldn't be listening to that voice. There was only one person who could get through to him in this moment, but she was off fighting her own battles. And she'd gut him herself if she knew what he was doing.

Willem grinned and raised his eyebrows. "I've heard stories about you, you know. They say you're one of the greatest swordsmen alive, but I don't believe that for a moment. If that were true, then why weren't you papa's favorite? Seems like while he was busy spoiling your brother, he placed you right in the path of those pesky radicals, hoping you'd abandon your duty to Akkinor. He knew you weren't suited for leadership, just like Aurelia."

"Don't you dare speak to me about my father," Jack growled.

"Fine, then. There's plenty of other things to talk about." Willem laughed. "I'll say, it was a good thing your wife gave herself to me when she did, because there was nothing *you* could've done for your daughter. Poor little Sisi asked for you so often that I was almost compelled to sew her lips together. I couldn't understand why she believed you'd come to save her—because of course, you're not *really* her father. And you couldn't have done a thing without your wife. But you already know that, don't you?"

Willem was circling Jack now. "You're helpless without Aurelia, just like you're helpless to protect your children. After I take her back, I'll have each of your children brought to me, too, and you won't be able to do a thing about it."

417

A ragged shout burst from Jack's chest as he swung his sword, but Willem skipped backward like a gazelle, missing the blade before it pierced his chest.

Willem *tsked* him and shook his head. "Terrible sportsmanship. It's improper to strike during conversation. Did you lose your manners to Carthe while you were running from your responsibilities, *Mister Sherbourne?*"

Jack swung again, and again, until finally, Willem met Jack's blade with his own. To Jack's surprise, Willem was stronger than he looked, and so comfortable with a sword that he was able to clasp one hand behind his back. The grin didn't fade from his lips for even a moment.

In all his years, Jack had never been pitted against a man smaller than him who fought him without breaking a sweat. Jack's strength and weight behind a sword almost always ensured that his blade met its mark—or, at the very least, that he disarmed his opponent. He never sparred for long before he emerged victorious, but now, he found himself practically dancing along the battlefield—and he didn't feel like he was leading.

"You're a worthy opponent. I'll give you that much." After sparring for a bit, Willem started circling again, prompting Jack to follow suit as both of them started to pant for air. "Still, I don't understand why your wife is so infatuated by the mere *idea* of you. You're a traitor, for one, and an untrained hound, for another. You bark and bark, but you never say anything of substance." He chuckled to himself. "You know why she married you, right? A very clever thing, she is. She needed a husband to appease her people, but one that could not rival her in power. And no Akkinorian would put a traitor on the throne, even if it meant replacing a woman. You were the only option she had that allowed her to keep her crown."

Jack flinched, and when Willem hooted with laughter, he knew the king had noticed. "I'd choose my next words carefully if I were you," Jack warned. "Your own mother made Aurelia promise to ensure your death today. I'm more than happy to fulfill that promise on her behalf."

"Was that meant to be a threat?" Willem shook his head, still grinning. "My word. You're a great grizzly of a man, but you have the mind of an *ant*, for gods' sakes. You fight to fulfill a prophecy you've never heard—one you'd probably never understand—told to your wife by an old witch you've never met. If you kill me, you'll damn the realm. It's that simple."

Jack gritted his teeth. "I may not know *exactly* what the prophecy says, but I do know that it speaks of a hero, not a pathetic king who lies to his people, kidnaps little girls to get what he wants, and can't stand the sight of his own reflection. You can say whatever the hell you want about me,

418

but you know as well as I do that there's someone else much more heroic than you—someone *else* with western blood."

Willem's eyes flashed, and Jack knew he'd struck a nerve. "Careful," Willem said darkly. "Say it any louder, and someone might hear you. I don't suppose Akkinor will stand for a Carthinian on the throne, and they'd probably kill her for her deception, too. Such a lie is considered treason in all corners of the world. They'd kill her for it, and you, and your children, too—just for good measure."

That was the last straw. Jack charged him with every bit of strength he could muster, relishing the brief glimmer of fear in Willem's green eyes, and brought his sword down over and over again until he was certain he'd never forget the sound of bronze against steel. When Willem's sword arm faltered, Jack socked him in the face, then kicked the king in the chest so hard he fell to the ground.

Before Jack could climb on top of him and punch him until the both of them blacked out, Willem jumped to his feet and swung his sword directly at Jack's throat. Jack ducked, narrowly missing the blade, and slammed the butt of his sword against Willem's back. The king howled in pain, then whirled around and tried to cut the backs of Jack's knees. When Jack swerved out of the way, Willem slashed at him again, and the side of his sword would've sliced through Jack's shoulder if his armor hadn't been in the way.

Using the same strategy, Jack brought his sword down on Willem's armor. The blade bounced off, but it was enough to reverberate Willem's bones. When the king dropped his sword, Jack grabbed him by the throat, putting every ounce of anguish Willem had caused him over the past few weeks toward squeezing the breath from the king's airway.

"I've been dreaming of this for weeks now," Jack growled. "Feeling the life leave your body has been the only thing I've craved so deeply in a very, *very* long time."

Red-faced and wide-eyed, Willem managed to grin and gasp, "So have I."

Jack's grip loosened when he felt a sudden heat spreading across his abdomen. When he looked down and saw the hilt of a dagger lodged in the one place his armor had slipped, protruding from a gap in his armor, his mind finally caught up to his body. As white-hot pain caused black spots to form in his vision, the dagger twisted, forcing Jack to drop the king to the ground.

Grimacing, Jack covered the wound with his hand, his fingers on either side of the blade as his flesh throbbed against it. He staggered backward, head spinning as blood oozed from between his fingers, and wondered why the roaring sounds of battle had suddenly become no louder than a murmur.

In the two seconds it took for him to look up, Willem was in front of him, and a gurgling sound escaped his throat when the king plunged his sword through the other side of Jack's abdomen—the only other gap in his armor. While the hilt of Willem's dagger throbbed against Jack's flesh, the king brought him into what felt like an embrace, only to whisper in his ear:

"Don't worry—I'll take care of Aurelia. Gods know I can't have another man's spawn looking to *my* wife and calling her *Mother*, so I'll send your children to meet you as quickly as I can. I promise."

Then he pulled his sword from Jack's gut and walked away as Jack fell to a heap on the ground, blackness corrupting his vision.

The last thing Jack heard before succumbing to a cold, dark silence was a woman's scream—though perhaps it was just an angel, on her way to greet him.

***

Who is screaming? Aurelia wondered. *Why won't they stop? Who is—*

It took her a moment to realize that she was the one screaming. It was a sound she'd never heard herself make before, but it was one she'd heard from someone else in the past: her mother, as she held her stillborn son in her arms. It was the primal, unmistakable scream of a woman who'd just lost a piece of her soul.

Willem hadn't even glanced in her direction when she started screaming. He hadn't looked around to see if anyone was watching, either. He didn't care if anyone saw him kill the King Consort of Akkinor: Willem had no interest in making a spectacle out of something that meant so little to him—unless, of course, Aurelia was the sole witness.

Jack couldn't be dead. He *couldn't* be. He was a survivor if nothing else, and far too stubborn to let himself die. He wouldn't leave her, and he wouldn't leave their children. He'd fight for his life as he always had, hanging on until the battle ended so a mage could find him and heal his injuries. He wouldn't let himself die when he knew help would come.

That's what she told herself, but as the seconds passed, she believed it less and less. Even from afar, she saw the light leave his eyes when Willem removed the blade. He'd lost far too much blood already, judging by the crimson pool seeping around his body, so even if he were still alive, he wouldn't regain consciousness for a *very* long time.

She knew running for him was a bad idea, but she did it anyway. She didn't care if Willem or Dayne noticed that she'd put herself within striking distance—if they took that opportunity to kill her, then so be it. In this moment, she'd rather be with her husband, wherever he was in the universe, than alone while he suffered.

She ran so fast that every part of her ached and burned, but before she was halfway to Jack, someone ran at her from the side and tackled her to the ground, forcing her to drop her sword. She hollered and thrashed while reaching around for her weapon until she saw Lord Zhoqa's face staring down at her.

"Get off of me!" she shouted, struggling against the weight of his knee on her abdomen. "I have to get to Jack! I have to—"

"You need to find your wits—for his sake, if not for everyone else's." He let her up, but when she tried to spring to her feet and run again, he grabbed her by the wrists and forced her to her knees, mirroring his position. "Don't let them see you break."

When they were eye-level, he set his hands on her shoulders while she kept her eyes trained on Jack's limp body about a dozen yards away. He was a ways away from the heart of the fighting, so nobody got close enough to potentially trample him, but that didn't make her feel any better. He was alone out there, like an embalmed body displayed in a coffin for mourners.

Lord Zhoqa blocked her view with his head. Only then did she snap out of her daze to acknowledge him fully, tears streaming down her face and mixing with the blood, dirt, and soot staining her cheeks. Even while his azurite gaze was wide with alarm, Lord Zhoqa brushed her tears away with his fingertips before squeezing her shoulders.

"Aurelia." It was the first time he'd ever used her first name, but it was out of urgency rather than friendship. "Don't look at him. Look at me." She obeyed, and to her surprise, she saw grief glimmering in his eyes. "I don't know where the others have gone, but Willem's cowering behind that blasted sorcerer, and killing the pair of them is the only way we can end this. The sooner we kill them, the sooner we can help your husband. We're of no use to him now. If Willem or Dayne sees you running to him, they'll kill you before you get the chance to help him—if he's still alive. If he's already dead...then there's nothing we can do anyway. I'm sorry, but we can't risk losing to Willem for Jack. We need you, even if I like to pretend otherwise."

Her mouth was so dry that she could hardly part her lips to speak. "Balor, I—"

"I know." His fingers clenched on her shoulders. "Between the two of us, you're the one who deserves to take his head. I'll keep the sorcerer busy, but...but I haven't any magic. I don't stand much of a chance against him. Do you understand what I'm saying to you?"

Swallowing, she reached into the too-tight base layer she wore underneath her loose top. The shirt had been keeping the amulet safely tucked against her chest throughout the battle, and until this moment, she'd completely forgotten about Edea's power.

As she removed the amulet, Lord Zhoqa helped her to her feet, hands hovering over her arms even as she regained her footing. She sniffed, used her free hand to wipe golden tears from her cheeks, and turned the moonrock over in her palm as she recalled everything Edea had said to her in her dream.

She swallowed the lump in her throat as visions of Jack's last moments replayed in her head. "He never liked the idea of this thing. He wouldn't want me to use it because I lost him."

Lord Zhoqa's eyebrows furrowed. "Your Grace—"

Inhaling sharply, Aurelia held her hand out and turned it over, watching as the amulet fell from her palm for what felt like the longest few seconds of her life. The ground at her feet had turned into massive puddles of blood and dirt, so the moment the amulet hit the ground, it sunk into a thick layer of crimson mud.

He cursed and bent over to retrieve it, but Aurelia stopped him. "Leave it."

"Are you *mad?*"

"In this moment? No." She wiped her running nose with her sleeve and looked behind him, where Willem and Dayne were observing the fighting from afar. "He may have powers, but he's still human—even a sorcerer can't survive without his head."

He furrowed his eyebrows. "Aurelia—"

"Aim for the neck," she advised, and then she was off.

Lord Zhoqa scrambled to follow her as the pair stalked toward their targets. As the battle raged behind them—and Jack lay alone and lifeless to their left—Aurelia pushed her emotions aside to focus every ounce of her energy on the promise she made to Maysa. She knew Jack wouldn't have wanted her to abandon her chance at killing Willem so she could cry over his body instead.

She could almost hear his voice in her head: *Don't waste your energy on me, Lily dear. I'm not going anywhere. I'll still be right here after you've finished gutting him.*

Willem and Dayne saw them coming, of course, and turned to them without a lick of fear or worry on their faces. In fact, the sight of Aurelia—battered, bloody, and blubbering—only made Willem grin.

"My blushing bride!" he mused. "I'm so glad you've found me! As I'm sure you've seen by now, the main threat to our happy union has been neutralized. But please, spare me from a mourning period—why should a widow need to mourn if she's already found a new husband?"

Aurelia spat at his feet. "You insufferable coward. I know you only defeated him because Dayne cast some sort of spell over you. Made you stronger, faster—I don't know, exactly, but I know he did *something*. You would've bragged about your combat skills from the moment we met if you had any." Jack's voice in her head made her smile and add, "You knew you couldn't best Jack as you are. It must eat you alive, knowing you're worthless without someone else's magic."

His face darkened. "Watch your tongue, my love, or you'll spend the rest of your life without one."

"Careful." Lord Zhoqa's words were directed at Willem, but his eyes were trained on Dayne. "If you lay a hand on her, every Akkinorian alive will make sure you suffer for it. The Bozari will, too."

Dayne sneered at him. "And what will *your* people do? Hmm? Throw books at us?"

That did it. Lord Zhoqa released a bellowing battle cry and charged the mage, and in the time it took Aurelia to blink, the two of them were sparring a few feet away from where she and the king stood face-to-face. Dayne wasn't using his magic yet, which wasn't a surprise—he probably wanted to taunt his opponent, weakening Lord Zhoqa by making him wonder when Dayne would strike him down with just a wave of his hand.

"Put your sword down, beautiful," Willem told her. "I don't wish to hurt you or ruin your pretty face."

Her fighting arm twitched, making his eyes flicker down to her sword, and that brief distraction gave her the chance to plant her fist on his mouth. He staggered backward, momentarily miffed by her diversion, before bringing a hand to his mouth and staring at the blood staining his fingertips. He met her eyes again, guffawed, and spit a mouthful of blood onto the ground to his left.

"It was a good shot, Your Grace, but that's the only one you'll get." He lifted his sword and grinned as a dark, malicious glint formed in his eyes. "Don't worry—I won't kill you. I'll aim for the non-vital organs, paying close attention to ensure your womb remains intact. You may wish you were dead, but you'll live a long life. The dungeons and the birthing bed will be your new home."

A low, growl-like sound emerged from her throat as she lunged at him, stumbling forward when he side-stepped her and hit her in the back with the hilt of his sword. She recovered and managed to block his next strike, but he was a far better swordsman than she'd expected. It all but confirmed her suspicion that Dayne had done something to ensure Willem's success in battle.

Her lungs strained and her entire body ached, but she refused to show weakness. The sight of him so close to her reminded her of everything he'd done to make her suffer: kidnapping her daughter, holding her hostage, forcing her friend to betray her, killing her husband—it all struck her like a tidal wave, threatening to swallow her whole, but it wasn't enough to give her the strength she needed.

As Willem forced their kissing blades to her throat, a sudden thought popped into her head. Or rather, a short passage from a children's story she knew like the back of her hand. It wasn't her own voice narrating in her head, either, but her father's—the first person who'd read the story to her when she was a girl.

I am the tempest. I am the sun. I am eternal.

She didn't realize she'd been saying the words out loud until Willem laughed, releasing his sword from hers and sending her staggering. "What gibberish are you blabbing about now? Some ridiculous words my idiot mother told you?"

Aurelia raised an eyebrow and smiled a bit. "Oh, darling, don't you remember?" Her words dripped with a sickly sweetness as she batted her eyelashes at him. "I read that story the first day I visited your library. You told me it was one of your favorites. You also told me you were the only person in my life who hadn't lied to me. Men really will say *anything* to break a dry spell, won't you?"

A ragged scream ripped from Willem's chest as he charged her, dropping the facade and revealing the person he really was: a cowardly, vile man with no love in his heart for anything but himself.

Just as she gained the upper hand by pushing her sword down on his, nicking his neck with his own blade, a powerful force whacked her in the chest and sent her flying several feet backwards. From the corner of her eye, she caught a glimpse of a Kanish mage loitering nearby, who'd seemingly intervened out of fear for his king. Willem glowered at the mage as if to say, *I don't need your help.* He ran a hand through his mahogany hair, spit out another mouthful of blood, then stalked over to where Aurelia gasped on the ground.

She could do nothing but wheeze as Willem towered over her, pointing the tip of his blade against her chest and glowering down at her with pure, unbridled hatred.

"What a pitiful queen you are," he spat. "You're as useless as every other woman, from a raging witch spouting lies, to that whore who chose the wrong brother to back. You'd have been much better off bearing my children and warming my bed, but you couldn't even do that. You never stood a chance."

Aurelia's chest heaved with every deep breath, so powerful that the tip of his sword dug deeper into her flesh with every rise and fall. Blood oozed from between her breasts, burning her skin like acid as it trailed down to her navel and stained her shirt.

"I am not a woman," Aurelia snapped, eyes burning holes into Willem's skull. "I am a dragon."

It happened so quickly that neither of them even saw the shadow approaching from the sky. In a matter of seconds, the ground beneath her shook like an earthquake, as Halvor settled in his rightful spot. The dragon craned his neck over Aurelia's body, roaring in Willem's face with so much rage that even Aurelia found herself shaking.

Willem dropped his sword as he fell to the ground, scooching backwards along the grass to get as far from Halvor as possible. His chest heaved and his eyes widened with panic as Halvor growled, saliva dripping from his mouth and pooling at Aurelia's feet. The king almost looked more shocked than afraid—he'd clearly believed that whatever his mages had done to Halvor had killed him.

When Willem's fingers twitched in the dirt, Halvor growled again, bringing his mouth even closer to the king's body. Willem's eyes bugged from his skull as he was forced to lay flat on the ground, Halvor's teeth only inches from Willem's chest. He was trembling like a dog during a thunderstorm, but he had no reason to fear Halvor—he only needed to fear Aurelia.

Without uttering a syllable, Aurelia urged Halvor to pull back. He obeyed, but not before snorting plumes of smoke from his nostrils and making a low rumbling sound in his throat. As Aurelia stood on wobbly legs, Halvor retreated.

As she took a few steps toward the king, while he lay on the ground with his eyes squeezed shut, she noticed something odd: the roots of his hair were turning gray. She frowned, watching as those roots slowly began to spread down the length of his hair, and saw that his face was changing, too. Wrinkles formed on his forehead and around his eyes, deep lines appeared on either side of his mouth, his under-eyes became puffy and swollen, and some of his teeth became rotted. His hands gained wrinkles and dark spots, his gut fell over the waistband of his pants, and the skin on his neck became loose and saggy.

Aurelia looked up at where Lord Zhoqa had been fighting Dayne. She smiled when she saw her ally sawing off one of Dayne's fingers with a dagger—likely to claim it as a trophy. Dayne's throat was slit so deeply that his head wasn't fully attached to his body anymore, and his eyes were still open and wide with terror.

Only then did she realize that the sun had begun to rise over the horizon line. It was almost dawn, meaning Willem's day-long glamour spell had broken; and without Dayne to cast another, the young man Willem claimed to be was gone forever.

"You know," she said to him, "it was never about how you looked. It was the fact that neither I, nor any woman, would want to be with someone as vainglorious as you, *Your Majesty.*"

While Halvor kept growling behind her, Willem continued to tremble. His hands were held up against his chest like a praying mantis, as if trying to keep her calm so she wouldn't command Halvor to eat him.

"Please" was all the king could say.

"The blood of the rider is the blood of the dragon." Aurelia smiled a bit as she wiped crimson liquid from her split lip. "So the stories say, anyway."

With that, she turned to the side, tossing one quick glance at Halvor before walking away. Not a second later, an incredible heat warmed her from behind as a shriek rattled her eardrums. Willem only screamed for a moment—as long as it took for Halvor's flames to turn the king's flesh into ashes.

The fire was so massive and intense that it distracted the soldiers on the battlefield. They stopped fighting each other to watch for a moment, but without any means of identifying the charred remains, they started sparring again—too afraid of or loyal to Willem to stop unless they knew for certain that he was dead.

Her eyes found Jack, but he wasn't alone anymore. Arian and a young female mage were kneeling beside him, working their magic to tend to his injuries. Just as she started running over to them, the fighting stopped again—but not because of Halvor or Willem. The soldiers lowered their swords, confused, and backed away from one another to create a path through the carnage. When they moved, Aurelia found herself standing directly across from a few hundred people who'd just arrived in Thurran Valley.

She frowned as the person leading them—a young man, no older than nineteen or twenty—met her eyes and walked toward her. She had no idea who he was until she saw the emblems on his shoulders: the one on the left was a lotus flower, symbolic of Krotis; and the one on the right was a bolas spider, symbolic of the Trevas family.

Lord Zhoqa appeared at Aurelia's side just as the man approached her. "And who might you be?" the nobleman demanded, Dayne's finger hanging from a cord around his neck.

The boy's eyes didn't leave Aurelia's. "Harryn Trevas."

XLVI

I'll stay with him," Arian promised Aurelia. His hands were stained not with his own blood or the blood of his enemies, but Jack's. "It'll take him a few days to recover, but he'll survive. Willem's blades met nothing but flesh—no organs. The only thing that concerns me is how much blood he lost, but Lucyra here has seen worse cases than his. He's in good hands." He leaned close to her ear and lowered his voice. "She's our cousin, you know."

Aurelia snapped her eyes over to the Taundosan mage behind him. The woman, Lucyra, was checking Jack's bandages as he lay atop an abandoned knight's cape on the ground. When she finished, four men lifted the cape—and Jack along with it—and she followed them from the battlefield as they carried him away.

Aurelia thanked her uncle and lingered for a moment while she watched him scurry to catch up with the others. He walked along Jack's left side, and a smile formed on her lips when Jack lifted a weak arm to clasp Arian's hand. That was the most he'd been able to do, other than smile and flutter his eyelids, since Lucyra and Arian began healing him.

She'd known deep in her soul that he wasn't dead, but until she saw his eyes again, she hadn't fully believed it. She'd bolted to him after leaving Harryn with Lord Zhoqa, and after only a few minutes of kneeling by his side and clutching his hand to her chest, he'd coughed, groaned, and slowly peeled his eyes open. She was the first thing he saw when his vision stabilized, and the way he'd smiled at the sight of her inspired the greatest feeling she'd ever known in her lifetime.

She'd wanted to stay with him and oversee his care herself, but he'd managed to nod in agreement with Arian when her uncle reminded her that she couldn't leave quite yet—her soldiers still needed a leader while they collected themselves and dealt with the aftermath of the battle. Before she left Jack with Arian and Lucyra, though, she'd kissed him on the forehead and whispered in his ear, "If you ever do anything like that again, I'll kill you myself." He hadn't been able to speak, but he'd smiled at her.

When Jack and Arian disappeared from view, she turned to find her allies. A weak Lord Zhaaran was sitting on a rock while holding a cloth to an oozing cut on his forehead, and Lord Zhoqa stood beside him with his hand on the old man's shoulder. Reyna stood with them, too, clutching what looked like a sprained wrist to her chest, and almost every inch of her dark skin was caked in dried blood that didn't belong to her.

At least they'd all made it out alive—for a while there, Aurelia wasn't so sure she'd see them all again.

The three of them were conversing with the person who'd unintentionally ended the battle: Harryn Trevas, Willem's nephew. The unexpected arrival had stalled the battle long enough for everyone to realize that Willem was dead, and after that, both the Kanish and the Kroti dropped their swords, like they'd been waiting for that moment since the fighting began.

Aurelia offered the group a weak smile when she joined them. "How are we?"

"Thriving," Lord Zhoqa said with a sardonic snort.

"Managing," Lord Zhaaran muttered.

"Glad to be alive." Reyna tore her eyes from Harryn to raise an eyebrow at Aurelia. "You did this, didn't you? You brought him here."

Aurelia smiled. "I only sent a message."

"I didn't see you send a raven."

"Who said anything about a raven?"

Harryn mirrored her smile. "A sprite visited me not too long ago. Coincidentally, I was on my way to Kanibar with a few troops to ask my uncle about my inheritance. I turned right instead of left when I reached the edge of the desert—just in time, apparently."

"Just in time," Aurelia repeated.

Reyna shook her head, dumbfounded. "You have incredible luck, Your Grace."

"I have the gods on my side. *Our* side. That's all."

In truth, she hadn't expected—or intended for—Harryn to meet them on the battlefield. The thought of him struck her when she arrived in Taundosa after her escape, as strategizing made her wonder about the future of Kanibar. She knew that even if Willem survived the battle and won, Harryn could challenge his claim to the throne as a legitimate Trevas heir, and the Kanish would be more inclined to support a just ruler over a war criminal. Harryn hadn't known what was happening with his uncle as of late, so Aurelia had simply taken it upon herself to tell him he could intervene if he wished to.

"Well," Lord Zhoqa said with a sigh, "I think that makes you the new King of Kanibar."

Harryn squared his shoulders and lifted his chin. He was the same age Aurelia had been when she took the throne, but he still looked like a boy: scrawny and lanky with a clean-shaven face, messy hair, and a certain innocence in his eyes. She didn't know what kind of man he was or what kind of king he would be, but she had to hope that anything was better than Willem. Besides, if he wasn't the right person for the job, Maysa wouldn't have given his name to Aurelia.

He raised an eyebrow at Aurelia. "My uncle put you through hell. Is there anything I can do to make amends for his crimes?"

She only smiled. "He's kept your grandmother prisoner in the temple at the palace for years now. Set her free. That's all I could ever ask of you."

"I would've done so regardless of your request." He ran a hand through his hair and sighed. "I'll have more reparations to make in the near future, and none so easily remedied as that."

"Go to your soldiers. They'll be expecting you," Lord Zhaaran said to him. "Collect your dead, arrest those who resist, and ensure everyone is escorted out of Dofell as soon as possible. Talk to them like you're already their king, and they won't disobey you."

Harryn nodded, sucked in a deep breath, and did as he was told. While they watched him go, Reyna muttered something about looking in the other direction. Aurelia and the others obeyed her, and relief coursed through Aurelia's veins when she spotted Diantha riding towards them with Rayan and a handful of other soldiers at her side. Diantha wasn't looking at the allies, but rather up at the sky, where Halvor was coasting overhead. They hadn't been summoned back to the battlefield since their departure, so something—more than likely Edom, who'd probably ignored Aurelia's commands so it could watch the battle unfold—had let them know that the fighting had ended.

While they approached, Aurelia saw something from the corner of her eye: a faint white glow on the ground. Frowning, she left the allies and followed the light, then crouched down and dug through the blood muck. A quiet, gurgling laugh caught in her throat when her fingers wrapped around the amulet.

Naturally, she thought to herself. *Such power won't disappear without a fight.*

She clutched the amulet in her fist as she returned to the allies. By the time she got there, Diantha was already with them, but Rayan and the soldiers had left to help the other survivors. Nobody said a word as Aurelia looked down at the amulet in her fist, using the pads of her thumbs to wipe mud from the moonstone.

"Even though I didn't use it as intended," she murmured, "I think I *did* use it, in a way."

Lord Zhaaran smiled weakly. "I understand now. You were never meant to find it—*it* was meant to find *you*." He lowered the cloth from his face to reveal a thick, open wound that just barely missed his eye. "She knew exactly what you'd do with it."

"Making the choice to dispose of unparalleled power deems you worthy in the gods' eyes," Reyna told her. "It was a bit like a sacrifice, wasn't it? A test you managed to pass."

"I suppose it was." Aurelia sighed. "I wish I could give it back to her."

Nobody answered for a moment. Then Lord Zhoqa scrubbed a tired hand over his face and said, "We'll figure out what to do with it later on. The gryphons fled when Halvor came back, so I'm certain Lady Swann will be expecting to hear from us when they return to her. Do we know why she finally decided to participate?"

"I think she had this planned from the start," Reyna muttered. "She couldn't risk the other Kroti leaders intercepting a message from her desk to ours. They would've been at odds over their loyalties, and she couldn't have that. But in the end, she was true to the oath she made to us, even if it wasn't always clear."

"Where do you suppose she's been keeping them?" Lord Zhoqa snorted. "She'll probably never tell us. I wonder what else the old woman's been hiding from us."

"I'm sure we'll find out eventually. We'll have to call for a meeting with all reigning Carthinians, anyway, to discuss—"

"What in the name of the Almighty is *that*?" Diantha interrupted.

Aurelia and the others followed her gaze to the sky just as everyone around them gasped, screamed, pointed, and ran about like headless chickens. Aurelia's heart pounded in her chest as she squinted to see through the most blinding, magnificent sphere of light she'd ever seen in her lifetime.

When the sphere collided with the ground, it didn't leave a crater in the earth or shake the ground beneath their feet. It fell at an incredible speed, but its landing was rather...*soft*. Gentle, even. For a moment, the light spread from the sphere as if it were scanning its surroundings, bathing everything in its vicinity in what felt like pure sunlight. The veil beamed so brightly that everyone had to look away to avoid having their eyeballs melt in their skulls.

As the veil of light faded, Aurelia and the others turned to face it again. The sphere lingered for a moment, pulsating, before morphing into a shape that reminded Aurelia of when Jack teased their children by running around with a sheet draped over him. The light retracted again until it was no larger than a pinpoint, then disappeared into layers of silver silk. In its place, a pale woman with white hair and silver eyes stood on the ground not ten feet from the allies.

It hadn't been sunlight at all—it'd been *moonlight*.

Lord Zhoqa fell to his knees, trembling, and began to pray. "Dhylo, give me strength, for I am your servant and a loyal student in the study of life, both then and now. I ask for your guidance, my Lord of Wisdom, as I trade my pride and ignorance for the pursuit of knowledge. I shall study what you allow me to observe, O Great Almighty, and I shall thank you humbly for the education I receive on a matter beyond what my human mind is worthy of comprehending."

Lord Zhaaran pulled himself from the stone he'd been sitting on, took a knee, and began to pray, too. So did Reyna, and Diantha, and every other soul who'd stopped what they were doing to gather around the mysterious arrival from the heavens. Only Aurelia remained standing, knowing that the object she held was the reason for all of this.

The figure from Aurelia's dream stood perfectly still, her fingers delicately interlinked over her abdomen, as her colorless hair dusted the ground—and was somehow spared from being stained with blood and filth. Her face was softer than Aurelia remembered, her cheeks bloomed with color, and her pink lips were curled into a soft, welcoming smile.

Swallowing the anxiety in her throat, Aurelia took a few steps forward and held out the amulet. "I believe this belongs to you," she said.

Edea's smile widened, revealing her pearly teeth, and held out a hand. Aurelia set the amulet on her palm, and when she did, Edea curled her fingers around both the moonrock and Aurelia's hand. Aurelia inhaled sharply and resisted the urge to pull away. It didn't feel like a human hand wrapped around hers, but rather like a cold, hollow darkness made tangible at will.

"Thank you," Aurelia whispered.

Edea only tipped her head in response. As she released Aurelia's hand, prompting the queen to step back again, she flicked her gaze over to where Diantha knelt on the ground. Diantha released a strangled gasp when she realized the moon goddess was looking at her, but the exchange didn't last long; Edea only needed to acknowledge Diantha to validate her new role as Dofell's Almighty.

Another pinprick of light appeared on Edea's abdomen, growing larger and larger by the second, until it enveloped her entire being in a fierce white glow. The glow condensed to form a sphere, the silhouette of Edea's body disappearing in the blink of an eye, and lifted into the sky.

Just like that, the goddess of the moon had returned to the heavens.

***

If Aurelia's allies hadn't been there to confirm Aurelia's story about Edea to Jack and Arian, she wasn't certain they would've believed her. But when they heard it from everyone who'd been in Thurran Valley to bear witness, what they couldn't believe was simply that they'd missed it.

"One of the Twelve arrives in the realm for the first time in over a thousand years, and I'm lying in a sickbed when it happens." Jack shook his head and scoffed. "Figures."

"It was phenomenal." Reyna hadn't stopped glowing since it happened, even with her wrist wrapped and dangling in a sling. "Do you suppose she'll come back?"

"If not Edea, then another deity. I'm certain of it." Lord Zhaaran smiled as he set his palm against Aurelia's cheek in a fatherly sort of way, like he'd forgotten she was a queen. "You did well, Your Grace."

"I told you," she teased. Reminded of Edmund, she briefly leaned her cheek against his touch before he dropped his hand. "Keeping the amulet wasn't a terrible idea."

"Not that any of us could've predicted this," Lord Zhoqa reminded her. He shook his head, eyebrows furrowed in confusion. "Does this mean the prophecy's been fulfilled? It can't be. The prophecy speaks of a hero of western blood, and Edea presented herself to an Akkinorian."

Aurelia felt Arian eyeing her, but she didn't acknowledge it. "Prophecies have always been told in ancient tongues," she offered. "Perhaps it was a mistranslation."

"It doesn't matter," Arian added, quick to change the subject. "A goddess returned to the realm today, my friends. If the prophecy hasn't yet been fulfilled, it will be—soon."

Silence rang out as Aurelia and her allies sat in a private room in the infirmary wing at the Palace of Taundosa. She was sitting on the edge of Jack's bed while the others either stood or claimed chairs around them. The rest of the injured were gathered in the main corridor of the infirmary, with the mages and healers paying special attention to the Akkinorians so they'd survive the voyage home.

By the time everyone returned to the palace, word had already spread of Edea's visit. Aurelia heard servants in passing whispering about what they thought they'd seen: a shooting star. That was over an hour ago, so by now, everyone would've known that it wasn't a shooting star, but the goddess of the moon.

"How's Halvor?" Diantha said suddenly.

Aurelia blinked at her. "Just fine. I still don't know what the mages did to him, but he seems to have recovered fully. Edom visited the place Halvor landed when he fell—apparently, there's a city-sized hole in the earth near the coastline. One village was demolished. I-I'm sorry about the damage."

Diantha waved a dismissive hand. "There hasn't been fresh drinking water in that part of Dofell in decades. Perhaps a water mage can assist me in turning the crater into a lake. The village was probably abandoned, anyway. It's practically uninhabitable over there."

"I'll send coin to help you rebuild the kingdom," Aurelia offered. The others muttered in agreement. "It won't be much, but it will help you get started. We promised to guide you through this process, and I intend on keeping that promise."

"We'll all do what we can," Lord Zhaaran added. "Dofell was once the heart of this continent. We'd all like to see it returned to such a status. Anything you might need, Your Majesty, Orestes will provide to you."

"And Taundosa." Reyna's eyes sparkled as she met Diantha's gaze. "Although, if our faith in Edea hasn't been misplaced, you may not need as much help as we think."

Aurelia grinned. While there were certain problems that couldn't be remedied without coin—like repairing or constructing homes, buildings, roads, and so on—others had a way of solving themselves now that the Phyres had handed Dofell over to Diantha. The curse had affected a number of things, and now that it was broken, each of those issues would be resolved on their own: fresh water would be safe for consumption again; sickness would stop plaguing livestock and, subsequently, humans; soil would become fertile again, allowing the Dofelli to grow and sell their own crops; and medicines would reach patients' hands instead of disappearing as soon as the vials were filled.

Those four things alone would give the Dofelli the strength they needed to find their footing. If Edea was kind, then perhaps she'd even bless them with a few unexpected gifts, too. Either way, Diantha would have more than enough to worry about in the near future, and the same woes would certainly be passed down to her eldest child after her death. Luckily for the Pharoses, the allies were prepared to help them—not because they owed anything to Dofell (quite the opposite), but because the kingdom's good, innocent people had suffered long enough.

"Lord Cristos will see to it that you and your family are settled here in Taundosa for the time being," Reyna said to Diantha. "It'll take some time for each of us to recover from the battle, but as soon as we have, we'll gather again to organize your coronation and assist in your transition. For now, though, we all need to rest. Dofell can wait a few days longer before official plans are set in motion."

Diantha smiled. "Thank you. And what of the Phyres?"

"Already handled." Aurelia smiled as Edom appeared on the other side of Jack's bed, sitting cross-legged against Jack's thigh. "Edom delivered a letter to the king on my behalf before we set out for the wall. I've invited the king and his family to live in a small earldom in the kingdom of Sadia. They'll always have a place to live and a hearth to keep them warm, but every other aspect of their lifestyle will be in their hands. That's what the king wishes for."

"They'll be all right," Jack said with a yawn. "Eventually."

Aurelia smiled and brushed a sweaty curl from his forehead. "Let's give you some time to rest."

He nodded, already groggy, as she pressed a light kiss to his lips. As soon as she stood, Edom zipped from the bed to perch on her shoulder while she and the others followed Reyna out of the infirmary.

Aurelia tried not to look at the wounded soldiers while they exited the infirmary wing. Half of the bodies on the beds had already been covered with sheets, and the ones still breathing hadn't stopped screaming or moaning in pain since they were injured. The mages and medics were doing their best, but the injuries were far more horrific than anyone had prepared for—a consequence of a battle fought with magic.

The casualties had been worse for the other side, but that wasn't Aurelia or her allies' concern. She hoped Harryn was adjusting to his new responsibilities and taking care of his people.

The group went their separate ways when they reached the foyer. Reyna was desperate to see her children, Arian needed to speak with the General of the Goldmen about their casualties, and the Bozari lords had to depart for their kingdom to update their counterparts. By the time they left, only Aurelia and Diantha remained.

Aurelia raised an eyebrow. "Care to promenade?"

"To where?"

"The washroom."

Diantha stifled a laugh. Aurelia offered her arm to Dofell's queen and turned toward the staircase, but just as they began to climb, a group of

Akkinorians passed them on their way to the main entrance. They'd clearly come from the infirmary, as they were carrying six bodies wrapped in sheets. The bodies were destined for wagons waiting outside, and the wagons were destined for two Akkinorian ships reserved for carrying the dead back home.

Aurelia's throat felt thick. "Jack arrived here with fifteen-hundred men. We're taking six hundred home with us, as of now."

"Anyone you know?"

"A few."

"I'm sorry."

"It could've been worse."

Diantha nodded, but her head quickly jerked up when Halvor's shrieking from outside rattled the palace. Aurelia studied her, but she was unable to decipher the look on Diantha's face.

"He takes a bit of getting used to," Aurelia said as they reached the top of the stairs. "He'd never harm you, though. He knows we're friends."

"Are we?"

Aurelia bristled. "Well, I—"

"I think I know what they did to him." Diantha's cheeks had turned pink by then, so Aurelia knew she was trying to change the subject. "I-I read about it once. There's a spell in the Book of Hega. It's a spell book that requires the use of dark magic."

Aurelia furrowed her eyebrows. "What's the spell?"

"It floods the veins of any living creature with a substance that's toxic to that particular species. For a fire dragon like Halvor, I assume they filled his veins with ice. That wouldn't have killed him, though. Not like King Willem expected. I read about one instance in which a nymph's veins were filled with wax. Any manmade substance—even composed of natural materials—was toxic to nymphs. Only natural products in their raw, untouched state were safe for them to touch or consume. The effects of the spell killed *her* instantly, but dragons are stronger than nymphs."

Aurelia opened the door to her suite and led Diantha into the washroom. Luckily, her handmaidens had already been there, and they'd left a basin of water and clean cloths behind. She motioned for Diantha to join her at the basin, as the both of them—even though Diantha hadn't fought—were covered in ashes, dirt, and blood.

As she thought about the spell, something else struck her as odd. "You called Halvor a *fire dragon*," she said as she dunked a cloth in the water. "What does that mean?"

Diantha's eyes flashed up to hers. "Not all dragons breathe fire. Some are...different," she muttered. Aurelia said nothing as she brought the cloth to her chest to clean the blood from Willem's sword. Diantha eyed her and did the same. "What kind of dragon is he, specifically?"

Aurelia's lips parted. "How do you mean?"

"Is he an ironwing, a longbelly—?"

"I, uh...I don't know."

Diantha blinked at her and retracted her hands from the basin. "You've had him all this time, and you don't know anything about him?"

Aurelia felt her cheeks warm, but she knew Diantha wasn't trying to shame or embarrass her, so she proceeded like the two were friends— exactly as she'd said earlier.

"The circumstances surrounding my bond with him are unique," Aurelia said carefully. "I haven't had the chance to learn more about dragonkind since I released him. I did a bit of research when I first learned about him, but the texts accessible to me were less about dragonkind and more about how humans interacted with dragons. I didn't...I didn't even know there were different species. How do *you* know that?"

Diantha flushed and averted her gaze. "I've been cleaning the Bank of Dofell for decades now. The library crumbled years ago, so they moved every surviving text to the bank for safekeeping. I taught myself to read during my breaks. There were quite a few texts about dragons and ancient magic."

"I see."

"I'm guessing you don't know much about dragonriding either, then?" Diantha pressed. Aurelia only stared in response, and to her surprise, Diantha released a somewhat sardonic chuckle. "You'll have to dedicate more time to researching your own power, Your Grace. You have no idea what you—and Halvor—are truly capable of."

"I—"

"Don't you have mages at your court? Priests at the monastery at your beck and call? They can tell you close to everything."

Aurelia fought the urge to snap when she replied, "Magic only returned to Akkinor five years ago, and it's been a painstakingly slow process. Even after Halvor was released...It's been difficult to find people willing to talk about magic and magical creatures. They still reject it, even now, after everything. I suppose I was wary of the backlash I'd face by asking such questions."

Diantha sighed in a way that was nothing short of pitiful. "You're desperate for magic to exist in Akkinor as it once did, but you've never lived with it. You didn't grow up with it. I'll bet your palace keeps limited records about magic, too, based on what I know about your country's participation in the persecution. You have the greatest magic in the world at your fingertips, yet you've refused to learn about it because it's foreign in your homeland. If you want to change things for the better, you have to swallow your discomfort and embrace magic for what it is. That's the only way you'll achieve what you want."

Aurelia's back stiffened as she dunked the now-filthy cloth into the basin again. The water was already murky, but she could still feel the blood of the dead staining her skin, and cleaning it off with dirty water was better than letting it linger.

When she flicked her hair over her shoulder to wash behind her ears, she realized Edom had left. She didn't know where the sprite went, but she knew that wherever it was, it was listening.

"Magic isn't as prevalent in Dofell as it used to be," Diantha continued, "but it's still there, if you know where to look. I've seen it almost every day from people who use my kingdom as a walking trail. They come from all around, never staying for long, and they're all capable of doing remarkable things. I was fortunate to have access to the texts at the bank, because just a glimpse of their abilities made me want to know more about them—and I wasn't in a position that required me to know everything about them."

If possible, Aurelia's face grew even hotter. "Your Majesty, I—"

"I'll leave you be."

Diantha set her used cloth on the table holding the basin, flashed a forced smile, and left without another word.

Somewhere in the distance, Halvor shrieked, and for the first time since the day they met, she wasn't sure what he was feeling. Aurelia couldn't help but wonder if he was trying to tell her something—something he was missing, that she hadn't bothered to consider until a queen born as a peasant forced her to acknowledge her ignorance.

XLVII

The next five days felt like the slowest of Aurelia's life—but at the same time, like they'd come and gone in the blink of an eye.

On the first full day after the battle ended, the allies tested their theory about the curse by visiting the Palace of Dofell. They'd all watched in silence, hearts pounding with nerves, as King Elrin trembled on the other side of the fractured wall separating Dofell from Taundosa. Dofelli and Taundosan civilians alike watched from their respective sides of the border, too, while exchanging frightened murmurs about the king's feet touching the ground. As Elrin took one wobbly step over the threshold, holding his breath, it felt like the entire realm was standing still.

He'd taken one step, and then another, and then another—all without blood seeping from his nose, eyes, and ears. He'd relaxed so much that he nearly fell to the ground and wept, but he'd managed to regain his composure while the rest of his family followed suit. In a matter of minutes, the entire Phyre family was standing on Taundosan soil, alive and well.

The whooping and cheering that followed was perhaps the only time in Elrin's life that he'd ever been celebrated for something. Aurelia had been glad to see it; he deserved that much after years of being scorned for something he'd had no part in.

The Phyres were then escorted to Reyna's palace, where they'd remain until they left with Aurelia and her troops to start new lives in Akkinor. Before they climbed into the carriage, though, Elrin had approached Diantha and knelt before her as best he could. He didn't meet her gaze until she took his chin and lifted his head, and even from several feet away, Aurelia saw tears streaming down the king's cheeks.

FORGED IN ASHES

He'd removed his crown and held it out for her. "I, Elrin Ophelos Phyre, Third of My Name, King of Dofell, humbly abdicate the throne in an effort to salvage what remains of my kingdom. I entrust the crown to Diantha Amarylla Pharos, First of Her Name, Queen of Dofell. May the Almighty Edea bless you as you lead our kingdom to greatness."

Smiling, Diantha urged him to rise. "Thank you, Your Majesty. Your faith in me means more than I can say."

"Dofell may not be the Great City any longer, but—"

"That's all right." Diantha curtsied to him as one last show of respect. "We are the City of Refuge now."

The grin that'd spread over the former king's face was nothing short of heart-wrenching, but in a good way.

As Elrin led his family to the carriage, looking ten years younger, he stopped in front of Aurelia when he saw her extended hands. He'd accepted her hands without a second thought, eyes still glassy with tears.

"Thank you," he'd whispered.

She'd squeezed his hands and smiled at him. "We keep our promises in Akkinor, my friend. You shall have the fresh start you requested all those weeks ago. I can't promise that life will be easy—"

"That's all right. I don't want it, or need it, to be happy." Elrin blushed when she leaned up on her toes to kiss his cheek, then released her hands so he could bow to her. "Thank you again, my queen."

When the Phyres left, the next phase began. Despite her insistence that her feet *would* touch the ground, regardless of custom, Dofelli soldiers helped Diantha onto a palanquin before carrying her over the border. This wasn't to respect the custom, though—it was merely to parade her around the kingdom so her subjects could catch a glimpse of their new queen, raised high in the air for all to see.

Diantha's husband and three children had trailed behind her, guarded on either side, while Aurelia and her allies followed. As they crossed the kingdom, Aurelia noticed a few oddities—oddities that filled her heart with warmth and hope.

Wildflowers had begun sprouting through thick layers of sludge. Patches of brown, stiff grass had started turning green and lush again. The dark clouds that seemed to hang over Dofell indefinitely had rolled away, revealing blue skies and warm sunlight. The kingdom's largest population of living creatures—rats—scurried out of homes and establishments, only to disappear into sewer grates like something was calling them away.

What'd caught Aurelia's eye more than anything, though, came from up above. While watching Halvor circle overhead, she spotted something near the sun: the outline of a crescent moon. She'd never seen the sun and

440

moon adjacent to one another before, and she'd certainly never seen the moon in broad daylight.

It was Arian who'd voiced what she already knew: "Edea and Gianla, the sun goddess, are twins. It's said that their divine entities were born as one, but they split into separate beings at some point. They're opposites in every way, so many scholars debate the nature of their relationship. Some believe they despise one another, and others believe their bond is unbreakable."

Aurelia's lips curled into a smile. "Is it a coincidence that they just so happen to be the Almighties of neighboring kingdoms?"

The childlike wonder she loved so much illuminated his dark eyes. "Nothing in this world is a coincidence, my dear. Everything has happened as it should've." A laugh shook his body. "'The sun never sleeps in the City of Gold.' What do you make of that now?"

Her answer had been immediate: "'The moon never wanes in the City of Refuge.'"

Arian had grinned unabashedly.

Not long after, Diantha had welcomed the allies into her new home— and none of them fell victim to a fit of madness when they crossed the threshold. There weren't many people in attendance other than those who'd fought for Dofell in battle, but they'd gathered in the palace's throne room for Diantha's crowning, anyway. Even in a near-empty room, a powerful aura fell over everyone while the Elder of Dofell officially proclaimed Diantha Pharos as Dofell's new queen.

"We shall have a proper ceremony—and a celebration—after we've recovered a bit," Reyna had said after the crowning. She'd curtsied to Diantha not out of obligation, but out of respect. "Congratulations, Your Majesty."

While Diantha beamed, Aurelia added, "While I won't be in attendance, I shall send tokens of my support from Akkinor, along with the coin I promised. Perhaps—"

"—we might come to an arrangement of sorts?" A clever, playful smile formed on Diantha's lips. Aurelia couldn't help but laugh at that. "I can't promise that it'll be a quick development, but I won't let it stray from my mind. An alliance with Akkinor is exactly what Dofell needs."

Before Aurelia could reply, Diantha surprised her by pulling her into an embrace. She hesitated to return it, unsure about Diantha's opinions of her after the last conversation they'd had about Halvor, but eventually wrapped her arms around the new queen. She was opening her mouth to say something when Diantha murmured in her ear:

"Remember what we talked about, Your Grace, and don't forget that a dragon is only as strong as the bond he shares with his rider." Her hands tightened on Aurelia's shoulders as Aurelia stiffened. "Your souls have always been united, but...he'll never fully understand you unless *you* understand *him*."

Then, in the time it took Aurelia to blink, Diantha released her and bounded across the room to reunite with her family. Aurelia was left standing there, agape, not fully able to comprehend what she'd just been told—or why the message had been delivered by Diantha, of all people.

It was the last time Aurelia would speak to Diantha face-to-face for over three years.

On the second day after the battle, Harryn Trevas met the allies at Reyna's palace to confirm that he'd been crowned King of Kanibar. He brought Aurelia a message from Maysa, too, but made her promise not to read it until she was home in Akkinor—an instruction sent by Maysa herself. In exchange, Aurelia gave something to Harryn to be delivered to Maysa as a thank-you for her guidance and support: Willem's family ring, which one of her soldiers recovered from the remains of the late king's body when it finally stopped smoldering. Though Maysa would undoubtedly hand the ring over to Harryn, Aurelia knew the oracle would understand the message behind it: *I did what you asked.*

The third day was a bit slower, so Aurelia took advantage of it by bringing her children on a day-long trip to Ardiham Castle in Agotia. They were too young to know that this was their ancestral home—they couldn't keep a secret if their lives depended on it, which, in this case, they did—but she'd wanted them to see it, nonetheless. She'd introduced them to Katryna, Dyron, and Sylvina Cristos only as Arian's sister and parents. One day, though, the children would stand across from the portraits and urns of their late relatives, knowing exactly who they were.

On the fourth day, Aurelia assisted Rayan in preparing for departure. Since the battle, the surviving soldiers had turned to Rayan for leadership—not on Aurelia's word, and not because Rayan had appointed himself as a commanding voice, but because the survivors *chose* to listen to him. He hadn't seemed to think anything of it, but Aurelia certainly did.

Aurelia helped him oversee the packing and equipping of Akkinor's fleet, mainly because she wanted the survivors to know that she was right there with them, instead of relaxing in a golden palace while they labored. With so many casualties, they were forced to abandon a few ships at the Taundosan harbor, as there weren't enough soldiers to crew all of them. One ship in particular carried several herds of Orestean sheep as a fulfillment of Lord Zhaaran's promise to Aurelia, and she'd used every ounce of strength in her body to command Halvor to ignore the ship instead of feasting on his prey.

The very same ship that would carry the royal family home to Akkinor would be carrying two other important individuals, too. Ansyl was removed from the Taundosan dungeon on the fourth day, then transferred to the ship's brig to await departure. He hadn't said a word when the soldiers escorted him to the ship, and when he'd passed Aurelia on his trek, the only thing he'd managed to do was hang his head in shame.

Aurelia had given Edom the choice to stay in Carthe with its kin or return to Akkinor, and it had chosen the latter. The sprite had only this to say when she asked why: "You are my home now."

She was glad Edom was staying with her, even if a sprite in Akkinor wasn't commonplace. Pesky little creature or not, Edom had become a member of her family.

By the time the sky darkened on that fourth day, the number of Akkinorian soldiers set to return home dropped from six hundred to less than five hundred. Aurelia didn't feel right about delivering stinking, decomposed bodies back to their families, so she decided to invent a new practice—one that she felt would've been easier on the mourners, even if it wasn't exactly customary.

At dawn on the morning of their departure, the deceased were placed on massive funeral pyres, while a Taundosan priest delivered a sermon to guide their souls into the heavens. After the sermon, Halvor ignited the pyres, and within an hour, nothing remained but smoldering wood and bones.

Every Akkinorian soldier, mage or mortal, was required to carry a bronze medallion engraved with their name, rank, and legion in the military. The medallions were carefully packaged with each soldier's suit of armor in individual wooden crates, which would be delivered to the families in place of bodies. Anyone with access to Aurelia's ear—even Jack—suggested repurposing the valuable Akkinorian bronze armor, but Aurelia wouldn't have it. Each suit belonged only to the person who'd worn it and died in it; it was only right, she thought, that she lay them to rest while honoring their service and sacrifice.

Luckily, Jack was well enough to sail by the time the funeral ended, the ships were prepared for departure, and everything was sorted out amongst the allies. Aurelia didn't wish to delay their return any longer, so after saying goodbye to Carthe and its people once more, she led her family aboard their ship: *The Dragon's Revenge*.

Now, Aurelia stood in her cabin aboard the ship, watching through the porthole as Taundosa grew smaller and smaller in the distance. Behind her, Jack was half asleep in their massive bed, taking advantage of the peacefulness while their children were above deck. It was fortunate that Rayan was traveling aboard *The Dragon's Revenge*, too: he continued to prove himself as a selfless, loyal subject when he observed Aurelia and Jack's exhaustion, then volunteered to mind the children while they explored the ship.

The door to their cabin had been cracked open, but it widened with an unforeseen breeze as a golden glow zipped inside. Jack grunted when Edom landed on his chest, but didn't bother scolding the creature for disturbing him.

"Sisi is very clever," Edom shared, sitting cross-legged on Jack's chest. "She speaks of Halvor's former mistresses and their adventures. Your people think she's telling tales."

Aurelia chuckled. "Of course they do. They'd never suspect..." Her face went slack when a realization struck her, prompting her to meet Jack's gaze. "Do you know what's odd? Willem had every opportunity to expose me on that battlefield. He could've told everyone about who my real parents are. He could've told them about Hyacinth, too, but he didn't. My own allies would've turned their backs on me for lying to them, and everything would've fallen apart. That alone could've ensured his success. Why do you think he kept quiet about it?"

"Does it matter?" Jack yawned. "He's dead, and his silence was probably the only decent thing he's ever done. Let's leave it at that."

Aurelia shook her head. "It doesn't make sense."

Jack scrubbed a hand down his face and sighed. "I don't know, my love. Maybe he was hoping to torture you."

"How so?"

"He knew that you knew everything he'd uncovered. He had complete control over you in that way. Perhaps he thought it would torment you, knowing he could expose you at any moment."

"I wasn't even thinking about it," she admitted. "It only just occurred to me. He knew I possessed the amulet, too, but he didn't do anything about *that*, either. Ser Rhys..."

She trailed off when she remembered the first life claimed on the battlefield. Halvor had reclaimed Rhys's body after the battle ended, and he'd been returned to Kanibar with the other remains, but Aurelia would have to send word to his sister—after all, Sora wouldn't know that Rhys was dead, because nobody in the capital knew that the pair were related.

"He chose to view you as weak, Aurelia. That was his downfall." Jack beckoned her over to him, so she crawled into bed beside him and took his hands. "If Ser Rhys told Willem what you instructed him to about the amulet...Would Willem really believe it? I don't think so. I think he'd choose to believe that you fed Rhys the kind of lie that would frighten a king. He'd never believe that such power would end up in your hands. It didn't fit the image he'd created of you—or himself, for the matter."

"I suppose. Something still doesn't feel right, though. Willem had so many opportunities to destroy me, and he didn't take them."

"It wasn't entertaining enough that way. Not for him. It was never about destroying you. It was always about becoming a god, a savior—a hero."

Aurelia sighed and stroked her thumb over his. "It was all one big game, wasn't it?"

"It was, but the gods chose you to win it. That's what matters."

For now, she thought.

"A part of me wishes I hadn't let Halvor kill him," she admitted. Jack scowled as his hands tensed beneath hers. "There are so many things I want to know that only he could tell me. I suppose Maysa might know some of it, but there's no telling how much she'll be willing to share."

"I'll admit," he said, yawning, "I found it odd that he didn't deploy the sprites. Kanibar is crawling with them, and while they're more useful as spies, they can also pose a great threat in battle." He looked around the room and exhaled, just now realizing that Edom had left his chest. "Come here, sprite."

Aurelia gave him a look. "It has a name."

He rolled his eyes. "Come here, *Edom.*" The sprite appeared on the edge of the bed, sitting cross-legged, and offered Jack a snarky grin. "Do you happen to know why your kin weren't summoned to battle?"

Edom shrugged. "They refused."

"He would've threatened them somehow if that were true."

As the sprite hissed at him, Aurelia shook her head. "They hid all those years to survive the persecution, and surely they would have done so again if it came down to it."

"Or, they're loyal to others in Kanibar who protected them," Jack offered. "We've seen that time and time again with Halvor, with Lady Swann's gryphons..."

"I'm sure more of them will emerge in the future, too. Creatures of all kinds." Aurelia smiled at the idea, but a part of her was uneasy about it. "Let's just hope that they come back to help us better the realm instead of helping us slaughter one another. I've had quite enough of that."

"We only want peace," Edom claimed.

"It doesn't matter what you want," Jack retorted. "A significant portion of magical species are known for bonding with humans. Dragons, phoenixes—even sprites. When loyalty has been assured, most creatures find themselves incapable of disobeying or betraying the human they've bonded to. Even if they disagree with commands given by their master or mistress...They'd rather die than break that bond."

Edom didn't answer, so Aurelia knew Jack was right. It got her thinking about what Diantha had said to her, too: *A dragon is only as strong as the bond he shares with his rider.* Diantha had given her an awful lot to think about since the battle ended, and still, Aurelia had no idea what to make of it.

When the time came, though, Halvor would help her understand what she was meant to do. She was sure of it.

***

"I'll take this one." Nyla wrapped her bony fingers around a polished, golden doorknob. "I'll be fine on my own. You can help the others with the late king's chambers."

Eira raised an eyebrow. "Are you sure?"

"Positive."

Eira nodded and scampered off, following the handful of other servants trickling into King Willem's former bedchamber. It'd only been a short time since news broke of his loss on the battlefield—and since the new king, a young man called Harryn, arrived at the Palace of Kanibar—but they'd been ordered to clear his things away immediately, nonetheless.

At least Harryn hadn't fired the lot of them. Maybe he would, eventually, but for now, the last thing he seemed to care about was what his new staff thought of his late uncle.

Nyla slipped into the room by her lonesome and locked the door behind her. She inhaled the familiar scent of musk and maple, and the lingering aroma of burnt nutmeg and citrus that seemed to have melted into the walls. When she spotted a cloak hanging over the back of a chair near the hearth, she lifted it and brought it to her nose, her eyes welling with tears as she bunched the fabric in her fists.

"Oh, Dayne." She closed her eyes and sniffled. "I'm so sorry, my love."

She took a moment to mourn him, but quickly remembered the task at hand. After dropping the coat on the chair, she followed the verbal instructions Dayne had given her before he left for battle. She stood with the back of her legs pressed against his bed, then took four steps forward until the floorboards squeaked beneath her. She bent down to lift two of them, where she found a small chest in the niche below.

Nyla knelt on the floor and reached into her corset, where an iron key rested between her breasts. She unlocked the chest, hoping to find some sort of gift from her beloved in addition to the object he'd told her about, and swallowed disappointment when she found nothing but a lone letter inside. She'd been carefully instructed to deliver the letter by her own hand—no messengers and no ravens—but when she saw who it was addressed to, she realized she should've asked Dayne for more information before agreeing to complete the task.

In King Willem's handwriting, five words were printed on the parchment: *Amarion Selle, Lord of Bruila.*

Nyla knew she wasn't meant to read the contents of the letter, but if she'd be risking her life to deliver it to Krotis, she *had* to know what was so important—important enough that King Willem needed to trust not only Dayne, but someone else, to deliver it in his place if he died in battle.

As she unfolded the parchment and read the brief message, a laugh gurgled in her throat. She fell from her knees and onto her bottom as she leaned against Dayne's nightstand, breathless, while folding the parchment into a square again.

"It looks like that wretched queen and her beast will get what they deserve soon enough." As if Queen Aurelia could hear her, Nyla grinned and added, "You're in for a treat, Your Grace."

XLVIII

Once more, Aurelia knew she was dreaming as soon as it began. She'd fallen asleep in her bed on the ship, and the next thing she knew, she was opening her eyes to find herself facing a blazing hearth in one of the palace's parlors. She was perched in an armchair, and Hyacinth was curled up in her arms, fast asleep. She blinked, not understanding how the pair of them got there, and gasped when a voice accompanied the sound of crackling firewood:

"I'm surprised you still have your pretty smile. I saw the Kanish giant plant his fist on your face."

She sucked in a sharp breath as she turned to the left. Archie was sitting in an armchair identical to hers, body swiveled so he was facing her, with his elbow propped on the armrest and his face leaning in his hand.

Aurelia shivered and held her daughter closer. "You saw that?"

"Mhm. She did, too."

His eyes flickered down to Hyacinth as Aurelia did the same. She wanted him to be wrong, but she knew he wasn't. Hyacinth had seen more than Aurelia knew, and more than a little girl ought to.

He dropped his hand from his face and raised an eyebrow. "Did you know her name means *sorrow?*"

"No, it doesn't."

"Yes, it does."

"It *doesn't.*"

"It *does.*"

She resisted the urge to smile at that. There they were, bickering like any other brother and sister might. As good as it felt for a moment, she couldn't forget their history, not even in a dream.

At her silence, he said, "*Your* name means *golden one.*"

Another shudder ravaged her. "I didn't know that."

"I did."

She felt like he'd punched her in the gut. It was strange, hearing him acknowledge that he was dead, but at the same time, she was glad that he sounded like he'd made peace with it.

"It's like Mother and Father forged the path to this destiny you've found yourself tethered to." He turned his gaze to the hearth as a distant, bitter look flashed over his face. "Like they knew exactly what you'd become."

Aurelia swallowed the lump in her throat. "Why have you come to see me again, brother?"

He grinned as his eyes flicked back to hers. "You could come see me, too, you know. I know I did horrible things to you, but would it kill you to visit once in a while?"

"That's ridiculous and you know it," she snapped. She softened when Hyacinth stirred in her lap. "You know I can't visit you, even if I wanted to."

"You can. You just haven't figured it out yet."

"What does *that* mean?"

He gave her a look as if to say, *Come on, Li. You can do better than that.*

"I think I'm being sent here to warn you." When he finally gave her an answer of substance, she straightened up as well as she could. He grimaced, averting his gaze from hers, and stared into the crackling flames. "There's something you ought to be ready for in the near future. It'll be a few years, but it'll come, and you'll need to be prepared."

Aurelia snorted. "Is that all?"

"That's all I'm permitted to know. I'm sure your friend can tell you more—the Queen Mother whose family line you nearly furthered."

Maysa. She cleared her throat and tucked a lock of hair behind her ear. "Why you? Of everyone in the afterlife, why were *you* sent here to warn me? It seems rather ironic, given the circumstances."

She'd almost expected him to laugh at that, but he didn't. He only looked at her in a way that chilled her to her bones.

"Because I'm the last person you'd expect to be here trying to save your life. So maybe, just maybe, you'll believe me."

Her lips parted. "A-Archie—"

"Three cycles after the moon falls from the sky, the Four Pillars shall emerge from the shadows, and their return shall mark the end of the beginning."

"*Archie—*"

Just then, Hyacinth's eyes snapped open, and before Aurelia knew what was happening, the little princess sat up and placed her hands on either side of her mother's face. Aurelia's neck whipped backwards as she gasped, and her vision was corrupted by flashing scenes of a battle yet to come. She only caught bits and pieces of it, but that was enough.

Silver claws against golden ones. A hurricane of flames swallowing a ship. A green, reptilian eye. A teenage girl with her face covered by a scarf. Boots marching across desert sand. A young woman with white hair kneeling before a tree. A golden cup on a stone pedestal. A crown drowning in a pool of blood.

Her brother's name was forming on her lips when the world around her faded to black, sucking her out of the land of dreams and throwing her back into the land of the living. She could almost feel herself reaching out to him as she was dragged through the darkness—reaching out in desperation for the last person she ever thought she would.

Aurelia woke with a gasp to the sound of blaring horns. She sat upright, panting for air, and realized she was back in her room on the ship with Jack beside her—not Archie. The horns blared again, making her flinch, but Jack only groaned and folded a pillow around his head to drown out the noise. He'd be sleeping again in seconds, but after talking to her brother, Aurelia had no desire to meet with the god of dreams again.

As she climbed out of bed and padded over to a porthole, she heard a female voice she vaguely recognized echoing in her head, humming the melody of a song she'd never heard. At the same time, the last sentence Archie had uttered played on a loop—almost like the two sounds were at war with one another.

She opened the porthole, a calm gust of wind blowing through her hair as she did so, and peered out at the ship's path ahead. The horns continued blaring as sailors above deck clamored in preparation to dock, having spotted their first glimpse of land in the near distance: Seaport.

As Archie's words and the woman's lullaby flooded her thoughts, Aurelia slipped her hand through the porthole and smiled when salty spray tickled her fingers. The air felt different now that the ship was inching closer to Akkinor—and yet, so did everything else. Nothing would be the same now that one of the Twelve had presented herself to Akkinor's queen.

***

"Where are you, Edom? Come out and play!"

Hyacinth giggled and scoured the carriage for the little creature, but it was impossible to find Edom when the sprite wasn't glowing. Aurelia chuckled when a lock of Hyacinth's hair lifted from her shoulder, making the young princess shriek in delight and grasp at the air. Beside her, Halle gasped when Edom landed atop her head, leading both girls to break out in fits of giggles when the sprite finally perched on Aurelia's knee.

Halle held a hand out, prompting Edom to scurry onto her palm. "You're silly, Edom," she said as the sprite teased her by dangling from her fingers. "Where were you hiding?"

"I visited Henry and baby Lena."

The heir to the Akkinorian throne poked her head through the window to examine the carriage trailing theirs. Aurelia mimicked her and smiled when she saw Henry dangling out the window of his carriage—held around the waist by Irina—and waving at his family.

"I want Henry to ride with us," Halle complained.

Jack snorted. "When we docked, the two of you were quarreling like feral animals. You begged us to separate you, and now you wish he were here?"

Halle muttered something under her breath as her parents chuckled. They hadn't made it to the carriages when they docked at Seaport before Halle and Henry started hollering at one another, so the Brentwoods separated into two carriages to ensure just a tiny bit of peace. Aurelia should've known her children would regret their decision, though—they always forgot what they'd been fighting about after a few minutes passed.

When the carriage jolted, likely having rolled over a stone, Jack grunted and brought a hand to his abdomen. Worried, Aurelia set her hand on his thigh and raised an eyebrow, but he merely waved a dismissive hand and offered her a reassuring—yet forced—smile.

"I'm all right," he promised. "Just a bit sore."

"You're not to do anything strenuous until the pain is completely gone." She ignored him when he scoffed at her. "I won't hear a word of your excuses. Arian and Lucyra may have prevented your death, but your recovery is yours alone to manage. If you push yourself too soon, you'll cause permanent damage."

"Heavens above, woman! *Must* you coddle me like a helpless babe?"

"You *are* a helpless babe sometimes," she retorted. Hyacinth and Halle giggled as the former held Edom on her palm between their ears, prompting Aurelia to raise an amused eyebrow. "Is something funny, girls?"

Their faces went slack as Edom disappeared from view. Halle, ever the obedient one, merely blushed and said, "Nothing, Mama."

"Fine, then. Keep it to yourselves."

Aurelia and Jack met eyes, suppressing laughter, before both turned to glance out the window to their left. They were halfway to the palace now, riding through the dense foliage separating Seaport from the heart of the

Folly. She'd traveled this path dozens upon dozens of times in the last five years alone. And yet, every time she saw it, she couldn't shake the feeling of being hunted by her brother's assassins as she fled through these trees.

When her family stepped onto the dock at Seaport, Aurelia didn't have a second to herself to bask in the joy of returning home. They were immediately surrounded by civilians—but instead of asking after their loved ones who fought in battle, this particular swarm was interested in hearing about Edea's arrival on Thurran Valley. A soldier had written a letter to his wife about the encounter, who then told their family, who then told their friends, neighbors, and coworkers. Everyone who heard of it had been relaying the message along in the weeks that'd passed since the troops began their voyage home, so if the whole of Akkinor didn't know about it yet, they would soon enough.

Aurelia was certain that everyone knew about who she'd brought home with her, too. Between the royal family's carriages and the sea of troops behind them, the Phyre family was riding to the Folly, where they'd stay for a few days until their new lodgings in Sadia were ready.

As soon as the carriages and the surviving soldiers left the forest behind, Aurelia spotted hundreds, if not thousands, of Follian civilians gathered on the streets. They would've done so regardless of Edea's visit as a means of welcoming their queen home after a great victory, but with a goddess involved now, they had something even greater to celebrate.

For the first time, the people of the Folly weren't gawking at Halvor flying over their heads, but rather marveling at the royal family, the Dofelli refugees, and the surviving war heroes as they waved and attempted to catch the favors thrown in their direction.

Flower petals lined the cobblestone road as civilians flanked every inch of the path, shouting adoring words and blessings until they were blue in the face. Children were perched on their fathers' shoulders and waving small flags bearing the new Akkinorian sigil. Women threw handkerchiefs at Rayan, who was leading the surviving soldiers on horseback, in hopes of gaining his favor. Men whistled through their teeth and cupped their hands over their mouths to whoop as loudly as they could. Even the elderly stood with the support of wooden canes, dabbing at their misty eyes with cloths and muttering prayers in Aurelia's name.

Some of them, she noticed, wore Akkinor's banners like blankets draped over their shoulders. Nearly every public establishment hung the banners over their doors, too—something she'd never seen before. What shocked her most, though, was the handful of people who waved more than one miniature flag: in their right hands, closest to their hearts, was the Akkinorian flag; and in their left hands were flags bearing the sigils of Taundosa, Orestes, Kazamir, and Runeia, too.

Her voice threatened to fail her when she stammered, "D-Do you see—?"

"The flags." Jack nodded, blue eyes twinkling, and continued waving at the commonfolk. "I think they've finally accepted Akkinor's partnership with Carthe. We have Edea to thank for that. It's fortunate she came when she did—Ansyl's betrayal could've persuaded them to hate Carthe even more." He nodded his head toward the window. "They may not know about the prophecy, but they *do* know that a goddess visited their queen in Carthe. That's worth about as much as knowing the prophecy has been fulfilled."

Aurelia cracked a smile. "Your ancestors must be beaming down upon us, *Mister Sherbourne*."

That made him laugh. "Oh, yes. They knew this day would come, even if I myself often doubted it."

The alias Jack had chosen for himself in Carthe—*Sherbourne*—meant *light-bringer* in the ancient tongue. His ancestors had utilized the word when speaking of a day of great promise when divinity returned to the realm. Though Jack never believed in that ideology, he knew the word held tremendous power in his family, even if he'd long since lost hope in the gods' return.

If only the Jack from ten years earlier could've been there now to see himself proven wrong.

By the time they reached the palace, the sea of people had thinned out, so only those who lived and worked in the palace were present on the bailey to welcome everyone home. The first faces Aurelia saw amongst the crowd gathered by the front steps were Thea and Mycah, who looked thrilled—if not slightly worried. They weren't certain if Ansyl had survived the battle, but they had absolutely no idea that his survival wasn't what they should've been worried about.

Aurelia had sent word about Ansyl to the Assembly members looking after Akkinor in her absence, but clearly, they hadn't relayed the message to the Bolas siblings.

"I'll take care of it." Jack spoke before Aurelia had the chance, having followed her gaze while she frowned at the siblings. "They shouldn't be here to watch him escorted to the dungeon, regardless of what he did. That's not an image they should have of their brother."

"Thank you." Aurelia sighed in relief before turning to her antsy daughters. "Follow your father inside, and help Irina and Celesse unpack your things."

They nodded as Edom perched itself on Halle's shoulder, making both girls giggle again. They met up with their siblings and governesses when they followed Jack out of the bailey, but separated from their father when he approached Thea and Mycah. Aurelia held her breath and watched as Jack turned the siblings away toward the palace doors, a hand on either of their shoulders, until all of them disappeared into the foyer.

When Aurelia exited the carriage, she immediately summoned the palace stewardess and instructed her to situate the Phyres in their temporary lodgings. As the Phyres were escorted into the palace, the very last carriage in the caravan—the only one that'd been trailing behind the surviving soldiers, not in front of them—rolled to a stop in the bailey. Three knights emerged first, followed by Ansyl, and the latter didn't so much as look up from the ground as the knights led him toward the dungeon.

As soon as Ansyl, the children, and the Phyres were gone, Aurelia turned to face her expectant soldiers. It was customary for troops to wait until their commander delivered a final address before they were dismissed from their duties and sent home, but she knew her speech would have to be a short one. They were visibly exhausted, battered, and grieving the many lives that'd been lost in battle.

Aurelia took a long, deep breath as the survivors knelt before her. "The men and women standing before me today have done something we never thought possible: defended a suffering kingdom from the most formidable enemy we've faced thus far, on a continent we Akkinorians have never treated with kindness or understanding." Her hands were trembling, so she clasped them behind her back. "Each of you volunteered to do so, and for that, I thank you. Thousands of people will be given a second chance at life because of your service. I grieve your brothers and sisters in arms alongside you, and I assure you, their memories will never be forgotten. You'll receive a generous reward for your service, and the families of the deceased will receive the same. Because of your contribution, a goddess returned to the realm this year—a miracle if there ever was one. Go home to your families, and take the time you need to recover, but please, don't allow the tragedy to overcome the wondrous things you helped accomplish."

The soldiers rose, either bowed or curtsied, and murmured responses she couldn't hear before leaving the bailey. As she turned to enter the palace, desperate to wash the smell of ocean from her hair and to sleep in her own bed, she realized one soldier was still lingering: Ser Rayan Haze.

He followed her to the front steps and bowed. "Your Grace. I'd best be off, but you dropped this when you exited the carriage."

454

She furrowed her eyebrows and accepted something nestled in his fist: a folded piece of parchment. It was the message Harryn had given her on Maysa's behalf.

"Thank you." She offered him a tired smile as he tipped his head in response. "I expect to see you here again soon, ser. We have a feast to plan."

That made him laugh. "I'd be most obliged."

Rayan bowed once more before rushing off to join his fellow soldiers. Aurelia watched him go for a moment, relieved that he'd emerged from the battle unscathed, before climbing the front steps and unsealing Maysa's note. She read as she walked, careful not to bump into anything, as the familiar smell and sounds of the palace welcomed her home.

My dear child,

Thank you for putting an end to Willem's schemes. He may have been my son once, but that can never excuse the things he did or the things he would've done, had he survived.

Remember what I said: we'll meet again in due time. I'm enjoying my newfound freedom, for now, while my grandson cleans up Willem's messes. The next few years will be interesting, for certain, but they'll lead us back together again, eventually. The gods aren't done with you yet, and when they call you to action once more, I'll be here to guide you through it.

Until we meet again, I'll leave you with this message: don't trust that everything is as it seems. Everyone in the realm has powerful secrets—even those we'd never bat an eye at. Be careful, Your Grace, and don't forget that you can't trust everyone who calls you a friend.

Yours in friendship,

Maysa.

XLIX

Three days later, the entire country had learned of what'd happened in Dofell, from the crowning of Queen Diantha, to the death of King Willem, to the arrival of the moon goddess on the battlefield. Aurelia thought her subjects would insist that she dive into her domestic responsibilities as soon as she was situated in the palace again, but nobody pressured her into doing anything—they were too delighted by what'd happened in Carthe.

Despite knowing she could take a few days to enjoy the peace, Aurelia was oddly energized, and she managed to cross a few items off of her engagement diary within those first three days. The first thing she did was sign off on the order to compensate both her surviving soldiers and the families of the fallen for their service in battle, and the second was to record the names of everyone who'd fought so they could be recognized by the realm—not only in documentation, but also with an engraved stone obelisk placed in the center of the Folly.

After that, she'd sent a few letters to Carthe: one for Lord Zhoqa, to confirm in their contract that their alliance would be broken if he attempted anything like what he'd done to retrieve the amulet; one for Maysa, to respond out of respect despite not fully understanding what the oracle's message meant; and one for Diantha, to remind the new queen that Akkinor was willing to discuss a potential alliance whenever Dofell was ready for it.

Finally, the most pressing matter of all arrived: Ansyl.

Aurelia knew she couldn't hold off any longer. The people would be demanding that she name a new Lord Hand as quickly as possible, and they wouldn't stand to have a traitor lingering in the dungeon for longer than necessary.

Early in the morning on their third day at home, Aurelia and Jack left the palace to meet five others on the bailey: Thea and Mycah; two Akkinorian knights; and Lord Julien Clay, a Sadian-born nobleman living in the Folly who oversaw all matters pertaining to the punishment, execution, and exiling of criminals.

As the front doors of the palace opened, the Bolas siblings sucked in sharp breaths while Aurelia tossed a glance over her shoulder. A wagon encased in bars on all sides—except for the coachman's seat, of course—stood behind her, carrying three other prisoners destined for exile to Quapebet at the border of Vilgh-Azhor. They were chained and shackled, their heads were bowed in shame, and not one of them had uttered a word since Aurelia joined them.

Tears burned in her eyes as two knights held Ansyl by the elbows and escorted him down the stairs. Nobody moved when he was stopped just a few feet from Aurelia and the others. He kept his head bowed, refusing to meet her eyes—or his siblings' eyes—and merely stared at his shackled wrists. It was almost hard to believe that this man, unable to maintain eye contact or clean the crumbs from his beard, had once been the second-most powerful person in Akkinor.

Aurelia inhaled sharply and squared her shoulders. "As you know, today you'll depart the Folly for Vilgh-Azhor. Lord Clay here will read the terms of your exile when you arrive at your destination. When he's finished reading, your restraints will be removed, and you'll be free to do as you please with the rest of your life—so long as you never step foot on Akkinorian soil again."

Ansyl's jaw clenched as he nodded. Sighing, she turned to face his siblings, who were watching him with glassy eyes and quivering lips. She felt horrible for putting them through such pain, but she knew this was the best, and only, option. Ansyl had sealed his own fate when he agreed to serve Willem instead of Aurelia.

"As for the two of you," she murmured, "I'll offer you a choice. You can accompany your brother to Quapebet if you wish to do so. You've done nothing wrong, so Akkinor will always welcome you back if you change your minds. But if you wish to stay here in Akkinor, you may."

Thea's lips parted. "B-But—"

"Stay." Ansyl's voice was hoarse and weak, but it was still his. He finally lifted his eyes as he took a step closer to his siblings, kneeling in front of them and setting a hand on either of their arms. He was smiling, but tears welled in his dark eyes. "If you come with me, I may never have peace of mind. We'll live like we did in Kanibar: me wasting away trying to keep you alive, and you resenting me for coddling you." They protested, but he shook his head and talked over them, his smile never fading. "Here, I know you'll be taken care of. You'll always have beds to sleep in and food in your bellies. You'll be educated, trained, and inspired. The opportunities at your fingertips are endless in Akkinor, but anywhere else...I'll never be certain that I can provide for you as a brother should. I can't let you come with me when I know your chances are better here."

Mycah sniffed. "What if we want to come with you?"

"What you want isn't as important as what you need, brother. You'll learn that eventually. And you, sister..." Ansyl's smile faltered for just a moment as he reached up to cup Thea's cheek. "I know that you know you need to stay. You just don't want to admit it."

She covered his hand with hers and used the other to wipe her tears away. "I know. We'll be all right here, Ansyl. You needn't worry for us."

"You needn't worry for me, either. I'll be just fine." He cleared his throat when his voice cracked. "We'll find each other again, one day. I know we will."

Ansyl pulled both of them into an embrace, squeezing his eyes shut as his chin wobbled, before releasing them and stepping away so they couldn't cling to him. When their tutor—who'd been watching the interaction from the front steps—came over to fetch them, he gave them an encouraging nod, then watched them walk away to the palace as they spared a few final glances in his direction.

His shoulders slumped as he turned to face Aurelia and Jack. "I...I hope you can find it in your heart to forgive me someday, Your Grace. And you, Your Highness. I deeply regret my actions, and I've made peace with my fate. You didn't have to spare me, but you did." A somber glint shimmered in his eyes when he met Aurelia's gaze. "You showed me great friendship these last five years, the same friendship I now know you showed Kaia. My deepest regret is not only that I betrayed you as your Hand, but as your friend."

Aurelia maintained her composure as Jack merely glowered. "Thank you," she replied. "I wish you safe travels, and I hope you make the most of your new life. I'll tell the children you said goodbye."

His face contorted with pain, but it was gone when she blinked. "Thank you."

The knights helped him climb into the back of the wagon as Lord Clay said his goodbyes to Aurelia and Jack. While the nobleman sat beside the coachman, Ansyl sat on the floor of the wagon with his back facing Aurelia, knees drawn to his chest and arms draped over his lap.

As the carriage jolted and rolled away, Aurelia just barely heard the other prisoners muttering to Ansyl about Edea's return to the realm. His head shot up as soon as they told him, shock stiffening his body, so Aurelia knew he hadn't been told about—or even overheard—what'd happened in Dofell.

Just before the carriage passed through the gates, Halvor shrieked from above, and Ansyl craned his neck backward to marvel at the dragon.

It was the last memory Aurelia would ever have of Kaia's brother.

"I know this probably isn't the right time, but..." Jack sighed as she furrowed her eyebrows at him. "The Assembly inspected the list of potential replacements Ansyl provided. They've reached out to most of those individuals—and others of their own choosing—and summoned them to the palace. They'll be here in a few hours to make their petitions."

Aurelia sighed. "All right."

He brushed a lock of hair from her face, worry creasing his forehead. "Are you sure you're all right?"

"I'll be fine." She chewed on her lower lip as he escorted her to the front entrance. "My father ruled for five-and-twenty years, and only one Hand ever served him."

"Linden's father."

"Yes." Her face crumpled as visions of Linden played in her head, memories of his laughter nearly drowning out her thoughts. "I thought Linden would be my Hand until the day of my death. I never imagined I'd have to replace him. And now here I am, searching for a *third* Hand."

That innocent, wicked smile she loved so much formed on his lips. "Third time's a charm. Isn't that what people say?"

That made Aurelia smile, too. "Let's hope it proves to be true."

***

"I fought beside you as a mortal in the battle against your brother, then again as a mage in the battle against Kanibar. My specialty is earth magic, but I'm proficient in a number of spells, thanks to my years studying at the monastery. I've lived here in the Folly for my entire life, though both of my parents immigrated from Myra—Eldford, in fact. My mother looked after yours when your parents stayed in Eldford many years ago. They were fond of one another."

Aurelia smiled. "Have you any experience in politics?"

The middle-aged lowborn man crumpled the brim of his hat in his hands as he swallowed. "N-Not exactly, Your Grace. I have more military experience, so I'm a strong leader, and I'm prepared to educate myself as you see fit."

"Thank you, Mister Fletcher. I'll take your application into consideration."

As the man bowed and scurried off, a woman took his place. Aurelia knew the woman's face immediately: Marina Tarre, the second-eldest child of the late Lady Beverly Tarre, and the younger sister of Lord Kallan of Holos.

Just like the many others who'd come before her, Marina outlined her strengths and qualifications, passionately trying to prove herself as a worthy candidate for Hand of the Queen. Unfortunately, like the others, Aurelia didn't feel the instant connection between Marina that she'd felt with Ansyl or Linden (though her best friend didn't exactly count).

In the hours that'd passed since Ansyl departed for exile, Aurelia had listened to petition after petition, and none had swayed her. Having no candidates in mind to fulfill the role, she was left with no choice but to interview anyone hoping for the job. The number of people—highborn and lowborn alike—who'd shown up was vast, but still, there were fewer of them than she'd expected.

When the next petitioner took Marina's place, Aurelia saw something from the corner of her eye: a new arrival slipping into the throne room and observing from the back wall. Eager to speak with her half-brother again, Aurelia waited for the next candidate to finish before announcing that she was done hearing petitions for the day, and she'd resume again at dawn the next morning.

She left her advisors (most of whom were clawing at the position, too) to send the candidates home, then met Rayan in the back of the room. He seemed surprised that she'd come for him, but when she asked if he'd like to take a walk with her, he didn't hesitate to offer his arm.

"I expected more of them," he admitted as they strolled through the halls. "Now that a goddess has presented herself to you, the entire country is looking for any excuse to earn your favor."

Aurelia grimaced. "They're motivated by fame and glory, not honor or devotion. I suppose that's why I haven't found anyone yet."

"You will, Your Grace. Soon enough." He returned her smile and turned his gaze to the foyer ahead. "I've come today to ask you to abandon the feast you wished to hold on my behalf. Akkinor has already found itself drowning in reparations and celebrations alike, so honoring me for winning a joust is the last thing you should concern yourself with. Respectfully, my queen."

"No disrespect taken. That's a very thoughtful thing to do."

"Thank you, Your Grace. I only wish to—"

"How would *you* like to be my Hand?" she blurted.

When he brought them to a screeching halt and stared down at her, wild-eyed, she finally realized what she'd said. She hadn't meant to say it, nor had she heard herself when the words spewed from her lips. It just...came out.

She felt her cheeks warm with embarrassment at her outburst, but as she thought about it—and as Rayan gawked at her, speechless—she realized it wasn't an *entirely* foolish thing to say. Rayan may not have been a politician, or a businessman, or even someone with basic knowledge of royal duties, but then again, Ansyl hadn't been any of those things, either. Ansyl had served her well and faithfully until Willem corrupted him, but there was nobody alive who'd ever have that effect on Rayan.

"Your Grace, I..." Rayan trailed off, cleared his throat, and released her arm so they were facing each other. "You honor me beyond words, but I must refuse. I have no qualifications for the role. There are others better suited for it than I."

"How so?" She smiled when he continued staring at her, flabbergasted. "You're a knighted soldier, just like my first Hand. You defended my name during the war with my brother, didn't you? You're educated, too, and you beautifully executed each of my commands throughout this latest conflict. Our soldiers looked to you for guidance and inspiration in Carthe, even though you weren't responsible for them. They chose you as much as I'm choosing you." She cleared her throat. "Ansyl Bolas has proven that one doesn't need highborn blood or experience to serve as Lord Hand, and despite what he did at the end, he served me well for many years. You're honorable, intelligent, strong, *kind*. Kindness is a trait my advisors are lacking for, and even my husband, on occasion. The palace—and all of Akkinor, for that matter—would do well with a good man like you ruling by my side."

"It's impossible." He looked around in search of potential eavesdroppers before lowering his voice. He closed his eyes and clenched his jaw, making her frown, as his face turned crimson. "I-I have broken my oath, Your Grace. More than once, and for many years now. I have a mistress and three children who I'm responsible for. They depend on me. I love them dearly, and I'd be unable to care for them or bring them with me if I accepted your offer. I'd be stripped of my knighthood, too, and lashed for treason. The country wouldn't accept me as Lord Hand."

"I'm sorry, what?"

Rayan blinked at her. "I broke my oath by siring children. I have a woman at home, waiting for me in our bed. I shouldn't even be wearing my cape or calling myself a knight, let alone serving as Hand of the Queen. It's disgraceful. *I'm* disgraceful."

"I didn't quite catch that. Come again?"

His eyebrows furrowed. "Your Grace?"

Then his eyes flicked down to her smiling lips, and a light seemed to burn brighter behind his eyes. He relaxed, his face returning to alabaster from crimson, and ran a hand through his hair as an awkward laugh gurgled in his throat.

"Tradition is tradition," Aurelia said, still smiling as she took his arm, "but I find one in particular to be rather silly. A knight can still perform his duties while living as a husband and a father. If I ever happen to meet a knight who desperately loves a woman and their children...Even if he isn't supposed to have them in his life, I'll choose to remain ignorant of it. It isn't right to have a man's honor stripped away simply because he loves too deeply to maintain a life of solitude."

When she looked up at him, she saw tears shining in his pale eyes. "You're the beating heart of this realm, Your Grace. Do you know that?"

"Sometimes." She raised an eyebrow and squeezed his arm. "What say you, Ser Rayan? Will you accept my offer?"

He took a long, deep breath before mirroring her smile. "If you're certain you'll have me, I'd be most obliged."

Grinning from ear to ear, Aurelia released him so she could throw her arms around his neck. He hesitated, body tensing with surprise, before gently settling his hands on her back and returning the embrace. She closed her eyes as she rested her chin on his shoulder, fighting the urge to cry when the comfort she felt in his arms instantly reminded her of Linden.

"You'll be perfect," she whispered. "I know you will."

"Thank you, Your Grace."

"Oh, enough of *that*." She released him, blinking the tears from her eyes, and grinned again. "You'll have to call me by name now. I'm afraid I'll be unable to respond to anything else."

"All right." Rayan's grin matched hers so well that anyone who didn't know them personally might assume they were siblings—because they were, even if only one of them knew it. "Thank you, Aurelia."

She offered him a playful curtsy. "The pleasure is mine."

L

I'm sorry your family couldn't make it for the ceremony. I know you would've loved for them to be there."

Rayan waved a dismissive hand. "It's all right. It's impossible to predict when a babe will make their arrival. They'll make it up to me once Ginny and little Olive are strong enough to travel."

Aurelia forced a smile as she turned to face the carriage window to her right. She'd never say it aloud, of course, but she was relieved the Haze family hadn't attended Rayan's coronation ceremony—she wasn't sure what she would've done if she saw her half-sister in the flesh, let alone her birth father. Meeting the infamous Eric Haze wasn't exactly something she'd prepared for.

Fortunately for her, Eric had set out for Holos two days before the ceremony after receiving word that his daughter, Ginevra, was in labor with her third child. Though he hadn't made it in time for the birth, he'd traveled the country to help care for Ginny while she recovered. Both Eric and Ginny sent word of how much they regretted missing Rayan's coronation as Hand of the Queen, but Aurelia knew Rayan was too wracked with nerves—and excitement—to miss them.

It'd been a week since Rayan's coronation, and today was his first official outing as Lord Hand. He was accompanying Aurelia and Jack to the heart of the Folly, a bolstering town called Wildewell, where a memorial obelisk had been erected to honor the soldiers who'd fought in Dofell. Aurelia was meant to reveal the obelisk to the masses and deliver a short speech, but she'd asked Rayan to help her—after all, what better way to introduce him to the lowborn than to request his assistance on such an important task?

The people were desperate to catch a glimpse of the new Lord Hand, so from the moment the carriage departed the palace bailey, it'd been flanked on either side by whooping, whistling civilians. They shouted Rayan's name and threw favors at the carriage—some of which made it inside—but they knew better than to approach the carriage. Soldiers marched alongside the carriage, anyway, while Halvor flew overhead. As excited and curious as the civilians were, they didn't dare try to fling themselves at the carriage while Halvor loomed above them.

"I received a letter from Julien Clay this morning," Rayan said after a moment of silence. Both Aurelia and Jack raised their eyebrows as Rayan winced. "It was a bit delayed, but he's confirmed that Ansyl crossed the Delorantis Bridge into Quapebet. His exile is now official."

A touch of guilt rattled Aurelia's heart, but it was gone in the blink of an eye. "That's good to know. Thank you."

He tipped his head. "I...I hope you don't mind, but I told Thea and Mycah before we departed the palace today. I thought it was right that they know, but please, accept my forgiveness if I overstepped."

"You've done nothing of the sort," she insisted. A smile graced her lips. "Your compassion is one of the many reasons I asked you to be my Hand. I'll never be displeased with you for being a good man." She elbowed Jack's arm. "You should take notes."

Her husband grunted. "I'm compassionate enough, thank you very much."

"You wanted Ansyl's head on a pike."

"Well, yes, but—"

Suddenly, the carriage jolted to a stop, nearly sending Aurelia flying forward and landing on Rayan's lap. The Lord Hand was already hollering at the coachmen by the time Jack helped Aurelia steady herself, but the poor driver was too distracted to reply until the reason for his sudden stop revealed itself to the passengers.

Edom appeared on the cushion beside Rayan as the coachmen yelled, "Apologies, Your Grace! The creature—"

"It's all right," Aurelia called back. "Give us a moment." As he grumbled something in response, she raised an eyebrow at the sprite. "What are you up to, Edom?"

"We must stop."

"What? Why would we do that? We can't just—"

"*Stop.*"

A bit frightened by the sprite's firmness, she nodded and told the coachmen they'd be taking a short break for the time being. She and Jack both questioned Edom as the whooping and cheering of the civilians died down, morphing into quiet, confused murmurings, but the creature refused to respond.

"Come" was all Edom said before zipping out of the carriage.

Muttering in frustration, she reached across Jack to open the door, ignoring protests from both he and Rayan as she climbed out. As soon as her shoes touched the road, every Follian in the vicinity bowed or curtsied to her, having gone completely mute by then. She smiled so they wouldn't sense her uneasiness as she scoured the area for Edom, and soon enough, she found the sprite perched on one of the carriage's wheels.

"Aurelia?" Rayan frowned as he and Jack joined her on the street. "Is something wrong?"

"That's yet to be determined." She furrowed her eyebrows as Edom glanced around at the village of Limewick, located just a few miles from their destination. "Edom? What's the matter?"

Without a word, the sprite zipped from the wheel and disappeared onto the street. Onlookers gasped in alarm and looked around for Edom, like Aurelia, but the sprite was far too tiny to see with ease—particularly when it muted its glow.

"I've said it before, and I'll say it again." Jack shook his head and sighed. "Rotten little things, sprites."

Aurelia ignored him, still searching for Edom, as the crowd rose to their feet again and exchanged puzzled whispers. They hadn't known that Edom had been with Aurelia for over a season now, so she didn't know if they thought the creature was a friend or a foe who'd followed her home. She hoped she found it—or that it managed to flee to the palace—before someone captured it.

Just then, a civilian yelled, "Over there! *Look!*"

Aurelia followed the man's pointed finger to a tree not far from where she stood. Edom was clinging to the trunk like a squirrel, and it appeared to be...knocking.

It didn't linger there for long, though. By the time she blinked, Edom had already moved on to another tree, where it appeared to knock again. Then the sprite climbed to the very edge of a wire-thin branch and moved its lips, as if speaking into the wind. After that, it hopped to the ground and stood beside a large puddle, stopping just long enough to dip its finger into the water.

As Edom zipped around the entire village, Aurelia's eyes stayed focused on the puddle. It was still rippling, even after many minutes had passed. That's when she saw something emerge from the water: a hand.

Thin, dainty fingers peeked out from within the puddle, before curling over the edge of where the water met the ground. Then a wrist, then a forearm, and then—gods be good, a *head*. As onlookers screamed in panic and fled from the streets, a woman with pale blonde hair, reptile-like blue eyes, and blue lips pulled herself from the puddle. Soon enough, she was standing as tall as any other human, wearing nothing but thin strips of blue cloth around her breasts and her waist. She looked around, but she didn't appear frightened—in fact, she looked relieved.

At the same time, another woman emerged from the first tree trunk Edom had knocked on. Her hand rippled through the trunk before she peeled her entire body from the bark to stand beside the tree. Her hair was a rich chestnut brown, her eyes the same color, and her green lips matched the leaf-like material she wore to cover her modesty. She glanced around for a bit, too—also unbothered—before approaching another tree and holding out a hand. When she did so, yet another female hand poked out from the bark and set its hand over hers.

"Gods above." Jack's voice wobbled in disbelief. "Those aren't—?"

Aurelia's breath caught in her throat. "Nymphs."

Joyous female laughter echoed in the wind as people hollered and pointed. Aurelia looked around, as if searching for a fly circling her head, and that's when she saw a faint pink glow zipping around the air. The pink ball of light, no larger than Edom, landed on the roof of a nearby cottage. When the light faded, a palm-sized woman with dainty wings covered her mouth and giggled from her seat on the roof, legs dangling over the edge and kicking like a child's.

"Look, Mama!" a child's voice exclaimed. "It's a fairy!"

A fairy, one of the first creatures to have gone extinct—as the stories claimed, anyway—during the persecution. A creature as fast and clever as sprites, but less driven by mischief. They had the ability to cast spells like mages, and often used their powers to bring joy to humans—like snatching neglected children from their beds and bringing them to better homes, as they were rumored to have done.

More screams came from the path ahead, cutting through the brief veil of silence that had fallen over the crowd as they watched the scene unfold. Aurelia met eyes with Jack and Rayan before the trio dashed forward, following the sounds of terror—or thrill, she couldn't be sure.

Several feet ahead of where they'd been standing moments earlier, the crowd had practically evaporated—and for good reason. The cobblestone road had caved in like a sinkhole had struck, creating a massive, horse-sized crater in the ground. As the dust and debris settled, another pair of hands appeared over the edge of the crater, but they were larger and meatier than the nymphs'.

Aurelia nearly fell to the ground when a mountain of a man pulled himself up from the hole. Though his size was staggering, what shocked her the most was the single eye resting on his forehead. When he was standing on solid ground, the Cyclops stretched his arms, yawned, and glanced around. His eyes quickly landed on Aurelia, and to her surprise, he *bowed* to her when he spotted her crown.

"Your Grace." His voice sounded sleepy, but it was strong and powerful. "How do you do?"

She opened her mouth to reply, but no sound emerged. Then Edom appeared on a disrupted chunk of earth at her feet, beaming at her, and she could do nothing but stare at it while every soul in Limewick fell silent once more.

"I told you." Edom grinned. "They've been sleeping."

"E-Edom, I—"

The sprite gasped. "Oh, my."

Aurelia followed its eyes to her right, where a tree nymph was gliding toward them. The remaining civilians fell to their bottoms and scooched away, creating a path for her as she walked by them, unable to do anything but stare at her in utter bewilderment.

Like the tree nymphs Aurelia had seen earlier, this woman wore nothing but leafy garments to cover her modesty, and she hadn't any shoes. Her lips and her eyes were both green, but her skin was a deep, rich brown, and her hair was darker than night as it hung in tight, coarse curls down her back. Leaves and twigs were caught in her hair, but they didn't look out of place—it was like they were a part of her.

As she approached, another female face appeared in the air beside her. The face was almost entirely transparent, but her features were visible enough for Aurelia to see the outline of eyes, lips, and a nose. Her laughter echoed for miles before her face faded from view, disappearing into the wind.

When the tree nymph held out a hand, Edom rushed over to sit on her palm. The pair muttered things to each other that Aurelia couldn't hear, but when she saw the joy and relief on Edom's face, she knew exactly who the nymph was.

"You're Laurel," Aurelia said before she could stop herself. "Aren't you?"

The nymph smiled at her. "Hello, Your Grace."

Aurelia mirrored her expression. "Welcome home."

When she sensed both Jack and Rayan staring at her, she explained who the nymph was: a friend of Edom's from the old days, who'd left Carthe to help her kin in Akkinor resist the persecution. Edom hadn't known if Laurel survived the persecution or went into hiding, and the sprite was beaming after finding that it was the latter.

Laurel approached Aurelia as Edom settled on the nymph's shoulder. Aurelia held her breath—anxious, but not frightened—as Laurel placed her hand behind her back before holding it out to the queen again. A shaky, nervous laugh bubbled up in Aurelia's throat when she saw what the nymph was offering her: a hyacinth.

"Thank you." She accepted the flower and inhaled its sweet scent. "How did—"

Laurel interrupted her: *"An era of uncertainty shall come to an end when, in the east, water runs thicker than blood. A period of peace and promise shall follow for five cycles, only to be broken when the sun burns hottest across the realm. Chaos and carnage shall return, demanding that a hero of western blood emerges from the shadows of men to restore the realm to glory. In the wake of such turmoil, the voice of the divine shall be heard across the realm once again through the falling of stars."*

As Aurelia gawked at her, Edom grinned and said, "The stars have fallen."

Edea.

Until now, Aurelia hadn't been *entirely* certain that Maysa's prophecy had been fulfilled. A part of her wondered if Willem's defeat, Dofell's revival, and Edea's return had only been the beginning of what was foretold. She'd assumed the prophecy had only existed within Maysa's lifetime, too, but that couldn't be right. Clearly, the prophecy had been passed down from oracle to oracle over the centuries, originating so early on in the realm's existence that even creatures of old knew what it spoke of.

They hadn't woken up because Edom wanted them to return. They'd woken up because they, like the sprite, knew the prophecy had been fulfilled. They knew the time had come for their voices to be heard across the realm again—the voices of the divine who'd created them, exactly like the prophecy stated.

Beside Aurelia, Rayan murmured, *"'A hero of western blood...'"*

She felt Jack eyeing her, but she ignored both of them while Halvor roared overhead. Now wasn't the time for analyzing what the prophecy meant—only for celebrating that it'd come to fruition.

Aurelia's lips parted as she gazed at her surroundings again, turning in a slow, complete circle to ensure she didn't miss a thing. There were over a dozen of them now—nymphs, fairies, the one Cyclops, and even a few sprites—yawning, stretching, and conversing. They were casually walking the streets like they'd been living in Limewick for their entire lives.

They probably have been, she reminded herself.

For the first time since taking the throne, when the people of the Folly fell to their knees, it wasn't out of praise or respect for their queen—it was for them, these creatures Edom had awoken, who hadn't seen the light of day since the persecution forced them into hiding; and no mage or mortal had known they were there.

Now, they were free.

Epilogue

1989 Post Creation

Thousands of miles from where magical creatures woke from their centuries-long slumber, a woman slipped out of her home late at night, avoiding the many soldiers tasked with ensuring her safety. She pulled on a billowing cloak, laced up tailored boots, then snatched a horse from the stables.

She still couldn't get used to the feel of smooth silk against her skin, or shoes that fit her perfectly. She sometimes longed for the rough wool or stiff loafers of her former life, before the realm needed her.

She set out for the east, riding through silence and moonlight, concealed by darkness. She knew the route better than she knew herself, even now when she was departing from a new, foreign home. There was a fierce tugging sensation in her chest guiding her path, like one end of a rope was wrapped around her soul and tethered to what awaited her.

The ride must've taken at least an hour or two, but it felt like only minutes had passed when she arrived. She dismounted her horse and tied the reins to a lone wooden post half-buried in the ground—the remains of an old fence—then wrapped her arms around herself to combat the bitter nighttime chill. She would be walking the rest of the way to her destination.

After a few moments, she spotted a familiar sight in the near distance: a series of large caves lining more than half of the eastern Dofelli border. Only a native of eastern Dofell would know that the caves—sitting high above sea level and forming something of a gate between the edge of the cliffs and the ocean below—were interconnected, leading down to an opening at sea that was completely concealed from view during high tide.

It was fortunate that she had the moon on her side. Without the white light beaming down from above, she might not have seen the opening of the largest cave, as it blended in with the darkness of the rock walls. She had to thank her own expertise with the area, too: many others who'd visited this place at nighttime were unaware of just how close they were to the edge of the cliffs, and far too many lives had been lost by taking one wrong step.

Humming an ancient song, she removed the hood of her cloak, letting her sleek black hair hang loose over her back, and bent down to collect two rocks from the ground at her feet. Holding them in one fist, she took a step closer to the cave's entrance and felt around in the darkness along the left side. She grinned when she felt cloth wrapped around something firm beneath her fingers, then removed it while thanking the gods for keeping the torch exactly where she'd left it when she last visited three seasons earlier.

She rubbed the stones together until sparks formed, holding them directly above the cloth that still stunk of whale fat. She carefully blew on the sparks when they landed on the cloth, and in a matter of minutes, the torch had been set ablaze, thanks to the whale oil ensuring the flames thrived in this damp place.

She grabbed the other end of the torch and took a few steps into the cave's entrance again. Swallowing the nerves that'd risen up in her throat, she tossed the torch into the cave, watching as it rolled along the dirt until it stopped several yards from where she stood. She stepped backwards and clasped her hands over her abdomen as she increased her volume, transforming her humming into singing.

The song spewing from her lips was one she knew like the back of her hand, first shared with her by her father, and his father before him. No other soul in the realm knew the words or the melody, and now that her father was dead, she was solely responsible for passing it onto the next generation.

As she sang, another sound chimed in: a low, eerie rumbling that almost sounded like the groaning of an old ship threatening to snap in two. As the rumbling grew louder, the ground began to tremble, and debris rained down from the roof of the cave, threatening to extinguish the flames illuminating the entrance.

Then a shadow appeared behind the torch, and something equally beautiful and terrifying glowed in the darkness: a pair of yellow, reptilian eyes blinking away grogginess.

Diantha Pharos, Queen of Dofell, smiled when a massive snout lowered over the flames, plumes of smoke wafting from hand-sized nostrils. Deep purple scales—so dark that the color could be mistaken for black, if one didn't look closely enough—and silver claws were the only colors breathing life into the cave, made more vibrant when the glow from the flames projected the colors onto the rocky walls.

Diantha took a few steps forward again, holding out a hand, and held her breath until a damp nose nudged her palm. She chuckled a bit, exhaling in relief, as she splayed her palm over the snout and rubbed her skin against cool, sleek scales.

"Hello again, my friend," she murmured.

The dragon chuffed and slowly blinked as if to say, *I'm glad to see you, too.*

"You got my message, didn't you?" Diantha said quietly. "About the other one. You managed to help him somehow." Rieza only rumbled in response, making the queen smile even wider. "I knew it." Diantha set her hands on either side of Rieza's snout, pressing her forehead to the scales between nostrils, and closed her eyes. "Well done, old girl. Well done."

Rieza made a sound that reminded Diantha of a child's coo. The Queen of Dofell knew what that sound meant, too: *It was my pleasure.*

***

Hundreds of miles to the south, another young woman—still a girl, really—sat alone in her bedchamber in her grand estate. She knelt on the floor along the side of her bed, arms folded on the edge of her mattress, and held her breath in anticipation. Her wide, round brown eyes refused to blink as she stared at the object nestled atop her favorite knitted blanket. The object emitted a strange type of heat that reminded the girl of the warmth of the earth. Until recently, it'd been buried in a deep grave, walked over dozens of times a day for over a thousand years by those who wouldn't think twice about what lies beneath the surface.

She'd been keeping it hidden in her wardrobe for days now, but when she went to sleep that night, she was quickly woken by the sound of rattling furniture. She'd seen her wardrobe trembling, and when she opened the doors, she found the object rumbling like something was trying to break out of it.

A gasp escaped her lips when a sudden crack formed along the center, wisps of earth-smelling smoke exhaling from the imperfection as liquid dripped over the edges. She held her breath as the crack spread, and before she knew it, a large chunk of emerald shell split from the egg and fell onto the blanket.

Shasta Selle, the only child of a Kroti lord, watched with wide, mesmerized eyes as something emerged from the goopy liquid inside of the egg: a green, scaly wing.

As Shasta's laughter echoed in her eardrums, a weak roar screeched from the egg, the sounds traveling in tandem throughout the province of Bruila.

While the newborn's voice reached out to the realm, both a purple beast in a cave and a blue beast in a garden craned their necks to the sky, mimicking the sound and answering the call.

THE GOLDEN ONE TRILOGY IS NOW COMPLETE! GET ALL THREE BOOKS ON AMAZON!

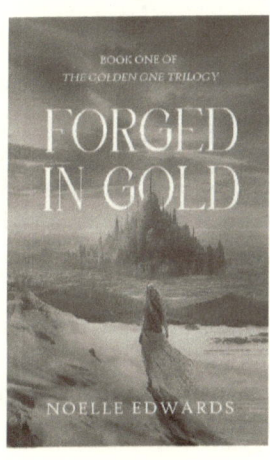  

Keep reading for a sneak peek of Book 3, Forged in Blood!

H e can't have that, Lena."

"Why?"

"Because he could choke on it."

"Why?"

"Because babes put things in their mouths when they aren't supposed to."

"But *why?*"

Halle sighed exasperatedly. "Because—"

Jack's chest rumbled with laughter. "All right, all right. Listen to your sister, Halyna, and don't be a nuisance with your questions."

Three-year-old Halyna huffed at him. Obeying her elder sister, she refrained from handing a gold-plated knucklebone to her one-year-old brother, Harlen. She moved like she wanted to hand it to Harlen's twin sister, Holly, but thought better of it when she saw the scolding look in Halle's eyes.

Jack grinned from ear to ear when Halle met his gaze and offered him a small, shy smile. The look of her eyes—a swirling combination of blue, green, and gray, like the sea during a storm—was identical to his, but the look *in* her eyes—authoritative, confident, and demanding respect—was a perfect match for her mother's.

Jack turned to his wife and chuckled when he saw her suppressing a smile. He knew they were thinking the same thing: Halle, Crown Princess of Akkinor, was already well on her way to becoming an exceptional queen.

She's learning from the best, after all, Jack thought to himself. He must've been giving Aurelia some sort of look while he thought it, because her pale cheeks quickly turned pink.

"Give it here, darling." Aurelia held out her hand, prompting Halyna to set the knucklebone on her mother's palm. Aurelia returned the piece to a linen bag with the others, then tossed a glance over her shoulder at the piano in the corner of the parlor. "That sounds lovely, Sisi. You're getting better every day."

Hyacinth turned and opened her mouth to respond, but Henry—perched on the bench alongside her—beat her to it: "I'm helping, Mama!"

"No, you're not." Hyacinth, eight years old like Halle, gave her brother a slight push. "Go play over there."

Jack snorted into a laugh as the five-year-old prince dragged his feet over to the floor, where Jack was sitting with the other four Brentwood children. Across from where they sat on the carpet, Aurelia was curled up on the couch watching Hyacinth play the pianoforte. Jack knew exactly what his wife was thinking: Hyacinth may not have inherited much from her biological father—Aurelia's brother, the late Prince Archie—but she'd certainly inherited his musical talent.

Ser Rayan Haze, Hand of the Queen, hummed along to the tune from his seat beside Aurelia. His position—head tilted back against the couch cushions, shoeless feet propped up on the tea table, and hands splayed over his stomach—made Jack envious while he strained his back on the floor. As if he could sense Jack watching him, Rayan cracked an eye open and stifled laughter when he met Jack's eyes.

"Would you like to trade seats?" Rayan teased.

Jack grunted and lay flat on his back, trying to find comfort on the hard floor. "I fear we've allowed you to grow too comfortable here, my Lord Hand."

Rayan guffawed, making both Jack and Aurelia grin, as Henry dashed over to Rayan. He set his small hands on Rayan's thigh, putting his entire body weight on his hands, as Rayan tousled the young prince's auburn hair—the same color as his.

"Uncle Rayan," Henry started, "would you like to play with me?"

"I would love to," the Hand replied, "but I feel I must remind you—again—that I'm not your uncle."

Jack's gaze snapped over to Aurelia's. Her smile faded a bit, the light in her eyes dimming, as she sighed and turned back to Hyacinth. Over three years had passed since Aurelia met Rayan Haze, and she still hadn't told him that they were born to the same father. It'd been a coincidence—or fate, Jack couldn't decide—when their paths crossed, but still, she didn't feel it was right to place such a burden on his shoulders. After all, learning the truth meant acknowledging that Aurelia wasn't the trueborn daughter of the last king, and such a secret was a damning one for Rayan to keep.

Halle sighed. "He thinks we have to call you *uncle* because of Uncle Arian."

"How so?" Rayan slid from the couch to sit on the floor with Henry, who immediately handed him a wooden ship to play with.

"Because Arian is a Hand of the Queen, too, and we call him *uncle*."

"That's not how it works, Henry," Hyacinth said from the piano, not bothering to look over her shoulder. "We didn't call Ansyl *uncle*, remember?"

The prince huffed and folded his arms over his chest. Before he could argue with his sisters, little Holly began to shriek, her twin brother following her lead. In response, Halyna covered her ears and whined, inching away from the twins while Jack swept them into his arms. At the same time, Halle and Henry began bickering over something, shouting so loudly that Hyacinth stopped playing so she could holler at them for interrupting her.

Jack met Aurelia's eyes as the pair struggled to contain their amusement. As frustrating—and, oftentimes, *annoying*—as their children were, it was entertaining to watch such tiny people express such fierce emotions.

The children quieted when Aurelia scolded them. As soon as they calmed down, she looked at Jack again, smirking, and said, "I don't recall there being so many of them. When did *that* happen?"

He laughed while Rayan chimed in, "Well, Omarans *are* known for being terrible breeders."

"Your sarcasm is less than appreciated," Jack teased, as they all knew that natives of Omara—Jack's home kingdom—tended to produce the largest broods in Akkinor.

As the adults laughed, a knock came at the door, and a servant entered shortly after. The messenger boy bowed as Aurelia rose to meet him by the door. She accepted a scroll and thanked him, then held the parchment between her fingers while she poured herself a glass of wine from a nearby table.

Jack turned his attention to the twins as they climbed on his legs until he heard something shatter on the floor. Everyone silenced, alarmed, and looked up at Aurelia while she stood beside the piano. Her goblet had fallen from her grasp, staining the beige carpet with burgundy liquid, and the unraveled scroll shook like a leaf in her trembling hands.

"Aurelia? What's happened?" Jack asked, climbing to his feet. "Is everything all right?"

Hyacinth gasped from her seat on the piano bench. "Oh, no."

Aurelia met Hyacinth's gaze and held it for a moment, then turned to Jack, an answer to his inquiry brewing on her lips. She didn't get the chance to speak, though: at that exact moment, her dragon, Halvor, shrieked from somewhere on the grounds. She bolted out of the parlor faster than a lightning strike, letting the scroll flutter to the ground as she did so.

"Follow her." Jack had given the command to Rayan before he knew what he was doing. As the Lord Hand scurried out of the parlor, Jack's eyes landed on Halle, who was holding a whimpering Halyna on her lap. "Irina and Celesse are in their quarters. Bring them here to mind your siblings. Quickly, now."

Halle set Halyna down, scampered to her feet, and dashed into the hallway to fetch the governesses. Jack was on his way out of the parlor, too—trusting Hyacinth to watch her younger siblings—when he spotted the fallen scroll and plucked it from the ground.

For the Queen of Akkinor:
You are not alone. Either of you.

Jack sucked in a sharp breath through his teeth, unintentionally meeting Hyacinth's eyes, exactly as Aurelia had just moments before. Hyacinth may not have known that her power to see glimpses of the past, present, and future meant that she was a mage, but she *did* understand that she had a special gift.

Jack's voice was nothing short of a whisper: "Sisi? What do you know?"

His daughter gulped, her hands trembling on the keys of the pianoforte. "There's more than one now."

His eyes widened, but before he could reply, he heard Halvor shriek again, louder and fiercer than before. Crumpling the message in his fist, he left the children in the parlor—passing Halle and the governesses as he ran through the halls—and followed the sound of Halvor's roars. He could hear his own heartbeat rattling his eardrums as he bolted toward the rear of the palace, where the doors to the gardens had been left wide open.

Aurelia was standing in the center of the gardens, the wind lifting her wild golden curls from her back, with her neck craned backward as she stared at the sky. Rayan stood a few feet behind her, mimicking her, with his hand resting on the hilt of his sword at his side.

Jack rushed to Aurelia's side, barely able to skid to a stop when his own momentum betrayed him, and stared at her face—whiter than a sheet, like she'd just seen the dead rise from the catacombs—before following her gaze.

Halvor was perched atop the stone walls surrounding the palace grounds, his long neck extended as high as it could go, roaring at something lost amongst the clouds. Jack spotted a tiny, faint golden glow on the very top of Halvor's head—Aurelia's sprite, Edom. He was opening his mouth to call for Edom, hoping the creature could explain the situation, but he didn't get the chance.

A shadow about the size of a small writing desk became visible from beyond the clouds. As the shadow descended, Jack saw a silhouette of wings, four limbs, and a reptile-like head attached to a long neck. Then the clouds parted, and Jack's heart plummeted to his knees when an emerald dragon swerved through the air while releasing a weak, somewhat juvenile screech.

The dragon wasn't large enough to bear a rider, but it was certainly large enough to pose a threat. And based on the contents of the message, it had a master or a mistress. What mattered more, though, was that another dragon of old existed in the realm, and Halvor was no longer the only one of his kind.

There's more than one now.

Jack snapped his gaze over to his wife again. Her jaw was clenched, and her lips were pressed in a thin, taut line. When she turned her head ever-so-slightly to follow the intruder's path, the moonlight illuminated the thick, silver scar along her cheekbone, making her look as menacing as the dragon whose soul she shared.

"Aurelia—" he started, unsure of what he was going to say.

Halvor shook the entire garden, interrupting Jack, when he released a bellowing shriek as the intruder flew just a bit too close for comfort. He must've succeeded in spooking the green dragon, because his tiny counterpart released one last screech before disappearing beyond the clouds again. Halvor growled and chuffed at the sky for a few moments longer, then roared one last time—telling the little one to stay far, far away.

Rayan appeared at Jack's side, gray and clammy. "W-Was that an innocent exploration of the Folly, or...was it a warning?"

Aurelia hadn't looked away from the sky since Jack found her outside. "I believe we'll be finding out soon enough. We need to send word to—"

Halvor interrupted her with another shriek, but this one was different. Before, he'd been warning an unexpected visitor to keep its distance, but he hadn't been violent. Now, the sound he emitted was the same one he'd made in the past while threatening—or devouring—enemy soldiers during wartime.

A battle cry.

Aurelia gasped when Halvor lifted off from the wall and soared into the clouds, his roars so terrifying that even she winced at the sound. Jack reached for her hand instinctively, squeezing, and started to speak—but he didn't get the chance to utter a single syllable before another shadow, much larger than the first, joined Halvor's behind the clouds.

The wind picked up, causing the trees in the gardens to sway and the birds to fly away in terror. Aurelia tightened her grip on Jack's hand, while setting her free hand on Rayan's forearm. The three of them stared up at the sky, having lost the shadows to the darkness, while the only sounds to be heard—for just a moment—were their pounding heartbeats.

A strangled scream escaped Aurelia's throat when Halvor plummeted through the clouds, just barely catching himself before he collided with the wall. He managed to land atop the wall, Edom now clinging to a spike on his back. Halvor's claws scraped the stone while he struggled to gain traction, then he craned his neck to release an enormous ball of fire from his throat. The flames didn't reach their destination, though—an unseen force, like the strongest gust of wind man had ever known, met the flames halfway, threatening to force the fire back against Halvor's face.

Just as the flames and the strange force subsided, another shriek echoed throughout the grounds. It was just as loud and terrifying as Halvor's, but it hadn't come from Aurelia's dragon. Jack caught a faint glimpse of the source—a purplish, scaly wing—before it disappeared even higher into the dark sky, camouflaging itself above the clouds.

Halvor shifted like he was prepared to follow it. Aurelia, trembling beside Jack, merely shook her head. Halvor hadn't even been looking at her, but the connection between their souls allowed him to receive and obey her command to stay put. He bellowed into the sky again, rattling the gardens, and growled as he turned to face the west, where the third dragon had disappeared into the night.

"Aur-Aurelia..." Jack sounded more like his five-year-old son than Henry did, unable to form the words. "That's—"

"Impossible." He barely heard her when she spoke, as the winds were still dying down and Halvor was still growling into the sky. "I..."

Just then, a flash of golden light appeared on her shoulder. Jack tried to listen to what Edom was whispering in her ear, but he couldn't make it out. He and Rayan merely watched as her face blanched and her lips parted. She muttered something to the sprite, making it nod, before the creature zipped off toward Halvor again.

Aurelia cleared her throat when she saw Jack and Rayan eyeing her. "Edom says the little one appears to be young—a few years old, at most— but the bigger one..." Her eyes fluttered shut. "The bigger one is ancient."

"Like Halvor," Rayan murmured.

For the first time in years, Aurelia looked at Jack with pure fear glistening in her pale blue eyes. He tried to reach for her, to bring her into his arms, but she took a step backward, clearly too shaken.

"Summon the Assembly," she croaked, flicking her gaze back to Halvor. "It would appear that we've made an enemy or two."

Acknowledgements

I've had most of Forged in Ashes written for a while now, and until recently, I never thought I'd see it in print. It was just the continuation of a book I'd written for my own pleasure, without any intention of sharing Aurelia's story with the world. When I made the decision to publish Forged in Gold, I knew the sequel would be more than something I'd just written for myself: it would be the second installment of Aurelia's journey, paving the way for an epic saga in which Aurelia Brentwood's story is only the beginning. That being said, I wouldn't have had the courage to commit to this trilogy—and the series—if not for the amazing people in my life who have supported me every step of the way.

Firstly, I want to thank my grandmothers, aunts, cousins, and the mothers of my close friends. After I lost my mom, each of you took care of me like I was your daughter, and you showed me the power a tribe of strong women has when the time comes to help someone in need. I'm one of a lucky few who knows what it feels like to belong to not one, but multiple families.

Thank you to my incredible friends for your constant love and support, endless laughter, and inspiration in all things. Whether we've known each other for fifteen years or two, every single one of you has left a permanent mark on me as a person and as an author. You remind me to have fun in life and to step away from my writing desk when I need it. You're the best allies I could ever hope for.

Thank you to my dad and my sister for so much, I could write an entire book dedicated to the two of you. Dad, you're the closest thing to a superhero there is in our world, and I wouldn't be here without your constant support. Chrissy, you taught me how to care about something more than myself from the day you came into this world, and you've been my rock for the last twenty years.

Thank you to the one I love for grounding me, always encouraging me to aim for the stars, and supporting my dreams so much that they feel like your dreams, too. When I doubt myself and my success as an author, you're always there to give me the push I need. Thank you for being my #1 fan from the first day we met.

To the two people who can't be here while I embark on this journey: my mom, Terrie, and my grandfather, Kenneth. I'm writing this because you believed in my dream from the time I was old enough to put pen to paper. Without you, none of this would've been possible. I wish you were here to see it, but I know you're cheering for me from heaven.

Thank you Katarina for another beautiful cover, and Aubrey for the lovely interior illustrations.

Thank you to my beta readers and ARC readers for pointing me in the right direction, supporting my work, and doing the absolute most to help me find my way through this industry.

To my readers, thank you from the bottom of my heart for following along on my journey and Aurelia's. I can't begin to tell you how much it means to me to have your support and the absolute outpouring of love you've sent my way. Hearing how much you love Aurelia's story fills me with so much hope and pride!

Lastly, thank you to the beautiful babies in my life: Emerson, Zuri, Amari, Addy, and Casey. Being your auntie is the best job I've ever had. One of the biggest reasons I decided to include Aurelia's children in this book was to honor how incredible it is to have kids in your life who you'd do anything for. I've never known love like the love I have for each of you. I've seen life differently every time one of you has joined us earthside, and there's nothing I want more than to hold your hands as you leave your marks on the world. You've become my reason for doing better, for becoming the best possible version of myself so you'll always be proud to call me your auntie.

P.S. Happy first birthday, Amari.

About the Author

Noelle is a pseudonym for a writer, beta reader, and editor from Boston who found her passion for writing early on and pursued it wholeheartedly. Although she is a young writer, she has been honing her craft for more than a decade, having written her first story in middle school!

While Noelle enjoys genres like romance, historical fiction, and science fiction, fantasy has always been her favorite. She fell in love with the genre at an early age after reading C.S. Lewis's *Narnia* series and William Goldman's *The Princess Bride*. Since then, her love of fantasy has only grown!

Much of Noelle's early career reflects her lifelong love of children, having worked as a nanny, infant/toddler daycare teacher, and substitute elementary teacher. However, since graduating with her BA in English Literature, she has immersed herself in the exciting realm of freelancing. When away from her writing desk, Noelle can often be found curled up with a novel or avidly working on expanding the world of her creation.

Noelle currently resides with her father, younger sister, and her feisty kitty, Nugget. *Forged in Gold* is her debut fantasy novel and marks the first of an exciting, heart-stopping series. She writes in honor of her beloved mother, who passed away from cancer in 2015.

Glossary

AGOTIA (Ah-goh-sha): Taundosan district bordering the Ngora Valley; governed by the Cristos family.

Ardiham Castle: Ancestral home of the Cristos family.

AKKINOR (Ack-inn-or): The largest populated continent of the east; the most powerful country in the realm; ruled by the Brentwood family; composed of six kingdoms:

Holos (Holl-os): Region in southeast Akkinor; ruled by the Tarre family.

Laynoa (Lay-noh-ah): Region in northeast Akkinor; ruled by the Stone family.

Myra (Meer-ah): Region in southwest Akkinor; ruled by the Crowland family; borders Quapebet.

Omara (Oh-mar-ah): Centermost Akkinorian territory; ruled by the Ashford family; the last kingdom seized by the Akkinorian monarchy.

Sadia (Sah-dee-uh): Mountainous northern region of Akkinor; ruled by the Normindi family.

Seaport: Small coastal town on the west coast of Akkinor; borders the Folly; ungoverned; the only international port in Akkinor.

The Folly: Capital of Akkinor; home to the palace and the royal family; ruled by the Brentwood family.

Elderhost: A town in the Folly.

Horscola: A small farming district in the Folly.

Mistcairn: A village in the Folly.

ALISTAIR ASHFORD: Former Lord of Omara; father of Arthur, Bryan, Cecelia, and Daniella; husband of Isobel; formerly exiled to Quapebet.

ANDREN NORMINDI: Lord of Sadia; elder brother of the late Queen Cressida.

ALKAMURA OCEAN: Also known as the Alka; massive ocean that lies between Carthe and Akkinor; corrupted by the Esposi following Oleander's Rebellion; formerly forbidden territory for Akkinorians.

ALKAMURA: Goddess of the seas; Almighty of Espos.

ALMIGHTY: The primary deity worshipped by individual cultures/civilizations.

ALORA CHERRANE: The last ruler of the Cherrane Dynasty in Akkinor; the last female monarch until Aurelia Brentwood.

ANSYL BOLAS: Native of Kanibar; elder brother of Kaia, Mycah, and Thea; former Kanish soldier; Hand of the Queen to Aurelia Brentwood.

ARCHIBALD BRENTWOOD (deceased): Former Prince of Akkinor; son of King Edmund II and Queen Cressida; younger brother and usurper of Queen Aurelia.

ARIAN CRISTOS: Lord of Agotia; Lord Hand to Queen Reyna; biological uncle of Aurelia Brentwood; water mage.

ARTHUR "JACK" ASHFORD: King Consort of Akkinor; husband of Queen Aurelia; father of Halle, Hyacinth, Henry, and Halyna; former heir to Lordship of Omara; alias: Jack Sherbourne.

AURELIA BRENTWOOD: Queen of Akkinor; adopted daughter of King Edmund II and Queen Cressida Brentwood; biological daughter of Katryna Cristos and Eric Haze; wife of Jack Ashford; mother of Halle, Hyacinth, Henry, and Halyna; mistress of the dragon Halvor; alias: Lily Linden.

BALOR ZHOQA II (Bay-lor Zoh-kah): Lord of Kazamir, Bozar; ally of Queen Aurelia.

BRYAN ASHFORD: Lord of Omara; younger brother of Jack Ashford.

BUEN (Bu-wen): God of prosperity; Almighty of Akkinor.

CARTHE: The largest populated continent in the west; a safe haven for mages and magical creatures; home to numerous civilizations:

> *Bozar* (Boh-zar): Kingdom east of the Ngora Valley; borders Taundosa and Khaba; ruled by four noble families: Zhaaran of Orestes, Zhoqa of Kazamir, Zoma of Iseppa, and Xada of Tucana.
>
> *Caedia* (Cay-dee-ah): Northernmost territory of Carthe; ungoverned port province frequented by travelers and merchants; borders the Violet Forest.
>
> *Dofell* (Doh-fell): Kingdom north of Taundosa and the Ngora Valley, south of the Violet Forest, and east of Kanibar; ruled by the Phyre family; formerly known as *the Great City*; the most impoverished kingdom in Carthe.
>
> *Kanibar* (Can-nih-bar): Kingdom north of the Ngora Valley; borders Dofell, Taundosa, and the Violet Forest; ruled by the Trevas family.
>
> *Khaba* (Cah-bah): Southernmost territory of Carthe; ungoverned port province; borders Bozar.

Krotis (Kroh-tis): Kingdom south of the Ngora Valley; borders Taundosa; governed by five noble families: Selle of Bruila, Keer of Mekya, Quagg of Osanad, Swann of Runeia, and Reesa of Vrurith.

Ngora Valley (Nih-gor-ah Valley): Vast desert that separates northern and southern Carthe; only accessible through Dofell and Taundosa.

Taundosa (Tawn-doh-sah): Kingdom east of the Ngora Valley and south of Dofell; the wealthiest Carthinian kingdom; ruled by the Caltheos family; known as *the City of Gold*.

> *Eight Kingdoms of Taundosa:* Agotia, Brorane, Cidour, Emerdes, Morvis, Thania, Trostall, and Vortea.

Violet Forest: Massive deciduous forest that lies between Caedia and the Carthinian kingdoms; home of nomadic native tribes; mostly frequented by travelers.

CERULEAN SEA: Body of water between Holos and Quapebet.

CHANGLING: A five-day celebration held in the Folly at the beginning/end of each season; attended by all highborn Akkinorians and citizens of the Folly; includes performances by jousters, theater actors, bards, jesters, etc.

CICELY POOLE (deceased): Close friend and lady-in-waiting to Queen Aurelia.

CRESSIDA BRENTWOOD (deceased): Former Queen Consort of Akkinor; wife of King Edmund II; mother of Queen Aurelia and Prince Archie.

CRYSTAL SEA: Body of water located between northwestern Akkinor and northeastern Carthe.

DHYLO (Die-loh): God of knowledge; Almighty of Bozar.

DIANTHA PHAROS: Lowborn successor of King Elrin III of Dofell.

EDEA (Ee-dee-ah): Goddess of the moon.

EDOM: A sprite befriended by Queen Aurelia.

EDMUND BRENTWOOD II (deceased): Former King of Akkinor; husband of Queen Cressida; father of Queen Aurelia and Prince Archie.

ELRIN PHYRE III: King of Dofell.

ERIC HAZE: Biological father of Aurelia Brentwood and Rayan Haze; native of Holos; former Cristos family soldier.

ESPOS: Island south of Carthe inhabited mainly by pirates.

GEMMA STONE: Lady of Laynoa; wife of Duke Lucan Stone; sister of Linden Elliot.

GIANLA (Gee-ahn-lah): Goddess of the sun; Almighty of Taundosa.

GLACIER BAY: Northernmost continent; home of the Isalders; ruled by the Styrmodr family.

GLACIER SEA: Northernmost body of water; Isalder territory.

GOLDMEN: An esteemed organization of soldiers loyal to the Taundosan monarchy.

HALLE BRENTWOOD: Eldest child of Aurelia Brentwood and Jack Ashford; Crown Princess of Akkinor.

HALVOR: (Hal-vohr): (1) God of protection; (2) Dragon of old loyal to Aurelia Brentwood and the Cristos family.

HALYNA BRENTWOOD: Youngest child of Aurelia Brentwood and Jack Ashford; Princess of Akkinor.

HENRY BRENTWOOD: Third child of Aurelia Brentwood and Jack Ashford; Prince of Akkinor.

HYACINTH BRENTWOOD: Second child and adopted daughter of Aurelia Brentwood and Jack Ashford; biological daughter of Archie Brentwood; Princess of Akkinor.

HZARL (His-arl): God of the hunt; Almighty of Glacier Bay.

IMMOR (Ee-mor): God of war.

INESIS (In-ness-iss): God of life and death; Almighty of Quapebet.

ISOBEL ASHFORD: Former Lady of Omara; mother of Arthur, Bryan, Cecelia, and Daniella; wife of Alistair; formerly exiled to Quapebet.

JALHOR ZHAARAN (Jall-or Zar-ran): Lord of Orestes in Bozar; air mage; ally of Queen Aurelia.

KAIA BOLAS (deceased): Native Kanish merchant; younger sister of Ansyl and elder sister of Thea and Mycah.

KATRYNA CRISTOS (deceased): Biological mother of Aurelia Brentwood; sister of Arian Cristos; native of Taundosa; fire mage.

LINDEN ELLIOT (deceased): Former Hand of the Queen and best friend of Aurelia Brentwood; murdered by Archie Brentwood.

LUKOS: Pirate captain of Espos.

LUNAR STAFF/STAFF OF EDEA: Ancient staff once wielded by the moon goddess; currently a small fragment of the original staff containing a piece of fallen moonrock.

MAGES: Humans with the ability to conjure magic from the gods.

MAGICAL PERSECUTION: The annihilation of mages and magical creatures during the old days that saw the extinction of numerous races and forced surviving mages into hiding.

MAROONER'S CHAIN: Archipelago off the western coast of Akkinor; mainly uninhabitable; serves as labor towns for low-ranking Akkinorians and criminals.

MAYSA: Kanish oracle; mother of King Willem.

MYENAR (My-enn-arr): God of judgement; Almighty of Dofell.

ODEYA SWANN: Lady of Runeia in Krotis; ally of Queen Aurelia.

OLEANDER BRENTWOOD: Usurper of Alora Cherrane during the old days; the first Brentwood king of Akkinor.

PHERENA (Ferr-ee-nah): Goddess of virtues; Almighty of Krotis.

QUAPEBET (Kwah-peh-bet): Continent south of Akkinor; ruled by the Kaplo family; shares the Cerulean Sea with Akkinor; connected to Myra by the neutral city of Vilgh-Azhor.

RAYAN HAZE: Akkinorian knight; Holosi-born; son of Eric Haze; biological half-brother of Aurelia Brentwood.

REYNA CALTHEOS: Queen of Taundosa.

ROBERT CHERRANE: The first King of Akkinor.

SILAS CROWLAND: Lord of Myra.

SPRITES: Tiny, mischievous magical creatures known for being tricksters and liars; found predominantly in Kanibar; fast-traveling and easily concealed; mainly used by humans as spies.

THE ASSEMBLY: An esteemed group of Akkinorian nobles serving as advisors to the monarch.

THE ELEMENTALS: The first four mages to walk among mankind, created directly by the hands of the gods to introduce magic to humanity:

> *Ceruleus* (Cerr-oo-lee-us): Elemental of air
> *Glacia* (Glah-see-uh): Elemental of water
> *Igneus* (Igg-nee-us): Elemental of fire
> *Terra* (Ter-rah): Elemental of earth

THE ONES FORGED IN GOLD: Humans said to be chosen by the gods to restore peace and harmony to the realm during times of peril; known to weep golden tears.

THE TWELVE: The global religion worshipped by all cultures of the realm; follows the twelve deities responsible for the Creation: Alkamura, Buen, Dhylo, Edea, Gianla, Hzarl, Immor, Inesis, Myenar, Pherena, Vyena, Xienia.

TULLWEINE (Tull-whey-inn): An island off the western coast of Quapebet; nicknamed "The Grin" because of small bodies of water within the island that form the shape of a smiling face.

VILGH-AZHOR (Vilg-Ah-zor): A neutral trading zone on the border of southern Akkinor and northern Quapebet; named for the Myran town of Vilgh and the Quenosi town of Azhor.

VYENA (Vee-enn-ah): Goddess of blessings; Almighty of Kanibar.

WILLEM TREVAS: King of Kanibar.

XIENIA (Zee-nee-ah): Goddess of love and beauty.